THE NEW PENGUIN BOOK
OF GAY SHORT STORIES

David Leavitt is the author of five novels (two of which, *The Lost Language of Cranes*, and *The Page Turner*, have been made into films), three collections of short stories, a book of novellas, and most recently a meditation on Florence for Bloombury's 'The Writer and the City' series. He teaches at the University of Florida.

Mark Mitchell is the author of, most recently, *Vladimir de Pachmann: A Piano Virtuoso's Life and Art*. The anthologies he has edited include *The Penguin Book of International Gay Writing* and, with David Leavitt, *Pages Passed from Hand to Hand*. He and Leavitt have also edited E. M. Forster's *Selected Stories* for Penguin Classics.

THE NEW PENGUIN BOOK OF
GAY SHORT STORIES

Edited by David Leavitt and Mark Mitchell

INTRODUCTION BY DAVID LEAVITT

PENGUIN BOOKS

PENGUIN BOOKS

Published by the Penguin Group
Penguin Books Ltd, 80 Strand, London WC2R 0RL, England
Penguin Group (USA) Inc., 375 Hudson Street, New York, New York 10014, USA
Penguin Books Australia Ltd, 250 Camberwell Road, Camberwell, Victoria 3124, Australia
Penguin Books Canada Ltd, 10 Alcorn Avenue, Toronto, Ontario, Canada M4V 3B2
Penguin Books India (P) Ltd, 11 Community Centre, Panchsheel Park, New Delhi – 110 017, India
Penguin Group (NZ), Cnr Airborne and Rosedale Roads, Albany, Auckland 1310, New Zealand
Penguin Books (South Africa) (Pty) Ltd, 24 Sturdee Avenue, Rosebank 2196, South Africa

Penguin Books Ltd, Registered Offices: 80 Strand, London WC2R 0RL, England

www.penguin.com

First published by Viking as *The Penguin Book of Gay Short Stories* 1994
Published in Penguin Books 1994
This new edition published as *The New Penguin Book of Gay Short Stories* 2003
Published in Penguin Books 2004
1

Copyright © David Leavitt and Mark Mitchell, 1994, 2003
All rights reserved

The moral right of the authors has been asserted

Pages 665–8 constitute an extension of this copyright page

Printed in England by Clays Ltd, St Ives plc

CONTENTS

PREFACE

The New Penguin Book of Gay Short Stories brings together twenty-one stories from the original anthology, published in 1994, with fifteen new stories. Eighteen selections have been excised, either because upon re-reading they seemed to us to 'date' – that is to say, to reflect too specifically the concerns and preoccupations of the historical moments at which they were written; because they were not short stories in the proper sense, but rather excerpts from longer works; or because we found other stories by the same authors that seemed to us more durable. The new stories are ones that we have discovered since putting the original anthology together. These include some older but little-known pieces – for example, Glenway Wescott's 'A Visit to Priapus' – as well as a sampling of works by newly emerging writers.

Of course, any revisionary undertaking of this kind invites retrospection. How have things changed since we submitted *The Penguin Book of Gay Short Stories* a decade ago? Reading over David Leavitt's original introduction, it occurred to us that the best way to answer that question was to annotate, offering commentary where necessary, in the form of both longer and shorter footnotes. These footnotes amount to a second introduction, at some points providing a corrective, at others clarification, and at still others a branching off into new territory.

D. L. and M. M.

INTRODUCTION

I

The first novel I ever read about gay men was called *The Lord Won't Mind*. I was sixteen at the time – 1977 – a high school junior growing up thirty miles south of San Francisco, in what was just becoming Silicon Valley. Palo Alto had a wonderful left-of-center bookstore in those days, Ploughshares, which actually maintained a gay section – just a few shelves, yet I knew their contents by heart. *The Lord Won't Mind*, by Gordon Merrick, published in 1970, caught my attention because its cover, on which two radiantly handsome blond men stared longingly into each other's eyes, suggested what seemed to me a promising combination of erotic heat and practical information. So I bought the book, slipping the copy I'd chosen between two innocuous magazines in case I ran into some-one I knew on the trip to the cash register. What I feared was being obliged to confess an identity to which my libido had already made an unwavering commitment. No one saw me, however. Now I wish someone had.*

Today, *The Lord Won't Mind* is out of print.† Turning up a copy took me ages, but I finally found one. The story concerns Charlie, just out of Princeton, and Peter, just about to start Princeton,‡ who are brought

---

* Why? So that the inevitable coming-out process could have been accelerated.

† No longer. Alyson Publications has since resurrected not only *The Lord Won't Mind* but many of its sequels.

‡ Edmund White is now the director of the Creative Writing program at Princeton – an irony that would no doubt surprise Charlie and Peter.

together by a wealthy woman of large gestures called C. B. Both are blond, muscular, stunningly handsome. In the first chapter Charlie seduces Peter by parading in front of him in only a towel, then suggesting that Peter undress so that they can compare their bodies in order to deduce whether they might share clothes. This titillating striptease leads, of course, to the inevitable revelation of male members 'extended to [their] fullest limits before actual erection, prodigious but blameless.' The words 'cock,' 'fuck,' 'suck' are never used; Merrick's pornography is insistently polite, even highbrow – just like his Princetonian protagonists.★ 'Before the staggering fact of Peter at last revealed, Merrick writes, 'Charlie thought for an instant that he had been surpassed. A quick glance for comparison reassured him. It was more slender than his and an inch or two shorter, just the way Charlie would have wished it, but without threatening his supremacy.'

What was my reaction to all this? First, hot arousal. Then, as hot arousal dissipated, bewilderment. Finally, after judicious effort, I had located a work of fiction that described the 'first time' experience I suspected (hoped) I would someday have. And yet this tale of bronzed gods with erections the size of tennis ball cans disturbed me as much as it excited me. Was sex between men, I wondered, the exclusive property of the beautiful, the muscular – the superhuman?

Of course I didn't know anything then about the history of the extremely negative way gay men have been portrayed in literature and in film: limp-wristed lispers, repressed sadists, psychopathic cross-dressers.†
Nor did I understand how Merrick and other homosexual writers of the early seventies, energized by Stonewall and the evolving gay liberation

---

★ At a recent dinner, an old Princetonian shared with us the story of how his son discovered he was gay: 'He found some documents in my glove compartment.' 'By documents do you mean porn?' someone asked. 'Porn is such a vulgar word,' he replied. 'But yes.'

† Perhaps the first television character to embody what would today be called 'queer empowerment' was one whom American audiences came to know relatively late: Mr Humphreys, played by John Inman in the British sitcom *Are You Being Served?* With his double-entendres (when told that there is a 'twelve-inch pouf in soft furnishings,' he replies, 'I thought he'd be in the novelty department') and adventurous antics, Mr Humphreys embodied a certain flaunting, queeny pride. Though sometimes the occasion for joking on the part of his colleagues, Mr Humphreys usually had the upper hand. More crucially, he seemed entirely happy in himself – a rarity for the late seventies.

movement, might have found this sort of glorification of the male body both invigorating and celebratory. Growing up near San Francisco, I knew nothing of what was going on *in* San Francisco.★ I knew only that I longed to read a novel in which the gay characters were neither reduced to a subhuman nor elevated to a superhuman level. I wanted to read a novel that told something like the truth.

Andrew Holleran's *Dancer from the Dance* (1978) was the second novel about gay men I read. This was a work of serious literature, even though it had a sexy cover. The novel followed the progress of a beautiful young man named Malone as he explores the gay Manhattan of the late seventies: a decadent, sex-driven, drunken, clothes-conscious orgy of a culture. The story is told in a voice that is literate, thoughtful, occasionally gothic, with a distinct Southern accent. (The ghosts of Tennessee Williams and Truman Capote hover in the white space.) It horrified me in ways the cartoon porn-boys in *The Lord Won't Mind* never could have. Here is a scene that exemplifies why.

An old queen called Sutherland is leading an innocent boy – an ephebe – on a sort of tour of the gay underworld. (Remember the song 'Disco Inferno'?) The boy sees a man with whom he falls instantly in love. 'Who is that?' he asks.

'His name is Alan Solis, he has *huge* balls and does public relations work for Pan Am . . . I used to be in love with Alan Solis, when I came to New York. I was so in love with him . . . that when he used the bathroom on the train to Sayville,† I used to go in right after him and lock the door, just to smell his farts! To simply breathe the gas of his very bowels!'

'You know,' said the boy, bending over as if in pain, his eyes on Alan Solis with all the intensity of a mongoose regarding a snake, 'if I can only find a flaw. If I can find a flaw in someone, then it's not so bad, you know? But that boy seems to be perfect!' he said. 'Oh, God, it's terrible!' And he put a hand to his forehead, stricken by that deadliest of forces, Beauty.

★ No book records with greater affection the lives of gay men in San Francisco in the seventies than Crawford Barton's extraordinary photo essay *Days of Hope* (Heretic Books, 1994).

† The train station for Fire Island.

'A flaw, a flaw,' said Sutherland, dropping his ash into the ashtray on his left, 'I understand perfectly.'

If I can just see a flaw, then it's not so hopeless and depressing,' said the boy, his face screwed up in agony, even though Solis, talking to a short, muscular Italian whom he wanted to take home that night, was completely oblivious to this adoring fan whose body was far too thin to interest him.

'I've got it,' said Sutherland, who turned to his companion now. 'I remember a flaw. His chest,' he said, 'his chest is so hairy that one can't really see the deep, chiselled indentation between the breasts. Will that do, darling?'

The boy gnawed on his lip and considered.

'I'm afraid it will have to. There isn't a thing else wrong with the man, other than the fact that he knows it.'

Chilly perfection. Inaccessibility. Disinterest. Were the only choices for gay men, I wondered, either to exude or suffer from these things? There is irony in Holleran's vision, of course, but I wasn't wise to it then; it didn't occur to me that he might, in some subtle way, have been mocking these exclusive rituals. (It is entirely possible to mock and romanticize simultaneously.) Instead I saw only, and with a kind of ashen horror, my future, or what I feared my future was going to amount to: relegation to some marginal role in a world where specimens of almost blinding physical perfection preened, dismissed, or simply ignored. Seventies gay male culture did not have very much patience for the ugly man, the old man, the man with a small dick or a potbelly or no hair on his head. (It has only slightly more these days.*) According to *Dancer from the Dance* and *The Lord Won't Mind*, only the most exceptionally beautiful were entitled to erotic fulfillment. The rest of us, it seemed, were destined to salivate in the wings, or at best, try to buy our way in.

A tendency to romanticize rejection – to romanticize the very farts deposited into the air by the object of idealization – characterizes the late Robert Ferro's 1983 novel *The Family of Max Desir* as well. (This

---

* In the years since this introduction was written, however, avenues have opened up – mostly via the Internet – both for those whose bodies fail to match these narrow criteria and for their admirers: chat rooms, bars, magazines and clubs testifying to the amplitude of the erotic imagination.

book I read later, when I had just graduated from college.) Here the author's obsession with the physical beauty of his hero – even Max's name suggests what he is the object of – overwhelms the eponymous family: the novel would be better titled *Desiring Max Desir*. For instance, in a long flashback, Ferro recalls Max's arrest in Florence after he makes a pass at a plainclothes policeman. Max ends up in jail, where he meets Nick Flynn, who becomes his lover. As in *The Lord Won't Mind*, their coupling is facilitated by a rich, theatrically self-dramatizing woman, this time an Italian named Lydia. Older men constantly fall for one or another of the pair; indeed, their beauty is such that at one point it quite literally kills an elderly monsignor who loves 'angels as they appeared in the form of young boys':*

> It had been his heart, concerning which this was the last of several incidents, but it seemed at the time, to Nick and Max, to be *them*. What strains had they put on the old man's failing health? Not that they had ever spent a moment alone with him, or thought of it. But it was death at close range, the first for either of them. And it seemed, like so much in their lives – as for instance their meeting in prison – to have some larger meaning. This impression was further developed a few weeks later when the host of a similar weekend house party, at which Lydia was not a guest, just as suddenly dropped dead, this time not actually in their presence but very soon after leaving it.

Talk about looks that kill! But as the novel progresses, the dreamlike tone of the Italian section gives way to a grittier American realism; more importantly, Ferro finally gets to the heart of the matter, namely Max's relationship with his father, John, particularly after his mother, Marie, has died. Nonetheless Max's erotic obsessiveness routinely intrudes on the family drama that is the novel's ostensible centerpiece, as in this scene, in which Max and his father fly to Vermont to supervise the erection of Marie's tombstone:

---

* The Catholic Ferro wrote this, obviously, many years before the current sex scandals that have riven his Church.

They drove to the airport, left the car in the lot, and had breakfast after checking in. A man behind the counter in the coffee shop was one of the most beautiful Max had ever seen. It was implausible that such a being had not conquered films, Seventh Avenue, or the Sultan of Oman, but was instead breaking eggs at La Guardia Marine. John did not notice. The man smiled back at Max. His was a body reserved for the transubstantiation of visiting angels, with the same perfect evenness, proportion and symmetry found in the beautiful face . . . While Max ate his breakfast John read the paper. The counterman had arranged the bacon on Max's plate in the shape of a question mark.★

The Family of Max Desire isn't *about* its hero's (or its author's) obsession with male beauty. Instead it's that rarity: a novel in which a gay man plays an integral role in the unfolding drama of family life. But the obsession with male beauty *is* a constant and intrusive element. What I found myself longing for, as I read the book, was a gay literature that transformed homosexual experience into human drama rather than fawning over angels made flesh; a gay literature that was literature first and gay second. Yes, writers might constantly be distracted by the sight of pretty boys behind breakfast counters; they could afford to be distracted; a work of literature cannot.

I had a conversation with a twenty-one-year-old friend of mine recently. When I told him I was planning to take on some sacred cows in this essay – most notably *Dancer from the Dance* – his response was swift and unhesitant. 'Thank God someone's doing it', he said; 'it's the first gay book most young American gay men read, and I can't think of another that's done as much damage.'† Damage is the key here: the voyeuristic fixation with beauty that powers the novel compels younger gay men who don't know better to wonder if *exclusion* is all there is to the business of being gay – exclusion from sex, from coupledom, from happiness itself.

★ On re-reading this passage, we recognized that Ferro was probably alluding here to the scene in E. M. Forster's *A Room with a View* in which George Emerson forms the food on his plate into a 'mark of interrogation,' which he then shows to Lucy Honeychurch.

† Today, *Dancer from the Dance* is no longer the first gay book most young American gay men read; nor can any one book be said to play that role.

To this question the answer is a resounding no (a no echoed by any number of lesser-known novels and stories). *Dancer from the Dance* exalted what is to many of us the dreariest aspect of gay experience. (It is curious that its publication so vastly overshadowed the almost simultaneous appearance of Larry Kramer's *Faggots*, a novel that savagely satirized the very bars and discos, Fire Island beaches and popper-hazed baths, about which Holleran writes so lushly – rudely shutting off the music, switching on the lights and forcing us to see things as they are.)

Although the gay section at Ploughshares didn't stock many books, it's to the credit of that sadly defunct place that a gay section existed at all.★ And what was in it? *The Lord Won't Mind* and its many interminable sequels. *The Front Runner*, by Patricia Nell Warren. *The Joy of Gay Sex*. John Rechy's *The Sexual Outlaw* with its seedy 'street' ambience and awkward neologisms ('youngman' as one word). And what wasn't in it that should have or could have been? *The Folded Leaf*, William Maxwell's tale of love between teenage boys, published in the late nineteen-forties. J. R. Ackerley's agonizingly honest autobiography *My Father and Myself*. Sanford Friedman's *Totempole*. John Cheever's *Falconer*. I knew about none

---

★ This was written before Barnes & Noble and Borders changed the face of American bookselling. Borders now relegates most fiction by gay men to a special 'gay men's fiction' section, emulating Ploughshares – but with results about which most writers are decidedly ambivalent. The problem is that being stocked under 'gay men's fiction' means *not* being stocked under 'literature'. A recent check at a Borders bookstore in Florida, for instance, found James Baldwin's books shelved under neither 'literature' nor 'gay men's fiction' but 'African-American literature.' Randall Kenan, by contrast, was in 'gay men's fiction' but not 'African-American literature.' Michael Cunningham was in 'literature.' Andrew Holleran, Armistead Maupin and Edmund White were in 'gay men's fiction.'

In any case, the market for literature about gay and lesbian experience has if anything shrunk in the years since the publication of *The Penguin Book of Gay Short Stories*. The 'Men on Men' series has lost its home at Plume, and moved to Attagirl Press. Mainstream publishers are doing fewer gay and lesbian books, leaving smaller specialized presses such as Alyson, Kensington and Harrington Park Press to pick up the slack. Most of the nation's gay and lesbian bookstores have gone out of business.

Whereas a decade ago books by women, gay men and lesbians, and minorities were in the ascendancy, we seem now to have returned to the world of the Big Important Novel, with straight white guys such as Jonathan Franzen, Rick Moody, Jeffrey Eugenides and Michael Chabon being given the vast bulk of the ever-shrinking space in our ever-shrinking book reviews.

of these books back then. I didn't know about them in 1984, when in direct response to the dearth of decent gay literature that characterized my adolescence I started my own first novel, *The Lost Language of Cranes*. It took years more to dig out the books I could have read when I was sixteen – books that neither prettified nor idealized gay experience, nor offered anything so simple as 'positive role models.' Instead the men who inhabited them were recognizably human. The impulse that fueled their creation was not the impulse to glorify; it was the impulse to articulate the process by which gay men went about their daily lives.

Still, even the luckiest young gay men and lesbians are isolated; even in places where people tell you it's okay to be gay, you have to tell *them* you're gay first, and that's rarely easy. Unlike young heterosexuals, for whom history, rituals of courtship and marriage, and codes of decorum – what Forster, in *Maurice*, called the 'beautiful conventions' – are handed out daily in the classroom, we must seek out, often privately, some sense of our connection to official history, not to mention some sense of our own history, which by definition is discontinuous, a series of stops and starts that begins again each time a young gay man or lesbian finds his or her way to the gay section at a bookstore – if indeed there is a gay section; if indeed there is a bookstore.

The assumption that an irrevocable gulf existed between 'them' and 'us' was characteristic of pre-eighties gay literature. Before *The Family of Max Desir*, few works of fiction about gay men represented an integration of the homosexual and heterosexual realms, which many portrayed as immutably hostile to each other. The gay underworld portrayed in Rechy's *City of Night* and *The Sexual Outlaw*, or in films like *Nighthawks* and *Taxi zum Klo*, existed as a parallel universe to the straight world, a shadowland where gay men by night led secret lives. Crucially, in these works night brought on the transformation not only of the men but of the world itself; a park where by day children played becomes by night the scene of orgiastic revels. Few novels portrayed the option of freeing oneself from this double life. Indeed, one of the only ones that did, *The Seraglio*, written in 1954 by the poet James Merrill, offered a protagonist whose liberation is achieved only by means of an act of extraordinary violence: he slices off his own penis. Afterward, quite literally 'cut off' from the heterosexual imperative his wealthy parents have demanded he obey, our hero reemerges a happy, bookish intellectual living in a brownstone in *louche* Greenwich Village. But at what cost?

If *Dancer from the Dance*, like the play and film *The Boys in the Band*, represented an important breakthrough, it was because its protagonists had freed themselves from the tyranny of the double life; indeed, they were made to suffer much more by each other than by heterosexual agents of oppression. The gay underworld now gave way to the gay ghetto, where men held hands and kissed in public and dared the 'public' to say a word about it. In those days, to come out was not merely to announce oneself, it was to change one's way of dressing, speaking, thinking; in many cases it required a literal relocation, to San Francisco's Castro district, or New York's Greenwich Village, or in the summer to Fire Island, Provincetown, the Russian River. These places became meccas for gay men eager to live free, though not always untroubled by the knowledge that in joining their fellow 'tribesmen' they were, in effect, accepting consignment to a realm that was separate and only perhaps equal.* As Susan Sontag put it in *AIDS and Its Metaphors*, in the 1970s 'many male homosexuals reconstituted themselves as something like an ethnic group, one whose distinctive folkloric custom was sexual voracity, and the institutions of urban homosexual life became a sexual delivery system of unprecedented speed, efficiency, and volume.' AIDS wasn't the only fallout; as Kramer's prophetic novel *Faggots* proclaims, such a life can destroy souls as well as T-cells.

I remember, in the early eighties, standing on the brink of coming out and being deterred not by fear of retribution so much as by fear of the culture into which coming out seemed inevitably destined to thrust me. Yes, I wanted to be openly gay; even so, my few forays into gay New York had left me shaken. This wasn't the world I wanted to live in, and I saw no advertised alternatives. More importantly, I flinched at the notion that coming out somehow meant that I would have not only to reimagine myself totally but to cut off my ties to my family, my heterosexual friends – indeed, the totality of the world I'd grown up in. To do so, it seemed to me, was to risk doing myself real psychic violence. Yes, I was gay, but I was also Jewish, a Leavitt, a writer: so many other things! Why should my sexual identity subsume all my other identities? I wondered. And then I saw the answer: because the 'straight' world, the 'normal' world, upon learning I was gay, would see me only as gay; because ghettos are invented

---

* In the late eighties, a gay male literary magazine called *Tribe* came and went, as the very *idea* of the 'tribe' lost favor among its putative members.

not by the people who live in them but by the people who don't live in them. A new level of liberation needed to be achieved, I saw then: one that would allow gay men and lesbians to celebrate their identities without having to move into a gulag.★

II

What makes a 'gay story' gay? This is a more complicated question than it may at first sound. Traditionally, anthologies of so-called gay fiction have collected stories by gay male writers writing about the lives of gay men. And yet, numerous gay male writers, from antiquity to the present day, have written fiction that at least explicitly has nothing to do with gay experience – even though it may exhibit a 'gay sensibility' or 'gay style'

★ Reading this paragraph over today, much in it seems false and falsely argued. While it is true that the dogma of the 'gay liberation' movement of the seventies prescribed a kind of social isolation from the wider world, that aspect of the movement proved in the end to be massively unpopular; indeed, the idea that coming out would necessitate cutting off all ties with one's family and straight friends would now strike many young gay people as ludicrous. Quite simply, for many young people, homosexuality is just not the big deal it used to be.

Also, while it is true that ghettos usually come into being thanks to the efforts of oppressors both economic and political, it would be disingenuous to accept at face value the claim that the men who elected to live in the urban gay ghettos of the seventies and eighties did so only because they were compelled to do so. Castro Street is a far cry from the Łódź ghetto; nor can New York's Chelsea, or Washington's Dupont Circle, or Philadelphia's 'Boystown' be compared in any way to the South Bronx. To a greater degree than many of us wanted to admit then, or want to admit today, most of the men who live in these neighborhoods do so by choice – and because they can afford to. Despite all the high-minded talk of 'community' that gay activists inject into their lectures, when we get down to brass tacks, it cannot be denied that most of the allure of these neighborhoods owes to their abundance of bars, gyms, escorts, discos, drug dealers, porn shops, liquor stores, and sex clubs.

Lastly, as any gay man who chooses not to live in New York or San Francisco soon discovers, the old slogan 'we are everywhere' is a true one. In fact, the vast majority of American gay men lead their lives outside the urban centers. When we moved to Gainesville, Florida, a couple of years ago, we discovered that one of our neighbors was Eric Garber, author – under the pseudonym 'Andrew Holleran' – of *Dancer from the Dance*. He lives in Keystone Heights, Florida.

(two more problematic terms). Likewise, numerous heterosexual writers have written fiction that deals eloquently with male homosexuality. What about them? And what about fiction by lesbians? The majority of gay anthologists have not only left out work by heterosexual and lesbian writers, they haven't even considered the possibility that the exclusion might diminish the value of their work. So rigid an ideology is, to our way of thinking, counterproductive. That said, certain limits must be agreed upon if an anthology is not to become so enormous as to defy practical publication.

For the purposes of this anthology, then, a gay story is defined as one that illuminates the experience of love between men, investigates the kinds of relationships gay men have with each other, their friends and their families, or explores the nature of homosexual identity. The sex or sexuality of the author is, according to this definition, irrelevant. Lastly, the anthology keeps itself to twentieth- and twenty-first century fiction originally written in English.★

We begin with a brief narrative of adolescent love, D. H. Lawrence's 'A Poem of Friendship,' published in 1911, and end with a brief narrative of adolescent love, A. M. Homes's 'The Whiz Kids,' published in 1992.† Comparing these two stories tells us a lot about how the lives of gay men have – and haven't – changed over the course of eighty years. In 'A Poem

---

★ Since the publication of the first *Penguin Book of Gay Short Stories*, a number of other anthologies and studies of the history of gay-themed literature have come into – and in at least one case out of – print. Mark Mitchell's *The Penguin Book of International Gay Writing* (Viking, 1995) collected only works in translation from languages other than English. Byrne Fone's *The Columbia Anthology of Gay Literature* (Columbia University Press, 1998) offers an encyclopedic survey. Two books of more specific focus are James Gifford's *Dayneford's Library: American Homosexual Fiction, 1900 to 1913* (University of Massachusetts Press, 1996) and our own *Pages Passed from Hand to Hand: The Hidden Tradition of Homosexual Literature in English from 1748 to 1914* (Chatto & Windus, 1997).

Important anthologies of lesbian literature published during the last decade include Margaret Reynolds's *The Penguin Book of Lesbian Short Stories* (Viking, 1994; unfortunately it excluded work by non-lesbian and male writers) and Lillian Faderman's *Chloe Plus Olivia: An Anthology of Lesbian Literature from the Seventeenth Century to the Present* (Viking, 1994).

† Although this is no longer true – for this edition, we have adopted a strictly chronological arrangement of the contents – these stories remain, respectively, near the beginning and near the end.

of Friendship,' the narrator and his beloved friend, George, swim and play, then dry off together:

> He saw I had forgotten to continue my rubbing, and laughing he took hold of me and began to rub me briskly, as if I were a child, or rather, a woman he loved and did not fear. I left myself quite limply in his hands, and to get a better grip of me, he put his arm round me and pressed me against him, and the sweetness of the touch of our naked bodies one against the other was superb. It satisfied in some measure the vague, indecipherable yearning of my soul; and it was the same with him. When he had rubbed me all warm, he let me go, and we looked at each other with eyes of still laughter, and our love was perfect for a moment, more perfect than any love I have known since, either for man or woman.

Similarly, in 'The Whiz Kids,' the narrator and his friend (unnamed) take a bath together:

> In the big bathtub in my parents' bedroom, he ran his tongue along my side, up into my armpits, tugging the hair with his teeth. 'We're like married,' he said, licking my nipples.
>
> I spit at him. A foamy blob landed on his bare chest. He smiled, grabbed both my arms, and held them down.
>
> He slid his face down toward my stomach, dipped it under the water, and put his mouth over my cock.
>
> My mother knocked on the bathroom door. 'I have to get ready. Your father and I are leaving in twenty minutes.'
>
> . . . Later, in the den, picking his nose, examining the results on his finger, slipping his finger into his mouth with a smack and a pop, he explained that as long as we never slept with anyone else, we could do whatever we wanted. 'Sex kills,' he said, 'but this,' he said, 'this is the one time, the only time, the chance of a life time.' He ground his front teeth on the booger.

The changes aren't only in the vernacular. In comparison to Lawrence, Homes's narration is shockingly direct, even pornographic. There's no apologizing here, no poeticizing for the sake of the uninitiated or faint of heart. More crucially, by 1991 AIDS has entered the picture. These sophisticated boys know that what they're experiencing together – sex free of complication, not to mention the threat of death – is something they can never again experience in their lives.★

In between these two stories there is every imaginable kind of gay story, written by every imaginable kind of writer. Some are already famous – Allan Gurganus's 'Adult Art,' Graham Greene's 'May We Borrow Your Husband?' Then there are surprises. Noël Coward? you may ask. Yes: this is an elegant and moving story about a gay man who has spent most of his life shepherding a group of showgirls around the world, and a joyous discovery for many reasons, not the least of which is its portrayal of gay men in long-term relationships – something rare in those days.† William Trevor's 'Torridge' is another surprise, primarily because its author, while generally recognized as a master of the short story, is not himself gay. Still, he has crafted an incendiary tale about hypocrisy at an English boys' school, a story that articulates more forcefully and effectively than any I can name the anger so many British gay men often feel toward those institutions that silently encourage homosexual behavior while simultaneously condemning homosexual identity.

There are, in these stories, gay parents (Ann Beattie's 'The Cinderella Waltz'), as well as gay children (Peter Cameron's 'Jump or Dive,' Christopher Coe's 'Gentlemen Can Wash Their Hands in the Gents''). The discoveries of the young (Richard McCann's 'My Mother's Clothes') elbow the ruefulness of the middle-aged and old (Edmund White's 'Reprise,' David Levinson's 'A Perfect Day for Swimming'). And the tragedy of AIDS is evoked in all its splendor and terror by writers as diverse as the late Allen Barnett, Dennis McFarland, and Peter Wells. As a subcategory, these stories constitute, it seems to me, the best collection of AIDS literature yet written. It is hard to emerge from Barnett's Fire Island

---

★ A decade later, we are witnessing a sudden rise in HIV infections among young gay men who claim not to have realized that they were at risk. Is this perhaps because they subscribed to the fallacy that the virus belonged exclusively to older generations?

† It remains rare today. Notwithstanding the documentary evidence that over the last century many gay men formed loving couples and stayed together for most of their lives, literature has remained curiously aloof from homosexual domesticity. James Gardiner's *A Class Apart: The Private Pictures of Montague Glover* (Consortium, 1999) is a moving photographic history of one long relationship, and includes some extraordinary love letters written from the front during the Great War.

unshaken, just as it is impossible to forget the erotic games played by the men in Stephen Greco's 'Good with Words,' for whom the threat of HIV infection turns out to be the source of surprising arousal. Nothing easy here, nothing status quo or politically correct. While most of these stories, moreover, are conventional in form, they are far from conventional in content. The traditional gay male distractions are avoided here – these writers have their fingers too firmly on the pulse of experience to waste time with any of that.★

★ In 1993, when we were editing the *Penguin Book of Gay Short Stories*, gay fiction was preoccupied with AIDS. Indeed, from every corner there came the cry, even the imperative, to write about AIDS. (Silence = Death.)

Although a small amount of literature about AIDS, driven by sincerity and outrage, came out of that day, much of what was written on the subject may be judged today, fairly, to have been mawkish or even calculated. Certainly few writers exploited the epidemic for the explicit purpose of furthering their own careers; and yet who could have failed to note that it was *Borrowed Time* – a memoir of the death of his lover and of his own discovery that he had AIDS – that brought Paul Monette the fame and commercial success that had eluded him through several novels and poetry collections? What critic would have dared give a negative review to a dying author, or to one who was lamenting the death of his lover? How could Tom Hanks *not* have won an Academy Award for his role as a gay man who dies of AIDS in *Philadelphia*? For not only writers, but publishing houses and movie studios, saw the advantages to be gained from exploiting the personal face of HIV. (A distinction must be drawn, of course, between the *cris de coeur* of writers who were themselves ill, and memoirs written by lovers, caregivers, friends, or relatives. Because the writers in this latter group – among them Clifford Chase, Mark Doty, and Fenton Johnson – *had* futures, they were able to benefit from the epidemic in ways that authors such as Barnett and Monette – whose books have outlived them – could not.)

Unfortunately, the overwhelming literary identification of gay men with AIDS contributed to the general perception that AIDS was an exclusively gay problem. If AIDS was really everyone's worry, then why were gay men virtually the only people to write about it? Presently, it was as if gay writers courted the tacit association of AIDS with homosexuality in order to win popularity with a heterosexual audience that had previously ignored them.

Significantly, the only openly gay writer to win the Pulitzer Prize for fiction, Michael Cunningham, did so for a novel, *The Hours*, in which the principal gay male character is suffering from AIDS-induced dementia and eventually commits suicide. By contrast, in Alan Hollinghurst's *The Spell*, published the same year, none of the gay male characters are dying (of AIDS or anything else), and all of them have a lot of sex. Which of these books won critical approbation? It was a depressing season, for it suggested that despite the illusion of gain, in fact the position of gay fiction had not

Literature confronts the perversity of individual experience. Its role has never been to promote or prescribe particular ways of being, but rather to expose the fine tension that exists between the way people actually are and the way the culture they live in would have them be.★ Thus the stories

---

improved much since the time when Forster elected not to try to publish *Maurice* – not because he was afraid to do so (although, in some measure, he was), but because no publisher in 1914 would have touched a gay book with a happy ending.

As is so often the case, pornography is the most potent register of social attitudes and changes in them. Coincident with the pressure to write about AIDS was the safe sex movement. At the beginning, practicing safe sex carried its own risks. If they were to make condom use a precondition of sex, many men feared, they would lose sexual opportunities – and, in fact, they often did so, since so many other men were willing to 'take the chance.' Then, once the methods of HIV transmission had been fairly clearly established, those who did not practice safe sex found themselves being condemned as irresponsible, violators of the sexual contract. The incidence of AIDS transmission began to diminish, and the advocates of safe sex breathed a collective sigh of relief – until something totally unforeseen occurred. Men in good health began to experience what was, in effect, survivor's guilt; that is to say, having watched so many of their friends and lovers die, they began to feel that life itself was a gift they did not deserve. It was at this moment that jerk-off clubs like the venerable 1808 Club in San Francisco had to close their doors. The need for intimacy without caution began to outweigh the fear of becoming sick. But had it ever been prudent to believe that safe sex would be a panacea?

In any case, with the transformation of AIDS from a major current of gay literature to the rivulet it is today, the very porn videos that had once promoted condom use and safe sex began to feature 'bareback' fucking as well as the oral ingestion of semen. (Astonishingly, a recent advertisement in *Advocate Men* sings the praises of 'Yummy Cum,' a pill that promises to make your partner 'want to perform fellatio all the way to orgasm without "spitting out." He is sure to come back for more and more. It works that well!') For some viewers, the evident 'incorrectness' of this behavior precludes its erotic appeal. For others, the very transgressiveness of the scene, its forbiddenness, is deeply erotic. Now that homosexuality is not, for most gay men and lesbians, tied up, as it once was, with rebellion, with rejection of the *status quo*, unsafe sex has become, in effect, a means of regaining – even at the cost of one's life – the sense of personal liberation that can be bought only by defiance.

If there was one thing safe sex refused to see, it was the erotics of death.

★ The use of the word 'culture' here today strikes us as simplistic. Yes, the dominant culture of heterosexuality has been pernicious and sometimes oppressive; but so is the 'one size fits all' approach to gay and lesbian identity sometimes promoted by such organs of gay culture as the mammoth www.gay.com, which owns both *The Advocate* and *Out* magazine.

collected in this anthology do not attempt to answer questions so much as to amplify, convolute, elaborate them; their purpose is not to solve a mystery but to illuminate its parameters. Most importantly, they resist the impulse to reduce gay experience to a set of clichés: what we as individuals are supposed to be as opposed to what we are. (And yet we must remember that as long as the society we live in despises us as a group, we *will* be a group, whether we like it or not.)

Many people ask me if I consider myself a 'gay writer.' My answer is that the question is irrelevant; as long as the culture I live in considers me a gay writer – and it considers every writer who tackles gay subject matter a gay writer – I'm stuck with the label. My sexual identity will subsume all other aspects of my identity – I might be a 'gay Jewish writer,' never a 'Jewish gay writer' – no matter how loudly I protest. The same people ask, with annoying frequency, why I always write about gay characters, which I don't. Well, I answer, if I were John Updike, would you ask, 'Mr Updike, why do you always write about *heterosexual* characters?'* They cough and get nervous. Because heterosexuality is the norm, writers have permission to explore its nuances without raising any eyebrows. To write about gay characters, by contrast, is always, necessarily, to make some sort of 'statement' about the fact of being gay. Stories in which a character's homosexuality is, as it were, 'beside the point' confuse us: why bring it up? asks the writing teacher in our heads.† Similarly, reviewers complain about books in which too many characters are gay. (Does anyone complain about too many characters in *Rabbit, Run* being straight?) The problem is that this kind of thinking gets into a writer's head; we begin to believe that the sexuality of our characters really does define them. This may be another reason why Forster, at the height of his career, chose to give up publishing fiction. On the one hand he longed to write fiction about homosexual experience. Wouldn't doing so, however, have diminished the illustrious author of *Howards End* and *A Passage to India*? Luckily for us, he continued writing; but his gay stories were not published until after his death.

That non-gay writers have agreed to have their work included in an anthology with a title like this surprises me and does my heart good.‡ I'm reminded of a performance I saw a few years back by the artist Holly

---

* He doesn't. See 'Scenes from the Fifties', in this anthology.

† Of course, why bring up *heterosexuality*, when it, too, is usually beside the point?

‡ In 2003, it surprises less, but still does the heart good.

Hughes. This was during the frightening days when the American right wing, led by Senator Jesse Helms, was attempting to use the National Endowment for the Arts as a weapon in its never-ending battle against sexual self-expression. A group of writers, singers, and performers – myself and Hughes among them – had gotten together to raise money for Harvey Gantt, the senatorial candidate then opposing Helms. Hughes was announced, but she did not appear; instead a young man and woman strode on to the stage, identified themselves as 'a fag' and 'a dyke,' and informally polled the audience. Would everyone who was gay please stand up? the young woman asked. Nervously, about a quarter of us did so. And now, the young man said, would everyone who does not consider him or herself to be gay but *has* slept with a member of the same sex stand up? A few more people stood, reluctantly. We were then instructed to sit down again. Now the young man and woman reminded us about what had happened in Denmark during World War II; how the king of Denmark, hearing that his Jewish subjects would be compelled to wear yellow stars, himself donned a yellow star; how indeed most Danes wore yellow stars, so that the Jews could not be distinguished from the non-Jews. Presumably everyone in the audience – given the evening's purpose – must have caught the allusion; I can't believe they failed to. And now, the young woman said, remembering what happened in Denmark, I ask you again: would all of you in the audience who are gay stand up?

About three-quarters of the people there did. As for the others, they remained in their seats, eyes grim and steadfast, clutching their armrests as if for dear life.

THE NEW PENGUIN BOOK OF
GAY SHORT STORIES

CHARLES KENNETH SCOTT-MONCRIEFF

EVENSONG AND MORWE SONG

'If Evensong and Morwe-song accorde'
—CHAUCER, *Prologue to the Canterbury Tales*, I, 380.

I

... 'And if we are found out?' asked Maurice. He was still on his knees in the thicket, and, as he looked up to where his companion stood in an awkward fumbling attitude, his face seemed even more than usually pale and meagre in the grey broken light. It was with rather forced nonchalance that Carruthers answered 'O, the sack, I suppose' – and he stopped aghast at the other's expression. Then as only at one other time in a long and well-rewarded life did he feel that a millstone round his neck might perhaps be less offensive than the picture of those small, startled features hung for all eternity before his eyes.

But all went well. Each returned to his house (they were at school at Gainsborough – this in the early eighties) without let or hindrance. When

CHARLES KENNETH SCOTT-MONCRIEFF (1889–1930): At the age of eighteen, Scott-Moncrieff (later to translate Marcel Proust's À la recherche du temps perdu into English) included his story 'Evensong and Morwe Song' in the pageant issue of New Field, the literary magazine of which he was editor at Winchester School. This accomplished piece of fiction revealed a young writer years ahead of his time. In contrast to most of his elders, Scott-Moncrieff was not only willing to write openly about homosexuality, but to publish the work under his own name. Nor was this decision without its consequences; the story caused such a scandal at Winchester that the magazine was immediately suppressed, and its editor expelled. 'Evensong and Morwe Song' was republished in the nineteen-twenties by Francis Edward Murray, in a limited edition – none of which was for sale.

Scott-Moncrieff died in Rome at the age of forty.

in the next autumn but one Carruthers went up to Oxford I doubt if he remembered his debt to the Creator of the soul of Edward Hilary Maurice. 'After all, had he been so scrupulous?' he argued, 'I am no worse than a dozen others and Maurice no better. Indeed, Maurice is getting quite a reputation. How dreadful all that sort of thing is!' And whatever he may have remembered at Oxford, we may be certain that when with his charming nonchalance he knelt before a golfer-bishop of no mean hysterical attractions to receive deacon's orders, he presented himself as a pure, sincere, and fragrant vessel, capable of containing any amount of truth.

II

William Carruthers turned a trifle uneasily in his stiff, new revolving chair as his victims entered. It was the last day of October. For a little more than a month he had occupied the headmaster's study at Cheddar, a school for which as a pious Gainsburgher he retained a profound contempt. This contempt was hardly diminished (to do him justice his salary was but moderate) by his having already to deal with one of those painful incidents which occur in second-rate schools almost as frequently as in the sacred Nine.

What he said to them is not our province. His weighty arguments (mainly borrowed from the boys' housemaster), his ears deaf to excuse or contradiction, his flaying sarcasm and his pessimistic prophecies drew great salt tears from the younger boy's eyes on to the gaudy new magisterial carpet before that unfortunate was sent away heavily warned against further outbreaks, and he was left free to damn the other in this world and disparage him in the next. He eyed him witheringly for some minutes, and then whispered: 'Ah, Hilary! It were better for thee that a millstone were hanged about thy neck, and thou cast into the sea, than that thou shouldest offend one of these little ones.' He had previously consulted a concordance, and in variously impressive tones rehearsed this and the parallel passages. Chance or inspiration might have prompted Hilary, whose whole life was being ruined to correct his first offence, to cite the following verses (read in Chapel an evening or two before) which enjoin that seven offences on the same day should be balanced by the offender's penitence. But he was silent. Carruthers, supposing him unrepentant and inveterate, lashed him with abuse that ranged from ribaldry to a little less than rhetoric; and finally dismissed him to remove his effects from his house and from Cheddar, whither he might, if well behaved, return in ten years' time.

These effectual workings over, the headmaster turned to the second part of the expulsion office – the letter to parent or guardian. It was then that he remembered his ignorance of the boy's address, and with some repugnance turned to a gaudy volume inscribed *Ordo Cheddarensis* in gold upon a red, blue and green back and sides, which had appeared there synchronically with himself. In the index he was faintly surprised to find: 'Hilary, see Maurice, J. E. H.'; and he was annoyed at the consequent delay. At last he found the reference, laid down the book (which crackled cheerily in its stiff, cheap binding), and read up his man:

'Maurice, James Edward Hilary (now J.E.H. Hilary). Born 13 Sept., 18—. Only son of Edward Hilary Maurice (now E.H. Hilary), of Leafsleigh, Co. Southampton, who on succeeding to that estate assumed the name of Hilary in lieu of that of Maurice. Addresses: 13 Worcester Gate Terrace, W.; Leafsleigh, Christchurch Road, R. S. O., Hants.'

As he was transcribing the address this most consummate of head-masters received an unpleasant shock. Its pages released, the book crackled inexpensively and closed itself. In its place lay or floated a picture of two boys in a thicket; of the one's charming nonchalance; of terror sickening the other, a child that had just lost its soul. When at Oxford Carruthers had received a letter in which Maurice said: 'It is not altogether because I must leave Gainsborough that I curse you now. But I can never send my sons there, nor to any decent school. Shorncliffe must receive them, or Milkmanthaite or even Cheddar – some hole that we have thought hardly worth our scorn. Because my sons will inherit the shame which you implanted, I now for the last time call you . . .' Carruthers' fine British reserve had elided the next words from his memory.

Before his ordination he had prayed for spiritual armour, and had received a coat of self-satisfaction which had so far held out against all assaults of man or woman. Now it felt rusty. Rather half-heartedly he rang and told the butler to send someone to Mr Herbertson's house to tell Mr Hilary that the headmaster wanted him again and at once. Then he picked up the sheet of tremendously coat-armoured school notepaper, upon which a laboured and almost illegible 'My dear Sir' was begun. On it he drew obscene figures for half-an-hour. Then the messenger returned. 'Please sir,' reported the butler, 'James that I sent up, sir, says he couldn't find no one in Mr Herbertson's house for him to speak to, leastways but Mrs Wrenn, the housekeeper. She said, sir, as how Mr Hilary had just gone off to the station in a fly with all his luggage.'

The Headmaster of Cheddar took up his mortarboard and went out, swearing indiscriminately.

D. H. LAWRENCE

A POEM OF FRIENDSHIP

The magnificent promise of spring was broken before the May-blossom was fully out. All through the beloved month the wind rushed in upon us from the north and northeast, bringing the rain fierce and heavy. The tender-budded trees shuddered and moaned; when the wind was dry, the young leaves flapped limp. The grass and corn grew lush, but the light of the dandelions was quite extinguished, and it seemed that only a long time back had we made merry before the broad glare of these flowers. The bluebells lingered and lingered; they fringed the fields for weeks like purple fringe of mourning. The pink campions came out, only to hang heavy

---

D. H. LAWRENCE (1885–1930): Although his tempestuous marriage to Frieda von Richthofen defined, if not fulfilled, Lawrence's erotic life, his work was not without a strong homoerotic component. That said, the bucolic 'A Poem of Friendship' – from his first book, The White Peacock – contrasts sharply with the famous 'Prologue' to Women in Love and 'The Prussian Officer,' which in its sadism recalls both Herman Melville's Billy Budd and Robert Müsil's novel of military school life, The Confusions of Young Törless.

   Cecil Gray wrote of Lawrence in Musical Chairs: 'The man who achieves complete and satisfying sexual experience in life is never obsessed with sex to the extent to which Lawrence was in his writings. Your strong, vital, satisfied male does not rapturously hymn the act of the flesh in his work – very much to the contrary, he is generally very quiet about it. The concupiscent, insatiable Tolstoi preaches austerity and asceticism; it is the Swinburnes and Nietzsches and Lawrences who persistently glorify and magnify the joys they have never really experienced in all their fullness, if at all.'

with rain; hawthorn buds remained tight and hard as pearls, shrinking into the brilliant green foliage; the forget-me-nots, the poor pleiades of the wood, were ragged weeds. Often at the end of the day, the sky opened, and stately clouds hung over the horizon infinitely far away, glowing, through the yellow distance, with an amber lustre. They never came any nearer, always they remained far off, looking calmly and majestically over the shivering earth, then, saddened, fearing their radiance might be dimmed, they drew away, and sank out of sight. Sometimes, towards sunset, a great shield stretched dark from the west to the zenith, tangling the light along its edges. As the canopy rose higher, it broke, dispersed, and the sky was primrose coloured, high and pale above the crystal moon. Then the cattle crouched among the gorse, distressed by the cold, while the long-billed snipe flickered round high overhead, round and round in great circles, seeming to carry a serpent from its throat, and crying a tragedy, more painful than the poignant lamentations and protests of the peewits. Following these evenings came mornings cold and grey.

Such a morning I went up to George, on the top fallow. His father was out with the milk – he was alone; as I came up the hill I could see him standing in the cart, scattering manure over the bare red fields; I could hear his voice calling now and then to the mare, and the creak and clank of the cart as it moved on. Starlings and smart wagtails were running briskly over the clods, and many little birds flashed, fluttered, hopped here and there. The lapwings wheeled and cried as ever between the low clouds and the earth, and some ran beautifully among the furrows, too graceful and glistening for the rough field.

I took a fork and scattered the manure along the hollows, and thus we worked, with a wide field between us, yet very near in the sense of intimacy. I watched him through the wheeling peewits, as the low clouds went stealthily overhead. Beneath us, the spires of the poplars in the spinney were warm gold, as if the blood shone through. Further gleamed the grey water, and below it the red roofs. Nethermere was half hidden, and far away. There was nothing in this grey, lonely world but the peewits swinging and crying, and George swinging silently at his work. The movement of active life held all my attention, and when I looked up, it was to see the motion of his limbs and his head, the rise and fall of his rhythmic body, and the rise and fall of the slow waving peewits. After a while, when the cart was empty, he took a fork and came towards me, working at my task.

It began to rain, so he brought a sack from the cart, and we crushed ourselves under the thick hedge. We sat close together and watched the rain fall like a grey striped curtain before us, hiding the valley; we watched it trickle in dark streams off the mare's back, as she stood dejectedly; we listened to the swish of the drops falling all about; we felt the chill of the rain, and drew ourselves together in silence. He smoked his pipe, and I lit a cigarette. The rain continued; all the little pebbles and the red earth glistened in the grey gloom. We sat together, speaking occasionally. It was at these times we formed the almost passionate attachment which later years slowly wore away.

When the rain was over, we filled our buckets with potatoes, and went along the wet furrows, sticking the spritted tubers in the cold ground. Being sandy, the field dried quickly. About twelve o'clock, when nearly all the potatoes were set, he left me and, fetching up Bob from the far hedge-side, harnessed the mare and him to the ridger, to cover the potatoes. The sharp light plough turned the soil in a fine furrow over the potatoes; hosts of little birds fluttered, settled, bounded off again after the plough. He called to the horses, and they came downhill, the white stars on the two brown noses nodding up and down, George striding firm and heavy behind. They came down upon me; at a call the horses turned, shifting awkwardly sideways; he flung himself against the plough and, leaning well in, brought it round with a sweep: a click, and they are off uphill again. There is a great rustle as the birds sweep round after him and follow up the new-turned furrow. Untackling the horses when the rows were all covered, we tramped behind them down the wet hillside to dinner.

I kicked through the drenched grass, crushing the withered cowslips under my clogs, avoiding the purple orchids that were stunted with harsh upbringing but magnificent in their powerful colouring, crushing the pallid lady smocks, the washed-out wild gillivers. I became conscious of something near my feet, something little and dark, moving indefinitely. I had found again the larkie's nest. I perceived the yellow beaks, the bulging eyelids of two tiny larks, and the blue lines of their wing quills. The indefinite movement was the swift rise and fall of the brown fledged backs, over which waved long strands of fine down. The two little specks of birds lay side by side, beak to beak, their tiny bodies rising and falling in quick unison. I gently put down my fingers to touch them; they were warm; gratifying to find them warm, in the midst of so much cold and wet. I became curiously absorbed in them, as an eddy of wind stirred the strands of down. When one fledgling moved uneasily, shifting his soft ball, I was quite excited; but he nestled down again, with his head close to his brother's. In my heart of hearts, I longed for someone to nestle against, someone who would come between me and the coldness and wetness of the surroundings. I envied the two little miracles exposed to any tread, yet so serene. It seemed as if I were always wandering, looking for something which they had found even before the light broke into their shell. I was cold; the lilacs in the mill garden looked blue and perished. I ran with my heavy clogs and my heart heavy with vague longing, down to the mill, while the wind blanched the sycamores, and pushed the sullen pines rudely, for the pines were sulking because their million creamy sprites could not fly wet-winged. The horse-chestnuts bravely kept their white candles erect in the socket of every bough, though no sun came to light them. Drearily a cold swan swept up the water, trailing its black feet, clacking its great hollow wings, rocking the frightened water hens, and insulting the staid black-necked geese. What did I want that I turned thus from one thing to another?

~ ~ ~

At the end of June the weather became fine again. Hay harvest was to begin as soon as it settled. There were only two fields to be mown this year, to provide just enough stuff to last until the spring. As my vacation had begun, I decided I would help, and that we three, the father, George, and I, would get in the hay without hired assistance.

I rose the first morning very early, before the sun was well up. The clear sound of challenging cocks could be heard along the valley. In the bottoms, over the water and over the lush wet grass, the night mist still stood white and substantial. As I passed along the edge of the meadow the cow-parsnip was as tall as I, frothing up to the top of the hedge, putting the faded hawthorn to a wan blush. Little, early birds – I had not heard the lark – fluttered in and out of the foamy meadow-sea, plunging under the surf of flowers washed high in one corner, swinging out again, dashing past the crimson sorrel cresset. Under the froth of flowers were the purple vetch-clumps, yellow milk vetches, and the scattered pink of the wood-betony, and the floating stars of marguerites. There was a weight of honeysuckle on the hedges, where pink roses were waking up for their broad-spread flight through the day.

Morning silvered the swaths of the far meadow, and swept in smooth, brilliant curves round the stones of the brook; morning ran in my veins; morning chased the silver, darting fish out of the depth, and I, who saw them, snapped my fingers at them, driving them back.

I heard Trip barking, so I ran towards the pond. The punt was at the island, where from behind the bushes I could hear George whistling. I called to him, and he came to the water's edge half dressed.

'Fetch a towel,' he called, 'and come on.'

I was back in a few moments, and there stood my Charon fluttering in the cool air. One good push sent us to the islet. I made haste to undress, for he was ready for the water, Trip dancing round, barking with excitement at his new appearance.

'He wonders what's happened to me,' he said, laughing, pushing the dog playfully away with his bare foot. Trip bounded back, and came leaping up, licking him with little caressing licks. He began to play with the dog, and directly they were rolling on the fine turf, the laughing, expostulating, naked man and the excited dog, who thrust his great head onto the man's face, licking, and, when flung away, rushed forward again, snapping playfully at the naked arms and breasts. At last George lay back, laughing and panting, holding Trip by the two forefeet, which were planted on his breast, while the dog, also panting, reached forward his head for a flickering lick at the throat pressed back on the grass, and the mouth thrown back out of reach. When the man had thus lain still for a few moments, and the dog was just laying his head against his master's neck to rest too, I called, and George jumped up, and plunged into the pond with me, Trip after us.

The water was icily cold, and for a moment deprived me of my senses. When I began to swim, soon the water was buoyant, and I was sensible of nothing but the vigorous poetry of action. I saw George swimming on his back laughing at me, and in an instant I had flung myself like an impulse after him. The laughing face vanished as he swung over and fled, and I pursued the dark head and the ruddy neck. Trip, the wretch, came paddling towards me, interrupting me; then, all bewildered with excitement, he scudded to the bank. I chuckled to myself as I saw him run along, then plunge in and go plodding to George. I was gaining. He tried to drive off the dog, and I gained rapidly. As I came up to him and caught him, with my hand on his shoulder, there came a laughter from the bank. It was Emily.

I trod the water and threw handfuls of spray at her. She laughed and blushed. Then Trip waded out to her, and she fled swiftly from his shower-bath. George was floating just beside me, looking up and laughing.

We stood and looked at each other as we rubbed ourselves dry. He was well proportioned, and naturally of handsome physique, heavily limbed. He laughed at me, telling me I was like one of Aubrey Beardsley's long, lean ugly fellows. I referred him to many classic examples of slenderness, declaring myself more exquisite than his grossness, which amused him.

But I had to give in, and bow to him, and he took on an indulgent, gentle manner. I laughed and submitted. For he knew how I admired the noble, white fruitfulness of his form. As I watched him, he stood in white relief against the mass of green. He polished his arm, holding it out straight and solid; he rubbed his hair into curls, while I watched the deep muscles of his shoulders and the bands standing out in his neck as he held it firm; I remembered the story of Annable.

He saw I had forgotten to continue my rubbing, and laughing he took hold of me and began to rub me briskly, as if I were a child, or rather, a woman he loved and did not fear. I left myself quite limply in his hands, and to get a better grip of me, he put his arm round me and pressed me against him, and the sweetness of the touch of our naked bodies one against the other was superb. It satisfied in some measure the vague, indecipherable yearning of my soul; and it was the same with him. When he had rubbed me all warm, he let me go, and we looked at each other with eyes of still laughter, and our love was perfect for a moment, more perfect than any love I have known since, either for man or woman.

We went together down to the fields, he to mow the island of grass he had left standing the previous evening, I to sharpen the machine knife, to mow out the hedge-bottoms with the scythe, and to rake the swaths from the way of the machine when the unmown grass was reduced to a triangle. The cool, moist fragrance of the morning, the intentional stillness of everything, of the tall bluish trees, of the wet, frank flowers, of the trustful moths folded and unfolded in the fallen swaths, was a perfect medium of sympathy. The horses moved with a still dignity, obeying his commands. When they were harnessed, and the machine oiled, still he was looking loth to mar the perfect morning, but stood looking down the valley.

'I shan't mow these fields any more,' he said, and the fallen, silvered swaths flickered back his regret, and the faint scent of the limes was wistful. So much of the field was cut, so much remained to cut; then it was ended.

This year the elder flowers were widespread over the corner bushes, and the pink roses fluttered high above the hedge. There were the same flowers in the grass as we had known many years; we should not know them any more.

'But merely to have mown them is worth having lived for,' he said, looking at me.

We felt the warmth of the sun trickling through the morning's mist of coolness.

'You see that sycamore,' he said, 'that bushy one beyond the big willow? I remember when father broke off the leading shoot because he wanted a fine straight stick, I can remember I felt sorry. It was running up so straight, with such a fine balance of leaves – you know how a young strong sycamore looks about nine feet high – it seemed a cruelty. When you are gone, and we are left from here, I shall feel like that, as if my leading shoot were broken off. You see, the tree is spoiled. Yet how it went on growing. I believe I shall grow faster. I can remember the bright red stalks of the leaves as he broke them off from the bough.'

He smiled at me, half proud of his speech. Then he swung into the seat of the machine, having attended to the horses' heads. He lifted the knife.

'Good-bye,' he said, smiling whimsically back at me. The machine started. The bed of the knife fell, and the grass shivered and dropped over. I watched the heads of the daisies and the splendid lines of the cocksfool grass quiver, shake against the crimson burnet, and drop over. The machine went singing down the field, leaving a track of smooth, velvet green in the way of the swath-board. The flowers in the wall of uncut grass waited unmoved, as the days wait for us. The sun caught in the up-licking scarlet sorrel flames, the butterflies woke, and I could hear the fine ring of his 'Whoa!' from the far corner. Then he turned, and I could see only the tossing ears of the horses, and the white of his shoulder, as they moved along the wall of the high grass on the hill slope. I sat down under the elm, to file the sections of the knife. Always as he rode he watched the falling swath, only occasionally calling the horses into line. It was his voice which rang the morning awake. When we were at work we hardly noticed one another. Yet his mother had said:

'George is so glad when you're in the field – he doesn't care how long the day is.'

Later, when the morning was hot, and the honeysuckle had ceased to breathe, and all the other scents were moving in the air about us, when all the field was down, when I had seen the last trembling ecstasy of the harebells, trembling to fall; when the thick clump of purple vetch had sunk; when the green swaths were settling, and the silver swaths were glistening and glittering as the sun came along them, in the hot ripe morning we worked together turning the hay, tipping over the yesterday's swaths with our forks, and bringing yesterday's fresh, hidden flowers into the death of sunlight.

It was then that we talked of the past, and speculated on the future. As the day grew older, and less wistful, we forgot everything, and worked on, singing, and sometimes I would recite him verses as we went, and sometimes I would tell him about books. Life was full of glamour for us both.

E. M. FORSTER

THE POINT OF IT

I

'I don't see the point of it,' said Micky, through much imbecile laughter. Harold went on rowing. They had spent too long on the sand-dunes, and now the tide was running out of the estuary strongly. The sun was setting, the fields on the opposite bank shone bright, and the farm-house where they were stopping glowed from its upper windows as though filled to the brim with fire.

'We're going to be carried out to sea,' Micky continued. 'You'll never win unless you bust yourself a bit, and you a poor invalid, too. I back the sea.'

They were reaching the central channel, the backbone, as it were, of the retreating waters. Once past it, the force of the tide would slacken, and they would have easy going until they beached under the farm. It was a glorious evening. It had been a most glorious day. They had rowed out to the dunes at the slack, bathed, raced, eaten, slept, bathed and raced and eaten again. Micky was in roaring spirits. God had never thwarted him

---

E. M. Forster (1879–1970): Shortly after the appearance of A Passage to India *in 1924, Forster made the decision no longer to publish fiction: he felt that he could not, in good conscience, continue to write novels and stories that took place in a heterosexual milieu. As he observed late in his life: 'I should have been a more famous writer if I had written or rather published more, but sex prevented the latter.'*

    'The Point of It' was published in 1911, and included in the collection The Eternal Moment.

hitherto, and he could not suppose that they would really be made late for supper by an ebbing tide. When they came to the channel, and the boat, which had been slowly edging upstream, hung motionless among the moving waters, he lost all semblance of sanity, and shouted:

> *It may be that the gulfs will wash us down,*
> *It may be we shall touch the Happy Isles,*
> *And see the great Achilles, whom we knew.*

Harold, who did not care for poetry, only shouted. His spirits also were roaring, and he neither looked nor felt a poor invalid. Science had talked to him seriously of late, shaking her head at his sunburnt body. What should Science know? She had sent him down to the sea to recruit, and Micky to see that he did not tire himself. Micky had been a nuisance at first, but common sense had prevailed, as it always does among the young. A fortnight ago, he would not let the patient handle an oar. Now he bid him bust himself, and Harold took him at his word and did so. He made himself all will and muscle. He began not to know where he was. The thrill of the stretcher against his feet, and of the tide up his arms, merged with his friend's voice towards one nameless sensation; he was approaching the mystic state that is the athlete's true though unacknowledged goal: he was beginning to be.

Micky chanted, 'One, two – one, two,' and tried to help by twitching the rudder. But Micky had imagination. He looked at the flaming windows and fancied that the farm was a star and the boat its attendant satellite. Then the tide was the rushing ether stream of the universe, the interstellar surge that beats for ever. How jolly! He did not formulate his joys, after the weary fashion of older people. He was far too happy to be thankful. 'Remember now thy Creator in the days of thy youth' are the words of one who has left his youth behind, and all that Micky sang was 'One, two'.

Harold laughed without hearing. Sweat poured off his forehead. He put on a spurt, as did the tide.

'Wish the doctor could see you,' cried Micky.

No answer. Setting his teeth, he went berserk. His ancestors called to him that it was better to die than to be beaten by the sea. He rowed with gasps and angry little cries, while the voice of the helmsman lashed him to fury.

'That's right – one, two – plug it in harder . . . Oh, I say, this is a bit stiff, though. Let's give it up, old man, perhaps.'

The gulls were about them now. Some wheeled overhead, others bobbed past on the furrowed waters. The song of a lark came faintly from the land, and Micky saw the doctor's trap driving along the road that led to the farm. He felt ashamed.

'Look here, Harold, you oughtn't to – I oughtn't to have let you. I – I don't see the point of it.'

'Don't you?' said Harold with curious distinctness. 'Well, you will some day', and so saying dropped both oars. The boat spun round at this, the farm, the trap, the song of the lark vanished, and he fell heavily against the rowlock. Micky caught at him. He had strained his heart. Half in the boat and half out of it, he died, a rotten business.

II

A rotten business. It happened when Michael was twenty-two, and he expected never to be happy again. The sound of his own voice shouting as he was carried out, the doctor's voice saying 'I consider you responsible', the coming of Harold's parents, the voice of the curate summarizing Harold's relations with the unseen – all these things affected him so deeply that he supposed they would affect him for ever. They did not, because he lived to be over seventy, and with the best will in the world, it is impossible to remember clearly for so long. The mind, however sensitive and affectionate, is coated with new experiences daily; it cannot clear itself of the steady accretion, and is forced either to forget the past or to distort it. So it was with Michael. In time only the more dramatic incidents survived. He remembered Harold's final gesture (one hand grasping his own, the other plunged deep into the sea), because there was a certain aesthetic quality about it, not because it was the last of his friend. He remembered the final words for the same reason. 'Don't you see the point of it? Well, you will some day.' The phrase struck his fancy, and passed into his own stock; after thirty or forty years he forgot its origin. He is not to blame; the business of life snowed him under.

There is also this to say: he and Harold had nothing in common except youth. No spiritual bond could survive. They had never discussed theology or social reform, or any of the problems that were thronging Michael's brain, and consequently, though they had been intimate enough, there was nothing to remember. Harold melted the more one thought of him. Robbed of his body, he was so shadowy. Nor could one imagine him as a departed spirit, for the world beyond death is surely august. Neither in heaven nor hell is there place for athletics and aimless good temper, and if these were taken from Harold, what was left? Even if the unseen life should prove an archetype of this, even if it should contain a sun and stars of its own, the sunburn of earth must fade off our faces as we look at it, the muscles of earth must wither before we can go rowing on its infinite sea. Michael sadly resigned his friend to God's mercy. He himself could do nothing, for men can only immortalize those who leave behind them some strong impression of poetry or wisdom.

For himself he expected another fate. With all humility, he knew that he was not as Harold. It was no merit of his own, but he had been born of a more intellectual stock, and had inherited powers that rendered him worthier of life, and of whatever may come after it. He cared for the universe, for the tiny tangle in it that we call civilization, for his fellow-men who had made the tangle and who transcended it. Love, the love of humanity, warmed him; and even when he was thinking of other matters, was looking at Orion perhaps in the cold winter evenings, a pang of joy, too sweet for description, would thrill him, and he would feel sure that our highest impulses have some eternal value, and will be completed hereafter. So full a nature could not brood over death.

To summarize his career.

Soon after the tragedy, when he in his turn was recruiting, he met the woman who was to become his helpmate through life. He had met her once before, and had not liked her; she had seemed uncharitable and hard. Now he saw that her hardness sprang from a morality that he himself lacked. If he believed in love, Janet believed in truth. She tested all men and all things. She had no patience with the sentimentalist who shelters from the world's rough and tumble. Engaged at that time to another man, she spoke more freely to Michael than she would otherwise have done, and told him that it is not enough to feel good and to feel that others are good; one's business is to make others better, and she urged him to adopt a profession. The beauty of honest work dawned upon the youth as she spoke. Mentally and physically, he came to full manhood, and, after due preparation, he entered the Home Civil Service – the British Museum.

Here began a career that was rather notable, and wholly beneficial to humanity. With his ideals of conduct and culture, Michael was not content with the official routine. He desired to help others, and, since he was gifted with tact, they consented to the operation. Before long he became a conciliatory force in his department. He could mollify his superiors, encourage his inferiors, soothe foreign scholars, and show that there is something to be said for all sides. Janet, who watched his rise, taxed him again with instability. But now she was wrong. The young man was not a mere opportunist. He always had a sincere opinion of his own, or he could not have retained the respect of his colleagues. It was really the inherent sweetness of his nature at work, turned by a woman's influence towards fruitful ends.

At the end of a ten years' acquaintance the two married. In the interval Janet had suffered much pain, for the man to whom she had been engaged had proved unworthy of her. Her character was set when she came to Michael, and, as he knew, strongly contrasted with his own; and perhaps they had already interchanged all the good they could. But the marriage proved durable and sufficiently happy. He, in particular, made endless allowances, for toleration and sympathy were becoming the cardinal points of his nature. If his wife was unfair to the official mind, or if his brother-in-law, an atheist, denounced religion, he would say to himself, 'They cannot help it; they are made thus, and have the qualities of their defects. Let me rather think of my own, and strive for a wider outlook ceaselessly.' He grew sweeter every day.

It was partly this desire for a wider outlook that turned him to literature. As he was crossing the forties it occurred to him to write a few essays, somewhat retrospective in tone, and thoughtful rather than profound in content. They had some success. Their good taste, their lucid style, the tempered Christianity of their ethics, whetted the half-educated public and made it think and feel. They were not, and were not intended to be, great literature, but they opened the doors to it, and were indubitably a power for good. The first volume was followed by 'The Confessions of a Middle-aged Man'. In it Michael paid melodious tribute to youth, but showed that ripeness is all. Experience, he taught, is the only humanizer; sympathy, balance and manysidedness cannot come to a man until he is elderly. It is always pleasant to be told that the best is yet to be, and the sale of the book was large. Perhaps he would have become a popular author, but his wife's influence restrained him from writing anything that he did not sincerely feel. She had borne him three children by now – Henry, Catherine, and Adam. On the whole they were a happy family. Henry never gave any trouble. Catherine took after her mother. Adam, who was wild and uncouth, caused his father some anxiety. He could not understand him, in spite of careful observation, and they never became real friends. Still, it was but a little cloud in a large horizon. At home, as in his work, Michael was more successful than most men.

Thus he slipped into the fifties. On the death of his father he inherited a house in the Surrey hills, and Janet, whose real interests were horticultural, settled down there. After all, she had not proved an intellectual woman. Her fierce manner had misled him and perhaps herself into believing it. She was efficient enough in London society, but it bored her, for she lacked her husband's pliancy, and aged more rapidly than he did. Nor did the country suit her. She grew querulous, disputing with other ladies about the names of flowers. And, of course, the years were not without their effect on him, too. By now he was somewhat of a valetudinarian. He had given up all outdoor sports, and, though his health remained good, grew bald, and rather stout and timid. He was against late hours, violent exercise, night walks, swimming when hot, muddling about in open boats, and he often had to check himself from fidgeting the children. Henry, a charming sympathetic lad, would squeeze his hand and say, 'All right, Father.' But Catherine and Adam sometimes frowned. He thought of the children more and more. Now that his wife was declining, they were the future, and he was determined to keep in touch with them, remembering how his own father had failed with him. He believed in gentleness, and often stood between them and their mother. When the boys grew up he let them choose their own friends. When Catherine, at the age of nineteen, asked if she might go away and earn some money as a lady gardener, he let her go. In this case he had his reward, for Catherine, having killed the flowers, returned. She was a restless, scowling young woman, a trial to her mother, who could not imagine what girls were coming to. Then she married and improved greatly; indeed, she proved his chief support in the coming years.

For, soon after her marriage, a great trouble fell on him. Janet became bedridden, and, after a protracted illness, passed into the unknown. Sir Michael – for he had been knighted – declared that he should not survive her. They were so accustomed to each other, so mutually necessary, that he fully expected to pass away after her. In this he was mistaken. She died when he was sixty, and he lived to be over seventy. His character had passed beyond the clutch of circumstance and he still retained his old interests and his unconquerable benignity.

A second trouble followed hard on the first. It transpired that Adam was devoted to his mother, and had only tolerated home life for her sake. After a brutal scene he left. He wrote from the Argentine that he was sorry, but wanted to start for himself. 'I don't see the point of it,' quavered Sir Michael. 'Have I ever stopped him or any of you from starting?' Henry and Catherine agreed with him. Yet he felt that they understood their brother better than he did. 'I have given him freedom all his life,' he continued. 'I have given him freedom, what more does he want?' Henry, after hesitation, said, 'There are some people who feel that freedom cannot be given. At least I have heard so. Perhaps Adam is like that. Unless he took freedom he might not feel free.' Sir Michael disagreed. 'I have now studied adolescence for many years,' he replied, 'and your conclusions, my dear boy, are ridiculous.'

The two rallied to their father gallantly; and, after all, he spent a dignified old age. Having retired from the British Museum, he produced a little aftermath of literature. The great public had forgotten him, but the courtliness of his 'Musings of a Pensioner' procured him some circulation among elderly and educated audiences. And he found a new spiritual consolation. *Anima naturaliter Anglicana*, he had never been hostile to the Established Church; and, when he criticized her worldliness and occasional inhumanity, had spoken as one who was outside her rather than against her. After his wife's death and the flight of his son, he lost any lingering taste for speculation. The experience of years disposed him to accept the experience of centuries, and to merge his feeble personal note in the great voice of tradition. Yes; a serene and dignified old age. Few grudged it to him. Of course, he had enemies, who professed to see through him, and said that Adam had seen through him too; but no impartial observer agreed. No ulterior motive had ever biassed Sir Michael. The purity of his record was not due to luck but to purity within, and his conciliatory manner sprang from a conciliated soul. He could look back on failures and mistakes, and he had not carried out the ideals of his youth. Who has? But he had succeeded better than most men in modifying those ideals to fit the world of facts, and if love had been modified into sympathy and sympathy into compromise, let one of his contemporaries cast the first stone.

One fact remained – the fact of death. Hitherto, Sir Michael had never died, and at times he was bestially afraid. But more often death appeared as a prolongation of his present career. He saw himself quietly and tactfully organizing some corner in infinity with his wife's assistance; Janet would be greatly improved. He saw himself passing from a sphere in which he had been efficient into a sphere which combined the familiar with the eternal, and in which he would be equally efficient – passing into it with dignity and without pain. This life is a preparation for the next. Those who live longest are consequently the best prepared. Experience is the great teacher; blessed are the experienced, for they need not further modify their ideals.

The manner of his death was as follows. He, too, met with an accident. He was walking from his town house to Catherine's by a short cut through a slum; some women were quarrelling about a fish, and as he passed they appealed to him. Always courteous, the old man stopped, said that he had not sufficient data to judge on, and advised them to lay the fish aside for twenty-four hours. This chanced to annoy them, and they grew more angry with him than with one another. They accused him of 'doing them', of 'getting round them', and one, who was the worse for drink, said, 'See if he gets round that', and slapped him with the fish in the face. He fell. When he came to himself he was lying in bed with one of his headaches.

He could hear Catherine's voice. She annoyed him. If he did not open his eyes, it was only because he did not choose.

'He has been like this for nearly two years,' said Henry's voice.

It was, at the most, ten minutes since he had fallen in the slum. But he did not choose to argue.

'Yes, he's pretty well played out,' said a third voice – actually the voice of Adam; how and when had Adam returned? 'But, then, he's been that for the last thirty years.'

'Gently, old boy,' said Henry.

'Well, he has,' said Adam. 'I don't believe in cant. He never did anything since Mother died, and damned little before. They've forgotten his books because they aren't first-hand; they're rearranging the cases he arranged in the British Museum. That's the lot. What else has he done except tell people to dress warmly but not too warm?'

'Adam, you really mustn't –'

'It's because nobody speaks up that men of the old man's type get famous. It's a sign of your sloppy civilization. You're all afraid – afraid of originality, afraid of work, afraid of hurting one another's feelings. You let anyone come to the top who doesn't frighten you, and as soon as he dies you forget him and knight some other figurehead instead.'

An unknown voice said, 'Shocking, Mr Adam, shocking. Such a dear old man, and quite celebrated, too.'

'You'll soon get used to me, nurse.'

The nurse laughed.

'Adam, it is a relief to have you,' said Catherine after a pause. 'I want you and your boy to help me with mine.' Her voice sounded dimmer; she had turned from her father without a word of farewell. 'One must profit by the mistakes of others . . . after all, more heroism . . . I am determined to keep in touch with my boy –'

'Larrup him,' said Adam. 'That's the secret.' He followed his sister out of the room.

Then Henry's delightful laugh sounded for the last time. 'You make us all feel twenty years younger,' he said; 'more like when –'

The door shut.

Sir Michael grew cold with rage. This was life, this was what the younger generation had been thinking. Adam he ignored, but at the recollection of Henry and Catherine he determined to die. If he chose, he could have risen from bed and driven the whole pack into the street. But he did not choose. He chose rather to leave this shoddy and ungrateful world. The immense and superhuman cynicism that is latent in all of us came at last to the top and transformed him. He saw the absurdity of love, and the vision so tickled him that he began to laugh. The nurse, who had called him a dear old man, bent over him, and at the same moment two boys came into the sick-room.

'How's grandpapa?' asked one of them – Catherine's boy.

'Not so well,' the nurse answered.

There was a silence. Then the other boy said, 'Come along, let's cut.'

'But they told us not to.'

'Why should we do what old people tell us? Dad's pretty well played out, and so's your mother.'

'Shocking; be off with you both,' said the nurse; and, with a little croon of admiration, Catherine's boy followed his cousin out of the room. Their grandfather's mirth increased. He rolled about in the bed; and, just as he was grasping the full irony of the situation, he died, and pursued it into the unknown.

III

Micky was still in bed. He was aware of so much through long melancholy dreams. But when he opened his mouth to laugh, it filled with dust. Choosing to open his eyes, he found that he had swollen enormously, and lay sunk in the sand of an illimitable plain. As he expected, he had no occasion greatly to modify his ideals; infinity had merely taken the place of his bedroom and of London. Nothing moved on its surface except a few sand-pillars, which would sometimes merge into each other as though confabulating, and then fall with a slight hiss. Save for these, there was no motion, no noise, nor could he feel any wind.

How long had he lain here? Perhaps for years, long before death perhaps, while his body seemed to be walking among men. Life is so short and trivial, that who knows whether we arrive for it entirely, whether more than a fraction of the soul is aroused to put on flesh? The bud and the blossom perish in a moment, the husk endures, and may not the soul be a husk? It seemed to Micky that he had lain in the dust for ever, suffering and sneering, and that the essence of all things, the primal power that lies behind the stars, is senility. Age, toothless, dropsical age; ungenerous to age and to youth; born before all ages, and outlasting them; the universe as old age.

The place degraded while it tortured. It was vast, yet ignoble. It sloped downward into darkness and upward into cloud, but into what darkness, what clouds! No tragic splendour glorified them. When he looked at them he understood why he was so unhappy, for they were looking at him, sneering at him while he sneered. Their dirtiness was more ancient than the hues of day and night, their irony more profound; he was part of their jest, even as youth was part of his, and slowly he realized that he was, and had for some years been, in Hell.

All around him lay other figures, huge and fungous. It was as if the plain had festered. Some of them could sit up, others scarcely protruded from the sand, and he knew that they had made the same mistake in life as himself, though he did not know yet what the mistake had been; probably some little slip, easily avoided had one but been told.

Speech was permissible. Presently a voice said, 'Is not ours a heavenly sky? Is it not beautiful?'

'Most beautiful,' answered Micky, and found each word a stab of pain. Then he knew that one of the sins here punished was appreciation; he was suffering for all the praise that he had given to the bad and mediocre upon earth; when he had praised out of idleness, or to please people, or to encourage people; for all the praise that had not been winged with passion. He repeated 'Most beautiful,' and the sky quivered, for he was entering into fuller torments now. One ray of happiness survived: his wife could not be in this place. She had not sinned with the people of the plain, and could not suffer their distortion. Her view of life had proved right after all; and, in his utter misery, this comforted him. Janet should again be his religion, and as eternity dragged forward and returned upon itself and dragged forward she would show him that old age, if rightly managed, can be beautiful; that experience, if rightly received, can lead the soul of men to bliss. Then he turned to his neighbour, who was continuing his hymn of praise.

'I could lie here for ever,' he was saying. 'When I think of my restlessness during life – that is to say, during what men miscall life, for it is death really – this is life – when I think of my restlessness on earth, I am overcome by so much goodness and mercy, I could lie here for ever.'

'And will you?' asked Micky.

'Ah, that is the crowning blessing – I shall, and so will you.'

Here a pillar of sand passed between them. It was long before they could speak or see. Then Micky took up the song, chafed by the particles that were working into his soul.

'I, too, regret my wasted hours,' he said, 'especially the hours of my youth. I regret all the time I spent in the sun. In later years I did repent, and that is why I am admitted here where there is no sun; yes, and no wind and none of the stars that drove me almost mad at night once. It would be appalling, would it not, to see Orion again, the central star of whose sword is not a star but a nebula, the golden seed of worlds to be? How I dreaded the autumn on earth when Orion rises, for he recalled adventure and my youth. It was appalling. How thankful I am to see him no more.'

'Ah, but it was worse,' cried the other, 'to look high leftward from Orion and see the Twins. Castor and Pollux were brothers, one human, the other divine; and Castor died. But Pollux went down to Hell that he might be with him.'

'Yes; that is so. Pollux went into Hell.'

'Then the gods had pity on both, and raised them aloft to be stars whom sailors worship, and all who love and are young. Zeus was their father, Helen their sister, who brought the Greeks against Troy. I dreaded them more than Orion.'

They were silent, watching their own sky. It approved. They had been cultivated men on earth, and these are capable of the nicer torments hereafter. Their memories will strike exquisite images to enhance their pain. 'I will speak no more,' said Micky to himself. 'I will be silent through eternity.' But the darkness prised open his lips, and immediately he was speaking.

'Tell me more about this abode of bliss,' he asked. 'Are there grades in it? Are there ranks in our heaven?'

'There are two heavens,' the other replied, 'the heaven of the hard and of the soft. We here lie in the heaven of the soft. It is a sufficient arrangement, for all men grow either hard or soft as they grow old.'

As he spoke the clouds lifted, and, looking up the slope of the plain, Micky saw that in the distance it was bounded by mountains of stone, and he knew, without being told, that among those mountains Janet lay, rigid, and that he should never see her. She had not been saved. The darkness would mock her, too, for ever. With him lay the sentimentalists, the conciliators, the peace-makers, the humanists, and all who have trusted the warmer vision; with his wife were the reformers and ascetics and all sword-like souls. By different paths they had come to Hell, and Micky now saw what the bustle of life conceals: that the years are bound either to liquefy a man or to stiffen him, and that Love and Truth, who seem to contend for our souls like angels, hold each the seeds of our decay.

'It is, indeed, a sufficient arrangement,' he said; 'both sufficient and simple. But answer one question more that my bliss may be perfected; in which of these two heavens are the young?'

His neighbour answered, 'In neither; there are no young.'

He spoke no more, and settled himself more deeply in the dust. Micky did the same. He had vague memories of men and women who had died before reaching maturity, of boys and unwedded maidens and youths lowered into the grave before their parents' eyes. Whither had they gone, that undeveloped minority? What was the point of their brief existence? Had they vanished utterly, or were they given another chance of accreting experiences until they became like Janet or himself? One thing was certain: there were no young, either in the mountains or the plain, and perhaps the very memory of such creatures was an illusion fostered by cloud.

The time was now ripe for a review of his life on earth. He traced his decomposition – his work had been soft, his books soft, he had softened his relations with other men. He had seen good in everything, and this is itself a sign of decay. Whatever occurred he had been appreciative, tolerant, pliant. Consequently he had been a success; Adam was right; it was the moment in civilization for his type. He had mistaken self-criticism for self-discipline, he had muffled in himself and others the keen, heroic edge. Yet the luxury of repentance was denied him. The fault was his, but the fate humanity's, for everyone grows hard or soft as he grows old.

'This is my life,' thought Micky; 'my books forgotten, my work superseded. This is the whole of my life.' And his agony increased, because all the same there had been in that life an elusive joy which, if only he could have distilled it, would have sweetened infinity. It was part of the jest that he should try, and should eternally oscillate between disgust and desire. For there is nothing ultimate in Hell; men will not lay aside all hope on entering it, or they would attain to the splendour of despair. To have made a poem about Hell is to mistake its very essence; it is the imaginations of men, who will have beauty, that fashion it as ice or flame. Old, but capable of growing older, Micky lay in the sandy country, remembering that once he had remembered a country – a country that had not been sand . . .

He was aroused by the mutterings of the spirits round him. An uneasiness such as he had not noted in them before had arisen. 'A pillar of sand,' said one. Another said, 'It is not; it comes from the river.'

He asked, 'What river?'

'The spirits of the damned dwell over it; we never speak of that river.'

'Is it a broad river?'

'Swift, and very broad.'

'Do the damned ever cross it?'

'They are permitted, we know not why, to cross it now and again.'

And in these answers he caught a new tone, as if his companions were frightened, and were finding means to express their fear. When he said, 'With permission, they can do us no harm,' he was answered, 'They harm us with light and a song.' And again, 'They harm us because they remember and try to remind.'

'Of what would they remind us?'

'Of the hour when we were as they.'

As he questioned a whisper arose from the low-lying verges. The spirits were crying to each other faintly. He heard, 'It is coming; drive it back over the river, shatter it, compel it to be old.' And then the darkness was cloven, and a star of pain broke in his soul. He understood now; a torment greater than any was at hand.

'I was before choice,' came the song. 'I was before hardness and softness were divided. I was in the days when truth was love, and I am.'

All the plain was convulsed. But the invader could not be shattered. When it pressed the air parted and the sand-pillars fell, and its path was filled with senile weeping.

'I have been all men, but all men have forgotten me. I transfigured the world for them until they preferred the world. They came to me as children, afraid; I taught them, and they despised me. Childhood is a dream about me, experience a slow forgetting: I govern the magic years between them, and am.'

'Why trouble us?' moaned the shades. 'We could bear our torment, just bear it, until there was light and a song. Go back again over the river. This is Heaven, we were saying, that darkness is God; we could praise them till you came. The book of our deeds is closed; why open it? We were damned from our birth; leave it there. O, supreme jester, leave us. We have sinned, we know it, and this place is death and Hell.'

'Death comes,' the voice pealed, 'and death is not a dream or a forgetting. Death is real. But I, too, am real, and whom I will I save. I see the scheme of things, and in it no place for me, the brain and the body against me. Therefore I rend the scheme in two, and make a place, and under countless names have harrowed Hell. Come.' Then, in tones of inexpressible sweetness, 'Come to me all who remember. Come out of your eternity into mine. It is easy, for I am still at your eyes, waiting to look out of them; still in your hearts, waiting to beat. The years that I dwelt with you seemed short, but they were magical, and they outrun time.'

The shades were silent. They could not remember.

'Who desires to remember? Desire is enough. There is no abiding home for strength and beauty among men. The flower fades, the seas dry up in the sun, the sun and all the stars fade as a flower. But the desire for such things, that is eternal, that can abide, and he who desires me is I.'

Then Micky died a second death. This time he dissolved through terrible pain, scorched by the glare, pierced by the voice. But as he died he said, 'I do desire', and immediately the invader vanished, and he was standing alone on the sandy plain. It had been merely a dream. But he was standing. How was that? Why had he not thought to stand before? He had been unhappy in Hell, and all that he had to do was to go elsewhere. He passed downwards, pained no longer by the mockery of its cloud. The pillars brushed against him and fell, the nether darkness went over his head. On he went till he came to the banks of the infernal stream, and there he stumbled – stumbled over a piece of wood, no vague substance, but a piece of wood that had once belonged to a tree. At his impact it moved, and water gurgled against it. He had embarked. Someone was rowing. He could see the blades of oars moving towards him through the foam, but the rower was invisible in cloud. As they neared mid-channel the boat went more slowly, for the tide was ebbing, and Micky knew that once carried out he would be lost eternally; there was no second hope of salvation. He could not speak, but his heart beat time to the oars – one, two. Hell made her last effort, and all that is evil in creation, all the distortions of love and truth by which we are vexed, came surging down the estuary, and the boat hung motionless. Micky heard the pant of breath through the roaring, the crack of muscles; then he heard a voice say, 'The point of it . . .' and a weight fell off his body and he crossed mid-stream.

It was a glorious evening. The boat had sped without prelude into sunshine. The sky was cloudless, the earth gold, and gulls were riding up and down on the furrowed waters. On the bank they had left were some sand-dunes rising to majestic hills; on the bank in front was a farm, full to the brim with fire.

WILLIAM PLOMER
LOCAL COLOUR

U pon certain kinds of Nordics the effect of living in Mediterranean
countries is the reverse of bracing. The freedom, warmth and glamour of their surroundings begin to sap their intellectual or artistic activity
and ambition. They drift into idleness and weaken in will. While constantly
talking about what they are going to do and accomplish, they do nothing
and make nothing, and at last discover that in gaining liberty and sunshine
they have lost purpose and virility. It is a matter of taste and temperament.
You can't have everything.

But when the Nordic, young, enterprising and healthy, first finds
himself enjoying freedom, warmth, and glamour, the effect upon him is
indescribably delightful. He is without responsibilities, he has a susceptible
body and an impressionable mind; the sun warms his skin and the blood
sings in his veins. Life is full of promise, he is ready for anything, and if
anybody asks him if he doesn't feel the heat he says, 'No, I love it.'

Two people in this happy condition were sitting in basket chairs on
the veranda of the best hotel in Athens. They were English undergraduates

*WILLIAM PLOMER (1903–1973): Although Plomer wrote novels (among them Tur-
bott Wolfe, The Case is Altered and Museum Pieces), short stories, poetry, biographies,
memoirs and libretti (for Benjamin Britten), the only piece of his work now in print is a limited
edition of the story 'Local Colour,' published by Elysium Press with an introduction by Mark
Mitchell. Peter F. Alexander is the author of an outstanding biography of Plomer — also,
regrettably, out of print.*

who had come to spend the long vacation in Greece. But they were not sitting there alone. They had a guest – nobody less than Madame Hélène Strouthokámelos.

'Don't you feel the heat?' she said, looking from one to the other.

'Not a bit,' said Grant.

'We love it,' said Spencer.

It *was* extremely hot, all the same. The glare was dazzling. It was just that hour when nothing seems likely ever to cast a shadow again, and the air itself buzzes like a cicada. The young men, neatly dressed in light summer clothing, sat in easy attitudes, but there was much more assurance in their voices than in their feelings. They had brought a letter of introduction to Madame Strouthokámelos and in delivering it had added an invitation to lunch. And here she was in the flesh, and they felt rather shy. Spencer, the English one, was uneasy because he was wearing rather too pretty a tie, which he had bought in Paris, and Madame Strouthokámelos kept glancing at it every now and again as if it offered a clue to his soul. Grant, the Scotch one, had begun looking at the toes of his shoes, and that was always a bad sign with him. Just then an important looking man in a straw hat came up the steps, and catching sight of Madame Strouthokámelos made her an obsequious bow, to which she replied with a cool nod. *Cool*, that was it. It was her coolness that was so disconcerting.

She was neither young nor middle-aged. She had dignity without stiffness, she was handsome, healthy, powerful. There was no powder on her face, she wore no jewellery, and her clothes were simple. She had taken off her little soft hat, just as a girl might have done, with a single gesture and laid it on the table at her side, and now she sat there with her head, most appropriately, against a white marble background. Spencer was facing her, Grant saw her in profile, and if they had been in the presence of Juno herself they could scarcely have been more impressed.

Before meeting her they had tried to imagine what she would be like, and they had invented a perspiring Levantine matron in black which the sun had faded, with a bluish moustache, bad teeth, and voluble French. And here was Juno at forty, or the Venus of Milo come to life, a woman of noble proportions, with naturally wavy hair, black, becomingly streaked with grey, and drawn back from a smooth forehead, from a face with regular features supported grandly on a firm neck like a cylinder of honey-coloured marble. Her skin was clear and honey-coloured too, and it made the white of her eyes and her fine teeth seem to be ever so slightly tinged with very pale blue. Her strong arms were bare, and her cool dress hung loosely over her firm breasts and clung against her hips and thighs. So much for her appearance. She had a manner to match it.

She had once had a baby – but rather a small one. It often happens with amazonian, mammoth, or merely muscular women that their off-spring comes into the world as an embodied protest against size and strength – in fact, the little Strouthokámelos weighed at birth no more than four pounds. It was, however, her husband rather than her child who had mainly disappointed her. Had he been dutiful, she would no doubt have worn him out, but he was casual, and she lost him. Strouthokámelos had been a little too Greek in his nature for her taste – she had been 'finished' in Paris and Vienna, but they hadn't prepared her for what happened. And when it *did* happen she took pains to inform herself about aspects of life, of Greek life, to which she had hitherto paid little attention. And having been informed, she was resentful. What she could no longer ignore she blamed, frowned upon, or affected not to notice, according to circumstances. And whenever any reflection happened to be cast by foreigners upon the Greeks in general she hastened to proclaim her countrymen's conformity with Christian morality, with the finishing-school view of human nature, failing altogether to remind herself that they are scarcely a European people.

Madame Strouthokámelos was not a fool. She was very much the reverse. Like so many citizens of the lesser European countries she was an excellent linguist, equally at home in English, French, German and Italian. She had read a great deal and was still reading. She was a capable housewife, a born organizer and to some extent a woman of the world. She could stride through thistles in Thessaly, hold her own at the bridge table, make a speech or sack a maid, was a personal friend of the prime minister, and of course was fully equal to the present occasion. She glanced in the direction of the dining-room, and then said:

'Do you specially want us to have lunch here?'

'No,' said Spencer.

'Not if you know of anywhere better,' said Grant.

'Ah, I see you're the practical one,' she said, displaying her classical, milk-blue teeth. 'I don't know about *better*, but hotels are all the same everywhere. I think while you are in Greece you ought to do as the Greeks do. I know a little place down by the sea, towards Vouliagméni, where we could get a nice *Greek* lunch. Do you think you would like that?'

'We should love it,' said Spencer.

'I'm all for local colour,' said Grant.

'Ah, that's just it,' she said. 'If we go there, it will be *Greek*, whereas *this* . . .' She shrugged her shoulders, but there was a delicious smell of food wafted from the dining-room. 'Then we may as well go at once?' she said, rising to her feet.

Her hosts got up obediently. She was used to obedience.

'You've left your book behind,' she said to Spencer. 'What is it? May I see? Ah, Proust.'

'Do you like Proust?' said Spencer.

'He's very clever, of course, but I don't much care for the atmosphere.' Spencer popped *Sodome et Gomorrhe* into his pocket.

'And now,' she said, leading the way, 'we'd better get into a taxi.'

The taxis, open touring cars, were lined up under some pepper trees on the opposite side of the road. Madame Strouthokámelos waved away the svelte hotel porter as if he was an insect, led the way, chose a taxi, instructed the driver brusquely, and climbed in. Spencer and Grant exchanged glances and followed. She made them sit one on each side of her, and the taxi drove off, rushing down the Boulevard Amalia towards the sea.

'She doesn't like men,' thought Spencer.

'She despises us,' thought Grant.

'It isn't many miles,' said Madame Strouthokámelos, and began asking them the usual questions about how long they were going to stay, where they were going, and so on.

'I'm afraid we Greeks are rather misunderstood or misrepresented,' she said. 'But there is a wonderful new spirit in the people. The refugees from Asia Minor have increased the population enormously, and have helped to consolidate the national feeling. The younger generation, the Greeks of your age, are manly and patriotic. I think there is great hope for the future.'

'*Manly*,' thought Spencer. 'She's thinking of my tie.'

'What is she getting at?' Grant wondered. 'Is this propaganda?'

It was propaganda.

'So I hope,' she went on, 'that although you'll be here such a short time you'll really be able to get in touch with the people a little and get an idea of what they're really like. That's one reason why I'm taking you to this place for lunch. I don't suppose any foreigner's ever been there before.'

'That's much more interesting than the hotel,' said Grant.

'Much,' said Spencer a little half-heartedly, remembering the smell of the hotel lunch.

'Hotels are *so* much the same everywhere,' she repeated.

They had passed Phaleron, and the conversation turned to Byron. They sped towards Glyphada, along what was then one of the only two decent roads in Greece, and the asphalt was like burnished steel. There was almost no traffic at this time of day. The sea was like a fiery glass and Byron had given place to the Greek language. The road was about to be very bad, when Madame Strouthokámelos, employing that language with great determination, brought the car to a standstill. They all got out, and she waited for her hosts to pay the fare. Then she led the way across a piece of waste land to a little white house by the sea.

There was no path. The way was through loose, burning sand which filled one's shoes. There were some prickly bushes about. They passed a pine tree, sighing to itself. The rays of the sun seemed to be vertical. Presently there was a crazy notice-board decorated with broken fairy-lamps and the inscription P A N T H E O N.

'Here we are,' said Madame Strouthokámelos as if she owned the place.

And immediately a man came out to welcome them. He treated his visitor with deference – she was known to have influence in important circles; her bearing would have demanded respect in any case; and she had brought two young foreigners with her. Well, three lunches meant three profits. He led the trio round to the seaward side of the 'Pantheon.'

'Now, surely this is better than the hotel!' cried Madame Strouthokámelos.

And indeed it was.

A veranda thatched with myrtle branches, and floored with the earth itself, on which stood three round tables covered with coarse but clean table-cloths, and chairs; and only a few yards away, the Aegean sparkling like a million diamonds. There was even a suggestion of a breeze.

The table at the far end was occupied. Four men, workmen or peasants apparently, were seated there, eating a cheerful meal. Beyond them were some rocks and bushes. At the corner of the house a single plant of maize had grown to a great height. It looked very green and was in flower. Beneath it some fowls were enjoying a dust-bath, and tied to one of the veranda-posts was a goat, recumbent in the shade. With clear yellow eyes which looked as though they missed nothing and saw through everything it watched what was going on. It looked so independent that one could not tell whether it was enjoying what it saw, enjoying a cynical attitude to what it saw, or simply indulging in sheer observation for its own sake.

The proprietor approached Madame Strouthokámelos for orders. She took off her little soft hat again with the characteristic sweeping gesture, and then, with a clean, capable hand on which the nails were cut short like a man's, she patted her hair, though its wiry waves had not lost their shape.

'There's not much to choose from,' she remarked. 'Of course they weren't expecting us.'

'We leave the choosing to you,' said Grant.

She ordered red mullets, black olives, white bread, a tomato salad, with yaghourt and coffee to follow.

'It sounds marvellous,' said Spencer.

'You'd better taste it first,' she said. 'At least everything here will be fresh.'

The fact that she never wore gloves aided the general impression that she was 'classical' in appearance.

'And what are we going to drink?' she said.

Spencer stole a glance at the other table.

'What are *they* drinking?' he said.

'*Retsina*, probably,' said Madame Strouthokámelos. 'Do you know what that is? White wine with resin in it. It's very nice. Would you like to try some?'

Spencer and Grant said they would, though somebody had told them that it was perfectly revolting.

'I adore the goat,' said Spencer.

'Isn't *adore* rather a strong word?' said Madame Strouthokámelos. 'It seems to me it stinks slightly.' She laughed.

'Exactly what are those people?' said Grant, looking at the other table.

'Oh, just country boys. It's a pity you can't talk to them. Very cheerful, aren't they? And they're really typical.'

They were, indeed, very cheerful, and had just ordered some more wine.

'Would you like to offer them some cigarettes?' said Madame Strouthokámelos. 'They would be very pleased.'

'Would they?' said Grant, and crossed rather shyly to the other table with an open cigarette case. The 'country boys,' even more shyly, helped themselves. And Madame Strouthokámelos, leaning forward graciously, addressed them in Greek.

'These are two young Englishmen,' she said, 'visiting Greece for the first time.'

The country boys expressed interest.

'So I've brought them down here to lunch, so that they can see a bit of the *real* Greece.'

The country boys registered approval and pleasure.

'I see you've got a guitar there,' said Madame Strouthokámelos. 'Won't you sing for these foreigners?'

The country boys laughed and looked at each other and then addressed themselves to one of their number who wore a lilac shirt, urging him to play. He took up the guitar just as the food arrived for the foreigners.

In spite of the heat Spencer and Grant were hungry, and the pleasant atmosphere and the pretty song that was now being sung to the guitar combined to whet their appetites.

'What a delicious lunch,' said Spencer.

'Perfect,' said Grant.

'I'm so glad you're enjoying it,' said Madame Strouthokámelos, and then, turning to the country boys, she suggested another tune for them to play. Her manner was gracious and patronizing and did not go down with them very well. However, the tune she suggested happened to be a favourite with Lilac Shirt, so he soon struck up with it. Drink had made him confident, and vanity made him self-conscious, so he became rather noisy, laughed, and now and then flashed a glance at Spencer and Grant. Madame Strouthokámelos wore an indulgent smile and nodded a gracious acknowledgment.

Conversation turned to the *retsina*. Grant thought it even more disgusting than he had anticipated – it tasted to him like pure turpentine, and he did his best not to make a wry face as he swallowed it. Spencer, who was rather romantic, pretended to himself and to the others that he liked it.

'It has such a nice *piny* sort of taste,' he said. 'But I don't think I could put away quite as much as *they* do – not in the middle of the day, at any rate.'

As he spoke he indicated the country boys, who had opened a fresh lot of wine and were getting very merry.

'Is that what they do every day?' said Grant.

'No, I think they must be celebrating rather a special occasion.'

The proprietor appeared in the doorway, looking genial above his apron. Somebody else had taken the guitar now and was playing a rapid syncopated tune. Lilac Shirt was looking rather flushed. His shirt had come unbuttoned, revealing a lean brown chest, very hairy. He was supporting the head of one of his companions in his lap, and making remarks which surely *must* be ribald. Spencer stole a glance at Madame Strouthokámelos. Yes, sure enough, she was looking at her plate, and a faint frown now marred her rather too regular features. Then Spencer looked at Grant, and Grant looked at Spencer and kicked him under the table, then they both looked at the other table, on which somebody was beating with a spoon just to add to the noise of the guitar and the laughing and the singing.

'They *are* getting gay,' said Spencer, in an affectedly innocent tone of voice.

'They have been drinking a little too much,' said Madame Strouthoká-melos with an expression of something like distaste. 'Have you had enough to eat, or shall I order some cheese?'

'Aha,' thought Grant, 'she's trying to hurry us away just when it's beginning to get interesting.' And he said, 'Yes, please. I should like to try the cheese. I expect it's very good here.'

With obvious reluctance Madame Strouthokámelos ordered cheese. The proprietor made a laughing comment on his other visitors, but she did not reply.

At this moment one of the country boys rose to his feet. He was very slender, with lank black hair and rather sleepy-looking eyes. He was going to dance. The others clapped and uttered cries of delight, encouragement and facetiousness. The dancer raised his arms and spread out his hands and began to dance to the guitar. He was skilful and kept excellent time and for a moment it seemed as if Madame Strouthokámelos' slightly disdainful expression might vanish.

'The cheese is excellent,' said Grant.

Spencer lighted a cigarette.

Just then Lilac Shirt rose to his feet, approached the other dancer and clasping one hand round his partner's waist and the other round his loins he called for a tune. Shouts of laughter, and one of the remaining two began again on the guitar. Madame Strouthokámelos frowned once more. The frown was deeper this time.

The tune was a tango. Lilac Shirt proceeded to sway his partner into a caricature of a tango. With absurdly languorous movements they danced, still keeping excellent time with the music. Lilac Shirt's white trousers were, however, a little too tight for really free movement.

'How well they dance,' said Spencer, smiling. 'I think we ought to join in.'

He got another kick under the table.

He then saw that Lilac Shirt's way of holding his partner was perhaps a little too daring, a little too intimate, for the open air, at midday, in public. As the dance continued the goat rose to its feet – as if to get a better view. It stared with its pale amber eyes at the dancers, then turned to look at Madame Strouthokámelos – it was a look that spoke volumes, but banned volumes – and then again fastened its keen, glassy, unblinking stare on the dancers.

The guitar-player paused. Lilac Shirt, leaning against his partner who was leaning against one of the veranda posts, embraced him and kissed him on the mouth. This brought loud cheers from the other two. All four of them had forgotten the two foreigners and Madame Strouthokámelos – a fact which made her next words rather wide of the mark.

'They have forgotten themselves,' she said in a tone of disgust. 'They have drunk too much.'

Lilac Shirt's kiss was so prolonged that she averted her eyes and rose abruptly to her feet.

'We had better go,' she said in a quiet and furious voice, and picking up her hat she went round to the landward side of the Pantheon to ask for the bill. Spencer and Grant followed to pay it. Glancing back, they saw Lilac Shirt and his partner disappear behind some rocks a few yards away.

'We live and learn,' said Grant, winking.

As for the goat, it had settled down again, and was quietly chewing the cud. Its yellow eyes were shut for the siesta.

GLENWAY WESCOTT

A VISIT TO PRIAPUS

Occasionally last winter Allen Porter would mention a young man of sonorous name and address, Mr Jaris Hawthorn of Clamariscassett, Maine, who as a lover had briefly amused but not satisfied him at all, and who thereafter bored him as a friend. He said that he would not think of introducing him to any of us because (a) he is a bad painter and a pseudo-intellectual, and so obtuse and pushing and clinging as to make any merely social relationship with him a nuisance; and (b) his sex is so monstrously large that sexual intercourse with him is practically impossible.

GLENWAY WESCOTT (1901–1987): Born in Wisconsin and educated, in his own words, 'in the baroque way, by the grand tour of the continent of Europe,' Wescott was the author of a small but exceptionally distinguished body of work including the novels The Grandmothers *and* The Pilgrim Hawk. *'A Visit to Priapus' was published only after his death.*

From Wescott's autobiographical note for Kunitz and Haycraft's Twentieth Century Authors: *'For a number of years it seemed to me that my ability had vanished into thin air; nothing that I could do was satisfactory. It must have seemed to others that there was something wrong with my character. Among other disabilities very grave for a novelist, I ceased to be able to take a real interest in anything fictitious. On mankind's account I believe in nothing but the truth, the naked truth; no other remedy or religion or dialectic. But can a novelist tell it? I myself have no exact knowledge of much of anything except sexual love and family relationships, and practically all in the first person singular. Is that worth telling? I now believe that it must be, if only to exercise the reader's sense of exactitude.'*

A biography of Wescott by Jerry Rosco was published in 2002 by University of Wisconsin Press.

I must say that neither the report of his monstrosity nor of his ambitious and sentimental spirit really dismayed me. For Allen in bed is easily affrighted; and when it comes to talk of art, excesses of friendliness, etc., he has less patience than anyone. With his lively and improper sense of humor, Allen presented this phenomenal fellow to Pavlik, on account of the obscene way Pavlik talks and the freakish pictures he has painted. But nothing came of that, he believed. Pavlik as a rule is unwilling to risk getting caught in such misdemeanor by his darling, Charles, who, I presume, would simply feel authorized by it to go and do likewise or worse.

When Allen heard of my trip to Maine he suggested that I see Hawthorn, *quand même*; we talked some sense and some nonsense about it, and I promised; but evidently he thought me too proud or prudent to do any such thing. Having taken stock of Sorrento and looked at the map, I wrote Hawthorn and proposed our meeting somewhere halfway. He did not reply promptly; and meanwhile Monroe had written that George's keeping company with young Chitwood worried him; so I had begun to worry again, to dream despairingly of Ignazio, and to write those above-mentioned letters. At last an answer came from Hawthorn, matter-of-fact and cordial: he would meet me on the verandah of the Windsor Hotel in Belfast at ten a.m. on Wednesday. I ruefully thought that I was no longer quite in the mood or in the pink of condition for such a meeting; but I did not let myself think much, one way or the other. For it might well turn out to be the sort of folly that I owe it to myself and even others to stoop to upon occasion, according to the rule of my health and my particular morality. And, even if no healthful pleasure was to be had of him at journey's end, no doubt the journey would be of interest. I should see some sea-captains' houses and some variations of the Maine landscape. And it seemed to me that I might turn to stone in Sorrento, to stone or to wood, if I did not go somewhere else, do something.

On Wednesday Ernest, the bright youth who tends Frances' furnaces, woke me at daybreak; and I gulped some potent warmed-over coffee; and he drove me to Ellsworth where I had to wait an hour for the bus. I was in my most absurd matutinal state, absent and giddy, like one strongly bestirring himself under hypnosis. The bus was of the vast and delectable streamlined type with powerful engine and terrible cry and springs like a dream. At first I thought its motion might make me sick. Maine highways are narrow, with very few motorists on them, but those few are plucky and stubborn. The bus would roar whenever we sighted one, and without slacking up in the least, descend upon him, then suddenly digress and swing around him, with two wheels off the pavement. South of Ellsworth there is a succession of long hills. As we flew down into the valleys between them – so delicately was every bit of shock mollified by the mattress-like suspension under us – we suddenly ceased to feel the road, resuming it with a slight tremor only when we began to climb again. After a certain term of chastity, to say nothing of particular discouragements such as this summer's, I always think of dying, with no very clear distinction between the longing for it and the dread of it. So I was frightened by this ride and somewhat fascinated by my fright. But I forced myself to entertain other thoughts; to admire the poor farms and the old towns through which we passed, and the successive waterways, the play of peculiar Maine light, and the wonderful absence of billboards: a sort of passion and chastity of landscape.

I arrived first at the rendezvous. No reference had been made in my letters or Hawthorn's to my spending the night; suddenly I felt ashamed to be taking all that for granted; therefore I hastily checked my bag inside the hotel. The porch agreed upon was half a block long, separated from the parked cars of Main Street by a jigsaw balustrade; and it had a neat alignment of rocking chairs on it. I sat in a rocking chair and read *Time*. No one else sat; a good many stepped briskly along the sidewalk, and a good many drove in and out of town, on more respectable business than mine, I thought. Then it occurred to me that neither of us had any idea of the other's appearance. I knew only one thing about him, and that one thing, of all I might have known, the least perceptible, the least practicable mark of identification. Which at least brought to my mind the fact that this constituted the worst behavior, the most grotesque episode, of my entire life. What, frankly speaking, was I sitting there waiting for, watching for? It might have been an obscene drawing in the style of El Poitevin or Vivant Denon: a giant phallus out for a ride in a car. And what part would it hold the wheel with, and how would it honk, I asked myself – ribald laughter all provoked but hushed in me, along with other more and more mixed emotion.

Naturally, bitter regret for my great days as a lover assailed me. Also a fresh and terrible kind of sense of devotion to the two whom I love, who love me, who cannot keep me happy, whom I torment and disappoint year in and year out, ached in my grotesque heart. With which my pride also started up, at its worst. To think that I should have come to this: sex-starved, in a cheap provincial hotel humbly waiting for a total stranger; and it should be so soon, at thirty-eight! But, I must say, then a certain good nature quickened in me as well, thank God; an amused appreciation of myself. Once more I summoned up courage to believe – scowling a little, grinning a little, gritting my teeth – that in the considerable brotherhood of middle-aged men in unlucky sexual plight, not many are my peers in this respect and that respect at least. G.D. on the Bowery. A.E.A. or B.K. in Turkish baths: my ventures no doubt are as undignified as theirs, my sensations probably less rapturous than theirs, but . . . But my life is the oddest. As a result of years of perfect intercourse, unforgettable, my self-consciousness is extraordinary. Living as I do, undivorced – with those I have most desired still the closest to me – I am embarrassed in the pursuit of pleasure by their alluring noble example; handicapped by trickery of my own spirit, my own flesh; impoverished by tribute. Nevertheless I have been able to keep a more level and subtle head than G.D., a more fearless temper than A.E.A., a soberer habit than B.K. In the very efficacy of my excitements there is something like a practical morality. My very sense of humor about it all seems somehow poetical. And if I ever have occasion to tell this tale, for example, I shall tell it well. So I said to myself, boasted to myself . . .

By that time, with mechanical eye, I had read *Time* from cover to cover. In any case I could not take any further interest in the sad international facts it so blithely reported, nor any other particular facts, not even the facts of my presence where I was, and why, and what would come of it. I was under an introspective spell. I was interested in only the wondrous tiresome way my mind works, always the same way, no matter what it has to do, incorruptible by what it has to deal with. It was fascination of only the sense of life in general, in the abstract, all of a piece: life of which, like everyone else alive, I am daily, gradually, dying . . . Which mystic fit, as it might be called – in almost entire forgetfulness of time and place and purpose and self – seemed the purest kind of experience of all. It can occur only when one's sense of reality has failed; when one's habitual way of thinking of one's self has broken down somehow. It occurs in sexual intercourse, but, alas, not often.

Then a young man drove up and parked his car, and I recognized him as my Hawthorn. With a sign of relief I noted that he was good-looking, respectable looking. He gazed at me but did not speak. I gazed at him. He turned away toward the main entrance of the hotel; so I waited a few seconds, from second to second, quiet as a mouse, while he went in and came out; and just as I was about to signal to him, he stepped into his car and drove away. That is to say, it was not he. And so it seemed to me that nothing in the world, no beauty, no monstrosity, could possibly stir me out of my absent-mindedness, sense of mysticism, and humiliation. For, said I to myself, I have lived too well; I have loved too truly, which now is all over; and I have thought too much, even in this half hour of Hawthorn's tardiness.

Then there Hawthorn was, in a more expensive car than the wrong young man's. There he was, and naturally he recognized me at once: I had forgotten that I am somewhat a celebrity. And he smiled at me and waved to me. I stepped down from the verandah to the curb, and we greeted each other as if we had been acquainted for years. I got in beside him. We drove a little way, then I remembered my valise, and we went after it. The back of his car was full of oil paintings for me to 'criticize': first indication of one of the peculiarities of which Allen had warned me. For a while naturally I wanted to forget about the other peculiarity.

First we went to visit the Marine Museum of Searsport, where I especially admired a ship's model all carved of the pith of the fig tree. That is the deadest-white substance on earth, whiter than marble, whiter than lard; but there is a slight parallel grain in it, a faintly yellow or flesh-colored thread, which shows in the sails, like fairy stitching. In its present home-made showcase it is drying and breaking; a bit of weather gets in; and gradually the tiny alternate storms of humidity and aridity undo the rigging; the tiny companionways all droop. The good gossipy Searsporter who acts as curator said that it could not be mended.

There are also fine antique chests of rosy wood trimmed with sallow brass, all smoothed by more or less intentional caresses of salty chapped hands of sailors dead and gone. There are also a few Oriental 'antiques,' including an astrological compass: a saucer of golden lacquer with a thousand minute scribbles on it – a gift to newly-weds, to determine the placement of their new house, the curator informed us. The handsomest object of all was a great pin or plug intended to be thrust into a hole in the gunwale of a whaler and entwined with some tackle: a thing of whittled whalebone, of a lovely flecked color, about the size of a policeman's club or a unicorn's horn, and indescribably shapely, perfectly tapering, with delicate flange near the top. Jaris Hawthorn, perhaps a bit proudly hinting at my real reason for being there with him, laughed at me for my admiration of it. But I believe that it did not particularly impress me as phallic; I usually know when I am thus impressed; I have not much subconscious. Apropos of which, he told me that the men of the Maine coast often carry little finely whittled wooden phalli which come in handy as thole-pins, and which they more or less honestly believe will also cause the lascivious opportunity to occur, and augment and safeguard their potency once it has occurred. There is a poem by Robert P. Tristram Coffin about this, entitled, 'Pocketpiece.' Jaris promised to discover and make me a present of one.

Then in the various coast towns, Belfast, Camden, Waldeboro, we devoted some time to what I had spoken of as my objective on this journey: the viewing of old domestic architecture, which must be America's richest heritage of art, and most lamentably unfulfilled tradition. The great residences of shipmaster and lumbermen disappointed me; they show the effect of the intercourse with southern seaports such as Charleston and Savannah, and too much honor has already been done them in the way of servile imitation: post offices, city halls, boarding schools. The small dwellings are the glamorous ones, particularly those of lovely local brick, blocky, with blunt roofs and a minimum of eaves; their austerely cut doors and door-jams and window-frames set in flush with the ruddy walls, just as in seaman's chests the brass locks and reinforcements are imbedded in the wood.

The modern architect is inclined to bully his client in the name of aesthetics. Let both of them consider this: everyone's evident determination in this part of the world a hundred years ago to have his individual habit and habit of mind and even foible respected and embodied in building. Habit forgotten long since, dead and buried; so what does it matter? It matters in that here in the inanimate lumber, the changeless mineral, there still is emotion, physiognomy, personality. This door-jam still smiles; that lintel looks haughtily important; this or that stairway has a philosophic or a melancholy or a gratified expression. It is a kind of beauty, and a quality of art, that formal aesthetics can never legislate into being.

One house that I particularly liked is in a precipitous street on a very narrow property. There was no ground on which to erect the horse stable except on a level with the second story; therefore the sympathetic builder ran a wide stairway up to it along the outside of the house, parallel to the sidewalk; and the combined effect, through the cheap and small, is as noble as Perugia. These retired mariners, having seen enough weather on their voyages, evidently dreaded getting wet; therefore most of the barns and woodsheds are under the same roof, continuations from the kitchen, which makes for grandeur as well as the beauty of compactness. Think of what a time I should have persuading modern architects Gropius or Lescage to respect my dislike of open doorways, opaque windows, and my light-shyness to boot, to complicate matters; my dread of overhearing the rest of the family in the next room converse, fidget, sigh.

In this part of Maine the true farmers' barns outside the villages, up on small simple hills, balmy with poor hay, surveying the august and brilliant inlets, are often shingled to the ground like old Long Island houses. In their present shabbiness every shingle catches its bit of light and casts a minute shadow; so they look as if they were bound in sharkskin.

At mid-day we stopped at an inn of the sort that ladies love, where the classic Maine menu was proudly served us: lobster in milk, hot biscuits, blueberry pie. Somewhat accustomed enough to my companion by that time, I improperly glanced at the antique four-poster beds spread with old hand-stitched coverlets but fitted, no doubt, with new 'beauty rest' mattresses. However, for us two, I felt, there would have been incongruity in that rich and dainty interior. Then with polite hypocrisy I told him a story that I had made up to explain my not returning to Sorrento that evening. With no hypocrisy at all he replied that he desired to spend the night with me. But it was his father's car that he was driving, and he had promised to be back with it before dinner. If I accompanied him as far as Clamariscassett it would make my return-trip on the bus only a little longer, that was all. So it was decided.

Next he sat me down cross-legged in the grass where the car was parked, and masterfully showed me all the oil paintings he had brought along to show me. And he had an air of profound respect for my opinion, but of difficulty in understanding it, or of determination not to understand it unfavorably. Usual provincial American landscapes; watercolor concep-tions executed in oil, and, alas, effortlessly executed, with a pretty bit here and a strange bit there, probably by accident . . . I kept thinking of Allen – how he must have hated this – with a certain soft hilarity.

Then Hawthorn and I strolled through a shabby meadow and an idyllic little grove, and lay there on the grass, ten or fifteen feet above sea level. The tide was out, leaving a few pools which winked and rippled, and rocks from which the seaweed hung in yellow braids and tangles, and a confetti of shells. The breeze brought up odors of ocean, an odor as herby as pubic hair, an odor as tepid and sweet as saliva . . . At last I felt at ease enough to stop talking. My Hawthorn lay, less at ease, fairly near me, with a mildly joyous grin now and then, and an occasional caress, not unmanly, not really indecent. His little eyes sparkled with perhaps one idea only, but we talked of this and that. Now it was he who was making me talk, questioning, teasing, which at any rate I preferred to my usual nervous, conscientious improvisation.

He was not beautiful. Yet there was nothing exactly unbeautiful about him except his teeth: they were not quite white, and there was one missing, on the right side of his grin. The line of his lips was indented in exact correspondence to the shape of his nostrils. His hair was coarsely wavy, and when the sun struck it, almost as yellow as the seaweed. I liked his hands which, oddly enough, were less ruddy than his face; good fleshy tapering fingers which were not hot, not cold, and not damp. Perhaps I did not like his eyes, in spite of their excitability. It is in hands and eyes that I particularly expect to observe what is called 'sex appeal'; that is to say, whenever they have failed to appeal to me and I have gone ahead anyway, I have had a sudden embarrassing disinclination to cope with myself at some point, or a particularly severe disenchantment at least. So I kept looking at these hands and eyes, questioning, whether to go ahead now or to stop.

One learns by experience that it is fatal to ask one's self that specific question too soon; and the right moment is infinitesimal; and therefore as a rule one asks it too late. Furthermore, except by the imaginary process of falling in love, how can one tell, how can one even prophecy, whether or not one will enjoy the body of another – until one has undressed it, touched it, tasted it? And apparently I am never to fall in love again, because I have not fallen out of the loves of my early manhood. Also I am the sort of person with whom no one is much inclined to go to bed without having been induced somehow to fall in love somewhat; which makes it all difficult for me, at least necessitates a certain hypocrisy . . . Now it was too late to try to be sincere. Before I left Sorrento, before I left New York, I had resolved not to stop; it was a matter of principle and a point of honor.

Now and then I withdrew a little distance on the flowery grass in order to take another good look at my man. As his trousers of Palm-Beach cloth were cut, the peculiarity of his physique which so impressed Allen did not appear, and with reference to that I quoted to myself the famous first line of Sterne's *Sentimental Journey*: 'They order, said I, these things better in France'; which amused me. All this, I also thought, was rather reminiscent of Sorrento, Italy, than of Sorrento, Maine; which was pleasant. And the very way my mind worked, immoral or mock-immoral, forever similizing and citing and showing off to itself, pleased me. Hawthorn of course had no notion what my several smiles meant, but replied to each with his little energetic self-conscious grin. I enjoyed lying there, comfortably fatigued and careless; perfectly willing but not at all anxious, not eager. For this I had come halfway across the state at the crack of dawn. What an odd mood; and it amounted to an odd attitude to take toward a young man reputed to be phenomenal: the oddest by-product of my wearisome dangerous passions all summer long . . .

Now Hawthorn had taken off his Palm-Beach coat and neatly folded it, lest this and that in the pockets disappear in the grass. He wore a loose shirt of silky finished fabric, very dressy in a provincial way. Very tight and bright-colored braces held up his roomy trousers. He lay propped on one elbow, vigilantly watching me, asking rather pointless questions, and giving bits of uninteresting information. I lay flat on my back with one arm up to keep the sun out of my eyes. I pulled blades of grass and chewed the juicy ends, and I teased my own nostrils with the stems of clover which had the plumpest, spiciest heads.

There was magic in the scene, but it was a humorous rather than a poetical or passionate magic. It reminded me of a chromolithograph that I used to have hanging over my desk in Paris; a scene of courtship about 1900, a young man and woman in boating attire on a river bank under a willow tree. He was in his shirt sleeves with bright braces, his hair parted in the middle, his eye lashes wonderful, his mustaches silkily drooping; and she lay flat on her back under a parasol; and he crouched facing her, no doubt with tremors of the mustaches and wonderful winks – to all intents and purposes my father and my mother, I used to think: a kind of epitomization of the mood in which in 1900 I must have been conceived. Monroe did not admire that chromolithograph, and left it behind in the Rue de Conde when he packed up our belongings . . . But the 1900 young man's eyes were dreamy, idle, cloudy, like a stallion's. Whereas my present young man's just slightly glittered now and then, with a look in the intervals between. Perhaps he as well as I was taking it for granted what deeds of darkness we should do when darkness fell. Yet those glitters were not what I should call sensual glances. His appetite, I gathered, was taking the form of a more and more intense friendliness and admiration. Well, I thought, that would suffice; or perhaps, as Allen had warned me, more than suffice. My appetite, it seemed, was not taking any form at all.

Meanwhile the cool noon sunlight came down the shore at an angle like that of the soft riptide; and hung like spray in the treetops; and rippled on a level with my head through the coarse bloom of the meadow. Down below in the returning water gulls worked or played, conversing a great deal. Their conversation here on the Penobscott, I fancied, was not the same as in Frenchman's Bay. Up there you might have thought them all in poor health or past their prime, retired from the strenuous and profitable business of the open ocean. They spoke tremulously, and with what was like effortlessly controlled temper, in the way of old ladies in a sanitarium complaining of what diet the nurses have brought them on trays . . . I told Hawthorn this; and he beamed, he always beamed, as if every utterance of mine were in perfect rhymed couplets. Also, I thought, there was something amorous about those Sorrento gulls, indecently gossiping, undignifiedly bewailing, like aging homosexuals at a cocktail party, comparing notes; but of course I did not mention this to Hawthorn. Instead I described to him the grief-stricken and perhaps crazy gull on the rock under my bedroom window, and I did so maliciously, to make sure of what I suspected: that it did not interest him; he knew nothing of grief, of true love.

Then some summer ladies wandered from the inn down through the grove with sudden piping voices, which made him blush and draw away from me. This gave me a welcome insight into his state of mind. For there had been nothing overtly improper in the relative positions of our recumbent persons there in the redolent and tickling grass where presently the ladies also would lie and gossip and giggle; but evidently his thoughts were amorous, his conscience bad. I took his embarrassment as a good excuse to bestir myself and get him started toward Clamariscassett. For this selfconscious and inactive felicity of mine would soon wear itself out, if it had not already done so.

When we reached Clamariscassett he introduced me to his family, friendly but not cheerful folk, evidently of modest fortune, somewhat shiftless. Then he asked me to criticize half a dozen more paintings. While I was thus occupied, thus embarrassed, the family terrier bit my ankle, but it did not hurt. Jaris, with money solicited from rich neighbors and vacationers, had built a little information bureau on the main street, which he and his sister administered; and I had to admire this next. The moral support and occasional friendliness of Maine celebrities such as Messieurs Colcord and Coffin, Madams Carrol and Chase, have been useful and gratifying to him, he explained; and now he is planning a small public park in a vacant lot on the waterfront; and we also inspected this lot. Then he marched me a good way up the Clamariscassett River to view its mysterious vast banks of oyster shells: residue of century-long banquets of a prehistoric people. All this tired me: I felt less and less equal to the opportunity that the night was to afford.

Jaris suggested that we sleep at his parents, although his mother would disapprove – the discomfort, not the immorality, he hastily explained; for we should have to share a single bed. I intensely agreed with her. His father needed the car early in the morning, but he offered to drive us to an inn at Pemaquid Point and to fetch us back next day at noon. Evidently it did not occur to these good people that I could be expected to spend the night at the inn alone, which complacence puzzled and amused me.

It was a new building, most absurdly planned and unattractively furnished. There were two double beds in the room over the kitchen assigned to us. The proprietress complained about this fact a little; she had hoped to rent it to two couples; the morals, that is the *moeurs*, of Americans, how odd! To reach the bathroom we had to go downstairs into the kitchen, and through the sitting-rooms, and back upstairs from the front hall. While I went on that expedition, then while I unpacked – as indeed all the day whenever I turned my back a moment – Jaris engaged a cook or a maid or another guest in the warmest conversation. This great sociability, I thought, must underlie his several semi-philanthropies, raising of funds, giving of information, etc.; and went well with other traits of his odd character: a sort of vacuity, and a sort of insincerity. It was evident also that he had confidence in his ability to obscure the issue of his homosexuality. A tireless indiscriminate friendliness no doubt is one good way; for these natives of Maine appear to be not fussily moral, but passionately neighborly, touchily democratic . . .

Then in my black waxed silk, exotic rather than erotic attire, I lay down on one of the double beds and waited for him. From the remote bathroom, and I know not what further conversation on the way there and back, he came at last and lay beside me. Still I could not think whether to like or dislike his eyes, so light-colored, so old-looking, and decidedly aslant, enclosed in numerous little intense wrinkles pointing out and pointing up. Suddenly I knew what I thought: they were half-animal eyes, metamorphosed eyes; the deadness in them was the legendary pathos of the satyr. His strong, thin, and slightly chapped mouth also pointed up. Most modern men smile downward; he smiled in Etruscan style. We gossiped some more; then he took me in his arms.

After a good many vigorous hugs and rough kisses, I observed that he was worrying about my response to them, that is, my lack of response. What was he doing that displeased me, or was it that I lacked temperament, or what? In fact the day had affected me as if it had been interminable, and I was waiting to forget my fatigue. Also our dinner had been of the grossest meat and potatoes and pie, and I was still aware of my digestion. Of course I was embarrassed to speak of these unromantic impediments. Instead I remarked that his Palm-Beach-cloth suit was uncomfortable, scratchy. He promptly removed it.

His hair was only warmly, rustily blond; but his flesh had the rather weak and precious texture, the hot-house pallor, that as a rule goes with red hair. This, in contrast with his sunburned face, made him appear very naked with his clothes off. The muscles of his back were admirable; the backbone in a deep indentation from the nape of his neck to his compact buttocks. He carried himself with a slight stoop, but his chest was round and stout enough to make up for it. The form and carriage of a young day-laborer . . . Having undressed in the opposite corner of the room with his back to me, briskly, methodically, he turned around and faced me with the strangest expression – somewhat joyously exhibiting himself, yet somewhat ashamed, and perhaps resentful of my interest, my amusement – and came to bed; and the seemingly interminable night's work or play began.

His sexual organ, the symbol of this silly pilgrimage, and also the cause of my severe self-consciousness and unromantic sense of humor, really was a fantastic object. No matter what infantile prejudice you might be swayed by, or pagan superstition, or pornographic habit of mind, you could not call it beautiful; it was just a desperate thickness, a useless length of vague awkward muscle. An unusual amount of foreskin covered it, protruded from the end of it, thickly pursed like a rose. In the other dimension also, around the somewhat flattened shaft, the skin was very coarse and copious. Neither in length nor breadth did it increase in the usual ratio, nor did it grow quite rigid, at least not until it had almost reached the point of its difficult orgasm. And at that point, as I presently found to my discomfiture, it was apt to fail suddenly, droop suddenly, lie useless half way down his thigh. But still in dull and futile flexibility it had a look of pompous, ominous erection. It was a thing which to a happy person of normal spirit would be a matter of indifference, an absurdity; which on the other hand, to a very sensual man or woman who happened to have a faulty understanding of his way of life, might be a cause of, or a pretext for, desperate bad habit and disappointment. And now here was I, certainly unhappy, and dangerously sensual, but no fool, and not afraid – here was I in bed with Priapus! A thing to frighten maidens with, and to frighten pillagers out of an orchard; a thing to be wreathed with roses, then forgotten . . .

The mind of poor Priapus in bed seemed to me no less exceptional and troubling than this classic bludgeon. You might have expected him to take pride in it as a kind of wonder of nature; or you might have expected him to hate or pity himself on account of it, or to have a horror of being desired for that and no other reason – expectations far too simple. Upon my referring to it he only conventionally and complacently demurred, as if that were a customary flattery, due tribute, and entirely agreeable. But when I paid attention to it more directly than by word of mouth, active attention, then its size and strength would suddenly decline: the flesh itself ashamed. You might think that such a thing, in its hour of exercise, must cast some spell upon the one of whom it is so disproportionate a part, upon his entire temperament, even his opinion and his emotion. It was not so. Never for an instant did my Hawthorn cease to be self-possessed, critical, and equivocally self-critical, and with the oddest air of begrudging, of calculatory cunning. A man of the purely mental type, pretending to be erotic . . . It absurdly occurred to me that he might be a man quite deficient physically to whom some wondrous physician, or compassionately inter- fering friend, or capricious deity, had simply attached this living, but rather spasmodically living, dildo.

And what a strange type: a mentality as busy as a bee, and forever blushing or turning pale; feeling devilish or feeling pure; and in an instant beginning to be sad or angry, but the next instant overcome by fond satisfaction, and self-satisfaction! All night long, throughout my own easy enjoyment and my laborious effort to please him, my falling asleep irresistibly and his waking me, and the rise and fall of that practically hopeless phallus, all night long he was evidently thinking, thinking, in that inconsistent way of his. Thinking, thinking: explaining himself a little, at least to himself; justifying himself a little, or trying to decide how to go about justifying himself if he should have to; and resenting little things I did or things I said, but losing track of his resentment at once, all absorbed in some sort of theory of love, or policy of being my lover, or dubious general scheme of lovableness. While the light bulb without a shade over the bed was on, I could not help seeing all this, kaleidoscopic in his face: all this disorderly rationalization, moralizing, this cold and interminable changing of his mind. I tried not to care; I looked away from his face, and my naturally erotic eyes were indeed otherwise fabulously occupied. I shut them; I turned off the light. But in the dark I could feel the same incongruity in the various emphasis of his fingertips, straining of his thighs, stiffening of his neck – an intellectual straining and stiffening.

I said to myself that he must so admire intellect that he encouraged himself to think as much as possible, no matter what; it was like being in bed with a kind of German philosopher. And probably his intelligence has never quite sufficed to put in order and clarify even for himself the incessant ejaculation of these pseudo-ideas. Certainly his speech never sufficed for an instant to convey to me anything that I could be quite sure of, or entirely respect. Every now and then he whispered something, but never a whole sentence: a word or two, then a silence, then a soft stammer, with a shrug, with a little grimace. Every now and then whatever I did obviously shocked him. But he was ashamed of himself for being shocked. So then almost instantly he would make up for it by an added word or two in explicit praise of my unembarrassed eroticism. Twice in the night he said that he hoped to be influenced by me and become like me in that respect. Evidently he assumed that this intimacy of ours, so rashly and improperly improvised – what for? – was to go on indefinitely like a marriage made in heaven . . .

Naturally at times I grew as inappropriately thoughtful as he. I simply wearied of lying in the dark, vainly clasping insensitive pseudo-Priapus; I despaired of ever understanding that petty morality, or ever discovering just what would undo and overcome that giant concupiscence. Therefore I would turn on the light again, and by some calculated caress keep him from speaking. Then I would see a sort of apathy, an expression of boredom and disinclination, gradually accumulate in his face, tight-mouthed, dead-eyed. Oh, that eye of his, retrospective even upon the present object, like the eye of a sea gull! If he noticed my observation of him, instantly he would respond with his little Etruscan grin, lips up, eyes up; and the impression that made was of entire insincerity, I think he must have sensed it; for he would kiss me with a fiercer approximation of appetite, or give me a special series of rapid and muscular hugs.

It was bound to be difficult, having to do with a physique such as that: a thing rather symbolic of sex in the abstract than apt to do the actual work of intercourse in any way that I know of. At a glance I could guess how long it would take, how lethargically, callously, it would function: which did not dismay me. What dismayed me little by little was to learn that it was very sensitive as well, more troubled than troublesome – like the sex of some shy wild animal, in incalculable kind of rut one minute, and a strange state of arbitrary chastity the next minute; or like the sex of a great will-o-the-wisp, shrinking away in the darkness. The abnormality, the practical or mechanical trouble, was bad enough; but it was the inability to concentrate, the subnormality of emotional temperature, which made it impossible. No matter, I said to myself; no doubt love or even lust would find a way in time; practice makes perfect . . .

But a certain uncomfortableness of spirit, obscurity of point of view, is likely to keep one from falling in love, and virtually discourage even the lesser or lower forms of desirous imagining; the spirit is prevented from going to work with any ardor to solve the problems of the body. In the case of male in love with male, this is serious, because homosexuality is somewhat a psychic anomaly, not exactly equipped with mechanism of flesh. At least at the start of such a relationship one must fumble and feel one's way amid a dozen improvised, approximative, substitutive practices. From start to finish many men find this a terrible disadvantage, a continuous punishment: the worry of what to do and what not to do, and why not and what next and what else; and the dread of the other's modesty or immodesty or other inexpressible sentiment; and the chill of sense of responsibility, the grievous anxiety of perhaps failing to do for the other what he needs to have done, even amid the fever and rejoicing of one's own success, at the last minute. In bed with such a fellow as my poor Priapus you would have to be phenomenally unkind or perverse not to suffer from this.

That fantastic plaything might have meant nothing to me at all; it was in fact almost good for nothing; it would have seemed only a fearful, comical, mythological, theoretical thing – unless I had been able to command myself to care about it extremely, unless I had deliberately yielded to a kind of drunkenness of caring: wild exercise of the sense of touch, and spurring on of every other nerve from head to foot around it, and intentional blindness to all else, and conscious fetishism, and so on I may say that I was quite successful in the management of myself in this respect. With a great store of sexual energy saved up in melancholy and inaction, I did care; I was drunken. But the more successful my excitement, naturally the more difficult it was to control myself, to bide my time, to keep from spending. I could continue with enthusiasm and without crisis for one hour, let us say, not for two; or perhaps for two hours, but not three. And whenever I made any special impatient effort to bring him to the point of felicity, or to keep my own pleasure going, or to distract my attention lest it go too far, then I would encounter suddenly the embarrassment of his mind, the defeatism of his flesh; then I would have to begin all over again. All night long in this way it was a little like nightmare: fighting an infinitude, or running infinitely nowhere. He reminded me of the old man of the sea, Proteus, becoming this and that and the other thing as one wrestled with him. I reminded myself of Tantalus in hell, thirsting to death up to his neck in fresh water, starving to death under a ripe fruit-tree . . . And whenever my mastery of myself foiled, the nightmare ended for the time being, that is to say whenever I succeeded in spending – there he was still, in his stubborn capricious pretentious condition, pretending that he was going to spend presently, and wildly enthusiastic about me, so he said: optimistic as a madman, energetic as a day-laborer.

Thus it went on all night, at least six hours of the night in action, clinging and pressing and striving. I spent three times, which I may say, surprised me. Twice he consented to go to his own bed and let me take a nap; but back he came, apologetic, conceited, coldly sweet. He did not spend until dawn; then so suddenly and softly that I did not notice it. Our room there above the kitchen was large and low: the ceiling drawn down shadowy like a tent to a pair of little windows knee-high. And I was noticing the daylight venturing just then in under those tent-flaps and horizontally across the rumpled beds toward my pillow in the corner. How glad I was to see it! Hours of the next morning sightseeing, hours of the next afternoon in the streamlined bus on my way back to Sorrento; how restful they would seem, after this peculiar darkness! For another hour or two, only an hour or two, this terrible companion would keep winding upon and around me like a great lively root of a tree, hungry, thirsty; and I felt more and more like a clod, like a stone, but with certain drops of moisture within me still, surprisingly. I noticed only a softening of his shoulders and his thighs, a soft kick such as an infant might give in sudden slumber. Then he whispered to me what it was. It was his orgasm; and it seemed in the nature of a weakness, a lapse, a breakdown; as if at last fatigue made him faint . . .

Evidently it had always been his habit to wield that superhuman phallus against one bent over in his crotch, head downward; so that when finally his moment approaches and he does just as he likes, and it must be in its entire bulk and strength, then precisely one feels it least. I scarcely felt it at all. This was the final instance of the alternation and confusion of too fanciful state of mind and too gross flesh which had characterized this intercourse from the start. Which at that point not only disappointed me; it worried me, in the way of an odd equivalent of bad conscience, a peculiar suspicion of my own honesty and sanity through this experience. The phallus of a demi-god, nightmarish bludgeon, vanishing at last, just as the day began to break . . . It was as if I had made it all up for myself, to please and cheat and defeat myself; and if I had done so in fact, indeed I might well have been ashamed or alarmed.

But what on earth is stranger than the benefit of sexual intercourse to those who feel the need of it? I honestly believe that it is not only politic but moral to comprehend and to admit that strangeness. For a long time I have had to live in wretched deprivation. Therefore I thanked God – and I mean, I really mean my own peculiar, exciting, painful, but certainly trustworthy god or gods – even for an oddity, even for an indecent comedy, like this. Having spent, my Hawthorn at last let me alone. Having slept a while, I began to turn restlessly this way and that in my double bed, so as to get out of line with the early blond rays of the sunrise; I began to hear the ready voices of the maids in the kitchen beneath us brewing weak coffee and frying cheap bacon; I woke up; I got up – feeling like a wild fowl, light and brave.

When I am happy, then I most sincerely wish to comprehend, to detect, to dissect. What man is not worth studying? Surely this young monster of Maine was, especially with strange myself in this curious combination . . . When I am happy, I am also as humble as can be. Therefore I did not conclude that he was simply somewhat impotent, although that fantastic grandeur of his sex might mean almost anything, and not improbably just that. But almost anyone may be impotent with someone. I am not an Adonis; I am the opposite of a Priapus; Maine Priapus simply may not have found me exciting. None of those I have gone to bed with just lately has. Only half a dozen all my life have – and then not really until I had a chance to deploy other aspects of myself than my sketchy, faulty physique; to devote a great amount of time and energy and intellect to their general advantage. I admit this, not complaining of it, but in order to conclude my disgraceful story with due scruple. The disgrace was more than mere physical indifference to me personally this time; there were complications.

In the course of the next morning I questioned him a little about his way of life, his past; and as I interpreted certain of his embarrassed but not in the least unwilling answers, they cleared up much of the mystery. He said that he has not been accustomed to being the beloved, that is, the one desired and labored over; therefore probably my positive active enthusiasm did not suit him. The lovers he has generally enjoyed have been young state-of-Mainers of an exceedingly simple manliness, fishermen and such. It is to be supposed that as a rule such young men never think of intercourse, certainly not of homosexual intercourse, until they are desirous to the point of overflowing. Therefore their excitement may be consummated, overcome, liquidated, in a jiffy. Then no doubt Hawthorn has gone on clinging to them in practically unselfish tribute of enthusiasm, and thrilled by fundamental incompatibility – which in fact affects many homosexuals as oppositeness of sex does not – until at last he has happened to spend, no matter how, as it were a swoon or a sweat or a shedding of tears: a culmination equivalent to exhaustion. Perhaps, truly juvenile, these youngsters have enjoyed his energy and obstination as a kind of nocturnal horse-play or rough-house. Or perhaps they have only allowed it, endured it. Poor ambitious boys, grateful for the fuss made over them, hopeful of advantage or advancement, often do serve their elders or supposed betters thus: with a kind of venality not quite cynical, not exactly economic. Or, if they have not even allowed it, then poor Hawthorn has had to fulfill the experience for himself at his leisure, in retrospect, in lonely fancy and worshipful dreams and memorial masturbations. And no doubt some new youth has come to his attention whenever retrospect has ceased to operate . . . In any case pleasure must have come to be associated in his mind with failure to have his own way. Desire must seem to him, not what the word ordinarily, exactly intends – the conception of, and strong instinctive urge toward – but an end in itself; felicity itself, whatever the outcome. Which is idealism in a way. And I, my bizarre mystic opinions notwithstanding, am a materialist.

This customary intercourse with facile, normal youngsters also explained that odd trick of tucking his terrible sex away down between his own thighs. A kind of involuntary coition; only impulsive hugging with an orgasm at the end by accident, not planned at all, not noticed much, an overflow, a pollution. At the age when the proletariat is prettiest, that suffices; and when it is a question of only a substitute for normal intercourse, more than that might give offense. Thus I put upon a vague set of unknown, otherwise innocent individuals a slight specific part of the onus of my disappointment . . . It is strange to think how, upon almost every first occasion of love, even every careless fornication, there is jealousy in a humble innocuous form, a token payment of that immense debt to nature – some such grudge against protagonists of the beloved's past; some vague objection to whatever, up to that point, has influenced him, educated him. But one unlucky human being, such as I, may not seriously blame another, such as my Hawthorn, for the gradual effect of the kind of sexual intimacy he has had a chance to engage in. For perhaps one may control the playing of one's own part in love and the like; but the casting of other actors with one is fate: one lives a good deal by accidental meetings.

However, I could not help thinking that in the way of important experience of love – such as my own, in the past, alas – my phenomenal young man's prospects were especially poor. Even in the midst of my enjoyment, it seemed to me: How unlikely that anyone would really wish to keep him for a lover long! Desirable he might appear, indeed, in so far as desire is distinguishable from hope; and in the long run, it is the recollection of delight that constitutes desire. The effect of a hopeless excitement in the end is to weaken one in amorous action; of which in fact I suppose that the sloth of his astonishing flesh is itself an example. Or perhaps the usage of that great fraudulent phallic symbol might just desperately intensify one's desire for someone else, someone less difficult. And I thought it would scarcely be worthwhile to be desired by him, labored over by him. Evidently his pleasures had not even been satisfactory enough, and probably never would be, to instruct him in the giving of pleasure. In any case it would take a long time for me to instruct him in that sense: night after night without a wink of sleep, month after month of exasperation. Thus my widowed, therefore loose imagination tried to peer into the winter months ahead, when he planned to be in New York.

The strangest thing, the worst complication, was that he evidently thought of himself — or at least wished me to think of him — as already seriously attached to me. Every now and then, all night in little truces of his stammering and self-censorship, he made the warmest protestation of his enjoyment of me, his admiration of me, and almost love. I could see almost-love as it were in the balance on his little strong thin lips: the shape of the words without sound. And the slight grimace with which he withheld it or withdrew it implied no uncertainty or insincerity; only a kind of etiquette, a strategical or political sense. Probably he had heard that one should never be the first to say it. No sign of common skepticism, common sense; in every way he seemed perfectly pleased and excited, that is, in every way except that which just then concerned me: the organic, the orgastic. And as I have already mentioned, he murmured optimistic and indeed presumptuous little plans of our continuing to make love regularly and as a matter of course all winter. But why, why, I wondered — since, especially in terms of his eroticism, it all seemed very nearly inefficacious.

Presently an answer occurred to me. It was that vague and no doubt lovely company of young fishermen which suggested it also. The mediocrity of his pleasure did not matter to him because he had an eye on a more important advantage. It was that same not exactly economic venality; that which must have inspired their beguilement of him, their indulgence of his interminable embraces. Indeed our inequality was more complex than that between them and him. In actual amorous effect, mine was the more youthful and potent and expeditious body. But I was the elder in fact; his social and economic superior. No restless boy in his teens was ever more intensely preoccupied with the future than he, more pathetically determined to get on in the world. And I personified the world: society and celebrity and luxury and, indeed, that worldly opinion which would be favorable or unfavorable to him as a painter.

Yes, I concluded his ardor in my arms, such as it was, had to do with all that, and with my poor physical person only associatively, and by courtesy, and on purpose. He desired me no more or less than a girl-crazy fisherman, a lovely whittler of thole-pins, a snobbish inquisitive parasitic adolescent, might desire him — rather less, probably: for of course he could easily give such a one the immediate satisfaction which I found it almost impossible to give him. Call this a sort of love if you like; surely it was the farthest thing in the world from lust. It was an intellectual effort, a moral embrace. There was indeed not the least indifference about it; but it was only admiration and ambition disguised as desire; in that sense it was fraudulent. It was wily Proteus impersonating Priapus . . . Happening to wear that ostentatious organ, that heavy heraldry of sex, that sacred-looking simulacrum, he more or less consciously would have it serve him as a means to an end, a pretext, an allurement; and as a substitute for what it symbolized, which was what he partially lacked. The entire night was booby-trap; and sex was the bait; and I was the booby. His worst anxiety was lest I perceived this. It evidently meant so much to him that, before I even tried to explain it to myself, instinctively I pretended not to perceive anything. Of course, for my own enjoyment, I needed to fool myself a little also; but only a little, and not all night, and certainly not next morning. During our last whispered conversation before daybreak, I ceased to pretend, in my naturally shameless fashion. His frigidity or difficulty must be my fault somehow, I said. All night long the contact with his body had kept mine in a state of extraordinary tension; therefore the failure or near-failure of our meeting must be due to a lack of physical magic on my part for him; and I said I was sorry. Whereupon he protested that it was not so, not so at all; there had been no frigidity, no difficulty, no failure. And he spoke with an accent of real despair and bad temper.

So I understood that I was not to be allowed to give him up as a bad job and regretfully retreat. He would follow with his peculiar ambitious infatuation, and no doubt self-pity and bitterness. It did not suit him to understand what I might mean by any politely insincere word of humility, apology. And at the last, when his orgasm so surprisingly occurred, it was my impression that he felt not only pleasant unusual sensation but a kind of sudden sadness, sorriness. For now, if we continued this intimacy next winter as he intended, there would be this precedent of his being able to have an orgasm at last; I might expect it of him; and I thought he was sorry about that. For he wished to bend and accustom me to the combination of exorbitance and inadequacy which characterized him physically. It did not suit him to have much of anything expected of him. He wished to compromise me, to engage me in a kind of collusion in the matter of his physical insensibility to me. He wished to feel free to disappoint me, if need be; and to be sincerely surprised by and resentful of my disappointment if I should so far forget myself as to voice any.

I concluded that in a more general sense also he might be a bad-tempered man; at least one of those who must make sure every instant, by hook or crook of their own opinion, of being entirely in the right. I was also reminded of a particular kind of ruthlessness and self-righteousness and spite that had nothing particularly to do with sex: that of many men brought up in hardship or in severe northern places when they arrive to seek their fortune amid those who appear to have been born undeservedly, effortlessly, in a sunny clime or in fortune's lap: New Englanders in New York, Scots in London, Germans everywhere. No doubt I should have trouble with this New Englander if and when I should attempt to cease to be friends with him. But no doubt he would not succeed in having his way with me; for he seemed not nearly pathetic enough to exercise the only intimidation as to which I am weak. Once or twice he frankly referred to his dread of perhaps being disappointed in me in the future. Never for an instant did he show the least interest in, or humility with respect to, the possibility of my having been disappointed by him, then and there, in the present nocturnal circumstances. It may have been only ignorance, innocence; but it vexed me, it warned me. Oh, woe, I exclaimed to myself, woe to whoever happens to be truly fascinated by the sight and the pseudo-promise of that supernatural private part of his! As for me, the characteristic laboriousness of my thought, all one incessant exorcization – to say nothing of my labors upon paper . . . My right hand, with pen in it, enables me not only to learn but to unlearn terrible things, in the long run.

At last we descended from that comical unlucky bedroom, and spent half the morning strolling along the ocean; and sitting on great shelves of vivid granite cross-hatched by the millennial waves; and watching two or three families of bathers, none glamorous, on a weedy strong-smelling beach; and chatting of our friends and of modern morality and modern art. It was gloriously sunny; and the little successive scene along shore and across estuary could not have been more beguiling, or more truly American in style: almost every shape in the foreground big and simple; almost everything in the distance little and distinct, speckled and spotted like birds' eggs; the light as specific as the hand of a miniature-painter. My Hawthorn, very proudly native to all this, told me which subjects he had already painted, which he had selected for future endeavor. I spoke encouragingly and suggestively, but it seemed a waste of time. His way of painting is not quite inappropriate for the simple reason that it is amateurish, literal. But with his shaving-brush brush work and muddy stirring together of miscellaneous squirts from inexpensive tubes of paint, how could he approximate all this American surface as of taffeta, this brilliance as of enamel, these clean lively shapes as of a school of fish?

The style of our more accomplished landscape-painters is inappropriate. For example, their preference for backgrounds of blurred air and fused foliage, inspired by the late Venetians, Rubens, Claude: I suppose they will never get anywhere until they cease that. Instead, surely, the right style for our scenery would derive from, or at least be comparable to, the bird's-eye of, let us say, Lucas van Leyden or even Patinir or, indeed, Brueghel: bright-colored as birds' eyes also. I do not think it essential for a painter to have much knowledge of the history of painting; but I soon run out of vocabulary, talking to one who has not.

Then we visited another marine museum, a small collection housed in a handsome old round fortress on Pemaquid Point, marine only in a manner of speaking, inclusive of unsorted bits of bone, stopped clocks, foxed engravings, tea-cups, and spindles – the ocean through tiny military windows shining in like crystal on fire. Finally the elder Hawthorn came for us; and back in Clamariscassett, we had a hearty meal of crustaceans and berries as usual.

Bit by bit then, Hawthorn told me what resulted from Allen's introduction of him to dear Pavlik: one of the latter's characteristic tyrannical, farcical, talkative little orgies . . . He came to their rendezvous accompanied by none other than, alas, his protégé Ignazio, George's Ignazio, my Ignazio; and then took them both to the flat of one Sylvester Dick, where he urged, or, perhaps, to be exact, ordered them to take all their clothes off. Which Hawthorn did with some unwillingness and misgiving, he told me. But, not having had much variety of sexual experience, he was interested to see what would happen and how it would affect him. And, as a provincial, he felt that in Rome one should do as the Romans do; that is, in New York, he should do as the Russians do. And it pleased him to participate a bit in the private life of so celebrated a painter.

Ignazio's beauty thrilled him, he said; and he assured me that Ignazio also somewhat fancied him. But they exchanged only a few caresses. Pavlik meanwhile not only poured forth his usual improper eloquence, but kept urging them to go ahead and do what they wished to do: which may have weakened their wishing. Also apparently he and Sylvester were all set to join in any amorous action they might commence: a prospect which, for all his admiration and good-sportsmanship, Hawthorn did not relish. Then Pavlik and Ignazio withdrew to a bedroom for twenty minutes. Hawthorn drew the natural conclusion, and was vexed and saddened by it. Upon their reappearance, Pavlik urged, that is, ordered, Hawthorn to stay there with Sylvester; and he and Ignazio departed. Then, upon specific and shameless request, phenomenal phallus was implanted phenomenally in Sylvester's person. My inexperienced provincial was even more surprised that it should be possible than I was to hear of it. He enjoyed it, but soon intensely disliked Sylvester, he said. Whereas he had not forgotten Ignazio's beauty; and Pavlik promised for them to meet again this winter.

To this coarse tale I listened with very mixed emotion, naturally. I replied with somewhat cunning characterization of dear Pavlik, cunning although honest: how he occasionally likes to maneuver his young acquaintances into awkward posture or scandalous relationship, to couple them, and avidly watch their courtship or intercourse, and perhaps slip a little in between them, and playfully uncouple them again – the wind of his strange spirit blowing where it listeth. It gratifies his terrible mental sensuality; or serves to furnish his great draughtsman's imagination; and flatters his sense of his own moral and social superiority. I refer not only to the occasional evenings of amorous fooling, indecent eye-witnessing; his general friendliness toward his inferiors, advising and interfering and gossiping, is in much the same spirit. And, as I warned Hawthorn, he does not as a rule show much respect or esteem for the young men in question, at least not unless they have seemed perfectly obedient.

My warning was perhaps unnecessary. For Hawthorn proceeded to congratulate himself warmly upon being altogether too idealistic and 'wholesome' for such goings-on. Also, Pavlik had taken no interest in him as a painter. Perhaps Pavlik would not wish to be friends with him. In any case, he guessed he did not care or dare to be friends with Pavlik. Needless to say, my rather heartsick and half-hearted malice was with reference to his possible future intimacy not with Pavlik, but with Ignazio.

For here I was back where I started, back in the trouble I had left behind in New York: desire for Ignazio and love of George, the first in a way a substitute for the second; and the present grotesque absurd intimacy only as it were a substitute for the substitute. Absurd and perhaps terrible error; anomalous idealism, idealism always mixed up now with immoral realism, and jealous or envious despairing; and the present little fit of jealousy of daft Pavlik and ridiculous Hawthorn with respect to beauteous Ignazio only a parody of my principle passions . . . Fortunately, when I have spent the night in anyone's arms, even cold-blooded Hawthorn's, I can regard practically anything with equanimity; practically nothing seems desperate.

Ignazio assured George that he never yielded to Pavlik; and it may be so. The twenty minutes at Sylvester's which made Hawthorn nervous may have been quite inactive. I can imagine my old friend just talking, talking, in his own honor, for his own entertainment; even preaching some, in his unique Manichaean manner; and certainly advising his protégé not to have much to do with Hawthorn, for this or that subtle reason. In fact, his established darling seems to satisfy him sufficiently; in any case he knows how to check him. As he himself once explained to me in a wonderful conversation, he deliberately encourages himself to think and talk as pornographically as possible and not as a preparation for active immortality or jazzy accompaniment, but as a substitute for it. With a mind excessive in everything, overwrought and over-optimistic, if he really did as a number of his close friends do, or if he did all that he himself would like to do, in fact he would lack strength and tranquility for his art. Year in and year out, at any hour of the day or night, especially after dinner, he is likely to get on the subject of sex, his hobby-horse, always with emphasis upon the actual or imagined magnitude of whatever private part comes in question: his very brain, in an extravagant correspondence to its theme, tumescent, erectible. Around and around and around he talks, and, you might say, all up in the air, like a witch astride a broomstick. Those of us who are not simply disgusted by this habit are often much alarmed by it; he might go crazy. But truly, so far, it has been in the nature of a sane wickedness rather than insanity. It is not degradation, but a 'sublimation'; not a mania but only idée fixe; not satyriasis, but a kind of cult worship . . . Also he likes to make people think that he fornicates tremendously, with all and sundry, harum-scarum. Many would make fun of him if they supposed that his bawdy was all smoke and no fire, all bark and no bite; he must prefer to seem abhorrent or alarming. Also the general credulity adds zest to his daydream of himself; throws a light of reality upon his purposeful fiction. I am sure that, as to the twenty minutes at Sylvester's, he wanted Hawthorn to think the worst. And, if I were to remind him of that occasion, I should not be surprised to be given to understand that he had enjoyed Hawthorn also, with wondrous abominable details.

I recount all this – not insisting upon the precision of any item, but, I think, generally veracious – as a sidelight upon my old friend's character and, indeed, his art. And the thought of him is helpful to me, enlightening. Indeed I must say that it is an enlightenment in wild disparate flashes, with bad awe-inspiring shadows. For in many respects his sex life has been like the sex lives of those I referred to while shamefully waiting for Hawthorn in the hotel at Belfast – of the kind that gives me an excuse to congratulate myself upon my own ventures, comparatively speaking; the repetitious, lowly, morbid, clownish kind. In other respects it is wonderfully symbolic of the terrible effort I too must make in my way; the policy of high thinking and low behavior to be pursued for art's sake and (in my case, not his), even for love's sake as well. He is a truly remarkable artist. He is certainly demented in a way, and not just figuratively speaking. But he suddenly stops the dancing prancing reeling progress of that dementia, right on the brink of his precipice. There on the brink he cheats it, and casts a beneficent spell upon himself, and turns some of it into art. That is why, when his art appears practically evil, then it is most beautiful, most important.

As for Ignazio, and whether or not he did make or might make love to Pavlik, or to others, even this latest 'lover' of mine who told me the above tale: it is a distinction which could not in any case make much difference to me. Even were I to begin caring for him again, hoping to have better luck with him presently in changed circumstances, the report of his mere lolling about and exhibiting himself at Pavlik's behest with that other incongruous couple would discourage me plenty. Hopeless as I am, perhaps I prefer to think the worst, whatever is worst; for George and I have already paid too dearly for our interest in him.

The meal of lobsters and huckleberries and the tale of bawdy ended, it was time to go to a certain drugstore and buy my ticket and wait for the bus back to Amalfi. It was not on schedule, because all morning there had been thunderstorms all up and down the coast.

The drugstore atmosphere troubled me with too many souvenirs of past waiting or loitering, even some pertaining to faraway adolescence: Wisconsin drugstores with Adelaide Bovery or with Roy Kilhart. That is perhaps the most universal and standardized atmosphere in this country. It was hard to believe that outdoors there was Maine's peculiar stormy brilliance, and a block or two away, vast commencement of a series of majestic waterways, and isles as shapely as the isle of Greece, and an intelligent architecture, and no billboards. Shadowy indoors full of twinkling of bottles and irritating imperative slogans; tableful of magazines glimmering with movie-star faces, platinum-blondes and redheads; odors of syrups and of chemicals; and the sullen chemist in his enclosed corner like a priest in the confessional or a witch-doctor ready to bewitch; and the lazy sweaty boy behind the soda fountain with a cold-sore on the left side of his smile, with platinum-blond hairs on his voluptuous forearm . . . I felt tired of it all, past and present; perhaps of this country; or tired of myself as part and parcel of the tiresome things I was tired of.

We ordered ice cream sodas to pass the time; and I carried mine to a table as far from the fountain as possible, to prevent Hawthorn's conversation with and getting me involved in conversation with the soda-jerker, a friend of his. He nudged me when a certain other young man came in and made a purchase and went out: one whose loveliness a year or two ago had preoccupied him. I could imagine it; but he had lost a number of his teeth; also his complexion bore witness to overindulgence in perhaps ice cream sodas. But now my interest in the not exactly imaginable things Hawthorn had to say about him was a bit forced.

My attention turned back to Hawthorn himself. Whether by night or day, whether on the seashore or in bed or in a restaurant or this drugstore, there was not the least sign of our intimacy's having had an effect on him. He was an inconsequential, that is, a nonsequential fellow, I thought; therefore he was incorrigible. And the incorrigible is practically the eternal. So then and there – in the drugstore, where there was no magic, no charm of scenery or uplifting interest of art or architecture; after lunch, when my desire had expired, and my wish to get away from him was as pronounced as a physical condition – he seemed more important to me than he had seemed before.

Proteus, Priapus: yes, I had thought of those great names, but only descriptively, with no sense of effect upon myself, no awe. Proteus the unknowable, old man of the sea, fish-blooded; personification of indecision and delusion and fraud. Great exciting unpleasant Priapus, embodiment of sex as it may have been set up eternally to intimidate us and to punish us with not pleasurable, no indeed, unendurable club . . . Religious I am, in a way; religious enough to respect and fear such concepts as those two when they come to mind – religious in the sense of a profound persuasion that everything must be significant, anything may matter. In which sense I fancied, as it were to pass the time, but with a great grave cold emotion, with a genuflection of all my intellect and every nerve from head to foot – there in the stuffy shadowy drugstore, amid the candy boxes and the patent medicines and the movie magazines – I fancied that those two divinities, oddly two-in-one in the priapic person and protean personality of my odd Hawthorn, perhaps had appeared in my life and come to my mind to show me something or do something to me.

The god of the orchard and the garden perhaps, according to Mediterranean tradition, to remind me to keep what little virginity I have left; to frighten me out of this particular orchard and garden, realm of pornographic imagining and make-believe love and substitute sex; to discourage any further thievery of this kind of exorbitant fruit, this not necessary unwholesome and not unnatural and in my opinion not immoral but forbidden – somehow, in the long run, by the nature of things, forbidden – fruit . . .

The opposite god, the god of metamorphoses and hopeless strife and vain labor, the opposite of animality and orgy – manifest in all my laborious attempt to understand my little man's odd, infinitely equivocal, perhaps meaningless character, and in the prospect of worse further difficulty if I should try to write an account of him and of our relationship – perhaps just to tire me out, wear me down; and to disgust me with the way I have been trying to live, trying to work and play at the same time, trying to love and not love at the same time. And to warn me of the terrible virtuosity and versatility and malleability of my imagination: my ability of disillusion with myself about no matter what in an instant, by one flourish of my hot spirit, one ejaculation of my sour wit; and my ability to embellish and dignify and even deify no matter who, for a while . . .

So I sat there more quietly gazing at my more or less deified fellow, Maine Priapus, Maine Proteus, over our two foamy beakers of ice cream, across the sticky little drugstore table of imitation onyx. And I felt sure that in any case our twenty-four-hour intimacy had been somehow a terminal rather than an initiatory or inaugurative experience. It marked the end, not the beginning of a bizarre chapter of myself; the signal to give up as a bad job one of my methods of managing my wretched temperament. No doubt I should not have been thinking of a written account of it, if it were not so. There probably would not be many more such fellows in my life; anyway my approach to them, my hail and farewell to them, would never be the same. And the expression on my face as I thought of this must have been terrible. For at last my poor Hawthorn seemed really respectful of me; he shut up, and ceased winking and grinning at me. He looked not at all extraordinary, not superhuman or subhuman; he was just an ordinary lonesome smalltown New Englander like his friend at the soda fountain or like his ex-darling with too few teeth.

Finally one of the thunderstorms hanging all around struck Clamariscassett, softly flashing, rumbling, and with thick tepid drops; and with it the bus arrived; and I clambered up into it. As I sat there waving goodbye to Hawthorn through the drenched window I observed that – so long and laborious had our night together been, our sensational and enjoyable but not joyous intercourse – one of my elbows had been chafed by the sheet under us until it had drawn blood. How extraordinary! And so I departed, somewhat smiling at this silly indecent valedictory idea; how much tougher his sex had proved than my elbow! Also I sillily wondered if in the figurative and spiritual sense I could call myself thin-skinned; and in spite of my various excitability, I thought not. In any case, I mend, I mend, I mend! – as fast as any young warrior or any incorrigible old tomcat.

Violent showers overtook us every few miles all the way to Ellsworth. At one point for half an hour we rode under a canopy of ashen and bluish cloud, trimmed with long funereal ostrich. Behind us in the west this rich drapery swung apart, constituting a great oblong window, through which we looked miles away to a very different skyscape, all summery azure, upon which rested a flock of diminutive cirrocumulus, lamb-like. And diagonally across the window, in front of the idyllic distance, there hung the voile of the rain in perfect little pleats.

Western skies are shinier, Mediterranean skies bluer; the characteristic thing about the Maine sky is its brilliance in a modest or intermediary or composite color: *grisaille*. Holland's in summer is like it, but less brilliant. The landscape also lends itself remarkably to strange light-effects. For there are almost no altitudes important enough or abrupt enough to wall one in; therefore the vistas are great, and as the road twines along the shore like a vine, they keep changing. Rock somewhat like alabaster and burnished hayfields and white architecture bend all along and baroquely frame the various bays and estuaries: ancient valleys submerged as the continent has tilted eastward; riverbeds flooded at whatever hour the moon has charmed the ocean. From these waters embedded in the countryside like looking-glass, an extraordinary cold refraction is always added to the sunlight; and a luxurious grayness like moonlight, ten times as strong, arises wherever the sun goes under a cloud.

Preoccupied with all this and the like, thus I returned from my escapade, to all intents and purposes delighted. I tried to make a few notes, to devise a few exact images, with my notebook on my jolted knees, my pencil jumping in my fingers. For the bus was traveling as fast as ever; the narrow highway was slippery; wind and showers kept rapidly and dimly enwrapping everything; now and then a little lightning snapped at us: it was fearful. The bus driver had struck up acquaintance with a pretty trained nurse in the seat next to his, somewhat behind him; so there was a good deal of turning of his head and rolling of his eyes away from the road, with modestly concupiscent small-talk. I could see that it was all a kind of play-acting, foolishness; she would not see him again, and he knew it. It might have been the death of us nevertheless.

But now I felt no fear: to that extent at least love had had an improving effect upon me. Properly speaking, of course, there had not been the least love about it. Love had nothing to do with it. I did not care to see that poor Hawthorn again; I hoped and prayed that I might never need to see him: to that extent the present need had been attended to. Month after month I appear to be living under an evil spell of chastity cast by Monroe and George, those two who need me most and whom I love best. Last night's exercise had enabled me to feel that it was not necessarily so. It had cured me for a while of being sorry for myself. It had cleared my imagination of the temptations like a sideshow, the nightmare as sad as Saint Anthony's, by which for lack of love it gets naturally inhabited. Now in my early middle age, these three little changes of state of mind constitute what I am willing to call happiness: which is the best excuse I can give for bad sexy behavior. I know that my life is a wonderfully fortunate one, but I cannot always be glad of it. Often, when I am chaste, I cannot be glad of it. I know that my maker, so to speak, made me wonderfully well; but I am often unable to feel any gratitude. I am ashamed of this; and in the vagueness and hypochondria of shame everything goes wrong or seems to go wrong or seems very like to go wrong. But now, as a result of just a little bout of disgraceful fornication, for the time being I felt willing to call myself happy, willing to be myself, glad to be myself, able to face my maker without grimacing – that is, in a fit state to die. How fantastic and wonderful! And readiness to die is equivalent to courage: therefore I did not mind how foolishly the bus driver flirted, how damnably he drove, all the way to Sorrento.

NOËL COWARD

ME AND THE GIRLS

Tuesday

I like looking at mountains because they keep changing, if you know what I mean; not only the colours change at different times of the day but the shapes seem to alter too. I see them first when I wake up in the morning and Sister Dominique pulls up the blind. She's a dear old camp and makes clicking noises with her teeth. The blind rattles up and there they are – the mountains I mean. There was fresh snow on them this morning, that is on the highest peaks, and they looked very near in the clear air, blue and pink as if someone had painted them, rather like those pictures you see in frame shops in the King's Road, bright and a bit common but pretty.

Today was the day when they all came in: Dr. Pierre and Sister Françoise and the other professor, with the blue chin and a gleam in his eye, quite a dish really he is, hairy wrists but lovely long slim hands. He was the one who actually did the operation. I could go for him in a big way if I was well enough, but I'm not and that's that, nor am I likely to be for a long time. It's going to be a slow business. Dr. Pierre explained it carefully and very very gently, not at all like his usual manner which is apt

NOËL COWARD (1899–1973): No doubt the candid, campy and tender 'Me and the Girls' will come as a surprise to those readers familiar only with Coward's work as a lyricist and playwright (Hay Fever, Blithe Spirit, Private Lives, and the one-act play from which the film Brief Encounter was adapted). Philip Hoare has written his biography.

to be a bit offish. While I was listening to him I looked at the professor's face: he was staring out at the mountains and I thought he looked sad. Sister Françoise and Sister Dominique stood quite still except that Sister Françoise was fiddling with her rosary. I got the message all right but I didn't let on that I did. They think I'm going to die and as they've had a good dekko inside me and I haven't, they probably know. I've thought of all this before of course, before the operation, actually long before when I was in the other hospital. I don't know yet how I feel about it quite, but then I've had a bit of a bashing about and I'm tired. It's not going to matter to anyone but me anyway and I suppose when it does happen I shan't care, what with being dopey and one thing and another. The girls will be sorry, especially Mavis, but she'll get over it. Ronnie will have a crying jag and get pissed and wish he'd been a bit nicer, but that won't last long either. I know him too well. Poor old Ron. I expect there were faults on both sides, there always are, but he was a little shit and no two ways about it. Still I brought it all on myself so I mustn't complain. It all seems far away now anyhow. Nothing seems very near except the mountains and they look as if they wanted to move into the room.

When they had all filed out and left me alone Sister D. came back because she'd forgotten my temperature chart and wanted to fill it in or something, at least that was what she said, but she didn't fool me: what she really came back for was to see if I was all right. She did a lot of teeth clicking and fussed about with my pillows and when she'd finally buggered off I gave way a bit and had a good cry, then I dropped off and had a snooze and woke up feeling quite spry. Maybe the whole thing's in my imagination anyhow. You never know really do you? – I mean when you're weak and kind of low generally you have all sorts of thoughts that you wouldn't have if you were up and about. All the same there *was* something in the way Dr. Pierre talked. The professor squeezed my hand when he left and smiled but his eyes still looked sad. It must be funny to be a doctor and always be coping with ill people and cheering them up even if you have to tell them a few lies while you're at it. Not that he said much. He just stood there most of the time like I said, looking at the mountains.

This is quite a nice room as hospital rooms go. There is a chintzy armchair for visitors and the walls are off-white so as not to be too glarey. Rather like the flat in the rue Brochet, which Ronnie and I did over just after we'd first met. If you mix a tiny bit of pink with the white it takes the coldness out of it but you have to be careful that it doesn't go streaky.

I can hardly believe that all that was only three years ago, it seems like a lifetime.

All the girls sent me flowers except Mavis and she sent me a bottle of Mitsouko toilet water which is better than flowers really because it lasts longer and it's nice to dab on at night when you wake up feeling hot and sweaty. She said she'd pop in and see me this afternoon just for a few minutes to tell me how the act's getting on. I expect it's a bit of a shambles really without me there to bound on and off and keep it on the tracks. They've had to change the running-order. Mavis does her single now right after the parasol dance so as to give the others time to get into their kimonos for the Japanese number. I must remember to ask her about Sally. She was overdue when I left and that's ten days ago. She's a silly little cow that girl if ever there was one, always getting carried away and losing her head. A couple of drinks and she's gone. Well if she's clicked again she'll just have to get on with it and maybe it'll teach her to be more careful in the future. I expect it was that Hungarian but she swears it wasn't. Anyway Mavis will know what to do, Mavis always knows what to do except when she gets what she calls 'emotionally disturbed,' then she's hell. She ought to get out of the act and marry somebody and settle down and have children, she's still pretty but it won't last and she'll never be a star if she lives to be a hundred, she just hasn't got that extra something. Her dancing's okay and she can put over a number all right but that dear little *je ne sais quoi* just isn't there poor bitch and it's no good pretending it is. I know it's me that stands in her way up to a point but I can't do anything about it. She knows all about me. I've explained everything until I'm blue in the face but it doesn't make any difference. She's got this 'thing' about me not really being queer but only having caught it like a bad habit. Would you mind! Of course I should never have gone to bed with her in the first place. That sparked off the whole business. Poor old Mavis. These girls really do drive me round the bend sometimes. I will say one thing though, they *do* behave like ladies, outwardly at least. I've never let them get off a plane or a train without lipstick and the proper clothes and shoes. None of those pony-tails and tatty slacks for George Banks Esq.: not on your Nelly. My girls have got to look dignified whether they like it or not. To do them justice they generally do. There have been one or two slip-ups, like that awful Maureen. She was a slut from the word go. I was forever after her about one thing or another. She always tried to dodge shaving under the arms because some silly bitch had told her that the men liked it.

Imagine! I told her that that lark went out when the Moulin Rouge first opened in eighteen-whatever-it-was but as she'd never heard of the Moulin Rouge anyway it didn't make much impression on her. At any rate she finally got mumps in Brussels and had to be sent home and I was glad to see the last of her. This lot are very good on the whole. Apart from Mavis there's Sally, blond and rather bouncy; Irma, skin a bit sluggish but comes up a treat under the lights; Lily-May, the best dancer of the lot but calves a bit on the heavy side; and Beryl and Sylvia Martin. They're our twins and they're planning to work up a sister act later on. They're both quite pretty but that ole debbil talent has failed to touch either of them with his fairy wings so I shouldn't think the sister act will get much further than the Poland Rehearsal Rooms. The whole show closes here next Saturday week then God knows what will happen. I wrote off to Ted before my operation telling him that the act would have to be disbanded and asking him what he could do for them, but you know what agents are, all talk and no do as a rule. Still he's not a bad little sod taken by and large so we shall see.

Wednesday

Mavis came yesterday afternoon as promised. I didn't feel up to talking for long but I did my best. She started off all right, a bit overcheerful and taking the 'Don't worry everything's going to be all right' line, but I could see she was in a bit of a state and trying not to show it. I don't know if she'd been talking to any of the sisters or whether they'd told her anything or not. I don't suppose they did, and her French isn't very good anyhow. She said the act was going as well as could be expected and that Monsieur Philippe had come backstage last night and been quite nice. She also asked if I'd like her to write to Ronnie and tell him about me being ill but I jumped on that double-quick pronto. It's awful when women get too understanding. I don't want her writing to Ronnie any more than I want Ronnie writing to me. He's got his ghastly Algerian *and* the flat so he can bloody well get on with it. I don't mind any more anyway. I did at first of course, I couldn't help myself, it wasn't the Algerian so much, it was all the lies and scenes. Fortunately I was rehearsing all through that month and had a lot to keep my mind occupied. It was bad I must admit but not so bad that it couldn't have been worse. No more being in love for me thank you very much. Not that I expect I shall have much chance. But if I do get out of this place all alive-o there's going to be no more of that caper. I've had it, once and for all. Sex is all very well in its way and I'm all for it but the next time I begin to feel that old black magic that I know so well I'll streak off like a bloody greyhound.

When Mavis had gone Sister Clothilde brought me my tea. Sister Clothilde's usually on in the afternoons. She's small and tubby and has a bit of a guttural accent having been born in Alsace-Lorraine; she also has bright bright red cheeks which look as if someone had pinched them hard just before she came into the room. She must have been quite pretty in a dumpy way when she was a girl before she took the veil or whatever it is you have to take before you give yourself to Jesus. She has quite a knowing look in her eye too as though she wasn't quite so far away from the wicked world as she pretended to be. She brought me a madeleine with my tea but it was a bit dry. When she'd gone and I'd had the tea and half the madeleine I settled back against the pillows and relaxed. It's surprising what funny things pop into your mind when you're lying snug in bed and feeling a bit drowsy. I started to try to remember everything I could from the very beginning like playing a game, but I couldn't keep dead on the beam: I'd suddenly jump from something that happened fifteen years ago to something that happened two weeks back. That was when the pain had begun to get pretty bad and Monsieur Philippe came into the dressing-room with Dr. Pierre and there was I writhing about with nothing but a jock-strap on and sweating like a pig. That wasn't so good that bit because I didn't know what was going to happen to me and I felt frightened. I don't feel frightened now, just a bit numb as though some part of me was hypnotised. I suppose that's the result of having had the operation. My inside must be a bit startled at all that's gone on and I expect the shock has made my mind tired. When I try to think clearly and remember things, I don't seem able to hold on to any subject for long. The thing is to give up to the tiredness and not worry. They're all very kind, the sisters and the doctors, even the maid who does the room every morning gives me a cheery smile as if she wanted to let me know she was on my side. She's a swarthy type with rather projecting eyes like a pug. I bet she'll finish up as a concierge with those regulation black stockings and a market-basket. There's a male orderly who pops in and out from time to time and very sprightly he is too, you'd think he was about to take off any minute. He's the one who shaved me before the operation and that was a carry-on if ever there was one. I wasn't in any pain because they'd given me an injection but woozy as I was I managed to make a few jokes. When he pushed my old man aside almost caressingly with his hand I said '*Pas ce soir Josephine, demain peutêtre*' and he giggled. It can't be much fun being an orderly in a hospital and have to shave people's privates and give them enemas and sit them on bed-pans from morning till night, but I suppose they must find it interesting otherwise they'd choose some other profession. When he'd finished he gave my packet a friendly little pat and said, '*Vive le sport.*' *Would* you mind! Now whenever he comes in he winks at me as though we shared a secret and I have a sort of feeling he's dead right. I suppose if I didn't feel so weak and seedy I'd encourage him a bit just for the hell of it. Perhaps when I'm a little stronger I'll ask him to give me a massage or something just to see what happens – as if I didn't know! On the other hand of course if what I suspect is true, I shan't get strong again so the question won't come up. Actually he reminds me a bit of Peter when we first met at Miss Llewellyn's Dancing Academy, stocky and fair with short legs and a high colour. Peter was the one that did the pas de deux from *Giselle* with Coralie Hancock and dropped her on her head during one of the lifts and she had concussion and had to go to St. George's Hospital. It's strange to think of those early days. I can see myself now getting off the bus at Marble Arch with my ballet shoes in that tatty old bag of Aunt Isobel's. I had to walk down Edgware Road and then turn to the left and the dancing academy was down some steps under a public house called the Swan. There was a mirror all along one wall with a *barre* in front of it and Miss Adler used to thump away at the upright while we did our bends and kicks and positions. Miss Llewellyn was a character and no mistake. She had frizzed-up fair hair, very black at the parting; a heavy stage make-up with a beauty spot under her left eye if you please and a black velvet band around her neck. She always wore this rain or shine. Peter said it was to hide the scar where someone had tried to cut her throat. She wasn't a bad old tart really and she did get me my first job, in a Christmas play called *Mr. Birdie*. I did an audition for it at the Garrick Theatre. Lots of other kids had been sent for and there we were all huddled at the side of the stage in practice clothes waiting to be called out. When my turn came I pranced on, followed by Miss Adler, who made a beeline for the piano, which sounded as if someone had dropped a lot of tin ashtrays inside it, you know, one of those diabolical old uprights that you only get at auditions. Anyhow I sang 'I Hear You Calling Me' – it was before the poor darlings dropped so I was still a soprano – and then I did the standard sailor's hornpipe as taught at the academy, a lot of hopping about and hauling at imaginary ropes and finishing with a few quick turns and a leap off. Mr. Alec Sanderson, who was producing *Mr. Birdie*, then sent for me to go and speak to him in the stalls. Miss Adler came with me and he told me I could play the heroine's little brother in the first act, a gnome in the second, and a frog in the third, and that he'd arrange the business side with Miss Llewellyn. Miss Adler and I fairly flew out into Charing Cross Road and on wings of song to Lyon's Corner House where she stood me tea and we had an éclair each. I really can't think about *Mr. Birdie* without laughing and when I laugh it hurts my stitches. It really was a fair bugger, whimsical as all get-out. Mr. Birdie, played by Mr. Sanderson himself, was a lovable old professor who suddenly inherited a family of merry little kiddos of which I was one. We were all jolly and ever so mischievous in act one and then we all went to sleep in a magic garden and became elves and gnomes and what have you for acts two and three. Some of us have remained fairies to this day. The music was by Oliver Bakewell, a rip-snorting old queen who used to pinch our bottoms when we were standing round the piano learning his gruesome little songs. Years later when I knew what was what I reminded him of this and he whinnied like a horse.

Those were the days all right, days of glory for child actors. I think the boys had a better time than the girls on account of not being so well protected. I shall never forget those jovial wet-handed clergymen queueing up outside the stage-door to take us out to tea and stroke our knees under the table. Bobby Clews and I used to have bets as to how much we could get without going too far. I once got a box of Fuller's soft-centres and a gramophone record of *Casse Noisette* for no more than a quick grope in a taxi. After my voice broke I got pleurisy and a touch of TB and had to be sent to a sanatorium near Buxton. I was cured and sent home to Auntie Iso after six months but it gave me a fright I can tell you. I was miserable for the first few weeks and cried my eyes out, but I got used to it and quite enjoyed the last part when I was moved into a small room at the top of the house with a boy called Digby Lawson. He was two years older than me, round about seventeen and a half. He died a short time later and I really wasn't surprised. It's a miracle that I'm alive to tell the tale, but I must say we had a lot of laughs.

It wasn't until I was nineteen that I got into the chorus at the Palladium and that's where I really learnt my job. I was there two and a half years in all and during the second year I was given the understudy of Jackie Foal. He was a sensational dancer and I've never worked so hard in my life. I only went on for him three times but one of the times was for a whole week and it was a thrill I can tell you when I got over the panic. One night I got round Mr Lewis to let me have the house seats for Aunt Iso and Emma, who's her sort of maid-companion, and they dressed themselves up to the nines and had a ball. Emma wore her best black with a bead necklace she borrowed from Clara two doors down and Auntie Iso looked as though she were ready for tiara night at the opera: a full evening dress made of crimson taffeta with a sort of lace overskirt of the same colour; a dramatic headdress that looked like a coronet with pince-nez attached and the Chinese coat Uncle Fred had brought her years ago when he was in the merchant navy. I took them both out to supper afterwards at Giovanni's in Greek Street. He runs the restaurant with a boy friend of his, a sulky-looking little sod as a rule but he played up that night and both he and Giovanni laid on the full VIP treatment, cocktails on the house, a bunch of flowers for the old girls, and a lot of hand kissing. It all knocked me back a few quid but it was worth it to see how they enjoyed themselves. They both got a bit pissed on Chianti and Emma laughed so much that her upper plate fell into the zabaglione and she had to fish it out with a spoon. Actually it wasn't long after that that Auntie Iso died and Emma went off to live with her sister in Lowestoft. I hated it when Auntie Iso died and even now after all these years it still upsets me to think of it. After all she was all I'd got in the way of relations and she'd brought me up and looked after me ever since I was five. After she'd gone I shared a flat with Bunny Granger for a bit in Longacre which was better than nothing but I'd rather have been on my own. Bunny was all right in his way; he came to the funeral with me and did his best to cheer me up but he didn't stay the course very long really if you know what I mean and that flat was a shambles, it really was. Nobody minds fun and games within reason but you can have too much of a good thing. There was hardly a night he didn't bring someone or other home and one night if you please I nipped out of my room to go to the bathroom which was up one flight and there was a policeman scuffling back into his uniform. I nearly had a fit but actually he turned out to be quite nice. Anyway I didn't stay with Bunny long because I met Harry and that was that. Harry was the first time it ever happened to me seriously. Of course I'd hopped in and out of bed with people every now and again and never thought about it much one way or another. I never was one to go off into a great production about being queer and work myself up into a state like some people I know. I can't think why they waste their time. I mean it just doesn't make sense does it? You're born either hetero, bi, or homo and whichever way it goes there you are stuck with it. Mind you people are getting a good deal more hep about it than they used to be but the laws still exist that make it a crime and poor bastards still get hauled off to the clink just for doing what comes naturally as the song says. Of course this is what upsets some of the old magistrates more than anything, the fact that it *is* as natural as any other way of having sex, leaving aside the strange ones who get excited over old boots or used knickers or having themselves walloped with straps. Even so I don't see that it's anybody's business but your own what you do with your old man providing that you don't make a beeline for the dear little kiddies, not, I am here to tell you, that quite a lot of the aforesaid dear little kiddies don't enjoy it tip-top. I was one myself and I know. But I digress as the bride said when she got up in the middle of her honeymoon night and baked a cake. That's what I mean really about the brain not hanging on to one thing when you're tired. It keeps wandering off. I was trying to put down about Harry and what I felt about it and got side-tracked. All right – all right – let's concentrate on Harry-boy and remember what he looked like and not only what he looked like, but him, him himself. To begin with he was inclined to be moody and when we first moved into the maisonette in Swiss Cottage together he was always fussing about whether Mrs. Fingal suspected anything or not, but as I kept explaining to him, Mrs. Fingal wouldn't have minded if we poked Chinese mice providing that we paid the rent regularly and didn't make a noise after twelve o'clock at night. As a matter of fact she was quite a nice old bag and I don't think nor ever did think that she suspected for a moment, she bloody well knew. I don't mean to say that she thought about it much or went on about it to herself. She just accepted the situation and minded her own business and if a few more people I know had as much sense the world would be a far happier place. Anyway, Harry-boy got over being worried about her or about himself and about us after a few months and we settled down, loved each other good and true for two and a half years until the accident happened and he was killed. I'm not going to think about that because even now it still makes me feel sick and want to cry my heart out. I always hated that fucking motor bike anyhow but he was mad for it, forever tinkering with it and rubbing it down with oily rags and fiddling about with its engine. But that was part of his character really. He loved machinery and engineering and football matches and all the things I didn't give a bugger about. We hadn't a thing in common actually except the one thing you can't explain. He wasn't even all that good-looking now I come to think of it. His eyes were nice but his face wasn't anything out of the ordinary: his body was wonderful, a bit thick-set but he was very proud of it and never stopped doing exercises and keeping himself fit. He never cared what the maisonette looked like and once when I'd bought a whole new set of loose covers for the divan bed and the two armchairs, he never even noticed until I pointed them out to him. He used to laugh at me too and send me up rotten when I fussed about the place and tried to keep things tidy. But he loved me. That's the shining thing I like to remember. He loved me more than anyone has ever loved me before or since. He used to have affairs with girls every now and again, just to keep his hand in, as he used to say. I got upset about this at first and made a few scenes but he wouldn't stand for any of that nonsense and let me know it in no uncertain terms. He loved me true did Harry-boy and I loved him true, and if the happiness we gave each other was wicked and wrong in the eyes of the Law and the Church and God Almighty, then the Law and the Church and God Almighty can go dig a hole and fall down it.

Thursday

I had a bad night and at about two in the morning Sister Jeanne-Marie gave me a pill and I got off to sleep all right and didn't wake until seven. I couldn't see the mountains at all because the clouds had come down and wiped them away. My friend the orderly came in at eight o'clock and gave me an enema on account of I hadn't been since the day before yesterday and then only a few goat's balls. He was very cheery and kiss-me-arse and kept on saying '*Soyez courageux*' and '*Tenez le*' until I could have throttled him. After it was all over he gave me a bath and soaped me and then, when he was drying me, I suddenly felt sort of weak and despairing and burst into tears. He at once stopped being happy-chappy and good-time-Charlie and put both his arms round me tight. He'd taken his white coat off to bathe me and he had a stringy kind of vest and I could feel the hairs on his chest against my face while he held me. Presently he sat down on the loo seat and took me onto his lap as though I were a child. I went on crying for a bit and he let me get on with it without saying a word or trying to cheer me up. He just patted me occasionally with the hand that wasn't holding me and kept quite still. After a while the tears stopped and I got hold of myself. He dabbed my face gently with a damp towel, slipped me into my pyjama jacket, carried me along the passage, and put me back into bed. It was already made, cool and fresh, and the flowers the girls had sent me had been brought back in their vases and put about the room. I leant back against the pillows and closed my eyes because I was feeling fairly whacked, what with the enema and the crying-jag and one thing and another. When I opened them he had gone.

I dozed on and off most of the morning and in the afternoon Sally came to see me. She brought me last week's *Tatler* and this week's *Paris Match*, which was full of Brigitte Bardot as usual. If you ask me, what that poor girl needs is less publicity and more discipline. Sally was wearing her beige two-piece with a camp little red hat. She looked very pretty and was in high spirits having come on after all nearly ten days late. She said the Hungarian had come to the show the night before last and given her a bottle of Bellodgia. I asked her if she'd been to bed with him again and she giggled and said, 'Of course not, for obvious reasons.' Then I asked her if she really had a 'thing' about him and she giggled some more and said that in a way she had because he was so aristocratic and had lovely muscular legs but that it wasn't serious and that anyhow he was going back to his wife in Vienna. She said he went into quite an act about this and swore that she would be forever in his heart but that she didn't believe a word of it. I told her that she'd better be more careful in the future and see to it that another time she got more out of a love affair than a near miss and a bottle of Bellodgia. She's a nice enough kid really, our Sally, but she just doesn't think or reason things out. I asked her what she was going to do when the act folds on Saturday week and she said she wasn't sure but she'd put a phone call through to London to a friend of hers who thinks he can get some modelling for her, to fill in for the time being. She said that all the girls sent me their love and that one or other of them was coming to see me every day, but Mavis had told them not more than one at a time and not to stay long at that. Good old Mavis. Bossy to the last.

Sally had brought me a packet of mentholated filter-tip cigarettes and when she'd gone I smoked one just for a treat and it made me quite dizzy because I've not been smoking at all for the last few days, I somehow didn't feel like it. During the dizziness the late afternoon sun came out and suddenly there were the mountains again, wobbling a bit but as good as new. I suppose I've always had a 'thing' about mountains ever since I first saw any, which was a great many too many years ago as the crow flies and I'd just got my first 'girl' act together and we had a booking on the ever so gay continent. Actually it was in Zurich in a scruffy little dive called Die Kleine Maus or something. There were only four girls and me and we shared a second-class compartment on the night train from Paris. I remember we all got nicely thank you on a bottle of red wine I bought at the station buffet and when we woke up from our communal coma in the early hours of the morning there were the mountains with the first glow of sunrise on them and everyone did a lot of ooh-ing and aah-ing and I felt as though suddenly something wonderful had happened to me. We all took it in turns to dart down the corridor to the lav and when we'd furbished ourselves up and I'd shaved and the girls had put some slap on, we staggered along to the restaurant car and had large bowls of coffee and croissants with butter and jam. The mountains were brighter then, parading past the wide windows and covered in snow, and I wished we weren't going to a large city but could stay off for a few days and wander about and look at the waterfalls. However we *did* go to a large city and when we got there we laid a great big gorgeous egg and nobody came to see us after the first performance. It was a dank little room we had to perform in with a stage at one end, then a lot of tables and then a bar with a looking-glass behind it so we could see our reflections, which wasn't any too encouraging I can tell you. A handful of square-looking Swiss gentlemen used to sit at the tables with their girl friends and they were so busy doing footy-footy and gropey-gropey that they never paid any attention to us at all. We might just as well not have been there. One night we finished the Punch and Judy number without a hand except from one oaf in the corner on the right, and he was only calling the waiter. There were generally a few poufs clustered round the bar hissing at each other like snakes, apart from them that was it. The manager came round after the third performance and told us we'd have to finish at the end of the week. He was lovely he was, bright red in the face and shaped like a pear. I had a grand upper and downer with him because we'd been engaged on a two weeks' contract. His English wasn't up to much and in those days I couldn't speak a word of German or French so the scene didn't exactly flow. There was a lot of arm waving and banging on the dressing-table and the girls sat round giggling, but I finally made him agree to pay us half our next week's salary as compensation. The next morning I had another upper and downer with Monsieur Huber, who was the man who had booked the act through Ted Bentley, my agent in London. Monsieur Huber was small and sharp as a needle, with a slight cast in his eye like Norma Shearer only not so pretty. As a matter of fact he wasn't so bad. At least he took our part and called up the red pear and there was a lot of palava in Switzer-Deutsch which to my mind is not a pretty language at all and sounds as if you'd got a nasty bit of phlegm in your throat and were trying to get rid of it. At any rate the upshot of the whole business was that he, Monsieur Huber, finally got us another booking in a small casino on the Swiss side of Lake Lugano and we all drove there in a bus on the Sunday and opened on the Monday night without a band call or even a dress rehearsal. I can't truthfully say that we tore the place up but we didn't do badly, anyway we stayed there for the two weeks we'd been booked for. We lived in a pension, if you'll excuse the expression, up a steep hill at the back of the town which was run by a false-blond Italian lady who looked like an all-in wrestler in drag. She wasn't a bad sort and we weren't worried by the other boarders on account of there weren't any. The girls shared two rooms on the first floor and I had a sort of attic at the top like *La Bohème*, which had a view, between houses, of the lake and the mountains. I used to watch them, the mountains, sticking up out of the mist in the early mornings, rather like these I'm looking at now. Madame Corelli, the all-in wrestler, took quite a fancy to us and came to see the show several times with her lover, who was a friend of the man who ran the casino. I wish you could have seen the lover. He was thick and short and bald as a coot and liked wearing very tight trousers to prove he had an enormous packet which indeed he had: it looked like an entire Rockingham tea service, milk jug and all. His name was Guido Mezzoni and he could speak a little English because he'd been a waiter in Soho in the dear dead days before the war. He asked us all to his place one night after the show and put on a chef's hat and made spaghetti Bolognese and we all got high as kites on vino rosso and a good time was had by *tutti* until just before we were about to leave when he takes Babs Mortimer, our youngest, into the bathroom, where she wanted to go and instead of leaving her alone to have her Jimmy Riddle in peace and quiet, he whisked her inside, locked the door, and showed her all he'd got. Of course the silly little cow lost her head and screamed bloody murder whereupon Madame Corelli went charging down the passage baying like a bloodhound. That was a nice ending to a jolly evening I must say. Nice clean fun and no questions asked. You've never heard such a carry-on. After a lot of banging on the bathroom door and screaming he finally opened it and Babs came flying into the room in hysterics and I had to give her a sharp slap in the face to quiet her, meanwhile the noise from the passage sounded as though the Mau Maus had got in. We all had another swig all round at the vino while the battle was going on and I couldn't make up my mind whether to grab all the girls and bugger off home or wait and see what happened, then I remembered that Madame Corelli had the front-door key anyhow so there wouldn't be much point in going back and just sitting on the kerb. Presently the row subsided a bit and poor old Guido came back into the room looking very hang-dog with a nasty red scratch all down one side of his face. Madame followed him wearing what they call in novels a 'set expression' which means that her mouth was in a straight line and her eyes looked like black beads. We all stood about and looked at each other for a minute or two because nobody could think of anything to say. Finally Madame hissed something to Guido in Italian and he went up miserably to Babs and said, 'I am sawry, so sawry, and I wish beg your pardon.' Babs shot me a look and I nodded irritably and she said 'Granted I'm sure' in a very grand voice and minced over to look out of the window which was fairly silly because it looked out on a warehouse and it was pitch dark anyway. Madame Corelli then took charge of the situation. Her English wasn't any too hot at the best of times and now that she was in the grip of strong emotion it was more dodgy than ever, however she made a long speech most of which I couldn't understand a word of, and gave me the key of the front door, from which I gathered that she was going to stay with Guido and that we were expected to get the hell out and leave them to it. I took the key, thanked Guido for the evening, and off we went. It was a long drag up the hill and there was no taxi in sight at that time of the morning so we had to hoof it. When we got to the house the dawn was coming up over the lake. I stopped to look at it for a moment, the air was fresh and cool and behind the mountains the sky was pale green and pink and yellow like a Neapolitan ice, but the girls were grumbling about being tired and their feet hurting so we all went in and went to bed.

The next day I had a little set-to with Babs because I thought it was necessary. I took her down to a café on the lake front and gave her an iced coffee and explained a few of the facts of life to her. Among other things I told her that you can't go through life shrieking and making scenes just because somebody makes a pass at you. There are always ways of getting out of a situation like that without going off into the second act of *Tosca*. In any case Guido hadn't really made a pass at her at all, he was obviously the type who's overproud of his great big gorgeous how-do-you-do and can't resist showing it to people. If he'd grabbed her and tried to rape her it would have been different, but all the poor little sod wanted was a little honest appreciation and probably if she'd just said something ordinary like 'Fancy' or 'What a whopper!' he wouldn't have wanted to go any further and all would have ended happily. She listened to me rather sullenly and mumbled something about it having been a shock and that she wasn't used to that sort of thing, having been brought up like a lady, to which I replied that having been brought up like a lady was no help in cabaret and that if she was all that refined she shouldn't have shoved her delicate nose into show business in the first place. Really these girls make me tired sometimes. They prance about in bikinis showing practically all they've got and then get hoity-toity when anyone makes a little pounce. What's so silly about it really is that that very thing is what they want more than anything only they won't admit it. Anyway she had another iced coffee and got off her high horse and confessed, to my great relief, that she wasn't a virgin and had had several love affairs only none of them had led to anything. I told her that it was lucky for her that they hadn't and that if at any time she got herself into trouble of any sort she was to come straight to me. After that little fireside chat we became quite good friends and when she left the act, which was about three months later, I missed her a lot. She finally got into the chorus of a musical at the Coliseum and then got married. I sometimes get a post-card from her but not very often. She must be quite middle-aged now. Good old Babs.

The other three were not so pretty as Babs but they danced better. Moira Finch was the eldest, about twenty-six, then there were Doreen March and Elsie Pendleton. Moira was tall and dark with nice legs and no tits to speak of. Doreen was mousey, mouse-coloured hair, mouse-coloured eyes, and a mouse-coloured character, she also had a squeaky voice just to make the whole thing flawless. I must say one thing for her though, she *could* dance. Her kicks were wonderful, straight up with both legs and no faking, and her turns were quick as lightning. Elsie was the sexiest of the bunch, rather pallid and languorous with the sort of skin that takes make-up a treat and looks terrible without it. They were none of them very interesting really, but they were my first lot and I can remember them kindly on the whole. We were together on and off for nearly a year and played different dance-halls and casinos all over Italy, Spain, Switzerland, and France. I learnt a lot during that tour and managed to pick up enough of the various languages to make myself understood. Nothing much happened over and above a few rows. Elsie got herself pregnant in Lyons, where we were appearing in a sort of nightclub-cum-knocking shop called Le Perroquet Vert. A lot of moaning and wailing went on but fortunately the old tart who ran the joint knew a character who could do the old crochet-hook routine and so she and I took Elsie along to see him and waited in a sitting-room with a large chandelier, a table with a knitted peacock-blue cloth on it, and a clanking old clock on the mantelpiece set between two pink china swans, the neck of one of them was broken and the head had been stuck on again crooked. After quite a long while during which Violette whatever-her-name-was told me a long saga about how she'd first been seduced at the age of thirteen by an uncle by marriage, Elsie came back with the doctor. He was a nasty piece of work if ever I saw one. He wore a greasy alpaca jacket with suspicious-looking stains on it and his eyes seemed to be struggling to get at each other over one of the biggest conks since Cyrano de Bergerac. Anyway I paid him what he wanted, which was a bloody sight more than I could afford, and we took Elsie back to the hotel in a taxi and put her to bed. She looked pale and a bit tearful but I suppose that was only to be expected. Violette said she'd better not dance that night so as to give her inside time to settle down after having been prodded about and so I had to cut the pony quartette which couldn't be done as a trio and sing 'The Darktown Strutters' Ball' with a faked-up dance routine that I invented as I went along. Nobody seemed to care anyway.

When we finally got back to London I broke up the act and shopped around to see if I could get a job on my own. I had one or two chorus offers but I turned them down. A small part, yes, even if it was only a few lines, but not the chorus again. I had a long talk with Ted Bentley and he advised me to scratch another act together, this time with better material. I must say he really did his best to help and we finally fetched up with quite a production. There was a lot of argle-bargle about how the act should be billed and we finally decided on 'Georgie Banks and His Six Bombshells.' Finding the six bombshells wasn't quite so easy. We auditioned hundreds of girls of all sorts and kinds until at long last we settled on what we thought were the best six with an extra one as a standby. In all fairness I must admit they were a bright little lot, all good dancers and pretty snappy to look at. Avice Bennet was the eldest, about twenty-seven, with enormous eyes and a treacherous little gold filling which only showed when she laughed. Then there was Sue Mortlock, the sort of bouncy little blonde that the tired businessmen are supposed to go for. Jill Kenny came next on the scroll of honour, she was a real smasher, Irish with black hair and violet blue eyes and a temper of a fiend. Ivy Baker was a redhead, just for those who like that sort of thing, she ponged a bit when she got overheated like so many redheads do and I was always after her with the Odorono, but she was a good worker and her quick spins were sensational. Gloria Day was the languid, sensuous type, there always has to be one of those, big charlies and hair like kapok, but she could move when she had to. (Her real name was Betty Mott but her dear old white-headed mum who was an ex-Tiller girl thought Gloria Day would look better on the bills.) The last, but by no means the least, was Bonny Macintyre, if you please. She was the personality kid of the whole troupe, not exactly pretty but cute – God help us all – and so vivacious that you wanted to strangle her, however she was good for eccentric numbers and the audiences always liked her. The standby, Myrtle Kennedy, was a bit horsey to look at but thoroughly efficient and capable of going on for anyone which after all was what she was engaged for. This was the little lot that I traipsed around the great big glorious world with for several years on and off, four and a half to be exact. Oh dear! On looking back I can hardly believe it. I can hardly believe that *Io stesso—Io mismo—Je, moi-même, Il signore*—El señor—Monsieur George Banks Esq. lying here rotting in a hospital bed really went through all that I did go through with that merry little bunch of egomaniacs. I suppose I enjoyed quite a lot of it but I'm here to say I wouldn't take it on again, not for all the rice in Ram Singh's Indian restaurant in the Brompton Road.

Friday

The loveliest things happen to yours truly and no mistake. I'm starting a bedsore! Isn't that sweet? Dr. Pierre came in to see me this morning and he and Sister Dominique put some ointment and lint on my fanny and here I am sitting up on a hot little rubber ring and feeling I ought to bow to people like royalty.

There was quite a to-do in the middle of the night because somebody died in number eleven, which is two doors down the passage. I wouldn't have known anything about it except that I happened to be awake and having a cup of Ovaltine and heard a lot of murmuring and sobbing going on outside the door. It was an Italian man who died and the murmuring and sobbing was being done by his relatives. Latins aren't exactly tight-lipped when it comes to grief or pain are they? I mean they really let go and no holds barred. You've never heard such a commotion. It kind of depressed me all the same, not that it was all that sad. According to Sister Jeanne-Marie the man who died was very old indeed and a disagreeable old bastard into the bargain, but it started me off thinking about dying myself and wondering what it would feel like, if it feels like anything at all. Of course death's got to come sometime or other so it's no use getting morbid about it but I can't quite imagine not being here any more. It's funny to think there's going to be a last time for everything; the last time I shall go to the loo, the last time I shall eat a four-minute egg, the last time I shall arrive in Paris in the early morning and see waiters in shirt-sleeves setting up the tables outside cafés, the last time I shall ever feel anybody's arms round me. I suppose I can count myself lucky in a way not to have anybody too close to worry about. At least when it happens I shall be on my own with no red-eyed loved ones clustered round the bed and carrying on alarming. I sometimes wish I was deeply religious and could believe that the moment I conked out I should be whisked off to some lovely place where all the people I'd been fond of and who had died would be waiting for me, but as a matter of fact this sort of wishing doesn't last very long. I suppose I'd like to see Auntie Iso again and Harry-boy but I'm not dead sure. I've got sort of used to being without them and they might have changed or I might have changed and it wouldn't be the same. After all nothing stays the same in life does it? And I can't help feeling that it's a bit silly to expect that everything's going to be absolutely perfect in the after-life, always providing that there is such a thing. Some people of course are plumb certain of this and make their plans accordingly, but I haven't got any plans to make and I never have had for the matter of that, anyway not those sort of plans. Perhaps there is something lacking in me. Perhaps this is one of the reasons I've never quite made the grade, in my career I mean. Not that I've done badly, far from it. I've worked hard and had fun and enjoyed myself most of the time and you can't ask much more than that can you? But I never really got to the top and became a great big glamorous star which after all is what I started out to be. I'm not such a clot as not to realise that I missed out somewhere along the line. Then comes the question of whether I should have had such a good time if I *had* pulled it off and been up there in lights. You never really know do you? And I'm buggered if I'm going to sit here on my rubber ring sobbing my heart out about what might have been. To hell with what might have been. What *has* been is quite enough for me, and what *will* be will have to be coped with when the time comes.

Another scrumptious thing happened to me today which was more upsetting than the bedsore and it was all Mavis's fault and if I had the strength I'd wallop the shit out of her. Just after I'd had my tea there was a knock on the door and in came Ronnie! He looked very pale and was wearing a new camel-hair overcoat and needed a hair-cut. He stood still for a moment in the doorway and then came over and kissed me and I could tell from his breath that he'd had a snifter round the corner to fortify himself before coming in. He had a bunch of roses in his hand and the paper they were wrapped in looked crinkled and crushed as though he'd been holding them too tightly. I was so taken by surprise that I couldn't think of anything to say for a minute then I pulled myself together and told him to drag the chintz armchair nearer the bed and sit down. He did what I told him after laying the flowers down very carefully on the bed-table as though they were breakable and said, in an uncertain voice, 'Surprise—surprise!' I said 'It certainly is' a little more sharply than I meant to and then suddenly I felt as if I was going to cry, which was plain silly when you come to analyse it because I don't love him any more, not really, anyhow not like I used to at first. Fortunately at this moment Sister Françoise came in and asked if Ronnie would like a cup of tea and when he said he didn't want anything at all thank you she frigged about with my pillows for a moment and then took the roses and went off to find a vase for them. This gave me time to get over being emotional and I was grateful for it I can tell you. After that we began to talk more or less naturally. I asked after the Algerian and Ronnie looked sheepish and said he wasn't with him any more, then he told me about the flat and having to have the bathroom repainted because the steam from the geyser had made the walls peel. We went on talking about this and that and all the time the feeling of emptiness seemed to grow between us. I don't know if he felt this as strongly as I did, the words came tumbling out easily enough and he even told me a funny story that somebody had told him about a nun and a parrot and we both laughed. Then suddenly we both seemed to realise at the same moment that it wasn't any good going on like that. He stood up and I held out my arms to him and he buried his head on my chest and started to cry. He was clutching my left hand tightly so I stroked his hair with my right hand and cried too and hoped to Christ Sister Françoise wouldn't come flouncing in again with the roses. When we'd recovered from this little scene he blew his nose and went over to the window and there wasn't any more strain. He stayed over an hour and said he'd come and see me again next weekend. He couldn't make it before because he was starting rehearsals for a French TV show in which he had a small part of an English sailor. I told him he'd better have a hair-cut before he began squeezing himself into a Tiddley suit and he laughed and said he'd meant to have it done ages ago but somehow or other something always seemed to get in the way. He left at about five-thirty because he was going to have a drink with Mavis at the L'Éscale and then catch the seven forty-five back to Paris. When he'd gone I felt somehow more alone than I had felt before he came so I had another of Sally's mentholated cigarettes just to make me nonchalant but it didn't really. Him coming in like that so unexpectedly had given me a shock and it was no good pretending it hadn't. I wriggled myself into a more comfortable position on the rubber ring, looked out at the view, and tried to get me and Ronnie and everything straight in my mind but it wasn't any use because suddenly seeing him again had started up a whole lot of feelings that I thought weren't there any more. I cursed Mavis of course for being so bloody bossy and interfering and yet in a way I was glad she had been. The sly little bitch had kept her promise not to write to him but had telephoned instead. I suppose it was nice of her really considering that she'd been jealous as hell of him in the past and really hated his guts. You'd have thought that from her point of view it would have been better to let sleeping dogs lie. She obviously thought that deep down inside I wanted to see him in spite of the way I'd carried on about him and the Algerian and sworn I never wanted to clap eyes on him again. After all she *had* been with me all through the bad time and I *had* let my hair down and told her much more than I should have. I don't believe as a rule in taking women too much into your confidence about that sort of thing. It isn't exactly that they're not to be trusted but it's hard for them to understand really, however much they try, and it's more difficult still if they happen to have a 'thing' about you into the bargain. I never pretended to be in love with Mavis. I went to bed with her every now and again mainly because she wanted me to and because it's always a good thing to lay one member of the troupe on account of it stops the others gabbing too much and sending you up rotten. I leant back against the pillows which had slipped down a bit like they always do and stared out across the lake at the evening light on the mountains and for the first time I found myself hating them and wishing they weren't there standing between me and Paris and the flat and Ronnie and the way I used to live when I was up and about. I pictured Mavis and Ronnie sitting at L'Éscale and discussing whether I was going to die or not and her asking him how he thought I looked and him asking her what the doctor had said and then of course I got myself as low as a snake's arse and started getting weepy again and wished to Christ I *could* die, nice and comfortably in my sleep, and have done with it.

I must have dropped off because the next thing I knew was Sister Françoise clattering in with my supper tray and the glow had gone from the fucking mountains and the lights were out on the other side of the lake and one more day was over.

Saturday

Georgie Banks and His Six Bombshells I am here to tell you began their merry career together by opening a brand-new night-spot in Montevideo which is in Uruguay or Paraguay or one of the guays and not very attractive whichever it is. The name of the joint was La Cumparsita and it smelt of fresh paint and piddle on account of the lavatories not working properly. We'd had one hell of a voyage tourist class in a so-called luxury liner which finished up in a blaze of misery with a jolly ship's concert in the first-class lounge. We did our act in its entirety with me flashing on and off every few minutes in my new silver lamé tail suit, which split across the bottom in the middle of 'Embraceable You.' The girls were nervous and Jill Kenny caught her foot in the hem of her skirt in the Edwardian quartette and fell arse over apple-cart into a tub of azaleas which the purser had been watering with his own fair hands for weeks. She let out a stream of four-letter words in a strong Irish brogue and the first-class passengers left in droves. The purser made a speech at the end thanking us all very much indeed but it didn't exactly ring with sincerity. Anyhow our opening at La Cumparsita went better and we got a rave notice in one local paper and a stinker in the other which sort of levelled things out. The Latin-Americanos were very friendly on the whole if a bit lecherous and the girls had quite a struggle not to be laid every night rain or shine. Bonny Macintyre, vivacious to the last, was the first to get herself pregnant. This fascinating piece of news was broken to me two weeks after we'd left Montevideo and moved on to Buenos Aires. Fortunately I was able to get her fixed up all right but it took a few days to find the right doctor to do it and those few days were a proper nightmare. She never stopped weeping and wailing and saying it was all my fault for not seeing that she was sufficiently protected. *Would* you mind! When it was all over bar the shouting she got cuter than ever and a bit cocky into the bargain and I knew then and there that out of the whole lot our Bonny was the only one who was going to cause me the most trouble, and baby was I right! The others behaved fairly well taken by and large. Jill was a bit of a trouble-maker and liable to get pissed unless carefully watched. Ivy Baker got herself into a brawl with one of the local tarts when we were working in the Casino at Vina del Mar. The tart accused her of giving the come-on to her boy friend and slapped her in the face in the ladies' john, but she got as good as she gave. Ivy wasn't a redhead for nothing. The manager came and complained to me but I told him to stuff it and the whole thing died away like a summer breeze.

On looking back on that first year with the bombshells I find it difficult to remember clearly, out of all the scenes and dramas and carry-ons, what happened where and who did what to who. It's all become a bit of a jumble in my mind like one of those montages you see in films when people jump from place to place very quickly and there are shots of pages flying off a calendar. This is not to be surprised at really because we did cover a lot of territory. It took us over seven months to squeeze Latin America dry and then we got a tour booked through Australia and New Zealand. By this time all the costumes looked as though we'd been to bed in them for years and so they had to be redone. We had a lay-off for a week in Panama City and we shopped around for materials in the blazing heat and then went to work with our needles and thread. Avice was the best at this lark. I know I nearly went blind sewing sequins onto a velvet bodice for Sue Mortlock, who had to do a single while we were all changing for 'The Darktown Strutters' Ball' which we had to do in home-made masks because there wasn't any time to black up.

The voyage from Panama City to western Australia was wonderful. The ship was quite small, a sort of freighter, but we had nice cabins and the food wasn't bad. It was the first time we'd had a real rest for months and we stopped off at various islands in the South Seas and bathed in coral lagoons and got ourselves tanned to a crisp all except poor Ivy, who got blistered and had to be put to bed with poultices of soda-bicarb plastered all over her. She ran a temperature poor bitch and her skin peeled off her like tissue-paper. All the girls behaved well nearly all the time and there were hardly any rows. There was a slight drama when Bonny was found naked in one of the lifeboats with the chief engineer. It would have been all right if only it hadn't been the captain who found them. The captain was half Norwegian and very religious and he sent for me to his cabin and thumped the table and said I ought to be ashamed of myself for traipsing round the world with a lot of harlots. I explained as patiently as I could that my girls were not harlots but professional artistes and that in any case I was not responsible for their private goings-on and I added that harlots were bloody well paid for what they did in the hay whereas all Bonny got out of the chief engineer was a native necklace made of red seeds and a couple of conch shells which were too big to pack. After a while he calmed down and we had two beers sitting side by side on his bunk. When he'd knocked back his second one he rested his hand a little too casually on my thigh and I thought to myself: 'Allo 'allo! Religious or not religious we now know where we are! From then on we lived happily ever after as you might say. It all got a bit boring but anything for a quiet life.

The Australian tour believe it or not was a wow, particularly in Sydney, where we were booked for four weeks and had to stay, by popular demand, for another two. It was in Sydney that Gloria Day fell in love with a life-guard she met on the beach, really in love too, not just an in and out and thank you very much. I must say I saw her point because he had a body like a Greek god. Unfortunately he also had a wife and two bouncing little kiddies tucked away somewhere in the bush and so there was no future in it for poor Gloria, and when we went away finally there was a lot of wailing and gnashing of teeth and threats of suicide. I gave her hell about this and reeled off a lot of fancy phrases like life being the most precious gift and time being a great healer etc., etc., and by the time we'd got to Singapore, which was our next date, she'd forgotten all about him and was working herself up into a state about the ship's doctor, who apart from being an alcoholic was quite attractive in a battered sort of way.

It was on that particular hop that things came to a head between me and Avice. We'd been in and out of bed together on and off for quite a long while but more as a sort of convenience than anything else. Then suddenly she took it into her head that I was the one great big gorgeous love of her life and that she couldn't live without me and that when we got back home to England we'd get married and have children and life would blossom like a rose. Now this was all cock and I told her so. In the first place I had explained, not in detail but generally, what I was really like and that although I liked girls as girls and found them lovely to be with they didn't really send me physically, anyway not enough to think of hitching myself up forever. Then of course there was a big dramatic scene during which she trotted out all the old arguments about me not really being like that at all and that once I'd persevered and got myself into the habit of sleeping with her regularly I'd never want to do the other thing again. After that snappy little conversation I need hardly say that there was a slight strain between us for the rest of the tour. Poor old Avice. I still hear from her occasionally. She finally married an electrician and went to Canada. She sent me a snapshot of herself and her family about a year ago. I could hardly recognise her. She looked as though she'd been blown up with a bicycle pump.

After Singapore we played various joints in Burma and Siam and one in Sumatra which was a bugger. It was there that Myrtle Kennedy, the standby, got amoebic dysentery and had to be left behind in a Dutch hospital where she stayed for nearly four weeks. She ultimately rejoined us in Bombay looking very thin and more like a horse than ever.

Bonny Macintyre's big moment came in Calcutta. She'd been getting more and more cock-a-hoop and pleased with herself mainly I think because her balloon dance always went better than anything else. It was our one unfailing show-stopper and even when there was hardly any-one in front she always got the biggest hand of the evening with it. In Calcutta she started ritzing the other girls and complaining about her hotel accommodation and asking for new dresses. She also had a brawl in the dressing-room with Jill and bashed her on the head so hard with her hair-brush that the poor kid had concussion and had to miss two perform-ances. This was when I stepped in and gave our Bonny a proper walloping. I don't usually approve of hitting women but this was one of those times when it had to be done. She shrieked bloody murder and all the waiters in the joint came crowding into the room to see what was going on. The next day all was calm again, or outwardly so at least. That night however when I arrived at the club in time to put my slap on I was met by Avice wearing her tragedy queen expression. She went off into a long rigmarole which I couldn't help feeling she was enjoying a good deal more than she pretended to. There was always a certain self-righteous streak in Avice. Anyway what had happened was that Bonny had bolted with a Parsee radio announcer who she'd been going with for the last ten days. She'd left me a nasty little note which she had put into Avice's box in the hotel explaining that she was never coming back again because I wasn't a gentleman and that she'd cabled home to her mother in High Wycombe to say she was going to be married. She didn't say where she and the Parsee had bolted to and so that was that. There really wasn't anything to be done. I knew she couldn't possibly leave India because I'd got her passport – one of the first rules of travelling around with a bunch of female artistes is to hang on to their passports – however we were all due to leave India in a few weeks' time and I couldn't see myself setting off to search the entire bloody continent for Bonny Macintyre. Nor could I very well leave her behind. I was after all responsible for her. It was a fair bitch of a situation I can tell you. Anyhow there I was stuck with it and the first thing to do was to get the show reorganised for that night's performance. I sent Avice hareing off to get Sue into the balloon dance dress; sent for the band leader to tell him we were altering the running order; told Myrtle to be ready to go on in all the concerted numbers. I then did a thing I never never do before a performance. I had myself a zonking great whisky and soda and pranced out gallantly onto the dance floor ready to face with a stiff upper lip whatever further blows destiny had in store for me.

The next week was terrible. No word from Bonny and frantic cables arriving every day from her old mum. Avice I must say was a Rock of Gibraltar. She kept her head and came with me to the broadcasting station where we tried to trace the Parsee. We interviewed lots of little hairy men with green faces and high sibilant voices and finally discovered that Bonny's fiancé – to coin a phrase – had been given two weeks off to go up to the hills on account of he'd had a bad cough. Nobody seemed to know or care what part of the hills he'd gone to. We sat about for a further few days worrying ourselves silly and wondering what to do. Our closing date was drawing nearer and we had all been booked tourist class on a homeward-bound P and O. Finally, to cut a dull story short, our little roving will-o'-the-wisp returned to us with a bang. That is to say she burst into my room in the middle of the night and proceeded to have hysterics. All the other girls came flocking in to see what the fuss was about and stood around in their night-gowns and dressing-gowns and pyjamas with grease on their faces looking like Christmas night in the whore-house. I gave Bonny some Three Star Martell in a tooth glass which gave her hiccups but calmed her down a bit. Presently, when Jill had made her drink some water backwards and we'd all thumped her on the back, she managed to sob out the garbled story of her star-crossed romance, and it was good and star-crossed believe me. Apparently the Parsee had taken her in an old Ford convertible which broke down three times to visit his family, a happy little group consisting of about thirty souls in all, including goats, who lived in a small town seventy miles away. The house they lived in was not so much a house as a tenement and Bonny was forced to share a room with two of the Parsee's female cousins and a baby that was the teeniest bit spastic. She didn't seem to have exactly hit it off with the Parsee's dear old mother who snarled at her in Hindustani whenever she came within spitting distance. There was obviously no room for fun and games indoors so whatever sex they had had to take place on a bit of waste-land behind the railway station. She didn't enjoy any of this very much on account of being scared of snakes, but being so near the railway station often *did* actually give her the idea of making a getaway. Finally after one of the usual cosy evenings *en famille* with mum cursing away in one corner and the spastic baby having convulsions in the other, she managed to slip out of the house without her loved one noticing and run like a stag to the station. It was a dark night but she knew the way all right having been in that direction so frequently. After waiting four hours in a sort of shed a train arrived and she got onto it and here she was more dead than alive.

By the time she'd finished telling us all this the dawn had come up like thunder and she began to get hysterical again so Avice forced a couple of aspirins down her throat and put her to bed. Three days after this, having given our last triumphant performance to a quarter-full house, we set sail for England, home, and what have you, and that was really the end of Georgie Banks and His Six Bombshells.

Sunday

It's Sunday and all the church bells are ringing and I wish they wouldn't because I had a bad night and feel a bit edgy and the noise is driving me crackers.

It wasn't a bad night from the pain point of view although I felt a little uncomfortable between two and three and Sister Clothilde came in and gave me an injection which was a new departure really because I usually get a pill. Anyway it sent me off to sleep all right but it wasn't really sleep exactly, more like a sort of trance. I wasn't quite off and I wasn't quite on if you know what I mean and every so often I'd wake up completely for a few minutes feeling like I'd had a bad dream and couldn't remember what it was. Then I'd float off again and all sorts of strange things came into my mind. I suppose it was thinking yesterday so much about me and the bombshells that I'd got myself kind of overexcited. I woke up at about eight-thirty with a hangover but I felt better when I'd had a cup of tea. The orderly came in and carried me to the bathroom and then brought me back and put me in the armchair with an eiderdown wrapped round me while the bed was being made and the room done. One of the nicest things about being ill is when you're put back into a freshly made bed and can lie back against cool pillows before they get hot and crumpled and start slipping. The orderly stayed and chatted with me for a bit. He's quite sweet really. He told me he'd got the afternoon and evening off and that a friend of his was arriving from Munich who was a swimming champion and had won a lot of cups. He said this friend was very '*costaud*' and had a wonderfully developed chest but his legs were on the short side. They were going to have dinner in a restaurant by the lake and then go to a movie. I wished him luck and winked at him and wished to God I was going with them.

Later. It's still Sunday but the bells have stopped ringing and it's started to rain. The professor with the blue chin came to see me after I'd had my afternoon snooze. He looked different from usual because he was wearing quite a snappy sports coat and grey-flannel trousers. He told me he'd had lunch in a little restaurant in the country and had only just got back. I watched him looking at me carefully while he was talking to me as though he wanted to find out something. I told him about having had the injection and how it made me feel funny and he smiled and nodded and lit a cigarette. He then asked me whether I had any particular religion and when I said I hadn't he laughed and said that he hadn't either but he supposed it was a good thing for some people who needed something to hang on to. Then he asked me if I had ever talked to Father Lucien who was a Catholic priest who was sort of attached to the clinic. I said he'd come in to see me a couple of times and had been quite nice but that he gave me the creeps. Then he laughed again and started wandering about the room sort of absent-mindedly as though he was thinking of something else, then he came back, stubbed his cigarette out in the ashtray on my bed-table, and sat down again, this time on the side of the bed. I moved my legs to give him a bit more room. There was a fly buzzing about and a long way off one of those bloody church bells started ringing again. I looked at him sitting there so nonchalantly swinging his legs ever so little but frowning as though something were puzzling him. He was a good-looking man all right, somewhere between forty and fifty I should say, his figure was slim and elegant and his face thin with a lot of lines on it and his dark hair had gone grey at the sides. I wondered if he had a nice sincere wife to go home to in the evenings after a busy day cutting things out of people, or whether he lived alone with a faithful retainer and a lot of medical books and kept a tiny vivacious mistress in a flashy little apartment somewhere or other or even whether he was queer as a coot and head over heels in love with a sun-tanned ski instructor and spent madly healthy weekends with him in cosy wooden chalets up in the mountains. He looked at me suddenly as though he had a half guess at what I was thinking and I giggled. He smiled when I giggled and very gently took my hand in his and gave it a squeeze, not in the least a sexy squeeze but a sympathetic one and all at once I realised, with a sudden sinking of the heart, what the whole production was in aid of, why he had come in so casually to see me on a Sunday afternoon, why he had been drifting about the room looking ill at ease and why he had asked me about whether I was religious or not. It was because he knew that I was never going to get well again and was trying to make up his mind whether to let me know the worst or just let me go on from day to day hoping for the best. I knew then, in a sort of panic, that I didn't want him to tell me anything, not in so many words, because once he said them there I'd be stuck with them in my mind and wake up in the night and remember them. What I mean is that although I knew that I knew and had actually known, on and off, for a long time, I didn't want it settled and signed and sealed and done up, gift wrapped, with a bow on top. I still wanted not to be quite sure so that I could get through the days without counting. That was a bad moment all right, me lying there with him still holding my hand and all those thoughts going through my head and trying to think of a way to head him off. I knew that unless I did something quickly he'd blurt it out that I'd be up shit creek without a paddle and with nothing to hang on to and no hope left and so I did the brassiest thing I've ever done in my life and I still blush when I think of it. I suddenly reared myself up on my pillows, pulled him towards me, and gave him a smacking kiss. He jumped back as if he'd been shot. I've never seen anyone so surprised. Then, before he could say anything, I went off into a long spiel – I was a bit hysterical by then and I can't remember exactly what I said – but it was all about me having a 'thing' about him ever since I'd first seen him and that that was the way I was and there was nothing to be done about it and that as he was a doctor I hoped he would understand and not be too shocked and that anyway being as attractive as he was he had no right to squeeze people's hands when they were helpless in bed and not expect them to lose control and make a pounce at him and that I'd obeyed an impulse too strong to be resisted – yes I actually said that if you please – and that I hoped he would forgive me but that if he didn't he'd just have to get on with it. I said a lot more than this and it was all pretty garbled because I'd worked myself into a proper state, but that was the gist of it. He sat there quite still while I was carrying on, staring at me and biting his lip. I didn't quite know how to finish the scene so I fell back on the old ham standby and burst into tears and what was so awful was that once I'd started I couldn't stop until he took out his cigarette-case, shoved a cigarette into my mouth, and lit it for me. This calmed me down and I was able to notice that he had stopped looking startled and was looking at me with one of his eyebrows a little higher than the other, quizzically as you might say, and that his lips were twitching as though he was trying not to laugh. Then he got up and said in a perfectly ordinary voice that he'd have to be getting along now as he had a couple more patients to see but that he'd come back and have a look at me later. I didn't say anything because I didn't feel I could really without starting to blub again, so I just lay puffing away like crazy at the cigarette and trying not to look too like Little Orphan Annie. He went to the door, paused for a moment, and then did one of the kindest things I've ever known. He came back to the bed, put both his arms round me, and kissed me very gently, not on the mouth but on the cheek as though he were really fond of me. Then he went out and closed the door quietly after him.

Monday

I woke up very early this morning having slept like a top for nearly nine hours. I rang the bell and when Sister Dominique came clattering in and pulled back the curtains it was a clear, bright morning again, not a bit like yesterday. When she'd popped off to get me my tea I lay quite still watching a couple of jet planes flying back and forth over the mountains and making long trails of white smoke in the pale blue sky. They went terribly quickly and kept on disappearing and coming back into view again. I tried to imagine what the pilots flying them looked like and what they were thinking about. It must be a wonderful feeling whizzing through the air at that tremendous speed and looking down at the whole world. Every now and then the sun caught one of the planes and it glittered like silver. I had some honey with my toast but it was a bit too runny. When the usual routine had been gone through and I was back in bed again I began to think of the professor yesterday afternoon and what I'd done and I felt hot with shame for a minute or two and then started to laugh. Poor love, it must have been a shock and no mistake. And then I got to wondering if after all it had been quite such a surprise to him as all that. Being a doctor he must be pretty hep about the so dainty facts of life, and being as dishy as he is, he can't have arrived at his present age without someone having made the teeniest weensiest pass at him at some time or other. Anyway by doing what I did I at least stopped him from spilling those gloomy little beans, if of course there were any beans to spill. Now, this morning, after a good night, I'm feeling that it was probably all in my imagination. You never know, do you? I mean it might have been something quite silly and unimportant that upset me, like those bloody church bells for instance. They'd been enough to get anybody down. Anyway there's no sense in getting morbid and letting the goblins get you. Maybe I'll surprise them all and be springing about like a mountain goat in a few weeks from now. All the same I shan't be able to help feeling a bit embarrassed when the professor comes popping in again. Oh dear – oh dear!

Here it is only half past eight and I've got the whole morning until they bring me my lunch at twelve-thirty to think about things and scribble my oh so glamorous memories on this pad which by the way is getting nearly used up so I must remember to ask Mavis to bring me another one. She'll probably be coming in this afternoon. It's funny this wanting to get things down on paper. I suppose quite a lot of people do if you only knew, not only professional writers but more or less ordinary people, only as a rule of course they don't usually have the time, whereas I have all the time in the world – or have I? Now then, now then, none of that. At any rate I've at least had what you might call an *interesting life* what with flouncing about all over the globe with those girls and having a close-up of the mysterious Orient and sailing the seven seas and one thing and another. Perhaps when I've finished it I shall be able to sell it to the *Daily Express* for thousands and thousands of pounds and live in luxury to the end of my days. What a hope! All the same it just might be possible if they cut out the bits about my sex life and some of the four-letter words were changed. Up to now I've just been writing down whatever came into my mind without worrying much about the words themselves. After all it's the thought that counts as the actress said to the bishop after he'd been bashing away at her for three hours and a half.

When I got back to London after that first tour with the bombshells I let them all go their own sweet ways and had a long talk to Ted about either working up an act on my own or trying to get into a West End show. Not a lead mind you. I wasn't so silly as to think I'd get more than a bit part, but if I happened to hit lucky and got a *good* bit part and was noticed in it then I'd be on the up and up and nothing could stop me. All this unfortunately came under the heading of wishful thinking. As a matter of fact I *did* get into a show and it *was* a good part with a duet in act one and a short solo dance at the beginning of act two, but the whole production was so diabolical that Fred Astaire couldn't have saved it and we closed after two weeks and a half. Then I decided that what I really needed was acting experience. After all nobody can go on belting out numbers and kicking their legs in the air forever whereas acting, legitimate acting that is, can last you a lifetime providing you're any good at it. Anyhow Ted managed to get me a few odd jobs in reps dotted over England's green and pleasant land and for two whole years, on and off, I slogged away at it. I had a bang at everything. Young juveniles – 'Anyone for tennis' – old gentlemen, dope addicts, drunks. I even played a Japanese prisoner-of-war once in a ghastly triple bill at Dundee. My bit came in the first of the three plays and I was on and off so quickly that by the end of the evening none of the audience could remember having seen me at all. Somewhere along the line during those two years it began to dawn on me that I was on the wrong track. Once or twice I did manage to get a good notice in the local paper but I knew that didn't count for much and finally

I found myself back in London again with two hundred and ten pounds in the bank, no prospects, and a cold. That was a bad time all right and I can't imagine now, looking back on it, how I ever lived through it. Finally, when I was practically on the bread line and had borrowed forty pounds from Ted, I had to pocket my pride and take a chorus job in a big American musical at the Coliseum which ran for eighteen months and there I was, stuck with it. Not that I didn't manage to have a quite good time one way or another. I had a nice little 'combined' in Pimlico – Lupus Street to be exact – and it had a small kitchenette which I shared with a medical student on the next floor. He was quite sweet really but he had a birth mark all down one side of his neck which was a bit off-putting, however one must take the rough with the smooth is what I always say. When the show closed I'd paid back Ted and got a bit put by but not enough for a rainy day by any manner of means, so back I went into the chorus again and did another stretch. This time it lasted two years and I knew that if I didn't get out and do something on my own again I'd lose every bit of ambition I'd ever had and just give up. Once you really get into a rut in show business you've had it. All this was nearly five years ago and I will say one thing for myself, I *did* get out of the rut and although I nearly starved in the process and spent all I'd saved, I was at least free again and my own boss. I owe a great deal to old Ted really. Without him I could never have got these girls together and now of course, just as we were beginning to do really nicely, I have to get ill and bugger up the whole thing. This is where I come to a full stop and I know it and it's no good pretending any more to myself or anybody else. Even if I do get out of this clinic it'll take me months and months to get well enough to work again and by that time all the girls will have got other jobs and I shall have to shop around and find some new ones and redo the act from the beginning, and while we're at it, I should like to know how I'm going to live during those jolly months of languid convalescence! This place and the operation and the treatment must be costing a bloody fortune. Ted and Mavis are the only ones who know exactly what I've got saved and they're coping, but it can't go on for much longer because there just won't be anything left. I tried to say something to Mavis about this the other day but she said that everything was all right and that I wasn't to worry and refused to discuss it any further. I've never had much money sense I'm afraid, Ted's always nagging me about it but it's no use. When I've got it I spend it and when I haven't I don't because I bloody well can't and that's that. All the same I have been careful during the last few years, more careful than I ever was before, and there must still be quite a bit in the bank, even with all this extra expense. I must make Mavis write to Ted and find out just exactly how things are. He's got power of attorney anyhow. Now you see I've gone and got myself low again. It's always the same, whenever I begin to think about money and what I've got saved and what's going to happen in the future, down I go into the depths. I suppose this is another lack in me like not having had just that extra something which would have made me a great big glamorous star. I must say I'm not one to complain much as a rule. I've had my ups and downs and it's all part of life's rich pattern as some silly bitch said when we'd just been booed off the stage by some visiting marines in Port Said. All the same one can't go on being a cheery chappie forever, can one? I mean there are moments when you have to look facts in the face and not go on kidding yourself, and this, as far as I'm concerned, is one of them. I wish to Christ I hadn't started to write at all this morning. I was feeling fine when I woke up, and now, by doing all this thinking back and remembering and wondering, I've got myself into a state of black depression and it's no use pretending I haven't. As a matter of fact it's no use pretending ever, about anything, about getting to the top, or your luck turning, or living, or dying. It always catches up with you in the end. I don't even feel like crying which is funny because I am a great crier as a rule when things get bad. It's a sort of relief and eases the nerves. Now I couldn't squeeze a tear out if you paid me. That really is funny. Sort of frightening. That's the lot for today anyway. The *Daily Express* must wait.

Tuesday

Mavis came yesterday afternoon as promised and I forgot to ask her about getting another writing pad, but it doesn't really matter because there's still quite a lot of this one left. I didn't feel up to talking much so I just lay still and listened while she told me all the gossip. Lily-May had sprained her ankle, fortunately in the last number, not a bad sprain really, not bad enough that is for her to have to stay off. She put on cold compresses last night and it had practically gone down by this morning. Beryl and Sylvia were taken out after the show on Saturday night by a very rich banking gentleman from Basle who Monsieur Philippe had brought backstage. He took them and gave them a couple of drinks somewhere or other and then on to an apartment of a friend of his which was luxuriously furnished and overlooked the lake except that they couldn't see much of it on account of it being pitch dark and there being no moon. Anyway the banker and his friend opened a bottle of champagne and sat Beryl and Sylvia down as polite as you please on a sofa with satin cushions on it and while they were sipping the champagne and being thoroughly piss-elegant, which they're inclined to be at the best of times, the banker, who'd gone out of the room for a minute, suddenly came in again stark naked carrying a leather whip in one hand and playing with himself with the other. The girls both jumped up and started screaming and there was a grand old hullabaloo for a few minutes until the friend managed to calm them down and made the banker go back and put on a dressing-gown. While he was out of the room he gave the girls a hundred francs each and apologised for the banker saying that he was a weeny bit eccentric but very nice really and that the whip was not to whack them with but for them to whack him, the banker, with, which just happened to be his way of having fun. Then the twins stopped screaming and got grand as all get-out and said that they were used to being treated like ladies. They didn't happen to mention who by. Then the banker came back in a fur coat not having been able to find a dressing-gown and said he was sorry if he had frightened them and would they please not say a word to Monsieur Philippe. They all had some more champagne and the banker passed out cold and the friend brought them home in a taxi without so much as groping them. Anti-climax department the whole thing. Anyway they got a hundred francs each whichever way you look at it and that's eight pounds a head for doing fuck all. I must say I couldn't help laughing when Mavis told me all this but she wasn't amused at all, oh dear me no. There's a strong governessy streak in our Mavis. She went straight to Monsieur Philippe and carried on as if she were a mother superior in a convent. This made me laugh still more and when she went she looked quite cross.

Friday

I haven't felt up to writing anything for the last few days and I don't feel any too good now but I suppose I'd better make an effort and get on with it. I began having terrible pains in my back and legs last Tuesday night I think it was, anyway it was the same day that Mavis came, and Dr. Pierre was sent for and gave me an injection and I've felt sort of half asleep ever since, so much so that I didn't even know what day it was. I've just asked Sister Dominique and she told me it was Friday. Imagine! That's two whole days gone floating by with my hardly knowing anything about it. I've been feeling better all day today, a bit weak I must admit, but no more pain. The professor came in to see me this afternoon and brought me a bunch of flowers and Mavis brought me a little pot of pâté-de-foie-gras, or maybe it was the other way round, anyway I know that they both came. Not at the same time of course but at different times, perhaps it was the day before yesterday that the professor came. I'm still feeling a bit woozy and can't quite remember. I know he held my hand for quite a long time so he can't have really been upset about me behaving like that. He's a wonderful man the professor is, a gentle and loving character, and I wish, I wish I could really tell him why I did what I did and make him understand that it wasn't just silly camping but because I was frightened. I expect he knows anyhow. He's the sort of man who knows everything that goes on in people's minds and you don't have to keep on saying you're sorry and making excuses to him any more than you'd have to to God if God is anything like what he's supposed to be. The act closes tomorrow night if today really is Friday, and all the girls have promised to come to say good-bye to me on Sunday before they catch the train, at least that's what Mavis said. I had the funniest experience last night. I saw Harry-boy. He was standing at the end of the bed as clear as daylight wearing his blue dungarees and holding up a pair of diabolical old socks which he wanted me to wash out for him. Of course I know I didn't really see him and that I was dreaming, but it did seem real as anything at the time and it still does in a way. Harry never could do a thing for himself, like washing socks I mean, or anything useful in the house. I'm not being quite fair because he did fix the tap in the lavatory basin once when it wouldn't stop running, but then he was always all right with anything to do with machinery, not that the tap in the lavatory basin can really be called machinery but it's the same sort of thing if you know what I mean. All the girls are coming to say goodbye to me on Sunday before they catch the train, at least that's what Mavis said. Good old Mavis. I suppose I'm fonder of her than anybody actually, anybody that's alive I mean. I must try to remember to tell her this the next time she comes. If she doesn't come before Sunday I can tell her then. The weather's changed with a vengeance and it's raining to beat the band which is a shame really because I can't see the mountains any more except every now and then for a moment or two when it lifts. I wonder whatever became of Bonny Macintyre. I haven't had so much as a post-card from her in all these years. She was a tiresome little bitch but she had talent and there's no doubt about it and nobody else ever did the balloon dance quite the way she did it. It wasn't that she danced all that brilliantly, in fact Jill could wipe her eye any day of the week when it came to speed and technique. But she had something that girl.

Sister Clothilde pulled the blinds down a few minutes ago just before Dr. Pierre and Father Lucien came in. Dr. Pierre gave me an injection which hurt a bit when it went in but felt lovely a few seconds later, a sweet warm feeling coming up from my toes and covering me all over like an eiderdown. Father Lucien leant over me and said something or other I don't remember what it was. He's quite nice really but there *is* something about him that gives me the creeps. I mean I wouldn't want him to hold my hand like the professor does. The act closes on Saturday night and the girls are all coming to say goodbye to me on Sunday before they catch the train. I do hope Mavis gets a job or meets someone nice and marries him and settles down. That's what she ought to do really. It isn't that she's no good. She dances well and her voice is passable, but the real thing is lacking. Hark at me! I should talk. I wish Sister Clothilde hadn't pulled the blinds down, not that it really matters because it's dark by now and I shouldn't be able to see them anyhow.

JOHN HORNE BURNS

MOMMA

Momma always lay a while in her bed when she awoke. Poppa was up four hours earlier and went out into the streets of Naples for a walk, to buy *Risorgimento* and to drink his caffè espresso. He said it made him nervous to lie beside her because she cooed to herself as she slept.

That love which Poppa no longer desired of her Momma showered on the clientele of her bar. One reason she cooed in her sleep was that she was one of the richest women in Naples. She could afford to buy black market food at two thousand lire a day. She ate better than the Americans. She had furs and lovely dresses and patent leather pumps which even the countesses in the Vomero couldn't afford. Momma had come from a poor family in Milan, but she'd made herself into one of the great ladies of Naples. And the merchants of Naples, when they sent her monthly bills, instead of writing signora before her name, wrote N.D., standing for nobil donna.

JOHN HORNE BURNS (1916–1953): 'There was a fellow who wrote a fine book and then a stinking book about a prep school, and then he just blew himself up.' So Ernest Hemingway summed up the career of John Horne Burns in an interview with Robert Manning. The 'fine' book was The Gallery, *from which 'Momma' is taken; the 'stinking' one was* Lucifer with a Book. (*A third novel,* A Cry of Children, *appeared in 1953.)*

Educated at Phillips Andover and Harvard, Burns spent a year and a half in Italy during World War II, and died in Florence, a probable suicide. John Mitzel's 'appreciative biography' of the writer was published by Manifest Destiny Books in 1974.

As the churches of Naples struck noon, Momma got out of her bed. She was wearing a lace nightie brought her from Cairo by an American flier. Momma knew that the flier had made money on the deal, but no other woman in Naples had one like it. In the old days she'd have driven Poppa mad with this lace nightie. But now he simply crawled in beside her, felt the sheer stuff, and clucked his tongue in disapproval. Poppa was first and last a Neapolitan. Even in the early days of their marriage he'd never grasped the fineness of Momma's grain. But she was beyond such bitterness now. She loved the world, and the world returned her love in her bar in the Galleria Umberto.

Beneath a colored picture of the Madonna of Pompei, flanked by two tapers and a pot of pinks, Momma said her morning prayers. She thanked the Virgin for saving her during the bombardments of Naples. But the Virgin hadn't spared that lovely appartamento in Piazza Garibaldi. And Momma prayed for all the sweet boys who came to her bar, that they might soon be returned to their families – but not too soon, for Momma loved their company. And she prayed also for the future of poor Italy, that the line up by Florence might soon be smashed by the American Fifth Army. And she prayed that Il Duce and his mistress Claretta Petacci might see the error of their ways. Finally Momma prayed that all the world might be as prosperous and happy as she herself was.

With the bombing of her apartment in Piazza Garibaldi in March, 1943, Momma'd been able to salvage only her frigidaire. Everything else had been destroyed – the lovely linens she'd brought Poppa with her dowry from Milan, her fragile plate, her genteel furniture. Only the frigidaire was to be found among the rubble, pert and smiling as a bomb shelter. Momma'd wept the whole day; then she and Poppa had moved into a dreary set of rooms on the third floor of the Galleria Umberto. Momma'd got the rooms cleaned, set the frigidaire in the kitchen, and bought secondhand furniture by cautious shopping in Piazza Dante. But her heart as a homemaker had died in the ruins of that appartamento to which Poppa had brought her as a bride.

She lived now only for her bar and for the Allied soldiers who came there every night except Sunday. In fact Momma was only treading water all day long until 1630 hours, at which time the provost marshal of Naples allowed her to open her bar. At 1930 MPs came to make sure it was closed. Three hours. Yet in those three hours Momma lived more than most folks do in twenty-four.

She'd opened her bar the night after Naples fell to the Allies, in October, 1943. Some American of the 34th Division had christened her Momma, and the name stuck. And because Momma had an instinctive knack for entertaining people, her bar was the most celebrated in Naples. Indeed a Kiwi had once told her that it was famous all over the world, that everyone in the Allied armies told everyone else about it. Momma rejoiced. Her only selfish desire was to be renowned as a great hostess. She was happy that she made money in her bar, but that wasn't her be-and-end-all. She knew that she was going down in history with Lili Marlene and the Mademoiselle of Armentières – though for a different reason.

～ ～ ～

Momma brushed her teeth with American dentrifice while the water ran into her tub. She studied her hair in the mirror. For ten years she'd been hennaing it. But she was too honest to go on kidding the world. She was forty-six. In the face of that sacred title, Momma, it seemed to her sacrilegious to sit every night behind her cash register with crimson hair glowing in the lights. So she'd stopped using the rinse. Now her hair was in that transitional stage, with gray and white and henna streaked through it. But the momentary ugliness of her hair was worth her title. At closing time in her bar, some of her boys, a bit brilli, would cry on her shoulder and tell her that she looked just like some elderly lady in Arkansas or Lyon or North Wales or the Transvaal or Sydney. Then she'd pat their hands and say:

'Ah, mio caro! Se fosse qui la Sua mamma! . . .'

She'd never been able to learn English, though she understood nearly everything that was said to her in it.

Momma climbed into the tub after she'd sprinkled in some salts a merchant seaman had brought her from New York. Her body was getting a little chunky, but she tried her best to keep it trim, the way a Momma's should be. At first she'd worn a pince-nez until Poppa had told her she looked like a Sicilian carthorse with blinders. So she had reverted to her gold-rimmed spectacles. She doted on American black market steaks, her pasta asciutta, her risotti, and her peperoni. She knew that a Momma mustn't be skinny either.

She dressed herself in black silk and laid out a quaint straw hat on which a stuffed bird sprawled eating cherries. She opened her drawerful of silk stockings. You could count on the fingers of one hand the women in Naples of August, 1944, who owned silk stockings – were they prosti-tutes on the Toledo or marchese in villas at Bagnoli. But Momma had em; she averaged a pair a week from her American admirers. Momma considered herself one of the luckiest ladies in the world. She knew that no woman gets presents for nothing.

Finally dressed and fragrant and cool in spite of the furnace that was Naples in August, 1944, Momma took up her purse and looked around the apartment before locking it. She checked the ice in the frigidaire. Sometimes, after she was compelled to close her bar, she invited her favorite boys up for extra drinks. She didn't charge for this hospitality.

She walked through the Galleria Umberto. At this hour it was empty of Neapolitans because of the heat. But the Allied soldiery was already out in full force. The bars weren't open, so they just loitered against the walls reading their *Stars and Stripes* or whistling at the signorine. A few waved to Momma, and she bowed to them. Then she went onto the Toledo, which Il Duce had vulgarized into Via Roma. Here she clutched her bag more tightly. Like anybody else born in Milan, she had no use for Neapolitans or Sicilians. They thought the world owed them a living, so they preyed on one another with a malicious vitality, like monkeys removing one another's fleas. And now that the Allies were in Naples, the Neapolitans were united in milking them. Momma knew that the Neapolitans hated her because she was rich and because she refused to speak their dialect. She walked through them all with her head in the air, clutching her purse. Some who knew her called out vulgar names in dialect and cracks about Napoli Milionaria, but she paid them no attention.

She and Poppa usually lunched together at a black market restaurant on Via Chiaia, patronized by Americans and those few Italians who could afford the price of a meal there. Today Poppa was out campaigning for public office at the Municipio, so Momma ate alone at her special table. Sometimes she suspected that Poppa had a mistress. But then he wouldn't stand a chance at snapping up anything really good, what with all the Allies in Naples.

The treatment Momma got at this restaurant was in a class by itself. Naturally the Americans got fawned on, but then they didn't know what the waiters said about them in the kitchen. Whereas Momma, as an Italian who'd made a success in the hardiest times Naples had ever known, always got a welcome as though she were Queen Margherita. There were flowers on her table and special wines rustled up from the cellar, although the

Allies got watered vino ordinario. And when Momma entered, the orchestra stopped playing American jazz, picked up their violins, and did her favorite tune, 'Mazzolin di Fiori.' Momma tapped her chin with her white glove and hummed appreciatively.

While she picked at her whitefish and sipped her white wine and peeped around the restaurant from under the shadow of the red bird that forever ate cherries on her hat, Momma observed an American sergeant wrestling with an American black market steak. He was quite drunk, and to Momma, who knew all the symptoms so well, he seemed ready to cry. She debated inviting him to her table and treating him to his lunch. But he gave her the I-hate-Italians scowl, so she thought better of it. He wasn't the sort who came to her bar anyhow. Momma was basically shy, except with people she thought needed affection. Then she'd open up like all the great hostesses of the world. However, she did take out of her purse a little pasteboard card advertising her bar. She sent it by a waiter over to the sergeant, plus a bottle of Chianti. He scowled at her again, and Momma decided basta, she'd gone more than halfway. Then he tore up her card and began to guzzle her wine.

She finished her lunch and smoked a cigarette. There seemed to be a rope about her neck pulled taut by all the evil fingers of the world. She wanted to go somewhere and have a good cry. She needed a friend. Poppa had never been close to her since, in the first year of their marriage, he discovered that she wasn't going to be fertile, like all the other women of Italy. Momma had conceived just once. In her Fallopian tubes. After the medico had curetted her out and she'd all but died, he'd told her she could never have a child of her own. And Poppa in disgust had taken to politics and reading the papers. Momma'd only begun to love again since the night in October, 1943, when she'd opened her bar in the Galleria Umberto . . .

She arose from table and drew on her white gloves. As she walked to the door, she saw herself pass by in the gilded mirror, a dumpy figure holding in its chin, a scudding straw hat under a bird chewing cherries. She knew that if she didn't get outside soon, she'd bawl right there in front of the waiters, and the drama she'd built up of a great lady would collapse forever. On Via Chiaia she debated what movie she'd go to. Since she went every afternoon, she'd seen them all. A few American films were beginning to dribble into Naples, and Momma'd enjoyed Greer Garson or Ginger Rogers with an Italian sound track. Yet movies bored her unless there was lots of music and color. The truth was that she went every afternoon because she'd nothing else to do; she was just killing time till the hour to open her bar. She decided on the Cinema Regina Elena off Via Santa Brigida.

She found a seat three-quarters of the way back from the screen, put on her glasses, and watched the show. It was an Italian film made in Rome on a budget of a few thousand lire. Momma was used to the tempo of American movies, so she found herself nodding. There wasn't even anything worth crying over. She eased her feet out of their patent leather pumps, cursed the pinching of her girdle, and settled down. Sometimes she drew a peppermint patty out of her bag and sucked it thoughtfully. Every half-hour the lights came up for an *intervallo*; the windows were opened, and people came in or out or changed their seats for various reasons. Momma'd have liked an Allied soldier to be sitting beside her. But to these the cinemas of Naples were off limits because of the danger of typhus and because of certain nuisances they'd committed in the dark just after the city fell. During the *intervalli* Momma stayed in her seat and smoked a cigarette. She wasn't going to force her feet back into her pumps.

The Italian film went on and on; Momma fell asleep and dreamed in the moldy dark. Her dreams were always the same, of the boys who came to her bar. There was a heterogeneous quality about them. They had an air of being tremendously wise, older than the human race. They understood one another, as though from France and New Zealand and America they all had membership cards in some occult freemasonry. And they had a refinement of manner, an intuitive appreciation of her as a woman. Their conversation was flashing, bitter, and lucid. More than other men they laughed much together, laughing at life itself perhaps. Momma'd never seen anything like her boys. Some were extraordinarily handsome, but not as other men were handsome. They had an acuteness in their eyes and a predatory richness of the mouth as though they'd bitten into a pomegranate. Momma dreamed that she was queen of some gay exclusive club.

She awoke and glanced at her watch. It was time to go. She'd seen almost nothing of the film. But she didn't care. She felt more rested than she did by Poppa's side. A silver hammer in her heart kept tapping out that in fifteen minutes more her life for the day would begin. She had the yearning hectic panic of a child going to a show. She shot her feet into her pumps. As the lights came up for the *secondo tempo* Momma left the theater. She looked a little disdainfully at the audience, contrasting it with what she'd shortly be seeing. Peaked Neapolitan girls on the afternoon of their giorno di festa, holding tightly to the arms of their fidanzati wearing GI undershirts; sailors of the Regia Marina and the Squadra Navale in their patched blue and whites; housewives from the vichi and the off-limits areas who'd come in with a houseful of children to peer at the screen and lose themselves in its shadowy life.

Her patent leather pumps hurt Momma's feet, but she sprinted up Santa Brigida. She turned left at Via Giuseppe Verdi. Once in the Galleria Momma all but flew. She wondered if she looked spruce, if her hat was chic. The Galleria was milling and humming, for all the bars opened within a few seconds of one another, just as clocks stagger their striking the hour throughout a great city. Momma had a presentiment that today was going to be especially glamorous.

The 1630 shift troie were coming into the arcade with the promptness of factory girls. From now until curfew time the Galleria would be a concentrated fever of bargaining and merchandising peculiar to Naples in August, 1944.

The rolling steel shutters of Momma's bar were already up. Gaetano was polishing the mirrors. He greeted Momma and went back to thinking about his wife and thirteen children and how it wasn't fair that a man who'd never signed the Fascist tessera should live like a dog under the Allies. Vincenzo was wearing a spotted apron, so Momma lashed him with her tongue and forced him into the gabinetto to put on a fresh one. She stitched them up herself out of American potato bags. Momma also inspected the glassware, the taps on the wine casks, the alignment of the bottles. She was kilometers ahead of the sanitation standards set by the PBS surgeon and the provost marshal.

She seated herself behind the cassa, unlocked the cash drawer, and counted her soldi. At this moment the old feeling of ecstasy returned. For Momma loved her bar: the mirrors in which everyone could watch everyone else, the shining Carrara marble, the urns for making caffè espresso. Behind her on the mirror she'd fastened a price list. She offered excellent white wine, vermouth, and cherry brandy. She hoped soon to be licenced to sell gin and cognac, which were what the Allies really wanted. When stronger liquors were available, the tone of her place would go sky-high, along with the moods of her clientele.

No one had yet turned up. Momma knew with racecourse certainty the exact order in which her habitués came. Her patrons were of three types: some came only to look, some with a thinly veiled purpose of meeting someone else, some just happened in.

A shadow cut the fierce light of the Galleria bouncing around the mirrors. It was Poppa treading warily and carrying his straw hat. Momma flinched. She had no desire to see Poppa now. If he addressed her in dialect, she'd refuse to answer. He had rings under his eyes, and through his brown teeth came the perfume of onions. Momma told him that there was half a chicken waiting in the frigidaire. But he seemed to want to talk. Momma got as peeved as though someone tried to explain a movie to her. So Poppa, after a few more attempts to talk, put on his straw hat and went out. But he called back to her from the entrance:

'Attenzione, cara . . .'

'Perchè?' Momma cried, but he was gone.

Nettled and distracted, she settled herself behind the cash register and folded her hands. Where *were* they? All behind schedule tonight. She began to wonder if some of the other bar owners had sabotaged her by passing around the rumor that she was selling methyl alcohol such as would cause blindness.

The husky figure of a major entered the bar. Momma smelled a rat because this major was wearing the crossed pistols of an MP officer. On his left shoulder he wore the inverted chamber pot with the inset blue star, symbolizing the Peninsular Base Section. The major set his jaw like one asking for trouble. He ran his hands through some of the wineglasses and blew on the wine spigots for dust.

'Ees clean the glass, the wine, everything!' Momma cried cheerily. 'Bar molto buono, molto pulito . . .'

The major advanced upon her. She was beginning to tremble behind her desk. He walked with the burly tread of one accustomed to cuff and kick. Momma remembered that some of the Germans, when they'd been in Naples, had walked like that.

'Lissen to me, signorina,' the major said, dropping a porky hand on her desk.

'Signora, scusi,' said Momma with dignity.

'I don't give a damn one way or the other,' the major said. 'But don't try an play dumb with me, see, paesan?'

'Ees molto buono my bar,' Momma twittered, offering the major a cigarette.

Vincenzo and Gaetano were watching the proceedings like cats.

'Molto buono, my eye. You're gettin away with murder in this joint . . . Now you can just take your choice. Either you get rid of most of the people who come here, or we'll put you off limits. And you know we damn well can, don't you?'

Momma quailed as she lit the major's cigarette. The words 'off limits' were understood by any Neapolitan who wanted to keep his shop open. Nothing could withstand the MPs closing a place, unless you were friendly with some colonel of PBS.

'You know as well as I do,' said the major. 'An old doll like yourself ain't as dumb as she looks. We don't want any more Eyeties comin in here to mix with the soldiers. Do I make myself clear? And you gotta refuse to serve some of the other characters . . . Don't come whining around that you ain't been warned.'

Momma motioned to Vincenzo and Gaetano to bring out a glass of that fine cognac from which she gave her favorites shots after closing time. It was set at the major's elbow. He drank it off, glaring at her the while, set down the glass with a click, and left.

'Capeesh?' he cried as he belched like a balloon out into the sunlight of the Galleria.

Momma couldn't decide what grudge the MPs had against her. There had been occasional fights in her bar, yet the other bars of Naples had even more of them. Her soldiers were gentle. All she was trying to do was run a clean bar where people could gather with other congenial people. Her crowd had something that other groups hadn't. Momma's boys had an awareness of having been born alone and sequestered by some deep difference from other men. For this she loved them. And Momma knew something of those four freedoms the Allies were forever preaching. She believed that a minority should be let alone . . .

In came the Desert Rat. He took off his black beret and pushed a hand through his rich inky hair. He said good evening to Momma and bought his quota of six chits for double white wines. It would take him three hours to drink these. He was always the first to arrive and the last to leave. He never spoke to a soul. He was the handsomest and silentest boy Momma'd ever seen. Why did he come at all? His manners were so perfect and soft that at a greeting from another, he'd reply and recede into himself. Momma wondered if at Tobruk or El Alamein someone in the desert night had cut his soul to pieces. He'd loved once – perfectly – someone, somewhere. Momma would cheerfully have slain whoever had hurt him so.

The face of the Desert Rat was an oval of light brown. His short-sleeved shirt showed the cleft in his neck just above the hair of his chest. He wore the tightest and shortest pair of shorts he could get into, and he leaned lost and dreaming against the bar with his ankles scraping one another in their low socks and canvas gaiters. Those legs were part of the poetry of the Desert Rat for Momma – the long firm legs of Germans, but tanned and covered from thigh to calf with thick soft hair. For three hours this English boy would stand in Momma's bar, doped and dozing in maddening relaxation and grace from the white wine.

Momma tore six chits out of the cash register and gave the Desert Rat four lire back out of his one hundred. Tonight she went so far as to pat his wrist, a thing she'd been longing to do for months.

'Ees warm tonight, no?'

'Oh very, madam,' the Desert Rat said.

It was the first time she'd seen his smile. And Momma suddenly saw him in someone's arms by moonlight in the Egyptian desert, in the midst of that love which had sliced the boy's heart in two . . . He left her and went to the bar. In the next three hours it was usually at him that Momma'd look when she wasn't making change. She saw him from all perspectives in the mirrors, all the loveliness of his majestic body.

Next to arrive was a Negro second lieutenant of the American quarter-master corps. Momma smiled to herself as the Negro made an entrance. He seemed to have the idea he was stepping onto some lighted stage. He moved his hips ever so slightly and carried his pink-insided hands tightly against his thighs. For some dramatic reason he wore combat boots, though Momma knew he'd never been farther north than the docks of Naples.

'Hulllllo, darling,' he said to Momma, kissing her fingers. He had a suave overeducated voice. 'You look simpppply wonderful tonight. Who does your hats? Queen Mary? . . . Uh-huh, uh-huh, uh-huh . . .'

Then he stationed himself at the bar quite close to the Desert Rat. They looked at each other for a swift appraising instant. Then the Negro lieutenant began to talk a blue streak at the Desert Rat.

'It's going to be brilliant here tonight, absolutely brrrrilliant. I feel it way down inside . . . My aunt, you know, is a social worker in Richmond, Virginia. But do you think I'm ever going back there? No, indeed, baby. I found a home in Italy, where the human plant can't help but thrive. I like the Italians, you know. They're like me, refined animals, which of course doesn't bar the utmost in subtlety and human development . . .

They talk about French love . . . Well, the Italians know all the French do, and have a tenderness besides . . . My God, why doesn't everybody just live for love? That's all there is, baby. And out of bed you have to be simply brilllllliant . . .'

Momma sometimes pondered to herself the reason for the wild rhetoric talk by some of the people who came to her bar. It wasn't like Italian rhetoric, which makes good Italian conversation a sort of shimmering badminton. At Momma's most of her customers talked like literate salesmen who cunningly invited you out to dinner – all the time you knew that they were selling something, but their propaganda was sparkling and insidious. At Momma's there were people who talked constantly for the whole three hours. There were others who simply listened to the talkers, smiling and accepting, as though they'd tacitly agreed to play audience. And Momma could tell the precise time in her bar by the level of the noise, by the speed with which the words shot through the air like molten needles, by the ever mounting bubbles of laughter and derision. Under this conversation Momma sensed a vacuum of pain, as though her guests jabbered at one another to get their minds off themselves, to convince themselves of the reality of something or other.

There now arrived the only two Momma didn't rejoice to see, two British sergeants wearing shorts draped like an old maid's flannels. They were almost twins, had peaked noses and spectacles that caused them to peer at everyone as though they were having difficulty in threading a needle from their rocking chairs. Momma wished they wouldn't stand so close to her desk, blocking her view. But stand there they did until the bar closed. Their conversation was a series of laments and groans and criticisms of everyone else present. They called this dishing the joint. Momma thought that they came to her bar because they couldn't stay away. They were disdainful and envious and balefully curious all at the same time. They reminded her of old women who take out their false teeth and contemplate their photograph of forty years ago. These sergeants bought some chits, took off their berets, and primped a little in the mirror behind Momma.

'Esther, my coiffure! Used to be so thick and lustrous . . . We're not getting any younger, are we? We'll have to start paying for it soon. Shall we live together and take in tatting?'

And the other sergeant said, giving himself a finger wave:

'Well, I've read that the end of all this is exhaustion and ennui.

As we've agreed steen times before, Magda, the problem is bottomless, simply bottomless. No one but ourselves understands it, or is even interested. You put your hand into a cleft tree to your own peril, Magda. When you take out the wedge, the tree snaps together and breaks your hand . . . And you cry your eyes out at night, but it doesn't do any good . . . It keeps coming back on you because it's in you. Even though you don't get any satisfaction, you go back to it like a dog to his vomit . . . That's what it is, Magda, vomit. Why kid ourselves and talk of love? Love is a constructive force . . . We only want to destroy ourselves in others because we hate ourselves . . .'

At 1700 hours Rhoda appeared after she'd had evening chow at the WAC-ery. Rhoda was the only woman who came to Momma's bar. No one ever spoke to Rhoda, who did her drinking standing at the far end of the counter, reading a thick book. She always made it a point to show Momma what she was reading. Rhoda worried about the state of the world. She studied theories of leisure classes and patterns behind governments.

'I'm not good for much of anything,' Rhoda once said, 'except to talk up a storm.'

To Momma's Italian ear Rhoda had a voice like a baritone; everything she said carried about a kilometer.

'What am I?' Rhoda said once. 'The reincarnation of L'Aiglon.'

It seemed to Momma that Rhoda was happy in her WAC uniform – the neat tie, the coat, the stripes on the sleeve, the skirt that didn't call attention to the fact that it was a skirt. Under her overseas cap Rhoda wore an exceptional hairdo. It was something like the pageboy bob of twenty years ago cut still more boyishly. And under this cropped poll were Rhoda's stark face, thin lips, weasel eyes. Rhoda looked as though she were lying in ambush for something. She bought a slew of tickets from Momma and went to her accustomed place, reading and drinking. She turned the pages by moistening her forefinger and looking quickly at the other persons in the bar.

Rhoda was the only American girl whom Momma knew well, but she was a symbol. Momma had a theory that romantic love was on the wane in America because if all the women were like Rhoda, American girls were mighty emancipated and intellectual. Since Rhoda was so cool and unfeminine, Momma foresaw a day in the United States when all the old graceful concepts of love would have perished. The women would have brought it on themselves by insisting on equality with the men. To Momma, thinking of her girlhood in Milan, this wasn't an inviting picture . . .

'Why don't signorine come here?' Rhoda asked authoritatively of Momma. 'Intellectual Italian women, I mean. I'd spread the gospel to them. I'm the best little proselytizer in the world. I'd make them socially conscious. We'd read the *Nation* and John Dos Passos. I might even pass out copies of *Consumers' Research* to help Italian girls buy wisely.'

Momma smiled. She knew quite well that if signorine started coming to her bar, most of her patrons would go away. It was an easy matter to get a signorina anywhere else in the Galleria Umberto or on the Toledo. Momma had indeed been ill at ease when Rhoda had first appeared, but the boys had accepted Rhoda while ignoring her. And so long as there was harmony, Momma didn't care who came to her bar . . .

'Oh this place of yours,' Rhoda boomed with a thick shiver. 'It's positively electric here, Momma. I get so much thinking and reading done in this stimulating atmosphere . . . Just like a salon.'

The two British sergeants eyed Rhoda. Momma'd been expecting them to accost one another for the past week. And tonight the bubble was going to burst.

'We've been asking one another why you come here,' the sergeant called Esther said. 'You must have a Saint Francis of Assisi complex. Or else you're a Messalina . . . If you want to give us a good laugh, why don't you bring one of your Warm Sisters with you and make a gruesome twosome? You shouldn't come here alone, darling. Momma's bar is like nature, which abhors vacuums and solitary people.'

'I'm not answerable to the likes of you,' Rhoda roared back, bristling with delight. 'But I will say I've always sought out milieux that vibrate in tune with me . . . So you two just get back to your knitting. Just because you two are jaded and joaded, that's no sign I should be too.'

'Magda, she's a tigress,' the other British sergeant said, 'but a veritable tigress. We must have her to our next Caserta party.'

'Don't think I don't know those parties,' Rhoda rumbled. 'The height of sterility. Everybody sits around tearing everybody else to pieces, thinking, My God, ain't we brilliant. Everybody gets stinking drunk. Then somebody makes an entrance down the stairs in ostrich feathers and a boa . . . No thank you, my pretty chicks.'

'Well, get you, Mabel,' the first British sergeant tittered.

Momma cleared her throat. She hated the turn things were taking by her cash desk. It was as though the three were armed with talons, raking at one another's faces.

'We understand one another all too well, don't we?' Rhoda said triumphantly. 'I pity you two from the bottom of my swelling heart. If you had a little more of what I have, or I had a little more of what you have, what beautiful music we could make . . . a trio . . .'

'Darling, I see you in London,' the second sergeant said. 'A sensation. But you aren't quite Bankhead, darling. But you are happy in the WACs, aren't you, dear? Your postwar plans are to run a smart little night club . . . wearing a white tuxedo . . . but darling, you just haven't the figger for it.'

'It's no use trying to scratch my eyes out,' Rhoda rumbled in her open diapason. 'I have a perfect armorplating against elderly queans.'

'Pleasa,' Momma murmured, clearing her throat again, 'pleasa . . .'

In her bar things moved by fits and starts. Incidents in the course of three hours followed some secret natural rhythm of fission and quiescence, like earthquakes and Vesuvio. Each time the climaxes grew fuller. This first was only a ripple to what she knew would happen later.

Rhoda and the two British sergeants glared at one another. She reopened her thick book and retreated into it like an elephant hulking off into the jungle. The two sergeants put arms about each other's waists and executed a little congratulatory dance.

After the first incident the Desert Rat raised his fine dark head, looked into the mirror, and ordered another white wine. The Negro second lieutenant stopped his monologue and called out:

'Everyone's still wearing their veil . . . but wait . . .'

An Italian contingent always came to Momma's on schedule. They entered with the furtive gaiety of those who know they aren't wanted, but have set their hearts on coming anyhow. They wore shorts and sandals and whimsical little coats which they carried like wraps around their shoulders, neglecting to put their arms into the sleeves. Momma knew that her Allied clientele didn't care for them. And besides they never drank more than two glasses apiece, if they drank that much. They just sat around and mimicked one another and sniggered and looked hard at the Allied soldiery. Each evening they had a fresh set of photos and letters to show one another. Momma thought of nothing so much as a bevy of Milan shopgirls having a reunion after the day's work. She knew them all so well. The Italians treated Momma with a skeptical deference, as though to say, Well, here we are again, dearie; your bar is in the public domain; so what are you going to do with us if we don't make a nuisance of ourselves?

There was Armando, who worked in a drygoods store. He was led in by his shepherd dog on a leather thong. This dog was Armando's lure for introduction to many people. He had tight curls like a Greek statue's, a long brown face, and an air of distinction learned from the films. He wore powder-blue shorts. It was Armando who translated all his little friends' English letters for them.

There was Vittorio, with the blue eyes of a doll and gorgeous clothes such as Momma'd seen on young ingegneri in the old days in Milan. Vittorio worked as a typist at Navy House on Via Caracciolo. He worked so well and conscientiously that the British gave him soap and food rations. Sunday afternoons he walked by the aquarium with an English ensign who murmured in his ear. Vittorio had arrogance and bitterness. He was the leader of the others. All evening long at Momma's he lectured on literature and life and the sad fate of handsome young Neapolitans in Naples of August, 1944. In Momma's hearing he said that he'd continue his present career till he was thirty. Then he'd marry a contessa and retire to her villa at Amalfi.

There was Enzo, who'd been a carabiniere directing traffic until the Allies had liberated Naples. Now Enzo led the life of a gaga, strolling the town in a T-shirt, inviting his friends to coffee in the afternoon, and singing at dusk in dark corners. Momma thought Enzo the apogee of brutal refinement. Over his shorts he wore shirts of scented silk or pongee. Under these the muscles of his back shimmered like salmon. The nostrils in his almost black face showed like pits, flaring with his breathing.

There was also a tiny sergente maggiore of the Italian Army. He held himself off from the rest, though he always came in with them. He used them as air-umbrella protection for his own debarking operations. The name of this sergente maggiore was Giulio. His eyes darted warily about, and once in a while he'd call out something in a barking voice, to show that he was accustomed to command. He insisted on wearing his smart fascist peaked cap, the visor of which he would nervously tug when he got an unexpected answer.

The last Italian to arrive at Momma's was the only one she respected. He was a count, but he permitted himself to be known only as Gianni.

Besides his title he had a spacious apartment in the Vomero. Momma respected his rank, and she hoped some day to be presented to his mother the countess. Momma liked Gianni as a person too. He was always dressed in black, with a white stiff collar and a black knitted tie. His black eyes smoldered with a remote nostalgia. For some months now he'd come to Momma's, drunk a little, and gone away. But tonight he seemed purposeful. He greeted Momma with a tender wretchedness. Momma knew his disease. He was a Neapolitan conte, dying of love. Gianni avoided the other Italians, who had perched themselves on a counter at the rear of the bar, and went straight up to the Desert Rat. Momma leaned over her cash desk and watched with popping eyes.

'May I speak to you, sir?' Gianni said to the Desert Rat.

His English was as slow and exquisite as that melancholy that lay over him like a cloud.

'Speak up, chum,' the Desert Rat said in his almost inaudible voice.

'Do you like me a little, sir?'

The Desert Rat didn't answer, but his tall body stiffened.

'I had a friend once,' Gianni said, almost crying. 'He was a German officer. He taught me German, you see. He was kind to me. And I think I was kind to him. I think I am a good person, sir. I am a rich count, but of course to you that does not import . . . I seek nothing from you, sir . . . like the others . . . You look so much like the German officer. I was happy with him. He said he was happy with me . . . Would you like sometimes to come to my house in the Vomero, sir?'

The two British sergeants set up a screaming like parrots. Gianni fled. Momma put her hand to her heart, which had given one vast jump. The Desert Rat quietly put down his wineglass. He took the two British sergeants and knocked their heads together. Then he ran out through the bar. Momma watched him stand outside, peering up and down the Galleria and shielding his eyes against the sun. After a while he returned to his place and fell into his old reverie. He seemed as stirred and angry as a true and passionate boy.

The two British sergeants were shrieking and sobbing and looking at their reddened faces in the mirror. Then they repaired to the gabinetto. Momma could hear them inside splashing water on their faces and gibbering like chickens being bathed by a hen.

Rhoda looked over her book at the silent Desert Rat. The second incident rolled through the bar like the aftertones of a bell. Momma just held onto her cash register and prayed, for she knew that this was going to be an evening. The Negro second lieutenant began to sing something about 'Strange Fruit.' The Italians footnoted the incident to one another. Momma's bar wasn't nearly full yet, but it was buzzing like a bomb.

Presently the two British sergeants swept out of the gabinetto, their faces swollen and their eyes flushed from weeping. They looked like hawks for someone to prey on. Enzo stepped easily up to them, placed a hand on his hip, and extended his powerful jeweled hand:

'Buona sera, ragazze.'

'You go straight to hell!' the first British sergeant screeched. 'Why do you come here at all, you sordid little tramps in your dirty old finery? Do you think we feel sorry for you? Go on Via Roma and peddle your stuff and stop trying to act like trade . . . We see through you, two-shilling belles. All of you get out, do you hear? Nobody here wants anything you've got. The Allies are quite self-sufficient, thank you. We did all right before Naples fell . . . Why the nerve of you wop queans! Glamor? Why you've all got as much allure as Gracie Fields in drag . . . Go find some drunken Yank along the port . . . But get the hell out of here!'

The Italians replied to the sally of the British sergeants in their own indirect but effective way. Momma decided that the Italians were more deeply rooted in life, that they accepted themselves. For the Italian contingent merely sent up a merry carol of laughter. If they'd had fans, they'd have retreated behind them. This laughter hadn't a hollow ring. It was based on the assumption that anything in life can be laughed out of existence. Momma had never admired the Italian element in her bar. Now she did. They shook with the silveriest laughter, lolling over one another like cats at play. Their limbs gleamed in their shorts. Even the tiny sergente maggiore joined in the badinage. And the two British sergeants stepped back by Momma's cash desk and resumed their jeremiad.

'What will become of us, Esther? When we were young, we could laugh off the whole business. You and I both know that's what camping is. It's a Greek mask to hide the fact that our souls are being castrated and drawn and quartered with each fresh affair. What started as a seduction at twelve goes on till we're senile old aunties, doing it just as a reflex action . . .'

'And we're at the menopause now, Magda . . . O God, if some hormone would just shrivel up in me and leave me in peace! I hate the thought of making a fool of myself when I turn forty. I'll see something gorgeous walking down Piccadilly and I'll make a pass and all England will read of my trial at the Old Bailey . . . Do you think we would have been happier in Athens, Magda?'

'Esther, let's face facts. You can't argue yourself out of your own time and dimension. You and I don't look like the Greeks and we don't think like them. We were born in England under a late Victorian morality, and so we'll die . . . The end is the same anyhow, Greek or English. Don't you see, Esther? We've spent our youth looking for something that doesn't really exist. Therefore none of us is ever at peace with herself. All bitchery adds up to an attempt to get away from yourself by playing a variety of poses, each one more gruesome and leering than the last . . . I'm sick to death of it, Esther. I can think of more reasons for not having been born than I can for living . . . Is there perhaps some nobility stirring in my bones?'

'Then is there no solution, Magda?' the second British sergeant asked wistfully.

He cast his eyes about the bar like a novice about to take the veil.

'Millions, Esther. But rarely in the thing itself. That's what tantalizes us all. We play with the thing till it makes of us what we swear we'll never become, cold-blooded sex machines, dead to love. There are so many ways of sublimating, Esther . . . But are they truly satisfying either? For some hours I've known, though they'll never come again, I'd cheerfully pass all eternity in hell.'

'And I too, Magda. That's the hell of it. We all have known moments, days, weeks that were perfect.'

'All part of the baggage of deceit, Esther. God lets us have those moments the way you'd give poisoned candy to a child. And we look back on those wonderful nights with far fiercer resentment than an old lady counting the medals of her dead son.'

'But we've had them, Magda; we've had them. No one can take them away from us.'

The two British sergeants lapsed into silence, for which Momma was grateful. Their conversation was a long swish of hissing *s*'s and flying eyebrows. They began to scratch their chevrons in a troubled and preoccupied way, and their faces fell into the same sort of introspective emptiness that Momma'd observed on old actresses sitting alone in a café. There was a lost air about them that made her prefer not to look at them, as though the devil had put her a riddle admitting of no solution, and a forfeit any way she answered it.

~ ~ ~

It was 1830 hours in Momma's bar, the time of the breathing spell. She was quite aware that, gathered under her roof and drinking her white wine and vermouth, there was a great deal of energy that didn't quite know how to spend itself. And since there's some rhythm in life, in bars, and in war, everybody at once stopped talking and ordered fresh drinks. She could see them all looking at their wrist watches and telling themselves: I have another hour to go – what will it bring me?

Momma's sixth sense told her there was trouble brewing. A group of soldiers and sailors entered her bar. From the way they shot around their half-closed eyes she knew that this wasn't the place for them. They had an easiness and a superiority about them as though they were looking for trouble with infinite condescension. Cigars lolled from their mouths.

'Gracious,' the Negro second lieutenant said, 'men!'

'Look, Esther,' said the first of the British sergeants, 'look at the essence of our sorrow . . . What we seek and can never have . . . And each side hates the other. The twain never meet except in case of necessity. And they part with tension on both sides.'

For there were two American parachutists who lounged insolently, taking up more cubic space than they should have. And with them were two drunken American sailors, singing and holding one another up. Momma now wished that Poppa were here to order this foursome out summarily, under threat of the MPs. Vincenzo and Gaetano were no help at all in such circumstances. Then what she feared happened. Someone of her regular clientele let up a soft scream like a pigeon being strangled. At once a parachutist stiffened, flipped a wrist, and bawled:

'Oh saaaay, Nellie!'

This was the moment the Italians had been waiting for. They picked themselves off the flat-topped counter where they'd been idling and padded toward the four newcomers. They were cajoling and tender and satiric and gay. They lit cigarettes for the parachutists and the sailors, and took some themselves. It became a swirling ballet of hands and light and rippling voices and the thickened accents of the sailors and the parachutists.

'Jesus, baby, those bedroom eyes!' someone said to Vittorio.

'I hateya and I loveya, ya beast,' one of the sailors said.

'Coo, it teases me right out of my mind,' one of the British sergeants said. 'So simple and complex. Masculine and feminine. All gradations and all degrees and all nuances.'

'The basis of life and love and cruelty and death,' said the other British sergeant, looking as though he would faint. 'And in the long run, Magda, who is master and who mistress?'

From a tension that was surely building up, Momma was distracted by the appearance of an assorted horde. In the final hour of the evening her bar filled until there were forty wedged in, six to eight deep from the mirrors to the bar. Her eyes had a mad skipping time to follow all that went on. It was like trying to watch a circus with a thousand shows simultaneous in as many rings.

First came an Aussie in a fedora hat, to which his invention had added flowers and feathers. Tonight he was more than usually drunk. He slunk in with the slow detachment of a mannequin modeling clothes. He waved a lace handkerchief at all:

'Oh my pets, my pets! Your mother's awfully late tonight, but she'll try and make it up to you!'

'Ella's out of this world,' some one said. 'She's brilliant, brilliant.'

A glazed look came over the sailors' eyes like snakes asleep. Ella the Aussie kissed their hands and bustled off while they were still collecting themselves.

'Don't call *me* your sister!' Ella shrieked, waving at his public while buying chits from Momma. He kissed Momma on both her cheeks, leaving a stench of alcohol and perfume.

There was a rich hollow thud. Momma at first feared that someone had planted a fist on someone else's chin. But it was only Rhoda, the WAC corporal, closing her book. That evening she read no further. It was getting too crowded in there even to turn pages.

Next to appear at Momma's was a British marine, sullen in his red and black, with a hulking beret. Momma knew he was a boxer, but not the sort who made trouble. He'd a red slim face, pockmarked and dour; the muscles in his calves stood out like knots. While drinking he teetered up and down on his toes and was a master at engineering newcomers into conversation. He observed everyone with a cool devotion. Often he'd invited Momma to his bouts at the Teatro delle Palme, but she hadn't gone because she couldn't bear to see him beating and being beaten in the ring. This British marine was on the most basic and genial terms with himself and the world.

Next came a plump South African lance corporal with red pips, and a Grenadier Guardsman, tall and reserved and mustached. The South African lance corporal was a favorite of Momma's because he made so much of her. She knew he didn't mean a word of it, but the whole ceremony was so much fun to her.

'Old girl, I've finally got married,' said the plump lance corporal, presenting her to the Grenadier Guardsman, who looked terrified and bulwarky at the same time. 'This is Bert. You'll love Bert. He saved my life in Tunisia. And he understands me. So he's not as stupid as he looks. And his devotion, darling! Coo! Just like a Saint Bernard Bert is. He knows how to cook, you know . . .' Bert's essence is in his mustaches. The traditionalism, the stolidity, and the stupidity of the British people produced those mustaches of Bert's.

Momma was in such a whirl of happiness that she gave the guardsman a chit for a drink on the house. Meanwhile the South African lance corporal whirled about the bar, burbling to everyone and formally announcing his marriage to Bert.

Momma was beginning to believe that she wasn't going to have any trouble from the parachutists and the sailors. They and the Italians were lazily drinking and mooing at one another. Momma tried to spell out for herself some theory of good and evil, but the older she got and the more she saw, the less clear cut the boundaries became to her. She could only conclude that these boys who drank at her bar were exceptional human beings. The masculine and the feminine weren't nicely divided in Momma's mind as they are to a biologist. They overlapped and blurred in life. This trait was what kept life and Momma's bar from being black and white. If everything were so clear cut, there'd be nothing to learn after the age of six and arithmetic.

~ ~ ~

Among the later comers to Momma's were certain persons from the port battalion that sweated loading and unloading ships in the Bay of Naples. They turned up in her bar in the Galleria Umberto as soon as the afternoon shift got off, just as the truck drivers make a beeline for coffee and doughnuts. They usually came with fatigues damp with their sweat, with green-visored caps askew on their knotted hair. Because they were out of uniform Momma feared trouble with the MPs. But some of these port battalion GIs were Momma's favorites since they brought her many odds and ends they'd taken from the holds of Liberty ships: tidbits destined for generals' villas and the like. They knew Momma's nature as a curio collector of things and people.

There was Eddie, an American corporal. Momma loved Eddie the way she'd love a child of her own who was born not quite all there. Eddie'd been a garage mechanic in Vermont. He squirmed with that twisted tenderness often acquired by people who spend their lives lying under motors and having axle grease drip on them. Eddie had misty lonely eyes; his mouth was that of one who has never made the transition out of babyhood. His red hair yielded to no comb, and there was always a thick mechanical residue under his fingernails, which Momma sometimes cleaned herself. Eddie was drunk on duty and off. As he bought his chits, he leaned over Momma and patted her clumsily on her hair.

'Come stai, figlio mio?' Momma asked.

'Bene, bene, Momma,' he replied.

Eddie would caress people in a soft frightened way and then run his tongue over his lips. After he'd got good and tight, he'd go through the crowded bar playing games, pulling neckties, snapping belt buckles, and thrusting his knee between people's legs. He was like a little dog that has got mixed up in society and desires to find a master.

Then there was a supply sergeant of the port battalion, with his vulture face. His every movement seemed to Momma a raucous suppression of some deeper inferiority sense. He talked constantly like a supply catalogue, reeling off lists of things in his warehouse for the potent music of their names. Then he would shoot out his jaw and the blood would capillate into his eyes. Momma got him rooms around Naples with spinster acquaintances of hers. He stayed in these rooms on his one night off a week. This sergeant loved to sally into off-limits areas and wet-smelling vichi.

'Color and glamour,' the sergeant said, 'all there is to life, baby . . .'

Eddie meanwhile had drunk three glasses of vermouth and came and stood by Momma, slipping cakes of soap into her hand behind the cash desk.

'Jees, I tink I got da scabies, Momma . . .'

The last delegate from the port battalion was one of its tech sergeants named Wilbur. He treated Momma like a serving girl and spent his time going over everyone with his eyes. Wilbur should have been born a lynx, for he draped his length over any available area with a slow rehearsed lewdness. Tonight he was growing a mustache, but it didn't camouflage his violet eyes that glowed like amethysts in his face. Momma could never get him to look her in the eyes. He simply drawled at everyone, and all the things he said lay around in gluey pools like melted lavender sherbet.

'Bonsoir, ducks,' Wilbur said to the two British sergeants. 'When is all this blah going to end? Because it is blah, and nobody knows it better than you . . . Done any one nice lately? What a town to cruise this is. All the belles in the States would give their eye-teeth to be in Naples tonight. And when they saw all there is here, they'd be so confused they wouldn't know what to do with it . . . Can you imagine the smell of their breaths? . . . Blah, that's all it is.'

Two of Momma's more distinguished patrons now entered from the Galleria. They did it every evening, but every evening a little hush fell over the drinkers. They came in a little flushed, as though they'd been surprised in a closet. Perhaps the momentary pall proceeded from a certain awe at their rank, or at their temerity in coming at all. For by now the party was well under way, susceptible to that hiatus in levels of euphoria when people come late to a group that is already from alcohol in a state of dubious social cohesion. One was a pasty-faced major of the American medical corps who gave Momma a free physical examination every month and got his dentist friends to clean her teeth gratis. The major's breath always boiled in an asthmatic fashion, as though he were in the last stages of love-making. With him was his crony, a not so young second lieutenant who'd been commissioned for valor in combat at Cassino. The major and the lieutenant both wore gold wedding bands on their fingers. Momma gathered that they preferred not to discuss their wives, since these little women were four thousand miles away.

'Poor pickins tonight,' said the major to the lieutenant.

'I don't waste any time any more,' the lieutenant grunted, paying for his chits. 'I just say do you and pushem into a dark corner . . . Piss on all introductions and flourishes . . . Who started this way anyhow? Not me, buddy . . .'

Momma looked at the half-bald head of the lieutenant under the crazy angle of his cap. She knew that he'd been most heroic in battle – that was how he'd got his commission. There was strife in his low grating voice. Once he'd told her of last winter in battle, of an Italian boy sewing by moonlight in the arch of a bombed house near Formia:

'I was drinking vino with my GIs . . . And he just sits there looking at me. Fifteen, he said he was . . . white skin. I remember his eyes over his needle . . . I wonder where he is now.'

As the lieutenant fumbled to pay her for their chits, a woman's picture fell on Momma's counter out of his pocket:

'Ees your wife in Stati Uniti?' Momma said, trying to turn the glossy print over.

He covered it from her gaze with a hand pocked with sandfly bites and umber with cigarette stains. His eyes were close to hers, yellow and protruding.

'Never mind that, Momma,' he said, restoring the picture to his pocket.

Momma knew that the bravest and coolest entered her bar alone. They entered with a curt functionalism that informed everyone that hadn't come just to drink or to watch or to brood. Still others came in specious twosomes, talked together a little, and spent most of the time ignoring one another and looking into the mirrors in a sort of reconnoitering restlessness. And a few came in groups of twos and threes for protection. When Momma's bar was full, it was like a peacock's tail because she could see nothing but eyes through the cigarette smoke. Restless and unsocketed eyes that wheeled all around, wholly taken up in the business of looking and calculating. Eyes of every color. Momma's bar when crowded was a goldfish bowl swimming with retinas and irises in motion.

Next there came two French lieutenants and two French sailors. The sailors were ubriachi and the lieutenants were icily sober. In the two French officers Momma'd always noted an excellence in the little braided pips through their shoulder loops, their American khaki shirts, and their tailored shorts. Their conversation played over the heads of their sailors with a silvery irony. Momma understood their tongue decently enough, that perfect language which gave all their remarks a literary quality beyond even the intelligence of the speakers.

'Ainsi je noie toute mon angoisse,' said the first French officer.

'C'est ma femme qui m'incite à de telles folies,' said the other.

'Tilimbom,' the drunken sailors said, clapping the pompons on their caps.

The French officers had a jeep which they parked at the steps of the Galleria. When Momma closed her bar, she knew that they whisked into this jeep an assorted and sparkling company and drove to the top of Naples to admire the August moonlight. Momma wondered if the

ripple of their epigrams and refinements ceased even when they were
making love.

'C'est une manie, Pierre.'

'Bon appétit, André.'

~ ~ ~

Momma had less than half an hour till closing time. Her bar, into which
people now must wedge themselves, was swimming in smoke and a terrific
tempo of talk and innuendo. Under its surface there was a force of madness
and a laughter of gods about to burst. Momma put her hand to her throat
and swallowed hard in the strangling ecstasy of one dropping down an
elevator shaft. For this was the time she loved best of her three hours: a
presentiment of infinite possibilities, of hectic enchantments, of the fleeting
moment that never could be again because it was too preposterous and
frantic and keyed up.

The Desert Rat was finishing his fifth white wine in his prison of
detachment and musing. Ella the Aussie was being removed by Gaetano
and Vincenzo from the top of the bar, where he was executing a cancan.
Rhoda was booming out a quotation from Spengler. The Negro second
lieutenant was examining his nail polish. Eddie had put his arms around
one of the French officers, talking about parlayvoo-fransay. And the two
British sergeants reared up like Savonarolas.

'I'm asking you, Esther, to take a good look at all these mad people.
For they are mad. And consider the subtle thread that brings them all
together here. Not so subtle as that either, Esther, since their personalities
are so deeply rooted in it. What an odd force to unite so many varied
personalities! Something they all want . . . and when they've had it, their
reactions will be different. Some will feel themselves defiled. Others will
want another try at it. Others will feel that they haven't found what they
were looking for and will be back here tomorrow night.'

'Does either of us know what these people are looking for, Magda?'
the second sergeant asked with thickened tongue.

'Don't be dull, Esther. They're all looking for perfection . . . and
perfection is a love of death, if you face the issue squarely. That's the
reason why these people live so hysterically. Since the desire to live, in its
truest sense of reproducing, isn't in them, they live for the moment more
passionately than most. That makes them brazen and shortsighted . . . In
this life, Esther, when you find perfection, you either die on the spot in

orgasm, or else you don't know what to do with it . . . These people are the embodiment of the tragic principle of life. They contain tragedy as surely as a taut string contains a musical note. They're the race's own question mark on its value to survive.'

'Is there any hope for them, Magda?' the second sergeant whimpered, wiping a mist from his glasses.

'In the exact measure that they believe in themselves, Esther. Depending on how they control their centripetal desires. Some hold back in their minds and distrust what they're doing. In them are the seeds of schizophrenia and destruction. Others give themselves wholly up to their impulses with a dizziness and a comic sense that are revolting to the more serious ones . . . Lastly there's a group which sees that they can profit by everything in this world. These are the sane. The Orientals are wiser in these matters than we or Queen Victoria. No phase of human life is evil in itself, provided the whole doesn't grow static or subservient to the part . . . But beware, Esther, of the bright psychiatrists who try to demarcate clearly the normal from the abnormal. In the Middle Ages people suffered themselves to be burnt as witches because it gave them such satisfaction to keep up their act. It was just a harmless expression of their ego. And children allow themselves to be pinked by hot stoves just to get a little sympathy out of their parents.'

'What does God think of all this, Magda?' mourned the second sergeant.

'Thank Him, if He exists, that we don't know . . . A new morality may come into existence in our time, Esther. That's one of the few facts that thrills me, old bitch that I am. Some distinction may be made between public and private sins, between economic and ethical issues. In 1944 you find the most incredible intermingling, a porridge of the old and the new, of superstition and enlightenment. How can we speak of sin when thousands are cremated in German furnaces, when it isn't wrong to make a million pounds, but a crime to steal a loaf of bread? Perhaps some new code may come out of all this . . . I hope so.'

'And if not?'

'Why then,' the first British sergeant said in drunken triumph, 'we shall have a chaos far worse than in Momma's bar this evening. This is merely a polite kind of anarchy, Esther. These people are expressing a desire disapproved of by society. But in relation to the world of 1944, this is just a bunch of gay people letting down their back hair . . . We mustn't go mad over details, Esther. Big issues are much more important. It is they which should drive us insane if we must be driven at all . . . All I say is, some compromise must and will be reached . . . Esther, I'm stinko.'

Momma watched the two British sergeants embrace each other with an acid tenderness. Then they slid to the floor unconscious, in a welter of battle dress and chevrons and spectacles. They lay with their eyes closed in the quiet bliss of two spinsters who have fought out their differences at whist, falling asleep over the rubber. And it was typical of Momma's at this time of the evening that no one paid any attention to the collapse, just pushed and wedged in closer to give the corpses room.

The talk was now at its full tide of animation, like a river ravenous to reach the sea, yet a little apprehensive to lose its identity in that amorphous mass which ends everything. Momma knew the secret of an evening's drinking, that life grows sweeter as the sun sets and one gets tighter. If only drinkers knew how to hold their sights on that yellow target bobbing on their horizons! For Momma understood the drunkenness of the Nordic better than most Italians did. They drank out of impatience with details, with personalities that were centrifugal, with a certain feminine desire to have a crutch for the spirit, with a certain sluggishness of their metabolism. Momma thought it weak of them to drink, but it was a weakness as amiable as modesty, courtesy, or the desire to live at all when the odds were against them.

In a delirium Momma leaned over her cash desk and strained her ear at the hurtling shafts of talk:

'How can you possibly like actors? Every goddam one of them is constantly playing a part. Off the stage too . . .'

'I am essentially an aristocrat. People must come to me. But I'm by no means passive . . .'

'My aunt, a refined colored woman, brought me up most circumspectly. I come from a long line of missionaries. So don't think I don't spread the good word among the Gentiles . . .'

'I don't know why our sort is always in the best jobs and the smartest . . .'

'First time for me, ya see. I'm not the lowered-eyelash kind . . .'

'So I told this Nellie to go peddle her fish somewhere else. And she did . . .'

'Do you remember loathing your father and doting on your teachers? . . . You didn't? . . .'

'. . . not responsible for anything I do tonight . . .'

'Il n'y a rien au monde comme deux personnes qui s'aiment . . .'

'Every time I think this is the real thing, the bottom falls right out from under me. Here I go again . . .'

'. . . un vero appassionato di quelle cose misteriose . . .'

'I could be faithful all night long . . .'

'Ciao, cara . . .'

'In the Pincio Gardens all I saw was flesh flesh flesh . . .'

'Sometime we'll read the *Phaedo* together. Then you'll see what I mean . . .'

'There's somethin in ya eyes. I dunno, I just know when I'm happy . . .'

'Let's you and me stop beating around the bush . . .'

'Don't feel you have to be elegant with me, Bella, cause your tiara's slippin over one ear . . .'

'For Chrissakes, what in hell do ya take me for? . . .'

'They're all suckin for a bruise . . . or somethin else . . .'

'. . . am frankly revolted with the spectacle of human beings with their bobbie pins flying all over the place . . .'

'And when they expect you to pay them for it . . .'

'Pussunally I tink da Eyetalians is a hunnert years behind da times . . .'

'Why do I wear a tie? Just to be different, that's why . . .'

'. . . simply no idea of the effect of Mozart coming over a loudspeaker at the edge of the desert. The Krauts simply lovedddd ittt! . . .'

'In a society predominantly militaristic . . .'

'Ciao, cara . . .'

'I looked at you earlier . . . but I didn't dare think . . .'

A sudden silence descended on Momma's bar. There was a movement of many bodies giving way to make space. She now knew exactly what time it was and who had come. It was Captain Joe and the young Florentine. This was the climax of every evening. Captain Joe stalked cool and somber in his tank boots, a green bandanna tucked round his neck in the negligence of magnificence. He had gold hair which caught the light like bees shuttling at high noon. He had a hard intense sunburned face that smoldered like a monk in a Spanish painting. Momma knew that he was a perfect law unto himself, though gentle and courteous with all. He came only in the company of the young Florentine, whose eyes never left his face. The captain smiled with amusement and understanding at all, but he spoke only to his friend. Their faces complemented one another as a spoon shapes what it holds. The Florentine had dark thoughtful eyes and olive skin. He seemed wholly selfless. He and Captain Joe shared a delight and a comprehension that couldn't be heard. But they gave out a peace, a wild tranquillity.

'Buona sera a Lei,' said Captain Joe to Momma. 'You keep a great circus at Naples, signora. And the miraculous thing about you is that you don't need the whip of a ringmaster . . . You and I and Orlando are the last of a vanishing tribe. We live in the sunshine of our own nobility. A perilous charge in these days. I wonder if our time will ever come again. We give because we have to. And others try to draw us into their own common mold, reading their own defects into our virtues.'

Momma signaled to Vincenzo and Gaetano to shut down the rolling steel shutter. It was closing time. Captain Joe lit her cigarette.

'Happiness,' Captain Joe said, 'is a compromise, signora, between being what you are and not hurting others . . . We smile, Orlando and I . . . Genius knows its own weaknesses and hammers them into jewels. All our triumphs come from within. We've never learned to weep . . .'

A shout, a thud, and screams tore the air.

'Ya will, willya!' a drunken voice roared, hoarse with murder. Fists began to fly and people retreated against the walls. There was kicking and petitioning and cursing. The Desert Rat roused from his torpor and leaped in to defend the fallen. In the narrow bar persons swirled back and forth in a millrace. There were bloody noses and snapping joints. And when Momma saw the MPs break in from the Galleria, flailing their night sticks, she knew that the time had come for her to faint. So almost effortlessly she fell out and across her cash desk. She'd been practicing mentally all evening long.

JOCELYN BROOKE

GERALD BROCKHURST

1

It must have been during my first term at Oxford that I became acquainted with Gerald Brockhurst; for I remember that our first meeting took place, over a pint of bitter, in the 'Trout' at Godstow. During those first weeks as a freshman, I had formed the habit of hiring a hack once or twice a week and riding out to Port Meadow; I did this partly because I liked it, and partly as an anti-social gesture – for, as a conscientious (and even a militant) aesthete, I had naturally refused to play any games. At the same time, I was not wholly immune to the fetish of 'exercise' – a hangover, no doubt, from my schooldays; and riding, though it might be anti-social, was admitted (even by athletes) to be as good a way as any other of shaking up one's liver.

Usually I rode in the afternoon: trotting cautiously – 'remote,

JOCELYN BROOKE (1908–1966): A distinguished fiction writer, poet and memoirist, Brooke was also a fireworks enthusiast, amateur botanist, and authority on orchids; his lesser-known titles include The Wild Orchids of Britain, The Flower in Season: A Calendar of Wildflowers, *and* The Wonderful Summer, *a children's novel that involves its young protaganists in fireworks-making and orchidaceous adventures. Brooke is better known for the semi-autobiographical trilogy consisting of* The Military Orchid, A Mine of Serpents, *and* The Goose Cathedral (*recently reissued by Penguin as* The Military Orchid and Other Novels), *and the novels* Conventional Weapons, The Image of a Drawn Sword, The Passing of a Hero, *and* The Scapegoat. *'Gerald Brockhurst' is taken from* Private View: Four Portraits.

unfriended, melancholy, slow' – through the outer suburbs, cantering a few times round Port Meadow, and returning, through the bleak November dusk, to tea and crumpets in my rooms. Now and again, however, a fine winter's morning would tempt me to cut lectures (I still went to lectures at that time) and ride out before lunch; and it was on one of these occasions that, having cantered dutifully, as usual, round the meadows, I tethered my horse outside the Trout and went into the bar for a drink. The keen, wintry air, the exercise and, perhaps, an agreeable sense of playing truant, had induced in me a mood of unaccustomed heartiness: I felt positively doggish, and a match for any athlete. I ordered a pint of bitter – not because I particularly liked beer, but because it seemed the drink most suited to the occasion. I exchanged a few remarks – of a suitable heartiness, as I supposed – with the landlord; then, as my eyes strayed round the room, I observed another young man dressed, like myself, in riding-kit, standing at the opposite end of the bar. I had noticed, when I came in, that another horse was tethered nearby; and it was almost inevitable, in the circumstances, that my fellow-rider and I should fall into conversation.

He was a very ordinary-looking young man: not very tall, but heavily built and stocky, with broad shoulders and a thick, muscular neck. His face was round, blunt-featured and in no way distinguished, though the expression was pleasant enough; he wore a little toothbrush moustache, which was perhaps a recent acquisition, for he was inclined to pull at it, rather self-consciously, as he talked. No doubt it was partly the moustache which made him seem older than he was; certainly it didn't occur to me that he could be an undergraduate – I put him down vaguely, I think, as an Army officer in mufti, or possibly a gentleman farmer. His accent was 'educated' yet not obtrusively so: there was about it the faintest suggestion of some regional 'burr'. I was not, in any case, particularly interested in his background; I was content to accept him as just an ordinary, quite pleasant young man, who happened to share my taste for riding. In my present elated mood I should have enjoyed talking to almost anybody; and this chance acquaintance, with his bluff, bucolic appearance, seemed (like the beer) entirely suited to the occasion.

I haven't the faintest recollection of what we talked about, though I should imagine that our conversation was mainly restricted to horses, beer and the weather. What I do remember is that we drank several pints of bitter – more than I was accustomed to – and that when the time came to start back, I found it uncommonly difficult to climb into the saddle, and even more difficult, once I had managed to do so, to remain there. My new acquaintance, fortunately, was also riding back to Oxford (he had hired his horse, as it turned out, from the same stable), and we set out together along the tow-path; more than once my horse stumbled, and only my companion's strong arm saved me from disaster. Before we parted, we arranged to go out together on an afternoon later in the same week.

When the time came, I half hoped he wouldn't turn up, for I was inclined to mistrust such chance acquaintanceships, formed under the influence of alcohol; for one thing, I didn't want to become involved with a bore, and being, moreover, an indifferent rider, I was more than a little afraid of making a fool of myself. Gerald, however (I had discovered that his name was Gerald Brockhurst), arrived punctually at the stables, and we started out towards Port Meadow. My qualms, as I soon realized, had been unjustified: for Gerald showed no disposition to laugh at my awkwardness; nor did he seem in the least the sort of person with whom one was likely to become tediously 'involved'. As a companion, I found him tactful and unexacting, and, despite the somewhat narrow and conventional range of his interests, I didn't, as I had half expected, find him a bore.

I discovered that he was, after all, a member of the university, only a year or two older than myself, and that he was studying medicine. This I found mildly distressing, for medical students were regarded as a slightly inferior breed at Oxford in those days. Gerald, as though guessing what was in my mind, explained that he would have preferred to go to Cambridge, but that his father had insisted upon Oxford.

'I always wanted to be a doctor, right from the word go,' Gerald confided. 'But the pater was dead against it – he wanted me to go into the family business. We had quite a bust-up just before I left school; finally, I sort of compromised, and said I'd come up here.'

'I suppose your father was up himself?' I asked, mildly curious.

Gerald chuckled.

'Not on your life – he started in business when he was sixteen. He's one of these self-made blokes, you see – civil engineer up at Northampton. He's retired now – got a little place in Surrey. I suppose,' Gerald added, turning to me with a shy smile, 'I suppose he'd got a sort of idea that Oxford was a bit more posh than the other place – you know, the kind of thing you see in the papers, gilded young aristocrats and all that.'

I realized, now, why Gerald hadn't seemed like an undergraduate: it wasn't only the moustache, or even the hint of a provincial accent, but something more deeply rooted – a kind of precocious maturity, an ability to get to grips with life, inherited from his father, and from the class from which his father had sprung. I began to suspect that Gerald was by no means so 'ordinary' as I had at first supposed; and his adult, realistic attitude, combined with his physical toughness and confidence, made me feel curiously unfledged and ineffectual.

He didn't say much more about himself that day, or, indeed, on the days which followed. For the rest of that term we rode together fairly regularly, and in a quiet, non-committal way we became very friendly; yet oddly enough it was never suggested, by either of us, that we should meet elsewhere. It didn't occur to me, for instance, to ask Gerald back to tea in college; nor did Gerald invite me to his rooms (which, I gathered, were somewhere out towards Iffley). If Gerald had other friends, he didn't talk about them; and I suspect that there was a tacit understanding between us that we belonged to different and perhaps mutually uncongenial 'sets'. In my own case, as it happened, this feeling was in no way justified, for I didn't – apart from one or two acquaintances in my own college – belong to any set at all. I was, in fact, extremely lonely during that first term, and should have been glad enough of Gerald's company at other times; yet our friendship remained limited to our afternoon rides, or an occasional morning jaunt when we would finish up, convivially, at the Trout, with a meal of bread-and-cheese and beer.

~ ~ ~

By the end of the term, Gerald had become, in a dim and unobtrusive way, a part of my life: I didn't think of him as a 'friend', but merely as someone quite pleasant whom I happened to see rather a lot of; rather like one's wine-merchant, or the head-waiter at a favourite restaurant – people with whom one was on the most amicable terms, yet never met elsewhere than in the particular ambience to which they belonged. In the case of Gerald, this ambience was the grey, frost-bound meadows beyond God-stow, the tow-path, and the bar at the Trout; to this day, when I think of him, it is against such a background that I imagine his squat, stocky figure, his rather podgy face, and his attractive, mildly ironic grin. I think of him as he was then – twenty or twenty-one, I suppose, yet giving an impression of being a good deal older; and indeed, Gerald was one of those people who, maturing early, alter very little between youth and middle age. Of some men one can say that they belong, by nature, to a characteristic, a 'typical' age-group: Gerald I should place at round about thirty; he changed remarkably little during the time I knew him, and if he seemed, when we first met, to be far older and more mature than myself, it was, oddly enough, his air of youth and *naïveté* which was to strike me most forcibly at our last encounter, nearly twenty years later.

Meanwhile – during these first weeks of our acquaintance – he remained for me a vague, almost impersonal presence: our association was primarily physical, a communion of bodily activity; and if I thought of Gerald at all, when I wasn't actually with him, it was his body that I chiefly remembered – the broad shoulders, the muscular neck, the cropped darkish hair. I hadn't, as yet, invested him with a 'personality': he remained, so to speak, on the wrong side of the counter – somebody with whom one passed the time of day and discussed the weather, but who ceased to exist, for all practical purposes, once one was out of the shop.

By the end of term, however, Gerald did begin to impinge upon me as a personality in his own right. Certain people seem never to become quite 'real' until one has observed them afresh through the eyes of a third person: viewed thus, from an unaccustomed angle, they acquire, so to speak, an added dimension, one sees them for the first time 'in the round', like a familiar photograph seen through a stereoscope. Gerald, I suppose, was such a person; up till now, he had remained for me, as it were, two-dimensional, like a 'flat' character in a novel; and, but for an accidental encounter with another of my friends, he might well, so far as I was concerned, have continued in the colourless and undistinguished rôle for which, with some injustice, I had originally cast him.

One afternoon after riding, as we were walking out of the stables in Walton Street, we ran straight into Eric Anquetil, with whom I had lately struck up a friendship. Seeing us, he hailed me across the street, and I was obliged to introduce him to Gerald. The situation was fraught, for me, with an absurdly disproportionate embarrassment: if Gerald had been one of the town prostitutes I couldn't have felt more self-conscious. I had not mentioned him to Eric – or, at most, had referred to him evasively as 'someone I went riding with'; nor, for that matter, had I mentioned Eric to Gerald. No two people, I felt, could have been more ill-assorted: Eric, on this occasion, was looking more than usually aesthetic, in a pale-grey suit, shantung tie and suède shoes; Gerald, I felt sure, would be embarrassed and perhaps morally outraged; and Eric, no doubt, would think Gerald impossibly dim and bourgeois.

As it happened, I couldn't have been more mistaken: expecting the worst, I was agreeably surprised to find that my two friends appeared, after a couple of minutes, to be on the best of terms. Soon they were chattering away nineteen to the dozen – about the latest film at the Super Cinema, about Fred Astaire, about the barmaids at the Clarendon: subjects which it would never have occurred to me to broach, and about which, in any case, I was profoundly ignorant. Eric, with a social aplomb which I could only helplessly envy, contrived to strike just the right note of heartiness combined with a touch of aristocratic *dandysme*; as for Gerald, I had never heard him so loquacious, and his manner had a vivacity and charm of which I had never supposed him capable. To be frank, I felt ever so slightly jealous: Gerald, after all, was *my* discovery; yet it had remained for Eric – improbably enough – to reveal his true 'personality', to put him, as they say nowadays, 'in the picture'.

Encouraged by the success of this encounter, I asked Gerald back to tea in my rooms. We gossiped amicably about trivialities over our crumpets and anchovy-toast; Gerald looked at my books, we played the gramophone (rather surprisingly, as I thought, Gerald was fond of music, with a special liking for Beethoven). Relaxed and euphoric after riding, I began to feel a new and more positive pleasure in his company; Gerald, I thought, if not particularly stimulating or glamorous, was an extremely pleasant and 'comfortable' person to be with.

~ ~ ~

As for Eric, he seemed to have taken an instant liking to Gerald, as I discovered that same evening when we met in Hall.

'I don't know why you've been keeping him under a bushel for so long,' he complained. 'I think he's very nice: I do so like that *sort* of athlete – so restful, don't you think? And it's odd and pleasing that his name should be Gerald.'

'Why odd – *or* pleasing?' I enquired with bewilderment.

'Oh, haven't you noticed? In novels, people like that are *always* called Gerald. There's one in E. M. Forster, and another in Lawrence – you know, the man in *Women in Love* – and I once read a novel by Gilbert Frankau, when I was at school, called *Gerald Cranston's Lady*; the hero was just the same type, terrifically hearty and military, with a moustache.'

'You ought to write a little monograph on the subject,' I suggested.

'Yes, I did think of it – or we might start some very queer, esoteric sort of society, and make Gerald Brockhurst the president.'

Thereafter, for some considerable time, Eric and I 'collected' Geralds; it was odd how often they seemed to support Eric's theory. Once we even went so far as to invite a totally unknown undergraduate to tea, merely on the strength of his Christian name (he had, I think, written a letter to the *Isis*). What pretext we invented for the invitation, I cannot remember; but the young man duly turned up (he was at Keble) and proved to be a person of singularly revolting aspect, with rimless glasses and false teeth.

'So much for your theory,' I said to Eric, when we had at last got rid of him.

'Not a bit of it,' Eric retorted, firmly, 'he was merely the exception which proves the rule.'

~ ~ ~

I rode once more with Gerald that term, and afterwards Eric invited us both to tea in his rooms. I was still a little nervous about Gerald's possible reactions to Eric (and vice versa); I need not have worried, for Eric had plainly laid himself out to be charming, and Gerald – as I was now beginning to realize – possessed a social flair which, though it differed in kind from Eric's more sophisticated code of manners, was not less adequate, and could indeed, on occasion, prove a good deal more effective.

There was something admirably solid and 'rooted' about Gerald: sitting back, lazily yet with an air of calm alertness, in his armchair, he seemed entirely at his ease; he spoke little, yet such remarks as he made were, if not brilliant, at least sensible and to the point. Our conversation was, to say the least, uninhibited: Eric, it was evident, had decided that Gerald was 'steeped' ('steeped in the highest philosophy') – or, if not positively steeped, at least faintly tinged with the appropriate greenery-yallery pigment. Once or twice I feared that Gerald, despite his apparent 'unshockableness', might jib at some of Eric's more outrageous remarks; yet he didn't, to my extreme relief, seem in the least perturbed. At the most he would raise his brows and give a slight shrug; then his face would relax again into a broad, tolerant grin – as though (it occurred to me) he were watching the undignified antics of a couple of naughty children. Once again, as when I had first met him, I was struck by his air of maturity; and I had an uneasy feeling that Eric and I were not, after all, quite so adult and sophisticated as we liked to suppose.

Gerald, as it happened, was quite a good Latin scholar, and was perfectly capable, in this respect, of meeting Eric upon his own ground: a fact by which (as I observed with a slight, ignoble relish) Eric was ever so slightly piqued. Gerald, moreover, rather surprisingly – or so it seemed to us – had read *Antic Hay* and even *Ulysses*.

'Of course,' he remarked of the latter, 'I enjoyed the dirty bits, just like anyone else; but if you want my honest opinion, I found it a bloody dull book' – a judgment which (though I wouldn't have openly admitted it) delighted me, for it coincided precisely with my own private opinion.

When Gerald left, I accompanied him as far as the porter's lodge. As we emerged into the street, Gerald paused, regarding me ruminatively; then said suddenly:

'What about coming to tea with *me*, sometime?'

For some reason the invitation startled me: somehow it had become a habit to think of Gerald as a guest rather than as a host; and it came as a slight shock to realize that Gerald, after all, had his own background – his rooms in the Iffley Road, his work and (presumably) those other friends whom he never referred to, but who must nevertheless exist.

'Make it tomorrow,' Gerald went on, before I could reply. 'We could have a high-tea – my landlady's rather good at that sort of thing – and then go out on the booze somewhere.'

It would be hard to say just why I refused Gerald's invitation; but refuse it I did. Tomorrow was the last day of term, and perhaps, with some idea of celebration in my mind, I was unwilling to tie myself to a definite engagement. I liked Gerald very much, but I didn't, as yet, regard him as an intimate – or even as a particularly valued – friend, and I wasn't prepared to run the risk of being saddled with a bore. At this period, moreover, I liked to imagine myself against a particular social background – a largely imaginary world of cocktails, smart people and witty conversation – and high-tea with a rather dim medical student in the Iffley Road didn't, I felt, quite fit into the picture. Nor did the prospect of subsequently 'going on the booze' seem specially attractive, for I hadn't at that time developed a taste for alcohol, except in the rarefied atmosphere of 'aesthetic' cocktail-parties, and Gerald, I had every reason to suppose, was almost exclusively a beer-drinker, with a preference for what, in those days, I would have snobbishly stigmatized as 'low pubs'.

I fabricated some vague excuse – a quite fictitious dinner-party – and I knew at once that Gerald wasn't taken in.

'Oh, come off it,' he said, with a disbelieving grin. 'Put 'em off – tell 'em you're going to your grandmother's funeral – you'd have much more fun on a pub-crawl. There's a decent little house I know in St Ebbe's – it's not often progged, and the beer's bloody good.'

For two pins I would have changed my mind; in my heart I knew that Gerald was right – I should have enjoyed a night out with him far more than an evening spent among my acknowledged 'friends'. Perversely, however, I stuck to my guns, and insisted that my imaginary dinner-party was an important occasion, and that my host would be mortally offended if I didn't turn up.

I saw Gerald's face fall, and knew that he was offended. Once again, I almost changed my mind; but I had left it too late.

'Oh well, if you won't, you won't,' Gerald said abruptly, his voice taking on a faint, unaccustomed edge of impatience. Then, suddenly, he grinned at me broadly and held out his hand.

'Well, so long,' he exclaimed cheerfully, 'see you next term.'

He grasped my hand with a painful violence, and turned away. The sudden gesture had taken me aback – partly, I daresay, because it wasn't 'done' to shake hands at Oxford in those days. I watched him walk away across Beaumont Street; as he reached the pavement, he turned and smiled again, raising his arm in a gesture of farewell.

'Hope you enjoy your dinner-party,' he shouted.

I waved back, rather feebly; then returned, guilty and disconsolate, to my rooms, where I sported my oak and tried, with a conspicuous lack of success, to read *The Brothers Karamazoff*. Later, after a penitential dinner in Hall, I wandered out by myself into the town: along the Cornmarket and down the High as far as Magdalen Bridge. It was a mild, damp evening; the lights gleamed feebly on the wet pavements, and a faint wind blew the rain against my face. A mood of romantic, Byronic melancholy descended upon me: leaning over the bridge, I was suddenly aware of the intolerable ache of loneliness – a sensation which had afflicted me, intermittently, for as long as I could remember, but which seemed, on this rainy autumnal night, more acute than ever before. I longed for friendship, yet I realized, with a gloomy clairvoyance, that I should almost certainly never achieve it. Too timid and repressed, myself, to make the first move, it seemed that I was ineluctably compelled, by some perverse instinct, to reject the kindly advances of others. Once, when I was six years old, I had longed above all things to become the friend of a little boy who was our neighbour; nothing, as it happened, could have been easier to arrange; yet when an opportunity occurred to go to a children's party at which he was to be present, I became terrified, and obstinately refused to go. It was just the same with my adult relations: no sooner did somebody I liked proffer me the hand of friendship, than I winced away as though at some threat of violence – horrified of committing myself, of 'giving myself away', and fatally mistrustful of my capacity to reciprocate, with genuine affection, the feelings of another.

Gerald Brockhurst, as I had come to realize during the last few weeks, was a thoroughly nice person, with whom I should have liked to be friends; moreover, he showed unmistakable signs of wanting to be friends with me – a fact which, in situations of this kind, never failed to surprise me. Yet I had recoiled, as usual, from his friendly approaches – and, which was worse, had recoiled so blatantly and with so little tact, that he had been quite justifiably offended, and in all probability would not renew his overtures. I cursed myself for my rudeness and – even more vehemently – for my snobbery and self-deceit. Gerald, I had told myself, was 'dim', a nobody, a potential bore; but I knew, in my heart, that he was nothing of the kind.

2

Surprisingly enough, I didn't see Gerald again till nearly halfway through the following term. During this comparatively short space of time, I had contrived almost to forget his existence; or at most I remembered him merely as a dim companion of my freshman days, whom I should in all probability never run across again. I suspect, in fact, that in thus banishing Gerald from my mind, I was trying to by-pass, as it were, my own feelings of guilt about him. At our last meeting, I had been tactless if not downright offensive; but there was, I think, another, more important reason for thus conveniently 'forgetting' him.

At this period of my life I was much troubled by the thought that I was 'escaping' from something which I was wont to refer to, with a portentous vagueness, as 'reality'; I was aware, in a dim and inchoate way, that my life was lived largely in terms of phantasy; somewhere, at the back of my mind, I envisaged a contrasted mode of existence which was not only more 'real' than my present one, but infinitely more desirable. This vision of the Good Life remained, it is true, exceedingly ill-defined; but it certainly included, among other essential requirements, a friendship with some nice, solid (and preferably 'unintellectual') person, a kind of elder brother to whom I could confide all my troubles, and who could be relied upon to share the burden of my own so difficult and delicately-adjusted temperament. I had already encountered one or two possible candidates for this singularly thankless rôle; so far, however, my attempts to enlist their sympathies had proved notably unsuccessful, and I had been forced, once again, to retire ignominiously into the cosy if somewhat depressing bolt-hole of my phantasy-life. In Gerald, I suppose, I had recognized yet another of these potential Big Brothers; but by this time I had developed a chronic fear of being humiliated; once bitten, twice shy – I wouldn't be 'had' again.

During these first few weeks of the Lent term, I had almost given up riding: partly because of the weather (which was particularly severe), and partly owing to one of those sudden and largely irrational fits of parsimony which are only possible to incorrigible spendthrifts like myself. Moreover, I had made a number of new acquaintances, with whom, as often as not, I would spend the afternoons listening to gramophone records at Acott's, followed by tea at the Cadena or the Super.

Yet the memory of Gerald did faintly persist, and once or twice, with a lingering sense of guilt, I almost decided to seek him out; other activities, however, intervened; and the fact that Gerald himself had made no sign seemed to indicate that he had no very urgent desire to renew the acquaintance.

One day, however, when I returned to college after a night in London, I was told by the porter that a gentleman had been asking for me – a Mr Brockhurst. Had he left any message? He had not. My sense of guilt began, once again, to assert itself: I really would go and look up Gerald – this very day; but then I remembered that I had promised to go to tea with a man at Oriel, and afterwards to a dance on Boar's Hill. For several days, indeed, I was kept busy with engagements of one sort or another, and soon the idea of Gerald had begun to recede, once again, into the background of my consciousness.

And then, one afternoon, I ran full-tilt into him in the Broad, outside Blackwell's. Overcome by a sudden and violent embarrassment, I blushed scarlet. Gerald, however, appeared perfectly self-possessed, and greeted me with his usual bluff bonhomie; from his manner one might have supposed that we had been seeing one another every day for the last two months.

'Where have you been hiding yourself?' he demanded. 'I came and looked you up last week, as a matter of fact, but you'd gone to Town.'

I muttered something about having been very busy – adding (with dubious relevance) that the weather had been too bad for riding. It was a feeble effort on my part, and I could see that Gerald didn't even pretend to take it seriously. I had half turned away, to hide my blushes, and was gazing, with a wholly assumed interest, at a new variorum edition of Keats in Blackwell's window; when I turned round again, it was to find Gerald's eyes fixed upon me with an expression of mildly contemptuous amusement. Suddenly his face broke into the broad, amiable grin which I remembered.

'Oh well, let's go and have some tea,' he suggested, with brusque geniality.

I could hardly refuse, and followed him, obediently, down the Broad towards the Cornmarket. I was still hot with embarrassment, and would have escaped if I could; yet I knew in my heart that I was genuinely glad to have met him again.

We went to the Moorish Tea-rooms, a gloomy and self-consciously arty establishment much frequented by visiting parents of undergraduates. Over our tea and scones we spoke vapidly of current topics; my embarrassment persisted, and I felt shy and tongue-tied, as though I were a schoolboy being taken out to tea by his housemaster. Nor were our surroundings calculated to increase my self-possession: the room was small and cramped, and the few other customers – mostly old ladies – spoke in sibilant undertones, as though they were in church. Gerald, perhaps realizing how I was feeling, chattered on about his college rugger-team, the weather, a 'bloody good show' (*Hit the Deck*) which he had taken his sister to in the vac ... Looking at him, I felt, with an inward detachment, what a remarkably nice person he really was: beneath the carapace of heartiness, the callow Wodehousian pose, he possessed, I thought, a kind of natural distinction – a quality which combined an innate sensitiveness with a knotty, unyielding strength. Tough as he was, there was nothing in the least oafish about him; above all (I thought) he gave an impression of cohesion, of being, more than most people, 'all-of-a-piece'. I was struck, once again, by his air of maturity: perhaps his clothes contributed to this effect – the old tweed coat with leather patches on the elbows, the plain, well-fitting shirt and school tie; I was reminded, suddenly, of my own elder brother, and for a moment my old, warm feeling for Gerald revived. I knew, as he sat placidly talking over his tea, that he was prepared to let bygones be bygones, and accept me as a friend; yet I knew, too, that I couldn't with any honesty accept his unspoken offer. I realized that I had left things too late: I was committed (or so it seemed) to a world and a way of life in which Gerald could have no part.

Tongue-tied, miserable, acutely aware of my own inadequacy, I longed to escape, to slink away into the dim, squalid phantasy-world which was (as I was beginning to realize) my natural habitat. *Non sum dignus*, I thought, with a mournful acquiescence; and, hardly aware of what Gerald was saying, allowed my eyes to stray across the room to a table in the centre, somewhat isolated from the rest, at which sat a very young man, obviously a freshman like myself, with a middle-aged woman whom I guessed to be his mother. They were quite evidently having one of those 'little talks' which are so liable to occur towards the end of one's first term at the university: the young man looked very unhappy – he was a colourless person, dressed unsuitably in silver-grey Oxford 'bags' and a crimson shantung tie. Plainly he was not enjoying his tea in the very least. Suddenly I heard his voice rise, in a plaintive falsetto, above the muted chatter of the old ladies.

'But don't you see, Mummy,' he wailed, nearly in tears, and raising both hands in an agonized though ineffectual gesture, 'don't you see, Life is so frightfully *difficult*.'

I looked at Gerald; he looked at me; and simultaneously, stricken by a sudden and quite uncontrollable hysteria, we burst out laughing. It was appalling, it was unpardonable: we stifled our laughter in our handkerchiefs, pretended to be coughing, tried with an increasing agony to control ourselves . . . It was useless: finally we bolted, incontinently, for the door; I suppose we paid our bill; all I can remember is that we managed to stumble down the stairs, still hooting and guffawing uncontrollably, into the street. On the pavement, we met each other's eyes, and our laughter was redoubled.

'Oh Mummy,' squeaked Gerald, in a wholly unsuccessful attempt at a 'nancy-boy' falsetto, 'Oh Mummy, Life is so frightfully *difficult*.'

An improbable *deus ex machina*, the poor, vapid undergraduate had succeeded, all unwittingly, in breaking the ice: suddenly the constraint of the past two months had vanished, Gerald and I were reunited, as though by magic, in the old, easy comradeship. Still laughing, we turned into the Cornmarket; by now our laughter had ceased to have any relation to its original cause – we laughed, quite simply, because we couldn't stop.

'Come on,' Gerald managed to mutter at last, through his giggles, 'let's go and have a drink at the Clarry – I'll go clean off my rocker if I don't get a pint inside me.'

I followed Gerald, without protest, into the bar of the Clarendon Hotel; nor did I raise any objection when he ordered two pints of bitter.

The Clarendon bar, in those days, had a somewhat dubious reputation: it was proggable (though the hotel lounge was not), and the undergraduates who, at their peril, frequented it, tended to be hearty, horsey and rather truculently heterosexual. This latter proclivity was admirably catered for by the barmaids, who were personable young women, and reputed to be of easy virtue. One of them was a tall, buxom brunette called Gladys: she must have been at least thirty-five, perhaps more, and (as I had heard Eric say) was doubtless a useful dumping-ground for a refractory Oedipus complex. The other, Kathleen, was younger, and affected a roguish, come-hither air borrowed, one would have guessed, from Miss Clara Bow. I had only once visited the bar before, and its atmosphere of raffish heartiness would have alarmed me if I had been with anybody but Gerald. I recognized one or two people I knew by sight: sporting types in loud checks, with very short hair and a pronounced tendency to acne; one associated them inevitably with high-powered sports-cars and week-ends at Maidenhead.

'Not a bad spot, this,' Gerald remarked, swallowing half his pint at a draught. 'And the beer's not bad. Come on, drink up – you're sipping it as if it was vintage port.'

With some difficulty I swallowed the rest of my pint.

'It's my turn, anyway,' I said, and ordered two more.

'This is the life,' Gerald said, with a satisfied sigh. 'You know,' he added suddenly, after a longish pause, and eyeing me quizzically across the table, 'you know, the trouble with *you* is you don't get around enough.'

'Get around?' I queried, feeling rather bewildered.

'Well, you know what I mean – getting around, seeing people, enjoying yourself.'

'But I *do* get around,' I protested, rather tartly. 'And I know any amount of people – more than you do, probably.'

'Oh well, yes – *those* sort of people –' Gerald retorted with a flicker of impatience, then checked himself, looking mildly embarrassed. 'What I mean is,' he continued, awkwardly, 'the people you know are all the same sort of type – awfully brainy and highbrow and all that, but they must be a bit of a strain, aren't they? Mind you,' he added, hastily, 'old Eric's all right – how is he by the way? – but most of the blokes I've seen you around with look a bit sissyfied, if you don't mind my saying so.'

With anybody but Gerald I should have lost my temper. I was extremely angry, but something in Gerald's face made me swallow down the cutting retort which rose to my lips.

'I didn't know you *had* seen me around,' I replied at last, with what I hoped was a just perceptible irony.

'Oh, I've caught sight of you once or twice, you know,' said Gerald casually. 'No, what I mean is –' he paused again, screwing up his face into a comical frown – 'what I mean is, you want taking out of yourself, if you see what I mean.'

I managed a rather sickly smile.

'I see,' I said. 'And do you propose to perform this interesting operation yourself?'

Gerald grinned.

'I wouldn't mind having a stab at it,' he said. 'No, what I mean is, you don't seem to know any ordinary sort of blokes – the sort of chap you can barge around and have a good time with, without all this highbrow talk.'

'I know *you*,' I retorted, stung at last into irritability.

Gerald gave a mocking smile.

'Yes, but you're not quite sure whether you want to or not, are you?'

I felt my face turn as red as a beetroot. That Gerald should thus suddenly decide to burn his boats – or, to be perfectly accurate, *my* boats – was the very last thing I had expected. I was profoundly shocked, and could only stare at him speechlessly. Gerald, for his part, looked perfectly composed, and continued to gaze at me calmly, his lips still parted in a half-smile.

'What *utter* nonsense,' I burst out at last. 'Why, I – I mean, you know perfectly well –' I broke off, knowing that it was worse than useless to defend myself: what Gerald had said was no more than the truth, and nothing I could say would convince him to the contrary.

'All right, all right, keep your hair on,' Gerald said hastily. 'Drink up, and I'll get the other half.'

Barely conscious of what I was doing, I emptied my glass. I felt outraged, unbearably humiliated: it was as though I had been stripped naked, and subjected to some shameful physical assault. Yet oddly enough I didn't feel any anger towards Gerald personally; I knew that my humiliation, however painful, was deserved; and I even began to feel, at the back of my mind, a curious sense of relief. My relationship with Gerald had, as I realized, been based on a lie; now the cat was out of the bag, and it was time to 'have things out'.

Soon Gerald came back with our refilled glasses.

'Bung-ho!' he exclaimed, with so exactly the air of a 'Sapper' hero that I had to laugh. He took a gulp of beer, then leaned over the table towards me. 'Sorry if I was a bit crude in my methods,' he said, 'but I'm no good at beating about the bush.'

With an effort, I met his clear, candid gaze, and felt suddenly more at ease.

'The fact is,' he went on, in halting tones, yet with a certain air of decision, 'the fact is, I think you're a pretty decent kind of bloke – I sort of took to you from the first, if you see what I mean, and I thought we were going to be pals, but of course –' Gerald paused, lowered his eyes, then looked up again with a shy and rather charming smile – 'of course, I realize you're quite a different type from me, and you probably find me a crashing bore and all that –'

'But I don't –'

'Shut up and let me finish,' Gerald cut in, with a sudden, half-comic violence. 'I know I'm not clever and artistic like all those friends of yours' (his tone was half-apologetic, half-contemptuous), 'but we do hit it off pretty well, after all – I mean, we like the same sort of things, riding and so on, and – oh, sod it,' he broke off, 'I can't say properly what I want to say, but you know what I mean.'

For a moment I could say nothing, struck dumb by Gerald's extraordinary outburst. My mind was a chaos of conflicting feelings: half-amused, half-touched, I was aware also of a sense of release, as though some obstruction in my mind had been suddenly removed.

'Yes,' I said at last, 'I think I understand.'

'Well, that's O.K. then,' Gerald exclaimed, brushing aside the subject with the brusque air of a chairman at a board-meeting disposing of some tiresome though essential item on the agenda. 'Let's have the other half – come on, drink up.'

'I'll be tight,' I protested.

'Never mind – does you good, once in a way,' Gerald grinned.

About the rest of that evening I remember very little; I know only that, by the time we staggered into the street at closing-time, I was in no state to go home by myself, and had to be escorted back to college by Gerald. I remember, too, that before we parted we had sworn vows of eternal friendship – or at any rate I had; Gerald, I suspect, had contented himself with shaking hands and muttering something about 'everything being O.K. now'. We had arranged, also, to resume our riding: Gerald had promised to book our horses, if possible, for the very next day. I tumbled into bed, at last, with a feeling that a new phase of my life had begun: at last – so I assured myself, as I drifted towards sleep – at long last I had escaped from my imprisoning Ego into the adult and exciting world of Real Life.

~ ~ ~

Real Life, alas, on the following morning, manifested itself in a form which I found too realistic by half: I woke with a splitting headache, and, having managed to stagger as far as the college bathroom, proceeded to be violently and embarrassingly sick.

After a bath and breakfast, however, I felt considerably better, and more able to confront the demands of the Reality Principle. I spent the morning at Acott's, listening to gramophone records of Debussy and Delius; returning to college, I found a note from Gerald saying that the horses were booked for that afternoon at half-past two.

The ride that afternoon was the first of many such outings, and it was, I think, during the next few weeks, that my friendship with Gerald attained to its happiest and most intimate phase. At first, it is true, I suffered from a slight sense of anticlimax: for Gerald's friendship didn't, after all, make me feel notably more 'real' than I had felt before. Yet the more I saw of him, the more likeable I found him: I began to accept him for what he was – an ordinary, unexciting but extremely nice person; and in a sense, I suppose, our association did, after all, aspire to that long-sought and ill-defined ideal of 'Reality' for which Gerald had seemed to provide so appropriate a symbol.

During the rest of that term, we spent a good deal of time together: sometimes I would visit Gerald at his rooms, sometimes we would meet at the Clarendon. He introduced me to one or two of his acquaintances – fellow-medical students, for the most part: pleasant enough, if a trifle dull, they seemed to have little importance in Gerald's life, and it struck me, for the first time, that Gerald was a surprisingly lonely person. I say 'surprisingly', for Gerald, after all, was not unsociable, nor was he lacking in charm; moreover, he played rugger, boxed occasionally, and belonged to one or two of the university clubs. Yet none of his social contacts seemed more than superficial; his attitude towards most of his acquaintances was one of mild and tolerant contempt. He despised what he called my 'smarty-arty' friends; but he seemed scarcely less censorious about people in his own circle. In his own way, I think, he was a perfectionist: he demanded certain qualities in people which they too seldom possessed, and he wasn't prepared (as I, alas, too often was) to make do with second-best. He wanted friendship – wanted it, perhaps, as much as I did – but it must be all or nothing: he wouldn't accept any sort of compromise, and a certain native pride made him scrupulous in concealing his emotional needs. The quality of self-sufficiency, inherited from his midland working-class forebears, afforded him a protection which was sadly lacking in myself, and which I secretly envied; Gerald, on occasion, could be hard, but he was never arrogant; his pride was offset by a natural humility which tempered even his harshest judgments with an element of forebearance. Thus, having roundly condemned some too-beautiful aesthete (an acquaintance of mine, as it happened) as a 'bloody nancy-boy', he would add, with a tolerant grin: 'Of course, you can't blame him, really – a bloke like that must have some sort of kink: something to do with his glands, probably – and come to that, we're all of us a bit homo when it comes to the point.'

As for women, Gerald viewed them with much the same tolerant disdain as he showed towards his male friends and towards the world in general. Like food, they were a physiological necessity – and about food (though he enjoyed it well enough) Gerald was not, as I had often noticed, over-particular. 'They're all the same in the dark,' he would say, or: 'I don't let them worry me much, but a chap's got to have his oats.' His attitude in this matter as in others seemed to me enviably adult, though the details of his conquests, when he related them, struck me as being squalid and rather tedious. Gerald, for his part, displayed little curiosity about my own amorous problems; on at least one occasion, however, I must have hinted, rather too obviously, at my private difficulties, for I found, to my horror, that Gerald – without consulting me – had arranged a joint outing with Gladys and Kathleen from the Clarendon ('It'll take you out of yourself,' said Gerald, with an avuncular benevolence). We were to take them to the cinema in the afternoon: 'And after that,' said Gerald, 'it's up to you: they have to be back at the Clarry at six o'clock, but I usually arrange to meet Kathleen at closing time, and take her home. She's rather sweet on me at the moment, so I'll leave Gladys to you, if you've no objection.'

I was appalled; but there seemed no possible escape. To back out at this stage would seem not only rude but ungrateful: for Gerald, I couldn't help feeling, had fixed up the jaunt entirely for my benefit. It was, I supposed, a kind of test of my virility: if I didn't go through with it, Gerald would despise me; and I valued Gerald's opinion, in such matters, more than I would have cared to admit.

We duly met the two girls, when the bar closed after lunch, and escorted them to the Super Cinema. I bought Gladys a box of chocolates, and, being well-fortified with beer, managed to adopt what I hoped was a suitably rakish manner. Gladys, for her part, behaved with a lady-like refinement which was calculated to discourage a far more hot-blooded lover than myself; when at last the lights went down and the film started, I heaved a sigh of relief; at least, I thought, one wouldn't be expected to talk. But what, I asked myself with growing horror, exactly what, in the circumstances, *was* one expected to do? I had gathered – partly from observation, partly from contemporary novels – that one began by holding hands . . . Tremulously, in the darkness, I edged my hand towards the spot where I supposed Gladys's hand to be; this opening gambit, however, was singularly inefficacious, for Gladys's hand proved to be grasping the box of chocolates. Supposing, very naturally, that the chocolates were what I was after, she thrust the box towards me; I clutched at it, but, in my extreme nervousness, contrived to drop it. Box and chocolates cascaded into the darkness at our feet: trembling with shame, I leaned forward and fumbled awkwardly in the narrow space between the seats; having managed to rescue at least some of the chocolates, I kept the box, this time, upon my own knee, and, after muttering my apologies, fixed my attention firmly upon the screen, where Ramon Novarro was engaged in passionately embracing a young woman whose plump cheeks were copiously gemmed with more than life-size glycerine tears. The moment seemed propitious for a renewed assault on my part; and once again I extended my hand, timorously, in the direction of Gladys. This time she did not misinterpret my intention, and immediately grasped my hand in a firm and somewhat sticky grip; I returned the pressure, less firmly, perhaps, but (I hoped) quite unequivocally. Gladys's eyes were fixed resolutely upon the screen: in the half-darkness I could just see her face – severe and matronly as the Demeter of Cnidos. Plainly she was far more interested in Ramon Novarro than in myself, and no wonder; she continued, none the less, to clasp my hand in a firm, enveloping grip which seemed not so much amorous as protective. I was reminded, indeed, of those occasions, in my childhood, when my Nannie, knowing that I was frightened of the dark, used to hold my hand during the showing of the magic lantern in the nursery.

Gladys, however, I reminded myself, was not a Nannie but (in the specialized and venal sense of the word) a Woman; and I knew that with Women one was expected to do rather more than just hold their hands. In comparable situations, in novels, young men's hands were apt to stray 'with apparent casualness' to other and more intimate parts of the female anatomy; but in the present circumstances this seemed much less easy of accomplishment than one might have supposed. For one thing, Gladys appeared to be quite genuinely absorbed in the film; for another, her hand continued to clasp mine with such a nannie-like firmness that it seemed almost impossible to withdraw it, without resorting to downright violence. Moreover, even supposing that I had been able to free my hand, I should have felt extremely uncertain as to which portion of Gladys's somewhat abundant anatomy to explore next; parts of it, I felt, were altogether too 'intimate', others perhaps not intimate enough. And in any case (I thought) Gladys herself showed no apparent desire for such explorations; she seemed perfectly content with her chocolates and with Ramon Novarro who, stripped to the waist and looking extremely handsome, now appeared to be bravely defending the heroine (registering 'horror', with her fist thrust firmly into her mouth) against a horde of hostile savages.

I had seldom, in my whole life, felt quite so miserable; but worse was to follow. The beer, with which I had managed to fortify (though imperfectly) my somewhat flaccid libido, now began to have other and less happy effects. For the next twenty minutes or so I managed to ignore the increasing discomfort; but Nature, at last, refused to be denied. Discomfort became agony: yet I dared not leave my seat. Conventions were stricter, at that period, than they are today: lavatories were presumed, for social purposes, not to exist; and I was, perhaps, more than normally sensitive in such matters. We were, furthermore, wedged firmly in the middle of the stalls, with at least a dozen pairs of legs between us and the gangway. Escape seemed impossible: I sweated, I began incontinently to fidget; and still Gladys kept my hand imprisoned, relentlessly, in hers. At last I could bear it no longer: muttering something about 'a breath of fresh air' I disengaged my hand, rose awkwardly to my feet, and stumbled past our indignant neighbours to the gangway.

Once outside, I was tempted to leave the cinema and return, ignominiously, to my rooms: I could always say that I had been taken ill – and indeed, at that moment, I was quite prepared to take to my bed for a week merely to substantiate my own story. Finally I decided to compromise, and stood up, uncomfortably, in the gangway, until the interval. The film dragged to its end at last, and I returned, covered with blushes, to my seat, to find Gladys engaged in an animated conversation with Gerald, and apparently not in the least perturbed by my absence. The lights went down again, and the second film began – a slapstick comedy featuring Harold Lloyd; on this occasion I made no attempt to renew my amorous advances; nor, to my relief, did Gladys offer me the slightest encouragement.

At last it was over, and we got up to go. My humiliation, I felt, was complete: and I carefully avoided Gerald's eyes as we made our way out into the foyer. Gerald, however, seemed perfectly unaware of the ordeal to which I had been subjected; waiting at the entrance, while the girls went to 'powder their noses', he winked at me conspiratorially.

'Old Gladys all right?' he asked.

I replied, with a feeble attempt to maintain my rakish pose, that I thought Gladys 'very nice'. At that moment I almost hated Gerald – hated him for his presumption, his obtuseness, and what seemed to me a gross lack of sensibility. My own humiliation, my sense of my own inadequacy, were suddenly kindled into a hot, vicious flame of hostility; with anybody but Gerald, I should without a doubt have lost my temper. Fortunately, I managed to check myself; the girls returned, and, as we accompanied them down the Cornmarket towards the Clarendon, I felt thankful that I had curbed my anger. The afternoon had been appalling; yet somehow, after that brief spurt of malice, I couldn't bring myself to blame Gerald; and I knew that, when it came to the point, I valued his friendship too highly to risk an open quarrel.

~ ~ ~

A week or two after this intimidating experience, Gerald and I went out riding. It was a day in early March, one of those brilliant, spring-like days which sometimes occur, miraculously, after a long spell of bad weather. We rode out, as usual, towards Godstow: the hedgerows and copses were furred with purple buds, coltsfoot and celandines blazed in the ditches. I noticed that Gerald, despite the fine weather, seemed in rather low spirits; he looked pale and drawn, and presently confessed that he had been working harder than usual. Apparently, too, he was having some sort of 'trouble' with his family – his father, I gathered, considered that Gerald was living too expensively, and had threatened to cut down his allowance.

'It's a bit tough,' Gerald commented, in that off-hand manner with which he habitually spoke of his own affairs. 'After all, I only came up to this lousy place to please him; and I'm not really an extravagant sort of bloke – my digs are about as cheap as you could find, and I don't have expensive tastes. What I mean is, a pint or two of an evening, and a bit of slap-and-tickle with Kathleen now and again – it's not a hell of a lot to ask, after all.'

Gerald fell silent, and, though I tried to keep up the conversation, seemed reluctant to pursue the subject. I had, as it happened, picked up quite a lot of information about Gerald's family during recent conversations with him, and what I had heard didn't sound very pleasant. The Brockhursts, I guessed, were both dim and pretentious: petty burgesses, newly enriched, and afflicted by the nastiest and most boring kind of snobbery. I could imagine, only too well, their 'place' in Surrey – somewhere between Woking and Camberley: a red Edwardian house among pine-trees, with a laurelled drive in front and a tennis-court at the back. Gerald's father was a great golfer, and the house was convenient for the links; his wife, it seemed, was a Christian Scientist – a fact to which Gerald referred with a slightly pitying contempt, rather as though his mother suffered from 'nerves', or some minor but embarrassing skin-disease. There was an elder brother named Kenneth, at present coffee-planting in Kenya, and a sister, Sheila, who had some sort of secretarial job in London; Gerald didn't seem particularly attached to either of them. Kenneth, it appeared, was the family favourite, and had already come into more than his fair share of the family fortune – the result, in part, of Gerald's decision to take up medicine against his father's wishes. In the circumstances, I couldn't help admiring the tolerant good nature with which Gerald regarded his brother and, indeed, his whole family.

'The fact is,' he said to me on one occasion, 'I'm the family blacksheep.

I always have been, and I suppose I always shall be. The pater was all for Ken from the start, and so was mother, and what with him and Sheila, I never got a proper look-in.'

Myself the runt of the litter, I could entirely sympathize, and said so; though Gerald was the last person I should ever have suspected of being a 'blacksheep'.

'Oh, I don't blame them,' Gerald went on, tolerantly. 'I suppose I'll get a little when the old man kicks the bucket, but I don't care much, either way. I'm glad I'll be independent, really – it's better that way, if you can manage it.'

'You're telling me,' I said, with feeling. I envied Gerald's independence as I envied his strength and stability. Of all the people I knew, he seemed the most securely armed against the world; there was something solid and unshakable about him which reminded me of those Russian toys, carved and painted to resemble *moujiks*, with a lead weight at the bottom, which, as often as one tries to knock them over, bob up again, serene and invincible, to face a fresh assault. Gerald, I thought, would never let life 'get him down'; whatever misfortunes he might encounter, he would, one felt, take them in his stride. He had his weaknesses – beer and (to a lesser extent) women, but I couldn't imagine that either of these would ever constitute a serious threat to his integrity. Some day, I supposed, he would fall in love and marry – a nice sensible girl who shared his tastes and his modest ambitions; it would all be rather un-romantic, but eminently suitable and cosy; they would settle (I decided) somewhere in the home-counties, and Gerald would ask me to be godfather to his children.

~ ~ ~

We rode, as usual, round the meadows, cantering for short distances on the dry stretches between the flooded levels. The sunshine, the keen March wind had induced in me a mood of gay irresponsibility: I decided that I would take Gerald out to dinner that night, and that we would get gloriously tight. Gerald himself, after a brisk canter or two, seemed in better spirits: 'There's nothing like it for shaking up the old liver,' he remarked. 'To tell you the truth, I wasn't feeling too good when we started out, but I'm feeling on top of the bloody world, now.'

Riding back, leisurely, through the fields, we came to a lonely back-water, half-hidden from view by pollard-willows. Suddenly Gerald pulled up his horse.

'Tell you what,' he exclaimed, 'let's have a swim.'

'Not on your life,' I said. 'The water'll be icy.'

'Ballocks to that,' Gerald retorted. 'The sun's lovely and warm – do you a world of good. Come on, you sissy old bastard.'

'I'm not quite dotty,' I replied. 'You bathe if you want to, but you won't get me in.'

We had pulled up our horses at the edge of the backwater and Gerald had already dismounted.

'You're coming in,' he said, peremptorily, scowling up at me with a sudden, half-playful ferocity.

'I'm not.'

'You bloody well are.'

'I tell you I'm not.'

'I'll bloody well force you to.'

'You won't.'

'Oh, come on, be a sport: just in and out – you'll feel grand after it.'

I protested that I hated the cold and wasn't going to risk pneumonia; Gerald, however, with an unaccustomed obstinacy, continued to badger me. His voice had taken on a curiously urgent tone, as though the question of whether I bathed or not were a matter of life or death; puzzled, I looked down at his scowling face, and wondered what exactly was in his mind. I had no intention of bathing; yet I felt, absurdly, that I was being subjected to some obscure and arbitrary test of loyalty. It was unlike Gerald to be so importunate; and I couldn't help suspecting that, consciously or otherwise, he had invested the occasion with some private and wholly disproportionate significance.

'Oh, all right then,' he said at last, 'if you won't you won't.'

His voice was suddenly sharp with exasperation, and as I met his eyes I could see that he was genuinely angry. With an impatient movement, he flung his horse's reins across my saddle.

'Here, hold my horse, then – I'm going in, even if you won't.'

He began at once to undress, stripping off his clothes with a curious air of urgency, almost of desperation, as though he were about to perform some heroic feat of life-saving. His face was still a sullen mask: I knew that, in some inexplicable way, I had deeply offended him, and for a moment I was half-tempted to change my mind and bathe after all. Yet the thought of the icy river-water held me back: I wasn't, when it came to the point, prepared to risk catching a chill merely to gratify a passing whim of Gerald's.

With a final, violent movement, he pulled his shirt over his head, and stood for a moment, naked, his arms hugged across his chest, the wind faintly stirring his short rumpled hair. Red-brown at the throat and wrists, the rest of his body was of a matt, milky whiteness: his nakedness seemed strangely incongruous and rather shocking against the background of this bleak wintry landscape. I watched him crouch forward, like a sprinter at the start of a race, the muscles rippling beneath his firm white flesh; for a moment he paused, balanced on his haunches; then, with a sudden savage shout like a battle-cry, he dashed down the grassy bank, raised his arms, and dived cleanly into the steel-blue, sunbright water. For several seconds I watched the ripples spread upon the waveless surface; suddenly panic gripped me: perhaps the pool was shallower than it appeared, perhaps Gerald had been seized by cramp . . . A moment later I saw his head emerge, a dark blob amid the sun-dazzle, twenty yards from shore. His hair hung in a grotesque fringe over his eyes; he tossed it back, treading water; then raised his arm and hailed me.

'Come on in,' he shouted, 'it's bloody lovely.'

I waved back, and shook my head discouragingly. Gerald threshed the surface with his legs, raising a fountain of bright foam. Again his voice came, resonant and commanding, across the glittering water.

'Tether the bloody horses and come on in . . . Buck up, or you'll lose the sun . . . Oh, come *on*, for Christ's sake . . .'

I shook my head again, and saw Gerald turn and swim vigorously away towards the opposite bank. Once again, I had the odd feeling that the whole occasion was in some way crucial, climacteric: it was as though life – in the shape of Gerald – was making some vast, implacable demand upon me which I knew that I couldn't satisfy. Once more, I felt the temptation to strip off my clothes and (risking pneumonia) plunge into the icy water; the impulse was accompanied by a perverse, almost erotic feeling of excitement; yet I knew that I couldn't do it. Over-cossetted in childhood, I was terrified of illness in general and of catching cold in particular. I knew that I lacked the guts to strip and swim in an English river in March; and I knew too, intuitively yet with no less certainty, that, because of my defection, because I had failed to pass the 'test', my relations with Gerald would never be quite the same again.

Sadly I watched him swim back to shore: a few yards from the bank, he began to thresh his limbs about, naïvely showing off for my benefit. I wished, by now, that I had taken the risk and bathed; but it was too late now. Gerald clambered up the muddy bank: I could see that his body was pocked with goose-flesh, and that he was shivering. He dabbed himself, inadequately, with a handkerchief, and scrambled rapidly into his clothes.

'Getting a bit nippy,' he remarked, as he pulled on his breeches; and indeed, though I had scarcely noticed it, a cloud had covered the westering sun, and a chilly wind had risen.

Gerald mounted his horse, and we rode back, almost in silence, along the tow-path. As we reached the town's outskirts, it began to rain – a cold, sleety downpour blowing straight in our faces. At the stables I remembered my plan to take Gerald out to dinner; but the mood of elation which had prompted the idea seemed already to belong to some remote, irrecoverable past. None the less, I proffered the suggestion: impelled less, perhaps, by convivial motives than by an obscure sense of guilt, a desire to make up to Gerald, in some way, for my own shortcomings.

'Not tonight, thanks all the same,' Gerald replied, in a curiously flat, conventional tone. 'Fact is, I really ought to do some work. Sorry, old boy – another time.'

I glanced at him with sudden disquiet: his face wore a remote, preoccupied expression, and he looked, as I had observed before, unusually pale. Nor was it usual for Gerald to address me as 'old boy', a hearty locution which (as I had often noticed) he was accustomed to employ only with comparative strangers, or in situations which required the exercise of a rather forced and bogus magnanimity – as, for example, when somebody trod on his toe in a crowded bar. In its present context, the phrase carried a wounding implication of indifference, perhaps even of hostility; and I parted from Gerald sadly, aware that I had offended him, yet unable – or perhaps unwilling – to analyse precisely the nature or extent of my offence. We hadn't, as we usually did, made a date for our next meeting: 'See you again soon,' Gerald had said, off-handedly, and without his usual smile; and I didn't, at that moment, feel much inclined to press the point.

~ ~ ~

A week passed – two weeks – and I heard nothing from Gerald. Once again, my latent sense of guilt took the form of a vague hostility, a feeling that Gerald himself was in some way to blame, and that he ought to make the first move. If he was silly enough to take offence merely because I had refused to bathe, that was his look-out . . . Considered rationally and in retrospect, the whole episode seemed trivial and even laughable; yet my uneasiness persisted, and I knew (however hard I might try to suppress the knowledge) that more had been at stake, on that sunlit afternoon at Godstow, than I was willing to admit.

The weeks slipped away, and still I heard nothing from Gerald. It was not till almost the last day of term that I decided, at last, to go and call on him at his digs.

I was greeted by his landlady with the news that he was in hospital: he had been there nearly a month, with pneumonia.

''E come in one day drenched to the skin,' she related, lugubriously, 'Been out 'orse-riding, 'e 'ad – it must be a month ago almost to the day. Told me 'e'd been swimmin' in the river – 'e ought to know better at 'is age,' etc. etc.

I hurried to the hospital, to find that Gerald had been discharged on the previous day. He had been very ill, but had made a remarkably rapid recovery, and had gone home to his family to convalesce.

I meant to write to him, but postponed the task from day to day. The news of his illness had increased my irrational sense of guilt, as though I myself had been in some way to blame: absurd, of course – for had I not warned him of the folly of bathing? And the mere fact of bathing myself, however pleasing to Gerald, could hardly have prevented him from catching pneumonia. I was sorry for him, of course; but there was no denying that I found him a remarkably easy person to banish from my mind . . . I thought about him more than once during the vac., but with a diminishing enthusiasm; other matters – and other people – claimed my interest. It would be nice to see him again next term – or so I assured myself; in actual fact, I looked forward to our next meeting with considerable disquiet; and perhaps half-hoped, unconsciously, that I should be able to avoid him altogether.

As it happened, I met him within a week or two of the beginning of term. He greeted me with his usual boisterous amiability – perhaps, indeed, he was just a little more boisterous than usual. I apologized for not writing, and for not coming to see him, explaining, rather lamely, that I hadn't known of his illness.

'Oh, that's all right, old boy,' he exclaimed, heartily. 'Glad you've turned up again – let's go and have a drink.'

We went and had a drink – several drinks – at the Clarendon. Gerald chattered away with what for him was an unaccustomed eloquence, telling me about his vac., which had been spent on Exmoor, and about the night-sister at the hospital who, he alleged, had been rather sweet on him, and whom he had once persuaded to kiss him goodnight ... Gerald, I guessed, was deliberately trying to spare me embarrassment: I was grateful to him, yet I felt sorry that it should be necessary. His tactfulness was a little too deliberate, a little too conscious and purposeful: for all his apparent friendliness, I knew that there was a barrier between us, and that the fault was mine.

His presence had revived all my old liking for him: I longed to penetrate his defences, to 'have things out'; but I knew that Gerald, for the present at any rate, would prefer that I should remain, as it were, on my own side of the fence. Rather sadly, I played the game as best I could – laughing at his jokes, and trying to think of things myself which would amuse him. To all outward appearance, he seemed perfectly recovered from his illness: a little thinner, but healthily sunburnt, and with an undiminished thirst for beer.

During the next few weeks, we met irregularly, and more or less on the same terms; mostly, I would encounter him in the Clarendon, and there was a tacit understanding that we shouldn't – except in the most general terms – refer to the happenings of the previous term. Our relationship had, in fact, become a wholly superficial one – an affair of beer, bawdy talk and a rather too conscious bonhomie; Gerald didn't come to my digs (I was now living in Beaumont Street), and I didn't go to his.

I realized that my friendship with him, like so many previous friendships, had failed; I regretted it, but accepted the fact – as I had learnt by now to accept such misfortunes – with a bleak, habitual fatalism. I should have minded more in earlier days, perhaps; now, however, I had more than enough friends – or at least acquaintances – to keep my days well-occupied. I had given up riding, so had Gerald: he was too busy, he said, working for his schools. As the term went on, I saw less and less of him; and after a time I ceased, except at rare moments of loneliness, to regret his absence.

I saw him for the last time in the Clarendon, just before his schools: he was already rather tight.

'I've been working too hard,' he announced, 'I need a break: I'm going to get properly sozzled. You'd better do the same.'

The evening was a riotous one, and ended – I forget exactly how or why – in somebody's rooms at the House, where, after drinking a quantity of green Chartreuse, I retired somewhat ungracefully into the *Ewigkeit*. I didn't see Gerald again: at the end of the term, I departed for Paris, and returned home to be greeted by the news that I had been sent down. In the months that followed, I lost touch almost entirely with my Oxford friends; and soon Gerald, like the rest, had receded into a past which seemed, already, as remote from my present way of life as the half-remembered events of childhood.

3

After my descent from the university, I worked for the next two years in the book-trade in London. The work bored me, but I wasn't particularly unhappy: I regarded my job, I suppose, as a kind of penance for the follies of Oxford – though such remorse as I felt was occasioned, I fear, less by genuine contrition than by the humiliating feeling that I might, if I had only been more enterprising, have indulged myself far more rewardingly. I couldn't but feel that such a lavish sowing of wild oats ought to have yielded a better crop: I had wasted too much time (I realized it now) on the wrong sort of people – second-rate charmers by whom, in my *naïveté*, I had been too easily beglamoured, and for whom, in reality, I had cared nothing. My time at Oxford had, in fact, been largely spent in a state of almost paranoiac self-delusion: I had thought (at any rate during my last term) that I was enjoying myself; but in reality I had been profoundly miserable.

I felt little regret for Oxford; but in my rare moods of nostalgia, it was Gerald Brockhurst to whom my thoughts would most often return, and I would wonder vaguely what had become of him. It didn't occur to me, however, to write to him for news; for he, like my other friends, had become already a kind of mythical figure, an inhabitant of that remote Olympus from which I myself had been so irrevocably and so ignomini-ously cast down. I remembered him with a mild elegiac affection tinged by remorse – a kind of Thyrsis, gone with 'the cuckoo's parting cry' into the 'world and wave of men'.

I was, in those days, extremely poor; yet I would contrive, as often as not, to save up a few shillings by the end of the week, and on Saturday night I would wander penuriously round the bars and *boîtes* of the west-end, hopeful of adventure or at least of encountering some acquaint-ance with more money than myself. Beer was cheap in those days, and one could get a good meal for half-a-crown or three-and-six; one could, moreover, buy a 'rover' ticket for two-and-fourpence at the Alhambra or the Coliseum.

~ ~ ~

It was on one such Saturday night, nearly two years after leaving Oxford, that, having dined cheaply and in solitude at a restaurant in Lisle Street, I decided to look in at the Alhambra. The theatre was unusually crowded, for Carnera, the giant Italian heavyweight, was billed for a sparring act. Reaching the Circle promenade, I edged my way through the shifting, close-packed crowd towards the front. A chorus-number was in progress: from the bright-lit stage the light was reflected with a vague, hallucinatory effect in the mirrors at the back of the promenade; here and there – in the stage-boxes or in the front row of the circle – a man's shirt-front or a woman's corsage glimmered faint and ghost-like, or a struck match would illuminate, suddenly, the outline of a face, imprinting the unknown features for an instant upon the darkness with the frightening vividness of those flashlight photographs by which some shy nocturnal animal is 'snapped' by the vigilant naturalist. Presently the chorus made their exit, the curtain descended to a blare of music, and rose again to reveal the figures of the Italian boxer and his sparring-partner. Focused by the spotlights, the giant's body seemed curiously unreal, like some top-heavy, ill-constructed model of a man; the performance itself was a farce – the two men danced awkwardly round the stage, tapping at each other in a ludicrous parody of violence, so that I was reminded of the ballet, *Le Boxing*, a performance of which I had recently seen at the Ballet Club. Around me, in the semi-darkness, the crowd pressed closer towards the balcony; I was aware, beneath the stifling reek of scent and tobacco, of the faint, sour odour of human bodies. Whispered remarks, little snirts of muffled laughter, eddied fitfully among the close-packed ranks; the glow of cigarettes, waxing and waning, lit one intent face after another with a vague rugose light. Half-turning to make my way to the bar, I saw the flare of a match a few feet from where I was standing, and a face was blazoned suddenly upon the darkness – a face which, though it seemed familiar, I couldn't, for a moment, quite place. The match flared again – the man, whoever he was, was smoking a pipe – and once more the features sprang into life: I saw a broad, blunt-featured face, a thatch of hair brushed smoothly back from the forehead. The match went out, the momentary vision was quenched again in the dim, anonymous twilight; but I was almost certain that the face which had gleamed so briefly and so indistinctly in the gloom was the face of Gerald Brockhurst.

The curtain descended, there was a burst of clapping, and I saw the figure of my neighbour move away from the balcony towards the bar. I followed him: for a few seconds, dazzled by the blaze of light after the darkness, I could see nobody who looked in the least like Gerald. Suddenly I felt my arm seized in a violent grip, and turned to see Gerald's face within six inches of my own.

'Well I *am* damned,' he shouted, pumping my hand up and down so violently that it hurt. 'Who'd have thought of seeing *you* here, of all people? It *is* you, isn't it? By God, what a lark – come and have a drink, for Christ's sake.'

The suddenness of the encounter had taken my breath away, and for a moment or two I could scarcely realize Gerald's presence: I was aware only of a figure larger than life, grasping my arm with a policeman-like firmness and propelling me towards the bar. It was not till he had ordered our drinks that Gerald reduced himself, as it were, to manageable proportions.

'Last place I expected to run into you,' he was saying. 'Thought I'd look in to see the boxing – bloody silly show, patting at each other like a couple of kittens – and you could have knocked me down with a feather when I saw you come in. Must be more than two years, isn't it? I was beginning to think you must be dead or something – I'm jolly glad you're not, though.'

Mastering my confusion, I looked for the first time directly at Gerald: he met my eyes with the candid yet faintly mocking gaze which I remembered. His pleasure at meeting me was obviously genuine; and as I looked at him I was overcome by a sudden, paralysing shyness, a sense that whatever I said or did must seem, in the circumstances, hopelessly inadequate. My own pleasure at seeing him was clouded by remorse: my old sense of defection and irrational guilt rose between us like a ghost. Gerald, however, if he noticed my perturbation, firmly disregarded it; and at last, encouraged by his total lack of self-consciousness, I felt my embarrassment suddenly dissipated in a warm impulse of renewed affection. In no time, it seemed, we were talking away as freely as in the first days of our acquaintance; and I knew that I had missed Gerald, during these last two years, more than I had realized.

'By God, we must celebrate,' Gerald exclaimed. 'Have another pint – no, let's have some whisky.'

I explained, with a slight return of my embarrassment, that I was broke: I had, in fact, exactly five shillings in my pocket. Gerald, however, swept my objections aside.

'Ballocks to that,' he retorted. 'I've got enough on me to get us both well and truly plastered – and that, I may tell you, is just what we're going to do.'

He ordered two double whiskies.

'Tell you what,' he suggested, 'let's get out of this place and go to some low dive.'

We went to several low dives: starting at Jack Bloomfield's pub round the corner, and moving on to a squalid and rather sinister club in Soho.

'And now let's have all the dirt,' said Gerald, when we were settled in a corner. 'What have you been up to all these years? Last time *I* saw you, you were passing out on Robin McQueen's floor at the House.'

I gave Gerald a brief account of my own dull doings, and afterwards he told me about himself. He was now at St Thomas's, and much occupied, at the moment, with midwifery cases in the slums of Lambeth. As he talked, I noticed that he seemed more self-confident and, perhaps, a trifle more opinionated than formerly; to look at, he was much the same – a little fuller in the face, but still possessing the healthy, bucolic good-looks of his undergraduate days. As so often in the past, I found myself envying his assurance and aplomb; and, despite his unaffected friendliness, I felt, as ever, a bit at a disadvantage with him. Gerald had always, ever since I had known him, seemed far more mature and 'grown-up' than myself; and I was now, more than ever, struck by his air of comparative adulthood. Gerald, in fact, had now shed the last vestiges of adolescence, and had emerged as a fully-fledged adult male, settled into the job of his choice, and apparently on the best of terms with life. By comparison, I felt myself a pretender – a mere overgrown schoolboy, playing at being grown-up, yet remaining still, to all intents and purposes, *in statu pupillari*.

Gerald was living in digs somewhere in Pimlico; his parents still inhabited their place near Woking. Gerald's relations with his family remained, so I gathered, amicable but a little strained.

'I manage to run down now and again,' he told me. 'As a matter of fact, I've just invested in a car – an awful old bus, I picked it up cheap from a bloke at Thomas's, but it's good enough for the likes of me. Tell you what, I thought of going down next weekend – why don't you come too? Breath of country air'ld do you a world of good.'

In my pleasure at meeting Gerald, and fortified with half-a-dozen whiskies, I was in no state to refuse such an invitation: though from what I remembered of Gerald's account of his family, the weekend hardly promised to be very enjoyable.

'And now,' Gerald announced, 'we're going to get stinking.'

We finished the evening in my bed-sitting-room in the King's Road, Chelsea. Gerald had bought a half-bottle of whisky at the last 'low dive', and we drank it, in turn, out of my tooth-glass. Gerald, rather to my surprise, became extremely drunk; I had seen him imbibe prodigious quantities at Oxford, but I had never before seen him the worse for it. At two o'clock in the morning he still seemed indisposed to go: dead-tired myself, I reminded him of the time, and hoped he would take the hint.

'Oh, sod it,' he protested. Then, glancing at my bed in the corner, he said: 'Can't I doss down here? There's plenty of room for two.'

'I should get home, if I were you,' I said, knowing that Gerald, in his present mood, was quite capable of sitting up for another hour or so. I was afflicted, moreover, by a spinsterly primness in such matters: I hated sharing my bed with anybody else, and I dreaded the crapulous squalor of tomorrow's awakening – lending Gerald my razor, explaining to the landlady, and so forth.

'Oh, all right,' Gerald agreed at last, heaving himself out of his chair. 'I'd better f— off, in that case.'

His voice had a sharp, resentful note, and I could see that he was offended.

'No, you'd better stay,' I said, impulsively. 'There's plenty of room really, if you don't mind me snoring.'

'No, no, I'll be off.' He moved towards the door; his face was set in a sullen, implacable frown.

'Honestly, I wish you'd stay,' I pleaded, miserable at having offended him.

'Thanks all the same, old boy – cheerioh, and thanks for a nice evening.'

I followed him down the stairs and into the street, where we managed to find a late taxi. He climbed into it without speaking. As the taxi drove off, he put his head through the window and shouted:

'Don't forget you're coming to stay with me for the weekend.'

~ ~ ~

Three days passed, I heard nothing from Gerald, and concluded (not without a certain relief) that the weekend was off. On the Friday, however, he rang me up: he sounded bluff and amiable as ever, and I knew that I was forgiven. Petty enough in itself, my prim refusal to put Gerald up for the night had, as I very well realized, provoked him to one of those sudden, inexplicable fits of resentment which I remembered from the past; and I was reminded, with a stab of nostalgia, of that March afternoon at Godstow when I had refused to bathe.

I met Gerald on the following day in a pub at Victoria, and in the afternoon we drove down, in a battered old Morris, to his home. It was a bright day in early autumn, and I was glad enough to escape from London, if it were only into the coniferous glooms of darkest Surrey. Gerald was in a gay, irresponsible mood; and I myself should have felt happy enough, but for my growing alarm at the prospect of meeting his family, whom I had every reason to suppose I should dislike; nor, indeed, were my fears to prove unjustified.

At Woking, we ran into rain, and arrived at Gerald's home, unpropitiously, in a downpour. I had imagined the house a red, Edwardian villa among pines; it proved to be a rather bleak-looking affair in stockbroker's Tudor, built, I suppose, in about 1924, and separated from its nearly identical neighbours by thickets of silver birch. The house was called 'Burnbrae'; a Sealyham yapped menacingly at us on the doorstep; in the hall, the fumed-oak fireplace was inscribed with a quotation from Omar Khayyam in Gothic script; and from the ceiling hung an enormous wrought-iron lantern in the Hollywood-baronial style. We were received, rather off handedly, by Gerald's sister, Sheila — a dark-browed, angry-looking girl who, I was convinced, loathed me at sight. Tea was ready, and we went into the drawing-room (Waring and Gillow, with 'jazz' cushions), where Mrs Brockhurst presided over an elaborate tea-tray, flanked by plates of exquisitely thin sandwiches and rather nasty-looking cakes; Mr Brockhurst, it seemed, was on the golf-links. Gerald's mother reminded me of the Cheshire cat: her smile — the persistent, hypnotic smile of the Christian Scientist — seemed to exist, so to speak, *in vacuo*, independently of the vague, characterless features which framed it. For the rest, she seemed amiable enough, if a little insipid; as we drank our tea, she kept up an intermittent fire of trivial and singularly pointless questions, mostly directed at myself: what was the weather like in London yesterday, did I prefer travelling by tube or bus, did I know Chiswick (where an aunt of hers, long dead and apparently unregretted, had once lived) – etc. etc. Sheila, I noticed, was inclined to bully her mother, and seemed chronically discontented with her family and, indeed, with life in general; her conversation consisted almost entirely of complaints – of the tea, of the weather, of her work in London, of the hostel where she lodged, of the plays or films which she had lately seen. Things or persons of which or of whom she disapproved were invariably described as 'absolutely foul'; anything unusual or outside her extremely narrow range of appreciation, was 'frightfully weird' or (with a deprecating little laugh) 'rather too highbrow for *me*, I'm afraid.' I disliked her as much as she only too obviously disliked me; partly to show my disapproval, partly out of pity for her victim, I tried to be as nice as possible to Mrs Brockhurst. My attempts to 'draw her out' were, however, notably unsuccessful: the more I talked, the more remotely unapproachable did she become, retreating behind her handsome and lavishly displayed dentures like some timid mollusc into the interior of its shell.

It was a considerable relief when Major Brockhurst (for thus he styled himself) returned from the links. I had been puzzled by the total lack of family likeness between Gerald and his mother and sister; it was now evident that Gerald took after his father, though even here the affinity was not markedly apparent. The Major (he had acquired some kind of temporary rank during the war, and still jealously retained it) looked what he was: a tough midland business-man who had done well out of the war, but not quite well enough. Beneath his bluff, slightly pompous façade, one could see that he was disgruntled and ill-at-ease, a man's man who, retired too early, was inclined to chafe at the padded, female ambience of his home. Plainly he was doing his best to live up to his honorary rank of Major and to the upper middle-class background which the title implied; yet his Harris tweed coat and knickerbockers and cloth cap seemed subtly wrong, the midland accent betrayed itself through the haw-haw of the stage colonel, and one felt that the assumed rôle was a perpetual effort, with which Major Brockhurst was becoming, already, just a trifle bored.

Presently Gerald suggested a 'run in the car' before dinner – an invitation which he accompanied by a significant wink at me. We drove to a pub a few miles away and drank beer.

'I'm afraid you won't get much at dinner-time,' Gerald apologized. 'Mother doesn't approve, you see, being a Christian Scientist, and the pater doesn't go beyond a couple of whiskies.'

The beer proved, indeed, to be a wise precaution, for dinner that night was a surprisingly inadequate affair – soup (obviously tinned) followed by cold beef and salad, carefully doled out by Mrs Brockhurst, whose smile, as she carved up the scraggy remnant of a sirloin, seemed to become more intense, more dazzlingly spiritual than ever. One was made to feel that the mere fact of taking nourishment was a regrettable (if necessary) concession to Mortal Mind; and we were not offered a second helping.

The next day, Sunday, was wet; at half-past ten, Mrs Brockhurst set off for the Christian Science church in Camberley, escorted with evident reluctance by her husband, a recent and somewhat half-hearted convert to the cult. Sheila spent the morning in what she ferociously described as 'stripping the Sealyham'; Gerald and I drove out to the pub at midday and drank beer among a crowd of pink, yapping subalterns.

'I'm afraid you're finding all this a crashing bore,' Gerald apologized, adding, with a shy smile: 'It's jolly nice of you to have come, anyway.'

'I'm not in the least bored,' I assured him – and oddly enough it was more than half true; for the Brockhurst *ménage* had begun to exercise a fascination of horror, I was both appalled and, in a curious way, attracted. I don't know quite what I had expected of Gerald's family; but the reality was certainly at variance with my anticipations. I had, I think, imagined the Brockhursts to be much more vulgarly prosperous, and it had surprised me to find that they were so unostentatious and, comparatively speaking, so poor. Not till long after did I hear that the Major had, in fact, lost a good deal of money since his retirement; he had wished to sell the house and buy a smaller one in a cheaper neighbourhood, but Mrs Brockhurst, with Christianly Scientific optimism, had refused to hear of it. The need for retrenchment appealed to her natural parsimoniousness, and, like so many middle-class women of her type, she was gallantly prepared to starve not only herself but the rest of her family rather than relinquish the outward trappings of gentility. It was hardly surprising that Gerald should spend as little time as possible at home; and I could only admire the tolerant, easy-going attitude which he adopted towards his parents and his sister. It was easy to see that he had little genuine affection for his family; yet his behaviour to his mother and father remained – unlike that of Sheila – impeccably restrained and courteous.

Sunday lunch – roast beef and apple pie – was a slight improvement upon the previous night's dinner, in quality if not in quantity. The Major even produced, with an air of reckless conviviality, a half-bottle of inferior

Graves for Gerald and me (he drank a small whisky-and-water himself). Afterwards, since it continued to rain, we sat in the bleak, unheated drawing-room, dozing over the Sunday papers. (The Major unashamedly covered his face with the *Observer* and snored.)

Gerald and I motored up to London after tea. Driving through the darkening countryside and the outlying suburbs, gleaming under the rain and loud with church-bells, I thought of the weekend, already, with the kind of perverse nostalgia with which one remembers an illness or some youthful unhappiness. Gerald's family background, if unenviable, had acquired for me a kind of poetry of its own: it was linked with Sapper's novels, old *Strand Magazine* stories by Wodehouse or Gilbert Frankau – a whole world of heroic phantasy which, in my prep-school days, had epitomized for me the mysterious and rather frightening prospect of being 'grown-up', and which now seemed bodied forth in the Brockhurst family and, to some degree, in the person of Gerald himself. The Brockhursts conformed perfectly to type, and, in a world in which such conformity was becoming increasingly rare, seemed to me to possess (like some primitive tribe which retains its customs and taboos despite the encroachments of an alien culture) an integrity which was lacking in most of the people I knew, and which, in a perverse and half-reluctant way, I admired.

4

My intermittent, rather uneasy friendship with Gerald was now once again resumed. Often I would meet him for a drink in a favourite pub of his at Lambeth, not far from St Thomas's; and one Saturday afternoon I went and watched him playing rugger for the hospital against Bart's. Our relationship had become a casual, comradely affair, without commitments on either side; Gerald, like myself, was lonely – he seemed by nature a man of few friends – and we were glad enough of one another's company. The barrier which had fallen between us during that last term at Oxford was, as I was dimly aware, still there; but I had long since relinquished any idea of a more intimate relation with Gerald, and I was perfectly prepared to accept him on his own terms. My feeling for him, at this time, was in fact rather of the sort which doggy people have for their favourite pet: I enjoyed his company, but I didn't expect him to share my interests; nor did it occur to me (and in this I differed from most dog-lovers) to introduce him to my other friends. I valued him, indeed, largely because of his refreshing unlikeness to most of the people I knew; very few of my acquaintances, I felt, would share my penchant for Gerald's amiable philistinism, still less would they appreciate his *Strand Magazine* background which, for me, provided an additional – if somewhat perverse – attraction. I preferred to keep my friendship with him a secret, rather as I might have concealed the fact that I was an impenitent addict of *Bulldog Drummond* or the novels of Dornford Yates.

Sometimes Gerald and I would meet for dinner and go to a cinema or a music-hall, finishing up (if we could afford it) at the Criterion brasserie or the Café Royal. It was on one such occasion that, greatly daring, I conceived the unlucky idea of taking Gerald to the Blue Lantern, of which I had lately become a member. I was naïvely proud of belonging to a Real Nightclub, and liked showing it off: I ought, of course, to have realized that the Lantern wasn't Gerald's cup of tea at all; he wouldn't feel at ease, and might easily be offended by the manners of the *habitués*, who belonged, for the most part, to the raffish fringes of that pseudo-'smart' Bohemia which was perhaps the most characteristic (and almost certainly the nastiest) social unit of that period. I ought to have known better: yet the idea of Gerald in such a milieu appealed to my taste for the incongruous; nor, perhaps, was I wholly innocent of a mischievous desire to *épater le bourgeois* – though Gerald, as I knew by now, despite certain well-defined prejudices, was by no means easy to shock.

~ ~ ~

The Blue Lantern that evening was quite as beastly as usual, and perhaps even beastlier. Gerald and I sat at a corner table downstairs and drank lager. Hugh Wade, the pianist, accompanied by drums and a saxophone, was discoursing the half-forgotten, nostalgic tunes of the first-war period; the dancefloor was crowded with painted and twittering young men whose partners, though technically of the female sex (for the Lantern was rather fussy about such conventions), appeared for the most part to be a good deal more virile than their cavaliers.

'God, what an awful crowd,' said Gerald. 'Tell you what, let's go round to the Forty-Three – I can always get in there, I know Ma Merrick. It's a stinking hole, but it doesn't stink as bad as this joint.'

By way of a compromise, I suggested going upstairs and having a drink at the bar. No sooner had we sat down and ordered our drinks than I heard a female voice addressing me by my Christian name, and turned to find myself face to face with Veriny Crighton-Jones.

'My dear,' she exclaimed, in her fashionably husky voice, 'it's utter heaven to see you. That *monster* Bertie Westmacott was meeting me, and I've been waiting here at *least* a thousand years, and I'm madly depressed. Do buy me a drink – here's some money, I know you're broke – and please introduce me to your boy-friend at *once*, I think he's a perfect lamb, and I'd like to eat him, d'you think he'd mind?'

It was thus, unavoidably and in the least propitious of circumstances, that I introduced Gerald to Veriny Crighton-Jones. I had known Veriny for some years: we had met, incongruously enough, at Bedales, where she had come, with her parents, to visit a cousin, who happened to be a friend of mine. I had immediately conceived a violent though almost wholly platonic passion for her: for Veriny, at that time, had seemed to me to typify the kind of woman whom I most fervently admired – a type which, it should be added, I had so far encountered only in fiction.

Veriny was strikingly beautiful in a style then becoming fashionable (the 'waif,' or *gamine*), and which, a few years later, would find its popular prototype in the *faux-naïf*, elfin charm of Fraülein Elisabeth Bergner. With her boyish figure, her blonde Eton crop and her street-arab's grin, Veriny not unnaturally seemed to me to belong to a wholly different species from the sort of girl to whom, at Bedales and in my home circle, I had been accustomed. There was something about her, I liked to think, of the Constant Nymph – an air of apparent innocence masking an illimitable sophistication (or did I, perhaps, mean the other way round?); her husky voice strongly suggested the 'death-bed' articulation of Mrs Viveash in *Antic Hay*, and her morals, from all I had heard about them, invited comparison with those of Iris Storm, that 'shameful, shameless lady' of Michael Arlen's celebrated novel. It seemed safe to infer, at least, that she had a number of lovers; probably she was a nymphomaniac, and quite possibly a drug-addict into the bargain ... In the novel which I immediately began to write about her, after her first visit to the school, she was all these things and more; and the sequel was to prove that Nature, in most respects (as is her habit), had once again imitated Art.

Like Firbank's Miss Sinquier, Veriny was the daughter of a country parson, who had outraged her family by 'going on the stage'. At the time I first met her, she was still at the R.A.D.A.; by the time I encountered her again in London, she had graduated to the chorus of the Cochran revue at the Pavilion; and, at the period when I introduced her to Gerald, she had lately scored a minor success in *revue intime* at the Little Theatre.

Veriny, if she didn't altogether live up to my idea of her as a nymphomaniac, certainly possessed (as I soon discovered) an embracing and, on the whole, undiscriminating fondness for young men. There was no conclusive evidence to show that she drugged; but she certainly drank like a fish, and, moreover, had learnt to hold her liquor a good deal better than most of her (or my own) male acquaintances. I should hardly have supposed that she was Gerald's cup of tea; indeed, I fully expected him to be as shocked by her behaviour as he had been by the antics of the dancers on the floor below. To my astonishment, however, it was perfectly evident that he found her irresistible; soon, indeed, I began to feel that my presence was superfluous, and wandered downstairs. Returning a quarter of an hour later, I saw that they were already shamelessly holding hands, and that Gerald was gazing into her eyes with a besotted, cow-like expression of which I should never before have supposed him capable.

Later, we all returned to the dance-room, and I sat, disconsolately, at a corner table, watching them as they danced. They made a handsome couple, I thought: and as I watched them I was overcome by a wild despairing envy of their beauty and of the shared happiness which transfigured their faces. Doomed, myself (as I was convinced), to a perpetual, frustrated celibacy, I could only wonder at the freakish ways of Providence, which had decreed that it should be myself, of all people, who had brought about this meeting. The sensation was, for that matter, all too familiar; for, on more than one occasion of late, I had found myself in precisely the same situation. I was destined, it seemed, to the perpetual rôle of unofficial (and unwitting) pander among the friends to whom I was most attached; in the chemistry of Love, my function was that of the catalyst – inert, sluggish, without inherent power of action, yet capable (it seemed) of precipitating the most violent and complex reactions in my immediate vicinity.

Presently, when Gerald and Veriny returned to our table, I said I was tired and wanted to go home.

'But my dears, you absolutely *must* come and have a drink with me,' Veriny insisted. 'They're just closing here' (the Lantern was strict about licensing hours), 'and I've got a delicious bottle of whisky and loads of gin.'

At any other time, I should probably have accepted this invitation; Veriny lived in a flat in St John's Wood, and I knew, from past experience, that her parties were apt (when she was 'resting', as she was at present) to be quite uninhibited, and to prolong themselves well into the small hours. Tonight, however, it was only too evident that I should be in the way; even as she spoke, Veriny was grasping Gerald's hand, possessively, beneath the table. My function as catalyst was, I decided with melancholy resignation, at an end; and I had no desire to assist at the chemical process which my introduction had so fatally initiated.

'Oh well, *you'll* come, won't you, my sweet?' Veriny said, turning to Gerald, and speaking in her huskiest, most Arlenish tones.

We left the club at last; Gerald and Veriny drove off in a taxi; and I was left to make my own way, solitary and disconsolate, along the empty reaches of Piccadilly towards my cheerless bed-sitting-room in the King's Road.

~ ~ ~

I saw nothing of Gerald for a fortnight or so: at the end of a week I rang him up and suggested a meeting, but he pleaded a previous engagement – I could guess only too easily with whom.

'Sorry, old boy' (I recognized the familiar, off-putting locution), 'I can't make it that night. Fact is, I'm meeting a dame.'

'Oh, you are, are you,' I said. Gerald's tone, over the telephone, had an assumed casualness beneath which I could detect a note of purring complacency. 'I suppose,' I added, guessing that he would be rather pleased than otherwise by my speculations, 'I suppose it wouldn't be Veriny Crighton-Jones, by any chance?'

'Right first time, old boy,' Gerald answered, still with the same purring intonation; and I could imagine the self-satisfied grin which overspread his face as he spoke. 'Gosh,' he went on, obviously quite unable to bottle up his feelings any longer, 'gosh, she's a grand girl . . . I've been seeing quite a bit of her, as it happens. To tell you the truth, I believe she's taken quite a fancy to me. Isn't it extraordinary?'

'Most,' I agreed.

'Well, I mean, I'm a pretty ordinary sort of bloke, and she's – well, she's a bit above my head, to tell you the truth – awfully sophisticated, and all that.'

'Bristling with sophistication, I should think.'

'*Exactly*. Of course, she's frightfully gay, and likes having a good time, but she's really awfully *innocent*, in a way.'

'She never struck me like that,' I said.

'Oh, but you don't know her as well as I – I mean, after all –' Gerald sounded suddenly embarrassed.

'I've known her for five years, on and off,' I said patiently.

'Yes, but what I mean *is* – the extraordinary thing is that Veriny's not like the rest of these good-time girls. She's *different*.'

'That's always a refreshing quality,' I replied.

'Sarcastic old bugger, aren't you?' Gerald retorted. 'Well, Abyssinia – I'll be giving you a ring next week, I shouldn't wonder.'

Gerald duly rang me up, and I could guess, from his voice, that he was still full of his new conquest, and longing to talk about it. We met in the pub at Lambeth; he was there before me and for a second or two, when I entered the bar, I hardly recognized him. Seldom, indeed, before or since, have I seen anybody so much changed in so short a time: Gerald had plainly lost weight, his face, beneath his tan, was paler than usual, and his eyes had an unaccustomed, a positively febrile brightness. One might have supposed him to be sickening of some fell disease, had it not been for the air of bubbling, uncontrollable happiness which he exhaled.

I was careful not to bring up the topic of Veriny, knowing perfectly well that he would be quite unable to keep off it for more than two minutes. Nor was I mistaken: no sooner had we ordered our drinks, than Gerald was launched upon an exhaustive (and to me somewhat exhausting) catalogue of Veriny's charms. Gerald had never been particularly reticent about his sexual life, and was willing enough, usually, to furnish any amount of clinical details about the progress of his affairs. Now, however, I noticed a difference: gone was the crude, medical student's approach, no longer did he refer to the loved one in such terms as he had been wont to employ, in the past, when describing such charmers as Kathleen and Gladys at the Clarendon. His praise was all for the beauty of Veriny's character: her essential simplicity, her capacity for hard work, her generosity ('She actually wanted to pay for dinner – you don't find many girls like that nowadays'). Above all, he extolled her 'difference' from other girls.

'It's wonderful, really, when you think of her being mixed up with all that beastly theatrical set . . . Most girls wouldn't have been able to stand the pace: it takes a real thoroughbred like Veriny to keep straight in that sort of set-up.'

I listened, with a kind of rueful amusement, to Gerald's ravings. I was tempted, at times, to laugh outright; at the same time, I felt genuinely concerned about him, for this, quite obviously, was no passing *béguin*, but – as Gerald himself never tired of assuring me – the 'real thing'. I rather prided myself, in those days, on being unshockable, and liked to think that no sexual vagary on the part of my friends could surprise me; but I was both astonished and distressed that Gerald – so level-headed, so commonsensical, so mature in his judgment – could be so utterly bamboozled. I was tempted to say outright what I knew to be true: that the only respect in which Veriny Crighton-Jones could be considered 'different' from other girls was in being more drunken, more lascivious and (to do her justice) more beautiful than most. If I refrained from speaking, it was chiefly from a natural reluctance to spoil Gerald's present happiness; it was, moreover, pretty obvious that no warning from me (or anybody else) would have the slightest effect upon him in his present besotted state. Perhaps, too, I was further restrained by a certain distrust of my own motives: the envy and frustration which I was wont to feel on such occasions could too easily (as I knew from past experience) add a sadistic relish to the most well-meant and high-minded of homilies.

Presently the flood of Gerald's eloquence began to subside, and I caught him looking at me with a shy, sidelong glance, as though he were trying to nerve himself to raise some less agreeable and perhaps embarrassing topic.

'By the way,' he managed to stammer out at last, 'd'you happen to know a chap called Bertie Westmacott?'

I said I knew Bertie fairly well.

'Well, the fact is, you see, that he's rather a friend of Veriny's . . . I haven't met him myself, mind you, but it seems that he and Veriny used to go around together rather a lot, and he still keeps ringing her up about twice a day, and – well, you know, I just wondered what sort of bloke he was.' Gerald paused a moment, then added, forcefully: 'Mind you, I'm not suggesting for a minute that Veriny – I mean, there couldn't really be anything of *that* sort, Veriny's not that kind of girl – but by God, if that chap's been pestering her, I'll have the bloody hide off him.'

As it happened, I was fairly well-informed about Veriny's relations with Bertie Westmacott, and had every reason to suppose that they were wholly innocent, since Bertie's love-life, from all accounts, was almost exclusively bound up with His Majesty's Brigade of Guards. It didn't, however, seem altogether prudent to tell Gerald this, and I consoled him, as best I could, by saying that Bertie was an old friend of Veriny's from her R.A.D.A. days; nor did I add (as I might well have done) that Gerald's threat to 'have the hide off him' would without a doubt have provided Bertie with the thrill of his life. It was perhaps as well (I reflected) that Gerald's jealousy had attached itself to so innocent an object; and I couldn't help suspecting that Veriny herself had been 'playing up' Bertie, quite deliberately, in order to throw Gerald off the scent of other and more blameworthy victims.

~ ~ ~

Shortly after this I was taken ill, and spent some months in the country; I didn't see or hear from Gerald again till my return to London, when I rang him up and suggested a meeting. We met, once again, in the Lambeth pub, for which we had both developed a fondness. Gerald greeted me genially enough, but I noticed at once that he was looking tired and rather worried, and that he had grown even thinner since our last encounter. For almost the first time since I had known him his geniality struck me as forced: there was a look of strain and, it seemed to me, concealed unhappiness behind the façade of conviviality. Once again I refrained from mentioning Veriny, and on this occasion it was some time before Gerald himself broached the subject.

'By the way,' he said at last, with a curious, rather rueful smile, quite unlike his usual candid grin, 'by the way, I suppose you ought to congratulate me.'

'Congratulate you?' I repeated, mechanically, with a vague, premonitory unease.

'Yes – I thought perhaps you'd have seen it in *The Times*. Veriny and I are being married next month.'

I gaped at him, idiotically, then, with a sudden and complete loss of control, burst out laughing.

'You don't *really* mean,' I gasped, incredulously, trying in vain to stifle my laughter, 'that you and Veriny are actually engaged to be *married*?'

'Yes, that's the idea – I popped the question a couple of months ago. We'd have been married by now, only Veriny didn't want to break her contract. She's in that Charlot show at the Vaudeville, you know – quite a decent little part – you ought to go and see it, if you haven't been . . .

Of course, she'll give up the stage when we're married – she didn't want to, but I put my foot down for once.'

As he spoke, Gerald's face had a curious expression which I had never seen there before: a kind of shy, animal defensiveness, the look of a normally good-tempered dog who has been ill-treated, and has learnt to distrust its owner. I knew (whatever might have happened between him and Veriny) that he was unhappy; and I felt deeply sorry for him. My ill-timed laughter had obviously distressed him, and I tried my best to make up for it.

'Of course I congratulate you,' I said, feeling my words and tone hopelessly inadequate. 'All the very best, and I hope you'll both be frightfully happy.'

'I hope so too,' said Gerald quietly; and there was something in his voice which implied, beyond any possible doubt, that he didn't expect the hope to be realized.

For the rest of that evening Gerald remained pointedly reticent about his forthcoming marriage; and it was not till I had met and talked to him on several future occasions that I began to have some idea of the sequence of events that had led up to his engagement. As it happened, I chanced to meet Veriny herself at about this time, at a party at which Gerald was not present; and bit by bit I was able to piece together, from one source and another, the not-very-edifying story.

Veriny, it seemed (and this much must be conceded in her favour), had quite genuinely fallen in love with Gerald – or at any rate had had (as she herself would have put it) a more than usually exclusive 'thing' about him. This, it appeared, had coincided rather conveniently with a desire on her part to 'settle down' – though I should have found this hard to credit if I had not elicited (from Bertie Westmacott, as it happened) the rather more cogent fact that Veriny had had one of her periodical 'scares': in other words, she had believed herself pregnant as the result of an affair with a young Guards officer, a close friend of Bertie's. More cogent still, perhaps, was the fact that Veriny, in the early days of their relationship, had acquired a wholly misleading impression of Gerald's financial resources. This had come about in a rather odd way: Gerald had introduced Veriny to his sister (who was still employed at her 'perfectly foul' secretarial job in London), and the two girls, so it seemed, had settled down to a nice cosy chat about Gerald's prospects. Sheila, perhaps dazzled by Veriny's smartness and by her rather deceptive air of luxury, and being, herself, extremely snobbish, had given her prospective sister-in-law to understand that Gerald would inherit an extremely comfortable little income. Not content with this, she had apparently implied – though without positively committing herself – that Gerald's father was a regular soldier, a scion of a minor but highly respectable county family, and the owner of a 'place' in Surrey which (it might be supposed from Sheila's description) he had inherited from distant – and even more distinguished – forebears.

It was, so I gathered, on the day following this conversation that Veriny had finally agreed to become engaged to Gerald. Shortly afterwards – at her own instigation, I inferred, rather than Gerald's – she spent a weekend with the Brockhursts at Woking; this had occurred shortly before my own meeting with Gerald, at which he had announced his engagement, and might in itself (as I guessed afterwards) have been quite enough to account for Gerald's defensive and unhappy state of mind on that occasion. It was soon after this that I myself encountered Veriny, and heard her account of the visit.

'My sweet, it's bliss to see you,' she exclaimed, disentangling herself, cocktail glass in hand, from a gaggle of young men among whom I recognized Bertie Westmacott and the Guards officer with whom, till lately, Veriny had been 'walking out'. 'I suppose you've *heard*,' she went on, 'about Gerry and me' (I had never heard Gerald called 'Gerry' before). 'He's such a sweetie-pie, and I'm madly happy – he's made me realize, you see, that I was just *made* to be a wife and mother' (here Veriny gave me one of her mischievous Constant Nymph grins). 'As a matter of fact, I was within *inches* of breaking it off only last week – my dear, that *family*! *Nobody* had warned me what I was marrying into – poor Gerry's terribly loyal, of course, and won't hear a *word* against them. Of course, I had met that bitchy sister – Moira, or Sheila, or whatever her ghastly name is – and she'd cracked them up as being stinking rich and ever so country, so you can imagine, my dear, my utter *horror*! That frightful house – like a *morgue*, my dear – and of course, the first thing that happened was that I was set on by that bloody dog of theirs – it bit me in the leg, and I swore like a trooper, which of course didn't exactly help to *endear* me . . . And the awful daughter said it was "only his fun", and the still more awful mother – a perfect *vampire* – said it was Mortal Mind, and my dear, if you can believe it, started to "demonstrate", there and then – clacking her teeth, and making a sort of cooing noise, like a wood-pigeon . . . My dear, it was all *too* frightful – except for the old man, who's rather a pet – madly common, of course, but really rather pathetic (my dear, the *way* that woman treats him!) and the brother – back on leave from some ghastly outpost of Empire, *oh* so pukka but rather handsome – I'm not sure I didn't make a tiny bit of a hit, but of course Gerry's *wildly* jealous, and always threatening to horsewhip anyone who comes within ten yards of me, which of course *is* rather bliss, though it does have its comic side, because he's always wanting to beat up the wrong people – I thought he was going to *murder* poor darling Bertie, who's as queer as a coot anyway, and only hangs round me because he's in love with Teddy Boscombe' (Teddy Boscombe was Veriny's guardee), 'and as I'm always telling him, he's wasting his time, because Teddy's practically stopped being queer since he met *me*, bless his little heart.'

5

Not long after this I retired once again into the country, and remained there for nearly two years; I didn't see either Gerald or Veriny during this period, and such news as I had of them was fragmentary and intermittent. I received an invitation to the wedding, but refused it on grounds of ill-health. I was, as it happened, genuinely ill; but I should have preferred, I think, in any case, not to be present at the ceremony. Since his marriage, Gerald had become for me (as one's friends, when they marry, are apt to become) slightly unreal; I thought of him as one thinks of a character in a novel with whose fortunes one has identified oneself, but in whom one loses all but a faint retrospective interest when the book is closed. Insofar as I remained objectively aware of his existence, I was inclined to take an extremely pessimistic view of his future; and the news of him which filtered through to me during the next two years was to justify only too abundantly my gloomy prognostications.

Once or twice I heard from him – brief, awkward but rather touchingly affectionate letters, in which he told me almost nothing which I really wanted to know. Veriny was seldom mentioned, and when her name did occur, it was in a context which gave no clue as to the present state of their relationship. Veriny had gone to a cocktail party, a tea-fight or a charity dance – and so forth; sometimes Gerald referred to her, with a curious impersonality as 'my wife' . . . One could have inferred anything or nothing from such references; Veriny herself never wrote to me, apart from a letter of thanks for my wedding present; this, however, didn't surprise me, for she had always been a poor correspondent.

Gerald had passed his final examinations shortly before his marriage, and had managed to obtain a junior partnership in a country practice near Edinburgh. Only one feature in his letters to me could have been construed as evidence that all was not well with his marriage: this was the growing frequency with which he complained of lack of money. At the time of his marriage, his father had apparently come up to the scratch, and helped him to buy his share in the practice; but the Brockhursts, as I knew, were far from rich, and indeed (despite Mrs Brockhurst's pious economies) were likely to be even less well-off in the future. Gerald was at present almost wholly dependent upon his job; as for Veriny, she had, so I gathered, only a small allowance – scarcely more than 'pin-money' – from her parents, who had strongly disapproved of the marriage. Knowing Veriny's habits and the standard of living to which she was accustomed, I found it hard to believe that she would settle down even for a week – let alone for a lifetime – to the dim, cheeseparing existence of a penurious country doctor's wife.

Poor Gerald, I thought – he had been well and truly 'caught' – trapped at the outset of his career, like many another promising young man, and doomed to a lifetime of near-failure; slogging away at the job at which, in other circumstances, he might have been a conspicuous success. With anybody else, it wouldn't have surprised me in the least; but Gerald, from the earliest days of our acquaintance, had seemed to me the very last person to suffer such a fate. With his toughness, his integrity of purpose, his basic indifference to the snares which beset the average young man, he had seemed destined for a career of solid if unspectacular achievement; that he should have been so easily – and so fatally – deflected from it, seemed to me a more than usually sadistic gesture on the part of 'whatever brute or blackguard made the world'.

Yet, if I am to be honest, I must confess that, beneath my genuine sorrow at his misfortunes, I was aware of a secret, inadmissible feeling of satisfaction. Doubtless I did possess a nasty streak – I am quite prepared to admit it; but Gerald, after all, had stood for me as the prototype of all those virtues which, since I didn't possess them myself, I was apt to envy – and often to resent – in other people. Much as I had liked and admired him, my feeling for Gerald had never been quite without the grain of malice engendered by my own sense of inferiority; and now Gerald, like many another, had been proved vulnerable, and unworthy of the trust which I had placed in him.

As the months passed, I began to acquire further scraps of information about him. Some of it came from a rather unlikely source: Eric Anquetil, teaching at a prep. school in Scotland, had encountered Gerald by chance in Edinburgh, and had been invited once or twice to his home.

'Your nice Gerald,' wrote Eric, 'seems changed beyond recognition – I hardly recognized him when we met in the Caley. He seems to be boozing pretty hard – I can put away a fair amount myself, as you may know, but I couldn't begin to keep up with him. He was very incoherent, and kept talking about someone called Boscombe – do you know him, and ought I to? I couldn't quite make out whether G. liked him very much or hated him like poison – he seemed rather ambivalent about the whole thing. I did rather gather, though, that G.'s horns were beginning to sprout, poor dear. It seems centuries since you and he used to go riding at Oxford, do you remember?'

'The Brockhurst home' (he wrote in another letter) 'I found very embarrassing: Veriny was tight as an owl at tea-time, and G. started nagging at her in front of me. I must say, my sympathies were rather on her side, though I was sorry, too, for poor G. He seems to be getting very tetchy and disgruntled, and kept saying how broke he was – at one moment I actually thought he was going to touch me for a fiver, but fortunately he didn't (I only had five bob on me, anyway). He's busy enough, it seems – plenty of patients – but Veriny has about as much idea as a chicken of keeping house, and obviously spends all the housekeeping money on the Demon.'

A further letter was even more explicit:

'Poor G.'s antlers are definitely burgeoning: I spent a night in Edinbro' at the Caley (having been offered a lift back in time for prayers the next morning), and Veriny B. was staying the night there too. G. was away at some medical function in Carlisle or somewhere, and V. introduced me to the ambivalent Mr Boscombe at tea-time. I made the obvious assumption, but was very tactful. Afterwards, we all had drinks in V.'s bedroom – champagne, I may say. (The wicked Mr B., by the way, is rather an Adonis, and I should guess crypto-musical – he seems to have been a great buddy of Hew Dallas at Oxford.) I got back very late from Francis's party (or rather very early – I had practically no sleep) and as I stumbled upstairs saw him (Mr B.) coming out of V.'s room. I'm sorry for poor Gerald – I give that marriage about another year at most.'

~ ~ ~

It was from Bertie Westmacott, nearly two years after Gerald's marriage, that I finally heard the news which, in the light of Eric's information, I had been expecting for some time: Gerald was getting a divorce – or rather, was allowing Veriny to divorce him.

'It's all madly complicated, as a matter of fact,' Bertie went on. 'You see, Gerald's known all about Teddy for ages, and was quite prepared to be the *mari complaisant* so long as they were reasonably tactful – in fact, Gerald must have found it quite convenient, seeing that he had such a thing about Teddy himself.'

'*Gerald* had?' I exclaimed, incredulously.

'My dear, it was common knowledge: they were terrific buddies – they went off fishing together one weekend, while *I* stayed with Veriny, and had the time of their lives. I must say, it came as a surprise to *me* when I first realized – I always thought Gerald was madly B.M. before he married, but *there* you are, dear, even an old bitch like me can make a bloomer sometimes.'

'What utter nonsense,' I exploded at last, 'I don't believe a word of it. Why, Gerald was no more like that than – than the Archbishop of Canterbury.'

Bertie's eyes widened.

'My dear, what do *you* know about the Archbishop? Anyway, as I was saying, it might have worked out all right – a sort of *ménage a trois*, you know – if only Veriny had stuck to Teddy, but knowing Veriny, what could you expect? You know how madly indiscreet she is . . . She was having a great walk-out with a Major in the Black Watch for quite a time – I don't think Gerald knew about it, though he may have had his suspicions. Well, Teddy knew this Major, *and*, my dear, one night Veriny asked them *both* back to dinner. Gerald was called out during the evening, to one of his gruesome patients, and they thought he'd be ages, because it was a rather sticky maternity case, apparently, but it turned out to be a false alarm, and Gerald was back in half-an-hour, my dear, and found all three of them in bed together . . . Well I do *rather* see Gerald's point, don't you? Cuckolded fore and aft, so to speak, and by the *Black Watch*, my dear . . . And after all, three in a bed *is* a bit of a crowd, and it *was* Gerald's bed, anyway. But *oh* –' and here Bertie drew a long sigh and raised his eyes to the ceiling – 'but oh, my dear, *isn't* our little Veriny a lucky girl?'

Soon after this encounter, I had a letter from Gerald – a brief, pathetic note, giving me the bare facts, and without any of the details (mostly apocryphal, as I preferred to believe) provided by Bertie Westmacott. 'I should like to see you,' the letter concluded. 'Will you be in Town next Wednesday? I shall be up, arranging about the divorce.'

I was staying down at Sandgate at the time – it was in the summer – and the letter had been forwarded from my London address; it was too late now to meet Gerald on the day he had suggested. I wrote to him – an awkward, unsatisfactory letter, in which my expressions of sympathy sounded absurdly pompous and stilted. I had scarcely posted it when Gerald himself walked into my room: he had tried to get me at my home, had heard I was at Sandgate, and had motored straight down the same day.

As Eric had said, he was barely recognizable: haggard, pale, and with a curiously seedy air about him, as though he had slept in his clothes. He came into the room breathing fast, and sat down heavily in an armchair, like a runner at the finish of a race.

'I had to see you,' he said, with a blurred, guttural intonation. At first I thought he had a cold; then I realized that he was drunk.

'Got anything to drink in the house?' he asked, with a shadow of his old, mischievous grin.

'I'm afraid I've only got a bottle of claret,' I said.

'That'll do. I can't talk till I've got a drink inside me.'

I brought the bottle of claret and a tumbler; Gerald poured out the wine impatiently, and took a long drink.

'That's better,' he said. 'Did you get my letter? Oh, you did – so you know what's up.' He paused, then threw his hands apart in a helpless, despairing gesture. 'You see,' he went on, in a flat expressionless tone, 'I'm finished – it's the bloody end of everything, as far as I'm concerned. I'm broke to the wide, for one thing – the practice has gone down the drain, and the divorce is going to cost a fortune, one way and another. I just don't know which way to turn – my people won't do a thing – they wouldn't even if they could, and they can't, anyway; the pater's lost a packet lately . . . I'm just about sunk, and that's a fact.'

Gerald poured out more claret, and drank down half a tumblerful at a gulp.

'You must wonder why I blew in on you,' he went on. 'I don't want to bore people with my troubles, but I had to see somebody, and – oh well, I don't know: you seem to be the person I've known longest, really, and I've always been rather fond of you, you know . . . I hope you don't mind – I feel a pretty thoroughgoing bastard at the moment, and I'm being a crashing bore.'

'Of course you're not,' I assured him. 'I only wish I could do something: I suppose there *isn't* anything I could do, is there?'

'Not a thing, thanks all the same: I'm in the shit, and I've just got to grin and bear it, I suppose.'

'Have some more claret,' I said.

Gerald laughed shortly.

'That's a sound suggestion, anyway,' he said, and poured out the remainder of the bottle. I was alarmed by his appearance: his eyes had a feverish, almost an insane glint in them, and his hands trembled pathetically as he poured out the wine. It was five o'clock in the afternoon, and I could hardly suggest that he went to bed; yet bed seemed the obvious place for him in his present condition.

I had reckoned, however, without Gerald's basic toughness, his ability to bounce up again, like a Russian toy, from the nadir of misfortune. The claret seemed suddenly to take effect: a flush overspread his cheeks, and he smiled at me with something of his own geniality.

'Tell you what,' he said, leaning forward with a sudden, purposeful air, 'let's go and have a swim.'

'All right,' I said, 'if you're sure you're not –' I checked myself, and added, lamely: 'if you're not too tired.'

'Tactful as ever,' Gerald retorted with a chuckle. 'It's all right – I've great powers of recuperation, and a swim'll just about set me up for the evening. Then we'll go out and get stinking . . . Think I could stay the night in this place?'

'I'll ask the landlady,' I said, and went to seek her out in the basement. There was no room vacant, but I could probably get one down the street, in the house of the landlady's sister.

'Oh, I can sleep anywhere,' Gerald said, when I returned with the news. He looked round the bed-sitting room, which possessed a fair-sized double bed. 'Mind if I cuddle up with you? I'd be damned grateful, actually – I've got into the sort of state when I can't stand being alone, especially at night.'

'I don't mind, as long as you don't,' I said, remembering another, far distant occasion when Gerald had asked me to put him up; I had a sudden, disquieting sense of duplication, as though the wheel of time and experience had come full circle.

'No,' said Gerald, glancing at me with a quick, sidelong smile, 'I didn't think you'd mind.'

We went down to the beach. The sun was still high, but a fresh wind had risen, and the sea didn't look particularly inviting; I was recovering, as it happened, from a bad cold, and decided not to bathe myself.

Gerald, already half-undressed, gave me a mocking grin.

'Not coming in, eh? All right, I won't try and force you . . .' He paused, then added, with a slight chuckle: 'You never would bathe when I asked you to, would you?'

Once again, it was as though Life had wheeled back upon itself, to that far-off, wintry afternoon in the flooded fields by Godstow; and I remembered, with a sudden backwash of emotion, that odd, crucial moment of decision, so heavily weighted with a sense of Gerald's destiny and of my own . . . But that, I thought, was in another country . . . A cloud covered the sun, and I began to shiver in the chilly sea wind.

I watched Gerald undress under a breakwater; his nakedness made him seem curiously vulnerable and rather pathetic. I noticed that, despite the haggard leanness of his face, his body was beginning to run to fat: the muscles were less firmly modelled, the flesh about the nipples had an almost feminine softness. I watched him run down the beach and plunge into the grey, muddy breakers: he swam out a long way, and I began to feel uneasy. In his present state he was likely to do something reckless: the sea was rough, and I knew that the currents could be dangerous. I ought to have warned him . . . I remembered his look of blank, unutterable misery as he spoke of his misfortunes; and the thought struck me, with a desolating horror, that he might, in a moment of sudden despair, cease to struggle with the strong, downward pull of the waves . . . But I had reckoned, once again, without Gerald's indomitable toughness and resilience. Soon I saw him swimming back; and in another three minutes he was standing by my side, rubbing his chilled body with a towel, and looking remarkably fresh and revivified after his bathe.

We drank some beers at a pub, and later dined at the Royal Kent Hotel. Astonishingly, Gerald seemed to have regained his normal poise almost completely: at dinner he was positively gay – laughing at old suddenly-remembered jokes from our shared past, and asking for news of people we used to know. It was only afterwards, when we returned to my room (with a bottle of whisky purchased by Gerald), that his mood of spurious, forced geniality seemed suddenly to leave him. He slumped down into the armchair, and for several minutes – while I uncorked and poured out the whisky – he brooded in silence. Suddenly he glanced across at me with a look of temporarily revived alertness.

'D'you know Teddy Boscombe?' he asked.

'Hardly at all,' I said, avoiding his eyes. 'I've met him at one or two parties.'

'Oh, I see – I just wondered,' he murmured vaguely, and lapsed again into silence. For a moment or two he closed his eyes, and I thought he had gone to sleep; presently, however, he began to talk again – haltingly and with many circumlocutions, running his words together, and stumbling over the consonants.

'Bloody done for, that's what I am . . . Properly scuppered. I don't blame Veriny, mind you – not her fault, poor bitch . . . It's just the way life bloody well treats people . . . D'you believe in God?'

'No, I'm afraid not.'

'Nor do I – never was much of a one for religion . . . I never wanted much for myself, y'know – I wasn't ambitious, like some of these go-getting bastards . . . I wasn't good enough for Veriny, that's the trouble – no money, no bloody prospects . . . Know what I'm goin' to do?' He darted the question at me suddenly.

'No, what?'

Gerald grinned at me rather sheepishly.

'You wouldn't guess . . . The bloody practice's down the drain – got to sell out. No more private practice for me . . . Only one thing to do now . . .'

His voice tailed off, as though he had once again lost interest in what he was saying.

'What do you think of doing?' I asked, as casually as I could.

He looked up at me, as if surprised, then suddenly burst out laughing.

'Why, I'm going for a soldier,' he said.

'D'you mean enlist in the ranks?' I asked, bewildered.

'No, Medical Corps – Rob-all-my-comrades, jolly old poultice-wallahs an' all that. 'Spect I can wangle some sort of commission – not a bad life, and it looks as if things are blowing up for a scrap, with this fellow Hitler and all . . . I'd rather fancy myself in uniform.'

'It seems a pretty good idea,' I said, cautiously.

'Might get sent abroad, y'know – India, Egypt . . . Suit me all ri' – fed up with this rotten country . . . Too small . . . Wide open spaces – that's the stuff to give the bloody troops . . . Wait till you see me in uniform . . .'

He rambled on, more and more incoherently: mostly about the R.A.M.C. and the prospects it offered, but reverting, now and again, with apparent inconsequence, to his divorce.

'S'pose I'll have to go for a weekend to Brighton – that'll be nice, won't it? Might take old Kathleen from the Clarry – wonder if she's still around . . . Good value, Kathy was. . . .' He broke off, and gave me a curiously sly, almost shifty look. 'Funny you didn't know Teddy Boscombe,' he went on. 'Thought everyone knew Teddy. Decent sort of chap . . . Sort of friend I always wanted . . . I was damned fond of him – used to go fishing together . . .' Gerald paused again, eyeing me speculatively. Suddenly he turned his eyes away. 'You didn't know I was like that, did you?' he queried.

'No, I suppose I didn't.'

'Always a bit that way, I s'pose, an' didn't know it . . . Remember that night at Oxford, when you passed out at the House? Last I saw of you . . . Chap called Dallas was there – asked me back to his digs . . . Stayed the night – all rather sordid, really. Hew had a photo of Teddy – told me all about him . . . Teddy was only half-queer . . . Liked women too, you know – sort of ambidextrous . . . Fancied me, though – went fishing together . . . Funny the way things turn out . . .'

Gerald's voice petered out into an inaudible mumble: I could see that he was already nearly asleep. I looked at him sadly: so Bertie, I thought, had been right after all; yet the fact refused to lodge itself in my consciousness, my mind rejected it as the queasy stomach rejects a bitter draught.

I roused Gerald at last, and suggested bed. His hand reached automatically for the whisky.

'I shouldn't have any more,' I said. 'Time you went to bed.' I had decided to put him in my bed and sleep in the armchair myself.

'Go and get f—ed,' Gerald retorted, grinning up at me drunkenly but with a sudden, surprising alertness. He poured out half a tumblerful of whisky, drank it off, and rose from his chair: to my astonishment, he seemed perfectly steady on his feet.

'Must go and see about the car,' he said. 'Got some things in the back – toothbrush, razor . . .'

'I should wait till the morning.'

'No, must go and get toothbrush – always clean teeth at night . . . You go to bed, ol' boy.'

I offered to go with him, but he seemed determined, for some reason, to go by himself. The car was parked outside, so he couldn't, I thought, come to much harm. I saw him out of the front-door, and returned to my room, where I undressed. Gerald, I thought, seemed an unconscionable long time finding his toothbrush . . . Anxious not to seem fussy and interfering, I waited for ten minutes; then, in my pyjamas and dressing-gown, went to the front-door and quietly opened it.

Gerald was standing on the other side of the road, beneath a street-lamp, deep in conversation with a private soldier. Hearing the click of the latch, he turned and saw me standing in the doorway. I watched him speak a final word to his companion, then turn and cross the road; he walked steadily enough, though with a certain stiff deliberation. I noticed that the soldier – a tough, rather good-looking young man – continued to stand on the opposite pavement, as though waiting for somebody.

'Sorry, ol' boy – just stayed out to have a breather.' Gerald pushed past me into my room, which was on the ground floor. As I followed him in, he turned and faced me, with the same sly, evasive expression which I had noticed earlier.

'Look here, ol' boy, if you don't mind frightfully, I think I'll push straight off tonight . . . Fact is, I ought really to be in Town at ten o'clock tomorrow, and it'll only hold things up if I'm not there.'

'I shouldn't go tonight if I were you,' I said, speaking with an unconcern which I was far from feeling. 'You must be tired after this afternoon, and it's one o'clock already. I'll see we're called early in the morning.'

I saw a flash of irritation cross Gerald's face.

'No, honestly, old boy, I'd rather get off if you don't mind.' His voice was suddenly sharp with impatience.

'But look here,' I said, deciding to risk his anger, 'it's absolute madness to drive after all that booze – nobody could. You'd much better stay.'

I saw his eyes blaze with anger: yet I was determined that he shouldn't go if I could prevent him, and I remained where I was, standing with my back to the door.

'Look here,' he said, mastering his temper with some difficulty, 'for

God's sake don't argue. I know you mean well, but I'm in that sort of state I just can't stand it. And anyway, I'm used to driving when I'm pissed-up – it's become rather a habit with me, lately. I've never had a smash yet – drunkard's luck, I suppose.'

'I'd rather you didn't go, all the same,' I said firmly.

For a moment I thought he was going to lose his temper and become violent: I saw him clench his hands, and his eyes were suddenly blank with rage.

'Oh for *Christ's* sake,' he muttered thickly. A moment later the spasm passed: his face relaxed, and he stared past me, evasively, at the door.

'Sorry, but I'm going . . . Fact is,' he added, with a carefully assumed casualness, 'I promised that soldier-bloke a lift up to the camp – it's all on my way, you see.'

He took a step forward, and suddenly seized me by both arms. The next moment, I was being half-pushed, half-carried across the room: for a drunken man, the action was performed with a remarkable power and dexterity. Gerald deposited me gently, as though I were an invalid, upon my bed: for a moment he leaned over me, his hands still firmly pinioning my arms.

'Sorry, old chap, but I'm afraid it's goodbye . . . I know I'm a rotten bastard, but try not to think too badly of me . . . And take care of yourself.'

A moment later, he was gone. I heard the front-door gently shut, and the noise of his footsteps, uncannily loud, as he walked towards the waiting soldier and the car.

~ ~ ~

Gerald's divorce went through with the usual interminable delays; meeting Bertie Westmacott shortly afterwards, I learned that he had applied successfully for a commission in the R.A.M.C., and was at present stationed at Catterick.

'I hear he's become a reformed character,' said Bertie. 'Strictly T.T., and quite drearily respectable – one asks oneself how long *that's* going to last . . . A friend of mine in the Brigade ran across him, and told me he was going bald and developing quite a paunch. Such a shame – Gerald was never really my tea, but I could see what people *meant* about him.'

Six months after the decree had been made absolute, I saw in *The*

Times the announcement of Veriny's engagement to the Hon. Edward Boscombe, of the Coldstream Guards.

~ ~ ~

In 1937 I received a letter, in a thin and much-smudged envelope, from Sierra Leone. To my astonishment, it proved to be from Gerald. It was so long since I had heard of him, that I half believed him dead, and his letter gave me a curious and not altogether pleasant shock.

'I've done a year out here, and have another year to do,' he wrote. 'It's a good place for the likes of me, and I manage to get quite a lot of fun.' The rest of the letter was taken up with rather dull details about native customs, hunting trips, etc. Enclosed was a photograph of himself, stripped to the waist, and looking comically like an Empire-builder in a tobacco advertisement.

I answered his letter, but he didn't write again, and I heard no more of him for over a year. Then, at Munich time, he suddenly rang me up at my home at Blackheath, and asked me to dinner at his club. At first I didn't catch his name, and the voice seemed wholly unfamiliar – a clipped, military accent which I should never have recognized as Gerald's. My first impulse was to avoid a meeting with him; our last farewell at Sandgate had seemed in some way final: it was as though the real Gerald – the Gerald I had known at Oxford – were dead, and the idea of meeting him again filled me with a curious, almost superstitious dread. Gerald, however, was insistent, and I duly met him, on the appointed evening, at the United Service Club.

His appearance, at least, as he bounced out of the smoking-room to meet me, was reassuring: he was tanned a dark brown, and looked alarmingly fit. I noticed, however, that his hair had receded a good deal, and was going grey at the sides. He greeted me with a rumbustious heartiness, and pushed me before him into the smoking-room. Drinks appeared – sherry for myself, a double gin for Gerald.

'Jolly good luck,' he exclaimed, raising his glass. 'It's grand to see you again. I'm only in Town for a day or two – thought I must look you up. I'll be buzzing down to Netley soon – great hoo-ha going on since this Munich business – matter of fact, I'm sweating on a rather good job – ought to be a bloody Major soon, if I'm lucky – been fart-arsing around with the war-house this last week – can't get a word of sense out of 'em – but here's hoping.'

Gerald drank to his own future, and ordered another round. I felt, suddenly, very ill-at-ease, and wished I had refused the invitation: there was something, it seemed to me, subtly and indefinably *wrong* about the occasion; I had the sense of some evil lurking, like a bad smell, among the solid, conventional trappings of the room. I looked at Gerald again, rather more closely: outwardly, he looked as fit as at any time since I had known him — if anything, fitter; yet, as I studied his face, it dawned upon me, suddenly and frighteningly, that he was a sick man. His nervous, staccato speech, his abrupt movements, a certain strained alertness in his whole manner, seemed somehow to give the lie to his air of bodily fitness.

During dinner, he continued his diffuse, self-centred monologue; only once or twice did he break off to enquire, briefly and perfunctorily, after my own doings. I began to suspect that the occasion was proving as much of a strain for Gerald as it was for myself; it was as though the spate of small-talk and reminiscence (so wholly uncharacteristic of Gerald as I remembered him) were a kind of defence-mechanism, like the ink-cloud secreted by the cuttlefish.

After dinner, in a corner of the smoking-room, Gerald produced from his note-case a bundle of photographs, mostly taken in Freetown. A few of them were of his brother officers, but most were of negroes; some were extremely indecent. I saw that one of the prints, unnoticed by Gerald, had fallen to the floor, and I bent down to pick it up; as I handed it to him, I caught a glimpse of a stalwart young man in bathing shorts, and recognized the face as that of Teddy Boscombe.

As the evening wore on, I became more and more depressed; I tried to appear interested in Gerald's talk, but I realized, sadly, that he had become — quite apart from anything else — a bore. I was thankful when I could at last, with a minimum of discourtesy, make my escape; and I felt pretty sure that Gerald was thankful too.

~ ~ ~

I had decided that I didn't want to see Gerald again: our long, equivocal and curiously inconclusive friendship seemed to have come to an end at last. Yet Gerald seemed destined to turn up in my life, like some wandering comet, whether I liked it or not. My next and — as it happened — penultimate meeting with him was a year later, during the first weeks of the war. On a flying visit to London, I ran into him in Whitehall, and we had a drink together. The drink led to a beery evening: it was, for Gerald, in the nature of a farewell party, for he was shortly to be drafted to the B.E.F., and seemed extremely pleased about it. He had changed, again, in the past year – this time, I thought, for the better; his nervous self-absorption was less marked, he seemed to have regained some of his old, confident bearing, and, in the nostalgic, war-time atmosphere, so poignant with its perpetual, unuttered sense of last farewells, I felt, in spite of myself, a faint recrudescence of my old affection for him.

'Soon be hanging out my washing on the Siegfried line,' he exclaimed breezily.

It was the sort of remark which, from anybody else, would have exacerbated me, but which, coming from Gerald, I accepted with the tolerance born of long habit. He was wearing the uniform of a Captain in the R.A.M.C., and, as he had predicted, obviously 'fancied himself' in it (he hadn't, it seemed, been able to wangle his majority, as he had hoped a year ago). In my civilian clothes, with a gas-mask slung on a piece of string over my shoulder, I realized that Gerald could still make me feel dim and inferior.

'I shouldn't wonder if it was over by Christmas,' said Gerald (it was the sort of remark that people like Gerald were fond of making at that time). 'By the bye, did you know Teddy Boscombe's been drafted? Oh yes, he went off a week ago – we had a farewell night together. He's probably having the time of his life in Gay Paree by this time . . .' Gerald paused, gave a sudden laugh, and added: 'He always did manage to work a flanker on poor muggins.'

It was Gerald's sole reference to the past during the whole course of the evening, apart from a few scraps of news about his own family (his father had died, his mother was living in a hotel in Devon, Sheila was in the A.T.S.). We drank a good deal of beer, and finished up at one of Gerald's 'low dives' in Soho, where I finally left him in the company of a dubious-looking character to whom, it appeared, he had 'taken a fancy'. Our farewells, when it came to the point, were hurried and perfunctory – 'Cheerioh, ol' boy, see you in Berlin' – and I wouldn't, in the circumstances, have had it otherwise. Yet I realized, rather to my surprise, after I had left him and was walking home, that I should be genuinely sorry if Gerald were killed. It was the first time that I had consciously felt like this about anybody, and it seemed to me that the war, which up till now had existed, so to speak, only on paper, was beginning at last to be less 'phoney' and more actual.

6

Three years later I was drafted to the Middle-East. I had heard almost nothing of Gerald and very little of anybody else during this period. Occasionally I would hear snippets of news about people I had known from Eric Anquetil, who was employed at the Air Ministry. So-and-so was dead, so-and-so was at the Min. of Inf.; Gerald Brockhurst, it appeared, was somewhere in the Middle-East, but Eric didn't know where. Teddy Boscombe had been killed at Dunkirk, and had apparently left a more than adequate provision for his widow.

'Veriny,' Eric wrote, 'seems to be having a pretty good war – I met her at a cocktail-party, surrounded by blond Adonises, and tight as a drum. She has some vague and not too exacting job with E.N.S.A. – "entertaining the troops" (mostly officers, if I know Veriny). She hardly seemed to be pining for the naughty Mr Boscombe, or for poor G. either, for that matter. There's something, I find, peculiarly refreshing about a thoroughgoing and perfectly uninhibited bitch, don't you agree?'

~ ~ ~

In the summer of 1943 I was stationed at Barce, in the green belt of Cyrenaica, whence I managed to get a week's leave to Alexandria; when I returned, I found that my unit had moved up westwards into the 'blue'. Probably, said the R.S.M. of the hospital to which we had been attached, probably it was Tripoli – but he couldn't be sure . . . The next fortnight was spent in a prolonged and rather Kafkaesque hitchhike across the Western Desert: it seemed highly improbable that I should ever reach Tripoli, or that my unit would be there if I did. Nevertheless I managed, in due course, to arrive at my destination, where I was absorbed into an enormous and overcrowded transit-camp. It was just after the Sicily landings, and the camp was in a state of chaos: the intakes during the previous week had been prodigious, and nobody seemed to have the faintest idea what anyone was supposed to do, or – which was more important – where anyone was supposed to go.

I was given a job in the cook-house. The day after my arrival a case of smallpox was reported in the town, and all new intakes were ordered to report immediately to the M.I. Room for vaccination. It was useless to protest that I had been vaccinated only a fortnight before: the M.O. simply refused to listen; so I was duly vaccinated all over again, for the second time in three weeks. Following the smallpox scare, came a craze for F.F.I.s. No less than three times, during my stay in the camp, was I forced to parade before an M.O., stark naked, in order to reassure him that I was not suffering from lice, scabies, gonorrhoea or syphilis. The last of these supererogatory inspections was carried out in particularly uncomfortable conditions; the day was exceptionally hot, a new draft had just arrived, and the M.I. tent, when I reached it, was already crowded with upwards of two-hundred naked, sweating soldiers.

For the benefit of those who have not experienced it, it should be explained that the procedure at an F.F.I. is as follows: other ranks queue up, stripped to the waist, and are examined, one by one (though in most cases rather cursorily) by the M.O. As your name is called, you step smartly forward to where the M.O. is sitting, drop your slacks, and raise your arms above your head as though offering a prayer to the sun (the purpose of this oddly hieratic gesture being, in fact, merely to enable the M.O. to make sure you haven't got crabs under the arm-pits).

I duly queued up; I was becoming accustomed, by now, to this particular form of exhibitionism. The tent was very hot, and I was a long way down the queue; the M.O., however, was plainly wasting no time over the job, and the long straggling line of men moved forward with more than usual rapidity. My turn came sooner than I had expected: I took two steps forward, beyond the flap which screened the M.O.'s table, dropped my trousers down to the ankle, and, like a priest officiating at some pre-Christian rite, raised my arms above my head.

For a moment I noticed nothing; then, glancing with the mildest curiosity at the top of the M.O.'s head, I was struck by something oddly familiar about it. The set of the hair, the particular way the ears projected from the sides of the head – surely this was somebody I had known before, years ago, before the war . . . The M.O. scrutinized conscientiously (though briefly) my pubic hair; then raised his face to the level of my arm-pits. As he did so, our glances met; and I found myself gazing into the eyes of Gerald Brockhurst.

For a moment we stared at one another as if spell-bound; my own surprise was reflected, comically, in the face of Gerald: his mouth fell open, his eyes bulged in helpless astonishment. Suddenly he leaned back in his chair, dropped his arms to his sides, and exclaimed, in a voice which sounded curiously exacerbated, almost angry:

'What the bloody hell are *you* doing here?'

I looked at the lined, weary face: Gerald had grown much thinner, and his hair was now quite grey; yet he still preserved the timeless, 'thirtyish' air which I remembered, and he looked, I thought, extraordinarily young for his age.

'I – well, I suppose I just happen to be here, sir,' I replied. For an instant, a sense of nightmare descended upon me: the heat was intolerable, and suddenly I began to tremble, afraid that I was going to faint.

'But look here,' Gerald rapped out, in the same exacerbated tone, 'what the hell are you *doing* in this outfit? I mean, it *is* you, isn't it?'

'Oh yes,' I replied, in no particular sort of voice, 'I suppose it's me all right.'

Suddenly Gerald leaned forward.

'Look here, I can't talk to you now,' he muttered (the other ranks behind me were becoming restive, and the medical orderly was casting curious glances at us). 'Stay behind afterwards, d'you mind?'

'Very good, sir,' I replied, stolidly, and, pulling up my trousers, shuffled out of the tent.

Afterwards, when the queue had dispersed, I returned, and talked to Gerald while the orderly cleaned up the mess in the M.I. Room.

'But look here,' Gerald kept repeating, 'what the hell are you doing as a private, anyway? Surely you could have got a commission of some sort.'

I assured him that I was perfectly happy where I was.

'But dammit, man, it's all nonsense – you ought to be doing something better than this . . . What *do* you do, anyway?'

I explained that I belonged to a V.D. treatment unit.

'A pox-wallah, eh? My Christ, that beats everything!' Gerald exclaimed, and burst into a violent fit of laughter. As he laughed, his face lost its look of strain and anxiety, and it was the old Gerald who, as his mirth subsided, grinned affectionately at me across the table.

'God, what a bloody awful war this is,' he said; and I noticed that he had suddenly become serious – almost gloomy – again. 'I suppose,' he added quietly, 'you heard about Teddy Boscombe?'

'Yes, I heard he was killed at Dunkirk.'

'It was a damned shame,' Gerald muttered, not looking at me. 'I was fond of Teddy, you know – fonder than I've ever been of anybody, I suppose.' He was silent for a moment, then added, conventionally: 'It's hard luck on Veriny.'

I said nothing: reflecting, sadly, that Teddy's death was not Veriny's tragedy but Gerald's.

'Look here, we must have a chin-wag,' Gerald exclaimed, with sudden briskness. 'The trouble is, though, it's going to be so damned difficult to – I mean, I can't very well ask you round to the mess, and – oh Christ,' – Gerald flung out his arm in a violent, futile gesture – 'what a bloody *hopeless* war this is!'

Suddenly he grinned at me, and held out his cigarette-case.

'You were always a bit of a dark horse, weren't you?' he chuckled. 'Tell me, why didn't you try for a commission?'

'I suppose because I didn't particularly want one,' I answered.

'Yes, but – oh, I dunno: you're probably better off in some ways . . . Being a bloody doctor, I wouldn't have had much choice, anyway . . . I haven't had much of a war, though. See here, can't I talk to you – properly, I mean? Trouble is, this camp is lousy with bloody officers and provost companies and what not . . .' Gerald grinned again, with a boyish embarrassment. 'Of course, I know it's all bullshit, but in a place like this–'

'Oh, that's all right,' I said quickly. 'It's just one of those things . . . Let's meet again after the war – we'll have a date in that pub at Lambeth, where we used to go when you were at Thomas's – d'you remember?'

A happy smile once again overspread Gerald's tired, harassed countenance.

'All right, we'll do just that: I'll keep you up to it . . . I'm expecting to be shifted in a day or two, anyway. By Christ, though, it's a lousy war, isn't it?'

'Yes,' I agreed, 'it's a lousy war.'

We were silent for a moment; and I was aware, in the hot, airless tent, of a sudden feeling of aloofness, as though I were gazing down at our two selves from some remote, Olympian height.

Gerald looked at his watch.

'Well, I suppose I must be pushing off,' he said, and I noticed that his voice had taken on an impersonal, faintly 'official' tinge. Taking the hint, I came to attention and saluted.

Gerald grinned as he returned my salute.

'Cheerioh, old boy,' he said, 'be seeing you sometime.'

I left the tent and walked through the blinding sunlight towards my own quarters.

~ ~ ~

I never kept my date with Gerald in the pub at Lambeth.

A year or two after the war, I happened to go into a bar off the Tottenham Court Road with which I had been familiar in the past. The first person I saw, as I entered, was Bertie Westmacott – older and balder, but with an air of perennial (if somewhat spurious) youthfulness.

He offered me a drink. He was working for the British Council, he told me, and expected soon to be sent to Greece – 'my spiritual home, definitely, my dear'. He was as full of gossip as ever, but I knew so few of the people to whom he referred, that I found his talk tedious. It occurred to me, suddenly, to ask for news of Gerald, of whom I had heard nothing since our meeting in Tripoli.

Bertie's eyes widened with incredulous astonishment.

'But d'you mean to say you haven't *heard*?'

I explained that I had spent the last few weeks in Italy, and had heard no news of anybody.

'Oh my dear, the most *ghastly* affair – splashed all over the *News of the World*, too squalid for *words*. I always *said* Gerald'd come to a sticky end, and *how* right I was.'

I felt my stomach contract with a sudden queasiness: knowing, before I put my next question, what the answer would be.

'Is he dead?' I asked.

Bertie nodded, his face suddenly grave.

'He got into trouble, you see – in Germany. You can guess what *sort* of trouble . . . The details all came out – they were pretty shaming, I must say, and *I'm* no prude, I'd have you know . . . Anyway, he was up for court-martial – under close arrest, and all that – but he must have bribed one of his guards, or something, because he managed to get hold of a service-revolver and blow his brains out. One only hopes that, being a doctor, he made a decent job of it.'

Oddly enough, after that first premonitory spasm, I found that I could feel no genuine emotion whatsoever. I was not really much surprised by the circumstances of Gerald's death, nor did I feel particularly shocked. The Gerald who had died – the ageing, unhappy Army officer – seemed to have so little real connection with the Gerald I had known that I found it all but impossible to connect the two; and the fact that a man bearing the same name had blown out his brains in a prison-cell in Germany, seemed irrelevant and without meaning.

I listened without very much interest as Bertie, with a certain macabre relish, related the details of the case. They were, as he had said, sufficiently squalid, and my curiosity was soon more than satisfied. I interrupted him at last to enquire after Veriny, about whom I had heard almost nothing since before the war.

'But where *can* you have been living?' Bertie exclaimed. 'My dear, she's madly notorious – she married that ghastly steel-millionaire, Vögelkraut, and came over all grand: she won't know *any* of us, nowadays. Stinking with money, of course – but *stinking* . . . Oh yes, young Veriny's done pretty well for herself – one of the hard-faced women who look as though they'd done well out of the war. Though I must say, filthy lucre *quite* apart, I can't think *how* she puts up with old Vögelkraut – bald as a coot, my dear, with at least half-a-dozen chins, and a simply *enormous* tummy. She used to have rather a pretty taste in husbands, after all . . . Poor Teddy – I simply wept *gallons* when he was killed. I never *really* took to Gerald, though – he always seemed to me madly ungay.' Bertie paused, eyeing me with a mild, reminiscent curiosity. 'You and he were rather buddies, at one time, weren't you?'

'Yes,' I said, 'I suppose, in a way, we were.'

I got away at last, and walked down the Tottenham Court Road, through the drenching, blustery weather of an English June; musing, with a remote, unpassionate sadness, upon Time's revenges and all the ruined years.

DONALD WINDHAM

SERVANTS WITH TORCHES

S ergio was thinking.

I am tired of pigeons, he was thinking. I am tired of their red feet
and orange eyes. I am tired of their feathers blowing about the court every
afternoon. I am bored.

He was standing guard at the entrance of the court to the caserma. The
caserma was a pink building on a side street. The court, which was paved
with stones, had a white marble well head in the centre, but nothing else.
At the far end, after lunch, Pancrazio had amused himself by tying a wad
of paper to the cat's back leg with a string and watching the cat run and
roll on its back, playing with the paper ball. And Luigi and Rosario had
amused themselves by hanging a piece of paper on Pancrazio's back while
he was absorbed with the kitten and then igniting the paper. Everyone,
except Sergio, had been amused with the results. He had seen them do
the same thing too many times. He was bored.

I may as well be a portiere, he thought. I did not become a carabiniere
to stand in a doorway all afternoon, or to sit at a table tearing pieces of
paper in half and then tearing the halves in quarters as I did all morning. I

DONALD WINDHAM (born 1920): A native of Atlanta, Windham is the author of five
novels (most notably Dog Star and Two People), memoirs of friends and acquaintances, and
an autobiography, Emblems of Conduct. 'Servants with Torches' is from his story collection,
The Warm Country, for which E. M. Forster wrote an introduction.

would like to do something important, or I would like at least to walk up and down the streets where I can see and be seen.

The court in which he was standing guard was deserted, but only a few feet away, Pancrazio, who was standing guard with him, was sitting in the small dark entrance to the office. Very few people came to the caserma except the carabinieri who worked there. Sometimes, however, tourists who had been robbed came, and Sergio wished that one would come now. He would ask her as many questions, talk to her as long and find out as much as possible before he let her go inside to see an officer who could help her. Pancrazio would not interfere; Pancrazio would only stand and listen. Besides, if the tourist spoke English he would speak English to her and Pancrazio would not understand. But I, Sergio thought, I was a prisoner in an American army camp in North Africa, and I can understand and speak English, which is more than most of the officers can do.

Walking to the small mirror which was stuck on the wall by the door, half concealed by the moulding, he looked at his reflection. In the light of the setting sun which poured through the portal, his skin glowed as though he were made of pink Venetian glass, and his small black moustache was very black and elegant over his mouth. He took off his cap, with its silver insignia of globe and flames, and holding it in one hand, he ran his other hand gently over the surface of his black hair and watched its reflection in the mirror. Then he frowned and thought: The one thing I like about working in the office is that I do not have to wear my cap there. And what I would not like about it if I were stationed outside is that I would have to wear my cap all the time.

He put his cap back on, walked to the portal again, and looked out. Maybe someone interesting was coming toward the caserma now. But only a group of boys passed, their arms about each other's waists, and a pigeon at his feet scurried a little distance away and then looked back expectantly. The street was almost dark, and Sergio felt the beginning of the restlessness which always rose in him as, from pastel day, the city sank to dark and brilliant night.

'Sergio.'

Pancrazio, who had gone into the building and returned, was calling him.

'What do you want?'

'The commissario has just spoken to me. You and I are to stand duty tonight in Campo Sant' Angelo, where there is to be the outdoor opera. Let's go, we must get ready.'

~ ~ ~

When it was dark, the half-moon over San Giorgio silvered the whole sky as though it were a great blue mirror suspended behind the city, and the lights above the piazza were like the many coloured threads of an agate curving across the mirror's surface.

This is the kind of world men should live in, Sergio thought as he stood in the entrance to the crowded square. From the women about him came the luxurious odour of perfume, making him visualise little glass bottles filled with liquids the tints of the lights in the sky, and on the men and women ornaments of gold flashed like the gold ornaments of gondolas. Nowhere did he see any of the poor or even any of the ordinary people of the city; here were only the rich, and among the rich there was nothing to do but to stand and wait.

Pancrazio had bought an ice cream and offered one to Sergio, but he had refused. Even though there was nothing for them to do, until the opera began he felt that it was their duty to stand at attention; so while Pancrazio retired into a corner and ate his ice cream with the firemen who were on duty there as they would have been in a theatre, although there did not seem to be much in the square which could burn, Sergio stood as near to the entrance as he could. The women brushed past him as they entered, some of them wearing jackets of fur, although their arms were bare and white, most of them talking and laughing, their voices as clear and light as the moonlight, and all of them so oblivious of him that he could not help thinking of the pleasure it would be to catch their elbows in his hand, turn them toward him, and smother their laughter, or at least demand, first roughly and then tenderly, why they were laughing. But the idea of disrespect to people of a better class appalled him as much as the other idea pleased him, and he watched silently until the lights dimmed for the opera to begin.

Then Pancrazio came up to him and took his arm, saying:

'Quick, let's go and find a seat before they are all taken.'

The opera was *Otello*, the story of a dark man loved by a fair woman. Sergio was extremely fond of it, and he hurried with Pancrazio and climbed toward the back benches near the electricians' booth, where the remaining free space was rapidly filling with sellers of drinks and candies. But he kept his eyes open for anyone slipping in, and even before they sat down he was watching a boy who had entered and was wandering back and forth through the seats below them. All the lower seats were taken, and as the boy mounted nearer, Sergio saw that he was well dressed, probably a foreigner, and in any case no one for him to question. He turned his attention to the stage, where, there before him, was the isle of Cyprus with the sail of a Venetian ship in the background.

He was aware, however, when the boy sat beside him, for the undivided wooden bench was crowded and the empty space beside Sergio would not comfortably have accommodated even a small child. But he did not object. He wanted to keep his attention on the stage, and he supposed that the boy had paid for a ticket and had more right to the space than he had.

There was no back to the seat, and after a while the boy, leaning back, spread himself out so that one of his hands was beneath Sergio's leg. Sergio had not objected to the boy's crowding him, but he was nevertheless determined not to give up his own space, and he did not move. Apparently the boy also was determined, for though he removed his hand several times he replaced it always in the same position, and it at last occurred to Sergio, in a sensation received together with the swell of the music, that the boy was touching him deliberately, for the pleasure of it. The idea rose in his mind without in the least distracting him from the music. In fact, he was so intent on the opera that it seemed to lessen his feeling of separation from the drama and to bring the music closer to him; and while he sat listening as though he were in the centre of the stage itself, his emotions rising and falling with Verdi's notes, he acted to discover if his idea was true. Not only did he refuse to make room but he pressed back, asserting his presence immovably. Then he turned his head and looked defiantly into the boy's face.

The boy was fair and blue-eyed, his face colder and calmer than an Italian's. But the boy showed no awareness of Sergio and, without removing his eyes from the stage, concealed whatever surprise Sergio had given him by taking a package of cigarettes from his pocket. For a moment Sergio thought that the boy was going to offer him a cigarette. But he did not. After taking one for himself, the boy returned the package to his pocket; and Sergio, seeing that the cigarettes were English, turned away with contempt. The English tourists since the war were notoriously stingy, and he had no use for them. He even thought of telling the boy that smoking was forbidden; but people were smoking all about them, so he turned his attention back to the stage, where Desdemona and the Moor were beginning their duet. Then the boy replaced his hand on the seat, and Sergio, swept away from himself by the music, was brought back again with his realisation of the hand's pressure.

This boy probably has a sister like Desdemona, he thought, only she would be feelingless, the way foreigners are, and would not deign to notice the people her brother comes and sits next to and touches. Or maybe he is travelling with his mother, who would still be young, and she is looking for another husband because his father has died. And if I should marry her and be his father, then I would put the fear of me into him. I would make him tell me what he means and if he often does this sort of thing when he goes out in the evening, and I would threaten to beat him if I found him among people of whom I did not approve. I would tie him in a chair for three days and give him only bread and water to eat. But even as it is, he remembered, I am a carabiniere and I can tell him that he cannot act in this manner in my country, that he must be careful how he acts with me.

For despite the ecstasy of the music, Sergio's awareness of the boy had increased, and it seemed to him that the very palm of the boy's hand was beneath his leg, motionlessly, almost tenderly waiting. The boy was touching him, yet like all foreigners who do not speak and assert themselves, the boy would not acknowledge Sergio and put himself under obligation to him.

Suddenly, Sergio hissed in a whisper:

'What do you want?'

The boy made no sign that he knew Sergio had spoken; but as low as Sergio's voice had been, Pancrazio on the other side of him had heard and asked:

'What, Sergio? What?'

Sergio shushed him and pointed to the stage. But he could not give all of his attention to the music now, as the boy seemed to be doing. If I had touched his sister or mother like that, he thought, when I was a soldier or before when I was a boy like him, they would not have allowed me simply to look as though nothing had happened. Not if I had put my hand on her white thigh. And she would be embarrassed to know that he has put his hand on mine, for I would show her just how he did it. He touched me here, I would say, and touch myself, looking at her. She would have to commit herself then, as he has not. She would have to say: But you are handsome, and because of this you must excuse him. He is a bad boy and

I shall send him to bed. But you must understand that this has happened because you are handsome, and you must excuse him. You must stay and have a glass of wine with me.

As the music ended and the applause drowned out his thoughts, he knew that that was not the way it would happen. But she would think of it, as he had thought of it, and that would please him.

'What did you say?' Pancrazio was asking.

But Sergio did not look at Pancrazio.

'Here,' he said, taking the boy's arm. 'You will have to come with me.'

The boy looked at him indignantly and tried to pull away. Then he said something which Sergio did not understand. But Sergio held on to his arm and repeated his own statement in English.

'Why?' the boy demanded.

'Because I have said so,' Sergio responded. 'And I am a carabiniere.'

And turning to Pancrazio, he added in Italian:

'Take his other arm.'

'Why?' Pancrazio asked.

'Do as I tell you,' Sergio told him. 'This is important.'

His tone was authoritative, and Pancrazio obeyed. Awkwardly, the three of them started down the steps, the boy in the middle, not resisting but not easily able to step from tier to tier of the seats with Sergio holding him in front and Pancrazio behind. When they reached the level of the piazza, Sergio said in English:

'Show me your documents.'

'What?'

'Your documents. Documents.'

'I don't have any documents,' the boy said. 'I'm not an Italian.'

'Then show me your passport.'

'I don't have my passport with me. Why should I?'

The boy tried to pull his arm away again, but Sergio held on to him.

'Where is your passport?' he asked.

'At the hotel.'

'What hotel?'

'I don't remember the name.'

Sergio became indignant.

'Do you tell me that you do not know where you live?'

'Certainly I know where I live,' the boy said. 'I can find my way there, but I do not remember the name.'

'With whom do you live in the hotel?' Sergio asked. 'Your father and mother?'

'I don't have to tell you all these things,' the boy replied. 'What have I done that's wrong? You have no right to treat me this way.'

'Perhaps you are staying with your sister,' Sergio suggested.

'I don't have to tell you with whom I am staying,' the boy insisted. 'What have I done that's wrong?'

Nearly everyone in the crowd was pouring obliviously toward the exit, but a few people around them were watching, and Sergio thought: This will be a good thing for me to report. If the commissario is here he will be pleased. He does not like foreigners who get in trouble like this, even with boys of the streets, and if they come to the caserma he laughs at them behind their backs. But I must do everything correctly.

'You watch him while I go and see if the commissario is on duty here,' he said to Pancrazio. 'I will be back soon.'

'Very well,' Pancrazio answered.

But Sergio had gone only a few steps when he heard Pancrazio shout, and turning around he saw that the boy had broken away and was running through the crowd toward the exit. He began to run also, knocking people from his path, and before the boy managed to reach the exit Sergio overtook him and grabbed hold of the arm of his jacket. The jacket tore, and the boy, the momentum of his run broken by the carabiniere's sudden grasp, swung around toward him with his feet completely off the ground and crashed against his body. The two of them stood close together and gasping. Pancrazio ran up and jerked the boy out of Sergio's grasp.

'Idiot!' Sergio cried, and slapped Pancrazio's hand from the boy's arm. 'If it had been up to you the boy would have escaped. I will take care of him from now on.'

Dragging the boy with him, he started toward the exit. But the boy fought back with anger.

'Look what you have done to my coat,' he shouted. 'You've torn my coat. What right have you to tear my coat? I haven't done anything wrong.'

Sergio stopped, also angry at the unfavourable attention which was beginning to centre on them, and demanded:

'No? If you had not done anything wrong, then why did you run?'

'Who wouldn't run,' the boy demanded, 'with a lot of carabinieri dragging him around and threatening to arrest him?'

'Very well,' Sergio said. 'But you must show your passport to a carabiniere when he asks to see it.'

The boy said nothing more; and Sergio, motioning for Pancrazio to follow, led the way alongside the strip of rough white cloth which was stretched at the back of the seats to screen off the view of the opera from passersby, and out into the narrow space between the cloth and the iron railing of the bridge which ran up and down several steps into a narrow street of closed shops. For a moment the three of them were only three more dark shapes in the crowd jamming its way through the narrow passage. Then they passed the aromatic stream of light from the open door of a pastry shop, on the sill of which a white cat was sitting, and came out into a long bright square filled with cafés and hung with paper lanterns. Sergio looked at the boy again, and even in the reflection of the coloured lanterns, curved in bright agate lines across the blue glass sky which roofed the crowded cafés, he could see that the boy was frightened and pale. He appeared even younger than Sergio had thought him, and despite his rather haughty coldness he had an air of nurtured innocence. Even with his jacket torn, he looked rich. He was wearing a beautiful shirt and tie.

They were almost to the middle of the square when someone called and the boy stopped. Sergio was alert, ready to grab the boy if he tried to escape again. But the boy merely stood where he was.

'Where are you going?' a man seated at an outdoor table of a café called to him.

'To the hotel with these carabinieri,' the boy replied. 'They say they are going to arrest me.'

'Oh, Christ, how stupid,' the man said. 'I'll come with you.'

And turning to the other person at the table, he added:

'You pay, please; I'm going with him.'

Hurriedly, the man rose from the table and joined them. He walked on the outside of Sergio and spoke across him to the boy. They spoke so rapidly that Sergio could not understand what they were saying, and he did not like the man's coming with them. The man was not old enough to be the boy's father, and it was the boy's family that he wanted to encounter.

At the middle of the square they turned into another dark passage, which led up and down over several bridges. The man, who spoke fair Italian, demanded of Sergio:

'What has my friend done that is wrong?'

'He behaved to me in a most insulting manner,' Sergio replied. 'He touched my leg with his hand.'

'Yes, but that is only an accident,' the man said. 'What is wrong with that?'

'You do not understand,' Sergio replied indignantly. 'He felt my leg, like this.'

And he improvised the most indecent gesture he could conceive.

'He says that you groped him,' the man said across Sergio to the boy.

'Then he's a liar,' the boy replied.

'Do you understand?' Sergio demanded.

'Yes, I understand,' the man said flatly. 'Well?'

'You may do things like that where you come from,' Sergio said with contempt, 'but we do not behave that way toward carabinieri in Italy.'

'In the first place,' the man replied, 'my friend says that he did not do what you said that he did. And in the second, even if he did, it isn't against the law to touch someone, as far as I know.'

'Your friend says that he did not touch me?' Sergio asked incredulously.

'Yes.'

'And I say that he did touch me. And my word is worth more than his.'

'Nevertheless,' the man replied, 'I believe him.'

'But I am a carabiniere. I am the law.'

'That is not my fault,' the man said.

'In your country do you not believe the word of the law?'

'I believe the word of whoever speaks the truth,' the man said smugly.

'Ha,' Sergio cried, 'and that is what I believe, also.'

They had arrived at the entrance of one of the most elegant hotels, and the boy stopped, bringing the others to a halt around him.

'Is this where you live?' Sergio demanded.

'Yes,' the boy answered.

'Very well, let us go inside.'

The lobby was enormous. The floors were of polished marble, the walls were hung with silks and decorated with great glass figures of gondoliers and masqueraders surrounded by exotic flowers. Sergio allowed the two foreigners to enter before him, then he followed, leaving Pancrazio to come behind. The lobby was empty except for a few employees in the distance and the portiere, who hurried from the desk to meet them as they entered. Sergio was impressed by the size and beauty of the hotel, in which he had never been before; but without allowing the foreigners to speak, he ordered the portiere to bring the key to the boy's room. When the portiere brought the key, Sergio saw with annoyance that the man accepted it. He had expected the boy to go up and return with his mother.

'It is the boy's passport that I want,' he said.

'Yes,' the man replied. 'I will bring it.'

'Go with him,' Sergio instructed Pancrazio, 'and have him bring his passport also.'

When they were gone Sergio removed his cap, and holding it in one hand, he smoothed his hair with the other. Then he put his cap under his arm and crossed to the portiere's desk.

'Show me the register,' he said. 'Is this boy with his family?'

'No,' the portiere replied. 'The two gentlemen are alone.'

Sergio turned the ledger around so that he could read it and looked across the column from the two names which the portiere pointed out. Under nationality he read: American.

'But they are not American,' he said. 'They are English.'

'No, they are American,' the portiere said. 'They have American passports.'

With a feeling more of unhappiness than of annoyance, Sergio turned and walked to the boy, who was standing in the middle of the lobby and watching him.

'You are American?' he asked.

'Certainly,' the boy replied. 'Isn't that why you are trying to make trouble for me? Because you are a communist and do not like Americans?'

'I am not a communist,' Sergio replied, 'and I like Americans very much. Our government is very friendly to Americans. Besides, I was a prisoner with the Americans in North Africa and they were very good to me.'

'Then maybe you don't like Americans because you were a prisoner of war,' the boy said. 'But you don't like us. I like the Italians, but you don't like us.'

'Ah, yes,' Sergio said sentimentally. 'You like the Italians too much.'

'Not any more,' the boy replied.

The elevator door opened. The man came across the lobby toward them, followed by Pancrazio, to whom Sergio held out his hand for the passports.

'He has them,' Pancrazio said, indicating the man. 'He would not give them to me.'

Sergio turned to the man, who gave him the passports. They were American. Sergio looked at the photographs and at the man and boy in turn. He did not know what to look for next, for although he could speak English he could not read it. Then he remembered the permesso di soggiorno, the police permit which all foreigners must have.

'Your permesso di soggiorno,' he said.

Without hesitating the man handed him the two folded papers which he was already holding in his hand.

With these Sergio knew what to look for, and he read them carefully while the others, aggregated now by a group of hotel employees at a short distance, stood and waited. He read on, hardly interested in what he was reading, wishing that there was some pleasant way in which the whole affair could be ended. Then, with an intense focusing of his attention, he realised that one of the permits was expired.

'Whose is this?' he asked, holding it out.

'Mine,' the man replied.

'It is expired,' Sergio said. 'It has been expired almost a month.'

'Yes, I know,' the man answered. 'I have requested a renewal, but it has not arrived yet.'

Sergio looked at the paper for several minutes, while everyone waited. It was not merely possible, it was proper now for him to take the man to the caserma, but he felt disinclined to do so.

'I am afraid I shall have to take you to the caserma,' he said.

'Why?' the man demanded. 'I have applied for a renewal.'

'It does not say here that a renewal has been applied for,' Sergio said, examining the piece of paper again.

'That is not my fault,' the man objected. 'I applied for it, and that is all that I can do. If I am to be taken anywhere, I wish to telephone the American consul first.'

'Excuse me, but that cannot be permitted,' Sergio said quickly. 'Besides, the consul's office would be closed now.'

'Very well, if he takes me away you telephone the American consul at his home and tell him what has happened, do you understand?' the man said to the boy.

Then, turning to the portiere, he added:

'And if he takes us both with him, I want you to telephone the

American consul for us and to continue telephoning until you receive an answer.'

'Yes, sir,' the portiere replied.

'Two minutes, please,' Sergio said.

Going into the corner of the lobby, away from the others, he called Pancrazio to him.

'This is a very complicated situation,' he began.

'Yes,' Pancrazio said.

'Yes, a very complicated situation,' Sergio repeated. 'One of the Americans has a permesso di soggiorno which is expired, but he has requested a renewal. It would be regular to take him to the commissario and report this, but I have already frightened both of the foreigners so much that I do not want to frighten them any more. After all, our government is friendly to the Americans and the E.R.P., and if we take them to the office we will have to report the other American's incivility to me and that will be most unpleasant for them. On the other hand, if we do not take them we must not mention the expired permesso di soggiorno. If we are asked, we must say that we examined the foreigners' documents and that they are in order. Do you understand?'

'Yes, I understand,' Pancrazio said.

'Very well. Then, if I do what I think is best and most civil to the foreigners, you will not say anything at the caserma which will get us into trouble with the commissario?'

'No, I will not say anything which will get us into trouble,' Pancrazio agreed.

'Very well.'

With an air of decision, Sergio returned to the group in the middle of the lobby.

'How long will you remain in Venice?' he asked the man.

'We intend to leave tomorrow,' the man replied.

'And where will you go?'

'To Rome, where I am staying.'

'Ah, in that case,' Sergio said happily, 'the matter of your permesso di soggiorno should be taken up there. If you will be sure to report to the Questura in Rome when you return and inquire if your renewal has been made, that will be all that is necessary.'

'Thank you,' the man said.

'And the other matter,' Sergio conceded, 'I will be willing to forget.'

'Thank you,' the man said.

'What about my coat that he tore?' the boy asked crossly. 'Is he just going to forget that too?'

'Really,' the man said. 'Let him go. Don't you know when you are well off?'

~ ~ ~

Out in the dark street again, Sergio heard the chimes of a nearby church ringing the hour. The half-moon was higher and smaller in the sky. Sergio turned back in the direction from which they had come and led the way toward the square in which the opera was being performed. Pancrazio walked at his side, waiting for him to say something, but he did not say anything. He was thinking.

It was very clever of me to be kind to them, he was thinking; it is better for everyone that way. But already he regretted that everything had not happened differently from the beginning. I am tired of nights at half-moon, he thought. I am bored with events which never come to a climax. I am bored with these dark narrow streets, up and down bridges. I am bored with these stupid pigeons. I hope that we get back to the opera in time to see Otello strangle Desdemona.

GRAHAM GREENE

MAY WE BORROW YOUR HUSBAND?

1

I never heard her called anything else but Poopy, either by her husband or by the two men who became their friends. Perhaps I was a little in love with her (absurd though that may seem at my age) because I found that I resented the name. It was unsuited to someone so young and so open – too open; she belonged to the age of trust just as I belonged to the age of cynicism. 'Good old Poopy' – I even heard her called that by the elder of the two interior-decorators (who had known her no longer than I had): a sobriquet which might have been good enough for some vague bedraggled woman of middle age who drank a bit too much but who was useful to drag around as a kind of blind – and those two certainly needed a blind. I once asked the girl her real name, but all she said was, 'Everyone calls me Poopy,' as though that finished it, and I was afraid of appearing too square if I pursued the question further – too middle-aged perhaps as well, so though I hate the name whenever I write it down, Poopy she has to remain: I have no other.

I had been at Antibes working on a book of mine, a biography of the

GRAHAM GREENE (1904–1991): It is Greene's arch humor and unblinkered apprehension of human deceit that give his novels and short stories – among the best of them The Quiet American, The Heart of the Matter, *and* The Power and the Glory – *their power to move. The brutal yet curiously touching 'May We Borrow Your Husband?' was made into a film with Dirk Bogarde in the role of the narrator.*

seventeenth-century poet, the Earl of Rochester, for more than a month before Poopy and her husband arrived. I had come there as soon as the full season was over, to a small ugly hotel by the sea not far from the ramparts, and I was able to watch the season depart with the leaves in the Boulevard Général Leclerc. At first, even before the trees had begun to drop, the foreign cars were on the move homeward. A few weeks earlier, I had counted fourteen nationalities, including Morocco, Turkey, Sweden and Luxembourg, between the sea and the Place de Gaulle, to which I walked every day for the English papers. Now all the foreign number-plates had gone, except for the Belgian and the German and an occasional English one, and, of course, the ubiquitous number-plates of the State of Monaco. The cold weather had come early and Antibes catches only the morning sun – good enough for breakfast on the terrace, but it was safer to lunch indoors or the shadow might overtake the coffee. A cold and solitary Algerian was always there, leaning over the ramparts, looking for something, perhaps safety.

It was the time of year I liked best, when Juan les Pins becomes as squalid as a closed fun-fair with Lunar Park boarded up and cards marked *Fermeture Annuelle* outside the Pam-Pam and Maxim's, and the Concours International Amateur de Striptease at the Vieux Colombiers is over for another season. Then Antibes comes into its own as a small country town with the Auberge de Provence full of local people and old men sit indoors drinking beer or pastis at the *glacier* in the Place de Gaulle. The small garden, which forms a roundabout on the ramparts, looks a little sad with the short stout palms bowing their brown fronds; the sun in the morning shines without any glare, and the few white sails move gently on the unblinding sea.

You can always trust the English to stay on longer than others into the autumn. We have a blind faith in the southern sun and we are taken by surprise when the wind blows icily over the Mediterranean. Then a bickering war develops with the hotel-keeper over the heating on the third floor, and the tiles strike cold underfoot. For a man who has reached the age when all he wants is some good wine and some good cheese and a little work, it is the best season of all. I know how I resented the arrival of the interior-decorators just at the moment when I had hoped to be the only foreigner left, and I prayed that they were birds of passage. They arrived before lunch in a scarlet Sprite – a car much too young for them, and they wore elegant sports clothes more suited to spring at the Cap. The elder man was nearing fifty and the grey hair that waved over his ears was too uniform to be true: the younger had passed thirty and his hair was as black as the other's was grey. I knew their names were Stephen and Tony before they even reached the reception desk, for they had clear, penetrating yet superficial voices, like their gaze, which had quickly lighted on me where I sat with a Ricard on the terrace and registered that I had nothing of interest for them, and passed on. They were not arrogant: it was simply that they were more concerned with each other, and yet perhaps, like a married couple of some years' standing, not very profoundly.

I soon knew a great deal about them. They had rooms side by side in my passage, though I doubt if both rooms were often occupied, for I used to hear voices from one room or the other most evenings when I went to bed. Do I seem too curious about other people's affairs? But in my own defence I have to say that the events of this sad little comedy were forced by all the participants on my attention. The balcony where I worked every morning on my life of Rochester overhung the terrace where the interior-decorators took their coffee, and even when they occupied a table out of sight those clear elocutionary voices mounted up to me. I didn't want to hear them; I wanted to work. Rochester's relations with the actress, Mrs. Barry, were my concern at the moment, but it is almost impossible in a foreign land not to listen to one's own tongue. French I could have accepted as a kind of background noise, but I could not fail to overhear English.

'My dear, guess who's written to me now?'

'Alec?'

'No, Mrs. Clarenty.'

'What does the old hag want?'

'She objects to the mural in her bedroom.'

'But, Stephen, it's divine. Alec's never done anything better. The dead faun . . .'

'I think she wants something more nubile and less necrophilous.'

'The old lecher.'

They were certainly hardy, those two. Every morning around eleven they went bathing off the little rocky peninsula opposite the hotel – they had the autumnal Mediterranean, so far as the eye could see, entirely to themselves. As they walked briskly back in their elegant bikinis, or some-times ran a little way for warmth, I had the impression that they took their bathes less for pleasure than for exercise – to preserve the slim legs, the flat stomachs, the narrow hips for more recondite and Etruscan pastimes.

Idle they were not. They drove the Sprite to Cagnes, Vence, St. Paul, to any village where an antique store was to be rifled, and they brought back with them objects of olive wood, spurious old lanterns, painted religious figures which in the shop would have seemed to me ugly or banal, but which I suspect already fitted in their imaginations some scheme of decoration the reverse of commonplace. Not that their minds were altogether on their profession. They relaxed.

I encountered them one evening in a little sailors' bar in the old port of Nice. Curiosity this time had led me in pursuit, for I had seen the scarlet Sprite standing outside the bar. They were entertaining a boy of about eighteen who, from his clothes, I imagine worked as a hand on the boat to Corsica which was at the moment in harbour. They both looked very sharply at me when I entered, as though they were thinking, 'Have we misjudged him?' I drank a glass of beer and left, and the younger said 'Good evening' as I passed the table. After that we had to greet each other every day in the hotel. It was as though I had been admitted to an intimacy.

Time for a few days was hanging as heavily on my hands as on Lord Rochester's. He was staying at Mrs. Fourcard's baths in Leather Lane, receiving mercury treatment for the pox, and I was awaiting a whole section of my notes which I had inadvertently left in London. I couldn't release him till they came, and my sole distraction for a few days was those two. As they packed themselves into the Sprite of an afternoon or an evening I liked to guess from their clothes the nature of their excursion. Always elegant, they were yet successful, by the mere exchange of one *tricot* for another, in indicating their mood: they were just as well dressed in the sailors' bar, but a shade more simply; when dealing with a Lesbian antique dealer at St. Paul, there was a masculine dash about their handker-chiefs. Once they disappeared altogether for the inside of a week in what I took to be their oldest clothes, and when they returned the older man had a contusion on his right cheek. They told me they had been over to Corsica. Had they enjoyed it? I asked.

'Quite barbaric,' the young man Tony said, but not, I thought, in praise.

He saw me looking at Stephen's cheek, and he added quickly, 'We had an accident in the mountains.'

It was two days after that, just at sunset, that Poopy arrived with her husband. I was back at work on Rochester, sitting in an overcoat on my balcony, when a taxi drove up – I recognized the driver as someone who plied regularly from Nice airport. What I noticed first, because the passengers were still hidden, was the luggage, which was bright blue and of an astonishing newness. Even the initials – rather absurdly PT – shone like newly-minted coins. There were a large suitcase and a small suitcase and a hat-box, all of the same cerulean hue, and after that a respectable old leather case totally unsuited to air travel, the kind one inherits from a father, with half a label still left from Shepheard's Hotel or the Valley of the Kings. Then the passenger emerged and I saw Poopy for the first time. Down below, the interior-decorators were watching too, and drinking Dubonnet.

She was a very tall girl, perhaps five feet nine, very slim, very young, with hair the colour of conkers, and her costume was as new as the luggage. She said, '*Finalmente*,' looking at the undistinguished façade with an air of rapture – or perhaps it was only the shape of her eyes. When I saw the young man I felt certain they were just married; it wouldn't have surprised me if confetti had fallen out from the seams of their clothes. They were like a photograph in the *Tatler*; they had camera smiles for each other and an underlying nervousness. I was sure they had come straight from the reception, and that it had been a smart one, after a proper church wedding.

They made a very handsome couple as they hesitated a moment before going up the steps to the reception. The long beam of the Phare de la Garoupe brushed the water behind them, and the floodlighting went suddenly on outside the hotel as if the manager had been waiting for their arrival to turn it up. The two decorators sat there without drinking, and I noticed that the elder one had covered the contusion on his cheek with a very clean white handkerchief. They were not, of course, looking at the girl but at the boy. He was over six feet tall and as slim as the girl, with a face that might have been cut on a coin, completely handsome and completely dead – but perhaps that was only an effect of his nerves. His clothes, too, I thought, had been bought for the occasion, the sports-jacket with a double slit and the grey trousers cut a little narrowly to show off the long legs. It seemed to me that they were both too young to marry – I doubt if they had accumulated forty-five years between them – and I had a wild impulse to lean over the balcony and warn them away – 'Not this hotel. Any hotel but this.' Perhaps I could have told them that the heating was insufficient or the hot water erratic or the food terrible, not that the English care much about food, but of course they would have paid me no attention – they were so obviously 'booked,' and what an ageing lunatic I should have appeared in their eyes. ('One of those eccentric English types one finds abroad' – I could imagine the letter home.) This was the first time I wanted to interfere, and I didn't know them at all. The second time it was already too late, but I think I shall always regret that I did not give way to that madness . . .

It had been the silence and attentiveness of those two down below which had frightened me, and the patch of white handkerchief hiding the shameful contusion. For the first time I heard the hated name: 'Shall we see the room, Poopy, or have a drink first?'

They decided to see the room, and the two glasses of Dubonnet clicked again into action.

I think she had more idea of how a honeymoon should be conducted than he had, because they were not seen again that night.

2

I was late for breakfast on the terrace, but I noticed that Stephen and Tony were lingering longer than usual. Perhaps they had decided at last that it was too cold for a bathe; I had the impression, however, that they were lying in wait. They had never been so friendly to me before, and I wondered whether perhaps they regarded me as a kind of cover, with my distressingly normal appearance. My table for some reason that day had been shifted and was out of the sun, so Stephen suggested that I should join theirs: they would be off in a moment, after one more cup . . . The contusion was much less noticeable today, but I think he had been applying powder.

'You staying here long?' I asked them, conscious of how clumsily I constructed a conversation compared with their easy prattle.

'We had meant to leave tomorrow,' Stephen said, 'but last night we changed our minds.'

'Last night?'

'It was such a beautiful day, wasn't it? "Oh," I said to Tony, "surely we can leave poor dreary old London a little longer?" It has an awful staying power – like a railway sandwich.'

'Are your clients so patient?'

'My dear, the clients? You never in your life saw such atrocities as we get from Brompton Square. It's always the same. People who pay others to decorate for them have ghastly taste themselves.'

'You do the world a service then. Think what we might suffer without you. In Brompton Square.'

Tony giggled. 'I don't know how we'd stand it if we had not our private jokes. For example, in Mrs. Clarenty's case, we've installed what we call the Loo of Lucullus.'

'She was enchanted,' Stephen said.

'The most obscene vegetable forms. It reminded me of a harvest festival.'

They suddenly became very silent and attentive, watching somebody over my shoulder. I looked back. It was Poopy, all by herself. She stood there, waiting for the boy to show her which table she could take, like a new girl at school who doesn't know the rules. She even seemed to be wearing a school uniform: very tight trousers, slit at the ankle – but she hadn't realized that the summer term was over. She had dressed up like that, I felt certain, so as not to be noticed, in order to hide herself, but there were only two other women on the terrace and they were both wearing sensible tweed skirts. She looked at them nostalgically as the waiter led her past our table to one nearer the sea. Her long legs moved awkwardly in the pants as though they felt exposed.

'The young bride,' Tony said.

'Deserted already,' Stephen said with satisfaction.

'Her name is Poopy Travis, you know.'

'It's an extraordinary name to choose. She couldn't have been *christened* that way, unless they found a very liberal vicar.'

'He is called Peter. Of an undefined occupation. Not Army, I think, do you?'

'Oh no, not Army. Something to do with land perhaps – there's an agreeable *herbal* smell about him.'

'You seem to know nearly all there is to know,' I said.

'We looked at their police *carnet* before dinner.'

'I have an idea,' Tony said, 'that PT hardly represents their activities last night.' He looked across the tables at the girl with an expression extraordinarily like hatred.

'We were both taken,' Stephen said, 'by the air of innocence. One felt he was more used to horses.'

'He mistook the yearnings of the rider's crotch for something quite different.'

Perhaps they hoped to shock me, but I don't think it was that. I really believe they were in a state of extreme sexual excitement; they had received a *coup de foudre* last night on the terrace and were quite incapable of disguising their feelings. I was an excuse to talk, to speculate about the desired object. The sailor had been a stop-gap: this was the real thing. I was inclined to be amused, for what could this absurd pair hope to gain from a young man newly married to the girl who now sat there patiently waiting, wearing her beauty like an old sweater she had forgotten to change? But that was a bad simile to use: she would have been afraid to wear an old sweater, except secretly, by herself, in the playroom. She had no idea that she was one of those who can afford to disregard the fashion of their clothes. She caught my eye and, because I was so obviously English, I suppose, gave me half a timid smile. Perhaps I too would have received the *coup de foudre* if I had not been thirty years older and twice married.

Tony detected the smile. 'A regular body-snatcher,' he said. My breakfast and the young man arrived at the same moment before I had time to reply. As he passed the table I could feel the tension.

'*Cuir de Russie*,' Stephen said, quivering a nostril. 'A mistake of inexperience.'

The youth caught the words as he went past and turned with an astonished look to see who had spoken, and they both smiled insolently back at him as though they really believed they had the power to take him over . . .

For the first time I felt disquiet.

3

Something was not going well; that was sadly obvious. The girl nearly always came down to breakfast ahead of her husband – I have an idea he spent a long time bathing and shaving and applying his *Cuir de Russie*. When he joined her he would give her a courteous brotherly kiss as though they had not spent the night together in the same bed. She began to have those shadows under the eyes which come from lack of sleep – for I couldn't believe that they were the 'lineaments of gratified desire.' Sometimes from my balcony I saw them returning from a walk – nothing, except perhaps a pair of horses, could have been more handsome. His gentleness towards her might have reassured her mother, but it made a man impatient to see him squiring her across the undangerous road, holding open doors, following a pace behind her like the husband of a princess. I longed to see some outbreak of irritation caused by the sense of satiety, but they never seemed to be in conversation when they returned from their walk, and at table I caught only the kind of phrases people use who are dining together for the sake of politeness. And yet I could swear that she loved him, even by the way she avoided watching him. There was nothing avid or starved about her; she stole her quick glances when she was quite certain that his attention was absorbed elsewhere – they were tender, anxious perhaps, quite undemanding. If one inquired after him when he wasn't there, she glowed with the pleasure of using his name. 'Oh, Peter overslept this morning.' 'Peter cut himself. He's staunching the blood now.' 'Peter's mislaid his tie. He thinks the floor-waiter has purloined it.' Certainly she loved him; I was far less certain of what his feelings were.

And you must imagine how all the time those other two were closing in. It was like a medieval siege: they dug their trenches and threw up their earthworms. The difference was that the besieged didn't notice what they were at – at any rate, the girl didn't, I don't know about him. I longed to warn her, but what could I have said that wouldn't have shocked her or angered her? I believe the two would have changed their floor if that would have helped to bring them closer to the fortress; they probably discussed the move together and decided against it as too overt.

Because they knew that I could do nothing against them, they regarded me almost in the role of an ally. After all, I might be useful one day in distracting the girl's attention – and I suppose they were not quite mistaken in that; they could tell from the way I looked at her how interested I was, and they probably calculated that my interests might in the long run coincide with theirs. It didn't occur to them that, perhaps, I was a man with scruples. If one really wanted a thing scruples were obviously, in their eyes, out of place. There was a tortoiseshell star mirror at St Paul they were plotting to obtain for half the price demanded (I think there was an old mother who looked after the shop when her daughter was away at a *boîte* for women of a certain taste); naturally, therefore, when I looked at the girl, as they saw me so often do, they considered I would be ready to join in any 'reasonable' scheme.

'When I looked at the girl' – I realize that I have made no real attempt to describe her. In writing a biography one can, of course, just insert a portrait and the affair is done: I have the prints of Lady Rochester and

Mrs. Barry in front of me now. But speaking as a professional novelist (for biography and reminiscence are both new forms to me), one describes a woman not so much that the reader should see her in all the cramping detail of colour and shape (how often Dickens's elaborate portraits seem like directions to the illustrator which might well have been left out of the finished book), but to convey an emotion. Let the reader make his own image of a wife, a mistress, some passer-by 'sweet and kind' (the poet required no other descriptive words), if he has a fancy to. If I were to describe the girl (I can't bring myself at this moment to write her hateful name), it would be not to convey the colour of her hair, the shape of her mouth, but to express the pleasure and the pain with which I recall her – I, the writer, the observer, the subsidiary character, what you will. But if I didn't bother to convey them to her, why should I bother to convey them to you, *hypocrite lecteur*?

How quickly those two tunnelled. I don't think it was more than four mornings after the arrival that, when I came down to breakfast, I found they had moved their table next to the girl's and were entertaining her in her husband's absence. They did it very well; it was the first time I had seen her relaxed and happy – and she was happy because she was talking about Peter. Peter was agent for his father, somewhere in Hampshire – there were three thousand acres to manage. Yes, he was fond of riding and so was she. It all tumbled out – the kind of life she dreamed of having when she returned home. Stephen just dropped in a word now and then, of a rather old-fashioned courteous interest, to keep her going. Apparently he had once decorated some hall in their neighbourhood and knew the names of some people Peter knew – Winstanley, I think – and that gave her immense confidence.

'He's one of Peter's best friends,' she said, and the two flickered their eyes at each other like lizards' tongues.

'Come and join us, William,' Stephen said, but only when he had noticed that I was within earshot. 'You know Mrs. Travis?'

How could I refuse to sit at their table? And yet in doing so I seemed to become an ally.

'Not *the* William Harris?' the girl asked. It was a phrase which I hated, and yet she transformed even that, with her air of innocence. For she had a capacity to make everything new: Antibes became a discovery and we were the first foreigners to have made it. When she said, 'Of course, I'm afraid I haven't actually *read* any of your books,' I heard the over-familiar remark for the first time; it even seemed to me a proof of her honesty – I nearly wrote her virginal honesty. 'You must know an awful lot about people,' she said, and again I read into the banality of the remark an appeal – for help against whom, those two or the husband who at that moment appeared on the terrace? He had the same nervous air as she, even the same shadows under the lids, so that they might have been taken by a stranger, as I wrote before, for brother and sister. He hesitated a moment when he saw all of us there and she called across to him, 'Come and meet these nice people, darling.' He didn't look any too pleased, but he sat glumly down and asked whether the coffee was still hot.

'I'll order some more, darling. They know the Winstanleys, and this is *the* William Harris.'

He looked at me blankly; I think he was wondering if I had anything to do with tweeds.

'I hear you like horses,' Stephen said, 'and I was wondering whether you and your wife would come to lunch with us at Cagnes on Saturday. That's tomorrow, isn't it? There's a very good racecourse at Cagnes . . .'

'I don't know,' he said dubiously, looking to his wife for a clue.

'But, darling, of course we must go. You'd love it.'

His face cleared instantly. I really believe he had been troubled by a social scruple: the question whether one accepts invitations on a honey-moon. 'It's very good of you,' he said, 'Mr. . . . .'

'Let's start as we mean to go on. I'm Stephen and this is Tony.'

'I'm Peter.' He added a trifle gloomily, 'And this is Poopy.'

'Tony, you take Poopy in the Sprite, and Peter and I will go by *autobus*.' (I had the impression, and I think Tony had too, that Stephen had gained a point.)

'You'll come too, Mr. Harris?' the girl asked, using my surname as though she wished to emphasize the difference between me and them.

'I'm afraid I can't. I'm working against time.'

I watched them that evening from my balcony as they returned from Cagnes and, hearing the way they all laughed together, I thought, 'The enemy are within the citadel: it's only a question of time.' A lot of time, because they proceeded very carefully, those two. There was no question of a quick grab which I suspect had caused the contusion in Corsica.

4

It became a regular habit with the two of them to entertain the girl during her solitary breakfast before her husband arrived. I never sat at their table again, but scraps of the conversation would come over to me, and it seemed to me that she was never quite so cheerful again. Even the sense of novelty had gone. I heard her say once, 'There's so little to do here,' and it struck me as an odd observation for a honeymooner to make.

Then one evening I found her in tears outside the Musée Grimaldi. I had been fetching my papers, and, as my habit was, I made a round by the Place Nationale with the pillar erected in 1819 to celebrate – a remarkable paradox – the loyalty of Antibes to the monarchy and her resistance to *les Troupes Etrangères*, who were seeking to re-establish the monarchy. Then, according to rule, I went on by the market and the old port and Lou-Lou's restaurant up the ramp towards the cathedral and the Musée, and there in the grey evening light, before the street-lamps came on, I found her crying under the cliff of the château.

I noticed too late what she was at or I wouldn't have said, 'Good evening, Mrs Travis.' She jumped a little as she turned and dropped her handkerchief, and when I picked it up I found it soaked with tears – it was like holding a small drowned animal in my hand. I said, 'I'm sorry,' meaning that I was sorry to have startled her, but she took it in quite another sense. She said, 'Oh, I'm being silly, that's all. It's just a mood. Everybody has moods, don't they?'

'Where's Peter?'

'He's in the museum with Stephen and Tony looking at the Picassos. I don't understand them a bit.'

'That's nothing to be ashamed of. Lots of people don't.'

'But Peter doesn't understand them either. I know he doesn't. He's just pretending to be interested.'

'Oh well . . .'

'And it's not that either. I pretended for a time too, to please Stephen. But he's pretending just to get away from me.'

'You are imagining things.'

Punctually at five o'clock the *phare* lit up, but it was still too light to see the beam.

I said, 'The museum will be closing now.'

'Walk back with me to the hotel.'

'Wouldn't you like to wait for Peter?'

'I don't smell, do I?' she asked miserably.

'Well, there's a trace of Arpège. I've always liked Arpège.'

'How terribly experienced you sound.'

'Not really. It's just that my first wife used to buy Arpège.'

We began walking back, and the mistral bit our ears and gave her an excuse when the time came for the reddened eyes.

She said, 'I think Antibes so sad and grey.'

'I thought you enjoyed it here.'

'Oh, for a day or two.'

'Why not go home?'

'It would look odd, wouldn't it, returning early from a honeymoon?'

'Or go on to Rome – or somewhere. You can get a plane to most places from Nice.'

'It wouldn't make any difference,' she said. 'It's not the place that's wrong, it's me.'

'I don't understand.'

'He's not happy with me. It's as simple as that.'

She stopped opposite one of the little rock houses by the ramparts. Washing hung down over the street below and there was a cold-looking canary in a cage.

'You said yourself . . . a mood . . .'

'It's not his fault,' she said. 'It's me. I expect it seems very stupid to you, but I never slept with anyone before I married.' She gulped miserably at the canary.

'And Peter?'

'He's terribly sensitive,' she said, and added quickly, 'That's a good quality. I wouldn't have fallen in love with him if he hadn't been.'

'If I were you, I'd take him home – as quickly as possible.' I couldn't help the words sounding sinister, but she hardly heard them. She was listening to the voices that came nearer down the ramparts – to Stephen's gay laugh. 'They're very sweet,' she said. 'I'm glad he's found friends.'

How could I say that they were seducing Peter before her eyes? And in any case wasn't her mistake already irretrievable? Those were two of the questions which haunted the hours, dreary for a solitary man, of the middle afternoon when work is finished and the exhilaration of the wine at lunch, and the time for the first evening drink has not yet come and the winter heating is at its feeblest. Had she no idea of the nature of the young man she had married? Had he taken her on as a blind or as a last desperate throw for normality? I couldn't bring myself to believe that. There was a sort of innocence about the boy which seemed to justify her love, and I preferred to think that he was not yet fully formed, that he had married honestly and it was only now that he found himself on the brink of a different experience. And yet if that were the case the comedy was all the crueller. Would everything have gone normally well if some conjunction of the planets had not crossed their honeymoon with that hungry pair of hunters?

I longed to speak out, and in the end I did speak, but not, so it happened, to her. I was going to my room and the door of one of theirs was open and I heard again Stephen's laugh – a kind of laugh which is sometimes with unintentional irony called infectious; it maddened me. I knocked and went in. Tony was stretched on a double bed and Stephen was 'doing' his hair, holding a brush in each hand and meticulously arranging the grey waves on either side. The dressing-table had as many pots on it as a woman's.

'You really mean he told you that?' Tony was saying. 'Why, how are you, William? Come in. Our young friend has been confiding in Stephen. Such really fascinating things.'

'Which of your young friends?' I asked.

'Why, Peter, of course. Who else? The secrets of married life.'

'I thought it might have been your sailor.'

'Naughty!' Tony said. 'But *touché* too, of course.'

'I wish you'd leave Peter alone.'

'I don't think he'd like that,' Stephen said. 'You can see that he hasn't quite the right tastes for this sort of honeymoon.'

'Now you happen to like women, William,' Tony said. 'Why not go after the girl? It's a grand opportunity. She's not getting what I believe is vulgarly called her greens.' Of the two he was easily the more brutal. I wanted to hit him, but this is not the century for that kind of romantic gesture, and anyway he was stretched out flat upon the bed. I said feebly enough – I ought to have known better than to have entered into a debate with those two – 'She happens to be in love with him.'

'I think Tony is right and she would find more satisfaction with you, William dear,' Stephen said, giving a last flick to the hair over his right ear – the contusion was quite gone now. 'From what Peter has said to me, I think you'd be doing a favour to both of them.'

'Tell him what Peter said, Stephen.'

'He said that from the very first there was a kind of hungry femininity about her which he found frightening and repulsive. Poor boy – he was really trapped into this business of marriage. His father wanted heirs – he breeds horses too, and then her mother – there's quite a lot of lucre with that lot. I don't think he had any idea of – of the Shape of Things to Come.' Stephen shuddered into the glass and then regarded himself with satisfaction.

Even today I have to believe for my own peace of mind that the young man had not really said those monstrous things. I believe, and hope, that the words were put into his mouth by that cunning dramatizer, but there is little comfort in the thought, for Stephen's inventions were always true to character. He even saw through my apparent indifference to the girl and realized that Tony and he had gone too far; it would suit their purpose, if I were driven to the wrong kind of action, or if, by their crudities, I lost my interest in Poopy.

'Of course,' Stephen said, 'I'm exaggerating. Undoubtedly he felt a bit amorous before it came to the point. His father would describe her, I suppose, as a fine filly.'

'What do you plan to do with him?' I asked. 'Do you toss up, or does one of you take the head and the other the tail?'

Tony laughed. 'Good old William. What a clinical mind you have.'

'And suppose,' I said, 'I went to her and recounted this conversation?'

'My dear, she wouldn't even understand. She's incredibly innocent.'

'Isn't he?'

'I doubt it – knowing our friend Colin Winstanley. But it's still a moot point. He hasn't given himself away yet.'

'We are planning to put it to the test one day soon,' Stephen said.

'A drive in the country,' Tony said. 'The strain's telling on him, you can see that. He's even afraid to take a siesta for fear of unwanted attentions.'

'Haven't you *any* mercy?' It was an absurd old-fashioned word to use to those two sophisticates. I felt more than ever square. 'Doesn't it occur to you that you may ruin her life – for the sake of your little game?'

'We can depend on you, William,' Tony said, 'to give her creature comforts.'

Stephen said, 'It's no game. You should realize we are saving *him*. Think of the life that he would lead – with all those soft contours lapping him around.' He added, 'Women always remind me of a damp salad – you know, those faded bits of greenery positively swimming . . .'

'Every man to his taste,' Tony said. 'But Peter's not cut out for that sort of life. He's very sensitive,' he said, using the girl's own words. There wasn't any more I could think of to say.

5

You will notice that I play a very unheroic part in this comedy. I could have gone direct, I suppose, to the girl and given her a little lecture on the facts of life, beginning gently with the régime of an English public school – he had worn a scarf of old-boy colours, until Tony had said to him one day at breakfast that he thought the puce stripe was an error of judgement. Or perhaps I could have protested to the boy himself, but, if Stephen had spoken the truth and he was under a severe nervous strain, my intervention would hardly have helped to ease it. There was no move I could make. I had just to sit there and watch while they made the moves carefully and adroitly towards the climax.

It came three days later at breakfast when, as usual, she was sitting alone with them, while her husband was upstairs with his lotions. They had never been more charming or more entertaining. As I arrived at my table they were giving her a really funny description of a house in Kensington that they had decorated for a dowager duchess who was passionately interested in the Napoleonic wars. There was an ashtray, I remember, made out of a horse's hoof, guaranteed – so the dealer said – by Apsley House to have belonged to a grey ridden by Wellington at the Battle of Waterloo; there was an umbrella stand made out of a shellcase found on the field of Austerlitz; a fire-escape made of a scaling ladder from Badajoz. She had lost half that sense of strain listening to them. She had forgotten her rolls and coffee; Stephen had her complete attention. I wanted to say to her, 'You little owl.' I wouldn't have been insulting her – she *had* got rather large eyes.

And then Stephen produced the master-plan. I could tell it was coming by the way his hands stiffened on his coffee-cup, by the way Tony lowered his eyes and appeared to be praying over his *croissant*. 'We were wondering, Poopy – may we borrow your husband?' I have never heard words spoken with more elaborate casualness.

She laughed. She hadn't noticed a thing. 'Borrow my husband?'

'There's a little village in the mountains behind Monte Carlo – Peille it's called – and I've heard rumours of a devastatingly lovely old bureau there – not for sale, of course, but Tony and I, we have our winning ways.'

'I've noticed that,' she said, 'myself.'

Stephen for an instant was disconcerted, but she meant nothing by it, except perhaps a compliment.

'We were thinking of having lunch at Peille and passing the whole day on the road so as to take a look at the scenery. The only trouble is there's no room in the Sprite for more than three, but Peter was saying the other day that you wanted some time to have a hair-do, so we thought . . .'

I had the impression that he was talking far too much to be convincing, but there wasn't any need for him to worry: she saw nothing at all. 'I think it's a marvellous idea,' she said. 'You know, he needs a little holiday from me. He's had hardly a moment to himself since I came up the aisle.' She was magnificently sensible, and perhaps even relieved. Poor girl. She needed a little holiday, too.

'It's going to be excruciatingly uncomfortable. He'll have to sit on Tony's knee.'

'I don't suppose he'll mind that.'

'And, of course, we can't guarantee the quality of food en route.'

For the first time I saw Stephen as a stupid man. Was there a shade of hope in that?

In the long run, of the two, notwithstanding his brutality, Tony had the better brain. Before Stephen had time to speak once more, Tony raised his eyes from the *croissant* and said decisively, 'That's fine. All's settled, and we'll deliver him back in one piece by dinner-time.'

He looked challengingly across at me. 'Of course, we hate to leave you alone for lunch, but I am sure William will look after you.'

'William?' she asked, and I hated the way she looked at me as if I didn't exist. 'Oh, you mean Mr Harris?'

I invited her to have lunch with me at Lou-Lou's in the old port – I couldn't very well do anything else – and at that moment the laggard Peter came out onto the terrace. She said quickly, 'I don't want to interrupt your work . . .'

'I don't believe in starvation,' I said. 'Work has to be interrupted for meals.'

Peter had cut himself again shaving and had a large blob of cottonwool stuck on his chin: it reminded me of Stephen's contusion. I had the impression, while he stood there waiting for someone to say something to him, that he knew all about the conversation; it had been carefully rehearsed by all three, the parts allotted, the unconcerned manner practised well beforehand, even the bit about the food ... Now somebody had missed a cue, so I spoke.

'I've asked your wife to lunch at Lou-Lou's,' I said. 'I hope you don't mind.'

I would have been amused by the expression of quick relief on all three faces if I had found it possible to be amused by anything at all in the situation.

6

'And you didn't marry again after she left?'

'By that time I was getting too old to marry.'

'Picasso does it.'

'Oh, I'm not quite as old as Picasso.'

The silly conversation went on against a background of fishing-nets draped over a wallpaper with a design of wine-bottles – interior decoration again. Sometimes I longed for a room which had simply grown that way like the lines on a human face. The fish soup steamed away between us, smelling of garlic. We were the only guests there. Perhaps it was the solitude, perhaps it was the directness of her question, perhaps it was only the effect of the *rosé*, but quite suddenly I had the comforting sense that we were intimate friends. 'There's always work,' I said, 'and wine and a good cheese.'

'I couldn't be that philosophical if I lost Peter.'

'That's not likely to happen, is it?'

'I think I'd die,' she said, 'like someone in Christina Rossetti.'

'I thought nobody of your generation read her.'

If I had been twenty years older, perhaps, I could have explained that nothing is quite as bad as that, that at the end of what is called 'the sexual life' the only love which has lasted is the love that has accepted everything, every disappointment, every failure and every betrayal, which has accepted even the sad fact that in the end there is no desire so deep as the simple desire for companionship.

She wouldn't have believed me. She said, 'I used to weep like anything at that poem about "Passing Away." Do you write sad things?'

'The biography I am writing now is sad enough. Two people tied together by love and yet one of them incapable of fidelity. The man dead of old age, burnt-out, at less than forty, and a fashionable preacher lurking by the bedside to snatch his soul. No privacy even for a dying man: the bishop wrote a book about it.'

An Englishman who kept a chandlers' shop in the old port was talking at the bar, and two old women who were part of the family knitted at the end of the room. A dog trotted in and looked at us and went away again with its tail curled.

'How long ago did all that happen?'

'Nearly three hundred years.'

'It sounded quite contemporary. Only now it would be the man from the *Mirror* and not a bishop.'

'That's why I wanted to write it. I'm not really interested in the past. I don't like costume-pieces.'

Winning someone's confidence is rather like the way some men set about seducing a woman; they circle a long way from their true purpose, they try to interest and amuse until finally the moment comes to strike. It came, so I wrongly thought, when I was adding up the bill. She said, 'I wonder where Peter is at this moment,' and I was quick to reply, 'What's going wrong between the two of you?'

She said, 'Let's go.'

'I've got to wait for my change.'

It was always easier to get served at Lou-Lou's than to pay the bill. At that moment everyone always had a habit of disappearing: the old woman (her knitting abandoned on the table), the aunt who helped to serve, Lou-Lou herself, her husband in his blue sweater. If the dog hadn't gone already he would have left at that moment.

I said, 'You forget – you told me that he wasn't happy.'

'Please, please find someone and let's go.'

So I disinterred Lou-Lou's aunt from the kitchen and paid. When we left, everyone seemed to be back again, even the dog.

Outside I asked her whether she wanted to return to the hotel.

'Not just yet – but I'm keeping you from your work.'

'I never work after drinking. That's why I like to start early. It brings the first drink nearer.'

She said that she had seen nothing of Antibes but the ramparts and the beach and the lighthouse, so I walked her around the small narrow backstreets where the washing hung out of the windows as in Naples and there were glimpses of small rooms overflowing with children and grandchildren; stone scrolls were carved over the ancient doorways of what had once been noblemen's houses; the pavements were blocked by barrels of wine and the streets by children playing at ball. In a low room on a ground floor a man sat painting the horrible ceramics which would later go to Vallauris to be sold to tourists in Picasso's old stamping-ground – spotted pink frogs and mauve fish and pigs with slits for coins.

She said, 'Let's go back to the sea.' So we returned to a patch of hot sun on the bastion, and again I was tempted to tell her what I feared, but the thought that she might watch me with the blankness of ignorance deterred me. She sat on the wall and her long legs in the tight black trousers dangled down like Christmas stockings. She said, 'I'm not sorry that I married Peter,' and I was reminded of a song Edith Piaf used to sing, '*Je ne regrette rien.*' It is typical of such a phrase that it is always sung or spoken with defiance.

I could only say again, 'You ought to take him home,' but I wondered what would have happened if I had said, 'You are married to a man who only likes men and he's off now picnicking with his boy friends. I'm thirty years older than you, but at least I have always preferred women and I've fallen in love with you and we could still have a few good years together before the time comes when you want to leave me for a younger man.' All I said was, 'He probably misses the country – and the riding.'

'I wish you were right, but it's really worse than that.'

Had she, after all, realized the nature of her problem? I waited for her to explain her meaning. It was a little like a novel which hesitates on the verge between comedy and tragedy. If she recognized the situation it would be a tragedy; if she were ignorant it was a comedy, even a farce – a situation between an immature girl too innocent to understand and a man too old to have the courage to explain. I suppose I have a taste for tragedy. I hoped for that.

She said, 'We didn't really know each other much before we came here. You know, weekend parties and the odd theatre – and riding, of course.'

I wasn't sure where her remarks tended. I said, 'These occasions are nearly always a strain. You are picked out of ordinary life and dumped together after an elaborate ceremony – almost like two animals shut in a cage who haven't seen each other before.'

'And now he sees me he doesn't like me.'

'You are exaggerating.'

'No.' She added, with anxiety, 'I won't shock you, will I, if I tell you things? There's nobody else I can talk to.'

'After fifty years I'm guaranteed shockproof.'

'We haven't made love – properly, once, since we came here.'

'What do you mean – properly?'

'He starts, but he doesn't finish; nothing happens.'

I said uncomfortably, 'Rochester wrote about that. A poem called "The Imperfect Enjoyment."' I don't know why I gave her this shady piece of literary information; perhaps, like a psychoanalyst, I wanted her not to feel alone with her problem. 'It can happen to anybody.'

'But it's not his fault,' she said. 'It's mine. I know it is. He just doesn't like my body.'

'Surely it's a bit late to discover that.'

'He'd never seen me naked till I came here,' she said with the candour of a girl to her doctor – that was all I meant to her, I felt sure.

'There are nearly always first-night nerves. And then if a man worries (you must realize how much it hurts his pride) he can get stuck in the situation for days – weeks even.' I began to tell her about a mistress I once had – we stayed together a very long time and yet for two weeks at the beginning I could do nothing at all. 'I was too anxious to succeed.'

'That's different. You didn't hate the sight of her.'

'You are making such a lot of so little.'

'That's what he tries to do,' she said with sudden schoolgirl coarseness and giggled miserably.

'We went away for a week and changed the scene, and everything after that was all right. For ten days it had been a flop, and for ten years afterwards we were happy. Very happy. But worry can get established in a room, in the colour of the curtains – it can hang itself up on coat-hangers; you find it smoking away in the ashtray marked Pernod, and when you look at the bed it pokes its head out from underneath like the toes of a pair of shoes.' Again I repeated the only charm I could think of. 'Take him home.'

'It wouldn't make any difference. He's disappointed, that's all it is.' She looked down at her long black legs; I followed the course of her eyes because I was finding now that I really wanted her and she said with sincere conviction, 'I'm just not pretty enough when I'm undressed.'

'You are talking real nonsense. You don't know what nonsense you are talking.'

'Oh no, I'm not. You see – it started all right, but then he touched me' – she put her hands on her breasts – 'and it all went wrong. I always knew they weren't much good. At school we used to have dormitory inspection – it was awful. Everybody could grow them big except me. I'm no Jayne Mansfield, I can tell you.' She gave again that mirthless giggle. 'I remember one of the girls told me to sleep with a pillow on top – they said they'd struggle for release and what they needed was exercise. But of course it didn't work. I doubt if the idea was very scientific.' She added, 'I remember it was awfully hot at night like that.'

'Peter doesn't strike me,' I said cautiously, 'as a man who would want a Jayne Mansfield.'

'But you understand, don't you, that if he finds me ugly, it's all so hopeless.'

I wanted to agree with her – perhaps this reason which she had thought up would be less distressing than the truth, and soon enough there would be someone to cure her distrust. I had noticed before that it is often the lovely women who have the least confidence in their looks, but all the same I couldn't pretend to her that I understood it her way. I said, 'You must trust me. There's nothing at all wrong with you and that's why I'm talking to you the way I am.'

'You are very sweet,' she said, and her eyes passed over me rather as the beam from the lighthouse which at night went past the Musée Grimaldi and after a certain time returned and brushed all our windows indifferently on the hotel front. She continued, 'He said they'd be back by cocktail-time.'

'If you want a rest first' – for a little time we had been close, but now again we were getting further and further away. If I pressed her now she might in the end be happy – does conventional morality demand that a girl remains tied as she was tied? They'd been married in church; she was probably a good Christian, and I knew the ecclesiastical rules: at this moment of her life she could be free of him, the marriage could be annulled, but in a day or two it was only too probable that the same rules would say, 'He's managed well enough, you are married for life.'

And yet I couldn't press her. Wasn't I after all assuming far too much?

Perhaps it was only a question of first-night nerves; perhaps in a little while the three of them would be back, silent, embarrassed, and Tony in his turn would have a contusion on his cheek. I would have been very glad to see it there; egotism fades a little with the passions which engender it, and I would have been content, I think, just to see her happy.

So we returned to the hotel, not saying much, and she went to her room and I to mine. It was in the end a comedy and not a tragedy, a farce even, which is why I have given this scrap of reminiscence a farcical title.

7

I was woken from my middle-aged siesta by the telephone. For a moment, surprised by the darkness, I couldn't find the light-switch. Scrambling for it, I knocked over my bedside lamp – the telephone went on ringing, and I tried to pick up the holder and knocked over a tooth-glass in which I had given myself a whisky. The little illuminated dial of my watch gleamed up at me marking 8:30. The telephone continued to ring. I got the receiver off, but this time it was the ashtray which fell over. I couldn't get the cord to extend up to my ear, so I shouted in the direction of the telephone, 'Hullo!'

A tiny sound came up from the floor which I interpreted as 'Is that William?'

I shouted, 'Hold on,' and now that I was properly awake I realized the light-switch was just over my head (in London it was placed over the bedside table). Little petulant noises came up from the floor as I put on the light, like the creaking of crickets.

'Who's that?' I said rather angrily, and then I recognized Tony's voice.

'William, whatever's the matter?'

'Nothing's the matter. Where are you?'

'But there was quite an enormous crash. It hurt my eardrum.'

'An ashtray,' I said.

'Do you usually hurl ashtrays around?'

'I was asleep.'

'At 8:30? William! William!'

I said, 'Where are you?'

'A little bar in what Mrs. Clarenty would call Monty.'

'You promised to be back by dinner,' I said.

'That's why I'm telephoning you. I'm being *responsible*, William. Do you mind telling Poopy that we'll be a little late? Give her dinner. Talk to her as only you know how. We'll be back by ten.'

'Has there been an accident?'

I could hear him chuckling up the phone. 'Oh, I wouldn't call it an accident.'

'Why doesn't Peter call her himself?'

'He says he's not in the mood.'

'But what shall I tell her?' The telephone went dead.

I got out of bed and dressed and then I called her room. She answered very quickly; I think she must have been sitting by the telephone. I relayed the message, asked her to meet me in the bar, and rang off before I had to face answering any questions.

But I found it was not so difficult as I feared to cover up; she was immensely relieved that somebody had telephoned. She had sat there in her room from half-past seven onwards thinking of all the dangerous turns and ravines on the Grande Corniche, and when I rang she was half afraid that it might be the police or a hospital. Only after she had drunk two dry Martinis and laughed quite a lot at her fears did she say, 'I wonder why Tony rang you and not Peter me?'

I said (I had been working the answer out), 'I gather he suddenly had an urgent appointment – in the loo.'

It was as though I had said something enormously witty.

'Do you think they are a bit tight?' she asked.

'I wouldn't wonder.'

'Darling Peter,' she said, 'he deserved the day off,' and I couldn't help wondering in what direction his merit lay.

'Do you want another Martini?'

'I'd better not,' she said, 'you've made me tight too.'

I had become tired of the thin cold *rosé* so we had a bottle of real wine at dinner and she drank her full share and talked about literature. She had, it seemed, a nostalgia for Dornford Yates, had graduated in the sixth form as far as Hugh Walpole, and now she talked respectfully about Sir Charles Snow, who she obviously thought had been knighted, like Sir Hugh, for his services to literature. I must have been very much in love or I would have found her innocence almost unbearable – or perhaps I was a little tight as well. All the same, it was to interrupt her flow of critical judgements that I asked her what her real name was and she replied, 'Everyone calls me Poopy.' I remembered the PT stamped on her bags, but the only real names that I could think of at the moment were Patricia and Prunella. 'Then I shall simply call you You,' I said.

After dinner I had brandy and she had a kümmel. It was past 10:30 and still the three had not returned, but she didn't seem to be worrying any more about them. She sat on the floor of the bar beside me and every now and then the waiter looked in to see if he could turn off the lights. She leant against me with her hand on my knee and she said such things as 'It must be wonderful to be a writer,' and in the glow of brandy and tenderness I didn't mind them a bit. I even began to tell her again about the Earl of Rochester. What did I care about Dornford Yates, Hugh Walpole or Sir Charles Snow? I was even in the mood to recite to her, hopelessly inapposite to the situation though the lines were:

> Then talk not of Inconstancy,
>   False hearts, and broken vows;
> If I, by miracle, can be
> This live-long minute true to thee,
>   'Tis all that Heaven allows.

when the noise – what a noise! – of the Sprite approaching brought us both to our feet. It was only too true that all that heaven allowed was the time in the bar at Antibes.

Tony was singing; we heard him all the way up the Boulevard Général Leclerc; Stephen was driving with the greatest caution, most of the time in second gear, and Peter, as we saw when we came out onto the terrace, was sitting on Tony's knee – nestling would be a better description – and joining in the refrain. All I could make out was

> Round and white
> On a winter's night,
> The hope of the Queen's Navee.

If they hadn't seen us on the steps I think they would have driven past the hotel without noticing.

'You *are* tight,' the girl said with pleasure. Tony put his arm round her and ran her up to the top of the steps. 'Be careful,' she said. 'William's made me tight too.'

'Good old William.'

Stephen climbed carefully out of the car and sank down on the nearest chair.

'All well?' I asked, not knowing what I meant.

'The children have been very happy,' he said, 'and very, very relaxed.'

'Got to go to the loo,' Peter said (the cue was in the wrong place), and made for the stairs. The girl gave him a helping hand and I heard him say, 'Wonderful day. Wonderful scenery. Wonderful . . .' She turned at the top of the stairs and swept us with her smile, gay, reassured, happy. As on the first night, when they had hesitated about the cocktail, they didn't come down again. There was a long silence and then Tony chuckled. 'You seem to have had a wonderful day,' I said.

'Dear William, we've done a very good action. You've never seen him so *détendu*.'

Stephen sat saying nothing; I had the impression that today hadn't gone quite so well for him. Can people ever hunt quite equally in couples or is there always a loser? The too-grey waves of hair were as immaculate as ever, there was no contusion on the cheek, but I had the impression that the fear of the future had cast a long shadow.

'I suppose you mean you got him drunk?'

'Not with alcohol,' Tony said. 'We aren't vulgar seducers, are we, Stephen?' But Stephen made no reply.

'Then what was your good action?'

'*Le pauvre petit Pierre*. He was in such a state. He had quite convinced himself – or perhaps she had convinced him – that he was *impuissant*.'

'You seem to be making a lot of progress in French.'

'It sounds more delicate in French.'

'And with your help he found he wasn't?'

'After a little virginal timidity. Or near virginal. School hadn't left him quite unmoved. Poor Poopy. She just hadn't known the right way to go about things. My dear, he has a superb virility. Where are you going, Stephen?'

'I'm going to bed,' Stephen said flatly, and went up the steps alone. Tony looked after him, I thought with a kind of tender regret, a very light and superficial sorrow. 'His rheumatism came back very badly this afternoon,' he said. 'Poor Stephen.'

I thought it was well then to go to bed before I should become 'Poor William' too. Tony's charity tonight was all-embracing.

8

It was the first morning for a long time that I found myself alone on the terrace for breakfast. The women in tweed skirts had been gone for some days, and I had never before known 'the young men' to be absent. It was easy enough, while I waited for my coffee, to speculate about the likely reasons. There was, for example, the rheumatism . . . though I couldn't quite picture Tony in the character of a bedside companion. It was even remotely possible that they felt some shame and were unwilling to be confronted by their victim. As for the victim, I wondered sadly what painful revelation the night would certainly have brought. I blamed myself more than ever for not speaking in time. Surely she would have learned the truth more gently from me than from some tipsy uncontrolled outburst of her husband. All the same – such egoists are we in our passions – I was glad to be there in attendance . . . to staunch the tears . . . to take her tenderly in my arms, comfort her . . . oh, I had quite a romantic day-dream on the terrace before she came down the steps and I saw that she had never had less need of a comforter.

She was just as I had seen her the first night: shy, excited, gay, with a long and happy future established in her eyes. 'William,' she said, 'can I sit at your table? Do you mind?'

'Of course not.'

'You've been so patient with me all the time I was in the doldrums. I've talked an awful lot of nonsense to you. I know you told me it was nonsense, but I didn't believe you and you were right all the time.'

I couldn't have interrupted her even if I had tried. She was a Venus at the prow sailing through sparkling seas. She said, 'Everything's all right. Everything. Last night – he loves me, William. He really does. He's not a bit disappointed with me. He was just tired and strained, that's all. He needed a day off alone – *détendu.*' She was even picking up Tony's French expressions second-hand. 'I'm afraid of nothing now, nothing at all. Isn't it strange how black life seemed only two days ago? I really believe if it hadn't been for you I'd have thrown in my hand. How lucky I was to meet you and the others too. They're such wonderful friends for Peter. We are all going home next week – and we've made a lovely plot together. Tony's going to come down almost immediately we get back and decorate our house. Yesterday, driving in the country, they had a wonderful discussion about it. You won't know our house when you see it – oh, I forgot, you never *have* seen it, have you? You must come down when it's all finished – with Stephen.'

'Isn't Stephen going to help?' I just managed to slip in.

'Oh, he's too busy at the moment, Tony says, with Mrs. Clarenty. Do you like riding? Tony does. He adores horses, but he has so little chance in London. It will be wonderful for Peter – to have someone like that because, after all, I can't be riding with Peter all day long, there will be a lot of things to do in the house, especially now, when I'm not accustomed. It's wonderful to think that Peter won't have to be lonely. He says there are going to be Etruscan murals in the bathroom – whatever Etruscan means; the drawing-room *basically* will be eggshell green and the dining-room walls Pompeian red. They really did an awful lot of work yesterday afternoon – I mean in their heads, while we were glooming around. I said to Peter, "As things are going now we'd better be prepared for a nursery," but Peter said Tony was content to leave all that side to me. Then there are the stables: they were an old coach-house once, and Tony feels we could restore a lot of the ancient character and there's a lamp he bought in St. Paul which will just fit . . . it's endless the things there are to be done – a good six months' work, so Tony says, but luckily he can leave Mrs. Clarenty to Stephen and concentrate on us. Peter asked him about the garden, but he's not a specialist in gardens. He said, "Everyone to his own métier," and he's quite content if I bring in a man who knows all about roses.

'He knows Colin Winstanley too, of course, so there'll be quite a band of us. It's a pity the house won't be all ready for Christmas, but Peter says he's certain to have wonderful ideas for a really original tree. Peter thinks . . .'

She went on and on like that; perhaps I ought to have interrupted her even then; perhaps I should have tried to explain to her why her dream wouldn't last. Instead, I sat there silent, and presently I went to my room and packed – there was still one hotel open in the abandoned fun-fair of Juan between Maxim's and the boarded-up Striptease.

If I had stayed . . . who knows whether he could have kept on pretending for a second night? But I was just as bad for her as he was. If he had the wrong hormones, I had the wrong age. I didn't see any of them again before I left. She and Peter and Tony were out somewhere in the Sprite, and Stephen – so the receptionist told me – was lying late in bed with his rheumatism.

I planned a note for her, explaining rather feebly my departure, but when I came to write it I realized I had still no other name with which to address her than Poopy.

JAMES PURDY

SOME OF THESE DAYS

W hat my landlord's friends said about me was in a way the gospel truth, that is he was good to me and I was mean and ungrateful to him. All the two years I was in jail, nonetheless, I thought only of him, and I was filled with regret for the things I had done against him. I wanted him back. I didn't exactly wish to go back to live with him now, mind you, I had been too mean to him for that, but I wanted him for a friend again. After I got out of jail I would need friendship, for I didn't need to hold up even one hand to count my friends on, the only one I could even name was him. I didn't want anything to do with him physically again, I had kind of grown out of that somehow even more while in jail, and wished to try to make it with women again, but I did require my landlord's love and affection, for love was, as everybody was always saying, his special gift and talent.

He was at the time I lived with him a rather well-known singer, and he also composed songs, but even when I got into my bad trouble, he was beginning to go downhill, and not to be so in fashion. We often quarreled over his not succeeding way back then. Once I hit him when he told me how much he loved me, and knocked out one of his front teeth. But that

JAMES PURDY (born 1923): Purdy's novels and story collections include Malcolm, 63: Dream Palace, In the Hollow of His Hand, and The Candles of Your Eyes. He lives in Brooklyn Heights, New York.

was only after he had also criticized me for not keeping the apartment tidy and clean and doing the dishes, and I threatened him with an old gun I kept. Of course I felt awful bad about his losing this front tooth when he needed good teeth for singing. I asked his forgiveness. We made up and I let him kiss me and hold me tight just for this one time.

I remember his white face and sad eyes at my trial for breaking and entering and possession of a dangerous weapon, and at the last his tears when the judge sentenced me. My landlord could cry and not be ashamed of crying, and so you didn't mind him shedding tears somehow. At first, then, wrote me, for as the only person who could list himself as nearest of kin or closest tie, he was allowed by the authorities to communicate with me, and I also received little gifts from him from time to time. And then all upon a sudden the presents stopped, and shortly after that, the letters too, and then there was no word of any kind, just nothing. I realized then that I had this strong feeling for him which I had never had for anybody before, for my people had been dead from the time almost I was a toddler, and so they are shadowy and dim, whilst he is bright and clear. That is, you see, I had to admit to myself in jail (and I choked on my admission), but I had hit bottom, and could say a lot of things now to myself, I guess I was in love with him. I had really only loved women, I had always told myself, and I did not love this man so much physically, in fact he sort of made me sick to my stomach to think of him that way, though he was a good-looker with his neat black straight hair, and his robin's-egg-blue eyes, and cheery smile . . . And so there in my cell I had to confess what did I have for him if it was not love, and yet I had treated him meaner than anybody I had ever knowed in my life, and once come close to killing him. Thinking about him all the time now, for who else was there to think about, I found I got to talking to myself more and more, like an old geezer of advanced years, and in place of calling on anybody else or any higher power, since he was the only one I had ever met in my twenty years of life who said he cared. I would find myself saying, like in church, *My landlord*, though that term for him was just a joke for the both of us, for all he had was this one-room flat with two beds, and my bed was the little one, no more than a cot, and I never made enough to pay him no rent for it, he just said he would trust me. So there in my cell, especially at night, I would say *My landlord*, and finally, for my chest begin to trouble me about this time and I was short of breath often, I would just manage to get out *My lord*. That's what I would call him for short. When

I got out, the first thing I made up my mind to do was find him, and I was going to put all my efforts behind the search.

And when there was no mail now at all, I would think over all the kind and good things he done for me, and the thought would come to me which was blacker than any punishment they had given me here in the big house that I had not paid him back for his good deeds. When I got out I would make it up to him. He had took me in off the street, as people say, and had tried to make a man of me, or at least a somebody out of me, and I had paid him back all in bad coin, first by threatening to kill him, and then by going bad and getting sent to jail . . . But when I got out, I said, I will find him if I have to walk from one ocean shore to the other.

And so it did come about that way, for once out, that is all I did or found it in my heart to do, find the one who had tried to set me straight, find the one who had done for me, and shared and all.

One night after I got out of jail, I had got dead drunk and stopped a guy on Twelfth Street, and spoke, *Have you seen my lord?* This man motioned me to follow him into a dark little theater, which later I was to know all too well as one of the porno theaters, he paid for me, and brought me to a dim corner in the back, and then the same old thing started up again, he beginning to undo my clothes, and lower his head, and I jumped up and pushed him and ran out of the movie, but then stopped and looked back and waited there as it begin to give me an idea.

Now a terrible thing had happened to me in jail. I was beat on the head by another prisoner, and I lost some of the use of my right eye, so that I am always straining by pushing my neck around as if to try to see better, and when the convict hit me that day and I was unconscious for several weeks and they despaired of my life, later on, when I come to myself at last, I could remember everything that had ever happened in my whole twenty years of life except my landlord's name, and I couldn't think of it if I was to be alive. That is why I have been in the kind of difficulty I have been in. It is the hardest thing in the world to hunt for somebody if you don't know his name.

I finally though got the idea to go back to the big building where he and I had lived together, but the building seemed to be under new management, with new super, new tenants, new everybody. Nobody anyhow remembered any singer, they said, nor any composer, and then after a time, it must have been though six months from the day I returned to New York, I realized that I had gone maybe to a building that just looked like the old building my landlord and I have lived in, and so I tore like a blue streak straight away to this 'correct' building to find out if any such person as him was living there, but as I walked around through the halls looking, I become somewhat confused all over again if this was the place either, for I had wanted so bad to find the old building where he and I had lived. I had maybe been overconfident of this one also being the correct place, and so as I walked the halls looking and peering about I become puzzled and unsure all over again, and after a few more turns, I give up and left.

That was an awesome fall, and then winter coming on and all, and no word from him, no trace, and then I remembered a thing from the day that man had beckoned me to come follow him into that theater, and I remembered something, I remembered that on account of my landlord being a gay or queer man, one of his few pleasures when he got an extra dollar was going to the porno movies in Third Avenue. My remembering this was like a light from heaven, if you can think of heaven throwing light on such a thing, for suddenly I knowed for sure that if I went to the porno movie I would find him.

The only drawback for me was these movies was somewhat expensive by now, for since I been in jail prices have surely marched upwards, and I have very little to keep me even in necessities. This was the beginning of me seriously begging, and sometimes I would be holding out my hand on the street for three fourths of a day before I got me enough to pay my way into the porno theater. I would put down my three bucks, and enter the turnstile, and then inside wait until my eyes got used to the dark, which because of my prison illness took nearly all of ten minutes, and then I would go up each aisle looking for my landlord. There was not a face I didn't examine carefully . . . My interest in the spectators earned me several bawlings-out from the manager of the theater, who took me for somebody out to proposition the customers, but I paid him no mind . . . But his fussing with me gave me an idea too, for I am attractive to men, both young and old, me being not yet twenty-one, and so I began what was to become regular practice, letting the audience take any liberty they was in a mind to with me in the hopes that through this contact they would divulge the whereabouts of my landlord.

But here again my problem would surface, for I could not recall the very name of the person who was most dear to me, yes that was the real sore spot. But as the men in the movie theater took their liberties with me, which after a time I got sort of almost to enjoy, even though I could barely see their faces, only see enough to know they was not my landlord, I would then, I say, describe him in full to them, and I will give them this much credit, they kind of listened to me as they went about getting their kicks from me, they would bend an ear to my asking for this information, but in the end they never heard of him nor any other singer, and never knowed a man who wrote down notes for a living.

But strange as it might seem to anybody who will ever see these sheets of paper, this came to be my only connection with the world, my only life — sitting in the porno theater. Since my only purpose was to find him and from him find my own way back, this was the only thoroughfare there was open for me to reach him. And yet I did not like it, though at the same time, even disliking it as much as I did, it give me some little feeling of a resemblance to warmth and kindness as the unknown men touched me with their invisible faces and extracted from me all I had to offer, such as it was. And then when they had finished me, I would ask them if they knew my landlord (or as I whispered to myself, my lord). But none ever did.

Winter had come in earnest, was raw in the air. The last of the leaves in the park had long blown out to sea, and yet it was not to be thought of giving up the search and going to a warmer place. I would go on here until I had found him or I would know the reason why, yes, I must find him, and not give up. (I tried to keep the phrase *My lord* only for myself, for once or twice when it had slipped out to a stranger, it give him a start, and so I watched what I said from there on out.)

And then I was getting down to the last of the little money I had come out of jail with, and oh the porno theater was so dear, the admission was hiked another dollar just out of the blue, and the leads I got in that old dark hole was so few and far between. Toward the end one man sort of perked up when I mentioned my landlord, the singer, and said he thought he might have known such a fellow, but with no name to go on, he too soon give up and said he guessed he didn't know after all.

And so I was stumped. Was I to go on patronizing the porno theater, I would have to give up food, for my panhandling did not bring in enough for both grub and movies, and yet there was something about bein' in that house, getting the warmth and attention from the stray men, that meant more to me than food and drink. So I began to go without eating in earnest so as to keep up my regular attendance at the films. That was maybe, looking back on it now, a bad mistake, but what is one bad mistake in a lifetime of them.

As I did not eat now but only give my favors to the men in the porno, I grew pretty unsteady on my feet. After a while I could barely drag to the theater. Yet it was the only place I wanted to be, especially in view of its being now full winter. But my worst fear was now realized, for I could no longer afford even the cheap lodging place I had been staying at, and all I had in the world was what was on my back, and the little in my pockets, so I had come at last to this, and yet I did not think about my plight so much as about him, for as I got weaker and weaker he seemed to stand over me as large as the figures of the film actors that raced across the screen, and at which I almost never looked, come to think of it. No, I never watched what went on on the screen itself. I watched the audience, for it was the living that would be able to give me the word.

'Oh come to me, come back and set me right!' I would whisper, hoping someone out of the audience might rise and tell me they knew where he was.

Then at last, but of course slow gradual like, I no longer left the theater. I was too weak to go out, anyhow had no lodging now to call mine, knew if I got as far as a step beyond the entrance door of the theater, I would never get back inside to its warmth, and me still dressed in my summer clothes.

Then after a long drowsy time – days, weeks, who knows? – my worse than worst fears was realized, for one – shall I say day? for where I was now there was no day or night, and the theater never closed its doors – one time, then, I say, they *come* for me, they had been studying my condition, they told me later, and they come to take me away. I begged them with all the strength I had left not to do so, that I could still walk, that I would be gone and bother nobody again.

When did you last sit down to a bite to eat? A man spoke this direct into my ear, a man by whose kind of voice I knew did not belong to the porno world, but come from some outside authority.

I have lost all track of time, I replied, closing my eyes.

All right, buddy, the man kept saying, and *Now, bud*, and then as I fought and kicked, they held me and put the straitjacket on me, though didn't they see I was too weak and dispirited to hurt one cruddy man jack of them.

Then as they was taking me finally away, for the first time in months I raised my voice, as if to the whole city, and called, and shouted, and explained: '*Tell him if he comes, how long I have waited and searched, that I have been hunting for him, and I cannot remember his name. I was hit in prison by another convict and the injury was small, but it destroyed my one needed memory, which is his name. That is all that is wrong with me. If you would cure me of this one little defect, I will never bother any of you again, never bother society again. I will go back to work and make a man of myself, but I have first to thank this former landlord for all he done for me.*'

'He is hovering between life and death.'

I repeated aloud the word 'hovering' after the man who had pronounced this sentence somewhere in the vicinity of where I was lying, in a bed that smelled strong of carbolic acid.

And as I said the word 'hovering' I knew his name. I raised up. Yes, my landlord's name had come back to me . . . It had come back after all the wreck and ruin of these weeks and years.

But then one sorrow would follow upon another, as I believe my mother used to say, though that is so long ago I can't believe I had a mother, for when they saw that I was conscious and in my right mind, they come to me and begun asking questions, especially what was my name. I stared at them then with the greatest puzzlement and sadness, for though I had fished up his name from so far down, I could no more remember my own name now when they asked me for it than I could have got out of my straitjacket and run a race, and I was holding on to the just-found landlord's name with the greatest difficulty, for it, too, was beginning to slip from my tongue and go disappear where it had been lost before.

As I hesitated, they begun to persecute me with their kindness, telling me how they would help me in my plight, but first of all they must have my name, and since they needed a name so bad, and was so insistent, I could see their kindness beginning to go, and the cruelty I had known in jail coming fresh to mind, I said, 'I am Sidney Fuller,' giving them you see my landlord's name.

'And your age, Sidney?'

'Twenty, come next June.'

'And how did you earn your living?'

'I have been without work now for some months.'

'What kind of work do you do?'

'Hard labor.'

'When were you last employed?'

'In prison.'

There was a silence, and the papers was moved about, then: 'Do you have a church or faith?'

I waited quite a while, repeating his name, and remembering I could not remember my own, and then I said, 'I am of the same faith as my landlord.'

There was an even longer silence then, like the questioner had been cut down by his own inquiry, anyhow they did not interrogate me any more after that, they went away and left me by myself.

After a long time, certainly days, maybe weeks, they announced the doctor was coming.

He set down on a sort of ice cream chair beside me, and took off his glasses and wiped them. I barely saw his face.

'Sidney,' he began, after it sounded like he had started to say something else first and then changed his mind. 'Sidney, I have some very serious news to impart to you, and I want you to try to be brave. It is hard for me to say what I am going to say. I will tell you what we have discovered. I want you, though, first, to swallow this tablet, and we will wait together for a few minutes, and then I will tell you.'

I had swallowed the tablet it seemed a long time ago, and then all of a sudden I looked down at myself, and I saw I was not in the straitjacket, my arms was free.

'Was I bad, Doctor?' I said, and he seemed to be glad I had broke the ice, I guess.

'I believe, Sidney, that you know in part what I am going to say to you,' he started up again. He was a dark man, I saw now, with thick eyebrows, and strange, I thought, that for a doctor he seemed to have no wrinkles, his face was smooth as a sheet.

'We have done all we could to save you, you must believe us,' he was going on as I struggled to hear his words through the growing drowsiness given me by the tablet. 'You have a sickness, Sidney, for which unfortunately there is today no cure . . .'

He said more, but I do not remember what, and was glad when he left, no, amend that, I was sad I guess when he left. Still, it didn't matter one way or another if anybody stayed or lit out.

But after a while, when I was a little less drowsy, a new man come in, with some white papers under his arm.

'You told us earlier when you were first admitted,' he was saying, 'that your immediate family is all dead . . . Is there nobody to whom you wish to leave any word at all? . . . If there is such a person, we would appreciate your writing the name and address on each of these four sheets of paper, and add any instructions which you care to detail.'

At that moment, I remembered my own name, as easily as if it had been written on the paper before me, and the sounds of it placed in my mouth and on my tongue, and since I could not give my landlord's name again, as the someone to whom I could bequeath my all, I give the inquirer with the paper my own real name:

James De Salles

'And his address?' the inquirer said.

I shook my head.

'Very well, then, Sidney,' he said, rising from the same chair the doctor had sat in. He looked at me some time, then kind of sighed, and folded the sheaf of papers.

'Wait,' I said to him then, 'just a minute . . . Could you get me writing paper, and fountain pen and ink to boot . . .'

'Paper, yes . . . We have only ballpoint pens, though . . .'

So then he brought the paper and the ballpoint, and I have written this down, asking another patient here from time to time how to say this, or spell that, but not showing him what I am about, and it is queer indeed, isn't it, that I can only bequeath these papers to myself, for God only knows who would read them later, and it has come to me very clear in my sleep that my landlord is dead also, so there is no point in my telling my attendants that I have lied to them, that I am really James De Salles, and that my lord is or was Sidney Fuller.

But after I done wrote it all down, I was quiet in my mind and heart, and so with some effort I wrote my own name on the only thing I have to leave, and which they took from me a few moments ago with great puzzlement, for neither the person was known to them, and the address of course could not be given, and they only received it from me, I suppose, to make me feel I was being tended to.

WILLIAM TREVOR

TORRIDGE

Perhaps nobody ever did wonder what Torridge would be like as a man – or what Wiltshire or Mace-Hamilton or Arrowsmith would be like, come to that. Torridge at thirteen had a face with a pudding look, matching the sound of his name. He had small eyes and short hair like a mouse's. Within the collar of his grey regulation shirt the knot of his House tie was formed with care, a maroon triangle of just the right shape and bulk. His black shoes were always shiny.

Torridge was unique in some way: perhaps only because he was beyond the pale and appeared, irritatingly, to be unaware of it. He wasn't good at games and had difficulty in understanding what was being explained in the classroom. He would sit there frowning, half smiling, his head a little to one side. Occasionally he would ask some question that caused an outburst of groaning. His smile would increase then. He would glance around the classroom, not flustered or embarrassed in the least, seeming to be pleased that he had caused such a response. He was naïve to the point where it was hard to believe he wasn't pretending, but his naïveté was real and was in time universally recognized as such. A master called

WILLIAM TREVOR (born 1928): Although Trevor is a prolific writer of short stories and novels alike, it is in the story form that he has emerged as a master. Since the publication of the Collected Stories in 1992, he has brought out two further collections, After Rain and The Hill Bachelors. The Irish-born Trevor has lived for many years in Devon, England.

Buller Yeats reserved his cruellest shafts of scorn for it, sighing whenever his eyes chanced to fall on Torridge, pretending to believe his name was Porridge.

Of the same age as Torridge, but similar in no other way, were Wiltshire, Mace-Hamilton, and Arrowsmith. All three of them were blond-haired and thin, with a common sharpness about their features. They wore, untidily, the same clothes as Torridge, their House ties knotted any old how, the laces in their scuffed shoes often tied in several places. They excelled at different games and were quick to sense what was what. Attractive boys, adults had more than once called them.

The friendship among the three of them developed because, in a way, Torridge was what he was. From the first time they were aware of him – on the first night of their first term – he appeared to be special. In the darkness after lights-out someone was trying not to sob and Torridge's voice was piping away, not homesick in the least. His father had a button business was what he was saying; he'd probably be going into the button business himself. In the morning he was identified, a boy in red and blue striped pyjamas, still chattering in the wash-room. 'What's your father do, Torridge?' Arrowsmith asked at breakfast, and that was the beginning. 'Dad's in the button business,' Torridge beamingly replied. 'Torridge's, you know.' But no one did know.

He didn't, as other new boys, make a particular friend. For a while he attached himself to a small gang of homesick boys who had only their malady in common, but after a time this gang broke up and Torridge found himself on his own, though it seemed quite happily so. He was often to be found in the room of the kindly housemaster of Junior House, an ageing white-haired figure called Old Frosty, who listened sympathetically to complaints of injustice at the hands of other masters, always ready to agree that the world was a hard place. 'You should hear Buller Yeats on Torridge, sir,' Wiltshire used to say in Torridge's presence. 'You'd think Torridge had no feelings, sir.' Old Frosty would reply that Buller Yeats was a frightful man. 'Take no notice, Torridge,' he'd add in his kindly voice, and Torridge would smile, making it clear that he didn't mind in the least what Buller Yeats said. 'Torridge knows true happiness,' a new young master, known as Mad Wallace, said in an unguarded moment one day, a remark which caused immediate uproar in a Geography class. It was afterwards much repeated, like 'Dad's in the button business' and 'Torridge's, you know.' The true happiness of Torridge became a joke, the particular property of Wiltshire and Mace-Hamilton and Arrowsmith. Furthering the joke, they claimed that knowing Torridge was a rare experience, that the private realm of his innocence and his happiness was even exotic. Wiltshire insisted that one day the school would be proud of him. The joke was worked to death.

At the school it was the habit of certain senior boys to 'take an interest in' juniors. This varied from glances and smiles across the dining-hall to written invitations to meet in some secluded spot at a stated time. Friendships, taking a variety of forms, were then initiated. It was flattering, and very often a temporary antidote for homesickness, when a new boy received the agreeable but bewildering attentions of an important fifth-former. A meeting behind Chapel led to the negotiating of a barbed-wire fence on a slope of gorse bushes, the older boy solicitous and knowledgeable. There were well-trodden paths and nooks among the gorse where smoking could take place with comparative safety. Farther afield, in the hills, there were crude shelters composed of stones and corrugated iron. Here, too, the emphasis was on smoking and romance.

New boys very soon became aware of the nature of older boys' interest in them. The flattery changed its shape, an adjustment was made – or the new boys retreated in panic from this area of school life. Andrews and Butler, Webb and Mace-Hamilton, Dillon and Pratt, Tothill and Goldfish Stewart, Good and Wiltshire, Sainsbury Major and Arrowsmith, Brewitt and King: the liaisons were renowned, the combinations of names sometimes seeming like a music-hall turn, a soft-shoe shuffle of entangled hearts. There was faithlessness too: the Honourable Anthony Swain made the rounds of the senior boys, a fickle and tartish *bijou*, desired and yet despised.

Torridge's puddingy appearance did not suggest that he had *bijou* qualities, and glances did not readily come his way in the dining-hall. This was often the fate, or good fortune, of new boys and was not regarded as a sign of qualities lacking. Yet quite regularly an ill-endowed child would mysteriously become the object of fifth- and sixth-form desire. This remained a puzzle to the juniors until they themselves became fifth- or sixth-formers and desire was seen to have to do with something deeper than superficial good looks.

It was the apparent evidence of this truth that caused Torridge, first of all, to be aware of the world of *bijou* and protector. He received a note from a boy in the upper fifth who had previously eschewed the sexual life offered by the school. He was a big, black-haired youth with glasses and a protruding forehead, called Fisher.

'Hey, what's this mean?' Torridge enquired, finding the note under his pillow, tucked into his pyjamas. 'Here's a bloke wants to go for a walk.'

He read the invitation out: '*If you would like to come for a walk meet me by the electricity plant behind Chapel. Half past four Tuesday afternoon. R.A.J. Fisher.*'

'Jesus Christ!' said Armstrong.

'You've got an admirer, Porridge,' Mace-Hamilton said.

'Admirer?'

'He wants you to be his *bijou*,' Wiltshire explained.

'What's it mean, *bijou*?'

'Tart, it means, Porridge.'

'Tart?'

'Friend. He wants to be your protector.'

'What's it mean, protector?'

'He loves you, Porridge.'

'I don't even know the bloke.'

'He's the one with the big forehead. He's a half-wit actually.'

'Half-wit?'

'His mother let him drop on his head. Like yours did, Porridge.'

'My mum never.'

Everyone was crowding around Torridge's bed. The note was passed from hand to hand. 'What's your dad do, Porridge?' Wiltshire suddenly asked, and Torridge automatically replied that he was in the button business.

'You've got to write a note back to Fisher, you know,' Mace-Hamilton pointed out.

'Dear Fisher,' Wiltshire prompted, 'I love you.'

'But I don't even —'

'It doesn't matter, not knowing him. You've got to write a letter and put it in his pyjamas.'

Torridge didn't say anything. He placed the note in the top pocket of his jacket and slowly began to undress. The other boys drifted back to their own beds, still amused by the development. In the wash-room the next morning Torridge said:

'I think he's quite nice, that Fisher.'

'Had a dream about him, did you, Porridge?' Mace-Hamilton enquired. 'Got up to tricks, did he?'

'No harm in going for a walk.'

'No harm at all, Porridge.'

In fact a mistake had been made. Fisher, in his haste or his excitement, had placed the note under the wrong pillow. It was Arrowsmith, still allied with Sainsbury Major, whom he wished to attract.

That this error had occurred was borne in on Torridge when he turned up at the electricity plant on the following Tuesday. He had not considered it necessary to reply to Fisher's note, but he had, across the dining-hall, essayed a smile or two in the older boy's direction: it had surprised him to meet with no response. It surprised him rather more to meet with no response by the electricity plant. Fisher just looked at him and then turned his back, pretending to whistle.

'Hullo, Fisher,' Torridge said.

'Hop it, look. I'm waiting for someone.'

'I'm Torridge, Fisher.'

'I don't care who you are.'

'You wrote me that letter.' Torridge was still smiling. 'About a walk, Fisher.'

'Walk? What walk?'

'You put the letter under my pillow, Fisher.'

'Jesus!' said Fisher.

The encounter was observed by Arrowsmith, Mace-Hamilton, and Wiltshire, who had earlier taken up crouched positions behind one of the chapel buttresses. Torridge heard the familiar hoots of laughter, and because it was his way, he joined in. Fisher, white-faced, strode away.

'Poor old Porridge,' Arrowsmith commiserated, gasping and pretending to be contorted with mirth. Mace-Hamilton and Wiltshire were leaning against the buttress, issuing shrill noises.

'Gosh,' Torridge said, '*I* don't care.'

He went away, still laughing a bit, and there the matter of Fisher's attempt at communication might have ended. In fact it didn't, because Fisher wrote a second time, and this time he made certain that the right boy received his missive. But Arrowsmith, still firmly the property of Sainsbury Major, wished to have nothing to do with R.A.J. Fisher.

When he was told the details of Fisher's error, Torridge said he'd guessed it had been something like that. But Wiltshire, Mace-Hamilton, and Arrowsmith claimed that a new sadness had overcome Torridge. Something beautiful had been going to happen to him, Wiltshire said: just as the petals of friendship were opening, the flower had been crudely snatched away. Arrowsmith said Torridge reminded him of one of Picasso's sorrowful harlequins. One way or the other, it was agreed that the experience would be beneficial to Torridge's sensitivity. It was seen as his reason for turning to religion, which recently he had done, joining a band of similarly inclined boys who were inspired by the word of the chaplain, a figure known as God Harvey. God Harvey was ascetic, seeming dangerously thin, his face all edge and as pale as paper, his cassock odorous with incense. He conducted readings in his room, offering coffee and biscuits afterwards, though not himself partaking of these refreshments. 'God Harvey's linnets' his acolytes were called, for often a hymn was sung to round things off. Welcomed into this fold, Torridge regained his happiness.

R.A.J. Fisher, on the other hand, sank into greater gloom. Arrowsmith remained elusive, mockingly faithful to Sainsbury Major, haughty when Fisher glanced pleadingly, ignoring all his letters. Fisher developed a look of introspective misery. The notes that Arrowsmith delightedly showed around were full of longing, increasingly tinged with desperation. The following term, unexpectedly, Fisher did not return to the school.

There was a famous Assembly at the beginning of that term, with much speculation beforehand as to the trouble in the air. Rumour had it that once and for all an attempt was to be made to stamp out the smiles and the glances in the dining-hall, the whole business of *bijou* and protectors, even the faithless behaviour of the Honourable Anthony Swain. The school waited, and then the gowned staff arrived in the Assembly Hall and waited also, in grim anticipation on a raised dais. Public beatings for past offenders were scheduled, it was whispered: the sergeant-major – the school's boxing instructor, who had himself told tales of public beatings in the past – would inflict the punishment at the headmaster's bidding. But that did not happen. Small and bald and red-skinned, the headmaster marched to the dais unaccompanied by the sergeant-major. Twitching with anger that many afterwards declared had been simulated, he spoke at great length of the school's traditions. He stated that for fourteen years he had been proud to be its headmaster. He spoke of decency and then of his own dismay. The school had been dishonoured; he would wish certain practices to cease. 'I stand before you ashamed,' he added, and paused for a moment. 'Let all this cease,' he commanded. He marched away, tugging at his gown in a familiar manner.

No one understood why the Assembly had taken place at that particular time, on the first day of a summer term. Only the masters looked knowing, as though labouring beneath some secret, but pressed and pleaded with, they refused to reveal anything. Even Old Frosty, usually a most reliable source on such occasions, remained awesomely tight-lipped.

But the pronounced dismay and shame of the headmaster changed nothing. That term progressed, and the world of *bijous* and their protectors continued as before, the glances, the meetings, cigarettes, and romance in the hillside huts. R.A.J. Fisher was soon forgotten, having never made much of a mark. But the story of his error in placing a note under Torridge's pillow passed into legend, as did the encounter by the electricity plant and Torridge's deprivation of a relationship. The story was repeated as further terms passed by; new boys heard it and viewed Torridge with greater interest, imagining what R.A.J. Fisher had been like. The liaisons of Wiltshire with Good, Mace-Hamilton with Webb, and Arrowsmith with Sainsbury Major continued until the three senior boys left the school. Wiltshire, Mace-Hamilton, and Arrowsmith found fresh protectors then, and later these new liaisons came to an end in a similar manner. Later still, Wiltshire, Mace-Hamilton, and Arrowsmith ceased to be *bijous* and became protectors themselves.

Torridge pursued the religious side of things. He continued to be a frequent partaker of God Harvey's biscuits and spiritual uplift, and a useful presence among the chapel pews, where he voluntarily dusted, cleaned brass, and kept the hymn-books in a state of repair with Sellotape. Wiltshire, Mace-Hamilton, and Arrowsmith continued to circulate stories about him which were not true: that he was the product of virgin birth, that he possessed the gift of tongues but did not care to employ it, that he had three kidneys. In the end there emanated from them the claim that a liaison existed between Torridge and God Harvey. 'Love and the holy spirit,' Wiltshire pronounced, suggesting an ambience of chapel fustiness and God Harvey's grey boniness. The swish of his cassock took on a new significance, as did his thin, dry fingers. In a holy way the fingers pressed themselves onto Torridge, and then their holiness became a passion that could not be imagined. It was all a joke, because Torridge was Torridge, but the laughter it caused wasn't malicious, because no one hated him. He was a figure of fun; no one sought his downfall, because there was no downfall to seek.

~ ~ ~

The friendship between Wiltshire, Mace-Hamilton, and Arrowsmith continued after they left the school, after all three had married and had families. Once a year they received the Old Boys' magazine, which told of the achievements of themselves and the more successful of their school-fellows. There were Old Boys' cocktail parties and Old Boys' Day at the school every June and the Old Boys' cricket match. Some of these occasions, from time to time, they attended. Every so often they received the latest rebuilding programme, with the suggestion that they might like to contribute to the rebuilding fund. Occasionally they did.

As middle age closed in, the three friends met less often. Arrowsmith was an executive with Shell and stationed for longish periods in different countries abroad. Once every two years he brought his family back to England, which provided an opportunity for the three friends to meet. The wives met on these occasions also, and over the years the children. Often the men's distant schooldays were referred to, Buller Yeats and Old Frosty and the sergeant-major, the little red-skinned headmaster, and above all Torridge. Within the three families, in fact, Torridge had become a myth. The joke that had begun when they were all new boys together continued, as if driven by its own impetus. In the minds of the wives and children the innocence of Torridge, his true happiness in the face of mockery, and his fondness for the religious side of life all lived on. With some exactitude a physical image of the boy he'd been took root: his neatly knotted maroon House tie, his polished shoes, the hair that resembled a mouse's fur, the pudding face with two small eyes in it. 'My dad's in the button business,' Arrowsmith had only to say to cause instant laughter. 'Torridge's, you know.' The way Torridge ate, the way he ran, the way he smiled back at Buller Yeats, the rumour that he'd been dropped on his head as a baby, that he had three kidneys, all this was considerably appreciated, because Wiltshire and Mace-Hamilton and Arrowsmith related it well.

What was not related was R.A.J. Fisher's error in placing a note beneath Torridge's pillow, or the story that had laughingly been spread about concerning Torridge's relationship with God Harvey. This would have meant revelations that weren't seemly in family circles, the explanation of the world of *bijou* and protector, the romance and cigarettes in the hillside huts, the entangling of hearts. The subject had been touched upon among the three husbands and their wives in the normal course of private conversation, although not everything had been quite recalled. Listening, the wives had formed the impression that the relationships between older and younger boys at their husbands' school were similar to the platonic admiration a junior girl had so often harboured for a senior girl at their own schools. And so the subject had been left.

One evening in June, 1976, Wiltshire and Mace-Hamilton met in a bar called the Vine, in Piccadilly Place. They hadn't seen one another since the summer of 1974, the last time Arrowsmith and his family had been in England. Tonight they were to meet the Arrowsmiths again, for a family dinner in the Woodlands Hotel, Richmond. On the last occasion the three families had celebrated their reunion at the Wiltshires' house in Cobham and the time before with the Mace-Hamiltons in Ealing. Arrowsmith insisted that it was a question of turn and turn about, and every third time he arranged for the family dinner to be held at his expense at the Woodlands. It was convenient because, although the Arrowsmiths spent the greater part of each biennial leave with Mrs. Arrowsmith's parents in Somerset, they always stayed for a week at the Woodlands in order to see a bit of London life.

In the Vine in Piccadilly Place, Wiltshire and Mace-Hamilton hurried over their second drinks. As always, they were pleased to see one another, and both were excited at the prospect of seeing Arrowsmith and his family again. They still looked faintly alike. Both had balded and run to fat. They wore inconspicuous blue suits with a discreet chalk stripe, Wiltshire's a little smarter than Mace-Hamilton's.

'We'll be late,' Wiltshire said, having just related how he'd made a small killing since the last time they'd met. Wiltshire operated in the import-export world; Mace-Hamilton was a chartered accountant.

They finished their drinks. 'Cheerio,' the barman called out to them as they slipped away. His voice was deferentially low, matching the softly lit surroundings. 'Cheerio, Gerry,' Wiltshire said.

They drove in Wiltshire's car to Hammersmith, over the bridge and on to Barnes and Richmond. It was a Friday evening; the traffic was heavy.

'He had a bit of trouble, you know,' Mace-Hamilton said.

'Arrows?'

'She took a shine to some guy in Mombasa.'

Wiltshire nodded, poking the car between a cyclist and a taxi. He wasn't surprised. One night six years ago Arrowsmith's wife and he had committed adultery together at her suggestion. A messy business it had been, and afterwards he'd felt terrible.

~ ~ ~

In the Woodlands Hotel, Arrowsmith, in a grey flannel suit, was not entirely sober. He, too, had run a bit to fat although, unlike Wiltshire and Mace-Hamilton, he hadn't lost any of his hair. Instead, it had dramatically changed colour: what Old Frosty had once called 'Arrows' blond thatch' was grey now. Beneath it his face was pinker than it had been, and he had taken to wearing spectacles, heavy and black-rimmed, making him look even more different from the boy he'd been.

In the bar of the Woodlands he drank whisky on his own, smiling occasionally to himself because tonight he had a surprise for everybody. After five weeks of being cooped up with his in-laws in Somerset, he was feeling good. 'Have one yourself, dear,' he invited the barmaid, a girl with an excess of lipstick on a podgy mouth. He pushed his own glass towards her while she was saying she didn't mind if she did.

His wife and his three adolescent children, two boys and a girl, entered the bar with Mrs. Mace-Hamilton. 'Hi, hi, hi,' Arrowsmith called out to them in a jocular manner, causing his wife and Mrs. Mace-Hamilton to note that he was drunk again. They sat down while he quickly finished the whisky that had just been poured for him. 'Put another in that for a start,' he ordered the barmaid, and crossed the floor of the bar to find out what everyone else wanted.

Mrs. Wiltshire and her twins, girls of twelve, arrived while drinks were being decided about. Arrowsmith kissed her, as he had kissed Mrs. Mace-Hamilton. The barmaid, deciding that the accurate conveying of such a large order was going to be beyond him, came and stood by the two tables that the party now occupied. The order was given; an animated conversation began.

The three women were different in appearance and in manner. Mrs. Arrowsmith was thin as a knife, fashionably dressed in a shade of ash grey that reflected her ash-grey hair. She smoked perpetually, unable to abandon the habit. Mrs. Wiltshire was small. Shyness caused her to coil herself up in the presence of other people, so that she often resembled a ball. Tonight she was in pink, a faded shade. Mrs. Mace-Hamilton was carelessly plump, a large woman attired in a carelessly chosen dress that had begonias on it. She rather frightened Mrs. Wiltshire. Mrs. Arrowsmith found her trying.

'Oh, heavenly little drink!' Mrs. Arrowsmith said, briefly drooping her blue-tinged eyelids as she sipped her gin and tonic.

'It *is* good to see you,' Mrs. Mace-Hamilton gushed, beaming at everyone and vaguely raising her glass. 'And how they've all grown!' Mrs. Mace-Hamilton had not had children herself.

'Their boobs have grown, by God,' the older Arrowsmith boy murmured to his brother, a reference to the Wiltshire twins. Neither of the two Arrowsmith boys went to their father's school: one was at a preparatory school in Oxford, the other at Charterhouse. Being of an age to do so, they both drank sherry and intended to drink as much of it as they possibly could. They found these family occasions tedious. Their sister, about to go to university, had determined neither to speak nor to smile for the entire evening. The Wiltshire twins were quite looking forward to the food.

Arrowsmith sat beside Mrs. Wiltshire. He didn't say anything, but after a moment he stretched a hand over her two knees and squeezed them in what he intended to be a brotherly way. He said without conviction that it was great to see her. He didn't look at her while he spoke. He didn't much care for hanging about with the women and children.

In turn Mrs. Wiltshire didn't much care for his hand on her knees and was relieved when he drew it away. 'Hi, hi, hi,' he suddenly called out, causing her to jump. Wiltshire and Mace-Hamilton had appeared.

The physical similarity that had been so pronounced when the three men were boys and had been only faintly noticeable between Wiltshire and Mace-Hamilton in the Vine was clearly there again, as if the addition of Arrowsmith had supplied missing reflections. The men had thickened in the same way; the pinkness of Arrowsmith's countenance was a pinkness that tinged the other faces too. Only Arrowsmith's grey thatch of hair seemed out of place, all wrong beside the baldness of the other two: in their presence it might have been a wig, an impression it did not otherwise give. His grey flannel suit, beside their pinstripes, looked like something put on by mistake. 'Hi, hi, hi,' he shouted, thumping their shoulders.

Further rounds of drinks were bought and consumed. The Arrowsmith boys declared to each other that they were drunk and made further *sotto voce* observations about the forming bodies of the Wiltshire twins. Mrs. Wiltshire felt the occasion becoming easier as Cinzano Bianco coursed through her bloodstream. Mrs. Arrowsmith was aware of a certain familiar edginess within her body, a desire to be elsewhere, alone with a man she did not know. Mrs. Mace-Hamilton spoke loudly of her garden.

In time the party moved from the bar to the dining-room. 'Bring us another round at the table,' Arrowsmith commanded the lipsticked barmaid. 'Quick as you can, dear.'

In the large dim dining-room, waiters settled them around a table with little vases of carnations on it, a long table beneath the chandelier in the centre of the room. Celery soup arrived at the table, and smoked salmon and pâté, and the extra round of drinks Arrowsmith had ordered, and bottles of Nuits St. Georges, and bottles of Vouvray and Anjou Rosé, and sirloin of beef, chicken à la king, and veal escalope. The Arrowsmith boys laughed shrilly, openly staring at the tops of the Wiltshire twins' bodies. Potatoes, peas, spinach, and carrots were served. Mrs. Arrowsmith waved the vegetables away and smoked between courses. It was after this dinner six years ago that she had made her suggestion to Wiltshire, both of them being the worse for wear and it seeming not to matter because of that. 'Oh, *isn't* this jolly?' the voice of Mrs. Mace-Hamilton boomed above the general hubbub.

Over Chantilly trifle and Orange Surprise the name of Torridge was heard. The name was always mentioned just about now, though sometimes sooner. 'Poor old bean,' Wiltshire said, and everybody laughed because it was the one subject they all shared. No one really wanted to hear about the Mace-Hamiltons' garden; the comments of the Arrowsmith boys were only for each other; Mrs. Arrowsmith's needs could naturally not be voiced; the shyness of Mrs. Wiltshire was private too. But Torridge was different. Torridge in a way was like an old friend now, existing in everyone's mind, a family subject. The Wiltshire twins were quite amused to hear of some freshly remembered evidence of Torridge's naïveté; for the Arrowsmith girl it was better at least than being questioned by Mrs. Mace-Hamilton; for her brothers it was an excuse to bellow with simulated mirth. Mrs. Mace-Hamilton considered that the boy sounded frightful, Mrs. Arrowsmith couldn't have cared less. Only Mrs. Wiltshire had doubts: she thought the three men were hard on the memory of the boy, but of course had not ever said so. Tonight, after Wiltshire had recalled the time when Torridge had been convinced by Arrowsmith that Buller Yeats had dropped dead in his bath, the younger Arrowsmith boy told of a boy at his own school who'd been convinced that his sister's dog had died.

'Listen,' Arrowsmith suddenly shouted out. 'He's going to join us. Old Torridge.'

There was laughter, no one believing that Torridge was going to arrive, Mrs. Arrowsmith saying to herself that her husband was pitiful when he became as drunk as this.

'I thought it would be a gesture,' Arrowsmith said. 'Honestly. He's looking in for coffee.'

'You bloody devil, Arrows,' Wiltshire said, smacking the table with the palm of his hand.

'He's in the button business,' Arrowsmith shouted. 'Torridge's, you know.'

As far as Wiltshire and Mace-Hamilton could remember, Torridge had never featured in an Old Boys' magazine. No news of his career had been printed, and certainly no obituary. It was typical, somehow, of Arrowsmith to have winkled him out. It was part and parcel of him to want to add another dimension to the joke, to recharge its batteries. For the sight of Torridge in middle age would surely make funnier the reported anecdotes.

'After all, what's wrong,' demanded Arrowsmith noisily, 'with old school pals all meeting up? The more the merrier.'

He was a bully, Mrs. Wiltshire thought: all three of them were bullies.

~ ~ ~

Torridge arrived at half past nine. The hair that had been like a mouse's fur was still like that. It hadn't greyed any more; the scalp hadn't balded. He hadn't run to fat; in middle age he'd thinned down a bit. There was even a lankiness about him now, which was reflected in his movements. At school he had moved slowly, as though with caution. Jauntily attired in a pale linen suit, he crossed the dining-room of the Woodlands Hotel with a step as nimble as a tap dancer's.

No one recognized him. To the three men who'd been at school with him the man who approached their dinner table was a different person, quite unlike the figure that existed in the minds of the wives and children.

'My dear Arrows,' he said, smiling at Arrowsmith. The smile was different too, a brittle snap of a smile that came and went in a matter-of-fact way. The eyes that had been small didn't seem so in his thinner face. They flashed with a gleam of some kind, matching the snap of his smile.

'Good God, it's never old Porridge!' Arrowsmith's voice was slurred.

His face had acquired the beginnings of an alcoholic crimson, sweat glistened on his forehead.

'Yes, it's old Porridge,' Torridge said quietly. He held his hand out towards Arrowsmith and then shook hands with Wiltshire and Mace-Hamilton. He was introduced to their wives, with whom he shook hands also. He was introduced to the children, which involved further hand-shaking. His hand was cool and rather bony: they felt it should have been damp.

'You're nicely in time for coffee, Mr. Torridge,' Mrs. Mace-Hamilton said.

'Brandy more like,' Arrowsmith suggested. 'Brandy, old chap?'

'Well, that's awfully kind of you, Arrows. Chartreuse I'd prefer, really.'

A waiter drew up a chair. Room was made for Torridge between Mrs. Mace-Hamilton and the Arrowsmith boys. It was a frightful mistake, Wiltshire was thinking. It was mad of Arrowsmith.

Mace-Hamilton examined Torridge across the dinner table. The old Torridge would have said he'd rather not have anything alcoholic, that a cup of tea and a biscuit were more his line in the evenings. It was impossible to imagine this man saying his dad had a button business. There was a suavity about him that made Mace-Hamilton uneasy. Because of what had been related to his wife and the other wives and their children, he felt he'd been caught out in a lie, yet in fact that wasn't the case.

The children stole glances at Torridge, trying to see him as the boy who'd been described to them, and failing to. Mrs. Arrowsmith said to herself that all this stuff they'd been told over the years had clearly been rubbish. Mrs. Mace-Hamilton was bewildered. Mrs. Wiltshire was pleased.

'No one ever guessed,' Torridge said, 'what became of R.A.J. Fisher.' He raised the subject suddenly, without introduction.

'Oh God, Fisher,' Mace-Hamilton said.

'Who's Fisher?' the younger of the Arrowsmith boys enquired.

Torridge turned to flash his quick smile at the boy. 'He left,' he said. 'In unfortunate circumstances.'

'You've changed a lot, you know,' Arrowsmith said. 'Don't you think he's changed?' he asked Wiltshire and Mace-Hamilton.

'Out of recognition,' Wiltshire said.

Torridge laughed easily. 'I've become adventurous. I'm a late developer, I suppose.'

'What kind of unfortunate circumstances?' the younger Arrowsmith boy asked. 'Was Fisher expelled?'

'Oh no, not at all,' Mace-Hamilton said hurriedly.

'Actually,' Torridge said, 'Fisher's trouble all began with the writing of a note. Don't you remember? He put it in my pyjamas. But it wasn't for me at all.'

He smiled again. He turned to Mrs. Wiltshire in a way that seemed polite, drawing her into the conversation. 'I was an innocent at school. But innocence eventually slips away. I found my way about eventually.'

'Yes, of course,' she murmured. She didn't like him, even though she was glad he wasn't as he might have been. There was malevolence in him, a ruthlessness that seemed like a work of art. He seemed like a work of art himself, as though in losing the innocence he spoke of he had re-created himself.

'I often wonder about Fisher,' he remarked.

The Wiltshire twins giggled. 'What's so great about this bloody Fisher?' the older Arrowsmith boy murmured, nudging his brother with an elbow.

'What're you doing these days?' Wiltshire asked, interrupting Mace-Hamilton, who had also begun to say something.

'I make buttons,' Torridge replied. 'You may recall my father made buttons.'

'Ah, here're the drinks,' Arrowsmith rowdily observed.

'I don't much keep up with the school,' Torridge said as the waiter placed a glass of Chartreuse in front of him. 'I don't so much as think about it, except for wondering about poor old Fisher. Our headmaster was a cretin,' he informed Mrs. Wiltshire.

Again the Wiltshire twins giggled. The Arrowsmith girl yawned, and her brothers giggled also, amused that the name of Fisher had come up again.

'You will have coffee, Mr. Torridge?' Mrs. Mace-Hamilton offered, for the waiter had brought a fresh pot to the table. She held it poised above a cup. Torridge smiled at her and nodded. She said:

'Pearl buttons d'you make?'

'No, not pearl.'

'Remember those awful packet peas we used to have?' Arrowsmith enquired. Wiltshire said:

'Use plastics at all? In your buttons, Porridge?'

'No, we don't use plastics. Leathers, various leathers. And horn. We specialize.'

'How very interesting!' Mrs. Mace-Hamilton exclaimed.

'No, no. It's rather ordinary really.' He paused, and then added, 'Someone once told me that Fisher went into a timber business. But of course that was far from true.'

'A chap was expelled a year ago,' the younger Arrowsmith boy said, contributing this in order to cover up a fresh outburst of sniggering. 'For stealing a transistor.'

Torridge nodded, appearing to be interested. He asked the Arrowsmith boys where they were at school. The older one said Charterhouse and his brother gave the name of his preparatory school. Torridge nodded again and asked their sister, and she said she was waiting to go to university. He had quite a chat with the Wiltshire twins about their school. They considered it pleasant the way he bothered, seeming genuinely to want to know. The giggling died away.

'I imagined Fisher wanted me for his *bijou*,' he said when all that was over, still addressing the children. 'Our place was riddled with fancy larks like that. Remember?' he added, turning to Mace-Hamilton.

'*Bijou*?' one of the twins asked before Mace-Hamilton could reply.

'A male tart,' Torridge explained.

The Arrowsmith boys gaped at him, the older one with his mouth actually open. The Wiltshire twins began to giggle again. The Arrowsmith girl frowned, unable to hide her interest.

'The Honourable Anthony Swain,' Torridge said, 'was no better than a whore.'

Mrs. Arrowsmith, who for some minutes had been engaged with her own thoughts, was suddenly aware that the man who was in the button business was talking about sex. She gazed diagonally across the table at him, astonished that he should be talking in this way.

'Look here, Torridge,' Wiltshire said, frowning at him and shaking his head. With an almost imperceptible motion he gestured towards the wives and children.

'Andrews and Butler. Dillon and Pratt. Tothill and Goldfish Stewart. Your dad,' Torridge said to the Arrowsmith girl, 'was always very keen. Sainsbury Major in particular.'

'Now look here,' Arrowsmith shouted, beginning to get to his feet and then changing his mind.

'My gosh, how they broke chaps' hearts, those three!'

'Please don't talk like this.' It was Mrs. Wiltshire who protested, to everyone's surprise, most of all her own. 'The children are quite young, Mr. Torridge.'

Her voice had become a whisper. She could feel herself reddening with embarrassment, and a little twirl of sickness occurred in her stomach. Deferentially, as though appreciating the effort she had made, Torridge apologized.

'I think you'd better go,' Arrowsmith said.

'You were right about God Harvey, Arrows. Gay as a grig he was, beneath that cassock. So was Old Frosty, as a matter of fact.'

'Really!' Mrs. Mace-Hamilton cried, her bewilderment turning into outrage. She glared at her husband, demanding with her eyes that instantly something should be done. But her husband and his two friends were briefly stunned by what Torridge had claimed for God Harvey. Their schooldays leapt back at them, possessing them for a vivid moment: the dormitory, the dining-hall, the glances and the invitations, the meetings behind Chapel. It was somehow in keeping with the school's hypocrisy that God Harvey had had inclinations himself, that a rumour begun as an outrageous joke should have contained the truth.

'As a matter of fact,' Torridge went on, 'I wouldn't be what I am if it hadn't been for God Harvey. I'm what they call queer,' he explained to the children. 'I perform sexual acts with men.'

'For God's sake, Torridge,' Arrowsmith shouted, on his feet, his face the colour of ripe strawberry, his watery eyes quivering with rage.

'It was nice of you to invite me tonight, Arrows. Our *alma mater* can't be too proud of chaps like me.'

People spoke at once, Mrs. Mace-Hamilton and Mrs. Wiltshire, all three men. Mrs. Arrowsmith sat still. What she was thinking was that she had become quietly drunk while her husband had more boisterously reached the same condition. She was thinking, as well, that by the sound of things he'd possessed as a boy a sexual urge that was a lot livelier than the one he'd once exposed her to and now hardly ever did. With boys who had grown to be men he had had a whale of a time. Old Frosty had been a kind of Mr. Chips, she'd been told. She'd never ever heard of Sainsbury Major or God Harvey.

'It's quite disgusting,' Mrs. Mace-Hamilton's voice cried out above the other voices. She said the police should be called. It was scandalous to have to listen to unpleasant conversation like this. She began to say the children should leave the dining-room, but changed her mind because it appeared that Torridge himself was about to go. 'You're a most horrible man,' she cried.

Confusion gathered, like a fog around the table. Mrs. Wiltshire, who knew that her husband had committed adultery with Mrs. Arrowsmith, felt another bout of nerves in her stomach. 'Because she was starved, that's why,' her husband had almost violently confessed when she'd discovered. 'I was putting her out of her misery.' She had wept then, and he had comforted her as best he could. She had not told him that he had never succeeded in arousing in her the desire to make love: she had always assumed that to be a failing in herself, but now for some reason she was not so sure. Nothing had been directly said that might have caused this doubt, but an instinct informed Mrs. Wiltshire that the doubt should be there. The man across from her smiled his brittle, malevolent smile at her, as if in sympathy.

With his head bent over the table and his hands half hiding his face, the younger Arrowsmith boy examined his father by glancing through his fingers. There were men whom his parents warned him against, men who would sit beside you in buses or try to give you a lift in a car. This man who had come tonight, who had been such a joke up till now, was apparently one of these, not a joke at all. And the confusion was greater: at one time, it seemed, his father had been like that too.

The Arrowsmith girl considered her father also. Once she had walked into a room in Lagos to find her mother in the arms of an African clerk. Ever since, she had felt sorry for her father. There'd been an unpleasant scene at the time; she'd screamed at her mother and later in a fury had told her father what she'd seen. He'd nodded, wearily seeming not to be surprised, while her mother had miserably wept. She'd put her arms around her father, comforting him; she'd felt no mercy for her mother, no sympathy or understanding. The scene formed vividly in her mind as she sat at the dinner table: it appeared to be relevant in the confusion and yet not clearly so. Her parents' marriage was messy, messier than it had looked. Across the table her mother grimly smoked, focusing her eyes with difficulty. She smiled at her daughter, a soft, inebriated smile.

The older Arrowsmith boy was also aware of the confusion. Being at a school where the practice which had been spoken of was common enough, he could easily believe the facts that had been thrown about.

Against his will, he was forced to imagine what he had never imagined before: his father and his friends as schoolboys, engaged in passion with other boys. He might have been cynical about this image, but he could not be. Instead, it made him want to gasp. It knocked away the smile that had been on his face all evening.

The Wiltshire twins unhappily stared at the white tablecloth, here and there stained with wine or gravy. They, too, found they'd lost the urge to smile and instead shakily blinked back tears.

'Yes, perhaps I'd better go,' Torridge said.

With impatience Mrs. Mace-Hamilton looked at her husband, as if expecting him to hurry Torridge off or at least to say something. But Mace-Hamilton remained silent. Mrs. Mace-Hamilton licked her lips, preparing to speak herself. She changed her mind.

'Fisher didn't go into a timber business,' Torridge said, 'because poor old Fisher was dead as a doornail. Which is why our cretin of a headmaster, Mrs. Mace-Hamilton, had that Assembly.'

'Assembly?' she said. Her voice was weak, although she'd meant it to sound matter-of-fact and angry.

'There was an Assembly that no one understood. Poor old Fisher had strung himself up in a barn on his father's farm. I discovered that,' Torridge said, turning to Arrowsmith, 'years later: from God Harvey actually. The poor chap left a note, but the parents didn't care to pass it on. I mean it was for you, Arrows.'

Arrowsmith was still standing, hanging over the table. 'Note?' he said. 'For me?'

'Another note. Why d'you think he did himself in, Arrows?'

Torridge smiled, at Arrowsmith and then around the table.

'None of that's true,' Wiltshire said.

'As a matter of fact it is.'

He went, and nobody spoke at the dinner table. A body of a school-boy hung from a beam in a barn, a note on the straw below his dangling feet. It hung in the confusion that had been caused, increasing the confusion. Two waiters hovered by a sideboard, one passing the time by arranging sauce bottles, the other folding napkins into cone shapes. Slowly Arrowsmith sat down again. The silence continued as the conversation of Torridge continued to haunt the dinner table. He haunted it himself, with his brittle smile and his tap dancer's elegance, still faithful to the past in which he had so signally failed, triumphant in his middle age.

Then Mrs. Arrowsmith quite suddenly wept and the Wiltshire twins wept and Mrs. Wiltshire comforted them. The Arrowsmith girl got up and walked away, and Mrs. Mace-Hamilton turned to the three men and said they should be ashamed of themselves, allowing all this to happen.

ANN BEATTIE

THE CINDERELLA WALTZ

Milo and Bradley are creatures of habit. For as long as I've known him, Milo has worn his moth-eaten blue scarf with the knot hanging so low on his chest that the scarf is useless. Bradley is addicted to coffee and carries a Thermos with him. Milo complains about the cold, and Bradley is always a little edgy. They come out from the city every Saturday – this is not habit but loyalty – to pick up Louise. Louise is even more unpredictable than most nine-year-olds; sometimes she waits for them on the front step, sometimes she hasn't even gotten out of bed when they arrive. One time she hid in a closet and wouldn't leave with them.

Today Louise has put together a shopping bag full of things she wants to take with her. She is taking my whisk and my blue pottery bowl, to make breakfast for Milo and Bradley; Beckett's *Happy Days*, which she has carried around for weeks, and which she looks through, smiling – but I'm not sure she's reading it; and a coleus growing out of a conch shell. Also, she has stuffed into one side of the bag the fancy Victorian-style nightgown her grandmother gave her for Christmas, and into the other she has tucked her octascope. Milo keeps a couple of dresses, a nightgown, a toothbrush, and extra sneakers and boots at his apartment for her. He got tired of

ANN BEATTIE (born 1947): An observant interpreter of contemporary American manners and mores, Beattie is the author, most recently, of Park City: New and Selected Stories *and the novel* The Doctor's House. *She teaches at the University of Virginia in Charlottesville.*

rounding up her stuff to pack for her to take home, so he has brought some things for her that can be left. It annoys him that she still packs bags, because then he has to go around making sure that she has found everything before she goes home. She seems to know how to manipulate him, and after the weekend is over she calls tearfully to say that she has left this or that, which means that he must get his car out of the garage and drive all the way out to the house to bring it to her. One time, he refused to take the hour-long drive, because she had only left a copy of Tolkien's *The Two Towers*. The following weekend was the time she hid in the closet.

'I'll water your plant if you leave it here,' I say now.

'I can take it,' she says.

'I didn't say you couldn't take it. I just thought it might be easier to leave it, because if the shell tips over, the plant might get ruined.'

'Okay,' she says. 'Don't water it today, though. Water it Sunday afternoon.'

I reach for the shopping bag.

'I'll put it back on my windowsill,' she says. She lifts the plant out and carries it as if it's made of Steuben glass. Bradley bought it for her last month, driving back to the city, when they stopped at a lawn sale. She and Bradley are both very choosy, and he likes that. He drinks French-roast coffee; she will debate with herself almost endlessly over whether to buy a coleus that is primarily pink or lavender or striped.

'Has Milo made any plans for this weekend?' I ask.

'He's having a couple of people over tonight, and I'm going to help them make crepes for dinner. If they buy more bottles of that wine with the yellow flowers on the label, Bradley is going to soak the labels off for me.'

'That's nice of him,' I say. 'He never minds taking a lot of time with things.'

'He doesn't like to cook, though. Milo and I are going to cook. Bradley sets the table and fixes flowers in a bowl. He thinks it's frustrating to cook.'

'Well,' I say, 'with cooking you have to have a good sense of timing. You have to coordinate everything. Bradley likes to work carefully and not be rushed.'

I wonder how much she knows. Last week, she told me about a conversation she'd had with her friend Sarah. Sarah was trying to persuade Louise to stay around on the weekends, but Louise said she always went to her father's. Then Sarah tried to get her to take her along, and Louise said that she couldn't. 'You could take her if you wanted to,' I said later. 'Check with Milo and see if that isn't right. I don't think he'd mind having a friend of yours occasionally.'

She shrugged. 'Bradley doesn't like a lot of people around,' she said.

'Bradley likes you, and if she's your friend I don't think he'd mind.'

She looked at me with an expression I didn't recognize; perhaps she thought I was a little dumb, or perhaps she was just curious to see if I would go on. I didn't know how to go on. Like an adult, she gave a little shrug and changed the subject.

~ ~ ~

At ten o'clock Milo pulls into the driveway and honks his horn, which makes a noise like a bleating sheep. He knows the noise the horn makes is funny, and he means to amuse us. There was a time just after the divorce when he and Bradley would come here and get out of the car and stand around silently, waiting for her. She knew that she had to watch for them, because Milo wouldn't come to the door. We were both bitter then, but I got over it. I still don't think Milo would have come into the house again, though, if Bradley hadn't thought it was a good idea. The third time Milo came to pick her up after he'd left home, I went out to invite them in, but Milo said nothing. He was standing there with his arms at his sides like a wooden soldier, and his eyes were as dead to me as if they'd been painted on. It was Bradley whom I reasoned with. 'Louise is over at Sarah's right now, and it'll make her feel more comfortable if we're all together when she comes in,' I said to him, and Bradley turned to Milo and said, 'Hey, that's right. Why don't we go in for a quick cup of coffee?' I looked into the back seat of the car and saw his red Thermos there; Louise had told me about it. Bradley meant that they should come in and sit down. He was giving me even more than I'd asked for.

It would be an understatement to say that I disliked Bradley at first. I was actually afraid of him, afraid even after I saw him, though he was slender, and more nervous than I, and spoke quietly. The second time I saw him, I persuaded myself that he was just a stereotype, but someone who certainly seemed harmless enough. By the third time, I had enough courage to suggest that they come into the house. It was embarrassing for all of us, sitting around the table – the same table where Milo and I had eaten our meals for the years we were married. Before he left, Milo had shouted at me that the house was a farce, that my playing the happy suburban housewife was a farce, that it was unconscionable of me to let things drag on, that I would probably kiss him and say, 'How was your day, sweetheart?' and that he should bring home flowers and the evening paper. 'Maybe I would!' I screamed back. 'Maybe it would be nice to do that, even if we were pretending, instead of you coming home drunk and not caring what had happened to me or to Louise all day.' He was holding on to the edge of the kitchen table, the way you'd hold on to the horse's reins in a runaway carriage. 'I care about Louise,' he said finally. That was the most horrible moment. Until then, until he said it that way, I had thought that he was going through something horrible – certainly something was terribly wrong – but that, in his way, he loved me after all. '*You don't love me?*' I had whispered at once. It took us both aback. It was an innocent and pathetic question, and it made him come and put his arms around me in the last hug he ever gave me. 'I'm sorry for you,' he said, 'and I'm sorry for marrying you and causing this, but you know who I love. I told you who I love.' 'But you were kidding,' I said. 'You didn't mean it. You were kidding.'

When Bradley sat at the table that first day, I tried to be polite and not look at him much. I had gotten it through my head that Milo was crazy, and I guess I was expecting Bradley to be a horrible parody – Craig Russell doing Marilyn Monroe. Bradley did not spoon sugar into Milo's coffee. He did not even sit near him. In fact, he pulled his chair a little away from us, and in spite of his uneasiness he found more things to start conversations about than Milo and I did. He told me about the ad agency where he worked; he is a designer there. He asked if he could go out on the porch to see the brook – Milo had told him about the stream in the back of our place that was as thin as a pencil but still gave us our own watercress. He went out on the porch and stayed there for at least five minutes, giving us a chance to talk. We didn't say one word until he came back. Louise came home from Sarah's house just as Bradley sat down at the table again, and she gave him a hug as well as us. I could see that she really liked him. I was amazed that I liked him too. Bradley had won and I had lost, but he was as gentle and low-key as if none of it mattered. Later in the week, I called him and asked him to tell me if any free-lance jobs opened in his advertising agency. (I do a little free-lance artwork, whenever I can arrange it.) The week after that, he called and told me about another agency, where they were looking for outside artists. Our calls to each other are always brief and for a purpose, but lately they're not just calls about business. Before

Bradley left to scout some picture locations in Mexico, he called to say that Milo had told him that when the two of us were there years ago I had seen one of those big circular bronze Aztec calendars and I had always regretted not bringing it back. He wanted to know if I would like him to buy a calendar if he saw one like the one Milo had told him about.

Today, Milo is getting out of his car, his blue scarf flapping against his chest. Louise, looking out the window, asks the same thing I am wondering: 'Where's Bradley?'

Milo comes in and shakes my hand, gives Louise a one-armed hug.

'Bradley thinks he's coming down with a cold,' Milo says. 'The dinner is still on, Louise. We'll do the dinner. We have to stop at Gristede's when we get back to town, unless your mother happens to have a tin of anchovies and two sticks of unsalted butter.'

'Let's go to Gristede's,' Louise says. 'I like to go there.'

'Let me look in the kitchen,' I say. The butter is salted, but Milo says that will do, and he takes three sticks instead of two. I have a brainstorm and cut the cellophane on a left-over Christmas present from my aunt – a wicker plate that holds nuts and foil-wrapped triangles of cheese – and sure enough: one tin of anchovies.

'We can go to the museum instead,' Milo says to Louise. 'Wonderful.'

But then, going out the door, carrying her bag, he changes his mind. 'We can go to America Hurrah, and if we see something beautiful we can buy it,' he says.

They go off in high spirits. Louise comes up to his waist, almost, and I notice again that they have the same walk. Both of them stride forward with great purpose. Last week, Bradley told me that Milo had bought a weather vane in the shape of a horse, made around 1800, at America Hurrah, and stood it in the bedroom, and then was enraged when Bradley draped his socks over it to dry. Bradley is still learning what a perfectionist Milo is and how little sense of humor he has. When we were first married, I used one of our pottery casserole dishes to put my jewelry in, and he nagged me until I took it out and put the dish back in the kitchen cabinet. I remember his saying that the dish looked silly on my dresser because it was obvious what it was and people would think we left our dishes lying around. It was one of the things that Milo wouldn't tolerate, because it was improper.

~ ~ ~

When Milo brings Louise back on Saturday night they are not in a good mood. The dinner was all right, Milo says, and Griffin and Amy and Mark were amazed at what a good hostess Louise had been, but Bradley hadn't been able to eat.

'Is he still coming down with a cold?' I ask. I was still a little shy about asking questions about Bradley.

Milo shrugs. 'Louise made him take megadoses of vitamin C all weekend.'

Louise says, 'Bradley said that taking too much vitamin C was bad for your kidneys, though.'

'It's a rotten climate,' Milo says, sitting on the living room sofa, scarf and coat still on. 'The combination of cold and air pollution . . .'

Louise and I look at each other, and then back at Milo. For weeks now, he has been talking about moving to San Francisco, if he can find work there. (Milo is an architect.) This talk bores me, and it makes Louise nervous. I've asked him not to talk to her about it unless he's actually going to move, but he doesn't seem to be able to stop himself.

'Okay,' Milo says, looking at us both. 'I'm not going to say anything about San Francisco.'

'*California* is polluted,' I say. I am unable to stop myself, either.

Milo heaves himself up from the sofa, ready for the drive back to New York. It is the same way he used to get off the sofa that last year he lived here. He would get up, dress for work, and not even go into the kitchen for breakfast – just sit, sometimes in his coat as he was sitting just now, and at the last minute he would push himself up and go out to the driveway, usually without a good-bye, and get in the car and drive off either very fast or very slowly. I liked it better when he made the tires spin in the gravel when he took off.

He stops at the doorway now, and turns to face me. 'Did I take all your butter?' he says.

'No,' I say. 'There's another stick.' I point into the kitchen.

'I could have guessed that's where it would be,' he says, and smiles at me.

~ ~ ~

When Milo comes the next weekend, Bradley is still not with him. The night before, as I was putting Louise to bed, she said that she had a feeling he wouldn't be coming.

'I had that feeling a couple of days ago,' I said. 'Usually Bradley calls once during the week.'

'He must still be sick,' Louise said. She looked at me anxiously. 'Do you think he is?'

'A cold isn't going to kill him,' I said. 'If he has a cold, he'll be okay.'

Her expression changed; she thought I was talking down to her. She lay back in bed. The last year Milo was with us, I used to tuck her in and tell her that everything was all right. What that meant was that there had not been a fight. Milo had sat listening to music on the phonograph, with a book or the newspaper in front of his face. He didn't pay very much attention to Louise, and he ignored me entirely. Instead of saying a prayer with her, the way I usually did, I would say to her that everything was all right. Then I would go downstairs and hope that Milo would say the same thing to me. What he finally did say one night was 'You might as well find out from me as some other way.'

'Hey, are you an old bag lady again this weekend?' Milo says now, stooping to kiss Louise's forehead.

'Because you take some things with you doesn't mean you're a bag lady,' she says primly.

'Well,' Milo says, 'you start doing something innocently, and before you know it it can take you over.'

He looks angry and acts as though it's difficult for him to make conversation, even when the conversation is full of sarcasm and double entendres.

'What do you say we get going?' he says to Louise.

In the shopping bag she is taking is her doll, which she has not played with for more than a year. I found it by accident when I went to tuck in a loaf of banana bread that I had baked. When I saw Baby Betsy, deep in the bag, I decided against putting the bread in.

'Okay,' Louise says to Milo. 'Where's Bradley?'

'Sick,' he says.

'Is he too sick to have me visit?'

'Good heavens, no. He'll be happier to see you than to see me.'

'I'm rooting some of my coleus to give him,' she says. 'Maybe I'll give it to him like it is, in water, and he can plant it when it roots.'

When she leaves the room, I go over to Milo. 'Be nice to her,' I say quietly.

'I'm nice to her,' he says. 'Why does everybody have to act like I'm going to grow fangs every time I turn around?'

'You were quite cutting when you came in.'

'I was being self-deprecating.' He sighs. 'I don't really know why I come here and act this way,' he says.

'What's the matter, Milo?'

But now he lets me know he's bored with the conversation. He walks over to the table and picks up a *Newsweek* and flips through it. Louise comes back with the coleus in a water glass.

'You know what you could do,' I say. 'Wet a napkin and put it around that cutting and then wrap it in foil, and put it in water when you get there. That way, you wouldn't have to hold a glass of water all the way to New York.'

She shrugs. 'This is okay,' she says.

'Why don't you take your mother's suggestion,' Milo says. 'The water will slosh out of the glass.'

'Not if you don't drive fast.'

'It doesn't have anything to do with my driving fast. If we go over a bump in the road, you're going to get all wet.'

'Then I can put on one of my dresses at your apartment.'

'Am I being unreasonable?' Milo says to me.

'I started it,' I say. 'Let her take it in the glass.'

'Would you, as a favor, do what your mother says?' he says to Louise.

Louise looks at the coleus and at me.

'Hold the glass over the seat instead of over your lap, and you won't get wet,' I say.

'Your first idea was the best,' Milo says.

Louise gives him an exasperated look and puts the glass down on the floor, pulls on her poncho, picks up the glass again and says a sullen goodbye to me, and goes out the front door.

'Why is this my fault?' Milo says. 'Have I done anything terrible? I –'

'Do something to cheer yourself up,' I say, patting him on the back.

He looks as exasperated with me as Louise was with him. He nods his head yes, and goes out the door.

~ ~ ~

'Was everything all right this weekend?' I ask Louise.

'Milo was in a bad mood, and Bradley wasn't even there on Saturday,' Louise says. 'He came back today and took us to the Village for breakfast.'

'What did you have?'

'I had sausage wrapped in little pancakes and fruit salad and a rum bun.'

'Where was Bradley on Saturday?'

She shrugs. 'I didn't ask him.'

She almost always surprises me by being more grown-up than I give her credit for. Does she suspect, as I do, that Bradley has found another lover?

'Milo was in a bad mood when you two left here yesterday,' I say.

'I told him if he didn't want me to come next weekend, just to tell me.' She looks perturbed, and I suddenly realize that she can sound exactly like Milo sometimes.

'You shouldn't have said that to him, Louise,' I say. 'You know he wants you. He's just worried about Bradley.'

'So?' she says. 'I'm probably going to flunk math.'

'No, you're not, honey. You got a C-plus on the last assignment.'

'It still doesn't make my grade average out to a C.'

'You'll get a C. It's all right to get a C.'

She doesn't believe me.

'Don't be a perfectionist, like Milo,' I tell her. 'Even if you got a D, you wouldn't fail.'

Louise is brushing her hair – thin, shoulder-length, auburn hair. She is already so pretty and so smart in everything except math that I wonder what will become of her. When I was her age, I was plain and serious and I wanted to be a tree surgeon. I went with my father to the park and held a stethoscope – a real one – to the trunks of trees, listening to their silence. Children seem older now.

'What do you think's the matter with Bradley?' Louise says. She sounds worried.

'Maybe the two of them are unhappy with each other right now.'

She misses my point. 'Bradley's sad, and Milo's sad that he's unhappy.'

I drop Louise off at Sarah's house for supper. Sarah's mother, Martine Cooper, looks like Shelley Winters, and I have never seen her without a glass of Galliano on ice in her hand. She has a strong candy smell. Her husband has left her, and she professes not to care. She has emptied her living room of furniture and put up ballet bars on the walls and dances in a purple leotard to records by Cher and Mac Davis. I prefer to have Sarah come to our house, but her mother is adamant that everything must be, as she puts it, 'fifty-fifty.' When Sarah visited us a week ago and loved the chocolate pie I had made, I sent two pieces home with her. Tonight, when I left Sarah's house, her mother gave me a bowl of Jell-O fruit salad.

The phone is ringing when I come in the door. It is Bradley.

'Bradley,' I say at once, 'whatever's wrong, at least you don't have a neighbor who just gave you a bowl of maraschino cherries in green Jell-O with a Reddi Whip flower squirted on top.'

'Jesus,' he says. 'You don't need me to depress you, do you?'

'What's wrong?' I say.

He sighs into the phone. 'Guess what?' he says.

'What?'

'I've lost my job.'

It wasn't at all what I was expecting to hear. I was ready to hear that he was leaving Milo, and I had even thought that that would serve Milo right. Part of me still wanted him punished for what he did. I was so out of my mind when Milo left me that I used to go over and drink Galliano with Martine Cooper. I even thought seriously about forming a ballet group with her. I would go to her house in the afternoon, and she would hold a tambourine in the air and I would hold my leg rigid and try to kick it.

'That's awful,' I say to Bradley. 'What happened?'

'They said it was nothing personal – they were laying off three people. Two other people are going to get the ax at the agency within the next six months. I was the first to go, and it was nothing personal. From twenty thousand bucks a year to nothing, and nothing personal, either.'

'But your work is so good. Won't you be able to find something again?'

'Could I ask you a favor?' he says. 'I'm calling from a phone booth. I'm not in the city. Could I come talk to you?'

'Sure,' I say.

It seems perfectly logical that he should come alone to talk – perfectly logical until I actually see him coming up the walk. I can't entirely believe it. A year after my husband has left me, I am sitting with his lover – a man, a person I like quite well – and trying to cheer him up because he is out of work. ('Honey,' my father would say, 'listen to Daddy's heart with the stethoscope, or you can turn it toward you and listen to your own heart. You won't hear anything listening to a tree.' Was my persistence willfulness, or belief in magic? Is it possible that I hugged Bradley at the door because I'm secretly glad he's down-and-out, the way I used to be? Or do I really want to make things better for him?)

He comes into the kitchen and thanks me for the coffee I am making, drapes his coat over the chair he always sits in.

'What am I going to do?' he asks.

'You shouldn't get so upset, Bradley,' I say. 'You know you're good. You won't have trouble finding another job.'

'That's only half of it,' he says. 'Milo thinks I did this deliberately. He told me I was quitting on him. He's very angry at me. He fights with me, and then he gets mad that I don't enjoy eating dinner. My stomach's upset, and I can't eat anything.'

'Maybe some juice would be better than coffee.'

'If I didn't drink coffee, I'd collapse,' he says.

I pour coffee into a mug for him, coffee into a mug for me.

'This is probably very awkward for you,' he says. 'That I come here and say all this about Milo.'

'What does he mean about your quitting on him?'

'He said . . . he actually accused me of doing badly deliberately, so they'd fire me. I was so afraid to tell him the truth when I was fired that I pretended to be sick. Then I really *was* sick. He's never been angry at me this way. Is this always the way he acts? Does he get a notion in his head for no reason and then pick at a person because of it?'

I try to remember. 'We didn't argue much,' I say. 'When he didn't want to live here, he made me look ridiculous for complaining when I knew something was wrong. He expects perfection, but what that means is that you do things his way.'

'I *was*. I never wanted to sit around the apartment, the way he says I did. I even brought work home with me. He made me feel so bad all week that I went to a friend's apartment for the day on Saturday. Then he said I had walked out on the problem. He's a little paranoid. I was listening to the radio, and Carole King was singing "It's Too Late," and he came into the study and looked very upset, as though I had planned for the song to come on. I couldn't believe it.'

'Whew,' I say, shaking my head. 'I don't envy you. You have to stand up to him. I didn't do that. I pretended the problem would go away.'

'And now the problem sits across from you drinking coffee, and you're being nice to him.'

'I know it. I was just thinking we look like two characters in some soap opera my friend Martine Cooper would watch.'

He pushes his coffee cup away from him with a grimace.

'But anyway, I like you now,' I say. 'And you're exceptionally nice to Louise.'

'I took her father,' he says.

'Bradley – I hope you don't take offense, but it makes me nervous to talk about that.'

'I don't take offense. But how can you be having coffee with me?'

'You invited yourself over so you could ask that?'

'Please,' he says, holding up both hands. Then he runs his hands through his hair. 'Don't make me feel illogical. He does that to me, you know. He doesn't understand it when everything doesn't fall right into line. If I like fixing up the place, keeping some flowers around, therefore I can't like being a working person too, therefore I deliberately sabotage myself in my job.' Bradley sips his coffee.

'I wish I could do something for him,' he says in a different voice.

This is not what I expected, either. We have sounded like two wise adults, and then suddenly he has changed and sounds very tender. I realize the situation is still the same. It is two of them on one side and me on the other, even though Bradley is in my kitchen.

'Come and pick up Louise with me, Bradley,' I say. 'When you see Martine Cooper, you'll cheer up about your situation.'

He looks up from his coffee. 'You're forgetting what I'd look like to Martine Cooper,' he says.

~ ~ ~

Milo is going to California. He has been offered a job with a new San Francisco architectural firm. I am not the first to know. His sister, Deanna, knows before I do and mentions it when we're talking on the phone. 'It's middle-age crisis,' Deanna says sniffily. 'Not that I need to tell you.' Deanna would drop dead if she knew the way things are. She is scandalized every time a new display is put up in Bloomingdale's window. ('Those mannequins had eyes like an Egyptian princess, and *rags*. I swear to you, they had mops and brooms and ragged gauze dresses on, with whores' shoes – stiletto heels that prostitutes wear.')

I hang up from Deanna's call and tell Louise I'm going to drive to the gas station for cigarettes. I go there to call New York on their pay phone.

'Well, I only just knew,' Milo says. 'I found out for sure yesterday, and last night Deanna called and so I told her. It's not like I'm leaving tonight.'

He sounds elated, in spite of being upset that I called. He's happy in the way he used to be on Christmas morning. I remember him once running into the living room in his underwear and tearing open the gifts we'd been sent by relatives. He was looking for the eight-slice toaster he was sure we'd get. We'd been given two-slice, four-slice, and six-slice toasters, but then we got no more. 'Come out, my eight-slice beauty!' Milo crooned, and out came an electric clock, a blender, and an expensive electric pan.

'When are you leaving?' I ask him.

'I'm going out to look for a place to live next week.'

'Are you going to tell Louise yourself this weekend?'

'Of course,' he says.

'And what are you going to do about seeing Louise?'

'Why do you act as if I don't like Louise?' he says. 'I will occasionally come back East, and I will arrange for her to fly to San Francisco on her vacations.'

'It's going to break her heart.'

'No it isn't. Why do you want to make me feel bad?'

'She's had so many things to adjust to. You don't have to go to San Francisco right now, Milo.'

'It happens, if you care, that my own job here is in jeopardy. This is a real chance for me, with a young firm. They really want me. But anyway, all we need in this happy group is to have you bringing in a couple of hundred dollars a month with your graphic work and me destitute and Bradley so devastated by being fired that of course he can't even look for work.'

'I'll bet he is looking for a job,' I say.

'Yes. He read the want ads today and then fixed a crab quiche.'

'Maybe that's the way you like things, Milo, and people respond to you. You forbade me to work when we had a baby. Do you say anything encouraging to him about finding a job, or do you just take it out on him that he was fired?'

There is a pause, and then he almost seems to lose his mind with impatience.

'I can hardly *believe*, when I am trying to find a logical solution to all our problems, that I am being subjected, by telephone, to an unflattering psychological analysis by my ex-wife.' He says this all in a rush.

'All right, Milo. But don't you think that if you're leaving so soon you ought to call her, instead of waiting until Saturday?'

Milo sighs very deeply. 'I have more sense than to have important conversations on the telephone,' he says.

~ ~ ~

Milo calls on Friday and asks Louise whether it wouldn't be nice if both of us came in and spent the night Saturday and if we all went to brunch together Sunday. Louise is excited. I never go into town with her.

Louise and I pack a suitcase and put it in the car Saturday morning. A cutting of ivy for Bradley has taken root, and she has put it in a little green plastic pot for him. It's heartbreaking, and I hope that Milo notices and has a tough time dealing with it. I am relieved I'm going to be there when he tells her, and sad that I have to hear it at all.

In the city, I give the car to the garage attendant, who does not remember me. Milo and I lived in the apartment when we were first married, and moved when Louise was two years old. When we moved, Milo kept the apartment and sublet it – a sign that things were not going well, if I had been one to heed such a warning. What he said was that if we were ever rich enough we could have the house in Connecticut *and* the apartment in New York. When Milo moved out of the house, he went right back to the apartment. This will be the first time I have visited there in years.

Louise strides in in front of me, throwing her coat over the brass coatrack in the entranceway – almost too casual about being there. She's the hostess at Milo's, the way I am at our house.

He has painted the walls white. There are floor-length white curtains in the living room, where my silly flowered curtains used to hang. The walls are bare, the floor has been sanded, a stereo as huge as a computer stands against one wall of the living room, and there are four speakers.

'Look around,' Milo says. 'Show your mother around, Louise.'

I am trying to remember if I have ever told Louise that I used to live in this apartment. I must have told her, at some point, but I can't remember it.

'Hello,' Bradley says, coming out of the bedroom.

'Hi, Bradley,' I say. 'Have you got a drink?'

Bradley looks sad. 'He's got champagne,' he says, and looks nervously at Milo.

'No one *has* to drink champagne,' Milo says. 'There's the usual assortment of liquor.'

'Yes,' Bradley says. 'What would you like?'

'Some bourbon, please.'

'Bourbon.' Bradley turns to go into the kitchen. He looks different; his hair is different – more wavy – and he is dressed as though it were summer, in straight-legged white pants and black leather thongs.

'I want Perrier water with strawberry juice,' Louise says, tagging along after Bradley. I have never heard her ask for such a thing before. At home, she drinks too many Cokes. I am always trying to get her to drink fruit juice.

Bradley comes back with two drinks and hands me one. 'Did you want anything?' he says to Milo.

'I'm going to open the champagne in a moment,' Milo says. 'How have you been this week, sweetheart?'

'Okay,' Louise says. She is holding a pale-pink, bubbly drink. She sips it like a cocktail.

Bradley looks very bad. He has circles under his eyes, and he is ill at ease. A red light begins to blink on the phone-answering device next to where Bradley sits on the sofa, and Milo gets out of his chair to pick up the phone.

'Do you really want to talk on the phone right now?' Bradley asks Milo quietly.

Milo looks at him. 'No, not particularly,' he says, sitting down again. After a moment, the red light goes out.

'I'm going to mist your bowl garden,' Louise says to Bradley, and slides off the sofa and goes to the bedroom. 'Hey, a little toadstool is growing in here!' she calls back. 'Did you put it there, Bradley?'

'It grew from the soil mixture, I guess,' Bradley calls back. 'I don't know how it got there.'

'Have you heard anything about a job?' I ask Bradley.

'I haven't been looking, really,' he says. 'You know.'

Milo frowns at him. 'Your choice, Bradley,' he says. 'I didn't ask you to follow me to California. You can stay here.'

'No,' Bradley says. 'You've hardly made me feel welcome.'

'Should we have some champagne — all four of us — and you can get back to your bourbons later?' Milo says cheerfully.

We don't answer him, but he gets up anyway and goes to the kitchen. 'Where have you hidden the tulip-shaped glasses, Bradley?' he calls out after a while.

'They should be in the cabinet on the far left,' Bradley says.

'You're going with him?' I say to Bradley. 'To San Francisco?'

He shrugs and won't look at me. 'I'm not quite sure I'm wanted,' he says quietly.

The cork pops in the kitchen. I look at Bradley, but he won't look up. His new hairdo makes him look older. I remember that when Milo left me I went to the hairdresser the same week and had bangs cut. The next week, I went to a therapist, who told me it was no good trying to hide from myself. The week after that, I did dance exercise with Martine Cooper, and the week after that the therapist told me not to dance if I wasn't interested in dancing.

'I'm not going to act like this is a funeral,' Milo says, coming in with the glasses. 'Louise, come in here and have champagne! We have something to have a toast about.'

Louise comes into the living room suspiciously. She is so used to being refused even a sip of wine from my glass or her father's that she no longer even asks. 'How come I'm in on this?' she asks.

'We're going to drink a toast to me,' Milo says.

Three of the four glasses are clustered on the table in front of the sofa. Milo's glass is raised. Louise looks at me, to see what I'm going to say. Milo raises his glass even higher. Bradley reaches for a glass. Louise picks up a glass. I lean forward and take the last one.

'This is a toast to me,' Milo says, 'because I am going to be going to San Francisco.'

It was not a very good or informative toast. Bradley and I sip from our glasses. Louise puts her glass down hard and bursts into tears, knocking the glass over. The champagne spills onto the cover of a big art book about the Unicorn Tapestries. She runs into the bedroom and slams the door.

Milo looks furious. 'Everybody lets me know just what my insufficiencies are, don't they?' he says. 'Nobody minds expressing himself. We have it all right out in the open.'

'He's criticizing me,' Bradley murmurs, his head still bowed. 'It's because I was offered a job here in the city and I didn't automatically refuse it.'

I turn to Milo. 'Go say something to Louise, Milo,' I say. 'Do you think that's what somebody who isn't brokenhearted sounds like?'

He glares at me and stomps into the bedroom, and I can hear him talking to Louise reassuringly. 'It doesn't mean you'll *never* see me,' he says. 'You can fly there, I'll come here. It's not going to be that different.'

'You lied!' Louise screams. 'You said we were going to brunch.'

'We are. We are. I can't very well take us to brunch before Sunday, can I?'

'You didn't say you were going to San Francisco. What *is* San Francisco, anyway?'

'I just said so. I bought us a bottle of champagne. You can come out as soon as I get settled. You're going to like it there.'

Louise is sobbing. She has told him the truth, and she knows it's futile to go on.

~ ~ ~

By the next morning, Louise acts the way I acted – as if everything were just the same. She looks calm, but her face is small and pale. She looks very young. We walk into the restaurant and sit at the table Milo has reserved. Bradley pulls out a chair for me, and Milo pulls out a chair for Louise, locking his finger with hers for a second, raising her arm above her head, as if she were about to take a twirl.

She looks very nice, really. She has a ribbon in her hair. It is cold, and she should have worn a hat, but she wanted to wear the ribbon. Milo has good taste: the dress she is wearing, which he bought for her, is a hazy purple plaid, and it sets off her hair.

'Come with me. Don't be sad,' Milo suddenly says to Louise, pulling her by the hand. 'Come with me for a minute. Come across the street to the park for just a second, and we'll have some space to dance, and your mother and Bradley can have a nice quiet drink.'

She gets up from the table and, looking long-suffering, backs into her coat, which he is holding for her, and the two of them go out. The waitress comes to the table, and Bradley orders three Bloody Marys and a Coke, and eggs Benedict for everyone. He asks the waitress to wait awhile before she brings the food. I have hardly slept at all, and having a drink is not going to clear my head. I have to think of things to say to Louise later, on the ride home.

'He takes so many *chances*,' I say. 'He pushes things so far with people. I don't want her to turn against him.'

'No,' he says.

'Why are you going, Bradley? You've seen the way he acts. You know that when you get out there he'll pull something on you. Take the job and stay here.'

Bradley is fiddling with the edge of his napkin. I study him. I don't know who his friends are, how old he is, where he grew up, whether he believes in God, or what he usually drinks. I'm shocked that I know so little, and I reach out and touch him. He looks up.

'Don't go,' I say quietly.

The waitress puts the glasses down quickly and leaves, embarrassed because she thinks she's interrupted a tender moment. Bradley pats my hand on his arm. Then he says the thing that has always been between us, the thing too painful for me to envision or think about.

'I love him,' Bradley whispers.

We sit quietly until Milo and Louise come into the restaurant, swinging hands. She is pretending to be a young child, almost a baby, and I wonder for an instant if Milo and Bradley and I haven't been playing house too – pretending to be adults.

'Daddy's going to give me a first-class ticket,' Louise says. 'When I go to California we're going to ride in a glass elevator to the top of the Fairman Hotel.'

'The Fairmont,' Milo says, smiling at her.

Before Louise was born, Milo used to put his ear to my stomach and say that if the baby turned out to be a girl he would put her into glass slippers instead of bootees. Now he is the prince once again. I see them in a glass elevator, not long from now, going up and up, with the people below getting smaller and smaller, until they disappear.

DESMOND HOGAN

JIMMY

Her office overlooked the college grounds; early in the spring they were bedecked with crocuses and snowdrops. Looking down upon them was to excel oneself. She was a fat lady, known as 'Windy' by the students, her body heaved into sedate clothes and her eyes somehow always searching despite the student gibes that she was profoundly stupid and profoundly academic.

She lectured in ancient Irish history, yearly bringing students to view Celtic crosses and round towers marooned in spring floods. The college authorities often joined her on these trips; one administrator insisted on speaking in Irish all the time. This was a college situated near Connemara, the Gaelic-speaking part of Ireland. Irish was a big part of the curriculum; bespectacled pioneer pin-bearing administrators insisted on speaking Irish as though it was the tongue of foolish crows. There was an element of mindlessness about it. One spoke Irish because a state that had been both severe and regimental on its citizens had encouraged it.

Emily delayed by the window this morning. It was spring, and foolishly

DESMOND HOGAN (born 1950): Hogan is the author of the story collections Diamonds at the Bottom of the Sea, The Mourning Thief, *and* Lebanon Lodge (*the latter two published in the United States in one volume under the title* A Link with the River), *and five novels, most recently* A Farewell to Prague; *also a volume of travel pieces and a play. He lives in County Clare, Ireland.*

she remembered the words of the blind poet Raftery. 'Now that it's spring the days will be getting longer. And after the feast of Brigid I'll set foot to the roads.' There was that atmosphere of instinct abroad in Galway today. Galway as long as she recalled was a city of travelling people: red-petticoated tinkers, clay-pipe-smoking sailors, wandering beggars.

In Eyre Square sat an austere statue of Pádraic Ó Conaire, an Irish scribe who'd once walked to Moscow to visit Chekhov and found him gone for the weekend.

In five minutes she would lecture on Brigid's crosses, the straw symbols of renewal in Ireland.

There was now evidence that Brigid was a lecher, a Celtic whore who was ascribed to sainthood by those who had slept with her, but that altered nothing. She was one of the cardinal Irish holy figures, the Isis of the spring-enchanted island.

Emily put words together in her mind.

In five minutes they'd confront her, pleased faces pushing forward. These young people had been to New York or Boston for their summer holidays. They knew everything that was to be known. They sneered a lot, they smiled little. They were possessed of good looks, spent most of the day lounging in the Cellar bar, watching strangers: even students had the wayward Galway habit of eyeing a stranger closely, for it was a city tucked away in a corner of Ireland, peaceable, prosperous, seaward-looking.

After class that day she returned to the college canteen, where she considered the subject of white sleeveless jerseys. Jimmy used to have one of those. They'd gone to college in the thirties, Earlsfort Terrace in Dublin, and Jimmy used to wear one of those jerseys. They'd sit in the dark corridor, a boy and a girl from Galway, pleased that the trees were again in bloom, quick to these things by virtue of coming from Galway, where nature dazzled.

Their home was outside Galway city, six miles from it, a big house, an elm tree on either side of it and in spring two pools of snowdrops like hankies in front of it.

Jimmy had gone to Dublin to study English literature. She had followed him in a year to study history. They were respectable children of a much-lauded solicitor, and they approached their lives gently. She got a job in the university in Galway. He got a job teaching in Galway city.

Mrs. Carmichael, lecturer in English, approached.

Mrs. Carmichael wore her grandmother's Edwardian clothes, because, though sixty, she considered it in keeping with what folk were wearing in Carnaby Street in London.

'Emily, I had trouble today,' she confessed. 'A youngster bit a girl in class.'

Emily smiled, half from chagrin, half from genuine amusement.

Mrs. Carmichael was a bit on the Anglo-Irish side, taut, upper-class, looking on these Catholic students as one might upon a rare and rather charming breed of radishes.

'Well, tell them to behave themselves,' Emily said. 'That's what I always say.'

She knew from long experience that they did not obey, that they laughed at her, and that her obesity was hallmarked by a number of nicknames. She could not help it, she ate a lot, she enjoyed cakes in Lydons' and more particularly when she went to Dublin she enjoyed Bewley's and country-shop cakes.

In fact the country shop afforded her not just a good pot of tea and nice ruffled cream cakes but a view of the green, a sense again of student days, here in Dublin, civilized, parochial. She recalled the woman with the oval face who became famous for writing stories and the drunkard who wrote strange books that now young people read.

'I'll see you tomorrow,' Mrs. Carmichael said, leaving.

Emily watched her. She'd sail in her Anglia to her house in the country, fleeing this uncivilized mess.

Emily put her handkerchief into her handbag and strolled home.

What was it about this spring? Since early in the year strange notions had been entering her head. She'd been half-thinking of leaving for Paris for a few days or spending a weekend in West Cork.

There was both desire and remembrance in the spring.

In her parents' home her sister, Sheila, now lived. She was married. Her husband was a vet.

Her younger brother, George, was working with the European Economic Community in Brussels.

Jimmy alone was unheard of, unlisted in conversation.

He'd gone many years ago, disappearing on a mail train when the war was waging in the outside world. He'd never come back; some said he was an alcoholic on the streets of London. If that was so he'd be an eloquent drunkard. He had so much, Jimmy had, so much of his race, astuteness, learning, eyes that danced like Galway Bay on mornings when the islands were clear and when gulls sparkled like flecks of foam.

She considered her books, her apartment, sat down, drank tea. It was already afternoon, and the Dublin train hooted, shunting off to arrive in Dublin in the late afternoon.

Tom, her brother-in-law, always said Jimmy was a moral retrograde, to be banished from mind. Sheila always said Jimmy was better off gone. He was too confused in himself. George, the youngest of the family, recalled only that he'd read him Oscar Wilde's *The Happy Prince* once and that tears had broken down his cheeks.

The almond blossom had not yet come and the war trembled in England and in a month Jimmy was gone and his parents were glad. Jimmy had been both a nuisance and a scandal. Jimmy had let the family down.

Emily postured over books on Celtic mythology, taking notes.

It had been an old custom in Ireland to drive at least one of your family out, to England, to the mental hospital, to sea, or to a bad marriage. Jimmy had not fallen easily into his category. He'd been a learned person, a very literate young man. He'd taught in a big school, befriended a young man, the thirties prototype with blond hair, went to Dublin one weekend with him, stayed in Buswell's Hotel with him, was since branded by names they'd put on Oscar Wilde. Jimmy had insisted on his innocence, but the boy had lied before going to Dublin, telling his parents that he was going to play a hurling match.

Jimmy had to resign his job; he took to drink, he was banished from home, slipping in in the afternoons to read to George. Eventually he'd gone. The train had registered nothing of his departure as it whinnied in the afternoon. He just slipped away.

The boy, Johnny Fogarthy, whom Jimmy had abducted to Dublin, himself left Ireland.

He went to the States, ended up in the antique trade, and in 1949, not yet twenty-seven, was killed in Pacifica. Local minds construed all elements of this affair to be tragic.

Jimmy was safely gone.

The dances at the crossroads near their home ceased, and that was the final memory of Jimmy, dancing with a middle-aged woman and she wearing earrings and an accordion bleating 'The Valley of Slievenamban.'

Emily heard a knock on the door early next morning. Unrushed, she went to the door. She was wearing a pink gown. Her hair was in a net.

She had been expecting no caller, but then again the postman knocked when he had a parcel.

For years afterwards she would tell people of the thoughts that had been haunting her mind in the days previously.

She opened the door.

A man aged but not bowed by age, derelict but not disarrayed, stood outside.

There was a speed in her eyes which detected the form of a man older than Jimmy her brother but yet holding his features and hiding nothing of the graciousness of which he was possessed.

She held him. He held her. There was anguish in her eyes. Her fat hands touched an old man.

'Jimmy,' she said simply.

Jimmy the tramp had won £100 at the horses and chosen from a variety of possibilities a home visit. Jimmy the tramp lived on Charing Cross Road.

Jimmy the tramp was a wino, yes, but like many of his counterparts near St.-Martin-in-the-Field in London was an eloquent one. Simply Jimmy was home.

News brushed swiftly to the country. His brother-in-law reared. His sister, Sheila, silenced. Emily, in her simple way, was overjoyed.

News was relayed to Brussels. George, the younger brother, was expected home in two weeks.

That morning Emily led Jimmy to a table, laid it as her own mother would have done ceremoniously with breakfast things, and near a pitcher, blue and white, they prayed.

Emily's prayer was one of thanksgiving.

Jimmy's too was one of thanksgiving.

Emily poured milk over porridge and dolled the porridge with honey from Russia, invoking for Jimmy the time Pádraic Ó Conaire walked to Moscow.

In the afternoon he dressed in clothes Emily bought for him, and they walked the streets of Galway. Jimmy by the Claddagh, filled as it was with swans, wept the tears of a frail human being.

'Emily,' he said. 'This should be years ago.'

For record he said there'd been no interest other than platonic in the young boy, that he'd been wronged and this wrong had driven him to drink. 'I hope you don't think I'm apologizing,' he said. 'I'm stating facts.'

Sheila met him, and Tom, his brother-in-law, who looked at him as though at an animal in the zoo.

Emily had prepared a meal the first evening of his return. They ate veal, drank rosé d'Anjou, toasted by a triad of candles. 'One for love, one for luck, one for happiness,' indicated Emily.

Tom said the EEC made things good for farmers, bad for businessmen. Sheila said she was going to Dublin for a hairdo.

Emily said she'd like to bring Jimmy to the old house next day.

Sure enough the snowdrops were there when they arrived, and the frail trees.

Jimmy said, as though in speed, he'd lived as a tramp for years, drinking wine, beating his breast in pity.

'It was all an illusion,' he said. 'This house still stands.'

He entered it, a child, and Tom, his brother-in-law, looked scared.

Jimmy went to the library, and sure enough the works of Oscar Wilde were there.

'Many a time *The Happy Prince* kept me alive,' he said.

Emily dressed newly; her dignity cut a hole in her pupils. They silenced and listened to talk about Romanesque doorways.

She lit her days with thoughts of the past: rooms not desecrated, appointments under the elms.

Her figure cut through Galway. Spring came in a rush. There was no dalliance. The air shattered with freshness.

As she lectured, Jimmy walked. He walked by the Claddagh, by Shop Street, by Quay Street. He looked, he pondered, his gaze drifted to Clare.

Once, Johnny Fogarthy had told him he was leaving for California on the completion of his studies. He left all right.

He was killed.

'For love,' Jimmy told Emily. He sacrificed himself for the speed of a car on the Pacific coast.

They dined together and listened to Bach. Tom and Sheila kept away.

Emily informed Jimmy about her problems. Jimmy was wakeful to them. In new clothes, washed, he was the aged poet, distinguished, alert to the unusual, the charming, the indirect.

'I lived in a world of craftsmen,' he told Emily. 'Most alcoholics living on the streets are poets driven from poetry, lovers driven from their beloved, craftsmen exiled from their craft.'

They assuaged those words with drink.

Emily held Jimmy's hand. 'I hope you are glad to be here,' she said.

'I am, I am,' he said.

The weekend in Dublin with Johnny Fogarthy he'd partaken of spring lamb with him on a white-lain table in Buswell's, he told Emily.

'We drank wine then too, rosé. Age made no difference between us. We were elucidated by friendship, its acts, its meaning. Pity love was mistaken for sin.'

Jimmy had gone during the war, and he told Emily about the bombs, the emergencies, the crowded air-raid shelters.

'London was on fire. But I'd have chosen anything, anything to the gap in people's understanding in Ireland.'

They drank to that.

Emily at college was noted now for a new beauty.

Jimmy in his days walked the streets.

Mrs. Kenny in Kenny's bookshop recognized him and welcomed him. Around were writers' photographs on the wall. 'It's good to see you,' she said.

He had represented order once, white sleeveless jumpers, fairish hair evenly parted, slender volumes of English poetry.

'Remember,' Mrs. Kenny said, 'the day O'Duffy sailed to Spain with the blueshirts, and you, a boy, said they should be beaten with their own rosary beads.'

They laughed.

Jimmy had come home not as an aged tramp but as a poet. It could not have been more simple if he'd come from Cambridge, a retired don. Those who respected the order in him did not seek undue information. Those puzzled by him demanded all the reasons.

Those like Tom, his brother-in-law, who hated him, resented his presence. 'I sat here once with Johnny,' Jimmy told Emily one day on the Connemara coast. 'He said he needed something from life, something Ireland could not give him. So he went to the States.'

'Wise man.'

'But he was killed.'

'We were the generation expecting early and lucid deaths,' he told Emily.

Yes. But Jimmy's death had been his parents' mortification with him, his friends' disavowal of him, Emily's silence in her eyes. He'd gone, dispirited, rejected. He'd gone, someone who'd deserted his own agony.

'You're back,' Emily said to him cheerily. 'That's the most important thing.'

His brother, George, came back from Brussels, a burly man in his forties.

He was cheerful and gangly at encountering Jimmy. He recognized integrity, recalled Jimmy reading him *The Happy Prince*, embraced the old man.

Over gin in Emily's he said, 'The EEC is like everything else, boring. You'll be bored in Tokyo, bored in Brussels, bored in Dublin.' Emily saw that Jimmy was not bored.

In the days, he walked through town, wondering at change, unable to account for it, the new buildings, the supermarkets. His hands were held behind his back. Emily often watched him, knowing that like De Valera he represented something of Ireland. But an element other than pain, fear, loneliness. He was the artist. He was the one forgone and left out in a rush to be acceptable.

They attended mass in the pro-cathedral. Jimmy knelt, prayed; Emily wondered, were his prayers sincere? She looked at Christ, situated quite near the mosaic of President Kennedy, asked him to leave Jimmy, for him not to return. She enjoyed his company as though that of an erstwhile lover.

Sheila threw a party one night.

The reasoning that led to this event was circumspect. George was home. He did not come home often. And when he did he stayed only a few days.

It was spring. The house had been spring-cleaned. A new carpet now graced the floor. Blossom threatened; lace divided the carpet with its shadows.

All good reasons to entertain the local populace.

But deep in Sheila, that aggravated woman's mind, must have been the knowledge that Jimmy, being home, despite his exclusion from all ceremony, despite his rather nebulous circumstances, his homecoming had by some decree to be both established and celebrated.

So neighbours were asked, those who'd borne rumour of him once, those who rejected him and yet were only too willing to accept his legend, young teacher in love with blond boy, affair discovered, young teacher flees to the gutters of London, blond boy ends up in a head-on collision in Pacifica, a town at the toe of San Francisco, California.

The first thing Jimmy noticed was a woman singing 'I Have Seen the Lark Soar High at Morn' next to a sombre ancient piano.

Emily had driven him from Galway, she beside him in a once-a-lifetime cape saw his eyes and the shadow that crossed them. He was back in a place which had rejected him. He had returned bearing no triumph but his own humility.

Emily chatted to Mrs. Connaire and Mrs. Delaney. To them, though a spinster, she was a highly erudite member of the community and as such acknowledged by her peers.

Emily looked about. Jimmy was gone. She thrust herself through the crowds and discovered Jimmy after making her way up a stairway hung with paintings of cattle marts and islands, in a room by himself, the room in which he had once slept.

'Jimmy.' He turned.

'Yes.'

'Come down.'

Like a lamb he conceded.

They walked again into the room where a girl aged seventeen sang 'The Leaving of Liverpool.'

It was a party in the old style, with pots of tea and whiskey and slender elegant cups.

George said, 'It's great to see the country changing, isn't it? It's great to see people happy.'

Emily thought of the miles of suburban horror outside Galway and thought otherwise.

Tom slapped Jimmy's back. Tom, it must be stated, did not desire this party, not at least until Jimmy was gone. His wife's intentions he suspected, but he let it go ahead.

'It's great having you,' he said to Jimmy, bitter and sneering from drink. 'Isn't it you that was the queer fellow throwing up a good job for a young lad.'

Emily saw the pain, sharp, smitten, like an arrow.

She would have reached for him as she would have for a child smitten by a bomb in the North of Ireland, but the crowd churned and he was lost from sight.

Tom sang 'If I Had a Hammer.' Sheila, plagued by the social success of her party, wearing earrings like toadstools, sang 'I Left My Heart in San Francisco.'

A priest who'd eyed Jimmy but had not approached him sang 'Lullaby of Broadway.'

George, Jimmy's young brother working in the EEC, got steadily drunker. Tom was slapping the precocious backsides of young women. Sheila was dancing attendance with cucumber sandwiches.

Jimmy was talking to a blond boy who if you stretched memory greatly resembled Johnny Fogarthy.

The fire blazed.

Their parents might have turned in their grave, hating Jimmy their child because he was the best of their brood and sank the lowest.

Emily sipped sherry and talked to neighbours about cows and sheep and daughters with degrees in medicine and foreign countries visited.

She saw her brother and mentally adjusted his portrait: he was again a young man, very handsome, if you like, in love in an idle way with one of his pupils.

In love in a way one person gives to another a secret, a share in their happiness.

She would have stopped all that was going to happen to him but knew that she couldn't.

Tom, her brother-in-law, was getting drunker and viler.

He said out loud, 'What is it that attracts men to young fellows?' surprising Jimmy in a simple conversation with a blond boy.

The party ceased, music ceased. All looked towards Jimmy, looked away. The boy was Mrs. McDonagh's son, going from one pottery to another in Ireland to learn his trade, never satisfied, always moving, recently taken up with the Divine Light, some religious crowd in Galway.

People stared. The image was authentic. There was not much sin in it but a lot of beauty. They did not share Tom's prejudice but left the man and the boy. It was getting late. The country was changing, and if there had been wounds, why couldn't they be forgotten?

Tom was slobbering. His wife attended him. He was slobbering about Jimmy, always afraid of that element of his wife's family, always afraid strange children would be born to him but none came anyway. His wife brought him to the toilet, where presumably he got sick.

George, drunk on gin, talked about the backsides of secretaries in Brussels, and Jimmy, alone among the crowd, still eloquent with drink, spoke to the blond teenager about circuses long ago.

'Why did you leave Ireland?' the boy asked him.

'Searching,' he said, 'searching for something. Why did you leave your last job?'

'Because I wasn't satisfied,' the boy said. 'You've got to go on, haven't you? There's always that sense that there's more than this.'

The night was rounded by a middle-aged woman who'd once met Count John McCormack singing 'Believe Me if All Those Endearing Young Charms.'

On the way back into Galway, Emily felt revered and touched by time, recalled Jimmy, his laughter once, that laughter more subdued now.

She was glad he was back; glad of his company and, despite everything, clear in her mind that the past was a fantasy. People had needed culprits then, people had needed fallen angels.

She said good night to Jimmy, touched him on the cheek with a kiss.

'See you in the morning,' she said.

She didn't.

She left him asleep, made tea for herself, contemplated the spring sky outside.

She went to college, lectured on Celtic crosses, lunched with Mrs. Carmichael, drove home in the evening, passing the sea, the Dublin train sounding distantly in her head. The party last night had left a strange colour inside her, like light in wine or a reflection on a saxophone.

What was it that haunted her about it? she asked herself.

Then she knew.

She remembered Jimmy on a rain-drenched night during the war coming to the house and his parents turning him away.

Why was it Sheila had thrown that party? Because she had to requite the spirit of the house.

Why was it Jimmy had come back to the house? Because he needed to reassert himself to the old spirits there.

Why was it she was glad? Because her brother was home and at last she had company to glide into old age.

She opened the door. Light fell, guiltily.

Inside was a note.

'Took the Dublin train. Thanks for everything. Love, Jimmy.'

The note closed in her hand like a building falling beneath a bomb, and the scream inside her would have dragged her into immobility had not she noticed the sky outside, golden, futuristic, the colour of the sky over their home when Easter was near and she, a girl in white, not fat, beautiful even, walked with her brother, a boy in a sleeveless white jersey, by a garden drilled in daffodils, expecting nothing less than the best life could offer.

PETER CAMERON

JUMP OR DIVE

Jason, my uncle's lover, sat in the dark kitchen, eating what sounded like a bowl of cereal. He had some disease that made him hungry every few hours – something about not enough sugar in his blood. Every night, he got up at about three o'clock and fixed himself a snack. Since I was sleeping on the living room couch, I could hear him.

My parents and I had driven down from Oregon to visit my uncle Walter, who lived in Arizona. He was my father's younger brother. My sister Jackie got to stay home, on account of having just graduated from high school and having a job at the Lob-Steer Restaurant. But there was no way my parents were letting me stay home: I had just finished ninth grade, and I was unemployed.

My parents slept in the guest room. Jason and Uncle Walter slept together in the master bedroom. The first morning, when I went into the bathroom, I saw Jason sitting on the edge of the big unmade bed in his jockey shorts. Jason was very tan, but it was an odd tan: his face and the bottom of three-quarters of his arms were much darker than his chest. It looked as if he was wearing a T-shirt.

The living room couch was made of leather and had little metal nubs

PETER CAMERON (born 1959): Cameron's novels and story collections include The Half You Don't Know, The Weekend, Andorra, and The City of Your Final Destination. He lives in New York City and is a recipient of a Guggenheim Foundation Fellowship.

stuck all over it. It was almost impossible to sleep on. I lay there listening to Jason crunch. The only other noise was the air conditioner, which turned itself off and on constantly to maintain the same, ideal temperature. When it went off, you could hear the insects outside. A small square of light from the opened refrigerator appeared on the dining room wall. Jason was putting the milk away. The faucet ran for a second, and then Jason walked through the living room, his white underwear bright against his body. I pretended I was asleep.

After a while, the air conditioner went off, but I didn't hear the insects. At some point in the night – the point that seems closer to morning than to evening – they stopped their drone, as though they were unionized and paid to sing only so long. The house was very quiet. In the master bedroom, I could hear bodies moving, and murmuring, but I couldn't tell if it was people making love or turning over and over, trying to get comfortable. It went on for a few minutes, and then it stopped.

~ ~ ~

We were staying at Uncle Walter's for a week, and every hour of every day was planned. We always had a morning activity and an afternoon activity. Then we had cocktail hour, then dinner, then some card game. Usually hearts, with the teams switching: some nights Jason and Walter versus my parents, some nights the brothers challenging Jason and my mother. I never played. I watched TV or rode Jason's moped around the deserted roads of Gretna Green, which was the name of Uncle Walter's condominium village. The houses in Gretna Green were called villas, and they all had different names – some for gems, some for colors, and some for animals. Uncle Walter and Jason lived in Villa Indigo.

We started each morning on the patio, where we'd eat breakfast and 'plan the day.' The adults took a long time planning the day so there would be less day to spend. All the other villa inhabitants ate breakfast on their patios too. The patios were separated by lawn and rock gardens and pine trees, but there wasn't much privacy: everyone could see everyone else sitting under uniformly striped umbrellas, but everyone pretended he couldn't. They were mostly old people, retired people. Children were allowed only as guests. Everyone looked at me as if I was a freak.

Wednesday morning, Uncle Walter was inside making coffee in the new coffee machine my parents had brought him. My mother told me that whenever you're invited to someone's house overnight you should bring something – a hostess gift. Or a host gift, she added. She was helping Uncle Walter make breakfast. Jason was lying on a chaise in the sun, trying to even out his tan. My father was reading the *Wall Street Journal*. He got up early every morning and drove into town and bought it, so he could 'stay in touch.' My mother made him throw it away right after he read it so it wouldn't interfere with the rest of the day.

Jason had his eyes closed, but he was talking. He was listing the things we could do that day. I was sitting on the edge of a big planter filled with pachysandra and broken statuary that Leonard, my uncle's ex-boyfriend, had dug up somewhere. Leonard was an archaeologist. He used to teach paleontology at Northern Arizona University, but he didn't get tenure, so he took a job with an oil company in South America, making sure the engineers didn't drill in sacred spots. The day before, I'd seen a tiny purple-throated lizard in the vines, and I was trying to find him again. I wanted to catch him and take him back to Oregon.

Jason paused in his list, and my father said, 'Uh-huh.' That's what he always says when he's reading the newspaper and you talk to him.

'We could go to the dinosaur museum,' Jason said.

'What's that?' I said.

Jason sat up and looked at me. That was the first thing I'd said to him, I think. I'd been ignoring him.

'Well, I've never been there,' he said. Even though it was early in the morning, his brown forehead was already beaded with sweat. 'It has some reconstructed dinosaurs and footprints and stuff.'

'Let's go there,' I said. 'I like dinosaurs.'

'Uh huh,' said my father.

My mother came through the sliding glass doors carrying a platter of scrambled eggs. Uncle Walter followed with the coffee.

'We're going to go to the dinosaur museum this morning,' Jason said.

'Please, not that pit,' Uncle Walter said.

'But Evan wants to go,' Jason said. 'It's about time we did something he liked.'

Everyone looked at me. 'It doesn't matter,' I said.

'Oh, no,' Uncle Walter said. 'Actually, it's fascinating. It just brings back bad memories.'

As it turned out, Uncle Walter and my father stayed home to discuss their finances. My grandmother had left them her money jointly, and they're always arguing about how to invest it. Jason drove my mother and me out to the dinosaur museum. I think my mother came just because she didn't want to leave me alone with Jason. She doesn't trust Uncle Walter's friends, but she doesn't let on. My father thinks it's very important we all treat Uncle Walter normally. Once, he hit Jackie because she called Uncle Walter a fag. That's the only time he's ever hit either of us.

The dinosaur museum looked like an airplane hangar in the middle of the desert. Inside, trenches were dug into the earth and bones stuck out of their walls. They were still exhuming some of the skeletons. The sand felt oddly damp. My mother took off her sandals and carried them; Jason looked around quickly and then went outside and sat on the hood of the car, smoking, with his shirt off. At the gift stand, I bought a small bag of dinosaur bone chips. My mother bought a 3-D panoramic postcard. When you held it one way, a dinosaur stood with a creature in its toothy mouth. When you tilted it, the creature disappeared. Swallowed.

On the way home, we stopped at a Safeway to do some grocery shopping. Both Jason and my mother seemed reluctant to push the shopping cart, so I did. In the produce aisle, Jason picked up cantaloupes and shook them next to his ear. A few feet away, my mother folded back the husks to get a good look at the kernels on the corncobs. It seemed as if everyone was pawing at the food. It made me nervous, because once, when I was little, I opened up a box of chocolate Ding Dongs in the grocery store and started eating one, and the manager came over and yelled at me. The only good thing about that was that my mother was forced to buy the Ding Dongs, but every time I ate one I felt sick.

A man in Bermuda shorts and a yellow cardigan sweater started talking to Jason. My mother returned with six apparently decent ears of corn. She dumped them into the cart. 'Who's that?' she asked me, meaning the man Jason was talking to.

'I don't know,' I said. The man made a practice golf swing, right there in the produce aisle. Jason watched him. Jason was a golf pro at a country club. He used to be part of the golf tour you see on television on weekend afternoons, but he quit. Now he gave lessons at the country club. Uncle Walter had been one of his pupils. That's how they met.

'It's hard to tell,' Jason was saying. 'I'd try opening up your stance a little more.' He put a cantaloupe in our shopping cart.

'Hi,' the man said to us.

'Mr. Baird, I'd like you to meet my wife, Ann,' Jason said.

Mr. Baird shook my mother's hand. 'How come we never see you down the club?'

'Oh . . ,' my mother said.

'Ann hates golf,' Jason said.

'And how 'bout you?' The man looked at me. 'Do you like golf?'

'Sure,' I said.

'Well, we'll have to get you out on the links. Can you beat your dad?'

'Not yet,' I said.

'It won't be long,' Mr. Baird said. He patted Jason on the shoulder. 'Nice to see you, Jason. Nice to meet you, Mrs. Jerome.'

He walked down the aisle and disappeared into the bakery section. My mother and I both looked at Jason. Even though it was cold in the produce aisle, he was sweating. No one said anything for a few seconds. Then my mother said, 'Evan, why don't you go find some Doritos? And some Gatorade too, if you want.'

Back at Villa Indigo, my father and Uncle Walter were playing cribbage. Jason kissed Uncle Walter on the top of his semi-bald head. My father watched and then stood up and kissed my mother. I didn't kiss anyone.

~ ~ ~

Thursday, my mother and I went into Flagstaff to buy new school clothes. Back in Portland, when we go into malls we separate and make plans to meet at a specified time and place, but this was different: it was a strange mall, and since it was school clothes, my mother would pay for them, and therefore she could help pick them out. So we shopped together, which we hadn't done in a while. It was awkward. She pulled things off the rack which I had ignored, and when I started looking at the Right Now for Young Men stuff she entered the Traditional Shoppe. We finally bought some underwear, and some orange and yellow socks, which my mother said were 'fun.'

Then we went to the shoe store. I hate trying on shoes. I wish the salespeople would just give you the box and let you try them on yourself. There's something about someone else doing it all – especially touching your feet – that embarrasses me. It's as if the person was your servant or something. And in this case the salesperson was a girl about my age, and I could tell she thought I was weird, shopping with my mother. My mother sat in the chair beside me, her pocketbook in her lap. She was wearing sneakers, with little bunny-rabbit tails sticking out the back from her socks.

'Stand up,' the girl said.

I stood up.

'How do they feel?' my mother asked.

'Okay,' I said.

'Walk around,' my mother commanded.

I walked up the aisle, feeling everyone watching me. Then I walked back and sat down. I bent over and unlaced the shoes.

'So what do you think?' my mother asked.

The girl stood there, picking her nails. 'They look very nice,' she said.

I just wanted to get out of there. 'I like them,' I said. We bought the shoes.

On the way home, we pulled into a gas station–bar in the desert. 'I can't face Villa Indigo without a drink,' my mother said.

'What do you mean?' I asked.

'Nothing,' she said. 'Are you having a good time?'

'Now?'

'No. On this trip. At Uncle Walter's.'

'I guess so,' I said.

'Do you like Jason?'

'Better than Leonard.'

'Leonard was strange,' my mother said. 'I never warmed to Leonard.'

We got out of the car and walked into the bar. It was dark inside, and empty. A fat woman sat behind the bar, making something out of papier-mâché. It looked like one of those statues of the Virgin Mary people have in their front yards. 'Hiya,' she said. 'What can I get you?'

My mother asked for a beer and I asked for some cranberry juice. They didn't have any, so I ordered a Coke. The woman got my mother's beer from a portable cooler like the ones you take to football games. It seemed very unprofessional. Then she sprayed Coke into a glass with one of those showerhead things. My mother and I sat at a table in the sun, but it wasn't hot, it was cold. Above us the air conditioner dripped.

My mother drank her beer from the long-necked green bottle. 'What do you think your sister's doing right now?' she asked.

'What time is it?'

'Four.'

'Probably getting ready to go to work. Taking a shower.'

My mother nodded. 'Maybe we'll call her tonight.'

I laughed, because my mother called her every night. She would always make Jackie explain all the noises in the background. 'It sounds like a party to me,' she kept repeating.

My Coke was flat. It tasted weird too. I watched the woman at the bar. She was poking at her statue with a swizzle stick – putting in eyes, I thought.

'How would you like to go see the Petrified Forest?' my mother asked.

'We're going to another national park?' On the way to Uncle Walter's, we had stopped at the Grand Canyon and taken a mule ride down to the river. Halfway down, my mother got hysterical, fell off her mule, and wouldn't get back on. A helicopter had to fly into the canyon and rescue her. It was horrible to see her like that.

'This one's perfectly flat,' she said. 'And no mules.'

'When?' I said.

'We'd go down on Saturday and come back to Walter's on Monday. And leave for home Tuesday.'

The bar woman brought us a second round of drinks. We had not asked for them. My Coke glass was still full. My mother drained her beer bottle and looked at the new one. 'Oh, dear,' she said. 'I guess we look like we need it.'

~ ~ ~

The next night, at six-thirty, as my parents left for their special anniversary dinner in Flagstaff, the automatic lawn sprinklers went on. They were activated every evening. Jason explained that if the lawns were watered during the day the beads of moisture would magnify the sun's rays and burn the grass. My parents walked through the whirling water, got in their car, and drove away.

Jason and Uncle Walter were making dinner for me – steaks, on their new electric barbecue. I think they thought steak was a good, masculine food. Instead of charcoal, their grill had little lava rocks on the bottom. They reminded me of my dinosaur bone chips.

The steaks came in packs of two, so Uncle Walter was cooking up four. The fourth steak worried me. Who was it for? Would we split it? Was someone else coming to dinner?

'You're being awfully quiet,' Uncle Walter said. For a minute, I hoped he was talking to the steaks – they weren't sizzling – so I didn't answer.

Then Uncle Walter looked over at me. 'Cat got your tongue?' he asked.

'What cat?' I said.

'The cat,' he said. 'The proverbial cat. The big cat in the sky.'

'No,' I said.

'Then talk to me.'

'I don't talk on demand,' I said.

Uncle Walter smiled down at his steaks, lightly piercing them with his chef's fork. 'Are you a freshman?' he asked.

'Well, a sophomore now,' I said.

'How do you like being a sophomore?'

My lizard appeared from beneath a crimson leaf and clicked his eyes in all directions, checking out the evening.

'It's not something you like or dislike,' I said. 'It's something you are.'

'Ah,' Uncle Walter said. 'So you're a fatalist?'

I didn't answer. I slowly reached out my hand toward the lizard, even though I was too far away to touch it. He clicked his eyes toward me but didn't move. I think he recognized me. My arm looked white and disembodied in the evening light.

Jason slid open the terrace doors, and the music from the stereo was suddenly loud. The lizard darted back under the foliage.

'I need a prep chef,' Jason said. 'Get in here, Evan.'

I followed Jason into the kitchen. On the table was a wooden board, and on that was a tomato, an avocado, and an apple. Jason handed me a knife. 'Chop those up,' he said.

I picked up the avocado. 'Should I peel this?' I asked. 'Or what?'

Jason took the avocado and sliced it in half. One half held the pit, and the other half held nothing. Then he pulled the warty skin off in two curved pieces and handed the naked globes back to me. 'Now chop it.'

I started chopping the stuff. Jason took three baked potatoes out of the oven. I could tell they were hot by the way he tossed them onto the counter. He made slits in them and forked the white stuffing into a bowl.

'What are you doing?' I asked.

'Making baked potatoes,' he said. He sliced butter into the bowl.

'But why are you taking the potato out of the skin?'

'Because these are stuffed potatoes. You take the potato out and doctor it up and then put it back in. Do you like cheese?'

'Yes,' I said.

'Do you like chives?'

'I don't know,' I said. 'I've never had them.'

'You've never had chives?'

'My mother makes normal food,' I said. 'She leaves the potato in the skin.'

'That figures,' Jason said.

After dinner, we went to the driving range. Jason bought two large buckets and we followed him upstairs to the second level. I sat on a bench and watched Jason and my uncle hit ball after ball out into the floodlit night. Sometimes the balls arched up into the darkness, then reappeared as they fell.

Uncle Walter wasn't too good. A few times, he topped the ball and it dribbled over the edge and fell on the grass right below us. When that happened, he looked around to see who noticed, and winked at me.

'Do you want to hit some?' he asked me, offering his club.

'Sure,' I said. I was on the golf team last fall, but this spring I played baseball. I think golf is an elitist sport. Baseball is more democratic.

I teed up a ball and took a practice swing, because my father, who taught me to play golf, told me always to take a practice swing. Always. My first shot was pretty good. It didn't go too far, but it went straight out and bounced a ways before I lost track of it in the shadows. I hit another.

Jason, who was in the next cubicle, put down his club and watched me. 'You have a great natural swing,' he said.

His attention bothered me, and I almost missed my next ball. It rolled off the tee. I picked it up and re-teed it.

'Wait,' Jason said. He walked over and stood behind me. 'You're swinging much too hard.' He leaned over me so that he was embracing me from behind, his large tan hands on top of mine, holding the club. 'Now just relax,' he said, his voice right beside my cheek.

I tried to relax, but I couldn't. I suddenly felt very hot.

'Okay,' Jason said, 'nice and easy. Keep the left arm straight.' He raised his arms, and with them the club. Then we swung through, and he held the club still in the air, pointed out into the night. He let go of the club and ran his hand along my left arm, from my wrist up to my shoulder. 'Straight,' he said. 'Keep it nice and straight.' Then he stepped back and told me to try another swing by myself.

I did.

'Looking good,' Jason said.

'Why don't you finish the bucket?' my uncle said. 'I'm going down to get a beer.'

Jason returned to his stall and resumed his practice. I teed up another ball, hit it, then another, and another, till I'd established a rhythm, whacking ball after ball, and all around me clubs were cutting the night, filling the sky with tiny white meteorites.

~ ~ ~

Back at Villa Indigo, the sprinklers had stopped, but the insects were making their strange noise in the trees. Jason and I went for a swim while my uncle watched TV. Jason wore a bathing suit like the swimmers in the Olympics: red-white-and-blue and shaped like underwear. We walked out the terrace doors and across the wet lawn toward the pool, which was deserted and glowed bright blue. Jason dived in and swam some laps. I practiced diving off the board into the deep end, timing my dives so they wouldn't interfere with him. After about ten laps, he started treading water in the deep end and looked up at me. I was bouncing on the diving board.

'Want to play a game?' he said.

'What?'

Jason swam to the side and pulled himself out of the pool. 'Jump or Dive,' he said. 'We'll play for money.'

'How do you play?'

'Don't you know anything?' Jason said. 'What do you do in Ohio?'

'It's Oregon,' I said. 'Not much.'

'I can believe it. This is a very simple game. One person jumps off the diving board – jumps high – and when he's at the very highest, the other person yells either "Jump" or "Dive," and the person has to dive if the other person yells "Dive" and jump if he yells "Jump." If you do the wrong thing, you owe the guy a quarter. Okay?'

'Okay,' I said. 'You go first.'

I stepped off the diving board, and Jason climbed on. 'The higher you jump, the more time you have to twist,' he said.

'Go,' I said. 'I'm ready.'

Jason took three steps and sprang, and I yelled, 'Dive.' He did.

He got out of the pool, grinning. 'Okay,' he said. 'Your turn.'

I sprang off the board and heard Jason yell, 'Jump,' but I was already falling forward headfirst. I tried to twist backward, but it was still a dive.

'You owe me a quarter,' Jason said when I surfaced. He was standing on the diving board, bouncing. I swam to the side. 'Here I go,' he said.

I waited till he was coming straight down toward the water, feet first, before I yelled, 'Dive,' but somehow Jason somersaulted forward and dived into the pool.

We played for about fifteen minutes, until I owed Jason two dollars and twenty-five cents and my body was covered with red welts from smacking the water at bad angles. Suddenly the lights in the pool went off.

'It must be ten o'clock,' Jason said. 'Time for geriatrics to go to bed.'

The black water looked cold and scary. I got out and sat in a chair. We hadn't brought towels with us, and I shivered. Jason stayed in the pool.

'It's warmer in the water,' he said.

I didn't say anything. With the lights off in the pool, the stars appeared brighter in the sky. I leaned my head back and looked up at them.

Something landed with a splat on the concrete beside me. It was Jason's bathing suit. I could hear him in the pool. He was swimming slowly underwater, coming up for a breath and then disappearing again. I knew that at some point he'd get out of the water and be naked, so I walked across the lawn toward Villa Indigo. Inside, I could see Uncle Walter lying on the couch, watching TV.

~ ~ ~

Later that night, I woke up hearing noises in the kitchen. I assumed it was Jason, but then I heard talking and realized it was my parents, back from their anniversary dinner.

I got up off the couch and went into the kitchen. My mother was leaning against the counter, drinking a glass of seltzer. My father was sitting on one of the barstools, smoking a cigarette. He put it out when I came in. He's not supposed to smoke anymore. We made a deal in our family last year involving his quitting: my mother would lose fifteen pounds, my sister would take Science Honors (and pass), and I was supposed to brush Princess Leia, our dog, every day without having to be told.

'Our little baby,' my mother said. 'Did we wake you up?'

'Yes,' I said.

'This is the first one I've had in months,' my father said. 'Honest. I just found it lying here.'

'I told him he could smoke it,' my mother said. 'As a special anniversary treat.'

'How was dinner?' I asked.

'Okay,' my mother said. 'The restaurant didn't turn around, though. It was broken.'

'That's funny,' my father said. 'I could have sworn it was revolving.'

'You were just drunk,' my mother said.

'Oh, no,' my father said. 'It was the stars in my eyes.' He leaned forward and kissed my mother.

She finished her seltzer, rinsed the glass, and put it in the sink. 'I'm going to bed,' she said. 'Good night.'

My father and I both said good night, and my mother walked down the hall. My father picked up his cigarette. 'It wasn't even very good,' he said. He looked at it, then held it under his nose and smelled it. 'I think it was stale. Just my luck.'

I took the cigarette butt out of his hands and threw it away. When I turned around, he was standing by the terrace doors, looking out at the dark trees. It was windy.

'Have you made up your mind?' he asked.

'About what?'

'The trip.'

'What trip?'

My father turned away from the terrace. 'Didn't Mom tell you? Uncle Walter said you could stay here while Mom and I went down to see the Petrified Forest. If you want to. You can come with us otherwise.'

'Oh,' I said.

'I think Uncle Walter would like it if he had some time alone with you. I don't think he feels very close to you anymore. And he feels bad Jackie didn't come.'

'Oh,' I said. 'I don't know.'

'Is it because of Jason?'

'No,' I said.

'Because I'd understand if it was.'

'No,' I said, 'it's not that. I like Jason. I just don't know if I want to stay here . . .'

'Well, it's no big deal. Just two days.' My father reached up and turned off the light. It was a dual overhead light and fan, and the fan spun around some in the darkness, each spin slower. My father put his hands on my shoulders and half pushed, half guided me back to the couch. 'It's late,' he said. 'See you tomorrow.'

I lay on the couch. I couldn't fall asleep, because I knew that in a while Jason would be up for his snack. That kept me awake, and the decision about what to do. For some reason, it did seem like a big deal: going or staying. I could still picture my mother, backed up against the wall of the Grand Canyon, as far from the cliff as possible, crying, her mule braying, the helicopter whirring in the sky above us. It seemed like a choice between that and Jason swimming in the dark water, slowly and nakedly. I didn't want to be there for either.

The thing was, after I sprang off the diving board I did hear Jason shout, but my brain didn't make any sense of it. I could just feel myself hanging there, above the horrible bright-blue water, but I couldn't make my body turn, even though I was dropping dangerously, and much too fast.

RICHARD McCANN

MY MOTHER'S CLOTHES: THE SCHOOL OF BEAUTY AND SHAME

He is troubled by any image of himself, suffers when he is named.
He finds the perfection of a human relationship in this vacancy of the
image: to abolish — in oneself, between oneself and others — adjectives;
a relationship which adjectivizes is on the side of the image, on the
side of domination, of death.

— ROLAND BARTHES, *Roland Barthes*

Like every corner house in Carroll Knolls, the corner house on our block was turned backward on its lot, a quirk introduced by the developer of the subdivision, who, having run short of money, sought variety without additional expense. The turned-around houses, as we kids called them, were not popular, perhaps because they seemed too public, their casement bedroom windows cranking open onto sunstruck asphalt streets. In actuality, however, it was the rest of the houses that were public, their picture windows offering dioramic glimpses of early-American sofas and Mediterranean-style pole lamps whose mottled globes hung like iridescent melons from wrought-iron chains. In order not to be seen walking across the living room to the kitchen in our pajamas, we had to close the venetian blinds. The corner house on our block was secretive, as though it had turned its back on all of us, whether in superiority or in

---

RICHARD McCANN (born 1949): From its first publication in The Atlantic, *McCann's 'My Mother's Clothes: The School of Beauty and Shame' has enjoyed something of a cult following. He is also the author of two poetry collections,* Ghost Letters *and* Nights of 1990. *McCann co-directs the MFA program in creative writing at American University in Washington, D.C.*

shame, refusing to acknowledge even its own unkempt yard of yellowing zoysia grass. After its initial occupants moved away, the corner house remained vacant for months.

The spring I was in sixth grade, it was sold. When I came down the block from school, I saw a moving van parked at its curb. 'Careful with that!' a woman was shouting at a mover as he unloaded a tiered end table from the truck. He stared at her in silence. The veneer had already been splintered from the table's edge, as though someone had nervously picked at it while watching TV. Then another mover walked from the truck carrying a child's bicycle, a wire basket bolted over its thick rear tire, brightly colored plastic streamers dangling from its handlebars.

The woman looked at me. 'What have you got there? In your hand.'

I was holding a scallop shell spray-painted gold, with imitation pearls glued along its edges. Mrs Eidus, the art teacher who visited our class each Friday, had showed me how to make it.

'A hatpin tray,' I said. 'It's for my mother.'

'It's real pretty.' She glanced up the street as though trying to guess which house I belonged to. 'I'm Mrs. Tyree,' she said, 'and I've got a boy about your age. His daddy's bringing him tonight in the new Plymouth. I bet you haven't sat in a new Plymouth.'

'We have a Ford.' I studied her housedress, tiny blue and purple flowers imprinted on thin cotton, a line of white buttons as large as Necco Wafers marching toward its basted hemline. She was the kind of mother my mother laughed at for cutting recipes out of *Woman's Day*. Staring from our picture window, my mother would sometimes watch the neighborhood mothers drag their folding chairs into a circle on someone's lawn. 'There they go,' she'd say, 'a regular meeting of the Daughters of the Eastern Star!' 'They're hardly even *women*,' she'd whisper to my father, 'and their *clothes*.' She'd criticize their appearance – their loud nylon scarves tied beneath their chins, their disintegrating figures stuffed into pedal pushers – until my father, worried that my brother, Davis, and I could hear, although laughing himself, would beg her, 'Stop it, Maria, please stop; it isn't funny.' But she wouldn't stop, not ever. 'Not even thirty, and they look like they belong to the DAR! They wear their pearls inside their bosoms in case the rope should break!' She was the oldest mother on the block, but she was the most glamorous, sitting alone on the front lawn in her sleek kick-pleated skirts and cashmere sweaters, reading her thick paperback novels, whose bindings had split. Her hair was lightly hennaed, so that when I saw her pillowcases piled atop the washer, they seemed dusted with powdery rouge. She had once lived in New York City.

After dinner, when it was dark, I joined the other children congregated beneath the streetlamp across from the turned-around house. Bucky True-blood, an eighth grader who had once twisted the stems off my brother's eyeglasses, was crouched in the center, describing his mother's naked body to us elementary school children gathered around him, our faces slightly upturned, as though searching for a distant constellation, or for the bats that Bucky said would fly into our hair. I sat at the edge, one half of my body within the circle of light, the other half lost to darkness. When Bucky described his mother's nipples, which he'd glimpsed when she bent to kiss him good night, everyone giggled; but when he described her genitals, which he'd seen by dropping his pencil on the floor and looking up her nightie while her feet were propped on a hassock as she watched TV, everyone huddled nervously together, as though listening to a ghost story that made them fear something dangerous in the nearby dark. 'I don't believe you,' someone said. 'I'm telling you,' Bucky said, '*that's what it looks like.*'

I slowly moved outside the circle. Across the street a cream-colored Plymouth was parked at the curb. In a lighted bedroom window Mrs. Tyree was hanging café curtains. Behind the chain-link fence, within the low branches of a willow tree, the new child was standing in his yard. I could see his white T-shirt and the pale oval of his face, a face deprived of detail by darkness and distance. Behind him, at the open bedroom window, his mother slowly fiddled with a valance. Behind me the children sat spellbound beneath the light. Then Bucky jumped up and pointed in the new child's direction – 'Hey, you, you want to hear something really *good*?' – and even before the others had a chance to spot him, he vanished as suddenly and completely as an imaginary playmate.

The next morning, as we waited at our bus stop, he loitered by the mailbox on the opposite corner, not crossing the street until the yellow school bus pulled up and flung open its door. Then he dashed aboard and sat down beside me. 'I'm Denny,' he said. Denny: a heavy, un-beautiful child, who, had his parents stayed in their native Kentucky, would have been a farm boy, but who in Carroll Knolls seemed to belong to no particular world at all, walking past the identical ranch houses in his overalls and Keds, his whitish-blond hair close-cropped all around except for the distinguishing, stigmatizing feature of a wave that crested perfectly just above his forehead, a wave that neither rose nor fell, a wave he trained with Hopalong Cassidy hair tonic, a wave he tended fussily, as though it were the only loveliness he allowed himself.

~ ~ ~

What in Carroll Knolls might have been described by someone not native to those parts — a visiting expert, say — as *beautiful*, capable of arousing terror and joy? The brick ramblers strung with multicolored Christmas lights? The occasional front-yard plaster Virgin entrapped within a chicken-wire grotto entwined with plastic roses? The spring Denny moved to Carroll Knolls, I begged my parents to take me to a nightclub, had begged so hard for months, in fact, that by summer they finally agreed to a Sunday matinee. Waiting in the back seat of our Country Squire, a red bow tie clipped to my collar, I watched our house float like a mirage behind the sprinkler's web of water. The front door opened, and a white dress fluttered within the mirage's ascending waves: slipping on her sunglasses, my mother emerged onto the concrete stoop, adjusted her shoulder strap, and teetered across the wet grass in new spectator shoes. Then my father stepped out and cut the sprinkler off. We drove — the warm breeze inside the car sweetened by my mother's Shalimar — past ranch houses tethered to yards by chain-link fences; past the Silver Spring Volunteer Fire Department and Carroll Knolls Elementary School; past the Polar Bear Soft-Serv stand, its white stucco siding shimmery with mirror shards; past a bulldozed red-clay field where a weathered billboard advertised IF YOU LIVED HERE YOU'D BE HOME BY NOW, until we arrived at the border — a line of cinder-block discount liquor stores, a traffic light — of Washington, D.C. The light turned red. We stopped. The breeze died and the Shalimar fell from the air. Exhaust fumes mixed with the smell of hot tar. A drunk man stumbled into the crosswalk, followed by an old woman shielding herself from the sun with an orange umbrella, and two teenaged boys dribbling a basketball back and forth between them. My mother put down her sun visor. 'Lock your door,' she said.

Then the light changed, releasing us into another country. The station wagon sailed down boulevards of Chinese elms and flowering Bradford pears, through hot, dense streets where black families sat on wooden chairs at curbs, along old streetcar tracks that caused the tires to shimmy and the car to swerve, onto Pennsylvania Avenue, past the White House, encircled by its fence of iron spears, and down Fourteenth Street, past the Treasury Building, until at last we reached the Neptune Room, a cocktail lounge in the basement of a shabbily elegant hotel.

Inside, the Neptune Room's walls were painted with garish mermaids reclining seductively on underwater rocks, and human frogmen who stared longingly through their diving helmets' glass masks at a loveliness they could not possess on dry earth. On stage, leaning against the baby grand piano, a *chanteuse* (as my mother called her) was singing of her grief, her wrists weighted with rhinestone bracelets, a single blue spotlight making her seem like one who lived, as did the mermaids, underwater.

I was transfixed. I clutched my Roy Rogers cocktail (the same as a Shirley Temple, but without the cheerful, girlish grenadine) tight in my fist. In the middle of 'The Man I Love,' I stood and struggled toward the stage.

I strayed into the spotlight's soft-blue underwater world. Close up, from within the light, the singer was a boozy, plump peroxide blonde in a tight black cocktail dress; but these indiscretions made her yet more lovely, for they showed what she had lost, just as her songs seemed to carry her backward into endless regret. When I got close to her, she extended one hand – red nails, a huge glass ring – and seized one of mine.

'Why, what kind of little sailor have we got here?' she asked the audience.

I stared through the border of blue light and into the room, where I saw my parents gesturing, although whether they were telling me to step closer to her microphone or to step farther away, I could not tell. The whole club was staring.

'Maybe he knows a song!' a man shouted from the back.

'Sing with me,' she whispered. 'What can you sing?'

I wanted to lift her microphone from its stand and bow deeply from the waist, as Judy Garland did on her weekly TV show. But I could not. As she began to sing, I stood voiceless, pressed against the protection of her black dress; or, more accurately, I stood beside her, silently lip-synching to myself. I do not recall what she sang, although I do recall a quick, farcical ending in which she falsettoed, like Betty Boop, 'Gimme a Little Kiss, Will Ya, Huh?' and brushed my forehead with pursed red lips.

~ ~ ~

That summer, humidity enveloping the landfill subdivision, Denny, 'the new kid,' stood on the boundaries, while we neighborhood boys played War, a game in which someone stood on Stanley Allen's front porch and machine-gunned the rest of us, who one by one clutched our bellies, coughed as if choking on blood, and rolled in exquisite death throes down the grassy hill. When Stanley's father came up the walk from work, he ducked imaginary bullets. 'Hi, Dad,' Stanley would call, rising from the dead to greet him. Then we began the game again: whoever died best in the last round got to kill in the next. Later, after dusk, we'd smear the wings of balsa planes with glue, ignite them, and send them flaming through the dark on kamikaze missions. Long after the streets were deserted, we children sprawled beneath the corner streetlamp, praying our mothers would not call us – '*Time to come in!*' – back to our ovenlike houses; and then sometimes Bucky, hoping to scare the elementary school kids, would lead his solemn procession of junior high 'hoods' down the block, their penises hanging from their unzipped trousers.

Denny and I began to play together, first in secret, then visiting each other's houses almost daily, and by the end of the summer I imagined him to be my best friend. Our friendship was sealed by our shared dread of junior high school. Davis, who had just finished seventh grade, brought back reports of corridors so long that one could get lost in them, of gangs who fought to control the lunchroom and the bathrooms. The only safe place seemed to be the Health Room, where a pretty nurse let you lie down on a cot behind a folding screen. Denny told me about a movie he'd seen in which the children, all girls, did not have to go to school at all but were taught at home by a beautiful governess, who, upon coming to their rooms each morning, threw open their shutters so that sunlight fell like bolts of satin across their beds, whispered their pet names while kissing them, and combed their long hair with a silver brush. 'She never got mad,' said Denny, beating his fingers up and down through the air as though striking a keyboard, 'except once when some old man told the girls they could never play piano again.'

With my father at work in the Pentagon and my mother off driving the two-tone Welcome Wagon Chevy to new subdivisions, Denny and I spent whole days in the gloom of my living room, the picture window's venetian blinds closed against an August sun so fierce that it bleached the design from the carpet. Dreaming of fabulous prizes – sets of matching Samsonite luggage, French Provincial bedroom suites, Corvettes, jet flights to Hawaii – we watched Jan Murray's *Treasure Hunt* and Bob Barker's *Truth or Consequences* (a name that seemed strangely threatening). We watched *The Loretta Young Show*, worshipping yet critiquing her elaborate gowns. When *The Early Show* came on, we watched old Bette Davis, Gene Tierney, and Joan Crawford movies – *Dark Victory*, *Leave Her to Heaven*, *A Woman's Face*. Hoping to become their pen pals, we wrote long letters to fading movie stars, who in turn sent us autographed photos we traded between ourselves. We searched the house for secrets, like contraceptives, Kotex, and my mother's hidden supply of Hershey bars. And finally, Denny and I, running to the front window every few minutes to make sure no one was coming unexpectedly up the sidewalk, inspected the secrets of my mother's dresser: her satin nightgowns and padded brassieres, folded atop pink drawer liners and scattered with loose sachet; her black mantilla, pressed inside a shroud of lilac tissue paper; her heart-shaped candy box, a flapper doll strapped to its lid with a ribbon, from which spilled galaxies of cocktail rings and cultured pearls. Small shrines to deeper intentions, private grottoes of yearning: her triangular cloisonné earrings, her brooch of enameled butterfly wings.

Because beauty's source was longing, it was infused with romantic sorrow; because beauty was defined as 'feminine,' and therefore as 'other,' it became hopelessly confused with my mother: Mother, who quickly sorted through new batches of photographs, throwing unflattering shots of herself directly into the fire before they could be seen. Mother, who dramatized herself, telling us and our playmates, 'My name is Maria Dolores; in Spanish, that means "Mother of Sorrows."' Mother who had once wished to be a writer and who said, looking up briefly from whatever she was reading, 'Books are my best friends.' Mother, who read aloud from Whitman's *Leaves of Grass* and O'Neill's *Long Day's Journey into Night* with a voice so grave I could not tell the difference between them. Mother, who lifted cut-glass vases and antique clocks from her obsessively dusted curio shelves to ask, 'If this could talk, what story would it tell?'

And more, always more, for she was the only woman in our house, a 'people-watcher,' a 'talker,' a woman whose mysteries and moods seemed endless: Our Mother of the White Silk Gloves; Our Mother of the Veiled Hats; Our Mother of the Paper Lilacs; Our Mother of the Sighs and Heartaches; Our Mother of the Gorgeous Gypsy Earrings; Our Mother of the Late Movies and the Cigarettes; Our Mother whom I adored and whom, in adoring, I ran from, knowing it 'wrong' for a son to wish to be like his mother; Our Mother who wished to influence us, passing the best of herself along, yet who held the fear common to that era, the fear that by loving a son too intensely she would render him unfit – 'Momma's boy,' 'tied to apron strings' – and who therefore alternately drew us close and sent us away, believing a son needed 'male influence' in large doses, that female influence was pernicious except as a final finishing, like manners; Our Mother of the Mixed Messages; Our Mother of Sudden Attentiveness; Our Mother of Sudden Distances; Our Mother of Anger; Our Mother of Apology. The simplest objects of her life, objects scattered accidentally about the house, became my shrines to beauty, my grottoes of romantic sorrow: her Revlon lipstick tubes, 'Cherries in the Snow'; her art nouveau atomizers on the blue mirror top of her vanity; her pastel silk scarves knotted to a wire hanger in her closet; her white handkerchiefs blotted with red mouths. Voiceless objects; silences. The world halved with a cleaver: 'masculine,' 'feminine.' In these ways was the plainest ordinary love made complicated and grotesque. And in these ways was beauty, already confused with the 'feminine,' also confused with shame, for all these longings were secret, and to control me all my brother had to do was to threaten to expose that Denny and I were dressing ourselves in my mother's clothes.

~ ~ ~

Denny chose my mother's drabbest outfits, as though he were ruled by the deepest of modesties, or by his family's austere Methodism: a pink wraparound skirt from which the color had been laundered, its hem almost to his ankles; a sleeveless white cotton blouse with a Peter Pan collar; a small straw summer clutch. But he seemed to challenge his own primness, as though he dared it with his 'effects': an undershirt worn over his head to approximate cascading hair; gummed hole-punch reinforcements pasted to his fingernails so that his hands, palms up, might look like a woman's – flimsy crescent moons waxing above his fingertips.

He dressed slowly, hesitantly, but once dressed, he was a manic Proteus metamorphosizing into contradictory, half-realized forms, throwing his 'long hair' back and balling it violently into a French twist; tapping his paper nails on the glass-topped vanity as though he were an important woman kept waiting at a cosmetics counter; stabbing his nails into the air as though he were an angry teacher assigning an hour of detention; touching his temple as though he were a shy schoolgirl tucking back a wisp of stray hair; resting his fingertips on the rim of his glass of Kool-Aid as though he were an actress seated over an ornamental cocktail – a Pink Lady, say, or a Silver Slipper. Sometimes, in an orgy of jerky movement, his gestures overtaking him with greater and greater force, a dynamo of theatricality unleashed, he would hurl himself across the room like a mad girl having a fit, or like one possessed; or he would snatch the chenille spread from my parents' bed and drape it over his head to fashion for himself the long train of a bride. 'Do you like it?' he'd ask anxiously, making me his mirror. 'Does it look *real*?' He wanted, as did I, to become something he'd neither yet seen nor dreamed of, something he'd recognize the moment he saw it: himself. Yet he was constantly confounded, for no matter how much he adorned himself with scarves and jewelry, he could not understand that this was himself, as was also and at the same time the boy in overalls and Keds. He was split in two pieces – as who was not? – the blond wave cresting rigidly above his close-cropped hair.

~ ~ ~

'He makes me nervous,' I heard my father tell my mother one night as I lay in bed. They were speaking about me. That morning I'd stood awkwardly on the front lawn – 'Maybe you should go help your father,' my mother had said – while he propped an extension ladder against the house, climbed up through the power lines he separated with his bare hands, and staggered across the pitched roof he was reshingling. When his hammer slid down the incline, catching on the gutter, I screamed, 'You're falling!' Startled, he almost fell.

'He needs to spend more time with you,' I heard my mother say.

I couldn't sleep. Out in the distance a mother was calling her child home. A screen door slammed. I heard cicadas, their chorus as steady and loud as the hum of a power line. *He needs to spend more time with you.* Didn't she know? Saturday mornings, when he stood in his rubber hip boots fishing off the shore of Triadelphia Reservoir, I was afraid of the slimy bottom and could not wade after him; for whatever reasons of his own – something as simple as shyness, perhaps – he could not come to get me. I sat in the parking lot drinking Tru-Ade and reading *Betty and Veronica*, wondering if Denny had walked alone to Wheaton Plaza, where the weekend manager of Port-o'-Call allowed us to Windex the illuminated glass shelves that held Lladró figurines, the porcelain ballerina's hands so realistic one could see tiny life and heart lines etched into her palms. *He needs to spend more time with you.* Was she planning to discontinue the long summer afternoons that she and I spent together when there were no new families for her to greet in her Welcome Wagon car? 'I don't feel like being alone today,' she'd say, inviting me to sit on their chenille bedspread and watch her model new clothes in her mirror. Behind her an oscillating fan fluttered nylons and scarves she'd heaped, discarded, on a chair. 'Should I wear the red belt with this dress or the black one?' she'd ask, turning suddenly toward me and cinching her waist with her hands.

Afterward we would sit together at the rattan table on the screened-in porch, holding cocktail napkins around sweaty glasses of iced Russian tea and listening to big-band music on the Zenith.

'You look so pretty,' I'd say. Sometimes she wore outfits I'd selected for her from her closet – pastel chiffon dresses, an apricot blouse with real mother-of-pearl buttons.

One afternoon she leaned over suddenly and shut off the radio. 'You know you're going to leave me one day,' she said. When I put my arms around her, smelling the dry carnation talc she wore in hot weather, she stood up and marched out of the room. When she returned, she was wearing Bermuda shorts and a plain cotton blouse. 'Let's wait for your father on the stoop,' she said.

Late that summer – the summer before he died – my father took me with him to Fort Benjamin Harrison, near Indianapolis, where, as a colonel in the U.S. Army Reserves, he did his annual tour of duty. On the prop jet he drank bourbon and read newspapers while I made a souvenir packet for Denny: an airsickness bag, into which I placed the Chiclets given me by the stewardess to help pop my ears during takeoff, and the laminated white card that showed the location of emergency exits. Fort Benjamin Harrison looked like Carroll Knolls: hundreds of acres of concrete and sun-scorched shrubbery inside a cyclone fence. Daytimes I waited for my father in the dining mess with the sons of other officers, drinking chocolate milk that came from a silver machine, and desultorily setting fires in ashtrays. When he came to collect me, I walked behind him – gold braid hung from his epaulets – while enlisted men saluted us and opened doors. At night, sitting in our BOQ room, he asked me questions about myself: 'Are you looking forward to seventh grade?' 'What do you think you'll want to be?' When these topics faltered – I stammered what I hoped were right answers – we watched TV, trying to preguess lines of dialogue on reruns of his favorite shows, *The Untouchables* and *Rawhide*. 'That Della

Street,' he said as we watched *Perry Mason*, 'is almost as pretty as your mother.' On the last day, eager to make the trip memorable, he brought me a gift: a glassine envelope filled with punched IBM cards that told me my life story as his secretary had typed it into the office computer. Card One: *You live at 10406 Lillians Mill Court, Silver Spring, Maryland.* Card Two: *You are entering seventh grade.* Card Three: *Last year your teacher was Mrs. Dillard.* Card Four: *Your favorite color is blue.* Card Five: *You love the Kingston Trio.* Card Six: *You love basketball and football.* Card Seven: *Your favorite sport is swimming.*

Whose son did these cards describe? The address was correct, as was the teacher's name and the favorite color; and he'd remembered that one morning during breakfast I'd put a dime in the jukebox and played the Kingston Trio's song about 'the man who never returned.' But whose fiction was the rest? Had I, who played no sport other than kickball and Kitty-Kitty-Kick-the-Can, lied to him when he asked me about myself? Had he not heard from my mother the outcome of the previous summer's swim lessons? At the swim club a young man in black trunks had taught us, as we held hands, to dunk ourselves in water, surface, and then go down. When he had told her to let go of me, I had thrashed across the surface, violently afraid I'd sink. But perhaps I had not lied to him; perhaps he merely did not wish to see. It was my job, I felt, to reassure him that I was the son he imagined me to be, perhaps because the role of reassurer gave me power. In any case, I thanked him for the computer cards. I thanked him the way a father thanks a child for a well-intentioned gift he'll never use — a set of handkerchiefs, say, on which the embroidered swirls construct a monogram of no particular initial, and which thus might be used by anyone.

~ ~ ~

As for me, when I dressed in my mother's clothes, I seldom moved at all: I held myself rigid before the mirror. The kind of beauty I'd seen practiced in movies and in fashion magazines was beauty attained by lacquered stasis, beauty attained by fixed poses — 'ladylike stillness,' the stillness of mannequins, the stillness of models 'caught' in mid-gesture, the stillness of the passive moon around which active meteors orbited and burst. My costume was of the greatest solemnity: I dressed like the *chanteuse* in the Neptune Room, carefully shimmying my mother's black slip over my head so as not to stain it with Brylcreem, draping her black mantilla over my bare shoulders, clipping her rhinestone dangles to my ears. Had I at that time already seen the movie in which French women who had fraternized with German soldiers were made to shave their heads and walk through the streets, jeered by their fellow villagers? And if so, did I imagine myself to be one of the collaborators, or one of the villagers, taunting her from the curb? I ask because no matter how elaborate my costume, I made no effort to camouflage my crew cut or my male body.

How did I perceive myself in my mother's triple-mirrored vanity, its endless repetitions? I saw myself as doubled – both an image and he who studied it. I saw myself as beautiful, and guilty: the lipstick made my mouth seem the ripest rose, or a wound; the small rose on the black slip opened like my mother's heart disclosed, or like the Sacred Heart of Mary, aflame and pierced by arrows; the mantilla transformed me into a Mexican penitent or a Latin movie star, like Dolores Del Rio. The mirror was a silvery stream: on the far side, in a clearing, stood the woman who was icily immune from the boy's terror and contempt; on the close side, in the bedroom, stood the boy who feared and yet longed after her inviolability. (Perhaps, it occurs to me now, this doubleness is the source of drag queens' vulnerable ferocity.) Sometimes, when I saw that person in the mirror, I felt as though I had at last been lifted from that dull, locked room, with its mahogany bedroom suite and chalky blue walls. But other times, particularly when I saw Denny and me together, so that his reality shattered my fantasies, we seemed merely ludicrous and sadly comic, as though we were dressed in the garments of another species, like dogs in human clothes. I became aware of my spatulate hands, my scarred knees, my large feet; I became aware of the drooping, unfilled bodice of my slip. Like Denny, I could neither dispense with images nor take their flexibility as pleasure, for the idea of self I had learned and was learning still was that one was constructed by one's images – '*When boys cross their legs, they cross one ankle atop the knee*' – so that one finally sought the protection of believing in one's own image and, in believing in it as reality, condemned oneself to its poverty.

(That locked room. My mother's vanity; my father's highboy. If Denny and I, still in our costumes, had left that bedroom, its floor strewn with my mother's shoes and handbags, and gone through the darkened living room, out onto the sunstruck porch, down the sidewalk, and up the street, how would we have carried ourselves? Would we have walked boldly, chattering extravagantly back and forth between ourselves, like drag queens refusing to acknowledge the stares of contempt that are meant to halt them? Would we have walked humbly, with the calculated, impervious piety of the condemned walking barefoot to the public scaffold? Would we have walked simply, as deeply accustomed to the normalcy of our own strangeness as Siamese twins? Or would we have walked gravely, a solemn procession, like Bucky Trueblood's gang, their manhood hanging from their unzipped trousers?

(We were eleven years old. Why now, more than two decades later, do I wonder for the first time how we would have carried ourselves through a publicness we would have neither sought nor dared? I am six feet two inches tall; I weigh 198 pounds. Given my size, the question I am most often asked about my youth is 'What football position did you play?' Overseas I am most commonly taken to be a German or a Swede. Right now, as I write this, I am wearing L. L. Bean khaki trousers, a LaCoste shirt, Weejuns: the anonymous American costume, although partaking of certain signs of class and education, and, most recently, partaking also of certain signs of sexual orientation, this costume having become the standard garb of the urban American gay man. Why do I tell you these things? Am I trying – not subtly – to inform us of my 'maleness,' to reassure us that I have 'survived' without noticeable 'complexes'? Or is this my urge, my constant urge, to complicate my portrait of myself to both of us, so that I might layer my selves like so many multicolored crinoline slips, each rustling as I walk? When the wind blows, lifting my skirt, I do not know which slip will be revealed.)

~ ~ ~

Sometimes, while Denny and I were dressing up, Davis would come home unexpectedly from the bowling alley, where he'd been hanging out since entering junior high. At the bowling alley he was courting the protection of Bucky's gang.

'Let me in!' he'd demand, banging fiercely on the bedroom door, behind which Denny and I were scurrying to wipe the make-up off our faces with Kleenex.

'We're not doing anything,' I'd protest, buying time.

'Let me in this minute or I'll tell!'

Once in the room, Davis would police the wreckage we'd made, the emptied hatboxes, the scattered jewelry, the piled skirts and blouses. 'You'd better clean this up right now,' he'd warn. 'You two make me *sick*.'

Yet his scorn seemed modified by awe. When he helped us rehang the clothes in the closet and replace the jewelry in the candy box, a sullen accomplice destroying someone else's evidence, he sometimes handled the garments as though they were infused with something of himself, although at the precise moment when he seemed to find them loveliest, holding them close, he would cast them down.

After our dress-up sessions Denny would leave the house without good-byes. I was glad to see him go. We would not see each other for days, unless we met by accident; we never referred to what we'd done the last time we'd been together. We met like those who have murdered are said to meet, each tentatively and warily examining the other for signs of betrayal. But whom had we murdered? The boys who walked into that room? Or the women who briefly came to life within it? Perhaps this metaphor has outlived its meaning. Perhaps our shame derived not from our having killed but from our having created.

~ ~ ~

In early September, as Denny and I entered seventh grade, my father became ill. Over Labor Day weekend he was too tired to go fishing. On Monday his skin had vaguely yellowed; by Thursday he was severely jaundiced. On Friday he entered the hospital, his liver rapidly failing; Sunday he was dead. He died from acute hepatitis, possibly acquired while cleaning up after our sick dog, the doctor said. He was buried at Arlington National Cemetery, down the hill from the Tomb of the Unknown Soldier. After the twenty-one-gun salute, our mother pinned his colonel's insignia to our jacket lapels. I carried the flag from his coffin to the car. For two weeks I stayed home with my mother, helping her write thank-you notes on small white cards with black borders; one afternoon, as I was affixing postage to the square, plain envelopes, she looked at me across the dining room table. 'You and Davis are all I have left,' she said. She went into the kitchen and came back. 'Tomorrow,' she said, gathering up the note cards, 'you'll have to go to school.' Mornings I wandered the long corridors alone, separated from Denny by the fate of our last names, which had cast us into different homerooms and daily schedules. Lunchtimes we sat together in silence in the rear of the cafeteria. Afternoons, just before gym class, I went to the Health Room, where, lying on a cot, I'd imagine the Phys Ed coach calling my name from the class roll, and imagine my name, unclaimed, unanswered to, floating weightlessly away, like a balloon that one jumps to grab hold of but that is already out of reach. Then I'd hear the nurse dial the telephone. 'He's sick again,' she'd say. 'Can you come pick him up?' At home I helped my mother empty my father's highboy. 'No, we want to save that,' she said when I folded his uniform into a huge brown bag that read GOODWILL INDUSTRIES; I wrapped it in a plastic dry cleaner's bag and hung it in the hall closet.

After my father's death my relationship to my mother's things grew yet more complex, for as she retreated into her grief, she left behind only her mute objects as evidence of her life among us: objects that seemed as lonely and vulnerable as she was, objects that I longed to console, objects with which I longed to console myself – a tangled gold chain, thrown in frustration on the mantel; a wineglass, its rim stained with lipstick, left unwashed in the sink. Sometimes at night Davis and I heard her prop her pillow up against her bedroom wall, lean back heavily, and tune her radio to a call-in show: '*Nightcaps, what are you thinking at this late hour?*' Sunday evenings, in order to help her prepare for the next day's job hunt, I stood over her beneath the bare basement bulb, the same bulb that first illuminated my father's jaundice. I set her hair, slicking each wet strand with gel and rolling it, inventing gossip that seemed to draw us together, a beautician and his customer.

'You have such pretty hair,' I'd say.

'At my age, don't you think I should cut it?' She was almost fifty.

'No, never.'

~ ~ ~

That fall Denny and I were caught. One evening my mother noticed something out of place in her closet. (Perhaps now that she no longer shared it, she knew where every belt and scarf should have been.)

I was in my bedroom doing my French homework, dreaming of one day visiting Au Printemps, the store my teacher spoke of so excitedly as she played us the Edith Piaf records that she had brought back from France. In the mirror above my desk I saw my mother appear at my door.

'Get into the living room,' she said. Her anger made her small, reflected body seem taut and dangerous.

In the living room Davis was watching TV with Uncle Joe, our father's brother, who sometimes came to take us fishing. Uncle Joe was lying in our father's La-Z-Boy recliner.

'There aren't going to be any secrets in this house,' she said. 'You've been in my closet. What were you doing there?'

'No, we weren't,' I said. 'We were watching TV all afternoon.'

'*We?* Was Denny here with you? Don't you think I've heard about that? Were you and Denny going through my clothes? Were you wearing them?'

'No, Mom,' I said.

'Don't lie!' She turned to Uncle Joe, who was staring at us. 'Make him stop! He's lying to me!'

She slapped me. Although I was already taller than she, she slapped me over and over, slapped me across the room until I was backed against the TV. Davis was motionless, afraid. But Uncle Joe jumped up and stood between my mother and me, holding her until her rage turned to sobs. 'I can't be both a mother and a father,' she said to him. 'I can't, I can't do it.' I could not look at Uncle Joe, who, although he was protecting me, did not know I was lying.

She looked at me. 'We'll discuss this later,' she said. 'Get out of my sight.'

We never discussed it. Denny was outlawed. I believe, in fact, that it was I who suggested he never be allowed in our house again. I told my mother I hated him. I do not think I was lying when I said this. I truly hated him – hated him, I mean, for being me.

For two or three weeks Denny tried to speak with me at the bus stop, but whenever he approached, I busied myself with kids I barely knew. After a while Denny found a new best friend, Lee, a child despised by everyone, for Lee was 'effeminate.' His clothes were too fastidious; he often wore his cardigan over his shoulders, like an old woman feeling a chill. Sometimes, watching the street from our picture window, I'd see Lee walking toward Denny's house. 'What a queer,' I'd say to whoever might be listening. 'He walks like a *girl*.' Or sometimes, at the junior high school, I'd see him and Denny walking down the corridor, their shoulders pressed together as if they were telling each other secrets, or as if they were joined in mutual defense. Sometimes when I saw them, I turned quickly away, as though I'd forgotten something important in my locker. But when I felt brave enough to risk rejection, for I belonged to no group, I joined Bucky Trueblood's gang, sitting on the radiator in the main hall, and waited for Lee and Denny to pass us. As Lee and Denny got close, they stiffened and looked straight ahead.

'Faggots,' I muttered.

I looked at Bucky, sitting in the middle of the radiator. As Lee and Denny passed, he leaned forward from the wall, accidentally disarranging the practiced severity of his clothes, his jeans puckering beneath his tooled belt, the breast pocket of his T-shirt drooping with the weight of a pack of Pall Malls. He whistled. Lee and Denny flinched. He whistled again. Then he leaned back, the hard lines of his body reasserting themselves, his left foot striking a steady beat on the tile floor with the silver V tap of his black loafer.

STEPHEN GRECO

GOOD WITH WORDS

Last night I dreamed I went back to the Mineshaft. I knew I had come home even before entering the unmarked door and climbing the flight of stairs to pay my five dollars. Outside, on the sidewalk – where I'd sometimes linger and survey the street action that was often hot enough to induce me to skip the bar entirely – I savored the exhaust that was being sucked out of the bar's downstairs suite by powerful industrial fans. Beer, piss, poppers, leather, sweat – the smells blended into a perfume more reassuringly familiar than the Bal à Versailles I remember from my mother's dressing table.

The first beer at the upstairs bar was just a formality. I gulped it down and immediately asked the tattooed bartender for another, the second one to sip – a prop, really, to keep my hands occupied until something better came along. Inside, a typical evening was under way: someone in the sling, ingeniously concealing someone else's arm up to the elbow; on-lookers rapt, then moving on casually, to survey some of the other attractions that were taking form in the shadows; assorted human undergrowth here and

STEPHEN GRECO (born 1950): *Originally published as a safe-sex porn story in the magazine* Advocate Men, *'Good with Words' has gone on to have a mythic life of its own; it is as unflinching and erotic a response to AIDS as has ever been written. The story is included in the collection* The Sperm Engine, *published in 2002. Greco is editor-at-large for* Trace *magazine and lives in Brooklyn.*

there, some of it inert and some gently undulating like deep-sea flora. On the platform toward the back, a tall blond man was getting blown. I stood nearby for a while and watched – evaluating his musculature with a touch, scrutinizing his gestures for a flaw in that impeccable attitude, observing the degree to which his arched posture expressed a belief in this kind of recreation – then I turned and went downstairs.

I always spit in the back stairway, as a sort of a ritual of purification, I suppose. Below, things were steamier, and I adjusted my fly accordingly. The piss room was packed, unnavigable, with dense clumps of flesh around each tub and growing outward from the corners. So noting who was doing what, I passed along the edge of it all, slowly, as if in a dream – which it was, of course – though even when it wasn't, back when the Mineshaft was open, it all seemed to be. A wet dream; some kind of prenatal fantasy, dark and sheltered; bathed in the music the management knew was perfect for down there, slowish, hazy waves of taped sound that always struck me as exactly what music would sound like if heard from inside the womb; a dream engulfed, as the evening built to its climax, by the fluids – no, the tides – of life itself.

I walked past the posing niche and entered the club's farthest recess, the downstairs bar. There, on his knees, was Paul. Known more widely than seemed possible as the Human Urinal, Paul had installed himself in one of his favorite spots for the early part of an evening, a relatively open and well-lighted place that invited inspection but did not permit extended scenes. Paul moved around, you see. As an evening progressed he would migrate to increasingly more auspicious locations until, around dawn, you would probably find him in what was by then a hub of the Mineshaft's hardest-core action, the upstairs men's room, where he planted himself efficiently, mouth gaping, eyes glazed, between the two nonhuman fixtures.

How I admired that man and his dedication! What fun we would have in the old days, both here and with the straight boys at the Hellfire Club! Paul is immobile as I pass, but I see by his slowly shifting eyes that he knows I've arrived. And he's glad: even in the dark I sense that his pupils have dilated a fraction when he notices I'm carrying a can of beer. I raise it slightly in his direction in a kind of toast. He understands. I stop for a moment opposite him, the constant flow of men between us. Then, because I feel I should follow through with a sympathetic gesture, I bring the can to my lips while pissing, almost incidentally, in my jeans.

I don't look down, of course, but I know that a dark patch has appeared at the top of my right thigh. And I know that Paul sees it too – but since manners are everything in affairs of the heart, we smile no acknowledgment. Burping unceremoniously, I move off toward the bar . . .

I was intending to return to Paul after getting another beer, but then I woke up. A garbage truck was roaring outside my bedroom window, and the dream was over.

~ ~ ~

Later that day I called my friend Albert, with whom I'd visited the Mineshaft on occasion. When I mentioned my dream he was unimpressed.

'Of course you're dreaming about the place, puss. It's because you can't go there anymore. What other options *do* we have nowadays for handling our genius, we who have dared to build a world that allowed us to encounter it repeatedly?'

It was like Albert to use the word *genius* that way, with overtones of 'essential spirit,' even 'demon.' Albert's good with words, which he says is lucky. He's one of those people who seem able to enjoy exchanging them during sex almost as much as he did those fluids that are now forbidden. Albert sighed and added that we should be thankful to have glimpsed the 'golden age.'

We discussed some of the old faces. It turns out that he'd been talking to the real Paul, whom I hadn't run into for quite some time. I was surprised to learn that my fastidious friend actually once traded phone numbers with the Human Urinal and recently has been indulging in a bit of phone J.O. with him. It was 'nothing kinky,' Albert insisted. 'We just chat for hours like schoolgirls, about choking body-builder cops with the severed penises of their teenage sons. What could be safer than that?'

I was happy to hear that Paul is still kicking. In fact, I was relieved, since it won't do to make assumptions anymore about people we used to see around. Yeah, Paul always maintained that he was exclusively oral, never anal, but the fact is that none of us is sure whether that or any particular limit is enough to guarantee someone's safety under present conditions. Wasn't one of Paul's favorite numbers, after all, to beg feverishly for 'clap dick' and to revel in the disgust this elicited from many men who took him literally? I don't know – maybe the request was meant literally; since gonorrhea was so readily curable, it never seemed to matter much. It was strange, I know, but I realized when talking to Albert how fond of Paul's creative perversity I'd become, how much I missed his 'genius' in a way that would be difficult to explain to someone who'd never experienced firsthand the catalytic charm of old-fashioned sex clubs.

I knew Paul slightly. Though not a chatty sort, he would sometimes expose a portion of his outside persona to me, especially if a biographical detail or two could help add luster to a scene we were building. He was thirty-five, the only child of Polish immigrant parents who were now retired. He lived alone in a tenement on the Lower East Side and was involved with a man he called his lover, a man who also had a live-in girlfriend. All three – Paul, lover, girlfriend – were somehow involved in big real estate deals and would often go jetting off for weekends in Europe or North Africa, though it was clear that Paul himself was not in the lucrative end of the business, since he spoke of having to take occasional jobs waiting on tables. Thin and darkly handsome, Paul was nonetheless at pains to downplay his appearance. I remember his pride when he arrived at the bar one night with a new haircut, a brutishly uneven head-shave that he said with a grin made him look 'even more' like a survivor of Auschwitz.

I was a little apprehensive about seeing this man again. Sure, I had gradually come to understand his unspoken language and to sense how far his attraction to dangerous things really went. But the world has changed. Who knew what mischief he might be up to these days, what I might have to frown upon sternly, what I might even find myself somehow drawn into doing? Yet things have been *so* dry lately, I whined to Albert. Could it do any harm to just *talk*? Albert laughed as he gave me Paul's number.

~ ~ ~

Paul was napping when I rang. A ballet gala the night before had kept him out until breakfast, and he confessed he was still in his tuxedo pants. After we brought each other up-to-date (and admitted indirectly that our health was fine), he said he'd be happy to get together again, 'to see what develops.' Nothing was said about conditions – more, I think, because neither of us wanted to queer an incipient liaison with ill-timed reality talk. We set a time for later that day. Paul suggested a secluded men's room on a downtown university campus. That's a good sign, I thought – if he's fooling around with those finicky college boys, he can't be too heedless.

When I arrived at the men's room I found a scene already in progress that would have seemed innocuous enough four or five years ago, but now, in the era of AIDS, took on a faintly unsettling quality. Paul and someone else had positioned themselves not in a stall but right out in the open, and they were talking about death.

The other guy, a bearded man in his forties whom I'd not seen before, was dressed in a beat-up leather jacket, no shirt, and a pair of those drab, baggy chinos that janitors wear. Out of his fly was hanging a cock that must be described as substantial as much for its apparent weight and density as for its obvious size. Semisoft and just at the point of unwrinkling, the thing had a thick, meandering vein down the top that looked more like an exhaust pipe than a detail of human anatomy. He was lighting a cigarette when I entered and seemed unconcerned that his twosome had just become a threesome. And he was wearing a wedding ring. Paul was kneeling in front of the guy, his head hung low, dressed only in a yellow-stained T-shirt and a pair of pulled-down sweatpants. After a moment I saw that his legs had been bound behind him with a length of rope, which struck me as risky, since someone else always could just walk in unannounced. His hands were tied too, though in front of him, so he was able to reach and clumsily manipulate his cock. The room reeked of pine cleanser.

I'd entered during a short lull – or maybe they'd been waiting for me. Instantly I found myself shedding the everyday state of mind that allows us to do things like hold jobs and get through city traffic and assuming a more intuitive, timeless disposition that's much better suited to the consumption of pleasure. Respectfully I approached. Understanding that this wasn't the time for a kiss and introduction, I grunted for them to continue.

'I want it, okay?' Paul said. It was that low, trancelike monotone I remember.

'Yeah? You like this fucker?' The other guy handled himself appreciatively.

'Uh-huh. I need it. Put it in my mouth?'

A pause. The other guy farted.

'Why do you need it?' he asked.

Paul did something obscene with his tongue.

Seeing that this was indeed going to work, I took out my own cock and began to pull on it. Already it felt pleasantly *intrusive*, like a complication worth solving. I couldn't have said exactly why, but there was something palpably right about our little scene, something perhaps reflected in subtle linguistic details like the register of Paul's voice and the rhythm of the other guy's responses, as well as in grosser ones like choice of vocabulary and subject matter. I know from experience that arranging these things is far from easy, and even after this preliminary exchange I understood perfectly why Paul had wanted me to meet this guy. The scene heated up rapidly.

'I live for that dick,' said Paul, his gaze fixed on it.

'Then tell me about it, man. Let me hear it.'

Paul's drone became more animated.

'Please, let me have your dick. Slip it into my head.'

Then he looked up at the guy's face.

'I'll take your load, okay? Let me suck it out of you. I don't care if I get sick.'

I guess that was what they both wanted to hear. The other guy narrowed his eyes.

'I don't give a fuck about you, cocksucker – I just wanna get off. You gonna eat my come?'

Paul nodded: 'Anything.'

Both were pumping faster.

'Okay, let me feel that pussy mouth on my meat. I'll feed you my fucking load and get out of this shithole.'

'If I get sick . . .,' Paul began.

'So you get sick,' was the reply. 'I guess you die, man.'

And at that moment – or one like it, since I was too deeply engaged by all this bad-boy stuff to remember more than the drift of the dialogue – the three of us shot. I think we'd all been close for a while, and we shot powerfully – me, off to the side, near the radiator; Paul, onto the floor in front of him, grazing my foot; the other guy, past Paul's shoulder and onto the wall and paper towel dispenser. It took only a couple of minutes for us to button up, undo Paul, and perform a thorough wordless cleanup. Then our guest silently signaled his farewell, pulling Paul toward him and grazing him on the cheek with an affectionate peck.

After he left I raised an eyebrow.

'I know,' Paul said. 'Sweet man.'

'Who is he?' I asked.

'Just a man,' was the answer.

As I stood drying my hands, I couldn't help thinking how dismal a conclusion a stranger would have drawn simply by reading a transcript of our encounter. And even if he'd been there himself, would a *Times* reporter or health department official have understood how loving it all was? Or how safe? Paul and his friend must have agreed fairly explicitly, though in their own language, to stay within certain limits. They wanted to raise a little hell, anyway.

I winked at myself in the mirror. Well, boys, I thought, we did it.

~ ~ ~

Hearing that word 'die' during sex did leave me feeling a little clammy, though. I've lost so many friends. So has Albert, I know, yet afterward he made light of my reservations.

'Isn't the best way to honor their memory to care for ourselves and the friends we've got left?' he asked. 'It sounds to me like the three of you were eminently careful. If you'd only invited me.'

But using death in that way. It felt so . . . odd.

'Look,' Albert explained, 'is it really so different from the old days, when we used to talk about things like getting worked over by a gang of Nazi motorcycle Satanists? Death by gang rape is hardly more attractive than death from AIDS. Sex is theater, darling, even now. And words are only words, even if they do bring the big, bad world into the bedroom, where we can play at controlling it.'

When I equivocated, he grew stern.

'Stephen, if you can't tell the difference between talking about something and the thing itself, then you belong in a cave, drawing bison on the wall.'

I thought of that remark sometime later, when I attended a play at which I was seated two rows away from someone who was so stirred up by an onstage murder that he began talking violently back to the actors . . .

DENNIS McFARLAND

NOTHING TO ASK FOR

Inside Mack's apartment, a concentrator — a medical machine that looks like an elaborate stereo speaker on casters — sits behind an orange swivel chair, making its rhythmic, percussive noise like ocean waves, taking in normal filthy air, humidifying it, and filtering out everything but the oxygen, which it sends through clear plastic tubing to Mack's nostrils. He sits on the couch, as usual, channel grazing, the remote-control button under his thumb, and he appears to be scrutinizing the short segments of what he sees on the TV screen with Zen-like patience. He has planted one foot on the beveled edge of the long oak coffee table, and he dangles one leg — thinner at the thigh than my wrist — over the other. In the sharp valley of his lap, Eberhardt, his old long-haired dachshund, lies sleeping. The table is covered with two dozen medicine bottles, though Mack has now taken himself off all drugs except cough syrup and something for heartburn. Also, stacks of books and pamphlets — though he has lost the ability to read — on how to heal yourself, on Buddhism, on Hinduism, on dying. In one pamphlet there's a long list that includes most human ailments, the personality traits and character flaws that cause these ailments, and the affirmations that need to be said in order to overcome them.

DENNIS McFARLAND (born 1950): McFarland is the author of the novels The Music Room, School for the Blind, A Face at the Window and Singing Boy. 'Nothing to Ask For' originally appeared in The New Yorker.

According to this well-intentioned misguidedness, most disease is caused by self-hatred, or rejection of reality, and almost anything can be cured by learning to love yourself – which is accomplished by saying, aloud and often, 'I love myself.' Next to these books are pamphlets and Xeroxed articles describing more unorthodox remedies – herbal brews, ultrasound, lemon juice, urine, even penicillin. And, in a ceramic dish next to these, a small waxy envelope that contains 'ash' – a very fine, gray-white, spiritually enhancing powder materialized out of thin air by Swami Lahiri Baba.

As I change the plastic liner inside Mack's trash can, into which he throws his millions of Kleenex, I block his view of the TV screen – which he endures serenely, his head perfectly still, eyes unaverted. 'Do you remember old Dorothy Hughes?' he asks me. 'What do you suppose ever happened to her?'

'I don't know,' I say. 'I saw her years ago on the nude beach at San Gregorio. With some black guy who was down by the surf doing cartwheels. She pretended she didn't know me.'

'I don't blame her,' says Mack, making bug eyes. 'I wouldn't like to be seen with any grown-up who does cartwheels, would you?'

'No,' I say.

Then he asks, 'Was everybody we knew back then crazy?'

What Mack means by 'back then' is our college days, in Santa Cruz, when we judged almost everything in terms of how freshly it rejected the status quo: the famous professor who began his twentieth-century-philosophy class by tossing pink rubber dildos in through the classroom window; Antonioni and Luis Buñuel screened each weekend in the dormitory basement; the artichokes in the student garden, left on their stalks and allowed to open and become what they truly were – enormous, purple-hearted flowers. There were no paving-stone quadrangles or venerable colonnades – our campus was the redwood forest, the buildings nestled among the trees, invisible one from the other – and when we emerged from the woods at the end of the school day, what we saw was nothing more or less than the sun setting over the Pacific. We lived with thirteen other students in a rented Victorian mansion on West Cliff Drive, and at night the yellow beacon from the nearby lighthouse invaded our attic windows; we drifted to sleep listening to the barking of seals. On weekends we had serious softball games in the vacant field next to the house – us against a team of tattooed, long-haired townies – and afterward, keyed up, tired and sweating, Mack and I walked the north shore to a place where we could watch the waves pound into the rocks and send up sun-ignited columns of water twenty-five and thirty feet tall. Though most of what we initiated 'back then' now seems to have been faddish and wrongheaded, our friendship was exceptionally sane and has endured for twenty years. It endured the melodramatic confusion of Dorothy Hughes, our beautiful shortstop – I loved her, but she loved Mack. It endured the subsequent revelation that Mack was gay – any tension on that count managed by him with remarks about what a homely bastard I was. It endured his fury and frustration over my low-bottom alcoholism and my sometimes raging (and *en*raging) process of getting clean and sober. And it has endured the onlooking fish eyes of his long string of lovers and my two wives. Neither of us had a biological brother – that could account for something – but at recent moments when I have felt most frightened, now that Mack is so ill, I've thought that we persisted simply because we couldn't let go of the sense of *thoroughness* our friendship gave us; we constantly reported to each other on our separate lives, as if we knew that by doing so we were getting more from life than we would ever have been entitled to individually.

In answer to his question – was everybody crazy back then – I say, 'Yes, I think so.'

He laughs, then coughs. When he coughs these days – which is often – he goes on coughing until a viscous, bloody fluid comes up, which he catches in a Kleenex and tosses into the trash can. Earlier, his doctors could drain his lungs with a needle through his back – last time they collected an entire liter from one lung – but now that Mack has developed the cancer, there are tumors that break up the fluid into many small isolated pockets, too many to drain. Radiation or chemotherapy would kill him; he's too weak even for a flu shot. Later today, he will go to the hospital for another bronchoscopy; they want to see if there's anything they can do to help him, though they have already told him there isn't. His medical care comes in the form of visiting nurses, physical therapists, and a curious duo at the hospital: one doctor who is young, affectionate, and incompetent but who comforts and consoles, hugs and holds hands; another – old, rude, brash, and expert – who says things like 'You might as well face it. You're going to die. Get your papers in order.' In fact, they've given Mack two weeks to two months, and it has now been ten weeks.

'Oh, my God,' cries Lester, Mack's lover, opening the screen door, entering the room, and looking around. 'I don't recognize this hovel. And what's that wonderful smell?'

This morning, while Lester was out, I vacuumed and generally straightened up. Their apartment is on the ground floor of a building like all the buildings in this southern California neighborhood – a two-story motel-like structure of white stucco and steel railings. Outside the door are an X-rated hibiscus (blood red, with its jutting yellow powder-tipped stamen), a plastic macaw on a swing, two enormous yuccas; inside, carpet, and plainness. The wonderful smell is the turkey I'm roasting; Mack can't eat anything before the bronchoscopy, but I figure it will be here for them when they return from the hospital, and they can eat off it for the rest of the week.

Lester, a South Carolina boy in his late twenties, is sick too – twice he has nearly died of pneumonia – but he's in a healthy period now. He's tall, thin, and bearded, a devotee of the writings of Shirley MacLaine – an unlikely guru, if you ask me, but my wife, Marilyn, tells me I'm too judgmental. Probably she is right.

The dog, Eberhardt, has woken up and waddles sleepily over to where Lester stands. Lester extends his arm toward Mack, two envelopes in his hand, and after a moment's pause Mack reaches for them. It's partly this typical hesitation of Mack's – a slowing of the mind, actually – that makes him appear serene, contemplative, these days. Occasionally, he really does get confused, which terrifies him. But I can't help thinking that something in there has sharpened as well – maybe a kind of simplification. Now he stares at the top envelope for a full minute, as Lester and I watch him. This is something we do: we watch him. 'Oh-h-h,' he says, at last. 'A letter from my mother.'

'And one from Lucy too,' says Lester. 'Isn't that nice?'

'I guess,' says Mack. Then: 'Well, yes. It is.'

'You want me to open them?' I ask.

'Would you?' he says, handing them to me. 'Read 'em to me too.'

They are only cards, with short notes inside, both from Des Moines. Mack's mother says it just makes her *sick* that he's sick, wants to know if there's anything he needs. Lucy, the sister, is gushy, misremembers a few things from the past, says she's writing instead of calling because she knows she will cry if she tries to talk. Lucy, who refused to let Mack enter her house at Christmastime one year – actually left him on the stoop in subzero cold – until he removed the gold earring from his ear. Mack's mother, who waited until after the funeral last year to let Mack know that his father had died; Mack's obvious illness at the funeral would have been an embarrassment.

But they've come around, Mack has told me in the face of my anger.

I said better late than never.

And Mack, all forgiveness, all humility, said that's exactly right: much better.

'Mrs. Mears is having a craft sale today,' Lester says. Mrs. Mears, an elderly neighbor, lives out back in a cottage with her husband. 'You guys want to go?'

Eberhardt, hearing 'go,' begins leaping at Lester's shins, but when we look at Mack, his eyelids are at half mast – he's half asleep.

We watch him for a moment, and I say, 'Maybe in a little while, Lester.'

~ ~ ~

Lester sits on the edge of his bed reading the newspaper, which lies flat on the spread in front of him. He has his own TV in his room, and a VCR. On the dresser, movies whose cases show men in studded black leather jockstraps, with gloves to match – dungeon masters of startling handsomeness. On the floor, a stack of gay magazines. Somewhere on the cover of each of these magazines the word 'macho' appears; and inside some of them, in the personal ads, men, meaning to attract others, refer to themselves as pigs. 'Don't putz,' Lester says to me as I straighten some things on top of the dresser. 'Enough already.'

I wonder where he picked up 'putz' – surely not in South Carolina. I say, 'You need to get somebody in. To help. You need to arrange it now. What if you were suddenly to get sick again?'

'I know,' he says. 'He's gotten to be quite a handful, hasn't he? Is he still asleep?'

'Yes,' I answer. 'Yes and yes.'

The phone rings, and Lester reaches for it. As soon as he begins to speak I can tell, from his tone, that it's my four-year-old on the line. After a moment, Lester says, 'Kit,' smiling, and hands me the phone, then returns to his newspaper.

I sit on the other side of the bed, and after I say hello, Kit says, 'We need some milk.'

'Okay,' I say. 'Milk. What are you up to this morning?'

'Being angry mostly,' she says.

'Oh?' I say. 'Why?'

'Mommy and I are not getting along very well.'

'That's too bad,' I say. 'I hope you won't stay angry for long.'

'We won't,' she says. 'We're going to make up in a minute.'

'Good,' I say.

'When are you coming home?'

'In a little while.'

'After my nap?'

'Yes,' I say. 'Right after your nap.'

'Is Mack very sick?'

She already knows the answer, of course. 'Yes,' I say.

'Is he going to die?'

This one too. 'Most likely,' I say. 'He's that sick.'

'Bye,' she says suddenly – her sense of closure always takes me by surprise – and I say, 'Don't stay angry for long, okay?'

'You already said that,' she says, rightly, and I wait for a moment, half expecting Marilyn to come on the line; ordinarily she would, and hearing her voice right now would do me good. After another moment, though, there's the click.

Marilyn is back in school, earning a Ph.D. in religious studies. I teach sixth grade, and because I'm faculty adviser for the little magazine the sixth graders put out each year, I stay late many afternoons. Marilyn wanted me home this Saturday morning. 'You're at work all week,' she said, 'and then you're over there on Saturday. Is that fair?'

I told her I didn't know – which was the honest truth. Then, in a possibly dramatic way, I told her that fairness was not my favorite subject these days, given that my best friend was dying.

We were in our kitchen, and through the window I could see Kit playing with a neighbor's cat in the backyard. Marilyn turned on the hot water in the kitchen sink and stood still while the steam rose into her face. 'It's become a question of where you belong,' she said at last. 'I think you're too involved.'

For this I had no answer, except to say, 'I agree' – which wasn't really an answer, since I had no intention of staying home, or becoming less involved, or changing anything.

Now Lester and I can hear Mack's scraping cough in the next room. We are silent until he stops. 'By the way,' Lester says at last, taking the telephone receiver out of my hand, 'have you noticed that he *listens* now?'

'I know,' I say. 'He told me he'd finally entered his listening period.'

'Yeah,' says Lester, 'as if it's the natural progression. You blab your whole life away, ignoring other people, and then right before you die you start to listen.'

The slight bitterness in Lester's tone makes me feel shaky inside. It's true that Mack was always a better talker than a listener, but I suddenly feel that I'm walking a thin wire and that anything like collusion would throw me off balance. All I know for sure is that I don't want to hear any more. Maybe Lester reads this in my face, because what he says next sounds like an explanation: he tells me that his poor old backwoods mother was nearly deaf when he was growing up, that she relied almost entirely on reading lips. 'All she had to do when she wanted to turn me off,' he says, 'was to just turn her back on me. Simple,' he says, making a little circle with his finger. 'No more Lester.'

'That's terrible,' I say.

'I was a terrible coward,' he says. 'Can you imagine Kit letting you get away with something like that? She'd bite your kneecaps.'

'Still,' I say, 'that's terrible.'

Lester shrugs his shoulders, and after another moment I say, 'I'm going to the Kmart. Mack needs a padded toilet seat. You want anything?'

'Yeah,' he says. 'But they don't sell it at Kmart.'

'What is it?' I ask.

'It's a *joke*, Dan, for chrissake,' he says. 'Honestly, I think you've completely lost your sense of humor.'

When I think about this, it seems true.

'Are you coming back?' he asks.

'Right back,' I answer. 'If you think of it, baste the turkey.'

'How could I not think of it?' he says, sniffing the air.

In the living room, Mack is lying with his eyes open now, staring blankly at the TV. At the moment, a shop-at-home show is on, but he changes channels, and an announcer says, 'When we return, we'll talk about tree pruning,' and Mack changes the channel again. He looks at me, nods thoughtfully, and says, 'Tree pruning. Interesting. It's just like the way they put a limit on your credit card, so you don't spend too much.'

'I don't understand,' I say.

'Oh, you know,' he says. 'Pruning the trees. Didn't the man just say something about pruning trees?' He sits up and adjusts the plastic tube in one nostril.

'Yes,' I say.

'Well, it's like the credit cards. The limit they put on the credit cards is . . .' He stops talking and looks straight into my eyes, frightened. 'It doesn't make any sense, does it?' he says. 'Jesus Christ. I'm not making sense.'

~ ~ ~

Way out east on University, there is a video arcade every half mile or so. Adult peep shows. Also a McDonald's, and the rest. Taverns — the kind that are open at eight in the morning — with clever names: Tobacco Rhoda's, the Cruz Inn. Bodegas that smell of cat piss and are really fronts for numbers games. Huge discount stores. Lester, who is an expert in these matters, has told me that all these places feed on addicts. 'What do you think — those peep shows stay in business on the strength of the occasional customer? No way. It's a steady clientele of people in there every day, for hours at a time, dropping in quarters. That whole strip of road is *made* for addicts. And all the strips like it. That's what America's all about, you know. You got your alcoholics in the bars. Your food addicts sucking it up at Jack-in-the-Box — you ever go in one of those places and count the fat people? You got your sex addicts in the peep shows. Your shopping addicts at the Kmart. Your gamblers running numbers in the bodegas and your junkies in the alleyways. We're all nothing but a bunch of addicts. The whole fucking addicted country.'

In the arcades, says Lester, the videos show myriad combinations and arrangements of men and women, men and men, women and women. Some show older men being serviced by eager, selfless young women who seem to live for one thing only, who can't get enough. Some of these women have put their hair into pigtails and shaved themselves — they're supposed to look like children. Inside the peep show booths there's semen on the floor. And in the old days, there were glory holes cut into the wooden walls between some of the booths, so if it pleased you, you could communicate with your neighbor. Not anymore. Mack and Lester tell me that some things have changed. The holes have been boarded up. In the public men's rooms you no longer read, scribbled in the stalls, 'All faggots should die.' You read, 'All faggots should die of AIDS.' Mack rails against the moratorium on fetal-tissue research, the most promising avenue for a cure. 'If it was legionnaires dying, we wouldn't have any moratorium,' he says. And he often talks about Africa, where governments impede efforts to teach villagers about condoms: a social worker, attempting to explain their use, isn't allowed to remove the condoms from their foil packets; in another country, with a slightly more liberal government, a field nurse stretches a condom over his hand, to show how it works, and later villagers are found wearing the condoms like mittens, thinking this will protect them from disease. Lester laughs at these stories but shakes his head. In our own country, something called 'family values' has emerged with clarity. '*Whose* family?' Mack wants to know, holding out his hands palms upward. 'I mean, we *all* come from families, don't we? The dizziest queen comes from a family. The ax murderer. Even Dan *Quayle* comes from a family of some kind.'

But Mack and Lester are dying, Mack first. As I steer my pickup into the parking lot at the Kmart, I almost clip the front fender of a big, deep-throated Chevy that's leaving. I have startled the driver, a young Chicano boy with four kids in the back seat, and he flips me the bird – aggressively, his arm out the window – but I feel protected today by my sense of purpose: I have come to buy a padded toilet seat for my friend.

~ ~ ~

When he was younger, Mack wanted to be a cultural anthropologist, but he was slow to break in after we were out of graduate school – never landed anything more than a low-paying position assisting someone else, nothing more than a student's job, really. Eventually, he began driving a tour bus in San Diego, which not only provided a steady income but suited him so well that in time he was managing the line and began to refer to the position not as his job but as his calling. He said that San Diego was like a pretty blond boy without too many brains. He knew just how to play up its cultural assets while allowing its beauty to speak for itself. He said he liked being 'at the controls.' But he had to quit work over a year ago, and now his hands have become so shaky that he can no longer even manage a pen and paper.

When I get back to the apartment from my trip to the Kmart, Mack asks me to take down a letter for him to an old high school buddy back in Des Moines, a country-and-western singer who has sent him a couple of her latest recordings. '*Whenever I met a new doctor or nurse,*' he dictates, '*I always asked them whether they believed in miracles.*'

Mack sits up a bit straighter and rearranges the pillows behind his back on the couch. 'What did I just say?' he asks me.

' "I always asked them whether they believed in miracles." '

'Yes,' he says, and continues. '*And if they said no, I told them I wanted to see someone else. I didn't want them treating me. Back then, I was hoping for a miracle, which seemed reasonable.* Do you think this is too detailed?' he asks me.

'No,' I say. 'I think it's fine.'

'I don't want to depress her.'

'Go on,' I say.

'*But now I have lung cancer,*' he continues. '*So now I need not one but two miracles. That doesn't seem as possible somehow.* Wait. Did you write "possible" yet?'

'No,' I say. ' "That doesn't seem as . . ." '

'Reasonable,' he says. 'Didn't I say "reasonable" before?'

'Yes,' I say. ' "That doesn't seem as reasonable somehow." '

'Yes,' he says. 'How does that sound?'

'It sounds fine, Mack. It's not for publication, you know.'

'It's not?' he says, feigning astonishment. 'I thought it was: "Letters of an AIDS Victim." ' He says this in a spooky voice and makes his bug eyes. Since his head is a perfect skull, the whole effect really is a little spooky.

'What else?' I say.

'*Thank you for your nice letter,*' he continues, '*and for the tapes.*' He begins coughing – a horrible, rasping seizure. Mack has told me that he has lost all fear; he said he realized this a few weeks ago, on the skyride at the zoo. But when the coughing sets in, when it seems that it may never stop, I think I see terror in his eyes: he begins tapping his breastbone with the fingers of one hand, as if he's trying to wake up his lungs, prod them to do their appointed work. Finally he does stop, and he sits for a moment in silence, in thought. Then he dictates: '*It makes me very happy that you are so successful.*'

~ ~ ~

At Mrs. Mears's craft sale, in the alley behind her cottage, she has set up several card tables: Scores of plastic dolls with hand-knitted dresses, shoes, and hats. Handmade doll furniture. Christmas ornaments. A whole box of knitted bonnets and scarves for dolls. Also, some baked goods. Now, while Lester holds Eberhardt, Mrs. Mears, wearing a large straw hat and sunglasses, outfits the dachshund in a bonnet and scarf. 'There now,' she says. 'Have you ever seen anything so *precious*? I'm going to get my camera.'

Mack sits in a folding chair by one of the tables; next to him sits Mr. Mears, also in a folding chair. The two men look very much alike, though Mr. Mears is not nearly as emaciated as Mack. And of course, Mr. Mears is eighty-seven. Mack, on the calendar, is not quite forty. I notice that Mack's shoelaces are untied, and I kneel to tie them. 'The thing about reincarnation,' he's saying to Mr. Mears, 'is that you can't remember anything and you don't recognize anybody.'

'Consciously,' says Lester, butting in. '*Sub*consciously you do.'

'Subconsciously,' says Mack. 'What's the point? I'm not the least bit interested.'

Mr. Mears removes his houndstooth-check cap and scratches his bald, freckled head. 'I'm not, either,' he says with great resignation.

As Mrs. Mears returns with the camera, she says, 'Put him over there, in Mack's lap.'

'It doesn't matter whether you're interested or not,' says Lester, dropping Eberhardt into Mack's lap.

'Give me good old-fashioned Heaven and Hell,' says Mr. Mears.

'I should think you would've had enough of that already,' says Lester.

Mr. Mears gives Lester a suspicious look, then gazes down at his own knees. 'Then give me nothing,' he says finally.

I stand up and step aside just in time for Mrs. Mears to snap the picture. 'Did you ever *see* anything?' she says, all sunshades and yellow teeth, but as she heads back toward the cottage door, her face is immediately serious. She takes me by the arm and pulls me along, reaching for something from one of the tables – a doll's bed, white with a red strawberry painted on the headboard. 'For your little girl,' she says aloud. Then she whispers, 'You better get him out of the sun, don't you think? He doesn't look so good.'

But when I turn again, I see that Lester is already helping Mack out of his chair. 'Here – let me,' says Mrs. Mears, reaching an arm toward them, and she escorts Mack up the narrow, shaded sidewalk, back toward the apartment building. Lester moves alongside me and says, 'Dan, do you think you could give Mack his bath this afternoon? I'd like to take Eberhardt for a walk.'

'Of course,' I say, quickly.

But a while later – after I have drawn the bath, after I've taken a large beach towel out of the linen closet, refolded it into a thick square, and put it into the water to serve as a cushion for Mack to sit on in the tub; when I'm holding the towel under, against some resistance, waiting for the bubbles to stop surfacing, and there's something horrible about it, like drowning a small animal – I think Lester has tricked me into this task of bathing Mack, and the saliva in my mouth suddenly seems to taste of Scotch, which I have not actually tasted in nine years.

There is no time to consider any of this, however, for in a moment Mack enters the bathroom, trailing his tubes behind him, and says, 'Are you ready for my Auschwitz look?'

'I've seen it before,' I say.

And it's true. I have, a few times, helping him with his shirt and pants after Lester has bathed him and gotten him into his underwear. But that doesn't feel like preparation. The sight of him naked is like a powerful, scary drug: you forget between trips, remember only when you start to come on to it again. I help him off with his clothes now and guide him into the tub and gently onto the underwater towel. 'That's nice,' he says, and I begin soaping the hollows of his shoulders, the hard washboard of his back. This is not human skin as we know it but something already dead – so dry, dense, and pleasantly brown as to appear manufactured. I soap the cage of his chest, his stomach – the hard, depressed abdomen of a greyhound – the steep vaults of his armpits, his legs, his feet. Oddly, his hands and feet appear almost normal, even a bit swollen. At last I give him the slippery bar of soap. 'Your turn,' I say.

'My poor cock,' he says as he begins to wash himself.

When he's done, I rinse him all over with the hand spray attached to the faucet. I lather the feathery white wisps of his hair – we have to remove the plastic oxygen tubes for this – then rinse again. 'You know,' he says, 'I know it's irrational, but I feel kind of turned off to sex.'

The apparent understatement of this almost takes my breath away. 'There are more important things,' I say.

'Oh, I know,' he says. 'I just hope Lester's not too unhappy.' Then, after a moment, he says, 'You know, Dan, it's only logical that they've all given up on me. And I've accepted it mostly. But I still have days when I think I should at least be given a chance.'

'You can ask them for anything you want, Mack,' I say.

'I know,' he says. 'That's the problem – there's nothing to ask for.'

'Mack,' I say. 'I think I understand what you meant this morning about the tree pruning and the credit cards.'

'You do?'

'Well, I think your mind just shifted into metaphor. Because I can see that pruning trees is like imposing a limit – just like the limit on the credit cards.'

Mack is silent, pondering this. 'Maybe,' he says at last, hesitantly – a moment of disappointment for us both.

I get him out and hooked up to the oxygen again, dry him off, and begin dressing him. Somehow I get the oxygen tubes trapped between his legs and the elastic waistband of his sweatpants – no big deal, but I suddenly feel panicky – and I have to take them off his face again to set them to rights. After he's safely back on the living room couch and I've returned to the bathroom, I hear him: low, painful-sounding groans. 'Are you all right?' I call from the hallway.

'Oh, yes,' he says. 'I'm just moaning. It's one of the few pleasures I have left.'

The bathtub is coated with a crust of dead skin, which I wash away with the sprayer. Then I find a screwdriver and go to work on the toilet seat. After I get the old one off, I need to scrub around the area where the plastic screws were. I've sprinkled Ajax all around the rim of the bowl and found the scrub brush, when Lester appears at the bathroom door, back with Eberhardt from their walk. 'Oh, Dan, really,' he says. 'You go too far. Down on your knees now, scrubbing our toilet.'

'Lester, leave me alone,' I say.

'Well, it's true,' he says. 'You really do.'

'Maybe I'm working out my survivor's guilt,' I say, 'if you don't mind.'

'You mean because your best buddy's dying and you're not?'

'Yes,' I say. 'It's very common.'

He parks one hip on the edge of the sink. And after a moment he says this: 'Danny boy, if you feel guilty about surviving . . . that's not irreversible, you know. I could fix that.'

We are both stunned. He looks at me. In another moment, there are tears in his eyes. He quickly closes the bathroom door, moves to the tub and turns on the water, sits on the side, and bursts into sobs. 'I'm sorry,' he says. 'I'm so sorry.'

'Forget it,' I say.

He begins to compose himself almost at once. 'This is what Jane Alexander did when she played Eleanor Roosevelt,' he says. 'Do you remember? When she needed to cry she'd go in the bathroom and turn on the water, so nobody could hear her. Remember?'

~ ~ ~

In the pickup, on the way to the hospital, Lester – in the middle, between Mack and me – says, 'Maybe after they're down there you could doze off, but on the *way* down, they want you awake.' He's explaining the bronchoscopy to me – the insertion of the tube down the windpipe – with which he is personally familiar: 'They reach certain points on the way down where they have to ask you to swallow.'

'*He's* not having the test, is he?' Mack says, looking confused.

'No, of course not,' says Lester.

'Didn't you just say to him that he had to swallow?'

'I meant *anyone*, Mack,' says Lester.

'Oh,' says Mack. 'Oh, yeah.'

'The general "you,"' Lester says to me. 'He keeps forgetting little things like that.'

Mack shakes his head, then points at his temple with one finger. 'My mind,' he says.

Mack is on tank oxygen now, which comes with a small caddy. I push the caddy, behind him, and Lester assists him along the short walk from the curb to the hospital's front door and the elevators. Nine years ago, it was Mack who drove *me* to a different wing of this same hospital – against my drunken, slobbery will – to dry out. And as I watch him struggle up the low inclined ramp toward the glass-and-steel doors, I recall the single irrefutable thing he said to me in the car on the way. 'You stink,' he said. 'You've puked and probably pissed your pants and you *stink*,' he said – my loyal, articulate, and best friend, saving my life, and causing me to cry like a baby.

Inside the clinic upstairs, the nurse, a sour young blond woman in a sky-blue uniform who looks terribly overworked, says to Mack, 'You know better than to be late.'

We are five minutes late to the second. Mack looks at her incredulously. He stands with one hand on the handle of the oxygen-tank caddy. He straightens up, perfectly erect – the indignant, shockingly skeletal posture of a man fasting to the death for some holy principle. He gives the nurse the bug eyes and says, 'And you know better than to keep me waiting every time I come over here for some goddamn procedure. But get over yourself: shit happens.'

He turns and winks at me.

Though I've offered to return for them afterward, Lester has insisted on taking a taxi, so I will leave them here and drive back home, where again I'll try – successfully, this time – to explain to my wife how all this feels to me, and where, a few minutes later, I'll stand outside the door to my daughter's room, comforted by the music of her small high voice as she consoles her dolls.

Now the nurse gets Mack into a wheelchair and leaves us in the middle of the reception area; then, from the proper position at her desk, she calls Mack's name, and says he may proceed to the laboratory.

'Dan,' Mack says, stretching his spotted, broomstick arms toward me. 'Old pal. Do you remember the Christmas we drove out to Des Moines on the motorcycle?'

We did go to Des Moines together, one very snowy Christmas – but of course we didn't go on any motorcycle, not in December.

'We had fun,' I say, and put my arms around him, awkwardly, since he is sitting.

'Help me up,' he whispers – confidentially – and I begin to lift him.

EDNA O'BRIEN

DRAMAS

W hen the new shopkeeper arrived in the village he aroused great curiosity along with some scorn. He was deemed refined because his fingernails looked as if they had been varnished a tinted ivory. He had a horse, or as my father was quick to point out, a glorified pony, which he had brought from the Midlands, where he had previously worked. The pony was called Daisy, a name unheard of in our circles for an animal. The shopkeeper wore a long black coat, a black hat, talked in a low voice, made his own jams and marmalades, and could even darn and sew. All that we came to know of, in due course, but at first we only knew him as Barry. In time the shop would have his name, printed in beautiful silver sloping script, above the door. He had bought the long-disused bakery, had all the ovens thrown out, and turned it into a palace which had not only gadgets but gadgets that worked: a lethal slicer for the ham, a new kind of weighing scale that did not require iron weights hefted onto one side but that simply registered the weight of a bag of meal and told it by a needle that spun round, wobbling dementedly before coming to a standstill. Even farmers praised its miraculous skills. He also had a meat safe with a

EDNA O'BRIEN (born 1932): 'Dramas' is from O'Brien's collection Lantern Slides, *the title story of which deserves particular attention: it is a kind of answer to James Joyce's* 'The Dead.' *She is, in fact, the author of a short biography of Joyce in the 'Penguin Lives' series.*

grey gauze door, a safe in which creams and cheeses could be kept fresh for an age, free of the scourge of flies or gnats.

Straightaway he started to do great business as the people reneged on the shops where they had dealt for years and where many of them owed money. They flocked to look at him, to hear his well-mannered voice, and to admire dainties and things that he had in stock. He had ten different-flavored jellies and more than one brand of coffee. The women especially liked him. He leant over the counter, discussed things with them, their headaches, their knitting, patterns for suits or dresses that they might make, and along with that he kept an open tin of biscuits so that they could have them if they felt peckish. The particular favorite was a tiny round biscuit, like a Holy Communion wafer with a thin skin of rice paper as a lining. These were such favorites that Barry would have to put his hand down beneath the ruffs of ink paper and ferret up a few from the bottom. The rice paper did not taste like paper at all but like a disk of some magical metamorphosed sugar. Besides that coveted biscuit, there were others, a sandwich of ginger with a soft white filling that was as sturdy as putty, and another in which there was a blend of raspberry and custard, a combination that engendered such ecstasy that one was torn between the pleasure of devouring it or tasting each grain slowly so as to isolate the raspberry from the custard flavour. There were also arrowroot and digestives, but these were the last to be eaten. He called the biscuits 'bikkies' and cigarettes 'ciggies.'

He was not such a favorite with the men, both because he raved to the women and because he voiced the notion of bringing drama to the town. He said that he would find a drama that would embody the talents of the people and that he would direct and produce it himself. Constantly he was casting people, and although none of us knew precisely what he meant, we would agree when he said, 'Rosalind, a born Rosalind', or, 'Cordelia, if ever I met one.' He did not, however, intend to do Shakespeare, as he feared that, being untrained, the people would not be able to get their tongues around the rhyming verse and would not feel at home in bulky costumes. He would choose something more suitable, something that people could identify with. Every time he went to the city to buy stock, he also bought one or two plays, and if there was a slack moment in the shop he would read a speech or even a whole scene, he himself acting the parts, the men's and the women's. He was very convincing when he acted the women or the girls. One play was about a young girl who saw a dead seagull, and in seeing it, her tragedy was predestined: she was crossed in love, had an illegitimate child, and drove a young man to suicide. Another time he read scenes about two very unhappy people in Scandinavia who scalded each other, daily, with accusation and counter-accusation, and to buoy himself up, the man did a frenzied dance. Barry did the dance too, jumping on and off the weighing scales or even onto the counter when he got carried away. He used to ask me to stay on after the shop closed, simply because I was as besotted as he was by these exotic and tormented characters. It was biscuits, sweets, lemonade, anything. Yet something in me trembled, foresaw trouble.

The locals were suspicious, they did not want plays about dead birds and illegitimate children, or unhappy couples tearing at each other, because they had these scenarios aplenty. Barry decided, wisely, to do a play that would be more heartening, a simple play about wholesome people and wholesome themes, such as getting the harvest in safely. I was always privy to each new decision, partly because of my mania for the plays and partly because I had to tell him how his pony was doing. The pony grazed with us, and consequently we were given quite a lot of credit. I shall never forget my mother announcing this good news to me flushed with pride, almost suave as she said, 'If ever you have the hungry grass on the way from school, just go into Barry and say you feel like a titbit.' By her telling me this so casually, I saw how dearly she would have loved to have been rich, to entertain, to give lunch parties and supper parties, to show off the linen tablecloths and the good cutlery which she had Vaselined over the years to keep the steel from rusting. In these imaginary galas she brandished the two silver salvers, the biscuit barrel, and the dinner plates with their bouquets of violets in the center and scalloped edging that looked like crochet work. We had been richer, but over the years the money got squandered.

Barry to her did not talk wisely about dramas but about the ornaments in our house, commenting on her good taste. It was the happiest half year in my life, being able to linger in Barry's shop and while he was busy read some of these plays and act them silently inside my head. With the customers all gone, I would sit on the counter, swing my legs, gorge biscuits, and discuss both the stories and the characters. Barry in his white shop coat and with a sharpened pencil in his hand would make notes of the things we said. He would discuss the scenery, the lights, the intonation of each line, and when an actor should hesitate or then again when an actor should let rip. Barry said it was a question of contrast, of nuance versus verve. I stayed until dark, until the moon came up or the first star. He walked home, but he did not try to kiss one or put his hand on the tickly part of the back of the knee, the way other men did, even the teacher's first cousin, who pretended he wasn't doing it when he was. Barry was as pure as a young priest and like a priest had pale skin with down on it. His only blemish was his thinning hair, and the top of his head was like an egg, with big wisps, which I did not like to look at.

Business for him was not quite as flush as in those first excitable weeks, but as he would say to my mother, things were 'ticking over,' and also he was lucky in that his Aunt Milly in the Midlands was going to leave him her farm and her house. Meanwhile, if there were debts she would come to the rescue, so that he would never be disgraced by having his name printed in a gazette where all the debtors' names were printed so that the whole country knew of it.

As it neared autumn Barry had decided on a play and had started auditions. 'All for Hecuba and Hecuba for me,' he said to the mystified customers. It was a play about travelling players, so that, as he said, the actors and actresses could have lots of verve and camp it up. No one knew quite what he meant by 'camp it up.' He mulled over playing the lead himself, but there were objections from people in the town. So each evening men and women went to the parlour that adjoined the shop, read for him, and often emerged disgruntled and threatening to start up a rival company because he did not give them the best part. Then an extraordinary thing happened. Barry had written on the spur of the moment to a famous actor in Dublin for a spot of advice. In the letter he had also said that if the actor was ever passing through the vicinity he might like 'to break bread.' Barry was very proud of the wording of this letter. The actor replied on a postcard. It was a postcard on which four big white cats adhered together, in a mesh. Spurred by this signal, Barry made a parcel of country stuffs and sent them to the actor by registered post. He sent butter, fowl, homemade cake, and eggs wrapped in thick twists of newspaper and packed in a little papier-mâché box.

Not long after, I met him in the street, in a dither. The most extraordinary thing had happened. The actor and his friend were coming to visit, had announced it without being invited, said they had decided to help Barry in his artistic endeavour and would teach him all the rudiments of theatre that were needed for his forthcoming production. 'A business lunch *à trois*' was how Barry described it, his voice three octaves higher, his face unable to disguise his fervid excitement. My mother offered to loan linen and cutlery, the Liddy girl was summoned to scrub, and Oona, the sacristan, was cajoled to part with some of the flowers meant for the altar, while I was enlisted to go around the hedges and pick anything, leaves, branches, anything.

'His friend is called Ivan,' Barry said, and added that, though Ivan was not an actor, he was a partner and saw to the practical aspect of things. How he knew this I have no idea, because I doubt that the actor would have mentioned such a prosaic thing. Preparations were begun. My mother made shortbread and cakes, orange and Madeira; she also gave two cockerels, plucked and ready for the oven, with a big bowl of stuffing which the Liddy girl could put in the birds at the last minute. She even put in a darning needle and green thread so that the rear ends of the chickens could be sewn up once the stuffing was added. The bath was scoured, the bathroom floor so waxed that the Liddy girl slipped on it and threatened to sue, but was pacified with the gift of a small packet of cigarettes. A fire was lit in the parlour for days ahead, so as to air it and give it a sense of being lived in. It was not certain if the actor and Ivan would spend the night, not clear from the rather terse bulletin that was sent, but, as Barry pointed out, he had three bedrooms, so that if they did decide to stay, there would be no snag. Naturally he would surrender his own bedroom to the actor and give Ivan the next-best one and he could be in the box room.

Nobody else was invited, but that was to be expected, since after all it was a working occasion and Barry was going to pick their brains about the interpretation of the play, about the sets and the degree to which the characters should exaggerate their plights. The guests were seen emerging from a big old-fashioned car with coupe bonnet, the actor holding an umbrella and sporting a red carnation in his buttonhole. Ivan wore a raincoat and was a little portly, but they ran so quickly to the hall door that only a glimpse of them was caught. Barry had been standing inside the door since after Mass, so that the moment he heard the thud of the knocker, the door was swung open and he welcomed them into the cold but highly polished corridor. We know that they partook of lunch because the Liddy girl told how she roasted the birds to a T, added the potatoes for roasting at the correct time, and placed the lot on a warmed platter with carving knife and carving fork to one side. She had knocked on the parlour door to ask if Barry wanted the lunch brought in, but he had simply told her to leave it in the hatch and that he would get it himself, as they were in the thick of an intense discussion. She grieved at not being able to serve the lunch, because it meant both that she could not have a good look at the visitors and that she would not get a handsome tip.

It was about four o'clock in the afternoon when the disturbance happened. I had gone there because of being possessed by a mad hope that they would do a reading of the play and that I would be needed to play some role, even if it was a menial one. I stood in the doorway of the drapery shop across the street, visible if Barry should lift the net curtain and look out. Indeed, I believed he would and I waited quite happily. The village was quiet and sunk in its after-dinner somnolence, with only myself and a few dogs prowling about. It had begun to spatter with rain. I heard a window being raised and was stunned to see the visitors on the small upstairs balcony, dressed in outlandish women's clothing. I should have seen disaster then, except that I thought they were women, that other visitors, their wives perhaps, had come unbeknownst to us. When I saw Barry in a maroon dress, larking, I ducked down, guessing the awful truth. He was calling, 'Friends, Romans, countrymen.' Already three or four people had come to their doorways, and soon there was a small crowd looking up at the appalling spectacle of three drunk men pretending to be women. They were all wearing pancake make-up and were heavily rouged. The actor also wore a string of pearls and kept hitting the other two in jest. Ivan was wearing a pleated skirt and a low-cut white blouse, with falsies underneath. The actor had on some kind of toga and was shouting wild endearments and throwing kisses.

The inflamed owner of the drapery shop asked me how long these antics had been going on.

'I don't know,' I said, my face scarlet, every bit of me wishing to vanish. Yet I followed the crowd as they moved, inexorably, towards the balcony, all of them speechless, as if the spectacle had robbed them of their reason. It was in itself like a crusade, this fanatic throng moving towards assault.

Barry wore a tam-o'-shanter and looked uncannily like a girl. It gave me the shivers to see this metamorphosis. He even tossed his neck like a girl, and you would no longer believe he was bald. The actor warmed to the situation and started calling people 'Ducky' and 'Cinders,' while also reciting snatches from Shakespeare. He singled people out. So carried away was he by the allure of his performance that the brunette wig he was wearing began to slip, but determined to be a sport about this, he took it off, doffed it to the crowd, and replaced it again. One of the women, a Mrs. Gleeson, fainted, but more attention was being paid to the three performers than to her, so she had to stagger to her feet again. Seeing that the actor was stealing the scene, Ivan did something terrible: he opened the low-cut blouse, took out the falsies, tossed them down to the crowd, and said to one of the young men, 'Where there's that, there's plenty more.' The young man in question did not know what to do, did not know whether to pick them up and throw them back or challenge the strangers to a fight. The actor and Ivan then began arguing and vied with each other as to who was the most fetching. Barry had receded and was in the doorway of the upper room, still drunk, but obviously not so drunk as to be indifferent to the calamity that had occurred.

The actor, it seemed, had also taken a liking to the young man whom Ivan had thrown the falsies to, and now holding a folded scroll, he leant over the wrought iron, looked down directly at the man, brandished the scroll, and said, 'It's bigger than that, darling.' At once the locals got the gist of the situation and called on him to come down so that they could beat him to a pulp. Enthused now by their heckling, he stood on the wobbly parapet and began to scold them, telling them there were some naughty skeletons in their lives and that they couldn't fool him by all pretending to be happily married men. Then he said something awful: he said that the great Oscar Wilde had termed the marriage bed 'the couch of lawful lust.' A young guard arrived and called up to the actor to please recognize that he was causing a disturbance of the peace as well as scandalizing innocent people.

'Come and get me, darling,' the actor said, and wriggled his fore-finger like a saucy heroine in a play. Also, on account of being drunk he was swaying on this very rickety parapet.

'Come down now,' the guard said, trying to humour him a bit, because he did not want the villagers to have a death on their hands. The actor smiled at this note of conciliation and called the guard 'Lola' and asked if he ever used his big baton anywhere else, and so provoked the young guard and so horrified the townspeople that already men were taking off their jackets to prepare for a fight.

'Beat me, I love it,' he called down while they lavished dire threats on him. Ivan, it seemed, was now enjoying the scene and did not seem to mind that the actor was getting most of the attention and most of the abuse. Two ladders were fetched, and the young guard climbed up to arrest the three men. The actor teased him as he approached. The doctor followed, vowing that he would give them an injection to silence their filthy tongues. Barry had already gone in, and Ivan was trying to mollify them, saying it was all clean fun, when the actor put his arms around the young guard and lathered him with frenzied kisses. Other men hurried up the ladder and pushed the culprits into the bedroom so that people would be spared any further display of lunacy. The French doors were closed, and shouting and arguments began. Then the voices ceased as the offenders were pulled from the bedroom to the room downstairs, so that they could be carted into the police van which was now waiting. People feared that maybe these theatrical villains were armed, while the women wondered aloud if Barry had had these costumes and falsies and things, or if the actors had brought them. It was true that they had come with two suitcases. The Liddy girl had been sent out in the rain to carry them in. The sergeant who now arrived on the scene called to the upper floor, but upon getting no answer went around to the back of the house, where he was followed by a straggle of people. The rest of us waited in front, some of the opinion that the actor was sure to come back onto the balcony, to take a bow. The smaller children went from the front to the back of the house and returned to say there had been a terrible crash of bottles and crockery. The dining room table was overturned in the fracas. About ten minutes later they came out by the back door, each of the culprits held by two men. The actor was wearing his green suit, but his makeup had not been fully wiped off, so that he looked vivid and startled, like someone about to embark on a great role. Ivan was in his raincoat and threatening aloud to sue unless he was allowed to speak to his solicitor. He called the guards and the people 'rabble.' The woman who had fainted went up to Barry and vehemently cursed him, while one of the town girls had the audacity to ask the actor for his autograph. He shouted the name of the theatre in Dublin to which she could send for it. Some said that he would never again perform in that or any theatre, as his name was mud.

When I saw Barry waiting to be bundled into the van like a criminal, I wanted to run over to him, or else to shout at the locals, disown them in some way. But I was too afraid. He caught my eye for an instant. I don't know why it was me he looked at, except perhaps he was hoping he had a friend, he was hoping our forays into drama had made a bond between us. He looked so abject that I had to look away and instead concentrated my gaze on the shop window, where the weighing scales, the ham slicer, and all the precious commodities were like props on an empty stage. From the corner of my eye I saw him get into the big black van and saw it drive away with all the solemnity of a hearse.

BERNARD COOPER

SIX FABLES

Atlantis

How did the barber pole originate? When did its characteristic stripes become kinetic, turning hypnotically, driven by a hidden motor, giving the impression of red and blue forever twining, never slowing? No matter. No icon or emblem, no symbol or sign, still or revolving, lit from within or lit from without, could in any way have prepared me for that haircut at Nick's Barber Shop, or for Nick himself. His thick Filipino accent obscured meaning, though the sound was mellifluous, and the sense, translated in the late afternoon light, was expressed in the movements of Nick's hands. He flourished a comb he never dropped, a soundless scissors, a razor which revealed, gently, gently, the nape of my neck, now so smooth, attuned to the wind and the wool of my collar.

After our initial exchange of misunderstood courtesies, Nick nudged me toward a wall, museum bright, on which hung a poster depicting the 'Official Haircuts for Men and Boys' from 1955. I understood immediately that I was to choose from among the Brush Cut, the Ivy League, the Flat Top with Fenders. To insure sanctity and a sense of privacy, Nick turned

BERNARD COOPER *(born 1951): Cooper's collection* Maps to Anywhere *won the PEN/Hemingway Prize in 1991. Part stories, part essays, part poems, these pieces defy and at the same time expand the parameters of fiction. Cooper is also the author of* A Year of Rhymes, Truth Serum, *and* Guess Again. *He lives in Los Angeles on the same street as Dennis Cooper, with whom he is infrequently confused.*

off the fan for a moment, lowered his head, and even the dust stopped drifting in abeyance. Above me, in every phase from profile to full front, were heads of hair, luxuriant, graphic, lacquer-black: outmoded curls like scrolls on entablature, sideburns rooted in the past, strands and locks in arrested motion, cresting waves styled into hard edges, like Japanese prints of typhoons.

None of the heads contained a face. One simply interjected his own face. These oval vessels waited to be filled again and again by men's imaginations. For decades, they absorbed the eyes and noses and lips of customers who stood on the checkerboard of old linoleum, or sat in salmon-pink chairs next to wobbling tables stacked with magazines featuring bikinis and ball games.

The haircut was over in no time. (Nick did a stint in the army, where expedience is everything.) I kept my eyes closed. But aware of strange and lovely afterimages – ghostly pay phone, glowing push broom – I seemed to be submerged in the rapture of the deep. The drone of the fan, the minty and intoxicating scent of Barbasol, pressed upon me; phosphene shimmered like minnows in the dark corners of my vision, and I found that this world, cigar stained, sergeant striped, basso profundo, was the lost world of my father, who could not love me. So when Nick kneaded my shoulders and pressed my temples (free scalp manipulation with every visit), I unconsciously grazed him like a cat in Atlantis. His fingers flowed over my forehead like water. I began to smile imperceptibly and see barber poles aslant like sunken columns and voluptuous mermaids in salmon-pink bikinis and bubbles the size of baseballs rising to the surface and bursting with snippets of Filipino small talk.

I can't tell you how odd it was when, restored by a splash of astringent tonic, I finally opened my eyes and saw a clump of my own hair, blown by the fan, skitter across the floor like a cat. For a moment the mirrors were unbearably silver, and the hand-lettered signs, reflected in reverse, seemed inscriptions in a long-forgotten language.

Indeed I looked better, contented. Older too in the ruddy light of sunset. And all of this, this seminal descent to the floor of the sea, this inundation of two paternal hands, this sudden maturation in the mirror, for only four dollars and fifty cents. But my debt of gratitude, beyond the dollar-fifty tip, will be paid here, in the form of Nick's actual telephone number, area code (213) 660–4876. Even his business card, adorned with a faceless haircut holding a phone, says, 'Call any time!' Nick means any time. He means day or night. I've driven by and glimpsed him asleep in the barber chair, his face turned toward the street, his combs soaking in blue medicinal liquid, the barber pole softly aglow like a night-light, the stripes cascading endlessly down, rivulets running toward a home in the ocean.

Capiche?

In Italy, the dogs say bow-bow instead of bow-wow, and my Italian teacher, Signora Marra, is not quite sure why this should be. When we tell her that here in America the roosters say cock-a-doodle-do, she throws back her head like a hen drinking raindrops and laughs uncontrollably, as if we were fools to believe what our native red rooster says, or ignoramuses not to know that Italian roosters scratch and preen and clear their gullets before reciting Dante to the sun.

In Venice there is a conspicuous absence of dogs and roosters, but all the pigeons on the planet seem to roost there, and their conversations are deafening. When the city finally sinks, only a thick dark cloud of birds will be left to undulate over the ocean, birds kept alive by pure nostalgia and a longing to land. And circulating among them will be stories, reminiscences, anecdotes of all kinds to help pass the interminable days. Even when this voluble cloud dissipates, the old exhausted birds drowning in the sea, the young bereft birds flying away, the sublime and untranslatable tale of the City of Canals will echo off the oily water, the walls of vapor, the nimbus clouds.

There were so many birds in front of Café Florian's, and mosquitoes sang a piercing song as I drank my glass of red wine. Waving them away, I inadvertently beckoned Sandro, a total stranger. With great determination, anxious to know me, he bounded around tables of tourists.

The Piazza San Marco holds many noises within its light-bathed walls, sounds that clash, are superimposed or densely layered like torte. Within that cacophony of words and violins, Sandro and I struggled to communicate. Something unspoken suffered between us. We were, I think, instantly in love, and when he offered me, with his hard brown arms, a blown-glass ashtray shaped like a gondola, all I could say, all I could recall of Signora Marra's incanting and chanting (she believed in saturating students in rhyme), was 'No capiche.' I tried to inflect into that phrase every modulation of meaning, the way different tonalities of light had changed the meaning of that city.

But suddenly this adventure is over. Everything I have told you is a lie. Almost everything. There is no lithe and handsome Sandro. I've never learned Italian or been to Venice. Signora Marra is a feisty fiction. But lies are filled with modulations of untranslatable truth, and early this morning when I awoke, birds were restless in the olive trees. Dogs tramped through the grass and growled. The local rooster crowed fluently. The Chianti sun was coming up, intoxicating, and I was so moved by the strange, abstract trajectories of sound that I wanted to take you with me somewhere, somewhere old and beautiful, and I honestly wanted to offer you something, something like the prospect of sudden love, or color postcards of chaotic piazzas, and I wanted you to listen to me as if you were hearing a rare recording by Enrico Caruso. All I had was the glass of language to blow into a souvenir.

Sudden Extinction

The vertebrae of dinosaurs, found in countless excavations, are dusted and rinsed and catalogued. We guess and guess at their huge habits as we gaze at the fossils which capture their absence, sprawling three-toed indentations, the shadowy lattice of ribs. Their skulls are a slight embarrassment, snug even for a head full of blunt wants and backward motives. The brachiosaurus's brain, for example, sat atop his tapered neck like a minuscule flame on a mammoth candle.

My favorite is triceratops, his face a hideous Rorschach blot of broad bone and blue hide. The Museum of Natural History owns a replica that doesn't do him justice. One front foot is poised in the air like an elephant sedated for a sideshow. And the nasal horn for shredding aggressors is as dull and mundane as a hook for a hat.

One prominent paleontologist believes that during an instantaneous ice age, glaciers encased these monsters midmeal – stegosaurus, podokesaurus, iguanadon – all trapped forever like spectrums in glass. But suppose extinction was a matter of choice, and they just didn't want to stand up any longer, like drunk guests at a party's end who pass out in the dark den. There are guys at my gym whose latissimus dorsi, having spread like thunderheads, cause them to inch through an ordinary door; might the dinosauria have grown too big of their own volition?

Derek speaks in expletives and swears that one day his back will be as big as a condominium. Mike's muscles, marbled with veins, perspire from ferocious motion, the taut skin about to split. When Bill does a bench press, the barbell bends from fifty-pound plates; his cheeks expand and expel great gusts of spittle and air till his face and eyes are flushed with blood and his elbows quiver, the weight sways, and someone runs over and hovers above him roaring for one more repetition.

Once, I imagined our exercise through X-ray eyes. Our skeletons gaped at their own reflection. Empty eyes, like apertures, opened onto an afterlife. Lightning-bright spines flashed from sacrums. Phalanges of hands were splayed in surprise. Bones were glowing everywhere, years scoured down to marrow, flesh redressed with white.

And I knew our remains were meant to keep like secrets under the earth. And I knew one day we would topple like monuments, stirring up clouds of dust. And I almost heard the dirge of our perishing, thud after thud after thud, our last titanic exhalations loud and labored and low.

Leaving

The statistical family stands in a textbook, graphic and unabashed. The father, tallest, squarest, has impressive shoulders for a stick figure. The mother, slighter, rounder, wears a simple triangle, a skirt she might have sewn herself.

A proud couple of generalizations, their children average 2.5 in number. One boy and one girl, inked in the indelible stance of the parents, hold each other's iconic little hands. But the .5 child is isolated, half a figure, balanced on one leg, one hand extended as if to touch the known world for the last time, leaving probable pounds of bread and gallons of water behind, leaving the norms of income behind, leaving behind the likelihood of marriage (with its orgasms estimated in the thousands), leaving tight margins, long columns, leaving a million particulars, without hesitation, without regret.

The Origin of Roget's Thesaurus
for Brian Miller

When Anne-Marie sidles up and bends slightly forward, her starched uniform crackles like a distant fire, and she discreetly, yet suggestively, offers potatoes with gravy to Dr. Roget. The smell of garlic assails his nose, and then the lilac smell of Anne-Marie, distinct odors fused into something mesmerizing, difficult to name. His nostrils flare. His eyes cloud up. His fork becomes inconceivably heavy. What precisely is this sensation, this suffusion of fragrance, appetite, lust? What rubric or term or adjective could capture it? He thinks *delicious*. No, *delightful*. Then the panorama of *pleasantness* opens in his brain: *pleasing, enchanting, appealing*, a vast and verdant country. But further inland, in the dark heart of Dr. Roget's confusion, lies the antonymous terrain of *unpleasantness*, its odious flora and horrible fauna, and he doesn't know where to turn.

'Peter?' murmurs Mrs. Roget, miles away at the end of the table.

'Daddy?' murmurs Peter junior, beneath a branching candelabrum.

Hush, hush. Doors are opening in Daddy's head, doors that lead to halls of doors that lead to other labyrinthine, musty halls of doors. Door by door, word by word, an entire lexicon will be discovered. A draft will begin to move through portals, the wind to whistle fluently, and someday Daddy will reach a door opening onto the sea.

~ ~ ~

The moment before we make love, I think about the sea at night. I'm clutching the sail of your broad warm back.

What tenuous connections, what tributaries of association brought me from the landscape in Roget's brain to your body beyond the limits of land? What convoluted currents of chance, what chain reaction of history took me drifting from my boyhood on the coast of California and propelled me to you, here in this bed in this vessel on the black undulating ocean, to this very second when I can't stop thinking, synapses flashing like stars, the doors in my head opening, opening, the wind of my words against your back: *supple, tractable, bendable, mutable* . . .

Childless

So I was talking to this guy who's the photo editor of *Scientific American*, and he told me he was having trouble choosing a suitable photograph of coral sperm for an upcoming issue. I was stunned because I'd always thought of coral as inanimate matter, a castle of solidified corpses, though corpses of what I wasn't sure. Of course, I had to find out what coral sperm looks like, and he told me it's round and fuchsia. I could see it perfectly, or so I supposed, as if through an electron microscope, buoyant and livid, pocked like golf balls, floating like dust motes. Still, I couldn't visualize the creature who constitutes female coral, as distinct from male, toward whom one seminal ball went bouncing, like a bouncing ball over lyrics to a song. It was kind of sad to think that, for all its flamboyant fans, osseous reefs, gaudy turrets, coral was one more thing, or species of thing, about which I knew almost nothing, except that it generates sperm, round, fuchsia.

The funny thing about being a man who is childless and intends to stay that way is that you almost never think of yourself as possessing spermatozoa. Semen, yes; but not those discrete entities, tadpoles who frolic in the microcosm of your aging anatomy, future celebrities who enter down a spiral staircase of deoxyribonucleic acid, infinitesimal relay runners who lug your traits, coloration, and surname from points remote and primitive. Certainly you don't believe that the substance you spill when you huff and heave in a warm tantrum of onanism could ever, given a million years and a Petri dish and an infrared lamp, could ever, come to resemble you. It would be like applauding wildly at a Broadway play and then worrying that you hurt the mites who inhabit the epidermis of your hands. Death is all around us, and we sometimes assist.

Anyway, there are so many varieties of life, and hardly enough Sunday afternoons to watch all those educational programs that teach you about the reproductive mechanisms of albino mountain goats with antlers that branch off and thin away like thoughts before you fall asleep. And sloths who move so slowly they never dry off from morning dew and so possess emerald coats of mold. And yonic orchids housing pools of perfume in which bees drink and wade and drown.

The first time I was alone in the wilderness, I walked through a field that throbbed with song and wondered whether crickets played their wings or their legs. My footfalls, instead of causing the usual thud, caused spreading pools of solemn silence. Sound stopped wherever I walked. And I walked and walked to hush the world, leaving silence like spoor.

ALLEN BARNETT

THE *TIMES* AS IT KNOWS US

Time will say nothing but I told you so,
Time only knows the price we have to pay.

—W. H. AUDEN

'With regard to human affairs,' Spinoza said, 'not to laugh, not to cry, not to become indignant, but to understand.' It's what my lover, Samuel, used to repeat to me when I was raging at the inexplicable behavior of friends or at something I had read in the newspaper. I often intend to look the quote up myself, but that would entail leafing through Samuel's books, deciphering the margin notes, following underlined passages back to where his thoughts were formed, a past closed off to me.

'Not to laugh, not to cry, not to become indignant, but to understand,' he would say. But I can't understand, I'd cry, like a child at the end of a diving board afraid to jump into the deep end of the pool.

'Then let go of it,' he would say. 'I can't,' I'd say about whatever had my heart and mind in an insensible knot. And he would come up behind me and put his arms around me. 'Close your eyes,' he'd say. 'Close them tight. Real tight. Tighter.'

Samuel would tell me to reach out my arms and clench my fists. 'Squeeze as hard as you can,' he would say, and I would, knowing that he believed in the physical containment of emotions in a body's gesture.

ALLEN BARNETT (1955–1991): Allen Barnett's The Body and Its Dangers *(In which this story is included) was the finalist for the 1991 PEN/Hemingway Prize. He once said that AIDS gave him something to write about and then took away the strength with which to write about it. He died not long after the publication of* The Body and Its Dangers, *his first and only book.*

'Now, let go,' he would say, and I did. If I felt better, though, it was because his mustache was against the back of my neck, and I knew full well that when I turned my head, his mouth would be there to meet mine.

The day that Samuel went into the emergency room, he took a pile of college catalogues with him, not suspecting this hospital was the only thing he would ever be admitted to again. I got to him just as a nurse was hanging a garnet-colored sack above his bed. Soon a chorus of red angels would be singing in his veins. He told me he wanted to go back to school to get a degree in Biomedical Ethics, the battlefront he believed least guarded by those most affected by Acquired Immune Deficiency Syndrome. 'Do you think you'll need an advanced degree?' I asked. His eyes opened, and his head jerked, as if the fresh blood had given him new insight, anagnorisis from a needle.

'That's not what I meant to say,' I said. He said, 'Not to worry.' He died before they knew what to treat him for, what an autopsy alone would tell them, before he could even be diagnosed.

Vergil said, 'Perhaps someday even this stress will be a joy to recall.' I'm still waiting.

I

Noah called Perry a 'fat, manipulative sow who doesn't hear anything he doesn't want to hear.'

The endearments 'fat' and 'sow' meant that the argument we were having over brunch was still on friendly terms, but 'manipulative' cued us all to get our weapons out and to take aim. Perry was an easy target, and we had been stockpiling ammunition since Tuesday, when an article on how AIDS had affected life in the Pines featured the seven members of our summer house. Perry had been the reporter's source. It was Saturday.

'What I resent,' Joe said, newspaper in hand, 'is when she writes, "They arrive at the house on Friday night to escape the city. When everyone is gathered, the bad news is shared: A friend died that morning. They are silent while a weekend guest, a man with AIDS, weeps for a few moments. But grief does not stop the party. Dinner that night is fettucine in a pesto and cream-cheese sauce, grilled salmon, and a salad created at one of New York's finest restaurants." '

Perry said, 'That's exactly what happened that night.'

'You made it sound as if we were hanging streamers and getting into party dresses,' said Enzo, who had cooked that meal. 'It was dinner, not the Dance of the Red Masque.' He put a plate of buttered English muffins in front of us, and four jars of jam from the gourmet shop he owned in Chelsea.

Joe said, 'I don't like the way she implies that death has become so mundane for us, we don't feel it anymore: Paul died today. Oh, that's too bad; what's for dinner? Why couldn't you tell her that we're learning to accommodate grief. By the way, Enzo, what's the black stuff on the pasta?'

'Domestic truffles. They're from Texas,' he answered from the kitchen counter, where he was mixing blueberries, nectarines, apricots, and melon into a salad.

Stark entered the fight wearing nothing but the Saks Fifth Avenue boxer shorts in which he had slept. 'Just because our lives overlap on the weekend, Perry, doesn't give you rights to the intimate details of our health.' His large thumb flicked a glob of butter and marmalade off the front of his shorts and into his mouth. Our eyes met. He smiled, and I looked away.

'What intimate details?'

Stark took the paper from Joe and read aloud, '"The house is well accustomed to the epidemic. Last year, one member died, another's lover died over the winter. This year, one has AIDS, one has ARC, and three others have tested positive for antibodies to the AIDS virus."'

'She doesn't identify anybody,' Perry protested.

'The article is about us, even if our names are not used,' Enzo said. He placed a cake ring on the coffee table. Noah, who had just had liposuction surgery done on his abdomen, looked at it nostalgically.

Perry, on the other hand, was eating defensively, the way some people drive a car. 'I was told this was going to be a human-interest piece,' he said. 'They wanted to know how AIDS is impacting on our lives –'

'Please don't use *impact* as a verb.'

'– and I thought we were the best house on the Island to illustrate how the crisis had turned into a lifestyle. But none of you wanted your name in the paper.'

I said, 'How we represent ourselves is never the way the *Times* does.'

'They officially started using the word *gay* in that article,' Perry said, pointing to the paper like a tour guide to the sight of a famous battle.

'It didn't cost them anything,' I said. Indeed, the *Times* had just started using the word *gay* instead of the more clinical *homosexual*, a semantic leap that coincided with the adoption of Ms. instead of Miss, and of publishing photographs of both the bride and the groom in Sunday's wedding announcements. And in the obituaries, they had finally agreed to mention a gay man's lover as one of his survivors.

'You're mad at me because she didn't write what you wouldn't tell her,' Perry said to me.

Noah said, 'We are mad at you because we didn't want to be in the piece and we are. And you made us look like a bunch of shallow faggots.'

'Me?' Perry screamed. 'I didn't write it.'

Noah slapped the coffee table. 'Yes, you, the media queen. You set up the interview because you wanted your name in the paper. If it weren't for AIDS, you'd still be doing recreation therapy at Bellevue.'

'And you'd still be stealing Percodan and Demerol from the nurses' station.'

'Yeah,' Noah shouted. 'You may have left the theater, but you turned AIDS into a one-man show. The more people die, the brighter your spotlight gets.'

'I have done nothing I am ashamed of,' Perry said. 'And you are going to be hard-pressed to find a way to apologize for that remark.' The house shook on its old pilings as Perry stamped out. Noah glared into space. The rest of us sat there wondering whether the weekend was ruined.

'I don't think that the article is so awful,' Horst said. He was Perry's lover. 'She doesn't really say anything bad about anybody.'

Horst was also the one in the article with AIDS. Every day at 4:00 A.M., he woke to blend a mixture of orange juice and AL721 – a lecithin-based drug developed in Israel from egg yolks and used for AIDS treatment – because it has to be taken when there is no fat in the stomach. For a while, he would muffle the blender in a blanket, but he stopped, figuring that if he woke us, we would just go back to sleep. He laughed doubtfully when I told him that the blender had been invented by a man named Fred who had died recently. It was also the way he laughed when Perry phoned to say their cat had died.

Stark asked Noah, 'Don't you think you were a little hard on Perry?'

Noah said, 'The next thing you know, he'll be getting an agent.'

I said, 'We're all doing what we can, Noah. There's even a role for personalities like his.'

He would look at none of us, however, so we let it go. We spoke of Noah among ourselves as not having sufficiently mourned Miguel, as if grief were a process of public concern or social responsibility, as if loss was something one just *did*, like jury duty, or going to high school. His late friend had been a leader at the beginning of the epidemic; he devised a training program for volunteers who would work with the dying; he devised systems to help others intervene for the sick in times of bureaucratic crisis. He was the first to recognize that AIDS would be a problem in prisons. A liberal priest in one of the city prisons once asked him, 'Do you believe your sexuality is genetic or environmentally determined?' Miguel said, 'I think of it as a calling, Father.' Dead, however, Miguel could not lead; dead men don't leave footsteps in which to follow. Noah floundered.

And we all made excuses for Noah's sarcasm and inappropriate humor. He once said to someone who had put on forty pounds after starting AZT, 'If you get any heavier, I won't be your pallbearer.' He had known scores of others who had died before and after Miguel, helped arrange their funerals and wakes. But each death was beginning to brick him into a silo of grief, like the stones in the walls of old churches that mark the dead within.

'Let's go for a walk,' his lover, Joe, said.

Noah didn't budge, but their dog, Jules, came out from under a couch, a little black Scottie that they had had for seventeen years. Jules began to cough, as if choking on the splintered bones of chicken carcass.

'Go for it, Bijou,' Noah said. (Even the dog in our house had a drag name.) One of his bronchial tubes was collapsed, and several times a day he gagged on his own breath. He looked up at us through button eyes grown so rheumy with cataracts that he bumped into things and fell off the deck, which was actually kind of cute. Taking one of the condoms that were tossed into the shopping bag like S & H green stamps at the island grocery store, Joe rolled it down the length of Jules's tail.

'Have you ever thought of having Jules put to sleep?' Stark asked.

'Yes, but Joe won't let me,' Noah said. But we knew it was Noah keeping Jules alive, or half-alive, stalling one more death.

Stark said, 'I noticed that his back is sagging so much that his stomach and cock drag along the boardwalk.'

'Yeah,' Joe said, 'but so do Noah's.'

~ ~ ~

I took The Living Section containing the offending article and threw it on the stack of papers I had been accumulating all summer. My role as a volunteer was speaking to community groups about AIDS, and I collected articles to keep up with all facets of the epidemic. But I had actually been saving them since they first appeared in the *Times* on a Saturday morning in July several years ago. RARE CANCER SEEN IN 41 HOMOSEXUALS, the headline of the single-column piece announced, way in the back of the paper. I read it and lowered the paper to my lap. 'Uh-oh,' I said.

I remember how my lover, Samuel, had asked from our bedroom, 'What is it?' He was wearing a peach-colored towel around his waist, from which he would change into a raspberry-colored polo shirt and jeans. There was a swollen bruise in the crook of his arm, where he had donated plasma the day before for research on the hepatitis vaccine. As he read the article, I put the lid on the ginger jar, straightened the cushions of the sofa we had bought together, and scraped some dried substance from its plush with my thumbnail. I looked at him leaning against the door arch. He was always comfortable with his body, whether he stood or sat. Over the years, we had slipped without thinking into a monogamous relationship, and space alone competed with me for his attention. No matter where he was, space seemed to yearn for Samuel, as if he gave it definition. He once stood me in the middle of an empty stage and told me to imagine myself being projected into the entire theater. From way in the back of the house, he said, 'You have a blind spot you're not filling above your right shoulder.' I concentrated on that space, and he shouted, 'Yes, yes, do you feel it? That's stage presence.' But I could not sustain it the way he did.

Samuel looked up from the article. 'It says here that there is evidence to point away from contagion. None of these men knew one another.'

'But they all had other infections,' I said. Hepatitis, herpes, amebiasis – all of which I had had. Samuel used to compare me to the Messenger in Greek tragedies, bearing news of some plague before it hit the rest of the populace.

'It also says cytomegalovirus,' he said. 'What's that?'

'*Cyto* means cell; *megalo* is large,' I said. 'That doesn't tell you much.'

'Well, if you haven't had it,' he said, 'there's probably nothing to worry about.'

~ ~ ~

Perry's guest for the week came in with the day's paper, a generous gesture, I thought, since our house's argument had embarrassed him into leaving through the back door. His name was Nils, but we called him Mr Norway, for that was where he was from, and where he was a crowned and titled body builder. By profession, he was an anthropologist, but he preferred being observed over observing, even if the mirror was his only audience. I didn't like him much. When he sat down and began to read the paper I assumed he had bought for us, I tried to admire him, since it was unlikely that I would read the Oslo *Herald* were I in Norway. I couldn't help thinking, however, that the steroids Nils took to achieve his award-winning mass had made him look like a Neanderthal man. On the other hand, I thought, perhaps that was appropriate for an anthropologist.

I picked up the last section of the paper and turned to the obituaries. 'Gosh, there are a lot of dead people today,' I said.

'You are reading the death notices every day,' Nils said. 'I thought so.'

'We all do,' said Stark, 'then we do the crossword puzzle.'

We deduced the AIDS casualties by finding the death notices of men, their age and marital status, and then their occupation. Fortunately, this information usually began the notice, or we would have been at it for hours. If the deceased was female, old, married, or worked where no one we knew would, we skipped to the next departed. A 'beloved son' gave us pause, for we were all that; a funeral home was a clue, because at the time, few of them would take an AIDS casualty – those that did usually resembled our parents' refinished basements.

Stark looked over my shoulder and began at the end of the columns. 'Here's a birthday message in the In Memoriams for someone who died thirty-six years ago. "Till memory fades and life departs, you live forever in my heart."'

'Who do people think read these things?' Enzo asked.

'I sometimes wonder if the dead have the *Times* delivered,' I said.

We also looked for the neighborhood of the church where a service would be held, for we knew the gay clergy. We looked at who had bought the notice, and what was said in it. When an AIDS-related condition was not given as the cause of death, we looked for coded half-truths: cancer, pneumonia, meningitis, after a long struggle, after a short illness. The dead giveaway, so to speak, was to whom contributions could be made in lieu of flowers. Or the lyrics of Stephen Sondheim.

It was good we had this system for finding the AIDS deaths, otherwise we might have had to deal with the fact that other people were dying too, and tragically, and young, and leaving people behind wondering what it was all about. Of course, the difference here was that AIDS was an infectious disease and many of the dead were people with whom we had had sex. We also read the death notices for anything that might connect us to someone from the past.

'Listen to this.' I read, ' "Reyes, Peter. Artist and invaluable friend. Left our sides after a courageous battle. His triumphs on the stage are only footnotes to the starring role he played in our hearts. We will deeply miss you, darling, but will carry the extra richness you gave us until we build that wall again together. Contributions in his name can be made to The Three Dollar Bill Theater. Signed, The people who loved you." '

Stark said, 'You learn who your friends are, don't you?'

Horst looked thoughtfully into the near distance; his eyes watered. He said, 'That is touching.'

'You know what I want my death notice to read?' Enzo asked. ' "Dead GWM, loved 1950s rock and roll, Arts & Crafts ceramics, back issues of *Gourmet* magazine. Seeking similar who lived in past for quiet nights leading to long-term relationship." '

'There's another one,' Stark said, his head resting on my shoulder, his face next to mine. 'Mazzochi, Robert.'

'Oh, God,' I said into the open wings of the newspaper.

The newsprint began to spread in runnels of ink. I handed the paper over to Stark, who read out loud, ' "Mazzochi, Robert, forty-four on July –, 1987. Son of Victor and Natalia Mazzochi of Stonington, Connecticut. Brother of Linda Mazzochi of Washington, D.C. Served as lieutenant in the United States Army. Came back from two terms of duty in Vietnam, unscarred and unblaming. With the Department of Health and Human Services NYC since 1977. A warm, radiant, much-loved man." '

'What a nice thing to say,' Horst said. 'Did you know him well?'

'He was that exactly,' I said.

There was another one for him, which Stark read. ' "Robert, you etched an indelible impression and left. Yes, your spirit will continue to enrich us forever, but your flesh was very particular flesh. Not a day will go by. Milton." '

The others sat looking at me as I stood there and wept. There was Stark, an investment banker from Scotland; Horst, a mountain peasant from a farm village in Switzerland; and Enzo, who grew up in Little Italy and studied cooking in Bologna (he dressed like a street punk and spoke like a Borghese); and there was Mr Norway on his biennial tour of gay America. They were waiting for a cue from me, some hint as to what I needed from them. I felt as if I had been spun out of time, like a kite that remains aloft over the ocean even after its string breaks. I felt awkward, out of time and out of place, like not being able to find the beat to music, which Samuel used to say that even the deaf could feel surging through the dance floor. Robert's funeral service was being held at that very moment.

The last time I had seen him was a Thursday afternoon in early October, a day of two funerals. Two friends had died within hours of one another that week. I went to the funeral of the one who had been an only child and whose father had died before him. I went, I guess, for his mother's sake. Watching her weep was the saddest thing I had ever seen.

Afterward, I made a bargain with myself. If Robert Mazzochi was still alive, I would go to work. If he was dead, I would take the day off. When he did not answer his home phone, I called the hospital with which his doctor was associated, and the switchboard gave me his room number. I visited him on my way to work, a compromise of sorts.

'How did you know I was here?' he asked.

'Deduction.'

Eggplant-colored lesions plastered his legs. Intravenous tubes left in too long had bloated his arms. Only strands were left to his mane of salt and pepper hair. He was in the hospital because thrush had coated his esophagus. The thrush irritated his diaphragm and made him hiccup so violently he could not catch his breath. Robert believed that he would have suffocated had his lover, Milton, not been there to perform the Heimlich maneuver. He was waiting for the nurse to bring him Demerol, which relaxed him and made it easier to breathe.

I finally said, 'I can't watch you go through this.'

He looked at me for a long moment. 'If I've learned anything through all this, it's about hope,' he said. 'Hope needs firmer ground to stand on than I've got. I'm just dangling here.'

' "Nothing is hopeless. We must hope for everything," ' I said. 'That's Euripides. It's a commandment to hope. It would be a sin not to.'

'Then why are you leaving me?' he asked, and I couldn't answer him. He said, 'Don't worry. I am surrounded by hopeful people. Milton's hope is the most painful. But I could be honest with you.'

'The truth hurts too,' I said.

'Yes, but you could take it.'

'For a while.'

We used to meet after work for an early supper before he went to his KS support group. One night he said to me, 'I never knew that I was handsome until I lost my looks.' He was still handsome as far as I was concerned, but when he pulled his wallet out to pay the check, his driver's license fell to the table. He snatched it back again, but I had seen the old picture on it, seen what must have told him that he had been a beautiful man.

The nurse came in and attached a bag of Demerol to the intravenous line feeding his arm. 'We might have been lovers,' Robert said to me, 'if it hadn't been for Milton.'

'And Samuel,' I said.

The Demerol went right to his head. He closed his eyes and splayed his fingers and smiled. 'My feet may never touch ground again,' he said, and floated there briefly. 'This is as good as it will ever get.'

~ ~ ~

The rest of the day passed slowly, like a book that doesn't give one much reason to turn the page, leaving the effort all in your hands. Perry was sulking somewhere. Stark and Nils had gone to Cherry Grove. A book of Rilke's poetry, which he was not reading, lay open on Horst's lap.

'Genius without instinct,' he said during the second movement of Mozart's *Jeunehomme* piano concerto. 'He knew exactly what he was doing.'

'Are you all right?' I asked Enzo, who was lying in the sun, in and out of a doze.

'It's just a cold,' he said. 'Maybe I'll lie down for a while.'

'You didn't eat breakfast today. I was watching you,' I said.

'I couldn't.'

'You should have something. Would you like some pasta al'burro?'

Enzo smiled. 'My mother used to make that for me when I was sick.'

'I could mix it with Horst's AL721. It might taste like spaghetti alla carbonara.'

Horst said, 'You should have some of that elixir my brother sent me from Austria. It has lots of minerals and vitamins.'

'Elixir?' Enzo asked.

'That potion that's in the refrigerator.'

Enzo and I worried what Horst meant by potion, for Horst went to faith healers, he had friends who were witches, he ate Chinese herbs by the fistful and kept crystals on his bedside. These he washed in the ocean and soaked in the sun to reinvigorate them when he figured they'd been overworked. He said things like 'Oh, I am glad you wore yellow today. Yellow is a healing color.' Around his neck, he wore an amulet allegedly transformed from a wax-paper yogurt lid into metal by a hermit who lived in Peru, and which had been acquired by a woman who had sought him out to discuss Horst's illness. 'You don't have to say anything,' the hermit told her at the mouth of his cave, 'I know why you're here.' Fabulous line, I said to myself, that should come in handy.

Enzo and I found a silver-colored canister in the refrigerator. Its instructions were written in German, which neither of us could read. I wet a finger and stuck it in the powder. 'It tastes safe,' I said.

'Athletes drink it after a workout,' Horst said.

'I'll have some after my nap,' Enzo said.

'If you have a fever, you sweat out a lot of minerals.'

'I'll mix it with cranberry juice,' Enzo assured him.

'You lose a lot of minerals when you sweat,' Horst said. He had been repeating himself a lot lately, as if by changing the order of the words in a sentence, he could make himself better understood.

'If you want me to cook tonight, I will,' I said.

Enzo said, 'The shopping's done already,' and handed me a large manila envelope from the city's health department, in which he kept his recipes. They were all cut from the *Times*, including the evening's menu: tuna steaks marinated in oil and herbs (herbs that Horst had growing in pots on the deck) and opma.

'What is opma?'

'It's an Indian breakfast dish made with Cream of Wheat.'

'We're having a breakfast dish for dinner?' I asked.

'If this gets out, we'll be ruined socially,' he said, and went to bed, leaving Horst and me alone.

Horst and I had been alone together most of the summer, except for a visit by his sister and brother, both of whom were too shy to speak whatever English they knew. Gunther cooked Horst's favorite meals. Katja dragged our mattresses, pillows, and blankets out on the deck to air. When she turned to me and said in perfect, unaccented English, 'I have my doubts about Horst,' I wondered how long it had taken her to put that sentence together. Gunther and I walked the beach early in the morning, before Horst was up. He wanted to know all he could about Horst's prognosis, but I was afraid to tell him what I knew, because I did not know what Horst wanted him to think. But fear translates, and hesitant truth translates instantly. I did not enjoy seeing them return to Switzerland, for when they thanked me for looking after their brother, I knew I had done nothing to give them hope.

'Remember my friend you met in co-op care?' I asked Horst. 'He has lymphoma. The fast-growing kind.'

'He should see my healer. Lymphoma is her specialty,' he said. 'Oh, I just remembered. Your office called yesterday. They said it was very important. Something about not getting rights for photographs. They need to put something else in your movie.'

'What time did they call?'

'In the morning.'

'Did you write it down?'

'No, but I remember the message. I'm sorry I forgot to tell you. I figured if it was important that they would have called back.'

'They are respecting my belated mourning period,' I said.

'What does this mean?'

'I'll have to go into town on Monday.'

'That's too bad. How long will you stay?'

'Three or four days.'

I began to look over the recipes that Enzo had handed me, angry at Horst for not telling me sooner but far more angry that I would have to leave the Island and go back to editing films I had thought were finished. Samuel had died when we were behind schedule and several hundred thousand dollars over budget on a documentary series titled *Auden in America*. Working seven-day weeks and twelve-hour days, it took a case of shingles to remind me of how much I was suffering the loss of what he had most fulfilled in me.

Perry came in while I was banging drawers and pans about the kitchen. 'What's with her?' he asked Horst.

'Oh, she's got a craw up her ass,' Horst said.

'I beg your pardon,' I said.

'He is mad at me for not taking a message, but I say to hell with him.' He raised a long, thin arm, flicked his wrist, and said, 'Hoopla.'

'I am not mad at you,' I said, although I was. I believed that he had been using his illness to establish a system of priorities that were his alone.

No one else's terrors or phone messages carried weight in his scheme of things. If he said something wasn't important, like the way he woke us up with the blender, knowing we would eventually go back to sleep, we had to take his word for it because he was dying.

And that was something we could not deny; the skeleton was rising in his face. Every two steps Death danced him backward, Horst took one forward. Death was the better dancer, and who could tell when our once-around-the-floor was next, when the terrible angel might extend a raven wing and say, 'Shall we?'

And then I was angry at myself for thinking that, for elevating this thing with a metaphor. What was I doing personifying Death as a man with a nice face, a way with the girls? This wasn't a sock hop, I thought, but a Depression-era marathon with a man in a black suit who probably resembled Perry calling, 'Yowsa, yowsa, yowsa, your lover's dead, your friends are dying.'

As I cleared aside the kitchen counter, I came across another note in Horst's spindly handwriting. I read it out loud: '"Sugar, your mother called. We had a nice chat. Love, Heidi."'

'Oh, I forgot again,' Horst said.

'It's all right,' I said, and paused. 'I'm more concerned with what you talked about.'

'We talked female talk for ten minutes.'

'Does that mean you talked about condoms or bathroom tiles?'

'We talked about you too.'

'What did you say?' I asked.

'I said that you were fabulous.'

'Oh, good. Did you talk about . . . yourself?'

'Yes, I told her about the herb garden,' he said. 'I'm going to bed now for a little nap. I want to preserve my energy for tonight's supper that you are cooking.' Then he went into his room and closed the door.

I looked at Perry, who registered nothing – neither about the exchange nor about the fact that his lover, who had been a bundle of energy for three days, was taking a nap.

'Aren't you out to your mother?' he asked.

'She probably knows. We just never talk about it.'

'I'm surprised you don't share this part of your life with her.'

'What part?' I asked.

'You shouldn't close yourself off to her, especially now.'

'It wouldn't be any different if AIDS hadn't happened,' I said.

'You'd have less to talk about.'

'I almost called her when Samuel died.'

Perry said, 'I think we should get stoned and drunk together.'

Horst came back out of his room. 'I forgot to show you these pictures of us my sister took when I was home for harvest last time.'

He showed me pictures of him and Perry carrying baskets and sitting on a tractor together. In my favorite, they were both wearing overalls, holding pitchforks, and smoking cigars.

'You two were never more handsome,' I said. I looked at Perry, who pulled the joint out of his pocket. He had recently taken up smoking marijuana again after three years of health-conscious abstinence.

'Look how big my arms were then,' Horst said. Then suddenly he pounded the counter with both his fists. Everything rattled. 'I hate this thing!' he said. And then he laughed at his own understatement.

'What time is dinner?' he asked.

'At nine, *liebchen*.'

Horst nodded and went to bed, closing the door behind him.

Perry looked at me. I poured the vodka that was kept in the freezer, while he lit the joint. I knew what was coming. It was the first time we had been alone together since Sam's death. Perry had known Sam from their days together working with a theater company for the deaf. Samuel loved sign language, which he attempted to teach me but which I would not learn, for it seemed a part of his life before we met, and I was jealous of the years I did not know him, jealous of the people as well, even the actors in their deafness, rumored to be sensuous lovers. When Samuel danced, he translated the lyrics of songs with his arms and fingers, the movement coming from his strong, masculine back and shoulders the way a tenor sings from his diaphragm. Sometimes I would leave the dance floor just to watch him.

'It was easier for you,' Perry said, referring to Sam's sudden death. 'It was all over for you fast.'

'You make it sound as if I went to Canada to avoid the draft.'

'You didn't have to force yourself to live in hope. It's hard to sustain all this denial.'

'Maybe you shouldn't make such an effort,' I said.

He looked at me. 'Do you want to hear some bad news?' Perry asked, knowing what the effect would be but unable to resist it. The Messenger in Greek tragedies, after all, gets the best speeches. 'Bruce was diagnosed this week. PCP.'

I heard a bullet intended for me pass through a younger man's lungs. I backed away from the kitchen counter for a few minutes, wiping my hands on a dish towel in a gesture that reminded me of my mother.

'Are you all right?' Perry asked.

'Actually, I'm not sure how much longer I can take this.'

'You're just a volunteer,' he said. 'I work with this on a daily basis.'

'I see,' I said. 'How does that make you feel when you pay your rent?'

There are people who are good at denying their feelings; there are those who are good at denying the feelings of others. Perry was good at both. 'Touché,' he said.

'Have you ever thought about leaving the AIDS industry for a while?' I asked him.

'I couldn't,' Perry said, as if asked to perform a sexual act he had never even imagined. 'AIDS is my mission.'

I finished my drink and poured myself another. 'Someone quoted Dylan Thomas in the paper the other day: "After the first death there is no other."'

'What does it mean?'

'I don't know, except that I believed it once.'

'We need more occasions to mourn our losses,' he said.

'What do you want, Grieve-a-thons?'

The *Times* had already done the article 'New Rituals Ease Grief as AIDS Toll Increases': white balloons set off from courtyards; midnight cruises around Manhattan; catered affairs and delivered pizzas. It was the 'bereavement group' marching down Fifth Avenue on Gay Pride Day bearing placards with the names of the dead that made me say, No, no, this has gone too far.

'I'm very distrustful of this sentimentality, this tendency toward willful pathos,' I said. 'A kid I met on the train was going to a bereavement counselor.'

'You've become a cynic since this all began.'

'That's not cynicism, that's despair.'

'I haven't been of much help to you,' Perry said. 'I never even called to see how you were doing when you had shingles.'

'I didn't need help,' I said, although I had mentioned this very fact in my journal: 'March 30. I am blistered from navel to spine. My guts rise and fall in waves. Noah paused a long time when I told him what I had and then asked about my health in general. Dr. Dubreuil said that shingles are not predictive of AIDS, but I know that the herpes zoster virus can activate HIV in vitro. So should that frighten me? We pin our hopes on antivirals that work in vitro. What should we fear? What should we draw hope from? What is reasonable? I worry: How much fear is choice of fear in my case? Horst has them now, as well. When I called Perry to ask him what shingles looked like, he said, "Don't worry, if you had them, you would know it." He hasn't called back, though the word is out.'

'I have a confession to make,' Perry said. 'I read your journal, I mean, the Reluctant Journal.'

That is what I called my diary about daily life during the epidemic: who had been diagnosed, their progress, sometimes their death. I wrote what I knew about someone who had died: what he liked in bed, his smile, his skin, the slope of his spine.

I asked Perry: 'Did you read the whole thing or just the parts where your name was mentioned?'

'I read the whole thing. Out loud. To the rest of the house when you weren't here,' he said. 'You just went white under your tan, Blanche.'

I laid Saran Wrap over the tuna steaks that I had been preparing. The oil made the cellophane adhere to the fish in the shape of continents; the herbs were like mountain ridges on a map.

'I was just joking,' Perry said.

'Right.'

'You had that coming to you.'

'I suppose I did.'

'I don't know what to say to you about Samuel that you haven't already said to yourself,' he said. 'I think of him every time you enter the room. I don't know how that makes me feel about you.'

'Sometimes I miss him so much I think that I am him.'

I took things to the sink in order to turn my back on Perry for a moment, squaring my shoulders as I washed the double blade of the food processor's knife. What connected the two of us, I asked myself, but Samuel, who was dead? What did we have in common but illness, sexuality, death? Perry had told himself that asking me to share the house this summer was a way of getting back in touch with me after Samuel died. The truth was that he could no longer bear the sole burden of taking care of Horst. He wanted Horst to stay on the Island all summer and me to stay with him. 'It would be good for you to take some time off between films, and Horst loves you,' he had said, knowing all along that I knew what he was asking me to do.

Perry was silent while I washed dishes. Finally, he said, 'I saw Raymond Dubreuil in co-op care last Friday night. He was still doing his rounds at midnight.'

'There aren't enough doctors like him,' I said, still unable to turn around.

'He works eighteen-hour days sometimes. What would happen to us if something should happen to him?'

'I asked him what he thought about that *Times* article that said an infected person had a greater chance of developing AIDS the longer he was infected. Ray said the reporter made years of perfect health sound worse than dying within eighteen months of infection.'

Perry had brought up a larger issue and placed it between us like a branch of laurel. I turned around. His hand was on the counter, middle two fingers folded under and tucked to the palm, his thumb, index, and little finger extended in the deaf's sign for 'I love you.' But he did not raise his hand. I thought of Auden's lines from *The Rake's Progress*, 'How strange! Although the heart dare everything/The hand draws back and finds no spring of courage.' For a passing moment, I loathed Perry, and I think the feeling was probably mutual. He had what I was certain was a damaged capacity to love.

Joe came in, followed by Stark and Nils. Joe kissed me and put his arm around my shoulder. 'Nils told me a friend of yours died. I'm sorry. Are you okay?'

Perry slapped the counter.

'Don't get me started,' I said. 'Where's Noah?'

'We've been visiting a friend with a pool,' Joe said. 'Here's something for your diary. This guy just flew all the way to California and back to find a psychic who would assure him that he won't die of AIDS.'

'Why didn't he just get the antibody test?' I asked.

'Because if it came out positive, he'd commit suicide. Anyway, Noah's coming to take you to tea. Where's Enzo?'

Stark came out of the room he shared with Enzo. 'His body's there, but I can't attest to anything else. Does this mean you're cooking dinner?'

Nils came out of my room, which had the guest bed in it. He had changed into a pastel-colored muscle shirt bought in the Grove. I stiffened as he put an arm around me. 'Come to tea and I will buy you a drink,' Nils said.

'We'll be there soon,' Perry said in a tone that implied wounds from the morning were being healed. Nils left to save us a place before the crowd got there. While the others were getting ready, Perry began to scour the kitchen counter. Someone was always cleaning the sink or dish rack for fear of bacteria or salmonella, mainly because of Horst, but you never know. Perry asked, 'You don't like Nils, do you?'

'No. He has ingrown virginity.'

'Meaning he wouldn't put out for you?'

'And another thing . . . all I've heard this week is that the Pines is going to tea later, that we're eating earlier, that there's more drag, fewer drugs, more lesbians, and less sexual tension. For an anthropologist, he sounds like *The New York Times*.'

Noah's long, slow steps could be heard coming around the house. When he saw Perry in the kitchen, he stopped in the center of the deck. Noah looked at Perry, raised his eyebrows, then turned and entered the house through the sliding door of his and Joe's room. Perry turned to the mirror and ran a comb through his mustache. From a tall vase filled with strings of pearls bought on Forty-second Street for a dollar, he selected one to wrap around his wrist. The pearls were left over from the previous summer, when the statistics predicting the toll on our lives were just beginning to come true; there were dozens of strands, in white, off-white, the colors of after-dinner mints. This will be over soon, my friend Anna says, they will find a cure, they have to. I know what she is saying. When it began, we all thought it would be over in a couple of years; perhaps the *Times* did as well and did not report on it much, as if the new disease would blow over like a politician's sex scandal. AIDS to them was what hunger is to the fed, something we think we can imagine because we've been on a diet.

From behind the closed door of their bedroom, I heard Joe whisper loudly to Noah, 'You're not going to change anything by being angry at him.' Perry stared at the door for a moment as if he should prepare to bolt. Instead, he asked, 'Are you still mad at me about the article?'

'I never was.'

'But you were angry.'

I looked over at the stack of papers accumulating near the couch, only then beginning to wonder what I achieved by saving them, what comfort was to be gained. 'I always expect insight and consequence from their articles, and I'm disappointed when they write on our issues and don't report more than what we already know,' I said. 'And sometimes I assume that there is a language to describe what we're going through, and that they would use it if there was.'

'You should have told me about your friend,' Perry said.

'This is one I can't talk about,' I said. 'As for your suggestion . . . I don't know how I would begin to tell my mother about my life as I know it now.'

'You could say, "I've got some good news and some bad news."'

'What's the good news?'

'You don't have AIDS.'

~ ~ ~

Noah was still taking a shower when the others left for tea. He came out of the bathroom with an oversized towel wrapped around his waist and lotion rubbed into his face and hands. I could see the tiny scar on his back where the liposuction surgery had vacuumed a few pounds of fat. Tall and mostly bald, older than he would confess to, he was certainly as old as he looked. For a moment, he regarded me as if I were a dusty sock found under the bed. Then his face ripened.

'Dish alert,' he said. 'Guess who's having an affair with a twenty-two-year-old and I'm not supposed to tell anyone?'

'Perry,' I said almost instantly. 'The bastard.'

'They were together in Washington for the international AIDS conference, supposedly in secret, but word has gotten back that they were making out in public like a couple of Puerto Rican teenagers on the subway.'

'Does Horst know?'

'Of course. Perry thinks that talking about dishonest behavior makes it honest. As far as I'm concerned, it's another distraction from Horst's illness. Perry distanced himself from everyone when it became obvious that they were dying. Last year it was Miguel, this year it's Horst. When I confronted him, he said, "Don't deny me my denial."'

'Oh, that's brilliant. As long as he claims to be in denial, he doesn't even have to appear to suffer,' I said. 'One of these days, all this grief he's avoiding is going to knock him on his ass.'

'But then he'll wear it around town like an old cloth coat so that everyone will feel sorry for him. He won't be happy until people in restaurants whisper "Brava" as he squeezes past them to his table.'

'What's the boyfriend like?'

'What kind of person has an affair with a man whose lover is dying of AIDS?' Noah asked.

I said, 'The kind that probably splits after the funeral.'

'He's what my Aunt Gloria would call a mayonnaise Jew, someone trying to pass for a WASP.'

'I don't know if I should be offended by that or not,' I said.

'But get this: He's had three lovers since he graduated from Harvard. The first one's lover died of AIDS. The second one had AIDS. Now there's Perry. So this kid gets the antibody test. It came back negative, and now he's got survivor's guilt.' Noah gave me one of his bland, expressionless looks. 'Perry acts as if this were the most misunderstood love affair since Abélard and Héloïse. He told me it was one of those things in life you just have no control over.'

'For someone so emotionally adolescent, he's gotten a lot of mileage out of this epidemic,' I said.

'Where else would he be center stage with a degree in drama therapy?' Noah asked. 'He even quoted your journal at the last AIDS conference.'

'What?'

'In Washington. He quoted you in a paper he presented. I knew he hadn't told you yet,' Noah said. 'He was certain you'd be honored. He would have been.'

'Do you know what he used?'

'Something about an air of pain, the cindered chill of loss. It was very moving. You wondered if there wasn't a hidden cost to constant bereavement. You know Perry, he probably presented your diary as the work of a recent widower whose confidentiality had to be protected. That way he didn't have to give you credit.'

I once went to an AIDS conference. Perry treated them like summer camp – Oh, Mary, love your hat, let's have lunch. I had seen him deliver papers that were barely literate and unprepared, and what was prepared was plagiarized. Claiming he was overwhelmed with work, he feigned modesty and said he could only speak from his heart. When social scientists provided remote statistics on our lives, Perry emoted and confessed. 'My personal experience is all I can offer as the essence of this presentation.' And it worked. It gave everyone the opportunity to cry and feel historic.

Noah asked, 'Are you coming to tea? There's someone I want you to meet.'

'Another widower?' I asked. 'More damaged goods?'

'I'll put it to you this way,' Noah said. 'You have a lot in common.'

With regard to human affairs, Noah was efficient. 'Let me count the ways,' I said. 'A recent death, the ache of memory, reduced T-cell functions, positive sero status . . .'

'Yes, well, there's that.'

'And maybe foreshortened futures, both of us wary of commitment should one or the other get sick, the dread of taking care of someone else weighed against the fear of being sick and alone.'

'I doubt that Samuel would like your attitude.'

'Samuel will get over it,' I said. 'And I'm not interested in a relationship right now. I'm only interested in sex.'

'Safer sex, of course.'

'I want to wake up alone, if that's what you mean.'

Noah raised his eyebrows and lowered them again, as if to say that he would never understand me. I said, 'Let me tell you a story. I hired a Swedish masseur recently because I wanted to be touched by someone, and no one in particular, if you get my innuendo. At one point, he worked a cramped muscle so hard that I cried out. And he said, "That's it, go ahead, let it out" – as if I was holding something back, you know, intellectualizing a massage. I asked him if he felt anything, and he said, "I feel" – long pause – "sorrow." I told him that I had been a little blue lately but it wasn't as bad as all that.'

Noah nodded. He said, 'The real reason I didn't want to be interviewed for the piece in the *Times* was because Perry invited the reporter for dinner and told her we'd all get into drag if she brought a photographer.'

Before I went down to the beach, I looked in on Enzo. Stark was right. The only time I'd ever seen anyone like this before was when Horst was first diagnosed. Perry had scheduled people just to sit with him, when none of us thought he would even survive. Enzo's skin was moist, his lips dry, his breath light. He was warm, but not enough for alarm.

These summer evenings I sat on the beach in a sling-back chair, listening to my cassette player and writing things about Samuel. I recalled our life together backward. The day he went into the hospital, he had cooked himself something to eat and left the dishes in the sink. Then he was dead, and washing his dishes was my last link to him as a living being.

This evening, the pages of my journal felt like the rooms of my apartment when I came home and found it burglarized. Like my apartment, I knew I had to either forsake it or reclaim it as my own. Though in this case something had been taken, nothing was missing. I was angry with Perry, but it was not the worst thing he could have done. The worst is not when we can say it is the worst.

I started to write about Robert. The words of his obituary, 'warm, radiant, much-loved man,' somewhat assuaged my remorse at having abandoned him to the attention of the more hopeful. The beach was nearly empty at this time of the day – as it was in the morning – except for those like me who were drawn by the light of the early evening, the color of the water, the sand, the houses seen without the protection of sunglasses. Others passed, and I nodded from my beach chair. We smiled. Everyone agreed that the Island was friendlier this year, as if nothing were at stake when we recognized one another's existence. Verdi's *Requiem* was on my Walkman, a boat was halfway between the shore and the horizon. One full sail pulled the boat across the halcyon surface of the water. Near me a man stood with his feet just in the waves. He turned and held his binoculars as if he were offering me a drink. 'They're strong,' he said. I found the sailboat in the glasses. I found a handsome and popular Episcopal priest who I knew from experience to be a fine lover in bed. He was in collar and was praying. There was another handsome man. He was indistinct, but I recognized his expression. He reached into a box and released his fist over the boat's rail. Another man and a woman repeated the gesture. *Libera me.* The surviving lover shook the entire contents of the cloth-wrapped box overboard. The winds that spin the earth took the ashes and grains of bones and spilled them on the loden-green sea. He was entirely gone now but for the flecks that stuck to their clothes and under their nails, but for the memory of him, and for the pleasure of having known him. The boaters embraced with that pleasure so intense they wept at it. *Dies magna et amara valde.* I returned the binoculars to the man. It was a beautiful day and it was wonderful to be alive.

II

Two old couches, one ersatz wicker, the other what my mother used to call colonial, sat at a right angle to one another in the middle of our living room. Enzo and Horst were lying on them with their heads close together, like conspiring convalescents. Horst's cheeks were scarlet.

'You aren't feeling well, are you?' I asked.

Horst said, 'No, but I didn't want to tell Perry and spoil his weekend.'

'How is Enzo doing?'

'He thinks he has a cold, but I don't think so.'

From where I stood, I could lay my hand on both their foreheads. I felt like a television evangelist. Enzo's forehead was the warmer of the two.

'I hear there's a flu going around,' Horst said.

'Where did you hear that? You haven't been in town in a week.'

'I had a flu shot,' he said. 'I think I'm not worried.'

Without opening his eyes, Enzo said, 'You had better get started if you are going to cook supper before everyone gets back. I put all the ingredients out for you.'

I heated oil as the recipe instructed. 'When the oil is very hot add mustard seeds,' it read. 'Keep the lid of the pan handy should the seeds sputter and fly all over.' In the first grade, I recalled giving a girl named Karen Tsakos a mustard-seed bracelet in a Christmas exchange, selecting it myself from the dollar rack at a store called Gaylord's. 'Aren't mustard seeds supposed to be a symbol of something?' I asked as they began to explode between me and the cabinet where the lids were kept.

'Hope, I think,' Enzo said.

'Perhaps I should put more in.'

'No, faith,' Horst said, lying down in his bedroom.

'Faith is a fine invention, as far as I can see, but microscopes are prudent, in case of emergency,' I said, approximating a poem by Emily Dickinson. Horst laughed, but Enzo showed no sign whatsoever that he knew what I was talking about. I wasn't so sure myself what Dickinson meant by an emergency: Could a microscope confirm one's belief in a crisis of faith, or, in a crisis of nature, such as an epidemic illness, was man best left to his own devices?

'How's dinner coming?' Stark asked, returning five minutes before it was to have been on the table.

'It's not ready,' I said.

'Why not?'

'I didn't start it in time,' I said.

'Why not?'

'Because I was at a funeral.'

He picked up one of Miguel's old porno magazines and disappeared into the bathroom with it. He emerged ten minutes later and asked, 'Is there anything I could be doing?'

'You can light the coals, and grill the tuna steaks. I've got to watch the opma,' I said. 'Enzo, what are gram beans?'

'The little ones.'

Perry returned next and kissed me. 'I forgot to tell you that Luis is in the hospital again,' he said loudly. 'His pancreas collapsed but he seems to be getting better.'

'Enzo, I think I burned the gram beans.'

'Luis's lover, Dennis, just took the antibody test,' Perry said. 'He was sero-negative.'

'Oh, that's good.'

'Yeah. Luis said, "Thank God for hemorrhoids." '

'Enzo, which of these is the cumin?'

'Don't cumin my mouth,' Perry said, going into his room to check on Horst. I watched him brush the hair off Horst's forehead and take the thermometer out of Horst's mouth to kiss him. Perry's face darkened when he read the thermometer, as if he didn't know what to think. I added the Cream of Wheat to the gram beans.

Nils came up to me and wrapped a huge arm around my shoulder. 'They told me down at tea that if dinner was scheduled for nine, that meant ten in Fire Island time.'

'Dinner would have been ready at nine o'clock if I hadn't been given this god-awful recipe to make,' I said, sounding more angry than I intended, and Nils hastened away. Noah came to the stove. 'You are bitter, aren't you?'

'He's like Margaret Mead on steroids,' I said.

'He's writing a book,' Noah said.

'Yeah, sure, *Coming of Age in Cherry Grove.*'

'What's this here?' Noah asked.

'Opma.'

'Where did you get the recipe?'

'From *The New York Times.*'

'I hate that paper.'

Stark came running into the kitchen with the tuna steaks and put them in the electric broiler. The recipe said to grill them four minutes on each side.

'The grill will never get hot enough,' he said. 'Is that opma?'

'In the flesh.'

'It looks like Cream of Wheat with peas in it.'

Noah found the radio station we always listened to during dinner on Saturday nights. 'Clark, what's the name of this song?' he asked, a game we played as part of the ritual. Enzo usually played along as he did the cooking.

' "The Nearness of You," ' I answered.

'Who's singing?'

'Julie London.'

'Who wrote it?'

'Johnny Mercer.' Enzo didn't say anything, though the correct answer was Hoagy Carmichael. Perry sang as he helped Joe set the table, making up his own lyrics as he went along, the way a child does, with more rhyme than reason. We were all aware that he and Noah were behaving as if the other were not in the room, but their orbits were getting closer. As the song closed, Perry and I turned to one another and imitated the deep voice of the singer: 'It's just the queerness of you.' Then I made everyone laugh by stirring the thickening opma with both hands on the spoon. Jules, the dog, began hacking in the center of the room.

'Did you have a productive cough, dear?' Joe asked. Horst laughed from his bedroom.

'Enzo, come tell me if the opma is done,' I said. He kind of floated up off the couch as if he was pleasantly drunk. I knew then that he was seriously ill. He took the wooden spoon from me and poked the opma twice. 'It's done,' he said.

We went to the table. I sat in the center, with Enzo on my right, Nils across from me, Joe on my left. Perry and Noah faced each other from the opposite ends, like parents. This was how we sat, each and every week. The guest was always in the same chair, whether he knew it or not. For the first several minutes of dinner, the table was a tangle of large arms passing the salad and popping open beer cans.

'Eat something, darling,' I said to Enzo, who was only staring at the fish on his plate. 'You haven't eaten anything all day.'

Perry said, 'This is the best opma I ever had.'

Horst looked up as if he had something to announce, his fork poised in the air. We all turned to him. His fork fell to his plate with a clatter, and he said, 'I think I have to lie down.'

Perry said, 'This opma will taste good reheated.'

'So Fred told me this story at tea about the last of the police raids on the Meat Rack in the early seventies,' Noah said.

'You're going to love this, Clark,' Perry said.

'The cops came in one night with huge flashlights and handcuffs. There were helicopters and strobe lights; they had billy clubs and German shepherds. And they started dragging away dozens of men. The queens were crying and screaming and pleading with the cops because they would get their names in the paper and lose their jobs, you know, this was when it was still illegal for two men to dance with one another. The guys that got away hid under the bushes until everything was clear. Finally, after everything was perfectly quiet, some queen whispered, "Mary, Mary!" And someone whispered back, "Shhh, no names!"'

'Nils, would you like this?' Enzo asked. I looked up at Nils, whose forearms circled his plate. Everyone looked at me looking at him. I picked up Enzo's tuna steak with my fork and dropped it on Nils's plate. Enzo got up and stumbled to the couch.

Stark and Joe cleared the table. Perry went outside and smoked a cigar. With his back turned toward the house, he was calling attention to himself. I sat on the arm of the couch, looking down at Enzo and looking out at Perry, wondering who needed me most. But Noah was also looking at Perry. I could see him in his room, a finger on his lip, looking through the doors that opened out onto the deck. He stepped back from my sight and called, 'Perry, this doesn't fit me. Would you like to try it on?'

The next thing I knew, Perry was wearing a black velvet Empress gown, like the one Madame X wears in the Sargent painting. In one hand, he held its long train, in the other, a cigar. Between the cleavage of the dress was Perry's chest hair, the deepest part of which was gray.

'Where'd you get that dress?' Stark asked.

'Noah inherited Miguel's hope chest. It was in the will.'

Enzo was smiling, but I knew he was faking it. I whispered, 'Do you need help to your bed?'

He clutched my hand and I helped him into his room. His forehead was scalding. 'I'll be right back,' I told him. I ran into the kitchen and pulled a dish towel from the refrigerator handle and soaked it under cold water. By this time, Noah was wearing the silver-lined cape that went with Perry's gown, a Frederick's of Hollywood merry widow, and silver lamé high heels. On his bald head was a tiny silver cap. I smiled as I passed through them, but they didn't see me.

Horst was sitting on Enzo's bed when I got back to him. This was the room in which Miguel had died the year before, and which Horst did not want this summer, though it was bigger and cooler than his own room and its glass doors opened onto the deck. 'I could hear his breathing over all the commotion,' Horst said. 'Have you taken any aspirin?'

'I've been taking aspirin, Tylenol, and Advil every two hours,' Enzo said, his voice strengthened by fear's adrenaline.

Horst asked, 'Did you take your temperature?'

'I don't have a thermometer.'

Horst got his own. 'I cleaned it with peroxide,' he said. 'I hope that is good enough.' Before I could ask him how to use it, he was on his way back to bed.

I pulled the thermometer from its case, pressed a little button, and placed it in Enzo's mouth. Black numbers pulsed against a tiny gray screen. I watched its numbers climb like a scoreboard from hell. Outside, Nils's arms were flailing because the high heels he was wearing were stuck between the boards of the deck. The thermometer beeped. Perry and Noah, in full drag, walked off with Nils between them.

'You have a temperature of a hundred and three point two,' I said. This was the first time in my life I had ever been able to read a thermometer. 'Do you want me to get the Island doctor?'

'Let's see if it goes down. Can you get me some cranberry juice?'

I went into the kitchen. Stark and Joe were reading. 'How's he doing?' Joe asked.

'I think we should get him to a doctor.'

'The number's on the ferry schedule,' Joe said, and went back to his book.

A machine at the doctor's office said in the event of an emergency, to leave a number at the sound of the beep. I could not imagine the doctor picking up messages that late at night. But what I really feared was the underlying cause of Enzo's fever. I put the phone in its cradle.

'Don't we know any doctors?' I asked.

Stark and Joe shook their heads. Joe said that Noah or Perry might. I suddenly realized how isolated the Island was at night. At this point, there was no way of getting Enzo off the Island short of a police helicopter.

He was asleep when I took him his juice. He was not the handsomest of men, but at this moment he was downright homely. He cooked all our meals for us, meals to which even Horst's fickle appetite responded. He overstocked the refrigerator with more kinds of foodstuff than we could identify. We wondered why he did it, even as we stored away a few extra pounds, telling ourselves we were delaying the sudden weight loss associated with the first signs of AIDS. Perry had put on so much weight, his posture changed. He tilted forward as he walked. If he should develop the AIDS-associated wasting-away syndrome, Noah told him, months might go by before anyone would notice. I took the towel off Enzo's head and soaked it in cold water again.

'You'll be sure to clean Horst's thermometer before you give it back to him,' he said, holding my hand, which held the towel to his face.

'Yes, of course.'

'I mean it.'

'Let me take your temperature again. This thermometer is really groovy.' His temperature had risen to just shy of 104. With all I knew about AIDS, I suddenly realized I did not even know what this meant. 'When was the last time you took some aspirin?'

'An hour ago. I'll give it another one.'

The house shook as Perry, Noah, and Nils returned, all aglow with the success of their outing. Perspiration hung off Perry's chest hair like little Italian lights strung about the Tavern on the Green. Nils got into a clean tank top and went dancing.

Noah snapped open a Japanese fan and waved it at his face. 'Dish alert,' he said. He could be charming. For a moment, I forgot Enzo, the thermometer in my hand.

Joe said, 'Clark thinks Enzo needs a doctor.'

Noah asked, 'What's his temperature?'

I stood in the doorway. 'It's one hundred and four,' I said, exaggerating a little.

'That's not too bad.'

'It isn't?'

'Is he delirious?' Noah asked.

'What if he's too sick to be delirious?'

Perry said, 'Miguel's temperature used to get much higher than that. He'd be ranting and raving in there sometimes.'

'Yes, but Miguel is dead,' I said.

When we opened the house this summer, I threw away his sheets, the polyester bathrobes, the towels from Beth Israel, St. Vincent's, Sloan-Kettering, and Mount Sinai, that filled our closets and dresser drawers from all of Miguel's hospital visits. Noah had watched me, neither protesting nor liking what I was doing. But I could not conceive of any nostalgia that would want to save such souvenirs. The hospital linen was part and parcel of the plastic pearls, the battery-operated hula doll, the Frederick's of Hollywood merry widow, five years' worth of porno magazine subscriptions – the measure of the extremes they went to for a laugh last year, the last summer of Miguel's life. Why did we need them when we were still getting post-dated birthday presents from Miguel: sweaters on our birthday, Smithfield hams at Christmas, magazine subscriptions in his name care of our address – anything he could put on his Visa card once he realized that he would expire before it did.

'If Enzo's temperature gets too high, we can give him an alcohol bath, or a shower, to bring it down,' Noah said.

'So can I go to bed now?' Stark asked.

'Sure,' I said. 'Just don't sleep too soundly.'

I went into my own room, which smelled of Nils's clothes, his sweat and the long trip, of coconut suntan lotion and the salty beach. I missed Samuel at moments like this, missed his balance of feelings, of moderated emotions as if he proportioned them out, the pacifying control he had over me. I fell asleep, woke and listened for Enzo's breath, and fell asleep again. I halfway woke again and sensed my longing even before Nils's presence woke me completely. In the next bed, a sheet pulled up to his nipples, Nils's chest filled the width of the bed.

Drunk one night on the beach, he had said to me, 'Perry doesn't think there's hope for anyone who is diagnosed in the next few years.'

'We've pinned our hopes on so many,' I said, aware that Nils was delving for useful information, 'that I don't know what role hope plays anymore. They're predicting as many deaths in 1991 alone as there were Americans killed in Vietnam. Some of those are bound to be people one knows.'

'Hope is the capacity to live with the uncertain,' he said.

I had read that line myself somewhere. 'Bullshit,' I said. Nils stepped back and looked at me as if I had desecrated the theology of some deified psychotherapist.

'You don't need hope to persevere,' I said.

'What do you need, then?' Nils asked.

'Perseverance,' I answered, and laughed at myself. And then I told him a story I had heard at a funeral service. It was the story of a Hasidic rabbi and a heckler. The rabbi had told his congregation that we must try to put everything into the service of God, even that which was negative and we didn't like. The heckler called out, 'Rabbi, how do we put a disbelief in God into His service?' The rabbi's answer made me think that God and hope are interchangeable. He told the heckler, 'If a man comes to you in a crisis, do not tell him to have faith, that God will take care of everything. Act instead as if God does not exist. Do what you can do to help the man.'

Nils put his arm around me and pulled me up close to him as we walked. There was a strong wind that night, and the waves were high. The moon was low across the water and illuminated the waves as they reached for it. I felt massive muscles working in Nils's thighs and loins, a deep and deeper mechanism than I had ever felt in a human body and which seemed to have as its source of energy that which lifted the waves and kept the moon suspended. He was that strong, and I would feel that secure. A bulwark against the insentient night, his body: if I did not need hope to persevere, I needed that. He stopped and held me, kissed my head politely, and pushed me out at arms' length. He made me feel like the canary sent down the mine to warn him of dangerous wells of feeling, wells that he could draw upon but needn't descend himself.

~ ~ ~

When I woke again, the oily surface of his back was glowing. The sky held more prophecy than promise of light. I got up to check on Enzo. He was not in bed. Stark was sitting up waiting for him to come out of the bathroom. He patted the bed next to him. I sat down and he put his arm around me.

'Has he been sleeping?' I asked.

'Like the dead.'

'Do you think we should have gotten a helicopter off the Island?'

'No, but I wish we had.'

Enzo could be heard breathing through the thin door. Stark said, 'It's been like that all night.'

The toilet flushed; we heard Enzo moan, then the thud of his body falling against the bathroom door.

Stark carefully pushed it open and looked in. 'All hell broke loose,' he said.

Enzo was lying in a puddle of excrement. In his delirium, he had forgotten to pull his pajamas down before sitting on the toilet. When he tried to step out of them, his bowels let go a spray of watery stool. His legs were covered, as were the rugs and the wall against which he fainted.

'You're burning up, darling,' Stark whispered to him.

'I'm afraid he'll dehydrate,' I said.

I pulled off Enzo's soiled pajamas, turned the shower on, and took off the old gym shorts I slept in. 'Hand him over,' I said from within the lukewarm spray.

Enzo wrapped his arms around my back and laid his hot head on my shoulder. Our visions of eternal hell must come from endless febrile nights like this, I thought. I gradually made the water cooler and sort of two-stepped with him so that it would run down his back, and sides, and front. The shower spray seemed to clothe our nakedness. If I closed my eyes, we were lovers on a train platform. We could have been almost anywhere, dancing in the sad but safe aftermath of some other tragedy, say the Kennedy assassinations, the airlift from Saigòn, the bombing of a Belfast funeral. Stark used the pump bottle of soap – bought to protect Horst from whatever bacteria, fungus, or yeast might accumulate on a shared bar – to lather Enzo's legs. I slowly turned the water cooler.

'Can we get your head under water a little bit?' I asked, though Enzo was barely conscious. 'Let's see if we can get your fever down.'

'I think we're raising it,' Stark murmured. He was washing Enzo's buttocks, and his hand would reach through Enzo's legs and wash his genitals almost religiously. He reached through Enzo's legs and lathered my genitals as well. He pulled on my testicles and loosened them in their sac. He pulled and squeezed them just to the pleasure point of pain. He winked at me, but he didn't smile. I noticed there were interesting shampoos on the shelf that I had never tried.

'I can't stand much longer, you guys,' Enzo whispered in my ear. 'I'm sorry.'

I maneuvered him around to rinse the soap off. Stark waited with huge towels. While I dried us both, Stark changed Enzo's bedclothes, tucking the fresh sheets in English style. Then he helped me carry him back to bed.

'Let's take his temperature before he falls asleep,' I said. Stark stared in my face as we waited. The thermometer took so long, I was afraid it was broken. It finally went off with a tremulous beep. 'Dear God,' I said.

'What is it?'

Despite the shower, his fever was over 105. 'Do we have any rubbing alcohol?' I asked.

Stark couldn't find any after checking both bathrooms. I said, 'Get the vodka, then.'

He returned with the ice-covered bottle from the freezer; the liquor within it was gelatinous. 'Do you think this wise?' he asked.

'Not the imported. Get the stuff we give the guests. Wait,' I said. 'Leave that one here and bring me a glass.'

Stark brought the domestic vodka and a sponge. 'Do you know what you're doing?' he asked.

'Alcohol brings a temperature down by rapidly evaporating off the body,' I said. 'Vodka happens to evaporate faster than rubbing alcohol. Other than that, no, I don't have the faintest idea.'

Stark watched me for a while, then took Enzo's temperature himself. It had fallen to 104.8. 'I think we should get some aspirin in him,' he said, which we woke Enzo to do. He drank a little juice. Fifteen minutes later, I took his temperature again. Enzo's temperature had gone down to 104.6. While waiting for this reading, Stark had fallen back asleep. I wondered whether he didn't want me in bed with him. That would have been pleasant, temporary; he was a solid man, like a park bench.

But instead I went out to the living room. My stack of newspapers was near the couch. I could look in on Enzo if I clipped the articles I intended to save. Just the night before, Noah had shaken his head at all the papers and said, 'It looks like poor white trash lives here.'

'My roots must be showing,' I said.

I clipped my articles and put them in an accordion file that I kept closed with an old army-issue belt. Sometimes margin notes reminded me why I was saving something, such as the obituary of an interior designer, in which, for the first time, the lover was mentioned as a survivor. Or the piece in which being sero-positive for HIV antibodies became tanta-mount to HIV infection, indicating that our language for talking about AIDS was changing. 'With the passage of time, scientists are beginning to believe that all those infected will develop symptoms and die,' the article said. It really doesn't sit well to read about one's mortality in such general terms.

In the magazine section, a popular science writer wrote that there was no moral message in AIDS. Over the illustration, I scrawled, 'When late is worse than never.' Scientists had been remiss, he said, for 'viewing it as a contained and peculiar affliction of homosexual men.' In the margin I wrote, 'How much did they pay you to say this?'

Then there were those living-out-loud columns written by a woman who had given up on actual journalism to raise her children. Some of them were actually quite perceptive, but I had never forgiven her for the one in which the writer confessed that she had been berated by a gay man in a restaurant for saying, 'They were so promiscuous – no wonder they're dying.'

Horst emerged from his bedroom to blend his AL721, which was kept in the freezer in ice-cube trays. He did not see me, and I did not say anything for fear of frightening him because he concentrated so severely on his task. If you did not know him, you would not think he was ill, but very, very old. He had always been a vulnerable and tender man, but now he was fragile. He hoped that the elixir in his blender could keep the brush of death's wings from crushing him entirely.

When Samuel called to tell me two years ago that Horst had been diagnosed, I began to weep mean, fat tears. My assistant editor sent me out for a walk. I wandered aimlessly around SoHo for a while, once trying to get into the old St. Patrick's, its small walled-in cemetery covered with the last of autumn's spongy brown leaves. I fingered cowhide and pony pelts hanging in a window; I bought a cheap stopwatch from a street vendor, some blank tapes, and spare batteries for my tape cassette. Eventually, hunger made me find a place to rest, a diner with high ceilings and windows looking onto a busy street. After I ordered, I thought of Horst again, and something odd happened: the room – no, not the room but my vision went, as when you've looked at the sun too long. All I could see was a glowing whiteness, like a dentist's lamp, or the inside of a nautilus shell. For a brilliant moment, I saw nothing, and knew nothing, but this whiteness that had anesthetized and cauterized the faculties by which one savors the solid world. Like a film dissolving from one scene to another, the room came back, but the leftover whiteness limned the pattern of one man's baldness, glittered off the earring of his companion, turned the white shirt my waitress wore to porcelain, fresh and rigid, as it was from the

Chinese laundry. She stood over me with a neon-bright plate in one hand and the beer's foam glowing in the other, waiting for me to lift my elbows and give her room to put down my lunch.

'Oh, shit,' Horst said, knocking the orange-juice carton over and spilling some into the silverware drawer.

'I'll clean it up,' I said softly.

'I knew you were there,' he said. 'I heard you in here. How is Enzolina?'

'His temperature was very high. We got it down a little bit.'

'You must sleep too.' He leaned over me and kissed my cheek. 'It's okay about Perry and his boyfriend,' he said, obviously having heard Noah speaking that afternoon. 'Perry is still affectionate and he takes care of me. And I don't feel so sexual anymore. But Noah shouldn't have told you, because it would only make you angry.'

Whether it was the lateness of the hour or the sensitive logic of pain, I thought I heard resignation in Horst's voice, as if he were putting one foot in the grave just to test the idea of it.

'Have you met the boyfriend?'

'Oh, yes. He's very bland. I don't know what Perry sees in him,' Horst said. 'Perry thinks the three of us should go into therapy together, but I'm not doing it. I don't have to assuage their guilt.'

'Where will Perry be when you get really sick?'

'Probably at a symposium in Central Africa.' He laughed and waved his hand like an old woman at an off-color joke. Horst used to be hardy, real peasant stock. He was the kind of man who could wear a ponytail and make it look masculine. Here was a man gang-banged for four days by a bunch of Turks on the Orient Express who lived to turn the memory into a kind of mantra. He said, 'Perry needs so many buffers from reality.'

'Most of us do.'

'Not you.'

'You're wrong,' I said. Then I showed him the article on the death of an iconoclastic theater director that had started on the front page of the *Times*. 'Look, there's a typo. It says he died of AIDS-related nymphoma.'

He laughed and laid his head in my lap. 'I am homesick for Switzerland,' he said. 'I'd like to go home, but I don't know if I could handle the trip. And I don't want to be a burden on my family.'

'You wouldn't be.'

'I've been thinking lately I don't want to be cremated. I want to be buried in the mountains. But it's so expensive.'

'Horst, don't worry about expenses,' I said.

'How is Samuel?' he asked.

'He's dead, honey. He died this winter.'

'Oh, I'm sorry,' he said, and covered his face with his hands. Memory lapses are sometimes part of the deterioration. I wondered whether Perry had noticed or ignored them. 'I forget these things,' he added.

'It's late, you're tired.' He started up. I said, 'Horst, I think you should go home if you want to. Just make sure you come back.'

My fingertips were pungent with the smell of newsprint, like cilantro, or the semen smell of ailanthus seeds in July. 'Did you see that piece in today's paper?' we asked one another over the phone when a point we held dear was taken up on the editorial page. 'Yes, haven't they come far and in such a short time,' we responded. I filed it all away, with little science and what was beginning to feel like resignation: *C* for condoms, *S* for Heterosexuals, *P* for Prevention and Safer Sex, *R* for Race and Minorities, *O* for Obits.

'I can't tell you how bored I am with this,' a man said to me on the beach one evening when he learned that another friend had gone down for the count. He said, 'Sometimes I wish there was something else to talk about,' which is what my mother used to say as she put her make-up on for a night out with my father. 'I just wish we could go out and talk about anything but you kids and the house,' she'd say with the vague longing I recall with numbing resonance. 'I just wish there was something else to talk about.'

They would eat at a place called D'Amico's Steak House, where the menus were as large as parking spaces. She would have frogs' legs, which she told me tasted like chicken but were still a leap toward the exotic, no matter how familiar the landing. Her desire had no specific object; she was not an educated woman; she did not even encourage fantasy in her children; but it still arouses whatever Oedipal thing there is left unresolved in me, and I often wish to be able to satisfy it – to give her nights and days of conversation so rooted in the present that no reference to when we were not happy could ever be made, and no dread of what to come could be imagined. But we both know that there's no forgetting that we were once unhappy. Our conversation is about my sisters' lives and their children. She ends our infrequent telephone conversations with 'Please take care of yourself,' emphasizing, without naming, her fear of losing me to an illness we haven't talked about, or to the ebbs of time and its hostilities that have carried me further and further away from perfect honesty with her.

But language also takes you far afield. Metaphors adumbrate; facts mitigate. For example, 'Nothing is hopeless; we must hope for everything.' I had believed this until I realized the lie of its intrinsic metaphor, that being without hope is not being, plunged into the abyss that nothingness fills. We have not come far since the world had one language and few words. Babel fell before we had a decent word for death, and then we were numb, shocked at the thought of it, and this lisping dumb word – *death*, *death*, *death* – was the best we could come up with.

And simply speak, disinterested and dryly, the words that fill your daily life: 'Lewis has KS of the lungs,' or 'Raymond has endocarditis but the surgeons won't operate,' or 'Howard's podiatrist will not remove a bunion until he takes the test,' or 'Cytomegalovirus has inflamed his stomach and we can't get him to eat,' or 'The DHPG might restore the sight in his eye,' or 'The clinical trial for ampligen has filled up,' or 'They've added dementia to the list of AIDS-related illnesses,' or 'The AZT was making him anemic,' or 'His psoriasis flaked so badly, the maid wouldn't clean his room,' or 'They found tuberculosis in his glands,' or 'It's a form of meningitis carried in pigeon shit; his mother told him he should never have gone to Venice,' or 'The drug's available on a compassionate basis,' or 'The drug killed him,' or 'His lung collapsed and stopped his heart,' or 'This is the beginning of his decline,' or 'He was *so* young.' What have you said and who wants to hear it?

'Oh, your life is not so awful,' a woman at my office told me. She once lived in India and knew whereof she spoke. At Samuel's funeral, a priest told me, 'I don't envy you boys. This is your enterprise now, your vocation.' He kissed me, as if sex between us was an option he held, then rode to the altar on a billow of white to a solitary place setting meant to serve us all.

Enzo's temperature remained the same through the night. I poured myself a drink – though I did not need it – to push myself over the edge of feeling. I took it down to the beach. There were still a few bright stars in the sky. Everything was shaded in rose, including the waves and the footprints in the sand, deceiving me and the men coming home from dancing into anticipating a beautiful day.

Since the deaths began, the certified social workers have quoted Shakespeare at us: 'Give sorrow words.' But the words we used now reek of old air in churches, taste of the dust that has gathered in the crevices of the Nativity and the Passion. Our condolences are arid as leaves. We are actors who have overrehearsed our lines. When I left the Island one beautiful weekend, Noah asked, 'Were you so close to this man you have to go to his funeral?' I told myself all the way to Philadelphia that I did not have to justify my mourning. One is responsible for feeling something and being done with it.

Give sorrow occasion and let it go, or your heart will imprison you in constant February, a chain-link fence around frozen soil, where your dead will stack in towers past the point of grieving. *Let your tears fall for the dead, and as one who is suffering begin the lament . . . do not neglect his burial.* Think of him, the one you loved, on his knees, on his elbows, his face turned up to look back in yours, his mouth dark in his dark beard. He was smiling because of you. You tied a silky rope around his wrists, then down around the base of his cock and balls, his anus raised for you. When you put your mouth against it, you ceased to exist. All else fell away. You had brought him, and he you, to that point where you are most your mind and most your body. His prostate pulsed against your fingers like a heart in a cave, *mind, body, body, mind,* over and over. Looking down at him, he who is dead and gone, then lying across the broken bridge of his spine, the beachhead of his back, you would gladly change places with him. *Let your weeping be bitter and your wailing fervent; then be comforted for your sorrow.* Find in grief the abandon you used to find in love; grieve the way you used to fuck.

~ ~ ~

Perry was out on the deck when I got back. He was naked and had covered himself with one hand when he heard steps on our boardwalk. With the other hand, he was hosing down the bathroom rugs on which Enzo had been sick. I could tell by the way he smiled at me that my eyes must have been red and swollen.

'There's been an accident,' he said.

'I was a witness. Do you need help?'

'I've got it,' he said, and waddled back inside for a bucket and disinfectant to do the bathroom floors.

Enzo opened the curtains on his room. I asked him how he was feeling.

'My fever's down a little. And my back hurts.'

Stark asked him, 'Do you think you can stay out here a couple of days and rest? Or do you want to go into the hospital?'

'You can fly in and be there in half an hour,' I said.

'One of us will go in with you,' Stark said.

'I'm not sure. I think so,' Enzo said, incapable of making a decision.

'What if I call your doctor and see what he says?' I asked.

The doctor's service answered, and I left as urgent a message as I could. I began breaking eggs into a bowl, adding cinnamon and almond concentrate. The doctor's assistant called me back before the yolks and egg whites were beaten together. 'What are the symptoms?' he asked.

'Fever, diarrhea.'

'Back pain?'

'Yes.'

'Is his breathing irregular?' the assistant asked.

'His breathing is irregular, his temperature is irregular, his pulse is irregular, and his bowel movement is irregular. My bet is he's dehydrated. What else do you need to know?'

'Has he been diagnosed with AIDS yet?'

'No,' I said, 'but he had his spleen removed two years ago. And Dr. Williams knows his medical history.'

'I'll call you back,' he said.

'How is he?' asked Noah. It was early for him to be out of bed. I began to suspect that no one had slept well.

'He's weak and now his back hurts. I think he'd like to go to the hospital.'

'It's Sunday. They aren't going to do anything for him. All they'll do is admit him. He might as well stay here, and I'll drive him in tomorrow.'

Horst came out of Enzo's room. 'That's not true. They can test oxygen levels in his blood for PCP and start treatment right away. And the sooner they catch these things, the easier they are to treat.'

Horst had said what none of us would say – PCP – for if it was *Pneumocystis carinii* pneumonia, then Enzo did have AIDS. One more person in the house would have it, one more to make it impossible to escape for a weekend, one more to remind us of how short our lives were becoming.

The phone rang. Dr. Williams's assistant told me to get Enzo in right away. 'Get yourself ready,' I said. 'Your doctor will be coming in just to see you. I'll call the airline to get you a seat on the seaplane.'

'Okay,' Enzo said, relieved to have the decision made for him. He put his feet on the floor and got his bearings. Stark helped him fill a bag. Then I looked outside and saw what appeared to be a sheet unfurling over the trees. Fog was coming through the brambles the way smoke unwraps from a cigarette and lingers in the heat of a lamp.

'Oh, my God, will you look at that,' Joe said. 'Another lousy beach day. This has been the worst summer.'

Perry called the Island airline. All flights were canceled for the rest of the morning. Visibility of three miles was needed for flight to the Island, and we couldn't even see beyond our deck. Even voices from the neighboring houses sounded muffled and far away, for the first time all summer.

'We're going to have to find someone who will drive him in,' Perry said. 'Unless he thinks he can handle the train.'

'He's too sick for the train,' I said.

'Who do we know with a car?' Perry asked. Joe took Jules out for a walk. Noah went behind the counter, where the batter for French toast was waiting. He began slicing challah and dipping it into batter, though no one was ready to eat.

Perry said, 'I wonder if Frank is driving back today.'

'Call him,' I said.

But Perry didn't get the response he expected. We heard him say, 'Frank, he's very sick. His doctor said to get him in right away.' He turned to us. 'Frank says he'll drive Enzo in if the fog doesn't clear up.'

'Well, I can understand why he would feel put upon,' Noah said. 'I wouldn't want to give up my weekend either.'

At that point, I said, 'I'm going in with Enzo.'

Noah said, 'He can go into the emergency room by himself. He doesn't need anyone with him.' I said nothing, but I did not turn away from him either. Perry looked at me and then to Noah. His lower lip dropped from under his mustache. Noah said, 'Well, doesn't he have someone who could meet him there?'

'Enzo,' I called, 'is there anyone who could meet you in the city?'

'I guess I could call my friend Jim,' he said.

'See,' Noah said.

'Jim's straight,' I said, not that I thought it really made any difference, but it sounded as if it did. We did, supposedly, know the ropes of this disease. 'Enzo, who would you rather have with you, me or Jim?'

'You.'

Noah raised his eyebrows and shrugged one shoulder. 'I don't know why you feel you have to go into the emergency room.'

'Because I am beginning to see what it will be like to be sick with this thing and not have anyone bring me milk or medication because it isn't convenient or amusing any longer.'

Noah said, 'I have been working at the Gay Men's Health Crisis for the past six years. I was one of the first volunteers.'

'Oh, good, the institutional response. That reassures me,' I said. Starting into my room to pack a bag, I bumped into Nils, who was coming out of the shower and didn't have any clothes on, not even a towel. Although Nils walked the beach in a bikini brief that left nothing to – nor satisfied – the imagination, he quickly covered himself and pressed his body against the wall to let me pass.

'I'm sorry if I kept you up last night,' he said to me.

'It wasn't you. I was worried about Enzo,' I said.

By eleven-thirty the fog was packed in as tight as cotton in a new jar of aspirin. Our friend with the car decided that since it was not a beach day, he could be doing things in the city. We were to meet him at the dock for the twelve o'clock ferry. He could not, however, take me as well, for he had promised two guests a ride and only had room for four in his jaunty little car.

Enzo and Perry seemed embarrassed by this. 'I don't mind taking the train,' I said. 'I'll be able to read the Sunday *Times*.'

Nils put his arm around me and walked me to the door. 'I'll be gone when you come back. I'd like to leave you my address.' I wanted to say a house gift would be more appropriate, something for the kitchen or a flowering plant. 'It's unlikely that I'll ever get that far north,' I said, 'but thanks all the same. Maybe I'll drop you a line.' The last thing I saw as I was leaving was his large head down over his plate, his arms on the table, a fork in a fist. He was a huge and odd-looking man. Stark said he had a face like the back of a bus, but it was actually worse than that. Nils was also the author of two books, was working on a third, about the Nazi occupation of Oslo. I saw the others join him around the table. He was probably ten times smarter than anyone there. Sharp words and arguments often defined the boundaries of personalities in this house, but Nils did not touch any of our borders. He simply did not fit in. And though tourists are insufferable after a point, I knew I should ask his forgiveness for my sin of inhospitality, but I couldn't make the overture to deserve it.

On the ferry, Enzo said, 'I'm glad you're coming.'

'I wanted out of that house,' I said.

'I know.'

We listened to our tape players so as not to speak about what was on our minds. People wore white sweaters and yellow mackintoshes. They held dogs in their laps, or the Sports section, or a beach towel in a straw purse; a man had his arm around his lover's shoulder, his fingertips alighted on the other's collarbone. No one spoke. It didn't seem to matter that the weekend was spoiled. We were safe in this thoughtless fog. The bay we crossed was shallow; it could hide neither monsters from the deep nor German submarines. It seemed all we needed to worry about was worrying too much; what we had to fear was often small and could be ignored. But as we entered the harbor on the other side, a dockworker in a small motorboat passed our ferry and shouted, 'AIDS!' And in case we hadn't heard him, shouted again, 'AIDS, AIDS!'

A man slid back the window and shouted back, 'Crib death!' Then he slunk in his seat, ashamed of himself.

I read the paper on the train. I listened to Elgar, Bach, Barber, and Fauré. An adagio rose to its most poignant bar; the soprano sang the Pie Jesù with a note of anger, impatient that we should have to wait so long for everlasting peace, or that the price was so high, or that we should have to ask at all. I filled the empty time between one place and another with a moderate and circumspect sorrow delineated by the beginning, middle, and end of these adagios. Catharsis is not a release of emotion; it is a feast. Feel this. Take that. And you say, Yes, sir, thank you, sir. Something hardens above the eyes and your throat knots and you feel your self back into being. Friends die and I think, Good, that's over, let go of these intolerable emotions, life goes on. The train ride passed; I finished mourning another one. The train ride was not as bad as people say it is.

And Enzo had arrived at the hospital only ten minutes before me. The nurses at the emergency desk said I couldn't see him.

'I'm his care partner from the Gay Men's Health Crisis,' I said, telling them more than they were prepared to hear. 'Can I just let him know I'm here?' The lie worked as I was told it would.

Dr. Williams was there as well, standing over Enzo's gurney, which was in the middle of the corridor. 'Was there any diarrhea?' he asked. Enzo said no, I said yes. 'Fever?' 'Over a hundred and five.' 'Did you have a productive cough?' he asked, and Enzo smiled. He pounded on the small of Enzo's back. 'Does that hurt?' It did. The doctor was certain that Enzo's infection was one to which people who have had their spleens removed are vulnerable. We were moved to a little curtained room in the emergency ward.

'I'm not convinced it isn't PCP,' Enzo said to me.

'Neither am I,' said the attending physician, who had been outside the curtain with Enzo's chart. 'Dr. Williams's diagnosis seems too logical. I want to take some tests just to make sure.'

He asked for Enzo's health history: chronic hepatitis; idiopathic thrombocytopenia purpura; the splenectomy; herpes. Enzo sounded as if he were singing a tenor aria from *L'Elisir d'Amore*. The attending physician leaned over him, listened for the high notes, and touched him more like a lover than a doctor.

'You don't have to stay,' Enzo said to me.

'I want to see if he comes back,' I said.

'He reminds you of Samuel.'

'A little bit.'

'Do you think he's gay?'

'I don't think he'd be interested in me even if he was. Maybe you, though,' I said.

Enzo smiled at that and fell asleep. The afternoon passed with nurses coming in to take more blood. He was wheeled out twice for X rays. A thermos of juice had broken in his overnight bag. I rinsed his sodden clothes and wrapped them in newspaper to take back to the house to wash. But his book about eating in Paris was ruined. He had been studying all summer for his trip to France the coming fall. Restaurants were highlighted in yellow, like passages in an undergraduate's philosophy book; particular dishes were starred.

He woke and saw me with it. 'My shrink told me that we couldn't live our lives as if we were going to die of AIDS. I've been putting off this vacation for years,' he said. 'If there's anything you want to do, Clark, do it now.'

'Do you want me to call anyone?' I asked.

'Have you called the house yet?'

'I thought I'd wait until we had something to tell them.'

'Okay,' he said, and went back to sleep. I read what I hadn't thrown away of the *Times*. In the magazine was an article titled 'She Took the

Test.' I began to read it but skipped past the yeasty self-examination to get to the results. Her test had come back negative. I wondered whether she would have written the piece had it come back positive.

Enzo woke and asked again, 'Have you called the house yet?'

'No, I was waiting until we knew something certain.'

'If I had PCP, you would tell them right away,' he said.

'Yes, Enzo, but we don't know that yet,' I said, but he had already fallen back asleep. He hadn't had anything to eat all day and hadn't been given anything to reduce the fever. Because he was dehydrated, they had him on intravenous, but he seemed to be sweating as quickly as the fluid could go into his body. I felt the accusation anyway, and it was just. I had not called the house precisely because they were waiting for me to call and because I was angry at them.

It was eight o'clock that evening before the handsome doctor returned again. 'There is too much oxygen in your blood for it to be PCP,' he told us. 'But we found traces of a bacterial pneumonia, the kind of infection Dr. Williams was referring to. Losing your spleen will open you up to these kinds of things, and there's no prevention. We'll put you on intravenous penicillin for a week, and you'll be fine.'

Enzo grinned. He would not have to cancel his trip to Paris. His life and all the things he had promised himself were still available to him. An orderly wheeled him to his room, and I followed behind with his bag. It was not AIDS, but it would be someday, a year from now, maybe two, unless science or the mind found prophylaxis. He knew this as well as I did. Not this year, he said, but surely within five. No one knows how this virus will affect us over the years, what its impact will be on us when we are older, ten years after infection, fifteen – fifteen years from now? When I was eleven years old, I never thought I would live to be twenty-six, which I thought to be the charmed and perfect age. I think fifteen years from now, and I come to fifty. How utterly impossible that seems to me, how unattainable. I have not believed that I would live to the age of forty for two years now.

'You'll call the house now,' he said as I was leaving.

'Yes.'

'I appreciate your being here.'

I turned in the doorway. Several responses came to mind – that I hadn't really done so much, that anybody would have done what I had done. Enzo saw me thinking, however, and smiled to see me paused in thought.

'I wanted to say that reality compels us to do the right thing if we live in the real world,' I said. 'But that's not necessarily true, is it?'

'It can put up a compelling argument,' Enzo said. 'Don't be mad at Noah. I didn't expect him to drive me in.'

With Enzo in his room, the penicillin going into his veins, feeling better simply at the idea of being treated, I submitted to my own exhaustion and hunger. I went home and collected a week's worth of mail from a neighbor. There was nothing to eat in the refrigerator, but on the door was a review from the *Times* of a restaurant that had just opened in the neighborhood and that I had yet to try. The light was flashing on my answering machine, but I could not turn it on, knowing the messages would be from my housemates. I called the man who drove Enzo in to tell him how much suffering he had saved Enzo from, exaggerating for the answering machine, which I was glad had answered for him. I turned my own off so that I couldn't receive any more messages and left my apartment with the mail I wanted to read.

Walking down a dark street of parking garages to the restaurant that had been reviewed, I saw a gold coin-shaped wrapper – the kind that chocolate dollars and condoms come in – embedded in the hot asphalt. Pop caps glittered in the street like an uncorked galaxy stuck in the tar.

~ ~ ~

Horst's prediction came true. While Horst was dying two years later, Perry was at an AIDS conference with his new little boyfriend. When confronted, he'd say, 'Horst wanted me to go.' Perry would include Horst's death notice with fund-raising appeals for the gay youth organization he volunteered for. Everyone who knows him learns to expect the worst from him. And Enzo would be right also. A year or so later, he was diagnosed with KS, then with lymphoma.

The *Times* would eventually report more on the subject and still get things wrong. Not journalism as the first draft of history, but a rough draft, awkward and splintered and rude and premeditated. They will do a cover story on the decimation of talent in the fashion industry and never once mention that the designers, stylists, illustrators, showroom assistants, make-up artists, or hairdressers were gay. How does one write about a battle and not give name to the dead, even if they are your enemy?

The dead were marching into our lives like an occupying army. Noah's defenses were weakening, but the illness did not threaten him personally.

He was sero-negative and would stay that way. Even so, he had found himself in a standstill of pain, a silo of grief, which I myself had not entered, though I knew its door well. Perry thought of Samuel every time he saw me and, in turn, probably thought of Horst. I suspected he saw his new boyfriend as a vaccine against loneliness and not as an indication that he had given up hope. We had found ourselves in an unacceptable world. And an unacceptable world can compel unacceptable behavior.

~ ~ ~

But that night, I turned around without my supper and went back home to listen to my messages. The first was from Horst, who would have been put up to call because he was the closest to me and the closest to death. 'Clark, are you there? It's Horst,' he said, as if I wouldn't have recognized his accent. 'We want to know how Enzolina is. Please call. We love you.'

For a long stretch of tape, there was only the sound of breathing, the click of the phone, over and over again. Perry's voice came next.

'I was very touched by your going into the hospital today and how you took care of Enzo last night. I want to tell you that now,' he said, in a low voice. 'I hope you understand that there was nothing to be done last night, and you were doing it. Sometimes I don't think Horst understands that the nights he is almost comatose that I am suffering beside him, fully conscious. I saw your face when Noah did not offer to drive Enzo in. I thought perhaps it was because they can't take the dog on the train, or because he had taken tomorrow off to spend with Joe. But I can't make any excuses for him. You are so morally strict sometimes, like an unforgiving mirror. Oh, let's see . . . Horst is feeling much better. Call us, please.'

Then Stark called to find out whether either Enzo or I needed anything, and told me when he would be home if I wanted to call. And then Joe. 'Where are you, Clark? Oh, God, you should have seen Noah go berserk today when he took the garbage out and found maggots in the trash cans. He screamed, "I can't live like this the rest of the summer." He's been cleaning windows and rolling up rugs. She's been a real mess all day. Oh, God, now he's sweeping under the bed. I can't decide if I should calm him down or stay out of his way. The house should look nice when you get back.'

Finally, Noah called. 'Clark, where are you, Superman? I have to tell you something. You know the novel you lent me to read? I accidentally threw it in the washing machine with my bedclothes. Please call.'

My lover Samuel used to tell a story about himself. It was when he was first working with the Theater of the Deaf. The company had been improvising a new piece from an outline that Samuel had devised, when he said something that provoked a headstrong and violent young actor, deaf since birth. 'I understand you,' Samuel said in sign, attempting to silence him, if that's the word. The young actor's eyes became as wild as a horse caught in a burning barn; his arms flew this way and that, as if furious at his own imprecision. Samuel needed an interpreter. 'You do not understand this,' the actor was saying, pointing to his ears. 'You will never understand.'

You let go of people, the living and the dead, and return to your self, to your own resources, like a widower, a tourist alone in a foreign country. Your own senses become important, and other people's sensibilities a kind of Novocaine, blocking out your own perceptions, your ability to discriminate, your taste. There is something beyond understanding, and I do not know what it is, but as I carried the phone with me to the couch, a feeling of generosity came over me, of creature comforts having been satisfied well and in abundance, like more than enough to eat and an extra hour of sleep in the morning. Though I hadn't had either, I was in a position to anticipate them both. The time being seeps in through the senses: the plush of a green sofa; the music we listen to when we attempt to forgive ourselves our excesses; the crazing pattern on the ginger jar that reminds us of why we bought it in the first place, not to mention the shape it holds, the blessing of smells it releases. The stretch of time and the vortex that it spins around, thinning and thickening like taffy, holds these pleasures, these grace notes, these connections to others, to what it is humanly possible to do.

ALLAN GURGANUS

ADULT ART

For George Hackney Eatman
and Hiram Johnson Cuthrell, Jr.

I've got an extra tenderness. It's not legal.

I see a twelve-year-old boy steal a white Mercedes off the street. I'm
sitting at my official desk – Superintendent of Schools. It's noon on a
weekday and I watch this kid wiggle a coat hanger through one front
window. Then he slips into the sedan, straight-wires its ignition, squalls
off. Afterward, I can't help wondering why I didn't phone the police. Or
shout for our truant officer just down the hall.

Next, a fifty-nine Dodge, black, mint condition, tries to parallel park
in the Mercedes' spot (I'm not getting too much paperwork done today).
The driver is one of the worst drivers I've ever seen under the age of
eighty. Three pedestrians take turns waving him in, guiding him back out.
I step to my window and hear one person yell, 'No, left, sharp *left*. Clown.'
Disgusted, a last helper leaves.

When the driver stands and stretches, he hasn't really parked his car,
just stopped it. I've noticed him around town. About twenty-five, he's
handsome, but in the most awkward possible way. His clothes match the
old Dodge. His belt's pulled up too high. White socks are a mistake. I
watch him comb his hair, getting presentable for downtown. He whips

*ALLAN GURGANUS (born 1947): A native of Rocky Mount, North Carolina, Gur-
ganus is the author of the novels* Oldest Living Confederate Widow Tells All *and* Plays
Well with Others. *His astute, unpredictable short stories and novellas have been collected in*
White People *and* The Practical Heart. *He lives in a small town in North Carolina.*

out a handkerchief and stoops to buff his shoes. Many coins and pens spill from a shirt pocket.

While he gathers these, a second boy (maybe a brother of the Mercedes thief?) rushes to the Dodge's front, starts gouging something serious across its hood. I knock on my second-story window – nobody hears. The owner rises from shoe-polishing, sees what's happening, shouts. The vandal bolts. But instead of chasing him, the driver touches bad scratches, he stands – patting them. I notice that the guy is talking to himself. He wets one index fingertip, tries rubbing away scrawled letters. Sunlight catches spit. From my second-floor view, I can read the word. It's an obscenity.

I turn away, lean back against a half-hot radiator. I admire the portrait of my wife, my twin sons in Little League uniforms. On a far wall, the art reproductions I change every month or so. (I was an art history major, believe it or not.) I want to rush downstairs, comfort the owner of the car, say, maybe, 'Darn kids nowadays.' I don't dare.

They could arrest me for everything I like about myself.

At five sharp, gathering up valise and papers, I look like a regular citizen. Time to leave the office. Who should pass? The owner of the hurt Dodge. His being in the Municipal Building shocked me, as if I'd watched him on TV earlier. In my doorway, I hesitated. He didn't notice me. He tripped over a new two-inch ledge in the middle of the hall. Recovering, he looked around, hoping nobody had seen. Then, content he was alone, clutching a loaded shirt pocket, the guy bent, touched the spot where the ledge had been. There was no ledge. Under long fingers, just smoothness, linoleum. He rose. I stood close enough to see, in his pocket, a plastic caddy you keep pens in. It was white, a gift from WOOTEN'S SMALL ENGINES, NEW AND LIKE-NEW. Four old fountain pens were lined there, name-brand articles. Puzzled at why he'd stumbled, the boy now scratched the back of his head, made a face. 'Gee, *that's* funny!' An antiquated cartoon drawing would have shown a decent cheerful hick doing and saying exactly that. I was charmed.

~ ~ ~

I've got this added tenderness. I never talk about it. It only sneaks up on me every two or three years. It sounds strange but feels so natural. I know it'll get me into big trouble. I feel it for a certain kind of other man, see. For any guy who's even clumsier than me, than *I*.

You have a different kind of tenderness for everybody you know.

There's one sort for grandparents, say. But if you waltz into a singles bar and use that type of affection, you'll be considered pretty strange. When my sons hit pop flies, I get a strong wash of feeling – and yet, if I turned the same sweetness on my Board of Education, I'd soon find myself both fired and committed.

~   ~   ~

Then he saw me.

He smiled in a shy cramped way. Caught, he pointed to the spot that'd given him recent trouble, he said of himself, 'Tripped.' You know what I said? When I noticed – right then, this late – how kind-looking he was, I said, 'Happens all the time. Me too.' I pointed to my chest, another dated funny-paper gesture. 'No reason.' I shrugged. 'You just *do*, you know. Most people, I guess.'

Well, he liked that. He smiled. It gave me time to check out his starched shirt (white, buttoned to the collar, no tie). I studied his old-timey overly wide belt, its thunderbird-design brass buckle. He wore black pants, plain as a waiter's brown wingtips with a serious shine. He took in my business suit, my early signs of graying temples. Then he decided, guileless, that he needed some quick maintenance. As I watched, he flashed out a green comb and restyled his hair, three backward swipes, one per side, one on top. Done. The dark waves seemed either damp or oiled, suspended from a part that looked incredibly white, as if my secretary had just painted it there with her typing correction fluid.

This boy had shipshape features – a Navy recruiting poster, forty years past due. Some grandmother's favorite. Comb replaced, grinning, he lingered, pleased I'd acted nice about his ungainly little hop. 'What say to a drink?' I asked. He smiled, nodded, followed me out. – How simple, at times, life can be.

~   ~   ~

I'm remembering: During football practice in junior high gym class, I heard a kid's arm break. He was this big blond guy, nice but out of it. He whimpered toward the bleachers and perched there, grinning, sweating. Our coach, twenty-one years old, heard the fracture too. He looked around: somebody should walk the hurt boy to our principal's office. Coach spied me, frowning, concerned. Coach decided that the game could do without me. I'd treat Angier right. (Angier was the kid – holding his arm, shivering.)

'Help him.' Coach touched my shoulder. 'Let him lean against you.'

Angier nearly fainted halfway back to school. 'Whoo . . .' He had to slump down onto someone's lawn, still grinning apologies. 'It's okay,' I said. 'Take your time.' I finally got him there. The principal's secretary complained – Coach should've brought Angier in himself. 'These *young* teachers.' She shook her head, phoning the rescue squad. It all seemed routine for her. I led Angier to a dark waiting room stacked with text-books and charts about the human body. He sat. I stood before him holding his good hand. 'You'll be fine. You'll see.' His hair was slicked back, as after a swim. He was always slow in class – his father sold fancy blenders in supermarkets. Angier dressed neatly. Today he looked so white his every eyelash stood out separate. We could hear the siren. Glad, he squeezed my hand. Then Angier swooned back against the bench; panting, he said something hoarse. 'What?' I leaned closer. 'Thank you.' He grinned, moaning. Next he craned up, kissed me square, wet, on the mouth. Then Angier fainted, fell sideways.

Five days later, he was back at school sporting a cast that everybody popular got to sign. He nodded my way. He never asked me to scribble my name on his plaster. He seemed to have forgotten what happened. I remember.

~ ~ ~

As we left the office building, the Dodge owner explained he'd been delivering insurance papers that needed signing – flood coverage on his mother's country property. 'You can never be too safe. That's Mother's motto.' I asked if they lived in town; I was only trying to get him talking, relaxed. If I knew his family, I might have to change my plans.

'Mom died,' he said, looking down. 'A year come March. She left me everything. Sure burned my sisters up, I can tell you. But they're both in Florida. Where were *they* when she was so sick? She appreciated it. She said she'd remember me. And Mom did, too.' Then he got quiet, maybe regretting how much he'd told.

We walked two blocks. Some people spoke to me; they gave my companion a mild look as if thinking, What does Dave want with *him*?

~ ~ ~

He chose the bar. It was called The Arms, but whatever word had been arched between the 'The' and the 'Arms' – six Old English golden letters – had been stolen; you could see where glue had held them to the bricks. He introduced himself by his first name: Barker. Palms flat on the bar, he ordered beers without asking. Then he turned to me, embarrassed. 'Mind reader,' I assured him, smiling, and – for a second – cupped my hand over the bristled back of his, but quick. He didn't seem to notice or much mind.

My chair faced the street. His aimed my way, toward the bar's murky back. Bathrooms were marked KINGS and QUEENS. Some boy played a noisy video game that sounded like a jungle bird in electronic trouble.

Barker's head and shoulders were framed by a window. June baked each surface on the main street. Everything out there (passersby included) looked planned, shiny and kind of ceramic. I couldn't see Barker's face that clearly. Sun turned his ears a healthy wax red. Sun enjoyed his cheekbones, found highlights waiting in the wavy old-fashioned hair I decided he must oil. Barker himself wasn't so beautiful – a knotty wiry kid – only his pale face was. It seemed an inheritance he hadn't noticed yet.

Barker sitting still was a Barker almost suave. He wasn't spilling anything (our beer hadn't been brought yet). The kid's face looked, backlit, negotiable as gems. Everything he said to me was heartfelt. Talking about his mom put him in a memory-lane kind of mood. 'Yeah,' he said. 'When *I* was a kid . . .' and he told me about a ditch that he and his sisters would wade in, building dams and making camps. Playing doctor. Then the city landfill chose the site. No more ditch. Watching it bulldozed, the kids had cried, holding on to one another.

Our barman brought us a huge pitcher. I just sipped; Barker knocked four mugs back fast. Foam made half a white mustache over his sweet slack mouth; I didn't mention it. He said he was twenty-nine but still felt about twelve, except for winters. He said after his mother's death he'd joined the Air Force but got booted out.

'What for?'

'Lack of dignity.' He downed a fifth mug.

'You mean . . . "lack of discipline"?'

He nodded. 'What'd I say?' I told him.

' "Dignity," "discipline." ' He shrugged to show they meant the same thing. The sadder he seemed, the better I liked it, the nicer Barker looked.

Women passing on the street (he couldn't see them) wore sundresses.

How pretty their pastel straps, the freckled shoulders; some walked beside their teenaged sons; they looked good too. I saw folks I knew. Nobody'd think to check for me in here.

Only human, under the table, my knee touched Barker's, lingered a second, shifted. He didn't flinch. He hadn't asked about my job or home life. I got the subject around to things erotic. With a guy as forthright as Barker, you didn't need posthypnotic suggestion to manage it. He'd told me where he lived. I asked wasn't that out by Adult Art Film and Book. 'You go in there much?'

He gave me a mock-innocent look, touched a fingertip to his sternum, mouthed Who, me? Then he scanned around to make sure nobody'd hear. 'I guess it's me that keeps old Adult Art open. Don't tell, but I can't help it, I just love that stuff. You too?'

I nodded.

'What kind?'

I appeared bashful, one knuckle rerouting sweat beads on my beer mug. 'I like all types, I guess. You know, boy/girl, girl/girl, boy/boy, girl/dog, dog/dog.' Barker laughed, shaking his fine head side to side. 'Dog/dog,' he repeated. 'That's a good one. *Dog*/dog!'

He was not the most brilliantly intelligent person I'd ever met. I loved him for it.

~ ~ ~

We went in my car. I didn't care to chance his driving. Halfway to Adult Art, sirens and red lights swarmed behind my station wagon. This is it, I thought. Then the white Mercedes (already mud-splattered, a fender dented, doing a hundred and ten in a thirty-five zone) screeched past. Both city patrol cars gave chase, having an excellent time.

We parked around behind; there were twelve or fourteen vehicles jammed back of Adult Art's single Dumpster; seven phone-repair trucks had lined up like a fleet. Adult's front asphalt lot, plainly visible from US 301 Business, provided room for forty cars but sat empty. This is a small town, Falls. Everybody sees everything, almost. So when you *do* get away with something, you know it; it just means more. Some people will tell you sin is old hat. Not for me. If, once it starts, it's not going to be naughty, then it's not worth wasting a whole afternoon to set up. Sin is bad. Sex is good. Sex is too good not to have a whole lot of bad in it. I say, Let's keep it a little smutty, you know?

Barker called the clerk by name. Barker charged two films — slightly discounted because they'd been used in the booths — those and about thirty bucks in magazines. No money changed hands; he had an account. The section marked LITERATURE milled with phone linemen wearing their elaborate suspension belts. One man, his pelvis ajangle with wrenches and hooks, held up a picture book, called to friends, 'Catch *her*, guys. She has got to be your foxiest fox so far.' Under his heavy silver gear, I couldn't but notice on this hearty husband and father, jammed up against work pants, the same old famous worldwide pet and problem poking.

~ ~ ~

I drove Barker to his place; he invited me in for a viewing. I'd hoped he would. 'World premiere.' He smiled, eyes alive as they hadn't been before. 'First show on Lake Drive anyways.'

The neighborhood, like Barker's looks, had been the rage forty years ago. I figured he must rent rooms in this big mullioned place, but he owned it. The foyer clock showed I might not make it home in time for supper. Lately I'd overused the excuse of working late; even as superintendent of schools there're limits on how much extra time you can devote to your job.

I didn't want to miff a terrific wife.

I figured I'd have a good hour and a half; a lot can happen in an hour and a half. We were now safe inside a private place.

The house had been furnished expensively but some years back. Mission stuff. The Oriental rugs were coated with dust or fur; thick hair hid half their patterns. By accident, I kicked a chewed rubber mouse. The cat toy jingled under a couch, scaring me.

In Barker's kitchen, a crockpot bubbled. Juice hissed out under a Pyrex lid that didn't quite fit. The room smelled of decent beef stew. His counter was layered with fast-food takeout cartons. From among this litter, in a clay pot, one beautiful amaryllis lily — orange, its mouth wider than the throat of a trombone, startled me. It reminded you of something from science fiction, straining like one serious muscle toward daylight.

In the dark adjacent room, Barker kept humming, knocking things over. I heard the clank of movie reels. 'Didn't expect company, Dave,' he called. 'Just clear off a chair and make yourself at home. Momma was a cleaner-upper. Me . . . less. I don't *see* the junk till I get somebody to . . . till somebody drops over, you know?'

I grunted agreement, strolled into his pantry. Here were cans so old you could sell them for the labels. Here was a 1950s tin of vichyssoise I wouldn't have eaten at gunpoint. I slipped along the hall, wandered upstairs. An archive of *National Geographics* rose in yellow columns to the ceiling. 'Dave?' he was hollering. 'Just settle in or whatever. It'll only take a sec. See, they cut the leaders off both our movies. I'll just do a little splice. I'm fast, though.'

'Great.'

~ ~ ~

On the far wall of one large room (windows smothered by outside ivy) a calendar from 1959, compliments of a now-defunct savings and loan. Nearby, two Kotex cartons filled with excelsior and stuffed, I saw on closer inspection, with valuable brown-and-white Wedgwood place settings for forty maybe. He really should sell them – I was already mothering Barker. I'd tell him which local dealer would give top dollar.

In one corner, a hooked rug showed a Scottie terrier chasing one red ball downhill. I stepped on it, three hundred moths sputtered up, I backed off, arms flailing before me. Leaning in the doorway, waiting to be called downstairs for movietime, still wearing my business clothes, I suddenly felt a bit uneasy, worried by a famous thought: What are you *doing* here, Dave?

Well, Barker brought me home with him, is what. And, as far back as my memory made it, I'd only wanted just such guys to ask me over. Only they held my interest, my full sympathy.

The kid with the terrible slouch but (for me) an excellent smile, the kid who kept pencils in a plastic see-through satchel that clamped into his loose-leaf notebook. The boy whose mom – even when the guy'd turned fourteen – *made* him use his second-grade Roy Rogers/Dale Evans lunchbox showing them astride their horses, Trigger and Buttermilk. He was the kid other kids didn't bother mocking because – through twelve years of schooling side by side – they'd never noticed him.

Of course, I could tell there were other boys, like me, studying the other boys. But they all looked toward the pink and blond Stephens and Andrews: big-jawed athletic officeholders, guys with shoulders like baby couches, kids whose legs looked turned on lathes, solid newels – calves that summer sports stained mahogany brown, hair coiling over them, bleached by overly chlorinated pools and an admiring sun: yellow-white-gold. But while others' eyes stayed locked on them, I was off admiring finer qualities of some clubfooted Wendell, a kindly bespectacled Theodore. I longed to stoop and tie their dragging shoestrings, ones unfastened so long that the plastic tips had worn to frayed cotton tufts. Math geniuses who forgot to zip up: I wanted to give them dating hints. I'd help them find the right barber. I dreamed of assisting their undressing – me, bathing them with stern brotherly care, me, putting them to bed (poor guys hadn't yet guessed that my interest went past buddyhood). While they slept (I didn't want to cost them any shut-eye), I'd just reach under their covers (always blue) and find that though the world considered these fellows minor minor, they oftentimes proved more major than the muscled boys who frolicked, unashamed, well-known, pink-and-white in gym showers.

What was I *doing* here? Well, my major was art history. I was busy being a collector, is what. And not just someone who can spot (in a museum with a guide to lead him) any old famous masterpiece. No, I was a detective off in the odd corner of a side-street thrift shop. I was uncovering (on sale for the price of the frame!) a little etching by Wyndham Lewis – futuristic dwarves – or a golden cow by Cuyp, one of Vuillard's shuttered parlors painted on a shirt cardboard.

Maybe this very collector's zeal had drawn me to Carol, had led me to fatherhood, to the underrated joys of community. See, I wanted everything – even to be legit. Nothing was so obvious or subtle that I wouldn't try it once. I prided myself on knowing what I liked and going shamelessly after it. Everybody notices grace. But appreciating perfect clumsiness, that requires the real skill.

'Won't be long now!' I heard Barker call.

'All *right*,' I hollered, exactly as my sons would.

~ ~ ~

I eased into a messy office upstairs and, among framed documents and pictures, recognized Barker's grandfather. He looked just like Barker but fattened up and given lessons. During the fifties, the granddad served as mayor of our nearby capital city. Back then, such collar-ad looks were still admired, voted into office.

A framed news photo showed the mayor, hair oiled, presenting horse-topped trophies to young girls in jodhpurs. They blinked up at him, four fans, giggling. Over the wide loud tie, his grin showed an actor's worked-at innocence. He'd been a decent mayor – fair to all, paving streets in the black district, making parks of vacant lots. Good till he got nabbed with his hand in the till. Like Barker's, this was a face almost too pure to trust. When you observed the eyes of young Barker downstairs – it was like looking at a *National Geographic* close-up of some exotic Asian deer – you could admire the image forever, it wouldn't notice or resist your admiration. It had the static beauty of an angel. Designed. That unaffected and willing to serve. His character was like an angel's own – the perfect gofer.

I heard Barker humming Broadway ballads, knocking around ice trays. I opened every door on this hall. Why not? The worse the housekeeping got, the better I liked it. The tenderer I felt about the guy downstairs. One room had seven floor lamps in it, two standing, five resting on their sides, one plugged in. Shades were snare-drum shaped, the delicate linings frayed and split like fabric from old negligees.

I closed all doors. I heard him mixing drinks. I felt that buzz and ringing you learn to recognize as the sweet warning sign of a sure thing. Still, I have been wrong.

I checked my watch. 'Ready,' he called, 'when you are.' I passed the bathroom. I bet Barker hadn't done a load of laundry since last March or April. A thigh-high pile made a moat around the tub. I lifted some boxer shorts. (Boxers show low self-esteem, bodywise; my kind of guy always wears them and assumes that every other man on earth wears boxers too.) These particular shorts were pin-striped and had little red New York Yankee logos rashed everywhere. They surely needed some serious bleaching.

~ ~ ~

There he stood, grinning. He'd been busy stirring instant iced tea, two tall glasses with maps of Ohio stenciled on them. I didn't ask, Why Ohio? Barker seemed pleased, quicker-moving, the host. He'd rolled up his sleeves, the skin as fine as sanded ashwood. The icebox freezer was a white glacier dangling roots like a molar's. From one tiny hole in it, Barker fished a gin bottle; he held the opened pint to one tea glass and smiled. 'Suit you?'

'Gin and iced tea? Sure.' Seducers/seducees must remain flexible.

'Say when, pal.' I said so. Barker appeared full of antsy mischief.

For him, I saw, this was still his mother's house. With her dead, he could do as he liked; having an illicit guest here pleased him. Barker cultivated the place's warehouse look. He let cat hair coat his mom's prized rugs; it felt daring to leave the stag-movie projector and screen set up in the den full-time, just to shock his Florida sisters.

I couldn't help myself. 'Hey, buddy, where *is* this cat?' I nodded toward the hallway's gray fluff balls.

'Hunh? Oh. There's six. Two mother ones and four kid ones. All super-shy but each one's really different. Good company.'

He carried our tea glasses on a deco chrome tray; the film-viewing room was just ten feet from the kitchen. Dark in here. Ivy vines eclipsed the sunset; leaf green made our couch feel underwater. I slumped deep into its dated scalloped cushions.

Sipping, we leaned back. It seemed that we were waiting for a signal: Start. I didn't want to watch a movie. But, also, I did. I longed to hear this nice fellow tell me something, a story, anything, but I worried: talking could spoil whatever else might happen. I only half knew what I hoped for. I felt scared Barker might not understand my particular kind of tenderness. Still, I was readier and readier to find out, to risk making a total fool of myself. Everything worthwhile requires that, right?

I needed to say something next.

'So,' is what I said. 'Tell me. So tell me something . . . about yourself. Something I should know, Barker.' And I added that, oh, I really appreciated his hospitality. It was nothing; he shrugged, then pressed back. He made a throaty sound like a story starting. 'Well. Something plain, Dave? Or something . . . kind of spicy?'

'Both,' I said. Education does pay off. I know to at least ask for everything.

~ ~ ~

'Okay.' His voice dipped half an octave. The idea of telling had relaxed Barker. I could see it. Listening to him relax relaxed me.

~ ~ ~

'See, they sent my granddad to jail. *For* something. I won't say what. He did do it; still, we couldn't picture prison – for him. My mom and sisters were so ashamed that at first they wouldn't drive out to see him. I wanted to. Nobody'd take me. I called up prison to ask about visiting hours. I made myself sound real deep, like a man, so they'd tell me. I was eleven. So when the prison guy gave me the times, he goes, "Well, thank you for calling, ma'am." I had to laugh.

'They'd put him in that state pen out on the highway, the work farm. It's halfway to Tarboro, and I rode my bike clear out there. It was busy, a Saturday. I had to keep to the edge of the interstate. Teenagers in two convertibles threw beer cans at me. Finally, when I got to the prison, men said I couldn't come in, being a minor and all. Maybe they smelled the beer those hoods'd chucked at my back.

'I wondered what my granddad would do in the same spot (he'd been pretty well known around here), and so I started mentioning my rights, *loud*. The men said "Okay, okay" and told me to pipe down. They let me in. He sat behind heavy-gauge chicken wire. He looked good, about the same. All the uniforms were gray, but his was pressed and perfect on him – like he'd got to pick the color of everybody else's outfit. You couldn't even hold hands with him. Was like going to the zoo except it was your granddaddy. Right off, he thanks me for coming and he tells me where the key is hid. Key to a shack he owned at the back side of the fairgrounds. You know, out by the pine trees where kids go park at night and do you-know-what?

'He owned this cottage, but seeing as how he couldn't use it – for six to ten – he wanted me to hang out there. Granddad said I should use it whenever I needed to hide or slack off or anything. He said I could keep pets or have a club, whatever I liked.

'He said there was one couch in it, plus a butane stove, but no electric lights. The key stayed under three bricks in the weeds. He said, "A boy needs a place to go." I said, "Thanks." Then he asked about Mom and the others. I lied: how they were busy baking stuff to bring him, how they'd be out soon, a carful of pies. He made a face and asked which of my sisters had driven me here.

'I said, "Biked it." Well, he stared at me. "Not nine miles and on a Saturday. No. I've earned this, but you shouldn't have to." He started crying then. It was hard, with the wire between us. Then, you might not believe this, Dave, but a black guard comes over and says, "No crying." I didn't know they could do that – boss you like that – but in jail I guess they can do anything they please. Thing is, Granddad stopped. He told me, "I'll make this up to you, Barker. Some of them say you're not exactly college material, Bark, but we know better. You're the best damn one. But listen, hey, you walk that bike home, you hear me? Concentrate on what I'm saying. It'll be dark by the time you get back to town, but it's worth it. Walk, hear me?"' I said I would. I left and went outside.

My bike was missing. I figured that some convict's kid had taken it. A poor kid deserved it more than me. Mom would buy me another one. I walked.'

~ ~ ~

Barker sat still for a minute and a half. 'What else?' I asked.

'You sure?' He turned my way. I nodded. He took a breath.

~ ~ ~

'Well, I hung out in my new cabin a lot. It was just two blocks from the busiest service station in town, but it seemed way off by itself. Nobody used the fairgrounds except during October and the county fair. You could smell pine straw. At night, cars parked for three and four hours. Up one pine tree, a bra was tied – real old and gray now – a joke to everybody but maybe the girl that'd lost it. Out there, pine straw was all litterbugged with used rubbers. I thought they were some kind of white snail or clam or something. I knew they were yucky; I just didn't know *how* they were yucky.

'I'd go into my house and I'd feel grown. I bought me some birds at the old mall with my own money. Two finches. I'd always wanted some Oriental type of birds. I got our dead parakeet's cage, a white one, and I put them in there. They couldn't sing; they just looked good. One was red and the other one was yellow, or one was yellow and one was red, I forget. I bought these seed balls and one pink plastic bird type of toy they could peck at. After school, I'd go sit on my man-sized sofa, with my birdcage nearby, finches all nervous, hopping, constant, me reading my comics – I'd never felt so good, Dave. I knew why my granddad liked it there – no phones, nobody asking him for favors. He'd take long naps on the couch. He'd make himself a cup of tea. He probably paced around the three empty rooms – not empty really: full of cobwebs and these coils of wire.

'I called my finches Huey and Dewey. I loved my Donald Duck comics. I kept all my funny books in alphabetical order in the closet across from my brown sofa. Well, I had everything I needed – a couch, comics, cups of hot tea. I hated tea, but I made about five cups a day because Granddad had bought so many bags in advance and I did like holding a hot mug while I read. So one day I'm sitting there curled up with a new comic – comics are never as good the second time, you know everything that's next – so I'm sitting there happy and I hear my back door slam wide open. Grownups.

'Pronto, I duck into my comics closet, yank the door shut except for just one crack. First I hoped it'd be Granddad and his bust-out gang from the state pen. I didn't believe it, just hoped, you know.'

'In walks this young service-station guy from our busy Sunoco place, corner of Sycamore and Bolton. I heard him say, "Oh yeah, I use this place sometimes. Owner's away awhile." The mechanic wore a khaki uniform that zipped up its front. "Look, birds." A woman's voice. He stared around. "I guess somebody else is onto Robby's hideaway. Don't sweat it." He heaved right down onto my couch, onto my new comic, his legs apart. He stared – mean-looking – at somebody else in the room with us. Robby had a reputation. He was about twenty-two, twice my age then – he seemed pretty old. Girls from my class used to hang around the Coke machine at Sunoco just so they could watch him, arm-deep up under motors. He'd scratch himself a lot. He had a *real* reputation. Robby was a redhead, almost a blond. His cloth outfit had so much oil soaked in, it looked to be leather. All day he'd been in sunshine or up underneath leaky cars, and his big round arms were brown and greasy, like . . . cooked food. Well, he kicked off his left loafer. It hit my door and about gave me a heart attack. It did. Then – he was flashing somebody a double-dare kind of look. Robby yanked down his suit's big zipper maybe four inches, showing more tanned chest. The zipper made a chewing sound.

'I sat on the floor in the dark. My head tipped back against a hundred comics. I was gulping, all eyes, arms wrapped around my knees like going off the high dive in a cannonball.

'When the woman sat beside him, I couldn't believe this. You could of knocked me over with one of Huey or Dewey's feathers. See, she was my best friend's momma. I decided, No, must be her identical twin sister (a bad one), visiting from out of town. This lady led Methodist Youth Choir. Don't laugh, but she'd been my Cub Scout den mother. She was about ten years older than Robby, plump and prettyish but real, real scared-looking.

'He says, "So, you kind of interested, hunh? You sure been giving old Rob some right serious looks for about a year now, ain't it? I was wondering how many lube jobs one Buick could take, lady."

'She studies her handbag, says, "Don't call me Lady. My name's Anne. Anne with an *e*." She added this like to make fun of herself for being here.

I wanted to help her. She kept extra still, knees together, holding on to her purse for dear life, not daring to look around. I heard my birds fluttering, worried. I thought: If Robby opens this door, I am dead.

'"Anne with a *e*, huh? An-nie? Like Little Orphan. Well, Sandy's here, Annie. Sandy's been wanting to get you off by yourself. You ready for your big red dog Sandy?"

'"I didn't think you'd talk like that," she said.

'I wanted to bust out of my comics closet and save her. One time on a Cub Scout field trip to New York City, the other boys laughed because I thought the Empire State Building was called something else. I said I couldn't wait to see the Entire State Building. Well, they sure ragged me. I tried to make them see how it *was* big and all. I tried to make them see the logic. She said she understood how I'd got that. She said it was right "original." We took the elevator. I tried to make up for it by eating nine hot dogs on a dare. Then I looked off the edge. That didn't help. I got super-sick, Dave. The other mothers said I'd brought it on myself. But she was so nice, she said that being sick was nobody's fault. Mrs . . . the lady, she wet her blue hankie at a water fountain and held it to my head and told me not to look. She got me a postcard, so when I got down to the ground I could study what I'd almost seen. Now, with her in trouble in my own shack, I felt like I should rescue her. She was saying, "I don't know what I expected you to talk like, Robby. But not like this, not cheap, please."

'Then he grinned, he howled like a dog. She laughed anyway. Huey and Dewey went wild in their cage. Robby held both his hands limp in front of him and panted like a regular hound. Then he asked her to help him with his zipper. She wouldn't. Well then, Robby got mad, said, "It's my lunch hour. You ain't a customer *here*, lady. It's your husband's silver-gray Electra parked out back. You brought me here. You've got yourself into this. You been giving me the look for about a year. I been a gentleman so far. Nobody's forcing you. It ain't a accident you're here with me. But hey, you can leave. Get out. Go on."

'She sighed but stayed put, sitting there like in a waiting room. Not looking, kneecaps locked together, handbag propped on her knees. Her fingers clutched that bag like her whole life was in it. "Give me that." He snatched the purse and, swatting her hands away, opened it. He prodded around, pulled out a tube of lipstick, said, "Annie, sit still." She did. She seemed as upset as she was interested. I told myself, She *could* leave. I stayed in the dark. So much was happening in a half-inch stripe of sunshine. The lady didn't move. Robby put red on her mouth – past her mouth, too much of it. She said, "Please, Robby." ' "Sandy," ' he told her, "You Annie, me Sandy Dog. Annie Girl, Sandy Boy. Sandy show Annie." He made low growling sounds. "Please," she tried, but her mouth was stretched from how he kept painting it. "I'm not sure," the lady said. "I wanted to know you better, yes. But now I don't feel . . . sure." "You will, Annie Mae. Open your Little Orphan shirt." She didn't understand him. ' "Blouse" then, fancy pants, open your "Blouse," lady.' She did it but so slow. "Well," she said. "I don't know about you, Robby. I really don't." But she took her shirt off anyhow.

'My den mother was shivering in a bra, arms crossed over her. First his black hands pushed each arm down, studying her. Then Robby pulled at his zipper so his whole chest showed. He put the lipstick in her hand and showed her how to draw circles on the tops of his – you know, on his nipples. Then he took the tube and made Xs over the dots she'd drawn. They both looked down at his chest. I didn't understand. It seemed like a kind of target practice. Next he snapped her bra up over her collarbones and he lipsticked hers. Next he threw the tube across the room against my door – but, since his shoe hit, this didn't surprise me so much. Robby howled like a real dog. My poor finches were just chirping and flying against their cage, excited by animal noises. She was shaking her head. "You'd think a person such as myself . . . I'm having serious second thoughts here, Robert, really . . . I'm just not too convinced . . . that . . . that we . . ."

'Then Robby got up and stood in front of her, back to me. His hairdo was long on top, the way boys wore theirs then. He lashed it side to side, kept his hands, knuckles down, on his hips. Mrs . . . the lady must have been helping him with the zipper. I heard it slide. I only guessed what they were starting to do. I'd been told about all this. But, too, I'd been told, say, about the Eiffel Tower (we called it the Eye-ful). I no more expected to have this happening on my brown couch than I thought the Eye-ful would come in and then the Entire State Building would come in and they'd hop onto one another and start . . . rubbing girders, or something.

'I wondered how Bobby had forced the lady to. I felt I should holler, "Methodist Youth Choir!" I'd remind her who she really was around town. But I knew it'd be way worse for her – getting caught. I had never given this adult stuff much thought before. I sure did now. Since, I haven't thought about too much else for long. Robby made worse doggy yips. He was a genius at acting like a dog. I watched him get down on all fours in front of the lady – he snouted clear up under her skirt, his whole noggin under cloth. Robby made rooting and barking noises – pig, then dog, then dog and pig mixed. It was funny but too scary to laugh at.

'He asked her to call him Big Sandy. She did. "Big Sandy," she said. Robby explained he had something to tell his Orphan gal but only in dog talk. "What?" she asked. He said it, part-talking, part-gargling, his mouth all up under her white legs. She hooked one thigh over his shoulder. One of her shoes fell off. The other – when her toes curled up, then let loose – would snap, snap, snap.

'I watched her eyes roll back, then focus. She seemed to squint clear into my hiding place. She acted drowsy then completely scared awake – like at a horror movie in the worst part – then she'd doze off, then go dead, perk up overly alive, then half dead, then eyes all out like being electrocuted. It was something. She was leader of the whole Methodist Youth Choir. Her voice got bossy and husky, a leader's voice. She went, "This is wrong, Robby. You're so low, Bobert. You are a sick dog, we'll get in deep trouble, Momma's Sandy. Hungry Sandy, thirsty Sandy. Oh – not that, not there. Oh Jesus Sandy God. You won't tell. How *can* we. I've never. What are we *doing* in this shack? Whose shack? We're just too . . . It's not me here. I'm not *like* this."

'He tore off her panties and threw them at the birdcage. (Later I found silky britches on top of the cage, Huey and Dewey going ga-ga, thinking it was a pink cloud from heaven.) I watched grownups do everything fast, then easy, back to front, speeding up. They slowed down and seemed to be feeling sorry, but I figured this was just to make it all last longer. I never heard such human noises. Not out of people free from jail or the state nuthouse. I mean, I'd heard boys make car sounds, "Uh-dunn. Uh-dunn." But this was like Noah's ark or every zoo and out of two white people's mouths. Both mouths were lipsticked ear to ear. They didn't look nasty but pink as babies. It was wrestling. They never got all the way undressed – I saw things hooking them. Was like watching grownups playing, making stuff up the way kids'll say, "You be this and I'll be that." They seemed friskier and younger, nicer. I didn't know how to join in. If I'd opened my door and smiled, they would have perished and *then* broke my neck. I didn't join in, but I sure was dying to.

'By the end, her pale Sunday suit had black grease handprints on the bottom and up around her neck and shoulders. Wet places stained both people where babies get stained. They'd turned halfway back into babies. They fell against each other, huffing like they'd forgot how grownups sit up straight. I mashed one hand over my mouth to keep from crying or panting, laughing out loud. The more they acted like slobbery babies, the older I felt, watching.

'First she sobbed. He laughed, and then she laughed at how she'd cried. She said, "What's come over me, Sandy?"

' "Sandy has." He stroked her neck. "And Annie's all over Sandy dog." He showed her. He blew across her forehead, cooling her off.

'She made him promise not to tell. He said he wouldn't snitch if she'd meet him and his best buddy someplace else. "Oh, no. No way." She pulled on her blouse and buttoned it. "That wasn't part of our agreement, Robert."

' "Agreement"? I like that. My lawyers didn't exactly talk to your lawyers about no agreement. Show me your contract, Annie with a *e*.' Then he dives off the couch and is up under her skirt again. You could see that he liked it even better than the service station. She laughed, she pressed cloth down over his whole working head. Her legs went straight. She could hear him snuffling down up under there. Then Robby hollered, he yodeled right up into Mrs . . . up into the lady.

'They sort of made up.

'After adults finally limped from sight and even after car doors slammed, I waited – sure they'd come back. I finally sneaked over and picked the pants off my birds' roof. What a mess my couch was! I sat right down on such wet spots as they'd each left. The room smelled like nothing I'd ever smelled before. Too, it smelled like everything I'd ever smelled before but all in one room. Birds still went crazy from the zoo sounds and such tussling. In my own quiet way, Dave, I was going pretty crazy too.

'After that I saw Robby at the station, him winking at everything that moved, making wet sly clicking sounds with his mouth. Whenever I bent over to put air into my new bike's tires, I'd look anywhere except Robby. But he noticed how nervous I acted, and he got to teasing me. He'd sneak up behind and put the toe of his loafer against the seat of my jeans. Lord, I jumped. He liked that. He was some tease, that Robby, flashing his hair around like Lash LaRue. He'd crouch over my Schwinn. The air nozzle in my hand would sound like it was eating the tire. Robby'd say, real low and slimy, "How you like your air, regular or hi–test, slick?" He'd make certain remarks – "Cat got your tongue, Too–Pretty–By–Half?" He didn't know what I'd seen, but he could smell me remembering. I dreaded him. Of course, Dave, Sunoco was not the only station in town. I worried Robby might force me into my house and down onto the couch. I thought: But he couldn't do anything to *me*. I'm only eleven. Plus, I'm a boy. But next I made pictures in my head, and I knew better. There were ways, I bet . . .

'I stayed clear of the cabin. I didn't know why. I'd been stuck not nine feet from everything they did. I was scared of getting trapped again. I wanted to just live in that closet, drink tea, eat M&Ms, praying they'd come back. Was about six days later I remembered: my birds were alone in the shack. They needed water and feeding every other day. I'd let them down. I worried about finches, out there by their lonesomes. But pretty soon it'd been over a week, ten days, twelve. The longer you stay away from certain things, the harder it is, breaking through to do them right. I told myself, "Huey and Dewey are total goners now." I kept clear of finding them – stiff, feet up, on the bottom of the cage. I had dreams.

'I saw my den mother uptown running a church bake sale to help hungry Koreans. She was ordering everybody around like she usually did, charming enough to get away with it. I thought I'd feel super-ashamed to ever see her again. Instead I rushed right up. I chatted too much, too loud. I wanted to show that I forgave her. Of course, she didn't know I'd seen her do all such stuff with greasy Robby. She just kept looking at me, part-gloating, part-fretting. She handed me a raisin cupcake, free. We gave each other a long look. We partly smiled.

'After two and a half weeks, I knew my finches were way past dead. I didn't understand why I'd done it. I'd been too lazy or spooked to bike out and do my duty. *I* belonged in prison – finch murderer. Finally I pedaled my bike in that direction. One day, you have to. The shack looked smaller, the paint peeled worse. I found the key under three bricks, unlocked, held my breath. I didn't hear one sound from the front room, no hop, no cheep. Their cage hung from a hook on the wall, and to see into it, I had to stand up on my couch. Millet seed ground between my bare feet and the cushions. Birds had pecked clear through the back of their plastic food dish. It'd been shoved from the inside out, it'd skidded to a far corner of the room. My finches had slipped out their dish's slot. Birds were gone – flown up a chimney or through one pane of busted window glass. Maybe they'd waited a week. When I didn't show up and treat them right, birds broke out. They were now in pinewoods nearby. I wondered if they'd known all along that they could leave, if they'd only stayed because I fed them and was okay company.

'I pictured Huey and Dewey in high pines, blinking. I worried what dull local sparrows would do to such bright birds, hotshots from the mall pet store. Still, I decided that being free sure beat my finches' chances of hanging around here, starving.

'Talk about relief. I started coughing from it, I don't know why. Then I sat down on the couch and cried. I felt something slippery underneath me. I wore my khaki shorts, nothing else – it was late August. I stood and studied what'd been written on couch cushions in lipstick, all caked. Words were hard to read on nappy brown cloth. You could barely make out "I will do what Robby wants. What Sandy needs worst. So help me Dog."

'I thought of her. I wanted to fight for her, but I knew that, strong as the lady was, she did pretty much what she liked. She wouldn't be needing me. I sat again. I pulled my shorts down. Then I felt cool stripes get printed over my brown legs and white butt. Lipstick, parts of red words stuck onto my skin – "wi" from "will," the whole word "help." I stretched out full length. My birds didn't hop from perch to perch or nibble at their birdie toy. Just me now. My place felt still as any church. Something had changed. I touched myself, and – for the first time, with my bottom all sweetened by lipstick – I got real results.

'Was right after this I traded in my model cars, swapped every single comic for one magazine. It showed two sailors and twin sisters in a hotel, doing stuff. During the five last pictures, a dark bellboy joined in. Was then that my collection really started. The End, I guess. The rest is just being an adult.'

~ ~ ~

Barker sat quiet. I finally asked what'd happened to his grandfather. How about Robby and the den mother?

'In jail. My granddad died. Of a broken heart, Mom said. Robby moved. He never was one to stay anyplace too long. One day he didn't show up at Sunoco and that was it. Mrs . . . the lady, she's still right here in Falls, still a real leader. Not two days back, I ran into her at the mall, collecting canned goods to end world hunger. We had a nice chat. Her son's a lawyer in Marietta, Georgia, now. She looks about the same, really – I love the way she looks, always have. Now, when we talk, I can tell she's partly being nice to me because I never left town or went to college and she secretly thinks I'm not too swift. But since I kept *her* secret, I feel like we're even. I just smile back. I figure, whatever makes people kind to you is fine. She can see there's something extra going on, but she can't name it. It just makes her grin and want to give me little things. It's one of ten trillion ways you can love somebody. We do, love each other. I'm sure. Nobody ever knew about Robby. She got away with it. More power to her. Still leads the Youth Choir. Last year they won the Southeast Chorus prize, young people's division. They give concerts all over. Her husband loves her. She said winning the prize was the most fulfilling moment of her life. I wondered. I guess everybody does some one wild thing now and then. They should. It's what you'll have to coast on when you're old. You know?' I nodded. He sat there, still.

'Probably not much of a story.' Barker shrugged. 'But back then it was sure something, to see all that right off the bat, your first time out. I remember being so shocked to know that men want to. *And* women. I'd figured that only one person at a time would need it, and they'd have to knock down the other person and force them to, every time. But when I saw that, no, everybody wants to do it and how there are no rules in it, I couldn't look straight at a grownup for days. I'd see that my mom's slacks had zippers in them, I'd near about die. I walked around town, hands stuffed deep in my pockets. My head was hanging, and I acted like I was in mourning for something. But hey, I was really just waking up. What got me onto all *that*? You about ready for a movie, Dave? Boy, I haven't talked so much in months. It's what you get for asking, I guess.' He laughed.

I thanked Barker for his story. I told him it made sense to me.

'Well, thanks for saying so anyhow.'

~ ~ ~

He started fidgeting with the projector. I watched. I knew him better now. I felt so much for him. I wanted to save him. I couldn't breathe correctly.

'Here goes.' He toasted his newest film, then snapped on the large and somehow sinister antique machine.

The movie showed a girl at home reading an illustrated manual, hand in dress, getting herself animated. She made a phone call; you saw the actor answering, and even in a silent film, even given this flimsy premise, you had to find his acting absolutely awful. Barker informed me it was a Swedish movie; they usually started with the girl phoning. 'Sometimes it's one guy she calls, sometimes about six. But always the telephones. I don't know why. It's like they just got phones over there and are still proud of them or something.' I laughed. What a nice funny thing to say. By now, even the gin and iced tea (with lemon and sugar) tasted like a great idea.

He sat upright beside me. The projector made its placid motorboat racket. Our couch seemed a kind of quilted raft. Movie light was mostly pink; ivy filtered sun to a thin green. Across Barker's neutral white shirt, these tints carried on a silent contest. One room away, the crockpot leaked a bit, hissing. Hallway smelled of stew meat, the need for maid service, back issues, laundry in arrears, one young man's agreeable curried musk. From a corner of my vision, I felt somewhat observed. Cats' eyes. To heck with caution. Let them look!

Barker kept elbows propped on knees, tensed, staring up at the screen, jaw gone slack. In profile against windows' leaf-spotted light, he appeared honest, boyish, wide open. He unbuttoned his top collar button.

~ ~ ~

I heard cars pass, my fellow Rotarians, algebra teachers from my school system. Nobody would understand us being here, beginning to maybe do a thing like this. Even if I went public, dedicated an entire Board of Education meeting to the topic, after three hours of intelligent confession, with charts and flannel boards and slide projections, I knew that when lights snapped back on I'd look around from face to face, I'd see they still sat wondering your most basic question:

Why, Dave, why?

I no longer noticed what was happening on-screen. Barker's face, lit by rosy movie light, kept changing. It moved me so. One minute, drowsy courtesy; next, a sharp manly smile. I set my glass down on a Florida-shaped coaster. Now, slow, I reached toward the back of his neck – extra-nervous, sure, but that's part of it, you know? My arm wobbled, fear of being really belted, blackmailed, worse. I chose to touch his dark hair, cool as metal.

'Come *on*.' He huffed forward, clear of my hand. He kept gazing at the film, not me. Barker grumbled, 'The guy she phoned, he hasn't even got to her *house* yet, man.'

I saw he had a system. I figured I could wait to understand it.

~ ~ ~

I felt he was my decent kid brother. Our folks had died; I would help him even more now. We'd rent industrial-strength vacuum cleaners. We'd purge this mansion of dinge, yank down tattered maroon draperies, let daylight in. I pictured us, stripped to the waist, painting every upstairs room off-white, our shoulders flecked with droplets, the hair on our chests flecked with droplets.

I'd drive Barker and his Wedgwood to a place where I'm known, Old Mall Antiques. I bet we'd get fifteen to nineteen hundred bucks. Barker would act amazed. In front of the dealer, he'd say, 'For *that* junk?' and, laughing, I'd have to shush him. With my encouragement, he'd spend some of the bonus on clothes. We'd donate three generations of *National Geographics* to a nearby orphanage, if there are any orphanages anymore and nearby. I'd scour Barker's kitchen, defrost the fridge. Slowly, he would find new shape and meaning in his days. He'd commence reading again – nonporn, recent worthy hardbacks. We'd discuss these.

He'd turn up at Little League games, sitting off to one side. Sensing my gratitude at having him high in the bleachers, he'd understand we couldn't speak. But whenever one of my sons did something at bat or out in center field (a pop-up, a body block of a line drive), I would feel Barker nodding approval as he perched there alone; I'd turn just long enough to see a young bachelor mumbling to himself, shaking his head yes, glad for my boys.

After office hours, once a week, I'd drive over, knock, then walk right in, calling, 'Barker? Me.'

No answer. Maybe he's napping in a big simple upstairs room, one startling with fresh paint. Six cats stand guard around his bed, two old Persians and their offspring, less Persian, thinner, spottier. Four of them pad over and rub against my pant cuffs; by now they know me.

I settle on the edge of a single bed, I look down at him. Barker's dark hair has fallen against the pillow like an open wing. Bare-chested, the texture of his poreless skin looks finer than the sheets. Under a blue blanket, he sleeps, exhausted from all the cleaning, from renewing his library card, from the fatigue of clothes shopping. I look hard at him; I hear rush-hour traffic crest, then pass its peak. Light in here gets ruddier.

A vein in his neck beats like a clock, only liquid.

– I'm balanced at the pillow end of someone's bed. I'm watching somebody decent sleep. If the law considers this so wicked – then why does it feel like my only innocent activity? Barker wakes. The sun is setting. His face does five things at once: sees somebody here, gets scared, recognizes me, grins a good blurry grin, says just, 'You.'

~ ~ ~

(They don't want a person to be tender. They could lock me up for everything I love about myself, for everything I love.)

~ ~ ~

Here on the couch, Barker shifted. 'Look *now*, Dave. Uh oh, she hears him knocking. See her hop right up? Okay, walking to the door. It's him, all right. He's dressed for winter. That's because they're in Sweden, right, Dave?'

I agreed, with feeling. Then I noted Barker taking the pen caddy from his pocket, placing it on the table before him. Next, with an ancient kind of patience, Barker's torso twisted inches toward me; he lifted my hand, pulled my whole arm up and around and held it by the wrist, hovering in air before his front side as if waiting for some cue. Then Barker, clutching the tender back part of my hand, sighed, 'Um-kay. *Now* they're really starting to.' And he lowered my whole willing palm – down, down onto it.

I touched something fully familiar to me, yet wholly new.

~ ~ ~

He bucked with that first famous jolt of human contact after too long, too long alone without. His spine slackened, but the head shivered to one side, righted itself, eager to keep the film in sight. I heard six cats go racing down long hallways, then come thumping back, relaxed enough to play with me, a stranger, in their house. Praise.

Barker's voice, all gulpy: 'I think . . . this movie's going to be a real good one, Dave. Right up there on my Ten Favorites list. And, you know? . . .' He *almost* ceased looking at the screen, he *nearly* turned his eyes my way instead. And the compliment stirred me. 'You know? You're a regular fellow, Dave. I feel like I can trust you. You seem like . . . one real nice guy.'

Through my breathing, I could hear him, breathing, losing breath, breathing, losing breath.

'Thank you, Barker. Coming from you, that means a lot.'

~ ~ ~

Every true pleasure is a secret.

PETER WELLS

PERRIN AND THE FALLEN ANGEL

Who has not been a slut has not been human.

Eric Westmore did not consider himself either a beauty or a gorgon. People did not run out of rooms gagging: but, on the other hand, not too many were driven to distraction by his glance. This did not preclude great explosions of attraction: yet such was Eric's nature, ironic, self-mocking – or was it merely self-doubting? – that he always put these frissons down to poor eyesight or a case of mistaken identity, which would almost inevitably catch up with him sooner or later.

He sat now in the brackish quiet of the Alexandra Hotel. It was 10 April 1986.

The Alex was a charmingly Edwardian hostelry on the outside, a wedding cake of plaster arranged, tastefully, to snare passersby on two back streets: it looked like the tiara, Eric always thought, of a minor Scottish peeress. It was the last week of it being a gay or, indeed, any kind of pub. It was going to be demolished. All over the city, in a speculative frenzy driven by the stock market, Edwardian and Victorian Auckland was being reduced to dust.

Even now, as Eric sat in the dullard moments of the quarter hour

PETER WELLS (born 1950): The New Zealander Peter Wells is the author of the story collections Dangerous Desires *and* The Duration of a Kiss. Boy Overboard, *his first novel, was published in 1997. He also wrote and directed the film* A Death in the Family.

before noon, demolition drills were attacking the air in nearby streets, a dull repetitive sound, drill to a toothache.

Yet it was a beautiful day, he said to himself, inclined to feel mellow (he was, after all, in the opening stages of, as he himself said, *a romance*, putting just the right ironic emphasis on what some might call a love affair and others might call a fuck). It was a superb day in early autumn: the crispness of winter had begun to lie like an essence over the lingering heat of summer. As if to symbolise his content, just as Eric walked down the street towards the pub, a yacht had serenely passed across the gap between two buildings, tightrope walker on his line of bliss.

Yet.

Eric, on the cusp of thirty-eight, aware that the tidal shifts of time were now beginning to run against him in a way that no amount of gym or artful haircuts could entirely alter, knew there always had to be a *yet*, a determinant in his bliss.

The *yet* he was thinking of now, as he sat in the pub gazing thoughtfully at a block of sun on the carpet – 'like winter butter set out on a white porcelain dish,' he memorised for his column – was the phone call from Perrin that morning.

The phone had gone off at seven-thirty, aggressive as an alarm.

Matthew was still in the shower, while Eric was standing in front of the stove, staring mindlessly at the milk he was scalding for caffè latte.

Perrin's voice cut through his groggy sleepiness. 'Can we meet today?'

'Today?' said Eric, who was still adjusting the sensuality of the night before to the demands of prosaic daylight.

'Yes, today,' said Perrin without any of his customary humour. He sounded pissed off – or was it sour?

Did he suspect already, Eric wondered, about Matthew?

Matthew, as if an apparition appearing on cue, walked into the kitchen stark naked. Eric admired his body – which, of course, he was meant to do: his freedom, his flanks, his beautiful tassel-like cock. Matthew did a small coquettish whirl, then sat down, forgetting Eric completely, and, picking up the morning's newspaper, began to study his horoscope.

'As soon as possible,' said Perrin's voice, again, in Eric's ear.

Eric had taken his eyes away from Matthew, unwillingly, and cast his mind ahead to his day. He thought of how much more work he had to do to get his daily food column readable. Then there was his guerrilla raid on an unsuspecting new restaurant, the one specialising in New Zealand game products.

'What about after six?' Eric suggested, looking tentatively at Matthew.

Matthew was, instead, investigating his pubic hairs with a mono-maniacal scrutiny.

'No. Earlier.' Perrin was being relentlessly persistent.

'You could meet me at that new place — Faringays. I've got to *cruelle* it.'

Perrin and he always called Eric's reviews 'to *cruelle de ville*' it.

A pause.

Perrin's response was definitive. 'I don't feel like food.'

Silence again as, in the background, Eric heard someone say good morning to Perrin and Perrin, crisply adjusting his tone to genial busy executive, batted back the greeting. Perrin said then, close to the phone: 'I want to see you, Eric. *I need to see you baby*,' he said in one long breath of confession.

Oh no, sweetheart, you haven't been seeing Sweet Sixteen *again*, Eric was about to whiplash back. Sweet Sixteen was a troublesome, if nubilely splendid, Niue Islander Perrin was being relentlessly pursued by. But something about Perrin's tone told him it was not going to be their usual enjoyable slanging match, in which mutual insult and hilarious parody mounted up until Perrin, almost inevitably, managed to cap Eric off with a flourish of obscene absurdity. Perhaps it was too early in the morning.

Or perhaps, Eric thought more reasonably, Perrin had a hangover. Or was it just that super-melodramatic flu which was casting Perrin into increasingly sombre moods: what Eric lightly dubbed his '*dame aux camellias*' complex.

'*Please*,' said Perrin, who was not one to beg.

Eric had quickly succumbed. They would meet at the Alex a few minutes before twelve. They would go on from there to somewhere 'quiet.'

Just as he put the receiver down, in that second before Perrin clicked off, Eric had an insane urge to put the phone back up to his ear, to listen harder, deeper, more faithfully to the textures of Perrin's silences, the underground music of his tone. But Eric was running late. His deadline for his food column was leering, the phone was already shrilling, and then, of course, he had had hardly any sleep after his night with Matthew.

Matthew.

It was true, a good seven eighths of his mind was given over to, willingly occupied by, thoughts of this young man who had suddenly, accidentally – impetuously – entered his life. Even as Eric now sat waiting at the Alex, eleven minutes before noon on that April day in 1986, he closed his eyes for a second, to reconnect with that world which still swirled, fragrantly as the scents of sex, through his consciousness.

Obligingly – or was it obediently? – he was wafted up to a serene and great height, as if he were in a glider which could not, would not, ever meet with catastrophe. And far below him he saw the body of Matthew, a vast landscape which stretched from horizon to horizon: a country he was beginning to be familiar with, his favourite destinations – Matthew's mouth, between his legs, his smooth buttocks like peeled grapes. Was it folly for a writer on food to conceptualise his new lover in terms of fruit, of vegetables? (His cock a courgette left on the vine too long and grown tautly too large, the pillows of his chest a perfectly ripe pawpaw he loved to lick and gnaw on, the cleft of his arsehole, well, not to be too ridiculous, moistly pink as perfectly cured Christmas ham. He could go on, his Matthew, his banquet, his feast.)

Perhaps this objectification, Eric lectured himself as he sat there, was simply defensive. It was part of his emotional defensiveness that he tried to picture Matthew in terms of appetite, keeping clear of that minefield, that scarred battleground of the emotions called love. Oh, keep me clear of that, sighed Eric, seasoned trooper of the wars of the heart.

With a conscious effort – but also with a pang of regret that he must leave such a perfumed landscape, one with its own laws, its own hegemony over his unconscious – he tried to focus on the exact present.

He dallied with his glass of tonic, looking for a moment at the bubbles. Then a faint smile of anticipation softened his face. He longed for Perrin to arrive, so he could gently, as if accidentally, spill the treasure of his new romance before Perrin's eyes.

He had been seeing Matthew for over three weeks, and though Perrin and he, old friends, well, *ancient* friends, touched base at least once a week, he had carefully screened the event from Perrin, until the romance, affair, the series of fucks – whatever it was – had some stable *emotional* basis.

Perrin, meanwhile, had noticed nothing: neither Eric's soaring spirits, nor his pleasurable languor, nor even, on the one occasion he had managed to coax Perrin down to the pool, the expressive love bites on the back of Eric's neck.

Perrin was inclined to be myopic anyway. His battles at the Equal Opportunities Commission, where he was a pugnacious lawyer, at times occupied all his fields of vision: when he wasn't, that is, pursuing remarkable pieces of Clarice Cliff, or unusually sensual young men whom he unearthed from unlikely situations, like post offices in small towns or half-empty laundromats – any of those situations which require a selective perception, tempered by endurance and fired by an almost fanatical flare of desire, and desirability. Or was it an unfillable capacity to be approved of, to be loved?

Perhaps that was why Eric wanted to torment Perrin, just slightly, at this moment. Perrin always had such spectacular success sexually (with, of course, its attendant moments of tedium, like courses of penicillin) that Eric felt drab and frowsy beside him. Eric always felt, in this situation, that his own desirability was diminished, a point he was not beyond getting petty about.

So now he carefully, and with a sense of epicurean enjoyment, selected his poisoned shafts. 'He (Matthew) is twenty-three (young), a student of architecture (a brain). He plays basketball (good body). And he's cute (rampant sexually).'

Eric toyed with the various ways he could casually, without undue emphasis, introduce this new persona to his and Perrin's life. Eric knew Perrin would want particulars: he would realise, as soon as Eric had introduced Matthew to him verbally, that it was merely a prelude to him meeting Matthew himself. Eric always regarded it as part of his lovers' educational process that they should meet someone as civilised, as exquisitely nuanced, as Perrin. Many a callow youth had learnt a correct table setting in his presence.

Perrin would, perhaps, have him and Matthew round for one of his delightfully casual, perfectly produced Thai meals. Other friends would be there. They would range over politics, personalities, fashion, food. In this way Matthew would enter a mutual zone of friendship, that *terra cognita* Eric had relied on ever since he had discovered it, tremblingly, in a state of hilarious ignorance, in what he now called, with sardonic quotation marks around it, *his youth*.

He looked around appreciatively. It was in a pub like this, Victorian, slightly seedy, scented with all the beers supped by many forgotten drinkers

– to drown what sorrows, evoke what dreams, nobody could any longer say – that he and Perrin had first met.

~ ~ ~

It had been Eric's first venture into a gay pub.

In a mood of determination which had about it the air of a suicide mission, Eric had bid farewell to his old self in his bedroom mirror and set out, one Friday night (15 May 1969, his old, deplorable diaries told him – marked with a significant X). He had presented himself, white-faced, at the bar. As far as he could see, there were only men there, apart from one extraordinary woman who appeared to be the hostess. She was dressed, head to foot, in a glittering black muumuu, her most pronounced feature a suntan so intense it appeared less her skin than a form of basted flesh on which pieces of gold were placed, ornamentally, to great advantage. This theme was carried into her mouth, where her teeth were bedizened in a similar precious metal. Overall she escaped, by a mere hair's breadth, being spectacularly gaudy.

Eric went straight to the bar and asked for something he took to be a typically sophisticated 'gay' drink. 'A Negroni, please.'

The barman had looked at him, was about to ask how old he was. Then something in Eric's face – his desperation, perhaps – made him hesitate and then, speaking almost *sotto voce*, say, 'Wait a sec.' He turned to serve two men who hung on each other's shoulders and, both casting conspicuous looks at Eric yet making him feel as if he wasn't quite there, continued to address each other in fluted tones.

Both men wore what Eric took to be a club uniform: white shoes, beige crimplene slacks, and hair which appeared to be both subtly teased and unsubtly lacquered. Their faces, variously wrinkled, were glaucous with moisturiser. 'Two double gin and tonics, love,' one of them asked the barman, in tones not quite so orchestral.

His companion smiled tentatively at Eric, and Eric felt his face crack a little as he smiled back. His heart was beating so hard he felt sure they could hear it.

The men departed, and the barman casually came back. 'Do you know how to make a Negroni,' he asked quietly, without any suggestion of aggression or even undue attention in his voice.

Eric flushed. He did. His throat was dry when he started speaking: he coughed up air over sandpaper.

The barman waited. Eric nodded. 'Yes,' he said, and told him.

While the man proceeded to make it, Eric said to him: 'I looked it up.' Then he said: 'I like reading recipes.' As he said this, he felt a swoon overtake him, a flush begin to rise up his face.

The barman had turned to look over his shoulder at him, not so much sharply but as if to check out the ingenuousness of the remark. Seeing Eric's discomfort, he slid the drink towards him and, shaking his head when Eric offered payment, solemnly withdrew.

Eric realised something nice had happened to him.

Safely in possession of something to hold, something to do, Eric slid his tongue into his drink experimentally. As soon as the alcohol hit his tongue, he had to try hard not to let his face react. It did not taste as he imagined the recipe would. Nevertheless, having obtained the drink in such special circumstances, he could hardly go back and ask for something else.

He must enjoy himself: that terrible imperative. He looked around the room to see who was looking at him. No one. It was extraordinary.

He looked around again, in panic. Nobody was taking the slightest bit of notice of him.

It was at this moment – this lacuna in his life – that Perrin McDougal walked in the door.

At this stage, before he had settled sublimely into his looks, wearing them with all the assurance of a bespoke jacket on carefully muscular shoulders, Perrin appeared a diffident, indifferent-looking youth. He was thin, high-nosed, dressed dramatically, head to toe, in black. He paused under a light, as if for dramatic effect, then threw his long amethyst scarf over his shoulder with a defiant emphasis.

This caused a momentary hush – almost of awe at someone contravening 'taste' so much. Then at the back a voice was heard to say something – thankfully, Eric thought, indistinct (it sounded like 'drama queen') – then there were guffaws or collapsed lungs of laughter.

Perrin, holding his profile in a distinctly Oscar Wilde manner (the young Oscar Wilde), as if he did not hear, obtained a drink and went into speedy exile – a miscalculation of effects? – by a wall.

Inevitably, it seemed, because they were the two people on their own, so spectacularly isolated, their eyes located each other. It was like radar – radar of the dispossessed.

It was Perrin who finally made the move across the room to him. Sidling up, he looked at Eric for a moment, radiant with silence.

Eric, panicking – was this his first pickup? – said, with a dry voice, 'There's quite a crowd here tonight, isn't there?'

His new companion turned on him an eye from which satirical emphasis was not entirely absent. 'I *hate* crowds,' Perrin pronounced.

'Why . . . why do you wear black?' Eric asked, racking his brain for clever, unusual things to say.

'I'm in mourning for the world, of course,' Perrin said superbly.

Eric, who was not *au fait* with Edith Sitwell's autobiography, believed he found himself in the presence of acerbic genius. 'Are you from out of town?' he asked, looking into Perrin's thin face, pimples just visible by his nose.

Perrin seemed uncomfortable, even nervous. Nevertheless, so convinced was he of his superiority that he looked Eric up and down, then said drily: 'The unpleasant fact of the matter is, I come from a Rue Morgue called Hamilton.'

Eric's eyes widened. 'That has a lake, doesn't it?'

'In which,' said Perrin, who spoke as if always between parentheses, 'the unhappy citizenry are driven to throw themselves, for their *divertissement*.'

Eric laughed, and Perrin congratulated him on his appreciation of wit, with a surprisingly shy, even tentative, smile. Then he turned to the room, sighing slightly.

'You see before you . . . a refugee. In fact, I clean dishes at the Hungry Horse.'

Eric saw that Perrin was by no means as self-assured as the turn of his scarf, the cut of his phrase. With this discovery, he felt himself to have attained a similar, happy refugee status.

A long, not unfriendly silence fell in which both did an inventory of the room, frequently and nervously sipping their drinks.

Eric was soon surprised to find his glass was empty: not a drop could be seduced from its shimmery viscous surface. Perrin's glass was similarly empty.

They both looked down at the diminution of their hopes and, as if in musical concert, sighed heavily together.

It was clear that, having created grand effects, neither had a penny.

'What were you drinking?' Perrin asked.

Eric, tentatively, told him. Perrin was thoughtfully silent (later he would admit he had never heard of the drink). 'I only ever drink Fallen Angels,' he said, with a high tilt to his nose which Eric read as instant glamour.

From that day on he would always think of Perrin – who later came to detest the drink as oversweet, the epitome of his early lack of sophistication, his suburban pretensions – as synonymous with that first occasion, when they had both tremblingly met and Perrin's mode of identification was, along with Edith Sitwell, a long amethyst scarf, a sense of the early Oscar Wilde, and a drink called Fallen Angel.

~ ~ ~

Later that night they left the pub, as if accidentally, together.

They walked to the bus stop still talking, and each, on the point of saying good-bye, speedily allowed the other to understand that he could be found at the pub the following Friday.

Neither confessed it was his very first visit.

~ ~ ~

Now, sitting in the Alex so many years later, more mature, filled out into his body in a way which made him feel he knew himself, Eric glanced around the bar. The men there all knew they were men: the few women's names bandied about were always used, as it were in quotation marks, knowingly camp. The barman, fleshily muscular, with a tightly trimmed moustache, looked for all the world like a rudimentary Tom of Finland sketch requiring a few master strokes for sublime completion.

This world of the Alex now was light-years away from that hotel, so long ago, in which Eric had nervously awaited his second meeting with Perrin.

That night Eric had allowed himself a small glass of beer. He was determined to keep sober. While he waited, anonymously, the crowd had swiftly grown. It was late summer, and there was that lax, overexcited air of sensuality – of louche possibilities – in the air.

Eric relaxed his body against the wall.

'Everything O.K. here, darlink?' a voice said to the side of him.

Eric turned. Pushing through the crowd towards him, like a beaver, was a small man with waved pale-blue hair and what looked like make-up on his face – or was it simply moisturiser? As he got nearer he closed his pink, slightly unguent lips together, cupid-fashion, and then laughed, revealing teeth which looked older than he was.

'Darlink! hold *onto* your funwig,' this man murmured to him, a mite melodramatically. His whole face was animated by a pleasantly puckish charm.

'Oh?' said Eric, not knowing quite how to reply. He broke out laughing.

Now, 'Call me Fay,' the little man said, pausing as if for breath. 'After the late great Fay Wray,' he murmured then, looking around the room in small darts and flicks, poisoned pricks of looks. 'We call her late,' whispered Fay, 'because she never comes on time! Famous for it!'

He looked around sharply, no longer smiling. 'Excuse me, dear, a dreadful clutch of old hags awaits,' declared Fay in a conspiratorial whisper, during which Eric felt his backside pinched, not unpleasurably – as if the man called Fay were a merchant and he was only taking a prudent feel of the fabric. Fay indicated with his head four men standing together, bodies turned, almost on display, to the constituents of the bar: 'We call them Boil, Toil, Struggle, and Poke.'

'Ciao,' he called then, melting back into the throng. Eric imagined the departing remark was a Chinese code-word.

At this point Perrin appeared beside him, unwinding himself out of his long purple scarf, sweating and bad-tempered. He had missed his bus and had to hitch a lift, he said. He intimated it had not been a pleasant adventure. When his lift found out the nature of the pub, he had turned threatening. Perrin had opened the door while the car was still moving and run, he said with superb dramatic emphasis, 'for my very life.'

But he still had in his hands a gift for Eric: a 'borrowed' library copy of Edith Sitwell's autobiography. 'The beginning of your *aesthetic* education, my dear,' he said expansively.

Eric bought a round of Fallen Angels, nonchalantly, as if this were an everyday drink for both. They drank these perhaps too quickly. Then Perrin bought a round.

By this time the room, as crowded as an audience at a boxing ring, had taken on a certain hectic tone: at any moment, it seemed, the bell would ping, the lights would lower, the main match would start. Obligingly, the bells began to shrill, urgent as the flutter of blood coursing through Eric's wrists.

Fay suddenly popped up beside him, almost with a suggestion of old-time vaudeville magic (later he found out that Fay had trained in Sydney as a show dancer before breaking his hip and ending up as a waiter). As the tidal swell of men swirled him past, Fay called out, 'Do you want to come to a party?'

'Oh,' said Eric, thinking.

'*Yes*,' said Perrin quickly. '*I* would.'

~ ~ ~

Everyone was spectacularly drunk. People were walking about, banging into walls. A middle-aged man, unwatched by most, was doing an impromptu, slightly wobbly strip on a chair. 'Oh, *trust* Fanny,' someone was saying acidly. 'One *whiff* of alcohol, and *off* come her easies.' Another fanatically serious man circulated through the crowd, wearing someone's mother's best ming-blue bri-nylon suit.

Eric and Perrin stood together in a crowded kitchen. Fay was surrounded by people, as if he were a great courtesan holding court.

'And yes, they put me on the overnight from Wellington,' Fay was saying, '*escorted* onto it by two large beasts. *Irish detectives*. They put me on and said, "Don't be in too much of a hurry to come back." Just to remind me they punched me. In turns.' There was silence. 'And then, after that, they said, "We've got some mates up in Auckland *waiting for you when you get in*. Just to make sure you don't cause any trouble up there, like."'

Fay left a brief, eloquent pause. 'So here I am, a poor helpless wretch,' he resumed, raising his eyes heavenward, in roguish imitation of a wilting Mary Pickford. He lisped softly, and with extraordinarily convincing pathos, 'just doing the best that I can.' A particularly wicked look passed over his face.

Fay then rose with great dignity, the dignity of an Empress Eugenie receiving the news of the fall of the Third Empire, the death of her only son. He turned and, in a spectacular wavering motion, as if tilting to follow the impulse of his feet, he listed towards the door, finding it open almost by accident, so that, faintly surprised, even vaguely nonplussed, the man called Fay disappeared into the halloo-ing night.

~ ~ ~

Eric and Perrin had to walk home, as the buses had long since stopped. They walked through suburbs of spectacular silence. To entertain themselves, each told the other a little about himself.

By the time they had parted – the first car was going to work – they had exchanged the same information: in order to cure them of their homosexuality, Perrin had had shock treatment, Eric aversion therapy.

They looked at each other, slowly smiling, in the diminishing night. It had not worked.

~ ~ ~

Outside, in the street, there was a sudden crumbling sound, as a tidal wave of masonry came crashing down. In a few seconds, all that was left was a cloud, a hideous perfume, a perforation of memory almost.

The entire structure of the Alex had shuddered in that moment, as if in apprehension. Outside the windows, the air became frail with grit.

Pneumatic drills took up their sound again, a drumroll at once curiously undramatic yet relentless.

At that moment, as if blown in by the gust of energy from the latest demolition, a figure arrived, tentatively, and hovered by the door. The light was behind him, yet Eric could see, immediately, the newcomer was not Perrin.

The man moved slowly out of the dust-filled sunlight, feeling his way, almost by toe, towards the bar. Eric felt a quiet claw of shock. The man was dressed with a certain hectic vivacity: his once-tight jeans were now winched in, painfully; over what was clearly a skeletal stomach, a belt with studs glinted with the eyes of a snake which had long ago lost its fury. And the man's face, gauntly handsome, haggard indeed, with deep heavy lines running from nose to chin, was shining with sweat, pale, white: he had not shaved, thus accentuating his dramatic pallor.

For one dreadful moment, Eric imagined he could remember the man: that is, he could recall a finer, fitter, indeed quite handsome man who seemed, now, like a distant, more healthy brother. *That* stranger – not *this* one, surely – had exchanged a few looks with Eric in the bar many years ago. Then *that* man, with his image of health and vigour, of whom this frail, too-old young man was a *doppelgänger*, had disappeared. He was rumoured to be in New York. He was either a waiter, according to one story, or, in the version preferred – because more apocryphal – he was the lover of someone very rich, very powerful, and, to the public at least, very heterosexual.

Now this man had returned home, and the sum of his voyage was making his way from the door to the bar in the Alex.

The occupants of the pub had grown briefly silent: then a series of falsely animated conversations broke out, like sweat on a forehead.

The newcomer reached a barstool, but suddenly relaxing his body against it, as if he had reached the end of what had become a too long and arduous mission, he misjudged its height so that, like a building collapsing sideways, his whole body began to topple down towards the carpet. At this moment, all pretence was abandoned.

The man beside him, a comfortable pool of flesh who propped up the bar from the minute it opened, getting slowly sozzled as the day went on, reached out an automatic arm, as if he had a spare limb set aside for the safety of drunks and others similarly incapacitated. Holding the falling man arrested for a moment, he got to his feet and, as if the other were a doll now, or a giddy child, plonked him down foursquare on the seat and held him secure.

At this the skeletal brother of the once-handsome man, once so much in command, the accruer of so many ardent looks, let out a wild laugh, its hilarity mocking everyone there in the gay pub, in its last days before being demolished. It was as if this man, so near his own end, clairvoyantly sensed that this place where so much life had gone on – where, indeed, rudimentary yet important transactions of a civilisation, a small branch of culture, had taken place – would be rendered faithlessly, by some dark law of anarchy, into a hole in the ground, an essential nothingness which might become, if it was lucky, the tarmac of a car park.

Eric threw the last drops of his tonic back. Where *was* Perrin, why was he late when he had been so bloody melodramatic on the phone in the morning? And what was so bloody pressing?

Eric's contemplative eye, as if a needle within a compass of anxiety, returned to the man at the bar.

He was talking with an eerie, rambling gusto, telling the story of his travels. Eric could see from the faces of the listeners that they did not know whether to believe what he was saying or believe something more profound, less acceptable.

Eric looked away quickly. He stared longingly out the door. The sun was still there, but it was gauzy with the dust of departing buildings. A huge demolition truck roared along the street, splicing everything abruptly into shadow.

He looked back into the room, quickly. He did not want to think of *that*.

He was prepared, of course, he used condoms, had studied the arcane codes of safe sex. (Come on him not into him, as the explicit ones said.) Yet, to Eric at that moment, the disease was still like a foreign war, happening, thankfully still, *over there*, a distant place from which occasional returned soldiers, like this one, emerged in the locals' midst, gnarled, bearing tales of defeat greater than anyone could possibly imagine. And to a certain extent it was unimaginable: this savage hewing down of men who had just climbed out of the darkness, emerging into light.

What the bloody hell was keeping Perrin? Suddenly Eric had an almost hysterical desire to flee the pub. He wanted to be outside, to be near the harbour or on top of one of the volcanoes, where he could look down at the city, make some sense of his life. What was Matthew but a diversion; he was fooling himself by saying he wasn't falling in love. Of course he fell in love every time. What the fuck do you expect from someone who grew up with the fateful tunes of *South Pacific*? '. . . across a crowded room . . .'

The drills suddenly swerved into closeness. Eric caught his own face in a mirror opposite: he was surprisingly, even insistently, physically *there* for someone who, at that moment, felt a peculiar seesaw of elation dipping down into black depression. He and Perrin had talked in the early days of having tests because, as Perrin had said, 'Let's face it, darling, we've both been utter sluts in our time . . . but then,' he had added thoughtfully, lifting his eyes up and looking towards a far distant point, as if he were delivering the eulogy for a generation, 'who has not been a slut has not been human.'

Eric had laughed.

Now he tried, with an almost fanatical need, to think of Matthew. He tried to conjure up in his mind those images of their lovemaking which acted, almost, as a way of banishing his anxieties. He began to wish, almost desperately, that Matthew were there with him, so that he might just casually brush by, knocking his body into Matthew's as if to recall what was real – against what could only be feared.

Yet at this moment, when he most needed him, Matthew refused to appear by osmosis.

It was now eight minutes past twelve, on 10 April 1986.

At that moment, as if exactly timed to an acme of pleasurable lateness, Eric saw another figure arrive at the door.

At first, because of the light behind him, Eric couldn't tell whether it was Perrin. It was certainly Perrin's height and approximate weight, but the person's body language was so different: slumped back, not pushing forward, standing there on the mat as if momentarily dazed, as if emerging out of a long black moment of introspection – thought – peregrination – a limning of the harsh white noon light, chalky almost, plashing and pouring down the side of, yes, it was Perrin's face.

He was still at the door, as if breaking off from some thought which possessed him. It was in his eyes as they searched the few people in the room, and the room went momentarily quiet *again* before, in quick shock waves, conversation took up, sealing over the startled apprehension that already, like an almost imperceptible drumroll, the words *again* and *again* and *again* were making themselves heard, explosions from the distant war landing closer and closer to that spot so that it was finally unavoidable that one day soon, or was it even now, a direct hit would be made and the whole culture, if it was not to be wiped out, would have to go underground again – disperse, change its nature – or else *fight*.

As if in the wake of this apprehension – or was it the beginnings of comprehension? – Perrin began to move slowly towards Eric. Each fraction of a centimetre closer he got, it was like a realisation being brought personally, without words, from Perrin to Eric, from Eric to Perrin, from Perrin to Eric.

Eric wanted to rise to his feet, he wanted to open his arms wide and put Perrin within them and hug him forever, till he could recover, get all right. The words were already forming in his mind, angry and furious: we will fight this bloody thing, it can't be allowed to win, *it won't, we won't let it*.

Yet already Perrin had raised his face to Eric's, as if he wished to intimate to him that he could sustain no thought, so deafened was he by the vast explosion which had, the day before, in a quiet doctor's room, blown away everything he believed in and held dear to his life.

So it was, in the pub, in the last weeks before its demolition, before the farewell party which everyone confidently expected to be halcyon, Perrin did what he would never have done, really, or only when completely drunk: he put his hand out, and Eric, as if by accident, caught it.

Together, they began to hold on.

DAVID WOJNAROWICZ

SELF-PORTRAIT IN TWENTY-THREE ROUNDS

S o my heritage is a calculated fuck on some faraway sun-filled bed while the curtains are being sucked in and out of an open window by a passing breeze. I'd be lying if I were to tell you I could remember the smell of sweat as I hadn't even been born yet. Conception's just a shot in the dark. I'm supposed to be dead right now but I just woke up this dingo motherfucker having hit me across the head with a slab of marble that instead of splitting my head open laid a neat sliver of eyeglass lens through the bull's-eye center of my left eye. We were coming through this four-and-a-half-day torture of little or no sleep. That's the breaks. We were staying at this one drag queen's house but her man did her wrong by being seen by some other queen with a vicious tongue in a darkened lot on the west side fucking some cute little puerto rican boy in the face and when me and my buddy knocked on the door to try and get a mattress to lay down on she sent a bullet through the door thinking it was her man – after three days of no sleep and maybe a couple of stolen donuts my eyes start separating: one goes left and one goes right and after four days of

DAVID WOJNAROWICZ (1954–1992): The author of Close to the Knives *and* Memories that Smell Like Gasoline, *Wojnarowicz was also an admired painter, film maker, sculptor, photographer, and performance artist.* Fever: The Art of David Wojnarowicz, *a catalogue accompanying a posthumous exhibition of his work at the New Museum in New York, was published by Rizzoli in 1998.*

sitting on some stoop on a side street head cradled in my arms seeing four hours of pairs of legs walking by too much traffic noise and junkies trying to rip us off and the sunlight so hot this is a new york summer I feel my brains slowly coming to a boil in whatever red-blue liquid the brains float in and looking down the street or walking around I begin to see large rats the size of shoeboxes; ya see them just outta the corner of your eyes, in the outer sphere of sight and when ya turn sharp to look at them they've just disappeared around the corner or down subway steps and I'm so sick my gums start bleedin' every time I breathe and after the fifth day I start seeing what looks like the limbs of small kids, arms and legs in the mouths of these rats and no screaming mommies or daddies to lend proof to the image, and late last night me and my buddy were walking around with two meat cleavers we stole from Macy's gourmet section stuck in between our belts and dry skin lookin' for someone to mug and some queer on the upper east side tried to pick us up but my buddy's meat cleaver dropped out the back of his pants just as the guy was opening the door to his building and clang clangalang the guy went apeshit his screams bouncing through the night off half a million windows of surrounding apartments we ran thirty blocks till we felt safe. Some nights we had so much hate for the world and each other all these stupid dreams of finding his foster parents who he tried poisoning with a box of rat poison when they let him out of the attic after keeping him locked in there for a month and a half after all dear it's summer vacation and no one will miss you here's a couple of jugs of springwater and cereal don't eat it all at once we're off on a holiday after all it's better this than we return you to that nasty kids home. His parents had sharp taste buds and my buddy spent eight years in some jail for the criminally insane even though he was just a minor. Somehow though he had this idea to find his folks and scam lots of cash off them so we could start a new life. Some nights we'd walk seven or eight hundred blocks practically the whole island of manhattan crisscrossing east and west north and south each on opposite sides of the streets picking up every wino bottle we found and throwing it ten feet into the air so it crash exploded a couple of inches away from the other's feet – on nights that called for it every pane of glass in every phone booth from here to south street would dissolve in a shower of light. We slept good after a night of this in some abandoned car boiler room rooftop or lonely drag queen's palace.

~ ~ ~

If I were to leave this country and never come back or see it again in films or sleep I would still remember a number of different things that sift back in some kind of tidal motion. I remember when I was eight years old I would crawl out the window of my apartment seven stories above the ground and hold on to the ledge with ten scrawny fingers and lower myself out above the sea of cars burning up eighth avenue and hang there like a stupid motherfucker for five minutes at a time testing my own strength dangling I liked the rough texture of the bricks against the tips of my sneakers and when I got tired I'd haul myself back in for a few minutes rest and then climb back out testing testing testing how do I control this how much control do I have how much strength do I have waking up with a mouthful of soot sleeping on these shitty bird-filled rooftops waking up to hard-assed sunlight burning the tops of my eyes and I ain't had much to eat in three days except for the steak we stole from the A&P and cooked in some bum kitchen down on the lower east side the workers were friendly to us that way and we looked clean compared to the others and really I had dirt scabs behind my ears I hadn't washed in months but once in a while in the men's room of a horn and hardart's on forty-second street in between standing around hustling for some red-eyed bastard with a pink face and a wallet full of singles to come up behind me and pinch my ass murmuring something about good times and good times for me was just one fucking night of solid sleep which was impossible I mean in the boiler room of some high-rise the pipes would start clanking and hissing like machine pistons putting together a tunnel under the river from here to jersey and it's only the morning 6:00 a.m. heat piping in to all those people up above our heads and I'm looking like one of them refugees in the back of life magazine only no care packages for me they give me some tickets up at the salvation army for three meals at a soup kitchen where you get a bowl of mucus water and sip rotten potatoes while some guy down the table is losing his eye into his soup he didn't move fast enough on the line and some fucked-up wino they hired as guard popped him in the eye with a bottle and I'm so lacking in those lovely vitamins they put in wonder bread and real family meals that when I puff one drag off my cigarette blood pours out between my teeth sopping into the nonfilter and that buddy of mine complains that he won't smoke it after me and in the horn and hardart's there's a table full of deaf mutes and they're the loudest people in the joint one of them seventy years old takes me to a nearby hotel once a month when his disability check comes in and he has me lay down on my belly and he dry humps me harder and harder and his dick is soft and banging against my ass and his arm is mashing my little face up as he goes through his routine of pretending to come and starts hollering the way only a deaf mute can holler like donkeys braying when snakes come around but somehow in the midst of all that I love him maybe it's the way he returns to his table of friends in the cafeteria a smile busted across his face and I'm the one with the secret and twenty dollars in my pocket and then there's the fetishist who one time years ago picked me up and told me this story of how he used to be in the one platoon in fort dix where they shoved all the idiots and illiterates and poor bastards that thought kinda slow and the ones with speeth spitch speeeeeeech impediments that means you talk funny he said and I nodded one of my silent yeses that I'd give as conversation to anyone with a tongue in those days and every sunday morning this sadistic sonofabitch of a sergeant would come into the barracks and make the guys come out one by one and attempt to publicly read the sunday funnies blondie and dagwood and beetle bailey and dondi with his stupid morals I was glad when some little delinquent punched his face in one sunday and he had a shiner three sundays in a row full color till the strip couldn't get any more mileage out of it and some cop busted the delinquent and put him back in the reform school he escaped from, and all the while those poor slobs are trying to read even one line the sergeant is saying lookit this stupid sonofabitch how the fuck do you expect to serve this country of yours and you can't even read to save your ass and he'd run around the barracks smacking all the guys in the head one after the other and make them force them to laugh at this guy tryin' to read until it was the next guy's turn, and when we got to this guy's place there was three cats pissing all over the joint crusty brown cans of opened cat food littering the floor window open so they could leave by the fire escape and he had this thing for rubber he'd dress me up in this sergeant's outfit but with a pair of rubber sneakers that they made only during world war two when it was important to do that I guess canvas was a material they needed for the war effort or something and anyway so he would have me put on these pure rubber sneakers and the sergeant's outfit and then a rubber trenchcoat and then he'd grease up his dick and he would start fucking another rubber sneaker while on his belly and I'd have to shove my sneaker's sole against his face and tell him to lick the dirt off the bottom of it and all the while cursing at him telling him how stupid he was a fuckin' dingo stupid dog ain't worth catfood where'd you get your fuckin' brains surprised they even let ya past the mp's on the front gate oughta call in the trucks and have you carted off to some idiot farm and where'd you get your brains and where'd you get your brains and when he came into his rubber sneaker he'd roll over all summer sweaty and say oh that was a good load musta ate some eggs today and I'm already removing my uniform and he says he loves the way my skeleton moves underneath my skin when I bend over to retrieve one of my socks.

EDMUND WHITE

REPRISE

A novel I'd written, which had flopped in America, was about to come out in France, and I was racing around, vainly trying to assure its success in translation. French critics seldom give nasty reviews to books, but they often ignore a novel altogether, especially one by a foreign writer, even one who like me lives in Paris.

In the midst of these professional duties I suddenly received a phone call. A stifled baritone voice with a Midwestern accent asked if I was 'Eddie.' No one had called me that since my childhood. 'It's Jim Grady. Your mother gave me your number.'

I hadn't seen him in almost forty years, not since I was fourteen and he twenty, but I could still taste the Luckies and Budweiser beer on his lips, feel his powerful arms closing around me, remember the deliberate way he'd folded his trousers on the crease rather than throwing them on the floor in romantic haste as I'd done.

I met Jim through our parents. My mother was dating his father, an arrangement she'd been falling back on intermittently for years, although

EDMUND WHITE (born 1940): White is one of a handful of living American authors who can genuinely be called a person of letters. He is the author of six novels (a seventh is in the works), biographies of Jean Genet and Marcel Proust, a story collection (Skinned Alive), a volume of non-fiction (The Burning Library), and two books about Paris, where he lived for many years. White is also the editor of The Faber Book of Gay Short Fiction. He lives in New York City and teaches at Princeton University.

she mildly despised him. She went out with him when there was no one better around. She was in her fifties, fat, highly sexed, hardworking, by turns bitter and wildly optimistic (now I'm all those things, so I feel no hesitation in describing her in those terms, especially since she was to change for the better in old age). My father and she had divorced seven years earlier, and she'd gone to work partly out of necessity but partly to make something out of herself. Her Texas relations expected great things from her, and their ambitions had shaped hers.

Before the divorce she'd studied psychology, and now she worked in the Chicago suburban public schools, traveling from one to another, systematically testing all the slow learners, problem cases, and 'exceptional' children ('exceptional' meant either unusually intelligent or retarded). She put great stock in making an attractive, even a stunning appearance at those smelly cinder-block schools and rose early in the morning to apply her make-up, struggle into her girdle, and don dresses or suits that followed the fashions better than the contours of her stubby body.

In the gray, frozen dawns of Chicago winters she would drive her new Buick to remote schools where the assistant principal would install her in an empty classroom and bring her one child after another. Shy, dirty, suspicious kids would eye her warily, wag their legs together in a lackluster parody of sex, fall into dumb trances, or microscopically assay the hard black riches they'd mined from their nostrils, but nothing could dim my mother's glittering determination to be cheerful.

She never merely went through the motions or let a more appropriate depression muffle her performance. She always had the highly colored, fatuously alert look of someone who is listening to compliments. Perhaps she looked that way because she was continuously reciting her own praises to herself as a sort of protective mantra. Most people, I suspect, are given a part in which the dialogue keeps running out, a supporting role for which the lazy playwright has scribbled in, 'Improvise background chatter' or 'Crowd noises off.' But my mother's lines had been fully scored for her (no matter that she'd written them herself), and she couldn't rehearse them often enough. Every night she came home, kicked off her very high heels, and wriggled out of her orthopedically strong girdle, shrinking and filling out and sighing, 'Whooee!' – something her Ranger, Texas, mother would exclaim after feeding the chickens or rustling up some grub in the summer heat.

Then our mother would pour herself a stiff bourbon and water, first of the many highballs she'd need to fuel her through the evening. 'I saw fifteen patients today – twelve Stanford-Binets, one Wexford, one House-Tree-Person. I even gave a Rorschach to a beautiful little epileptic with high potential.' On my mother's lips, 'beautiful' meant not a pretty face but a case of grimly classic textbook orthodoxy. 'The children loved me. Several of them were afraid of me – I guess they'd never seen such a pretty, stylish lady all smiling and perfumed and bangled. But I put them right at ease. I know how to handle those backward children; they're just putty in my hands.'

She thought for a moment, regarding her hands, then lit up. 'The assistant principal was so grateful to me for my fine work. I guess she'd never had such an efficient, skilled state psychologist visit her poor little school before. She accompanied me to my automobile, and boy, you should have seen her eyes light up when she realized I was driving a fine Buick.' Mother slung her stocking feet over the arm of the upholstered chair. 'She grabbed my hand and looked me right in the eye and said, "Who *are* you?"' This was the part of the litany I always hated, because it was so obviously a lie. '"Why, whatever do you mean?" I asked her. "You're no ordinary psychologist," she said. "I can see by your fine automobile and your beautiful clothes and your fine mind and lovely manners that you are a real lady."' It was the phrase 'fine automobile' that tipped me off, since only Southerners like my mother said that. Chicagoans said 'nice car.' Anyway, I'd never heard any Midwesterner praise another in such a gratifying way; only in my mother's scenarios were such heady scenes a regular feature.

As the night wore on and my sister and I would sit down to do our homework on the cleared dining room table, as the winter pipes would knock hypnotically and the lingering smell of fried meat would get into our hair and heavy clothes, our mother would pour herself a fourth high-ball and put on her glasses to grade the tests she'd administered that day or to write up her reports in her round hand, but she'd interrupt her work and ours to say, 'Funny, that woman simply couldn't get over how a fine lady like me could be battling the Skokie slush to come out to see those pitiful children.' The note of pity was introduced only after the fourth drink, and it was, I imagine, something she felt less for her patients than for herself as the telephone stubbornly refused to ring.

At that time in my mother's life she had few friends. Going out with other unmarried women struck her as a disgrace and defeat; she was convinced couples looked down on her as a divorcée, and those single men who might want to date a chubby, penniless middle-aged woman with two brats hanging around her neck were, as she'd say, scarce as hen's teeth.

That's where Mr. Grady came in. He was forty-five, going on sixty, overweight and utterly passive. He, too, liked his drinks, although in his case they were Manhattans; he fished the maraschino cherries out with his fingers. He didn't have false teeth, but there was something weak and sunken around his mouth as he mumbled his chemically bright cherries. His hairless hands were liver-spotted, and the nails were flaky, bluish, and unusually flat, which my mother, drawing on her fragmentary medical knowledge, called 'spatulate,' although I forget which malady this symptom was supposed to indicate. His wife had left him for another man, much richer, but she considerately sent Mr. Grady cash presents from time to time. He needed them. He lived reasonably well, and he didn't earn much. He worked on the city desk of a major Chicago daily, but he'd been there for nearly twenty years, and in that era, before the Newspaper Guild grew strong, American journalists were badly paid unless they were flashy, opinionated columnists. Mr. Grady wrote nothing and had few opinions. He occasionally assigned stories to reporters, but most of the time he filled out columns that ran short with curious scraps of information. These items were called, for some reason, 'boilerplate' and were composed weeks, even months in advance. For all I know, they were bought ready-made from some Central Bureau of Timeless Information. Although Mr. Grady seldom said anything interesting and was much given to dithering over the practical details of his daily life, his work furnished him with the odd bit of startling knowledge.

'Did you realize that Gandhi ate meat just once in his life and nearly died of it?' he'd announce. 'Did you know there is more electric wire in the Radio City Music Hall organ than in the entire city of Plattsburgh?'

He was capable of going inert, like a worm that poses as a stick to escape a bird's detection (I have my own stock of boilerplate). When my mother would hector him for not demanding a raise or for not acting like a man, his face would sink into his jowls, his chin into his chest, his chest into his belly, and the whole would settle lifelessly onto his elephantine legs. His eyes behind their thick glasses would refuse all contact. In that state he could remain nearly indefinitely, until at last my mother's irritation would blow over and she would make a move to head off for Miller's

Steak House, a family restaurant with a menu of sizzling T-bones, butter and rolls, French-fried onions, hot fudge sundaes, that would contribute to Mr. Grady's early death by cardiac arrest.

In September 1954 the Kabuki Theater came from Tokyo to Chicago for the first time, and my mother and Mr. Grady bought tickets for themselves and me and Mr. Grady's son, Jim, whom we had never met (my sister didn't want to go; she thought it sounded 'weird,' and the prospect of meeting an eligible young man upset her).

The minute I saw Jim Grady I became sick with desire – sick because I knew from my mother's psychology textbooks, which I'd secretly consulted, just how pathological my longings were. I had looked up 'homosexuality' and read through the frightening, damning diagnosis and prognosis so many times with an erection that finally, through Pavlovian conditioning, fear instantly triggered excitement, guilt automatically entailed salivating love or lust or both.

Jim was tall and tan and blond, with hair clipped soldier-short and a powerful upper lip that wouldn't stay shaved and always showed a reddish-gold stubble. His small, complicated eyes rapidly changed expression, veering from manly impenetrability to teenage shiftiness. He trudged rather than walked, as though he were shod with horseshoes instead of trim oxford lace-ups. He wore a bow tie, which I usually associated with chipper incompetence but that in Jim's case seemed more like a tourniquet hastily tied around his large, mobile Adam's apple in a makeshift attempt to choke off its pulsing maleness. If his Adam's apple was craggy, his nose was small and thin and well made, his bleached-out eyebrows so blond they shaded off into his tanned forehead, his ears small and neat and red and peeling on top and on the downy lobes.

He seemed eerily unaware of himself – the reason, no doubt, he left his mouth open whenever he wasn't saying 'Yes, ma'am' or 'No, ma'am' to my mother's routine questions, although once he smiled at her with the seductive leer of a lunatic, as though he were imitating someone else. He had allergies or a cold that had descended into his larynx and made his monosyllables sound becomingly stifled – or maybe he always talked that way. He could have been a West Point cadet, so virile and impersonal did his tall body appear, except for that open mouth, those squirming eyes, his fits of borrowed charm.

Someone had dressed him up in a hairy alpaca suit jacket and a cheap white shirt that was so small on him that his red hands hung down out of the cuffs like hams glazed with honey, for the backs of his hands were brushed with gold hair. The shirt, which would have been dingy on anyone less tan, was so thin that his dark chest could be seen breathing through it like a doubt concealed by a wavering smile. He wasn't wearing a T-shirt, which was unusual in those days, even provocative.

Mr. Grady was seated at one end, my mother next to him, then Jim, then me. My mother took off her coat and hat and combed her hair in a feathery, peripheral way designed to leave the deep structure of her permanent intact. 'You certainly got a good tan this summer,' she said.

'Thank you, ma'am.'

His father, heavily seated, said tonelessly, without lifting his face from his chin or his chin from his chest, 'He was working outside all summer on construction, earning money for his first year in med school.'

'Oh, really!' my mother exclaimed, suddenly fascinated by Jim since she had a deep reverence for doctors. I, too, felt a new respect for him as I imagined the white surgical mask covering his full upper lip. 'I want you on your hands and knees,' I could hear him telling me. 'Now bend forward, cross your arms on the table, turn your face to one side, and lay your cheek on the back of your forearm. Arch your back, spread your knees still wider.' He was pulling on rubber gloves, and from my strange, sideways angle I could see him dipping his sheathed finger into the cold lubricant . . .

'Have you chosen a specialty already?' my mother asked as the auditorium lights dimmed.

'Gynecology,' Jim said – and I clamped my knees together with a start.

Then the samisens squealed, kotos thunked dully, and drums kept breaking rank to race forward faster and faster until they fell into silence. A pink spotlight picked out a heavily armored and mascaraed warrior frozen in mid-flight on the runway, but only the scattered Japanese members of the audience knew to applaud him. The program placed a Roman numeral IV beside the actor's name, which lent him a regal importance. Soon Number IV was stomping the stage and declaiming something in an angry gargle, but we hadn't paid for the earphones that would have given us the crucial simultaneous translation, since my mother said she always preferred the Gestalt to the mere details. 'On the Rorschach I always score a very high W,' she had coyly told the uncomprehending and uninterested Mr. Grady earlier over supper. I knew from her frequent elucidations that a high W meant she saw each inkblot as a whole rather than as separate parts and this grasp of the Gestalt revealed her global intelligence, which she regarded as an attribute of capital importance.

A mincing, tittering maiden with a homely powdered white face and an impractical hobble skirt (only later did I read that the performer was a man and the fifth member of his improbable dynasty) suddenly metamorphosed into a sinister white fox. With suicidal daring I pressed my leg against Jim's. First I put my shoe against his, sole planted squarely against sole. Then, having staked out this beachhead, I slowly cantilevered my calf muscles against his, at first just lightly grazing him. I even withdrew for a moment, proof of how completely careless and unintended my movements were, before I sat forward, resting my elbows on my knees in total absorption, leaning attentively into the exotic squealing and cavorting on stage – an intensification of attention that of course forced me to press my slender calf against his massive one, my knobby knee against his square, majestic one.

As two lovers rejoiced or despaired (one couldn't be sure which) and tacky paper blossoms showered them, Jim's leg held fast against mine. He didn't move it away. I stole a glance at his profile, but it told me nothing. I pulsed slightly against his leg but still didn't move away. I rubbed my palms together and felt the calluses that months of harp practice had built up on my fingertips.

If I kept up my assaults would he suddenly and indignantly withdraw, even later make a remark to his father, who would feel obliged to tip off my mother about her son the fairy? I'd already been denounced at the country club where I'd worked as a caddy last summer. While waiting on the benches in the stifling hot caddy house for golfers to arrive, I'd pressed my leg in just this way against that of an older caddy named Mikey, someone who until then had liked shooting the shit with me. Now he stood up and said, 'What the hell are you anyway, some sort of fuckin' Liberace?' He'd tried to pull away several times, but I'd ignored his hints.

This time I'd wait for reciprocal signals. I wouldn't let my desire fool me into seeing mutual longing where only mine existed. I was dreading the intermission because I didn't know if I could disguise my tented crotch or the blush bloom that was slowly drifting up my neck and across my face.

I flexed my calf muscle against Jim's, and he flexed back. We were football players locked into a tight huddle or two wrestlers, each struggling to gain the advantage over the other (an advantage I was only too eager to concede). We were about to pass over the line from accident into intention. Soon he'd be as incriminated as I. Or did he think this dumb show was just a joke, indicative of other intentions, anything but sexual?

I flexed my calf muscles twice, and he signaled back twice; we were establishing a Morse code that was undeniable. On stage, warriors were engaged in choreographed combat, frequently freezing in mid-lunge, and I wondered where we would live, how I would escape my mother, when I could kiss those full lips for the first time.

A smile, antic with a pleasure so new I scarcely dared to trust it, played across my lips. Alone with my thoughts but surrounded by his body, I could imagine a whole long life with him.

When the intermission came at last, our parents beat a hasty retreat to the bar next door, but neither Jim nor I budged. We had no need of highballs or a Manhattan; we already had them and were already in New York or someplace equally magical. The auditorium emptied out. Jim looked at me matter-of-factly as his Adam's apple rose and fell and he said, 'How are we ever going to get a moment alone?'

'Do you have a television set?' I asked (they were still fairly rare).

'Of course not. Dad never has a damn cent; he throws his money away with both hands.'

'Why don't you come over to our place on Saturday to watch the Perry Como show, then drink a few too many beers and say you're too tight to drive home and ask to stay over. The only extra bed is in my room.'

'Okay,' he said in that stifled voice. He seemed startled by my efficient deviousness as much as I was by his compliance. When our much livelier parents returned and the lights went back down, I wedged a hand between our legs and covertly stroked his flexed calf, but he didn't reciprocate and I gave up. We sat there, knee to knee, in a stalemate of lust. I'd been erect so long my penis began to ache and I could see a precome stain seeping through my khakis. I turned bitter at the prospect of waiting three whole days till Saturday. I wanted to pull him into the men's room right now.

Once at home, my mother asked me what I thought of Jim and I said he seemed nice but dumb. When I was alone in bed and able at last to strum my way to release (I thought of myself as the Man with the Blue Guitar), I hit a high note (my chin), higher than I'd ever shot before, and I licked myself clean and floated down into the featherbed luxury of knowing that big tanned body would soon be wrapped around me.

Our apartment was across the street from the beach, and I loved to jump the Lake Michigan waves. Now I'm astonished I enjoyed doing anything that athletic, but then I didn't think of it as sport so much as opera, for just as in listening to 78 records I breasted one soaring outburst after another sung by Lauritz Melchior or Flagstad, in the same way I was thrilled by the repeated crises staged by the lake in September – a menacing crescendo that melted anticlimactically away into a creamy glissando, a minor interval that swelled into a major chord, all of it as abstract, excited, and endless as Wagner's *Ring*, which I'd never bothered to dope out motif by leitmotif since I, too, preferred an ecstatic Gestalt to tediously detailed knowledge. We were careless in my family, careless and addicted to excitement.

Jim Grady called my mother and invited himself over on Saturday evening to watch the Perry Como show on television. He told her he was an absolute fanatic about Como, that he considered Como's least glance or tremolo incomparably cool, and that he specially admired his long-sleeved golfer's sweaters with the low-slung yoke necks, three buttons at the waist, coarse spongy weave, and bright colors. My mother told me about these odd enthusiasms; she was puzzled by them because she thought fashion concerned women alone and that its tyranny even over women extended only to clothes, certainly not to ways of moving, smiling, or singing. 'I wouldn't want to imitate anyone else,' she said with her little mirthless laugh of self-congratulation and a disbelieving shake of her head. 'I like being me just fine, thank you very much.'

'He's not the first young person to swoon over a pop star,' I informed her out of my infinite world-weariness.

'Men don't swoon over men, dear,' Mother reminded me, peering at me over the tops of her glasses. Now that I unscramble the signals she was emitting, I see how contradictory they were. She said she admired the sensitivity of a great dancer such as Nijinsky, and she'd even given me his biography to read to make sure I knew the exact perverse composition of that sensitivity. ('What a tragic life. Of course, he ended up psychotic, with paranoid delusions, a martyr complex, and degenerative ataxia.') She'd assure me just as often, with snapping eyes and carnivorous smile, that she liked men to be men and a boy to be all boy (as who did not), although the hearty heartlessness of making such a declaring to her willowy, cake-baking, harp-playing son thoroughly eluded her. Nor would she have tolerated a real boy's beer brawls, bloody noses, or stormy fugues.

She wanted an obedient little gentleman to sit placidly in a dark suit when he wasn't helping his mother until, at the appropriate moment and with no advance fuss, he would marry a plain Christian girl whose unique vocation would be the perpetual adoration of her *belle-mère*.

At last Jim Grady arrived after our dispirited Saturday night supper, just in time for a slice of my devil's food cake and the Perry Como show. My sister skulked off to her room to polish her hockey stick and read through fan magazine articles on Mercedes McCambridge and Barbara Stanwyck. Jim belted back the six-pack he'd brought along and drew our attention with repulsive connoisseurship to every cool Como mannerism. I now realize that maybe Como was the first singer who'd figured out that the TV lens represented twenty million horny women dateless on Saturday night, and he looked searchingly into its glass eye and warbled with the calm certainty of his seductive charm.

As a homosexual I understood the desire to possess an admired man, but I was almost disgusted by Jim's ambition to imitate him. My mother saw men as nearly faceless extras who surrounded the diva, a woman; I regarded men as the stars; but both she and I were opposed to all forms of masculine self-fabrication, she because she considered it unbecomingly narcissistic, I because it seemed a sacrilegious parody of the innate superiority of a few godlike men. Perhaps I was just jealous that Jim was paying more attention to Como than to me.

Emboldened by beer, Jim called my mother by her first name, which I'm sure she found flattering since it suggested he saw her as a woman rather than as a parent. She drank one of her many highballs with him, sitting beside him on the couch, and for an instant I coldly appraised my own mother as a potential rival, but she lost interest in him when he dared to shush her during a bit of the singer's studied patter. In those days before the veneration of pop culture, unimaginative highbrows such as my mother and I swooned over opera, foreign films of any sort, and 'problem plays' such as *The Immoralist* and *Tea and Sympathy*, but we were guiltily drawn to television in spite of ourselves with a mindless, vegetable-like tropism best named by the vogue word of the period, 'apathy.' We thought it beneath us to study mere entertainment.

Jim was so masculine in the way he held his Luckies cupped between his thumb and middle finger and kept another, unlit cigarette behind his ear, he was so inexpressive, so devoid of all gesture, that when he stood up to go, shook his head like a wet dog, and said, 'Damn! I've had one too many for the road,' he was utterly convincing. My mother said, 'Do you want me to drive you home?' Jim laughed insultingly and said, 'I think you're feeling no pain yourself. I'd better stay over, Delilah, if you have an extra bed.'

My mother was much more reluctant to put Jim up than I'd anticipated. 'I don't know, I could put my girdle back on . . .' Had she picked up the faint sex signal winking back and forth between her son and Jim? Or was she afraid he might sneak into her bedroom after lights-out? Perhaps she worried how it might look to Mr. Grady – drunk son spends night in lakeside apartment, and such a son, the human species at its peak of physical fitness, mouth open, eyes shifting, Adam's apple working.

At last we were alone, and operatically I shed my clothes in a puddle at my feet, but Jim, undressing methodically, whispered, 'You should hang your clothes up, or your mother might think we were up to some sort of monkey business.' Hot tears sprang to my eyes, but they dried as I looked at the long torso being revealed, with its small, turned waist and the wispy hairs around the tiny brown nipples like champagne grapes left to wither on a vine gone pale. His legs were pale because he'd worn jeans on the construction site, but he must have worn them low. For an instant he sat down to pull off his heavy white socks, and his shoulder muscles played under the overhead light with all the demonic action of a Swiss music box, the big kind with its works under glass.

He lay back with a heavy-lidded cool expression I suspected was patterned on Como's, but I didn't care; I was even pleased he wanted to impress me as I scaled his body, felt his great warm arms close over me, as I tasted the Luckies and Bud on his lips, as I saw the sharp focus in his eyes fade into a blur. 'Hey,' he whispered, and he smiled at me as his hands cupped my twenty-six-inch waist and my hot penis planted its flag on the stony land of his perfect body. 'Hey,' he said, hitching me higher and deeper into his presence.

Soon after that I came down with mononucleosis, the popular 'kissing disease' of the time, although I'd kissed almost no one but Jim. I was tired and depressed. I dragged myself with difficulty from couch to bed, but at the same time I was so lonely and frustrated that I looked down from the window at every man or boy walking past and willed him to look up, see me, join me, but the will was weak.

Jim called one afternoon and we figured out he could come by the next evening, when my mother was going somewhere with my sister. I warned him he could catch mono if he kissed me, but I was proud that after all he did kiss me, long and deep. Until now the people I'd had sex with were boys at camp who pretended to hypnotize each other or married men who cruised the Howard Street Elevated toilets and drove me down to the beach in a station wagon filled with their children's toys. Jim was the first man who took off his clothes, held me in his arms, looked me in the eye, and said, 'Hey.' He who seemed so stiff and ill at ease otherwise became fluent in bed.

I was bursting with my secret, all the more so because mononucleosis had reduced my world to the size of our apartment and the books I was almost too weak to hold (that afternoon it had been Oscar Wilde's *Lady Windermere's Fan*). In the evening my mother was washing dishes and I was drying, but I kept sitting down to rest. She said, 'Mr. Grady and I are thinking of getting married.' The words just popped out of my mouth: 'Then it will have to be a double wedding.' My brilliant repartee provoked not a laugh but an inquisition, which had many consequences for me over the years, both good and bad. The whole story of my homosexual adventures came out, my father was informed, I was sent off to boarding school and a psychiatrist – my entire life changed.

My mother called up Jim Grady and boozily denounced him as a pervert and a child molester, although I'd assured her I'd been the one to seduce him. I never saw him again until almost forty years later in Paris. My mother, who'd become tiny, wise, and sober with age, had had several decades to get used to the idea of my homosexuality (and my sister's, as it turned out). She had run into Jim Grady twice in the last three years; she'd warned me he'd become maniacally stingy, to the point that he'd wriggle out of a drinks date if he thought he'd have to pay.

And yet when he rang me up from London, where he was attending a medical conference, he didn't object when I proposed to book him into the pricey hotel next door to me on the Île St. Louis.

He called from his hotel room and I rushed over. He was nearly sixty years old, with thin gray hair, clear glasses frames he'd mended with black electrician's tape, ancient Corfam shoes, an open mouth, a stifled voice. We shook hands, but a moment later he'd pulled me into his arms. He said he knew, from a magazine interview I'd given, that this time I was infected with a virus far more dangerous than mononucleosis, but he kissed me long and deep, and a moment later we were undressed.

Over the next four days with him I had time to learn all about his life.

He hadn't become a gynecologist after all but a sports doctor for a Catholic boys' school, and he spent his days bandaging the bruised and broken bodies of teenage athletes. His best friend was a fat priest nicknamed 'The Whale,' and they frequently got drunk with one of Jim's soldier friends, who'd married a real honey, a little Chinese gal. Jim owned his own house. He'd always lived alone and seemed never to have had a lover. His father had died from an early heart attack, but Jim felt nothing but scorn for him and his spendthrift ways. Jim himself had a tricky heart, and he was trying to give a shape to his life. He was about to retire.

It was true he'd become a miser. He bought his acrylic shirts and socks in packs of ten. His glasses came from public welfare. At home he went to bed at sunset to save on electricity. We spent hours looking for prints that would cost less than five dollars, as presents for The Whale, the army buddy, and the Chinese gal. He wouldn't even let me invite him to a good restaurant. We were condemned to eating at the Maubert Self, a cafeteria, or nibbling on cheese and apples we'd bought at the basement supermarket next to the Métro St. Paul. He explained his economies to me in detail. Proudly he told me he was a millionaire several times over and that he was leaving his fortune to the Catholic Church, although he was an atheist.

I took him with me to my literary parties and introduced him as my cousin. He sat stolidly by like an old faithful dog as people said brilliant, cutting things in French, a language he did not know. He sent every hostess who'd received us a thank-you letter, which in English was once so common it's still known as a 'bread-and-butter note,' although in French it was always so sufficiently rare as to be called a *lettre de château*. The same women who'd ignored him when he sat at their tables were retrospectively impressed by his New World courtliness.

During his trip to Paris I slept with him just that first time in his hotel room, but then, as we kissed, he removed his smudged, taped welfare glasses and revealed his darting young blue eyes. He undressed my sagging body and embraced my thirty-six-inch waist and bared his own body, considerably slimmer but just as much a ruin with its warts and wattles and long white hair. And yet, when he hitched me into his embrace and said, 'Hey,' I felt fourteen again. 'You were a moron to tell your mom everything about us,' he said. 'You made us lose a lot of time.' And if we had spent a life together, I wondered, would we each be a bit less deformed now?

As his hands stroked my arms and belly and buttocks, everything the years had worn down or undone, I could hear an accelerating drum and see, floating just above the rented bed, our young, feverish bodies rejoicing or lamenting, one couldn't be sure which. The time he'd come over when I had mono ('glandular fever,' as the English call it), my hot body had ached and shivered beside his. Now each time I touched him I could hear music, as though a jolt had started the clockwork after so many years. We watched the toothed cylinder turn under glass and strum the long silver notes.

A. M. HOMES

THE WHIZ KIDS

In the big bathtub in my parents' bedroom, he ran his tongue along my side, up into my armpits, tugging the hair with his teeth. 'We're like married,' he said, licking my nipples.

I spit at him. A foamy blob landed on his bare chest. He smiled, grabbed both my arms, and held them down.

He slid his face down my stomach, dipped it under the water, and put his mouth over my cock.

My mother knocked on the bathroom door. 'I have to get ready. Your father and I are leaving in twenty minutes.'

Air bubbles crept up to the surface.

'Can you hear me?' she said, fiddling with the knob. 'Why is the door locked? You know we don't lock doors in this house.'

'It was an accident,' I said, through the door.

'Well, hurry,' my mother said.

And we did.

Later, in the den, picking his nose, examining the results on his finger,

---

A. M. HOMES *(born 1961): Despite her ambiguous moniker and flair for writing with great accuracy from the vantage point of adolescent boys, Homes is in fact a woman. Her works include the story collections* The Safety of Objects *(made into a film directed by Rose Troche) and* Things You Should Know *and the novels* Jack, In a Country of Mothers, The End of Alice, *and* Music for Torching.

slipping his finger into his mouth with a smack and a pop, he explained that as long as we never slept with anyone else, we could do whatever we wanted. 'Sex kills,' he said, 'but this,' he said, 'this is the one time, the only time, the chance of a life time.' He ground his front teeth on the booger.

We met in science class. 'Cocksucker,' he hissed. My fingers were in my ears. I didn't hear the word, so much as see it escape his mouth.

~ ~ ~

The fire alarm was going off. Everyone was grabbing their coats and hurrying for the door. He held me back, pressed his lips close to my ear, and said it again, Cocksucker, his tongue touching my neck. Back and forth, he shook a beaker of a strange potion and threatened to make me drink it. He raised the glass to my mouth. My jaws clamped shut. With his free hand, he pinched my nostrils shut and laughed like a maniac. My mouth fell open. He tilted the beaker toward my throat. The teacher stopped him just in time. 'Enough horsing around,' she said. 'This is a fire drill. Behave accordingly.'

'Got ya,' he said, pushing me into the hall and toward the steps, his hard-on rubbing against me the whole way down.

My mother came in, stood in front of the television set, her ass in Peter Jennings's face, and asked, 'How do I look?'

He curled his lip and spit a pistachio shell onto the coffee table.

'Remember to clean up,' my mother said.

'I want you to fuck me,' he said, while my father was in the next room, looking for his keys.

'Have you seen them?' my father asked.

'No,' I said.

'I want your Oscar Mayer in my bun,' he said.

He lived miles away, had gone to a different elementary school, was a different religion, wasn't circumcised.

My father poked his head into the room, jiggled his keys in the air, and said, 'Got 'em.'

'Great tie,' I said.

My father tweaked his bow tie. 'Bye, guys.'

The front door closed, the lock turned. My father's white Chrysler slid into the street.

'I want you to give it to me good.'

'I want to watch *Jeopardy*,' I said, going for the remote control.

'Ever tasted a dick infusion?' he asked, sipping from my glass of Dr Pepper.

He unzipped his fly, fished out his dick, and dropped it into the glass. The ice cubes melted, cracking the way they do when you pour in something hot. A minute later, he put his dick away, swirled the soda around, and offered me a sip.

'Maybe later,' I said, focusing on the audio daily double. '"Tie a Yellow Ribbon."'

'I'm bored,' he said.

'Play along,' I said. 'I've already got nine thousand dollars.'

He went to the bookcase and started handling the family photos. 'Wonder if he ever sucked a cock,' he said, picking up a portrait of my father.

'Don't be a butt plug.'

He smiled. 'I love you,' he said, raising his T-shirt, pulling it off over his head.

Dark hair rose in a fishbone up and out of his jeans.

I turned off the television.

'We need something,' he said, as I led him down the hall toward my room.

'Something what?'

'Slippery.'

I ducked into the bathroom, opened the cabinet, and grabbed a tube of Neosporin.

'Brilliant,' he said. 'An antibiotic lube job, fights infection while you're having fun.'

Piece by piece I undressed with him, after him. He peeled off his socks, I peeled off mine. He unzipped his jeans and I undid mine. He slipped his fingers into the band of his underwear, snapped the elastic, and grinned. I pulled mine down. He slipped the tube of ointment into my ass, pinched my nipples, and sank his teeth deep into the muscle above my collarbone.

My parents got back just after midnight. 'It was so nice of you to spend the evening,' my mother said. 'I just hate to leave you-know-who home alone. I think he gets depressed.'

'Whatever,' he said, shrugging, leaving with my father, who was giving him a ride home.

'You don't have to come with us,' my father said to me. 'It's late. Go to bed.'

'See you in school tomorrow,' I said.

'Whatever.'

A week later he sat in my desk chair, jerking off, with the door open.

'Stop,' I said. 'Or close the door.'

'Danger excites me.'

'My mother isn't dangerous,' I said, getting up and closing the door myself.

'What we've got here,' he said, still jerking, 'is virgin sperm. People will pay a load for this shit.' He laughed at himself. 'Get it – pay a load.' Come shot into the air and landed on the glass of my fish tank.

'Very funny,' I said. I was working out an algebra problem on my bed. He came over to me, dropped his pants, and put his butt in my face. 'Your luck, I haven't used it for anything except a couple of farts all day. Lick it,' he said, bending over, holding his cheeks apart. It was smelly and permanently stained. His testicles hung loose and low, and I took them in my hand, rolling them like Bogart's *Caine Mutiny* balls. 'Get in,' he said. I buried my face there, tickled his asshole with the tip of my tongue and made him laugh.

Saturday, on her way to the grocery store, my mother dropped us off at the park. 'Shall I come back for you when I'm finished?' she asked.

'No,' he said, flatly.

'No, thanks,' I said. 'We'll find our way.'

'Ever fuck a girl?' he asked, as we cut across the grass, past the playground, past the baseball fields and toward the woods.

'No.'

'Ever want to?'

'No.'

'Wanna watch?' he said, taking me to a picnic table, where a girl I recognized from school was standing, arms crossed in front of her chest. 'It's twelve-thirty, you're late,' she said. The girl looked at me and blinked. 'Oh, hi. We're in history together, right?'

I nodded and looked at my shoes.

'Miss me?' he asked, kissing the girl's neck, hard.

My eyes hyperfocused and zeroed in on his lips, on her skin, on the feathery blond hair at the base of her skull. When he pulled away, the hair was wet, the skin was purple and red. There were teeth marks.

She stood in the clearing, eyes closed. He reached for her hand and led her into the woods. I followed, keeping a certain distance between them and me.

In the trees, he pulled his T-shirt off over his head. She ran her fingernails slowly up and down the fishbone of fur sticking out of his Levi's. He tugged at the top of her jeans.

'Take 'em off,' he said, in a familiar and desperate voice.

'Who do you think you're kidding,' she said.

'Show me yours,' he said, rubbing the front of his Levi's with an open palm, 'and I'll show you mine.'

'That's okay, thanks,' she said, backing away.

He went toward her, she stepped back again. He stuck his leg behind her, tripping her. She fell to the ground. He stepped on her open palms, holding her down with his Nikes.

'This isn't funny,' she said.

He laughed.

He unzipped his pants and peed on her. She screamed, and he aimed the river at her mouth. Her lips sealed and her head turned away. Torrent released, he shook it off on her, put it away, and stepped from her hands.

She raised herself. Urine ran down her cheeks, onto her blouse, down her blouse and into her jeans. Arms spread, faces twisted, together she and I ran out of the woods, screaming as though doused in gasoline, as though afire.

CHRISTOPHER COE

GENTLEMEN CAN WASH THEIR HANDS IN THE GENTS'

The day after I am arrested, my father invites me to lunch. He called this morning, first thing, at ten-thirty. I was in bed and had no plans not to be. This isn't a school day, not that it would matter if it were. I told my father, 'Daddy, I don't eat lunch, I never eat lunch, I despise lunch.'

He said he doesn't give a good goddamn if I eat or not, just be there at one o'clock sharp. He hung up before I could argue.

~ ~ ~

I was arrested in the library, the public one. Now we are in this private one, the library of my father's club, and my father orders me a Dubonnet. This is the first time I have been to my father's club since I've been old enough to have a drink. I'm not talking legal age, which I have yet to reach. I am talking about my father's laws. According to my father, I am of age for a Dubonnet. This is to be the kind of lunch at which the father will order the son a Dubonnet. This will be the kind of lunch where the son enters languidly forty-five minutes late, blows smoke at the father, and looks sullen.

CHRISTOPHER COE (1953–1994): Coe was the author of the novels I Look Divine *and* Such Times *– one of the fiercest and most powerful literary responses to AIDS (from which he died) ever published.*

It will be that kind of lunch, because today I am going to be that kind of son. Today I will be the son with the short fuse, who looks sullen and goes as far as he can to be the kind of son no father wants.

As poses go, sullen comes naturally.

My father's pose is not posing. He is a master of the pose that doesn't show. He heard of my arrest from my mother; now he is being unflappable.

My mother could not wait to tell him about it. She is one of those bothersome women who don't know what they're going to say until they say it. She was on the phone to my father, straight from the precinct. She spoke to him before she spoke to me. My mother loves having a reason to call my father. She doesn't need any particular reason, though lately I have given her a few.

To my mother, to my father, the library episode is the worst one yet. It's not the worst at all, really, but it's the one my father will hate; for him it will be the worst. When I stole a horse at the beach and kept it overnight, my father said it was just a natural, boyish thing to do. The man whose horse it was admitted the animal hadn't been abused. To the contrary, I fed that horse not only carrots but raw asparagus; it declined, with quiet, equine disdain, a six-pound Porterhouse.

I burned a deserted beach house, but my father never questioned me about it. No one could prove I'd set the fire, and my father never brought it up. The house did not burn *down*. A few windows gave in to the heat, that was all. Maybe a rug or two were charred, but no one died, because the house was deserted.

Life went on after the deserted house. I'm not sure how it will go on after the library. I haven't told the bad part yet, the part my father will hate. Here it is. Yesterday, when I was in the library, I wasn't arrested in the open stacks. Where I was when I was arrested is what my father calls the 'gents'.'

I call it the little boys', sometimes the powder room; I seldom call it the men's. My grandfather used to call it the 'can,' which is what I'd call it, if that didn't have so much the ring of my grandfather.

The 'gents',' the 'little boys',' the 'can,' call it what you will – it's where I was when the policeman kicked open the stall. It wasn't as bad as it sounds, but no one is going to believe my version. My mother didn't believe me. Neither will my father. That's why I don't know how life will go on after this lunch.

The 'gents'' is the reason for this lunch.

So is the 'little boys'.'

~ ~ ~

At the table, so far, life goes on. My father doesn't shout. This is his club. He has to come here again, so he doesn't say what the policeman did. My father does not speak of 'lewd and disorderly conduct,' and he does not use the prissy gerund of the verb 'to loiter.' For a while the only words my father says are 'calves' liver.' He says them to the waiter, says his son will have calves' liver, and without consulting me, he tells the waiter I will have it rare.

Actually, I won't have calves' liver, and I will not have it rare. I will blow smoke at my father, I'll look sullen, and I am not going to eat one bite at this lunch.

The truth is it wasn't so lewd. It wasn't even disorderly. In fact, as such things go, it was so damned orderly it was downright impeccable.

My father does not say disorderly conduct, but he does say that there is no need to hold a cigarette so flamboyantly. There is no need whatever, my father tells me, to be flamboyant now. I want another Dubonnet.

As a matter of fact, I'm not being flamboyant. I am being sullen. If my father thinks *this* is flamboyant, he should have seen me yesterday in the gents'.

It wasn't as though the fellow was someone I just picked up at the card catalogue. I'd known Pierre for more than a year. I'd noticed him at a place across the river where, every Friday evening, men and women go to folk-dance. I noticed Pierre in the dance where the men break from a circle of women and form inside it a circle of their own. They bear down with their arms upon each other's shoulders, and when the music cues them to, they all squat quickly on their haunches, touch knees to the floor, and, on cue, rise again in unison.

This dance was new to me, and I watched it with some curiosity, though the only part of it worth watching was Pierre. He was hard-boned handsome, had purposeful loins and the body of what I call a man.

When the dance was repeated, I joined the circle, just opposite Pierre. He looked at me as much as I did at him, which was exactly what I wanted. I managed to be at the bus stop the same time as he, and as we waited together we said a few words. The bus came; no one was on it. We sat together in the back, as though every other seat were taken. Our shoulders pressed together as they would have if we had been the last two men on earth.

I learned quickly that Pierre was from Monterey, California, was twenty-six, and had worked on fishing boats or in the cannery or in gas stations all his life, until he read *On the Road* and decided that drifting was the noble way to live.

He was living in a transient hotel, in a part of town I'd been driven through only to get to the airport. Pierre didn't have the money to live at the Y, though he told me he went there every day to lift weights. He didn't need to tell me he lifted weights. He said he lived on protein, which was another thing he didn't need to tell me. We walked to his hotel. He didn't invite me to his room, and I couldn't tell if I was too young for him or if he was ashamed of living where he did.

The next day I joined the Y. I didn't lift any weights, but I went every day unfailingly, and after swimming thirty laps I'd always detour through the weight room on the way to the showers. I had rehearsed at least five hundred times how surprised I'd be to see him, and in doing this I learned how many different inflections can be affixed to the greeting 'Hello.'

When I finally saw Pierre, not one of these inflections helped me at all.

We left together that day, but only after Pierre had made a point of not taking a shower. He said he didn't want me to see him naked. What he said was, 'I don't want you to see my penis.'

It was my reflex to say 'Perish the thought.' In truth, I could handle the thought. What I'd meant was perish the *word*.

Pierre looked at me in surprise.

What I said was that I didn't want to see anything that goes by that name. As soon as I'd said this, I knew it hadn't made the impression I'd wanted, and for a minute I was afraid this pillar of manly pulchritude would ditch me for being a word snob. He didn't, though. What he did was buy me freshly pressed carrot juice and advise me never to eat raisins or any dried fruit that has been treated with sulfur dioxide. He said that people who eat food with preservatives might just as well be drinking embalming fluid. I liked the carrot juice. I liked that he had bought it for me. It tasted like romance.

This time he did invite me to his room and then went about doing things as I imagined he would if I hadn't been there. He took off his socks but nothing else, tuned in a radio station that played songs from the sixties, and slapped a thick slab of beef liver onto a hot plate. He said that beef liver, cooked just until it's hot, is the best source of protein. He meant, I knew, animal protein. I stopped myself from saying that I'd rather be anemic than eat anything that smelled so alive.

Pierre sat cross-legged on the bed, eating the liver in big chunks, chewing thoroughly as he flipped through a fitness magazine. On the floor by the bed I saw a battered paperback he'd checked out from the library. I picked it up and turned to the index. The book was *Kiss, Kiss, Bang, Bang* by Pauline Kael, and it had just about the best index I had ever seen. There were seven entries for Elizabeth Taylor alone.

Pierre finished the liver and asked me if I wanted to take off my shoes. I did and sat at the foot of the bed.

'Come here,' he said.

'Where?' I asked. It scared me how much I wanted to do what he said.

'Here,' he said, and pointed to himself. 'I didn't want this to happen,' and when he said this, I believed him. He hesitated a second or so, as though seeking the clearest word, and then said, 'I'm sort of bisexual, and I like you more than I wanted to.'

I thought, This is it. I will now either melt or explode.

I'd always thought that when people liked each other the way Pierre was talking about, the first thing they did was pull each other out of their clothes, but I wasn't going to be the one to begin.

I didn't know what we could do without his giving me a look, then I remembered something I'd read about Jewish men cutting holes in sheets in order to have at their wives. This was not, thank God, what Pierre had in mind. Everything we did for the next two hours we did with our clothes on, but Pierre laid down no restrictions as to what we could do with our hands. It was with my hands, then, that I could ascertain that there was nothing whatever inadequate about any part of Pierre. I was certain that I would soon know this with my eyes.

The next day and the day after, Pierre wasn't at the Y. I spent every day that week leaning against parked cars across the street from his hotel. I'd walk around the block, hoping we'd collide. It was two weeks before I learned that Pierre had taken his hot plate and vanished. The man at the hotel told me, without my asking, that Pierre had paid his bill to the end of the week. I was glad he told me that.

The longer I thought about it, the more it struck me that Pierre's disappearance was inevitable. Pierre was a prince in disguise and could not stay long in one place. I did wonder every day, constantly, what it was that he didn't like about his body.

I hate untidy endings. I hate tidy endings. I hate endings.

It was a year later that I saw Pierre upstairs in the library. He was at the other end of the great two-story reading room, sitting at a long table with a stack of atlases. He looked up at the exact instant I saw him, and without any readable expression he rose from his chair and came all the way across the room to me. He seized my hand and pulled me from the room without any discretion whatever. He pulled me down the wide marble stairs, and with my hand in his he led me, all this without a word, into the gents'. No one was in it – the library had just opened – and he pushed me into the stall, locked the door, and grabbed me around my waist. He pressed himself against me, front to front, and forced his tongue into my mouth. I reached between us and grabbed a handful of him. I didn't care about seeing it; I only wanted to contain it.

I thought it was all going to happen there, and I knew then as clearly as I ever will that it is not without reason that so much of the world fears and hates this, opposes it and calls it wrong and worse than wrong, and the reason is that so few people ever get to have it, even for an instant.

Pierre was going to show me, and I was just about to see, when an ugly-sounding voice rose out of hell, accompanied by black ugly boots, and told us the fun was over.

'Beat it, buddy,' Pierre said to the outsider.

I didn't want the intruder to see my eyes. 'Can't you please just go away for a minute?' I asked.

The policeman's answer was to kick in the door. I knew that all this policeman cared about was his quota. I also knew this was the last time I'd see Pierre.

~ ~ ~

Maybe it was a little lewd, but it was nowhere near as lewd as it could have been. For an instant, there was potential.

What my father says about lewd conduct, a phrase he doesn't use, what he says about loitering, a word he doesn't use, what he says about the gents', instead of anything else, is that nothing needs be uncivilized.

My father says, 'You have an allowance. Don't you have an allowance?'

I concede that I have an allowance.

'You can afford a hotel,' my father says. 'Can't you afford a hotel?'

He's right, of course, in his way. I signal the waiter for another Dubonnet and admit that I could have taken the fellow to a hotel. I call Pierre 'the fellow' rather than kill my father more with the fact that Pierre was more to me than a fellow. Pierre was a man who had wanted me enough to take a risk. My father would say something moronic about what a sissy name Pierre is, and I would have to hate him for that. I dislike my father enough. I don't want to hate him.

I knew it would be less than prudent to tell my father that I hadn't wanted to take Pierre to a hotel, that what I'd wanted was to take him in hand. I didn't even get to do that, to take Pierre in hand. We hadn't reached a point where safety would have been an issue.

I'm not sure it would have been one if we had.

'A hotel would have been better,' my father says. 'Wouldn't a hotel have been better than the gents'?'

Better for *what* is not a question to raise.

'I want to know,' my father says, 'what would make you do this thing. Why in the library, of all places, why in the gents'.'

'What can I tell you, Daddy?' I ask. 'Can I tell you that I did it in the library because the library is where I was? Can I tell you that I happened to be in the neighborhood? What do you want to hear?'

My father says quietly that all he wants to hear is my answer.

'Daddy, why would I pay a hotel for what can be done in five minutes in the gents'?'

'Maybe to keep the police out of your hair,' my father answers, and I do have to admit this is a sensible reply. 'And to be civilized. To be comfortable. In a hotel, you can be a civilized man. You can lie on clean sheets, you can take a shower, you can clean up.'

I assume my father means clean up *after*, although he could just as easily mean before. I do not point out to my father that in a hotel you can also get a shirt pressed, order room service, drink too much, make conversation, take a fucking bubble bath, and in no time at all forget what it is you are there for.

You do not forget in the gents', but this is one other thing I do not tell my father today.

'Good God,' my father groans. 'In a hotel you can excuse yourself. In a hotel, you can wash your hands.'

This is not the time to point out to my father that gentlemen can wash their hands in the gents'.

~ ~ ~

This is a place to be sullen, this club. I look around the dining room, at all the fathers and sons. Some of the sons are my father's age.

You don't need to know much to know that every table has a problem. Every table has a reason for lunch. Since when have fathers and sons had lunch because they want to? No one here wants lunch; no one has an appetite here.

I know some of the sons, a few of the fathers. In a corner I see a son, a young man about my age. Half the men in the room must know what this son did a year or so ago, just as a few men here today have probably heard some version of what happened yesterday in the gents', the men's, the little boys'. What the son in the corner did makes lewd and disorderly conduct sound like a prayer meeting, especially lewd and disorderly conduct without so much as a nipple exposed. And the son in the corner isn't the worst. This room is full of more disappointing, more heartbreaking sons, much worse sons than he, worse than I, and my father should know this, should know that some of these sons are worse than any son he could ever have produced.

Most of the time I don't think this way, but today I'm thinking that there is never a time when you could not be worse than you are.

My father tells me again not to hold my cigarette flamboyantly. Where have I learned my gestures, my father wants to know. He thinks he can ask me a question like this. What the hell does he expect, Steve fucking McQueen?

Some things are easy to ignore. All you have to do is ignore them. I wish this lunch were one of them.

Another thing I don't say to my father, although it is what I'm thinking, is that he was the one who wanted this lunch, and I will give it to him.

And now, God help me, here comes the liver. The waiter carries it aloft, through the swinging door. There is no mistaking what it is. It's coming right at me, across the room, and I can tell from here how rare it's going to be.

My father wanted this lunch. He can have it with the kind of son whose disorderly conduct is failed and prim. He can have his lunch with a son who has learned his gestures from where it's none of his business.

He can have this lunch with a son who strikes a sullen pose, strikes a flamboyant one, and then offers a pose both sullen and flamboyant at once.

At least *my* poses show. I cut into the liver, only for a look. It's so rare it doesn't even bleed.

My father invited me to this lunch. Now he can have it with the worst son he could have.

JOHN UPDIKE

SCENES FROM THE FIFTIES

Yes. Time does pass. The other day I read that Harold 'Doc' Humes had died. I knew Doc slightly; hundreds of people did. He was a writer and conversationalist famous, or bucking for fame, in the Fifties – a short man with a merry, thin-skinned face and more intellectual energy and love of life than a writer needs, perhaps. He had published a long novel, *The Underground City*, in 1957, and then, in 1959, a shorter one, *Men Die*. That title, described by a friend of mine at the time as 'bald and bad,' was not untrue, as his own death shows. The last time I saw him he was playing chess with Marcel Duchamp at the party that sealed my departure from New York City.

It was 1959, and my vision of the moment seems now very time-specific – this living relic of High Modernism seated at a chessboard like some surreal raft upon which he had washed up on the breadfruit island of Eisenhower's America. Around him, dozens of artistic aspirants and operators drank and nibbled and chattered, hungrily circling in search of the immortality Duchamp already enjoyed. Art was big in the Fifties. We

JOHN UPDIKE (born 1932): This distinguished American writer is most famous for his chronicling of heterosexual marriage and its discontents – happens to be the author of one of the great gay short stories. 'Scenes from the Fifties' was first published as a limited edition chapbook on the occasion of Penguin's sixtieth anniversary and subsequently included in the collection Licks of Love.

were full of peacetime's rarefied ambitions and uncurtailed egos. I, who have become a silver-haired antique-dealer in Boston, picture that party – held in the high-ceilinged duplex of an art-patronizing couple called Berman – as a display window organized around its most precious ware, the inventor of the descending nude and some other deathless, celebrated trinkets of ironic disaffection. Duchamp was a handsome man, ascetically slender, with an anvil-shaped head. He might have been wearing socks and sandals. There certainly were a pipe, large and hairy ears, and a silk foulard.

I remember wondering if Doc's chess was up to this. 'Howie, hi,' Doc said to me affably. 'You probably know Marcel.'

'*Of* him, of course,' I said. As I shook both men's hands, I made a youthfully conceited, slyly ostentatious attempt to appraise their positions. In my agitated celebrity-consciousness the board looked like a jumble. I did have the decency to move away quickly, genuinely regretting any disturbance that holding out his hand to me had wrought in the great man's cogitations. The popular journals, which in the Fifties still devoted considerable space to the arts, had reported how Duchamp, elegantly disdaining to create any more art, was concentrating his powers, for the remainder of his life, on chess, much as Rimbaud abandoned poetry for gun-smuggling. I could not believe Doc was giving him much of a game, but had to admire the way my bumptious contemporary had thrust himself forward into the radius of greatness and was cheerfully basking there.

The Paris Review, of which Humes had been a founder, reported in its fond obituary that his own abstention, after his two novels, from artistic practice had stemmed from a supposed run-in, in the early Sixties, with British intelligence, which had implanted in one of his teeth a microscopic radio device that rendered him painfully, obsessively privy to the secrets and subtle clangor of the Cold War. The CIA and KGB had both, he thought, bugged his room, and he would sit swivelling his head to address first one and then the other of the hidden microphones, narrowly averting, with his remarks, an impending cataclysm. He spoke of a black box, called Fido, sent aloft by MIT engineers, which broadcast warnings that only he could interpret. He grew a gauzy big beard, I see on the obituary photograph. He ceased to write. The low thrum of global anxiety became for Doc a deafening static; he was as much a martyr to Cold War tensions as, say, Gary Powers.

Myself, nothing bores me more than conspiracy theories, international espionage, or novels in the portentous paranoid mode. For me, the long stretch of history between Churchill's Iron Curtain speech and the fall of the Berlin Wall, containing most of my adult life, was a blessed interim, a Metternichian remission of the usual savageries – which have been, I notice, resumed. The Cold War deprived men of the infernal heroic options. I deal in antiques, on Charles Street, with a longtime partner, and the peace of my fragilely loaded shop is what I gratefully owe to the atom bomb, the Marshall Plan, the SAC, and Soviet tanks. Believe it or not; readers of the year 2000, the 1950s were a sweet time of self-seeking, brimming, like my shop, with daily expectancy and quiet value.

In New York, Abstract Expressionism was happening, Pop was about to happen, and my wife and I, who had met in art school, were on the verge of happening, or so we felt for three years. It was as if we gave a party and no one came. We had the loft, the devotion and asceticism, the paints, brushes, canvases, and welding equipment (I painted, she sculpted) – everything, in short, but the patrons, the audience, the profit. We had, in one of our few sexual successes, added a female infant to our baggage, and in a drastic attempt to lighten our expenses had moved to a seaside hamlet north of Boston, where once-thriving boat yards building wooden clipper ships had dwindled to a row of clam shacks and, along the hamlet's central causeway, a kind of perpetual yard sale. Here, amid magnificent salt marshes and taciturn Yankee yeomen, my wife and I would definitely ripen our talents. In time, in triumph, we would return to New York. I had temporarily returned on this occasion for two days to close out the legal details of our sublease, and to arrange for the shipment of our horribly bulky, sadly unwanted works of art.

It all sounds more dismal than it was. I was twenty-five and felt that virtually all of my life was ahead of me. Just being in the same high-ceilinged room with Marcel Duchamp made everything seem possible and worth any amount of trouble. There was also at the party a woman I imagined I was falling in love with. We talked together a good hour, posing this way and that on the arm of a giant chrome-frame sofa covered in nubbly Haitian cotton. I forget the woman's name but not the tint of her skin, a neutral calm color like that of a plaster cast 'from the antique,' as they called it in art school. She was a Venus de Milo with arms. She wore a low-cut dress of bottle green, in one of those shiny stiff fabrics – taffeta, I suppose – considered sexy in the Fifties. Everything was in place, including my geographical distance from my wife and a nagging, hostile sense of insufficiency that had entered our marriage with its northern move. Yet I couldn't quite deliver the punch, the pass, that might have made this Venus mine for the night. Instead we agreed I would swing by her workplace tomorrow; she was an underling in the newly opened Guggenheim Museum. When I arrived, blushing and baggage-laden, she was out to lunch, the front desk informed me; I wandered up the ramp, looking at the big smeared canvases. Abstraction was getting tired, but there seemed nothing else to do – like the void at the center of Wright's magnificent, hollow temple.

When the lady returned, wearing black stockings and carrying a pocketbook over her shoulder, she waved me into her office, a tiny room in the crammed basement. I sat on a blue canvas director's chair and she perched at her desk, waiting for me to make my move. She knew I was married, and fleeing the city; I had said that much when our intercourse had been lubricated by the party. Now my gears were sticking. We smoked, gingerly talked about the art market, and gossiped about our hosts the night before. She knew Sally Berman well enough to say firmly, 'She is not happy.'

I was startled, and somehow took it personally. 'What should she do about it?'

'That's for her to figure out.'

'Well,' I said lamely, 'I'm sure she will.'

'What's in your little paper bag?' she asked.

'Oh – a toy for my daughter. A toy brush and comb. She's not quite three, and has just learned to brush her hair.'

'She sounds ravishing, Howard. I wonder if I'll ever have a child – they say it's worth it.'

'It's wonderful, but it doesn't solve problems. It *adds* problems.'

She grew a bit more distant at my implication that she had problems. I, her woman's eye could see, was the one with problems. 'Good luck up there,' she said stoutly in parting, like a headmistress wishing me well. 'I hope it's not too lonely.' She had that Manhattan faith that only New York people were real, and the rest were laughable phantoms.

'Oh – there are a few congenial spirits, even up there.'

'How often do you plan to get back to New York?'

'I don't know. Not often. It's a long way.'

'Please come see me when you do.'

'Yes, I'd like to. Very much.' But, though she held out a bare, plaster-pale arm toward me with almost a beseeching grace, we hadn't happened, just as New York hadn't happened for me.

~ ~ ~

Airlines existed in those days, yes, but one didn't think of flying what would become a shuttle route, a bus in the sky for gray suits. One took trains back and forth, a five-hour trip with the layover in New Haven while they switched engines. From Boston's South Station I took a cab to North Station, and found it would be nearly two hours for the next train to my town on the North Shore. But a train for Haverhill was leaving in five minutes, and in my ignorance of New England geography – we had moved just a month ago – I thought that, since Haverhill was also to the north, it would be a time-saving move to get there and then telephone my wife.

I boarded the train and for an hour stared out of a black window at inscrutable, hurrying lights and at my own flickering, murky reflection. It was night; my awkward call at the Guggenheim had delayed my escape until three. New York is always sticky to get away from, like a party where something wonderful may happen the minute after you leave. In the grand and largely empty Haverhill railroad station, there were several pay telephones, but none of them worked. When I made the call from a drugstore a block away, my wife was incredulous. 'Haverhill! Sweetie, who ever told you to go *there*?'

It was after nine o'clock and I was groggy and irritable with sitting and swaying in overheated railroad cars. I had brought to read only the Everyman's edition entitled *The Travels of Mungo Park*, and the jiggling small print had hurt my eyes. 'Nobody did. It was my own idea. I thought you'd like it; I thought it showed real powers of acclimation.' She was a New England native; I was from Maryland. Moving here had been in part an attempt to make her happier.

'Pookie,' she said, 'Haverhill's twenty miles away, it's the end of the world. I can't possibly come get you – Annie's had a fever both days you've been gone and I don't want to get her out of bed and put her in the cold car. But don't give up. Malcolm's right here, he cooked us our dinner. Let me ask him. He probably wouldn't mind, he's up till all hours anyway, listening to music.' She covered the mouthpiece but I overheard her say, 'Would you believe it?' and then a short length of laughter, wound of two strands, male and female.

Malcolm lived in Manchester-by-the-Sea, next to our less fashionable Essex. He was a friend of a slight New York acquaintance, and thus far our only cultural companion in this briny fastness. We had both taken to him, my wife more readily than I. To me he seemed a little fey. He had enough money, evidently, to avoid regular employment. He painted watercolors of marsh and dune, played a harpsichord he had made, listened to records of classical music and Forties jazz, read several books a week. He was *dying*, he said, to write a novel about his awful parents, but they were still alive, in their giant summer house on Coolidge Point. Somewhat older than we, with soft muscles and very white skin, a keen cook and domestic decorator, Malcolm made my wife laugh and even purr, as he sat there in our living room, slowly soaking up bourbon and letting his hair down, so to speak. His hair was romantically black but thinning, with a bald spot in the back. As with the late Doc Humes, there was nothing he didn't know or at least wasn't willing to talk about. Bubbly, smooth-tempered Malcolm made me uneasy, a little, but he was all we had, and my wife needed company. He and she half sincerely discussed opening, together, an antique shop on the Essex strip, which already held several. 'Malcolm says allow forty minutes, it's all back roads,' she said. 'He's being a saint, I think. Haverhill, really, darling – nobody goes to Haverhill!'

Maryland was full of places nobody went to; I wasn't bothered. I had a Coke and doughnut at the drugstore, which was closing up, and walked back through the cold to the railroad station. I suppose it's gone now, long torn down; I have never been back to see. It was a piece of the nineteenth century marooned in mid-twentieth, scaled, like the city's churches, to disappointed expectations. Inside, vandalized telephone booths and coin-operated lockers blocked out sections of the beaded wainscoting and flourishes of carpenter Gothic. Above the lovingly wrought grille of the ticket windows a rough sign was nailed: CLOSES 6 P.M. I was alone with pews of ghosts, travellers that would not return. From far off, somebody was complaining, in the carrying tones of a railroad conductor. Two men passed through the waiting room's great space and went into the lavatory together. Beneath the stained-glass windows brown radiators clunked and sang, warming the varnished boards behind them. Settling to enjoy the stretch of privacy ahead of me, I sat in the center of an empty pew, placed my suitcase at my feet, and opened up the Mungo Park. I was near the end, in the journal of his fatal second trip:

We kept ascending the mountains to the south of Toniba till three o'clock, at which time having gained the summit of the ridge which separates the Niger from the remote branches of the Senegal, I went on a little before; and coming to the brow of a hill, I *once more saw the Niger* rolling its immense stream along the plain!

Yet I could not keep my mind's eye on the African scenery. I could not shake a sensation for which my present predicament supplied a metaphor: my life was *off the tracks*. My high-rise ambitions and hopes had evaporated somewhere around New London. I would have to get a job, something repetitive and demeaning, to support my painting. Which would wither away. And my marriage: it, too, through no one's fault, was one of those things that were not happening. My wife's excited attraction to Malcolm was indication of that. And my little girl: Annie's very wonderfulness frightened me. So proud now of being able to brush her own hair, she would stroke it clumsily until it fanned out from her head in long floating wands, and then come to me, imagining it was beautifully smooth, her face fat with conceit, saying, 'Lookit, Daddy. Lookit.'

I was not totally alone in the station. Mine must have been the last train for hours. One of the men who had been in the lavatory had not left the waiting room, and he stood by the door staring out into the dingy small-city darkness. A car wheeled its lights through the station lot and bit the curb with a screech; I glimpsed several heads, including the tufted shadow of a woman's, and imagined that my wife and daughter had relented and driven here with Malcolm. They had been quicker than predicted – miraculously quick.

But it was a young man in an old athletic jacket who slammed through the double doors and raced into the lavatory. Too much beer, I supposed. He had left his motor running and his lights burning. Light poured into the face of the man waiting by the door, washing a halo into the rim of his flimsy fair hair. *Lookit. Lookit.*

The athlete dashed back to his car, the motor roared, and the lights backed off and sped away. The man by the door said to me, 'Not bad, huh? Two guys and one cunt.' He shuffled forward a few steps, a slender man with a stooped neck. He was not young, and yet not old either – merely hard-used, and poor.

'Yeah,' I said, and fixed my eyes pointedly on the book.

It was in the afternoon, and we fastened it to the tree close to the tent, where all the asses were tied. As soon as it was dark the wolves tore its bowels out, though within ten yards of the tent door where we were all sitting.

The little shuffling steps came closer. 'How d'ya bet she'll take care of 'em both?'

I refused to answer. I was trembling hideously inside. 'I bet she blows one of 'em.' Stoop-neck shuffled by close to my knees, paused, shuffled around the back of the pew, paused, and moaned as if to himself, 'Nothin' doin' around here tonight.' Then, to my immense relief, he went out the double doors into the night.

For all of its Victorian elaboration, the interior of the station lacked a clock. Surely Malcolm's forty minutes was used up. It was one of my artistic affectations in those years not to wear a watch. I kept on reading:

We saw on one of the islands, in the middle of the river, a large elephant; it was of a red clay color with black legs.

The sad stoop-necked man came back through the station doors, with their brass crashbars polished by generations of hands. 'Gettin' to be a cold night out there.' Shyly keeping his eyes fastened above my head, he wandered closer, his feet scuffling grittily on the marble floor and his little head tilted to one side. 'Nothin' doin' around here tonight,' he repeated.

I explained, 'I'm waiting for somebody. I wish to hell they'd come.'

'Yeah, well,' the other replied, with an oddly cynical, reedy lilt.

I realized that my responding, whatever the words, was a mistake – encouragement. Stoop-neck had paused ten feet away, transfixed by some scent. I stared rigidly into the book, as if like a campfire its white page made a circle of safety. A foot scratched one step closer, and then the man had seated himself beside me. 'You like books, huh?' The thighs of his unpressed cotton trousers were inches from mine. 'Hey,' he continued, on the same conversational level, 'was you ever blowed?'

I jumped to my feet and ran out of the station, abandoning my suitcase. My heart was swollen bigger than an elephant's and pounding with terror and indignation. Remember, I was very young. Not quite twenty-six – a stranger to myself. I restrained myself from running up the stony valley between the railroad embankment and a row of dark shops. The drugstore where I had had the doughnut was at the end of this row, and itself dark. But a taxi-stand shelter opposite the drugstore was still lit inside, waiting for whatever scrap the dying railroads might throw it. Behind a dirty picture window, in a little room papered with calendars, two old men sat on opposite sides of a worn desk that held a telephone and a radio. The radio, with a crackle of static, was playing, I seem to remember, a Benny Goodman quintet. One of the men, wearing a lumberjack shirt, pushed open the door to ask me, 'You want a cab, son?'

I said no, I was being picked up by a friend, was it O.K. if I waited outside here? My voice sounded boyish and tinny, and I knew I must look queer, in my big-city suit and artistically shaggy hair and with my finger still marking my place in the Everyman's volume that was still in my hand.

~ ~ ~

Yes. How young we were, how little it took to stir us up, in 1959. Malcolm came not long afterwards, in his marine-blue MG convertible. Foreign cars were still unusual then – what we now call a statement. I had edged halfway down the hill toward the front of the station, so as not to miss him. Pantingly I described how I had been assaulted and had fled, and he looked at me rather incredulously, there in the half-light, on the steep cold street. He parked in front of the station and went in with me to retrieve my suitcase. The stoop-necked man was gone, but my suitcase was there, in the center of that spread of empty pews, while rusty radiators knocked and hissed along the wainscoted walls. Even the little paper bag with Annie's toy hairbrush and comb in it was still there.

As we began the ride home, Malcolm did not seem his usual blithe self. 'Howard,' he said, in almost a scolding tone, 'that kind of man was no threat to you. They are almost never violent. Violence is not the problem, and in any case the problem was his, not yours.'

I felt chastised, and silly for having felt such terror. Everywhere I had gone, on these travels of mine, people had been sending me messages, though my teeth weren't wired to receive them.

Malcolm didn't let go of the subject; he seemed to have given it a lot of thought. He cited to me, from a book he had read, statistics in regard to male homosexuals: their unaggressiveness, their low crime rate, their creativity and forbearance. They were the model citizens, it turned out, of the liberated, diverse, depuritanized world to come. His voice, with its exotic New England twang, held something I had not heard before, an earnest edge. With my wife present, he was all flirtatiousness and idle fun.

'Yeah, well,' I said. 'That's all very fine. But why *me*? Why did he pick on me?'

Malcolm said, 'The obvious answer is, because you were there.'

Then, uncharacteristically, he said no more. Was there an unobvious answer? The dim lights of Haverhill sped by; we crossed a river into Groveland. The inside of the convertible was as surprisingly warm as the inside of the station had been, and I relaxed into it. He was wearing a little fuzzy checked hat, perhaps to protect his bald spot. I was touched, and dimly felt my relative youth, my full head of hair, as an advantage, a plume, a source of power. I told him about meeting Duchamp at the party, about Doc Humes having somehow inserted himself at the great man's chessboard. Malcolm laughed, and pressed me for details; I supplied them, but left out my attraction to Venus, and my visit to her after lunch hour, and the gesture of her long arm that benignly released me from my attraction. Malcolm volunteered that last week he and his sister had been present at a local dinner that included John Marquand, who had been handsome and gracious. Marquand was a big name back then.

Memory fades, but it must be that, after the long cozy drive through the winding wintry dark, over the back roads, through Groveland and Georgetown and Ipswich, Malcolm delivered me safely to my house and my wife. Somehow embarrassed about it, as if the fault had been mine, I didn't tell her about the man in the train station. It stayed a secret between Malcolm and me. Years went by, in which he continued as a friend of both of us, seductive to us equally, gently exerting the pressure of love against the one of us who would fall. Nothing happens overnight. By the time he and I had moved to Boston together and opened the shop on Charles Street, the Sixties were well advanced.

LORRIE MOORE

WHAT YOU WANT TO DO FINE

Mack has moved so much in his life that every phone number he comes across seems to him to be one he's had before. 'I swear this used to be *my* number,' he says, putting the car into park and pointing at the guidebook: 923–7368. The built-in cadence of a phone number always hits him the same personal way: like something familiar but lost, something momentous yet insignificant – like an act of love with a girl he used to date.

'Just call,' says Quilty. They are off Route 55, at the first McDonald's outside of Chicago. They are on a vacation, a road trip, a 'pile, stuff in, and go' kind of thing. Quilty has been singing movie themes all afternoon, has gotten fixated on 'To Sir with Love,' and he and Mack now seemed destined to make each other crazy: Mack passing buses too quickly while fumbling for more gum (chewing the sugar out fast, stick by stick), and Quilty, hunched over the glove compartment, in some purple-faced strain of emotion brought on by the line 'Those schoolgirl days of telling tales and biting nails are gone.' 'I would be a genius now,' Quilty has said three times already, 'if only I'd memorized Shakespeare instead of Lulu.'

LORRIE MOORE (born 1957): Moore is one of the boldest and bravest writers working today. The author of the story collections Self-Help, Like Life, *and* Birds of America *and the novels* Anagrams *and* Who Will Run the Frog Hospital?, *she teaches at the University of Wisconsin in Madison.*

'If only,' says Mack. Mack himself would be a genius now if only he had been born a completely different person. But what could you do? He'd read in a magazine once that geniuses were born only to women over thirty; his own mother had been twenty-nine. Damn! So fucking close!

'Let's just get a hotel reservation someplace and take a bath-oil bath,' Quilty says now. 'And don't dicker. You're always burning up time trying to get a bargain.'

'That's so wrong?'

Quilty grimaces. 'I don't like what comes after "dicker."'

'What is that?'

Quilty sighs. '*Dickest*. I mean, really: it's not a contest!' Quilty turns to feel for Guapo, his Seeing Eye dog, a chocolate Lab too often left panting in the backseat of the car while they stop for coffee. 'Good dog, good dog, yes.' A 'bath-oil bath' is Quilty's idea of how to end a good day as well as a bad. 'Tomorrow, we'll head south, along the Mississippi, then to New Orleans, and then back up to the ducks at the Peabody Hotel at the end. Does that sound okay?'

'If that's what you want to do, fine,' says Mack.

~ ~ ~

They had met only two years ago at the Tapston, Indiana, Sobriety Society. Because he was new in town, recently up from some stupid quickie job painting high-voltage towers in the south of the state, and suddenly in need of a lawyer, Mack phoned Quilty the next day. 'I was wondering if we could strike a deal,' Mack had said. 'One old drunk to another.'

'Perhaps,' said Quilty. He may have been blind and a recovering drinker, but with the help of his secretary, Martha, he had worked up a decent legal practice and did not give his services away for free. Good barter, however, he liked. It made life easier for a blind man. He was, after all, a practical person. Beneath all his eccentricities, he possessed a streak of pragmatism so sharp and deep that others mistook it for sanity.

'I got myself into a predicament,' Mack explained. He told Quilty how difficult it was being a housepainter, new in town to boot, and how some of these damn finicky housewives could never be satisfied with what was true professional work, and how, well, he had a lawsuit on his hands. 'I'm being sued for sloppy house painting, Mr Stein. But the only way I can pay you is in more house painting. Do you have a house that needs painting?'

'Bad house painting as both the accusation and the retainer?' Quilty hooted. He loved a good hoot – it brought Guapo to his side. 'That's like telling me you're wanted for counterfeiting but you can pay me in cash.'

'I'm sorry,' said Mack.

'It's all right,' Quilty said. He took Mack's case, got him out of it as best he could – 'the greatest art in the world,' Quilty told the judge at the settlement hearing, 'has been known to mumble at the edges' – then had Mack paint his house a clear, compensatory, cornflower blue. Or was it, suggested a neighbor, in certain streaky spots *delphinium*? At lunchtime, Quilty came home from his office up the street and stopped in the driveway, Guapo heeled at his feet, Mack above them on the ladder humming some mournful Appalachian love song, or a jazzed-up version of 'Taps.' Why 'Taps'? 'It's the town we live in,' Mack would later explain, 'and it's the sound of your cane.'

Day is done. Gone the sun.

'How we doing there, Mack?' asked Quilty. His dark hair was long and bristly as rope, and he often pulled on it while speaking. 'The neighbors tell me my bushes are all blue.'

'A little dripping couldn't be avoided,' Mack said unhappily. He never used tarps, the way other painters did. He didn't even own any.

'Well, doesn't offend me,' said Quilty, tapping meaningfully at his sunglasses.

But afterward, painting the side dormer, Mack kept hearing Quilty inside, on the phone with a friend, snorting in a loud horselaugh: 'Hey, what do *I* know? *I* have blue bushes!'

Or 'I'm having the shrubs dyed blue: the nouveau riche – look out – will always be with you.'

When the house was almost finished, and oak leaves began to accumulate on the ground in gold-and-ruby piles the color of pears, and the evenings settled in quickly and disappeared into that long solvent that was the beginning of a winter night, Mack began to linger and stall – over coffee and tea, into dinner, then over coffee and tea again. He liked to watch Quilty move deftly about the kitchen, refusing Mack's help, fixing simple things – pasta, peas, salads, bread and butter. Mack liked talking with him about the Sobriety Society meetings, swapping stories about those few great benders that sat in their memories like gorgeous songs and those others that had just plain wrecked their lives. He watched Quilty's face as fatigue or fondness spilled and rippled across it. Quilty had been born blind and had never acquired the guise and camouflage of the sighted; his face remained unclenched, untrained, a clean canvas, transparent as a baby's gas, clear to the bottom of him. In a face so unguarded and unguarding, one saw one's own innocent self – and one sometimes recoiled.

But Mack found he could not go away – not entirely. Not really. He helped Quilty with his long hair, brushing it back for him and gathering it in a leather tie. He brought Quilty gifts lifted from secondhand stores downtown. A geography book in Braille. A sweater with a coffee stain on the arm – was that too mean? Cork coasters for Quilty's endless cups of tea.

'I am gratefully beholden, my dear,' Quilty had said each time, speaking, as he sometimes did, like a goddamn Victorian valentine and touching Mack's sleeve. 'You are the kindest man I've ever had in my house.'

And perhaps because what Quilty knew best were touch and words, or perhaps because Mack had gone through a pig's life of everything tearing at his feelings, or maybe because the earth had tilted into shadow and cold and the whole damned future seemed dipped in that bad ink, one night in the living room, after a kiss that took only Mack by surprise, and even then only slightly, Mack and Quilty became lovers.

Still, there were times it completely baffled Mack. How had he gotten here? What soft punch in the mouth had sent him reeling to this new place?

Uncertainty makes for shyness, and shyness, Quilty kept saying, is what keeps the world together. Or, rather, is what *used* to keep the world together, used to keep it from going mad with chaos. Now – now! – was a different story.

A different story? 'I don't like stories,' said Mack. 'I like food. I like car keys.' He paused. 'I like pretzels.'

'Okaaaay,' said Quilty, tracing the outline of his own shoulder and then Mack's.

'You do this a lot, don't you?' asked Mack.

'Do what? Upgrade in the handyman department?'

'Bring into your bed some big straight guy you think's a little dumb.'

'I never do that. Never have.' He cocked his head to one side. 'Before.' With his flat almond-shaped fingertips, he played Mack's arm like a keyboard. 'Never before. You are my big sexual experiment.'

'But you see, you're *my* big sexual experiment,' insisted Mack. In his life before Quilty, he could never have imagined being in bed with a skinny naked guy wearing sunglasses. 'So how can that be?'

'Honey, it *be*s.'

'But someone's got to be in charge. How can both of us survive on some big experimental adventure? Someone's got to be steering the ship.'

'Oh, the ship be damned. We'll be fine. We are in this thing together. It's luck. It's God's will. It's synchronicity! Serendipity! Kismet! Camelot! Annie, honey, Get Your Fucking Gun!' Quilty was squealing.

'My ex-wife's name is Annie,' said Mack.

'I know, I know. That's why I said it,' said Quilty, trying now not to sigh. 'Think of it this way: the blind leading the straight. It can work. It's not impossible.'

In the mornings, the phone rang too much, and it sometimes annoyed Mack. Where were the pretzels and the car keys when you really needed them? He could see that Quilty knew the exact arm's distance to the receiver, picking it up in one swift pluck. 'Are you *sans* or *avec*?' Quilty's friends would ask. They spoke loudly and theatrically — as if to a deaf person — and Mack could always hear.

'*Avec*,' Quilty would say.

'Oooooh,' they would coo. 'And how *is* Mr Avec today?'

'You should move your stuff in here,' Quilty finally said to Mack one night.

'Is that what you want?' Mack found himself deferring in ways that were unfamiliar to him. He had never slept with a man before, that was probably it — though years ago there had been those nights when Annie'd put on so much makeup and leather, her gender seemed up for grabs: it had been oddly attractive to Mack, self-sufficient; it hadn't required him and so he'd wanted to get close, to get next to it, to learn it, make it need him, take it away, make it die. Those had been strange, bold nights, a starkness between them that was more like an ancient bone-deep brawl than a marriage. But ultimately, it all remained unreadable for him, though reading, he felt, was not a natural thing and should not be done to people. In general, people were not road maps. People were not hieroglyphs or books. They were not stories. A person was a collection of accidents. A person was an infinite pile of rocks with things growing underneath. In general, when you felt a longing for love, you took a woman and possessed her gingerly and not too hopefully until you finally let go, slept, woke up, and she eluded you once more. Then you started over. Or not.

Nothing about Quilty, however, seemed elusive.

'Is that what I want? Of course it's what I want. Aren't I a walking pamphlet for desire?' asked Quilty. 'In Braille, of course, but still. Check it out. Move in. Take me.'

'Okay,' said Mack.

Mack had had a child with Annie, their boy, Lou, and just before the end, Mack had tried to think up words to say to Annie, to salvage things. He'd said 'okay' a lot. He did not know how to raise a child, a toothless, trickless child, but he knew he had to protect it from the world a little; you could not just hand it over and let the world go at it. 'There's something that with time grows between people,' he said once, in an attempt to keep them together, keep Lou. If he lost Lou, he believed, it would wreck his life completely. 'Something that grows whether you like it or not.'

'Gunk,' Annie said.

'What?'

'Gunk!' she shouted. 'Gunk grows between people!'

He slammed the door, went drinking with his friends. The bar they all went to — Teem's Pub — quickly grew smoky and dull. Someone, Bob Bacon, maybe, suggested going to Visions and Sights, a strip joint out near the interstate. But Mack was already missing his wife. 'Why would I want to go to a place like that,' Mack said loudly to his friends, 'when I've got a beautiful wife at home?'

'Well, then,' Bob said, 'let's go to *your* house.'

'Okay,' he said. 'Okay.'

And when they got there, Annie was already gone. She had packed fast, taken Lou, and fled.

~ ~ ~

Now it is two and a half years since Annie left, and here Mack is with Quilty, traveling: their plan is to head through Chicago and St Louis and then south along the Mississippi. They will check into bed-and-breakfasts, tour the historic sights, like spouses. They have decided on this trip now in October in part because Mack is recuperating from a small procedure. He has had a small benign cyst razored from 'an intimate place.'

'The bathroom?' asked Quilty that first day after the surgery, and reached to feel Mack's thick black stitches, then sighed. 'What's the unsexiest thing we can do for the next two weeks?'

'Go on a trip,' Mack suggested.

Quilty hummed contentedly. He found the insides of Mack's wrists, where the veins were stiff cords, and caressed them with his thumbs. 'Married men are always the best,' he said. 'They're so grateful and butch.'

'Give me a break,' said Mack.

The next day, they bought quart bottles of mineral water and packets of saltines, and drove out of town, out the speed-way, with the Resurrection Park cemetery on one side and the Sunset Memories Park cemetery on the other – a route the cabbies called 'the Bone Zone.' When he'd first arrived in Tapston, Mack drove a cab for a week, and he'd gotten to know the layout of the town fast. 'I'm in the Bone Zone,' he used to have to say into the radio mouthpiece. 'I'm in the Bone Zone.' But he'd hated that damn phrase and hated waiting at the airport, all the lousy tips and heavy suitcases. And the names of things in Tapston – apartment buildings called Crestview Manor, treeless subdivisions called Arbor Valley, the cemeteries undisguised as Sunset Memories and Resurrection Park – all gave him the creeps. *Resurrection Park!* Jesus Christ. Every damn Hoosier twisted words right to death.

But cruising out the Bone Zone for a road trip in Quilty's car jazzed them both. They could once again escape all the unfortunateness of this town and its alarming resting places. 'Farewell, you ole stiffs,' Mack said.

'Good-bye, all my clients,' cried Quilty when they passed the county jail. 'Good-bye, good-bye!' Then he sank back blissfully in his seat as Mack sped the car toward the interstate, out into farm country, silver-topped silos gleaming like spaceships, the air grassy and thick with hog.

'I'd like to make a reservation for a double room, if possible,' Mack now shouts over the noise of the interstate traffic. He looks and sees Quilty getting out of the car, leaving Guapo, feeling and tapping his way with his cane, toward the entrance to McDonald's.

'Yes, a double room,' says Mack. He looks over his shoulder, keeping an eye on Quilty. 'American Express? Yes.' He fumbles through Quilty's wallet, reads the number out loud. He turns again and sees Quilty ordering a soda but not finding his wallet, since he'd given it to Mack for the call. Mack sees Quilty tuck his cane under his arm and pat all his pockets, finding nothing there but a red Howe Caverns handkerchief.

'You want the number on the card? Three one one two . . .'

Quilty now turns to leave, without a soda, and heads for the door. But he chooses the wrong door. He wanders into the Playland by mistake, and Mack can see him thrashing around with his cane amid the plastic cheeseburgers and the french fry swings, lit up at night for the kids. There is no exit from the Playland except back through the restaurant, but Quilty obviously doesn't know this and first taps, then bangs his cane against the forest of garish obstacles.

'. . . eight one zero zero six,' repeats the reservations clerk on the phone.

By the time Mack can get to him, Quilty is collapsed on a ceramic chicken breast. 'Good night, Louise. I thought you'd left me,' Quilty says. 'I swear, from here on in, I'll do whatever you want. I've glimpsed the abyss, and, by God, it's full of big treacherous pieces of patio furniture.'

'We've got a room,' says Mack.

'Fantastic. Can we also get a soda?' Mack lets Quilty take his elbow and then walks Quilty back inside, where they order Pepsis and a single apple pie the size of an eyeglass pouch – to split in the car, like children.

'Have a nice day,' says the boy at the counter.

'Thanks for the advice,' says Quilty.

~ ~ ~

They have brought along the game Trivial Pursuit, and at night Quilty likes to play. Though Mack complies – if that's what you want to do, fine – he thinks it's a dumb game. If you don't know the answer, you feel stupid. And if you do know the answer, you feel just as stupid. *More* stupid. What are you doing with that stupid bit of information in your brain? Mack would prefer to lie in the room and stare at the ceiling, thinking about Chicago, thinking about their day. 'Name four American state capitals named after presidents,' he reads sleepily from a card. He would rather try to understand the paintings he has seen that afternoon, and has almost understood: the Halloween hues of the Lautrecs; the chalky ones of Puvis de Chavannes; the sweet finger paints of the Vuillards and Bonnards, all crowded with window light and commodes. Mack had listened to the buzzing voice coming from Quilty's headphones, but he hadn't gotten his own headphones. Let a blind man be described to! Mack had his own eyes. But finally, overwhelmed by poor Quilty's inability either to see or touch the paintings, he had led Quilty downstairs to the statuary, and when no one was looking, he'd placed Quilty's hands upon the naked marble figure of a woman. 'Ah,' Quilty had said, feeling the nose and lips, and then he grew quiet and respectful at her shoulders, at her breasts, and hips, and when he got down past the thighs and knees to her feet, Quilty laughed out loud. Feet! These he knew best. These he liked.

Afterward, they went to a club to hear a skit called 'Kuwait Until Dark.'

'Lincoln, Jackson, Madison, Jefferson City,' says Quilty. 'Do you think we will have a war?' He seems to have grown impatient with the game. 'You were in the service once. Do you think this is it? The big George Bush showdown?'

'Nah,' says Mack. He had been in the army only during peacetime. He'd been stationed in Texas, then in Germany. He'd been with Annie: those were good years. Only a little crying. Only a little drinking. Later, he'd been in the reserves, but the reserves were never called up – everyone knew that. Until now. 'Probably it's just a sales demo for the weapons.'

'Well, they'll go off, then,' says Quilty. 'Won't they? If it's a demonstration, things will be demonstrated.'

Mack picks another card. 'In the song "They Call the Wind Maria," what do they call the rain?'

'It's Mar-eye-a, not Maria,' says Quilty.

'It's Mar-eye-a?' asks Mack. 'Really?'

'Really,' says Quilty. There is something wicked and scolding that comes over Quilty's face in this game. 'It's your turn.' He thrusts out his hand. 'Now give me the card so you don't cheat.'

Mack hands him the card. 'Mar-eye-a,' says Mack. The song is almost coming back to him – he recalls it from somewhere. Maybe Annie used to sing it. 'They call the wind Mareye-a. They call the rain . . . Okay. I think it's coming. . . .' He presses his fingers to his temples, squinting and thinking. 'They call the wind Mar-eye-ah. They call the rain . . . Okay. Don't tell me. They call the rain . . . Pariah!'

'*Pariah?*' Quilty guffaws.

'Okay, then,' says Mack, exasperated. 'Heavy. They call the rain Heavy Rain.' He reaches aggressively for his minibar juice. Next time, he's just going to look quickly at the back of the card.

'Don't you want to know the right answer?'

'No.'

'Okay, I'll just go on to the next card.' He picks one up, pretending to read. 'It says here, "Darling, is there life on Mars? Yes or no."'

Mack has gone back to thinking about the paintings. 'I say no,' he says absently.

'Hmmm,' says Quilty, putting the card down. 'I think the answer is yes. Look at it this way: they're sure there are ice crystals. And where there is ice, there is water. And where there is water, there is waterfront property. And where there is waterfront property, there are Jews!' He claps his hands and sinks back onto the acrylic quilting of the bedspread. 'Where are you?' he asks finally, waving his arms out in the air.

'I'm here,' says Mack. 'I'm right here.' But he doesn't move.

'You're here? Well, good. At least you're not at my cousin Esther's Martian lake house with her appalling husband, Howard. Though sometimes I wonder how they're doing. How are they? They never come to visit. I frighten them so much.' He pauses. 'Can I ask you a question?'

'Okay.'

'What do I look like?'

Mack hesitates. 'Brown eyes, brown eyebrows, and brown hair.'

'That's it?'

'Okay. Brown teeth, too.'

'Really!'

'Sorry,' says Mack. 'I'm a little tired.'

~ ~ ~

Hannibal is like all the river towns that have tried recently to spruce themselves up, make antique shops and bed-and-breakfasts from the shoreline mansions. It saddens Mack. There is still a despondent grandeur to these houses, but it radiates out, in a kind of shrug, onto a drab economy of tidbit tourism and health-care facilities. A hundred years of flight and rehab lie on the place like rain. Heavy rain! The few barges that still push this far upriver seem quaint and ridiculous. But Quilty wants to hear what all the signs say – the Mark Twain Diner, the Tom 'n Huck Motel; it amuses him. They take the tour of Sam Clemens's houses, of Mr. Clemens's office, of the little jail. They get on a tiny train Quilty calls 'Too, Too Twain,' which tours the area and makes the place seem even more spritely and hopeless. Quilty feels along the wide boards of the whitewashed fence. 'This is modern paint,' he says.

'Latex,' says Mack.

'Oooh, talk to me, talk to me, baby.'

'Will you stop?'

'Okay. All right.'

'Pretty dog,' a large woman in a violet dress says to them in the Tom

Sawyer Diner. The diner is situated next to a parking lot and a mock-up of the legendary fence, and it serves BLTs in red plastic baskets with stiff wax paper and fries. Quilty has ordered his usual glass of milk.

'Thank you,' says Quilty to the woman, who then stops to pet Guapo before heading for her car in the parking lot. Quilty looks suddenly annoyed. '*He* gets all the compliments, and *I* have to say thank you.'

'You want a compliment?' asks Mack, disgusted. 'Okay. You're pretty, too,' says Mack.

'*Am* I? Well, how will I ever know, if everyone just keeps complimenting my dog!'

'I can't believe you're jealous of your goddamn dog. Here,' Mack says. 'I refuse to talk to someone with a milk mustache.' He hands Quilty a napkin, touching the folded edge of it to his cheek.

Quilty takes it and wipes his mouth. 'Just when we were getting so good at being boring together,' he says. He reaches over and pats Mack's arm, then reaches up and roughly pets his head. Mack's hair is thin and swept back, and Quilty swipes at it from behind.

'Ow,' says Mack.

'I keep forgetting your hair is so Irish and sensitive,' he said. 'We've gotta get you some good tough Jew hair.'

'Great,' says Mack. He is growing tired of this, tired of them. They've been on these trips too many times before. They've visited Mother Goose's grave in Boston. They've visited the battlefield at Saratoga. They've visited Arlington. 'Too many cemeteries!' said Mack. 'It's the goddamn Bone Zone wherever we go!' They visited the Lincoln Memorial ('I imagine it's like a big marble Oz,' said Quilty. 'Abraham Oz. A much better name, don't you think?'). Right next door, they visited the Vietnam War Memorial, mind-numbing in its bloodless catalog of blood, Mack preferring instead the alternative monument, the buddy statue put up by the vets, something that wanted less to be art than to be human. 'It's about the guys, not just the *names of the guys*,' he said. '*Guys* died there. A list didn't die there.' But Quilty, who had spent an hour feeling for friends who'd died in '68 and '70, had sighed in a vaguely disgusted, condescending way.

'You're missing it totally,' he said. 'A list did die. An incredible heartbreaking list.'

'Sorry I'm not such an intellectual,' said Mack.

'You're jealous because I was feeling around for other men.'

'Yeah. I'm jealous. I'm jealous I'm not up there. I'm jealous because – stupid me – I waited until peacetime to enlist.'

Quilty sighed. 'I almost went. But I had a high draft number. Plus, guess what? Flat feet!'

At that, they both broke, feebly, into loud, exhausted laughter, like two tense lunatics, right there by the wall, until someone in a uniform asked them to leave: other people were trying to pray.

Trying to go someplace without cemeteries, they once flew to Key West, ate a lot of conch chowder and went to Audubon's house, which wasn't Audubon's house at all, but a place where Audubon had stayed once or something, shooting the birds he then painted. 'He shot them?' Mack kept asking. 'He shot the damn birds?'

'Revolting,' said Quilty loudly. 'The poor birds. From now on, I'm going to give all my money to the *Autobahn* Society. Let's make those Mercedes go fast, fast, fast!'

To prevent Mack's drinking in despair, they later found an AA meeting and dropped in, made friends and confessed to them, though not exactly in that order. The following day, new pals in tow, they strolled through Hemingway's house in feather boas – 'just to taunt Papa.'

'Before he wrote about them,' said Quilty, pretending to read the guidebook out loud, 'Hemingway shot his characters. It was considered an unusual but not unheard-of creative method. Still, even within literary circles, it is not that widely discussed.'

The next morning, at the request of a sweet old man named Chuck, they went to an AIDS memorial service. They sat next to Chuck and held his hand. Walt Whitman poems were read. Cello suites were played so exquisitely that people fell forward onto their own knees, collapsed by the beauty of grief. After the benediction, everyone got solemnly into their cars and drove slowly to the grave site. No matter how Mack and Quilty tried to avoid cemeteries, there they were again. A boneyard had its own insistent call: like rocks to sailors, or sailors to other sailors. 'This is all too intense,' whispered Mack in the middle of a prayer; at the grave site, Mack had positioned them farther off from the mourners than Quilty knew. 'This is supposed to be our vacation. When this prayer is over, let's go to the beach and eat cupcakes.' Which is what they did, letting Guapo run up and down the sand, chasing gulls, while the two of them lay there on a towel, the sea air blasting their faces.

Now, on this trip, Mack is in a hurry. He wants to leave the chipping white brick of Hannibal, the trees and huckleberries, the local cars all parked in the lot of some Tony's Lounge. He wants to get on to St. Louis, to Memphis, to New Orleans, then back. He wants to be done with touring, this mobile life they embark on too often, like old ladies testing out their new, sturdy shoes. He wants his stitches removed.

'I hope there won't be scars,' he says.

'Scars?' says Quilty in that screechy mockery he sometimes puts on. 'I can't believe I'm with someone who's worried about having a good-looking dick.'

'Here is your question. What American playwright was imprisoned for her work?'

'*Her* work. Aha. Lillian Hellman? I doubt it. Thornton Wilder –'

'Mae West,' blurts out Mack.

'Don't do that! I hadn't answered yet!'

'What does it matter?'

'It matters to me!'

There is only a week left.

~ ~ ~

'In St. Louis' – Quilty pretends again, his old shtick, to read from the guidebook as they take the bumpy ride to the top of the arch – 'there is the famous gateway, or "arch," built by the McDonald Corporation. Holy Jesus, America, get down on your knees!'

'I am, I am.'

'Actually, that's true. I heard someone talking about it downstairs. This thing was built by a company named McDonald. A golden arch of gray stone. That is the gateway to the West. At sunset very golden. Very arch.'

'Whaddyaknow.' Gray stone again. There's no getting away from it.

'Describe the view to me,' says Quilty when they get out at the top.

Mack looks out through the windows. 'Adequate,' he says.

'I said describe, not *rate*.'

'Midwestern. Aerial. Green and brown.'

Quilty sighs. 'I don't think blind men should date deaf-mutes until the how-to book has been written.'

Mack is getting hungry. 'Are you hungry?'

'It's too stressful!' adds Quilty. 'No, I'm not hungry.'

They make the mistake of going to the aquarium, instead of to an early dinner, which causes every sea creature to look delicious to Mack. Quilty makes the tour with a group led by a cute schoolteacherish guide named Judy, but Mack ventures off on his own. He feels like a dog set loose among schoolchildren: Here are his friends! The elegant nautilus, the electric eel, the stingray with its wavy cape and idiot grin, silently shrieking against the glass – or is it feeding?

When is a thing shrieking and when is it feeding – and why can't Mack tell?

It is the wrong hour of the day, the wrong hour of life, to be around sea creatures. Shrieking or feeding. Breaded or fried. There is a song Mack's aunt used to sing to him when he was little: 'I am a man upon the land. I am a Silkie on the sea.' And he thinks of this now, this song about a half man, half seal or bird – what was it? It was a creature who comes back to fetch his child – his child by a woman on the land. But the woman's new husband is a hunter, a good shot, and kills him when he tries to escape back to the sea with the child. Perhaps that was best, in the end. Still the song was sad. Stolen love, lost love, amphibious doom – all the transactions of Mack's own life: I am a Silkie on the sea. 'My life is lucky and rich,' he used to tell himself when he was painting high-voltage towers in Kentucky and the electric field on those ladders stood the hairs of his arms on end. Lucky and Rich! They sounded like springer spaniels, or two unsavory uncles. Uncle Lucky! Uncle Rich!

I am a man upon the land, he thinks. But here at sea, what am I? Shrieking or feeding?

Quilty comes up behind him, with Guapo. 'Let's go to dinner,' he says.

'Thank you,' says Mack.

After dinner, they lie in their motel bed and kiss. 'Ah, dear, yes,' murmurs Quilty, his 'dears' and 'my dears' like sweet compresses in the heat, and then there are no more words. Mack pushes close, his cool belly warming. His heart thumps against Quilty's like a water balloon shifting and thrusting its liquid from side to side. There is something comforting, thinks Mack, in embracing someone the same size as you. Something exhilarating, even: having your chins over each other's shoulders, your feet touching, your heads pressed ear-to-ear. Plus he likes – he loves – Quilty's mouth on him. A man's full mouth. There is always something a little desperate and diligent about Quilty, poised there with his lips big and searching and his wild unshaded eyes like the creatures of the aquarium, captive yet wandering free in their enclosures. With the two of them kissing like this – *exculpatory*, *specificity*, *rubric* – words are foreign money. There is only the soft punch in the mouth, the shrieking and feeding both, which fills Mack's ears with light. This, he thinks, this is how a blind man sees. This is how a fish walks. This is how rocks sing. There is nothing at all like a man's strong kiss: apologies to the women of Kentucky.

~ ~ ~

They eat breakfast at a place called Mama's that advertises 'throwed rolls.'

'What are those?' asks Quilty. They turn out merely to be warm buttermilk rolls thrown at the clientele by the waiters. Mack's roll hits him squarely in the chest, where he continues to clutch it, in shock. 'Don't worry,' says the waiter to Quilty. 'Won't throw one at you, a blind man, but just maybe at your dawg.'

'Good God,' says Quilty. 'Let's get out of here.'

On the way out, by the door, Mack stops to read the missing-child posters. He does not look at the girls. He looks at the boys: Graham, age eight; Eric, age five. So that's what five looks like, thinks Mack. Lou will be five next week.

~ ~ ~

Mack takes the slow southerly roads. He and Quilty are like birds, reclaiming the summer that left them six weeks before in the north. 'I'll bet in Tapston they've all got salt spats on their boots already,' says Mack. 'Bet they've got ice chunks in their tires.' Quilty hates winter, Mack knows. The frozen air makes things untouchable, unsmellable. When the weather warms, the world comes back. 'The sun smells like fire,' Quilty says, and smiles. Past the bleached doormat of old wheat fields, the land grows greener. There is cotton harvested as far north as Missouri, the fields spread out like bolts of dotted swiss, and Mack and Quilty stop on the shoulder once, get out to pick a blossom, peel back the wet bud, feel the cotton slowly dry. 'See what you miss, being a Yankee,' says Mack.

'Missing is all I do,' says Quilty.

~ ~ ~

They come upon a caravan of Jeeps and Hummers painted beige and headed south for a ship that no doubt will take them from one gulf to another. Mack whistles. 'Holy shit,' he says.

'What?'

'Right now, there're about two hundred army vehicles in front of us, freshly painted desert beige.'

'I can't bear it,' says Quilty. 'There's going to be a war.'

'I could have sworn there wouldn't be. I could have sworn there was just going to be a television show.'

'I'll bet there's a war.' They drive to Cooter along with the Jeeps, then swing off to Heloise to look at the river. It is still the same slow mongoose brown, lacking beauty of some kind Mack can't quite name. The river seems to him like a big ticky dog that doesn't know its own filth and keeps following your car along on the side as you drive.

They get out of the car to stretch. Mack lights a cigarette, thinking of the Jeeps and the Saudi desert. 'So there it is. Brown and more brown. Guess that's all there is to a river.'

'You're so . . . *Peggy Lee*,' says Quilty. 'How about a little Jerome Kern? It don't plant taters. It don't plant cotton. It just keeps rolling along.'

Mack knows the song but doesn't even look at Quilty.

'Smell the mud and humidity of it,' says Quilty, breathing deeply.

'I do. Great humidity,' says Mack. He feels weary. He also feels sick of trying, tired of living, and scared of dying. If Quilty wants musical comedy, there it is: musical comedy. Mack drags on his cigarette. The prospect of a war has seized his brain. It engages some old, ongoing terror in him. As a former soldier, he still believes in armies. But he believes in armies at rest, armies relaxing, armies shopping at the PX, armies eating supper in the mess hall. But armies as TV-network football teams? The quick beginning of the quick end.

'I hear the other side doesn't even have socks,' says Quilty when they are back in the car, thinking of the war. 'Or rather, they have *some* socks, but they don't all match.'

'Probably the military's been waiting for this for years. Something to ace — at last.'

'Thank God you're not still in the reserves. They're calling up all the reserves.' Quilty reaches up under Mack's shirt and rubs his back. 'Young people have been coming into my office all month to have their wills drawn up.'

Mack was in the reserves only a year before he was thrown out for drunkenness on one of the retreats.

'The reserves used to be one big camping trip,' Mack says.

'Well, now it's a camping trip gone awry. A camping trip with aspirations. A *big* hot camping trip. Kamp with a *K*. These kids coming in for wills: you should hear the shock in their voices.'

Mack drives slowly, dreamy with worry. 'How you doing back there, Miss Daisy?' Quilty calls over his shoulder to Guapo. Outside of Memphis, on the Arkansas side, they stop at a Denny's, next to a warehouse of dinettes, and they let Guapo out to run again.

Dinettes, thinks Mack. That's just what this world needs: a warehouse of dinettes.

'I once tried to write a book,' says Quilty, seated cozily in his booth, eating an omelette.

'Oh, yeah?'

'Yeah. I had these paragraphs that were so huge, they went on for pages. Sentences that were also just enormous – two or three pages long. I had to shrink things down, I was told.'

Mack smiles. 'How about words? Did you use big words, too?'

'Huge words. And to top it off, I began the whole thing with a letter I razored off a billboard.' He pauses. 'That's a joke.'

'I get it.'

'There *was* a book, though. I was going to call it *Dating My Sofa: A Blind Man's Guide to Life.*'

Mack is quiet. There is always too much talking on these trips.

'Let's hit Memphis on the way back,' says Quilty irritably. 'For now, let's head straight to New Orleans.'

'That's what you want to do? Fine.' Mack has no great fondness for Memphis. Once, as a boy, he'd been chased by a bee there, down a street that was long and narrow and lined on one side with parked cars. He'd ducked into a phone booth, but the bee waited for him, and Mack ended up stepping out after twenty minutes and getting stung anyway. It wasn't true what they said about bees. They were not all that busy. They had time. They could wait. It was a myth, that stuff about busy as a bee.

'That way, coming back,' adds Quilty, 'we can take our time and hit the Peabody when the ducks are out. I want to do the whole duck thing.'

'Sure,' says Mack. 'The duck thing is the thing.' On the way out of Denny's, Mack pulls slightly away from Quilty to look at another missing-child poster. A boy named Seth, age five. The world – one cannot drive fast or far enough away from it – is coming at him in daggers.

'What are you looking at?'

'Nothing,' says Mack, then adds absently, 'a boy.'

'Really?' says Quilty.

Mack drives fast down through the small towns of the Delta: Eudora, Eupora, Tallula – the poorest ones with names like Hollywood, Banks, Rich. In each of them, a Baptist church is nestled up against a bait shop or a Tina's Touch of Class Cocktails. The strawy weeds are tall as people, and the cotton puffs here are planted in soils grown sandy, near shacks and burned-out cars, a cottonseed-oil factory towering over the fields, the closest hamburger at a Hardee's four miles away. Sometimes the cotton fields look like snow. Mack notices the broken-down signs: EAT MAID-RITE EATS or CAN'T BEAT DICK'S MEAT. They are both innocent and old, that peculiar mix, like a baby that looks like a grandmother, or a grandmother that looks like a girl. He and Quilty eat lunch and dinner at places that serve hush puppies and batter-fried pickles; it reminds Mack of his aunt's cooking. The air thickens and grows warm. Sinclair brontosauruses and old-style Coke signs protrude from the road stops and gas stations, and then, closer to Baton Rouge, antique stores sell the same kinds of old Coke signs.

'Recycling,' says Mack.

'Everyone's recycling,' says Quilty.

'Someone told me once' – Mack is thinking of Annie now – 'that we are all made from stars, that every atom in our bodies was at one time the atom of a star.'

'And you believed them?' Quilty hoots.

'Fuck you,' says Mack.

'I mean, in between, we were probably also some cheese at a sorority tea. Our ancestral relationship to stars!' says Quilty, now far away, making his point before some judge. 'It's the biological equivalent of hearsay.'

They stay in an antebellum mansion with a canopy bed. They sit beneath the canopy and play Trivial Pursuit.

Mack once again reads aloud his own questions. 'Who was George Bush referring to when reminiscing: "We've had some triumphs; we've made some mistakes; we've had some sex"?'

Mack stares. The canopy bed looks psychotic. Out the window he sees a sign across the street that says SPACE FOR LEASE AT ABSOLUTELY YOGURT. Next to it, a large white woman is hitting a small black dog with a shopping bag. What is wrong with this country? He turns the card over and looks. 'Ronald Reagan,' he says. He has taken to cheating like this.

'Is that your answer?' asks Quilty.

'Yes.'

'Well, you're probably right,' says Quilty, who often knows the answer before Mack has read it to him. Mack stares at the bed again, its canopy like the headdress the Duchess wore in *Alice in Wonderland*. His aunt would sometimes read that book to him, and it always made him feel queasy and confused.

On the nightstand, there are sachets of peach and apricot pits, the sickly sweet smell of a cancer ward. Everything here now in this room reminds him of his aunt.

'What former Pittsburgh Pirates slugger was the only player inducted into the Baseball Hall of Fame in 1988?' Mack reads. It is Quilty's turn.

'I've landed on the damn *sports* category?'

'Yup. What's your answer?'

'Linda Ronstadt. She was in *The Pirates of Penzance*. I know it went to Pittsburgh. I'm just not sure about the Hall of Fame part.'

Mack is quiet.

'Am I right?'

'No.'

'Well, you never used to do that – land me on those sports questions. Now you're getting difficult.'

'Yup,' says Mack.

~ ~ ~

The next morning, they go to a Coca-Cola museum, which the South seems to be full of. 'You'd think Coca-Cola was a national treasure,' Mack says.

'It's not?' says Quilty.

Individual states, Georgia and Mississippi and whichever else, are all competing for claims: first served here, first bottled there – first thirst, first burst – it is one big corporate battle of the bands. There is a strange kind of refuge from this to be found in driving through yet another cemetery, this one at Vicksburg, and so they do it, but quickly, keeping the trip moving so they will not feel, as they might have in Tapston, the irretrievable loss of each afternoon, the encroaching darkness, each improvised day over with at last – only to start up again, in the morning, oppressively identical, a checker in a game of checkers, or a joke in a book of jokes.

'They seem to have all this organized by state,' says Mack, looking out over the Vicksburg grounds, the rolling green dotted as if with aspirins.

He looks back at the park map, which he has spread over the steering wheel. Here he is: back in the Bone Zone.

'Well, let's go to the Indiana part,' says Quilty, 'and praise the Hoosier dead.'

'Okay,' says Mack, and when he comes upon a single small stone that says *Indiana* – not the proper section at all – he slows down and says, 'Here's the section,' so that Quilty can roll down the window and shout, 'Praise the Hoosier dead!' There are kindnesses one can perform for a blind man more easily than for the sighted.

Guapo barks and Mack lets loose with an incongruous rebel yell.

'Whose side are you on?' scolds Quilty, rolling his window back up. 'Let's get out of here. It's too hot.'

They drive some distance out of the park and then stop at the Civil War Museum they saw advertised the day before.

'Is this a fifty?' Quilty whispers, thrusting a bill toward Mack as they approach the entrance cashier.

'No, it's a twenty.'

'Find me a fifty. Is this a fifty?'

'Yeah, that's a fifty.'

Quilty thrusts the fifty toward the cashier. 'Excuse me,' he says in a loud voice. 'Do you have change for a great American general?'

'Do believe I do,' says the cashier, who chuckles a bit, taking the fifty and lifting up the drawer to his register. 'You Yankees are always liking to do that.'

Inside, the place is dark and cool and lined with glass display cases and mannequins in uniforms. There are photographs of soldiers and nurses and 'President and Mrs. Jefferson.' Because almost everything is behind glass and cannot be touched, Quilty grows bored. '"The city of Vicksburg,"' Mack reads aloud, '"forced to surrender to Grant on the Fourth of July, refused to celebrate Independence Day again until 1971."'

'When no one cared anymore,' adds Quilty. 'I like a place with a strong sense of grudge – which they, of course, call "a keen acquaintance with history."' He clears his throat. 'But let's get on to New Orleans. I also like a place that doesn't give a shit.'

In a restaurant overlooking the river, they eat yet more hush puppies and catfish. Guapo, unleashed, runs up and down the riverbank like a mad creature.

In the dusk, they head south, toward the Natchez Trace, through

Port Gibson: 'TOO BEAUTIFUL TO BURN' – ULYSSES S. GRANT, says the WELCOME sign. Quilty is dozing. It is getting dark, and the road isn't wide, but Mack passes all the slow-moving cars: an old VW bus (northern winters have eliminated these in Tapston), a red pickup piled with hay, a Plymouth Duster full of deaf people signing in a fantastic dance of hands. The light is on inside the Duster, and Mack pulls up alongside, watching. Everyone is talking at once – fingers flying, chopping, stretching the air, twining, pointing, touching. It is astonishing and beautiful. If only Quilty weren't blind, thinks Mack. If only Quilty weren't blind, he would really like being deaf.

~ ~ ~

There are, in New Orleans, all manner of oysters Rockefeller. There is the kind with the spinach chopped long and coarse like seaweed, scabs of bacon in a patch on top. Then there is the kind with the spinach moussed to a bright lime and dolloped onto the shell like algae. There is the kind with spinach leaves laid limply off the edge like socks. There is the kind with cheese. There is the kind without. There is even the kind with tofu.

'Whatever happened to clams casino?' asks Mack. 'I used to get those in Kentucky. Those were great.'

'Shellfish from a landlocked place? Never a great idea, my dear,' says Quilty. 'Stick with Nawlins. A city no longer known for its prostitutes quickly becomes known for its excellent food. Think about it. There's Paris. There's here. A city currently known for its prostitutes – Las Vegas, Amsterdam, Washington, D.C. – is seldom a good food city.'

'You should write a travel book.' Was Mack being sarcastic? Mack himself couldn't say.

'That's what *Dating My Sofa* was going to be. A kind of armchair travel book. For the blind.'

'I thought *Dating My Sofa* was going to be a novel.'

'Before it was a novel, it was going to be a travel book.'

~ ~ ~

They leave behind the wrought-iron cornstalk fence of their little inn for a walk through the Quarter. Soon they are at the wharf, and with little else to do, they step aboard a glittering paddle wheeler for a Plantation River cruise. Quilty trips on a slightly raised plank on the ramp. 'You know, I find this city neither big nor easy,' he says. The tour is supposed to be beer and sun and a little jazz band, but there is also a stop at Chalmette, the site of the Battle of New Orleans, so that people can get off and traipse through the cemetery.

Mack takes Quilty to a seat in the sun, then sits beside him. Guapo lifts his head and smells the swampy air. 'No more cemeteries,' says Mack, and Quilty readily agrees, though Mack also wonders whether, when they get there, they will be able to resist. It seems hard for them, when presented with all that toothy geometry of stone and bone, not to rush right up and say hi. The two of them are ill-suited to life; no doubt that is it. In feeling peculiar, homeless, cursed, and tired, they have become way too friendly. They no longer have any standards at all.

'All the graves are on stilts here anyway,' says Mack. 'The sea level and all.' The calliope starts up and the paddle wheel begins to revolve. Mack tips his head back to rest it against the seat and look at the sky all streaked with stringy clouds, bird blue cracked fuzzily with white. To the right, the clouds have more shape and against the blue look like the figures of a Wedgwood dish. What a fine fucking bowl beneath which they have all been caught and asked to swim out their days! 'Look at it this way,' people used to say to Mack. 'Things could be worse' – a bumper sticker for a goldfish or a bug. And it wasn't wrong – it just wasn't the point.

He falls asleep, and by the time the boat returns to the wharf, ten thousand anesthesiologists have invaded the town. There are buses and crowds. 'Uh-oh. Look out. A medical convention,' says Mack to Quilty. 'Watch your step.' At a turquoise kiosk near the pier, he spots more missing-children posters. He half-expects to see himself and Quilty posted up there, two more lost boys in America. Instead, there is a heart-breaking nine-year-old named Charlie. There is a three-year-old named Kyle. There is also the same kid from Denny's up north: Seth, age five.

'Are they cute?' asks Quilty.

'Who?' says Mack.

'All those nice young doctors,' says Quilty. 'Are they good-looking?'

'Hell if I know,' says Mack.

'Oh, don't give me that,' says Quilty. 'You forget to whom you are speaking, my dear. I can *feel* you looking around.'

Mack says nothing for a while. Not until after he's led Quilty over to a café for some chicory coffee and a beignet, which he feeds pieces of to Guapo. The people at the table next to them, in some kind of morbid theatrical contest, are reading aloud obituaries from the *Times-Picayune*.

'This town's wacko,' says Mack. Back at the hotel, someone in the next room is playing 'The Star-Spangled Banner' on the kazoo.

They speed out the next day – across the incandescent olive milk of the swamps, leafless, burned trees jutting from them like crosses. 'You're going too fast,' says Quilty. 'You're driving like goddamn Sean Penn!' Mack, following no particular route, heads out toward the salt marshes: grebes, blackbirds, sherbet-winged flamingos fly in low over the feathery bulrushes. It is all pretty, in its bleak way. Lone cattle are loose and munching cordgrass amid the oil rigs.

'Which way are we going?'

He suddenly swings north toward Memphis. 'North. Memphis.' All he can think of now is getting back.

'What are you thinking of?'

'Nothing.'

'What are you looking at?'

'Nothing. Scenery.'

'Hot bods?'

'Yeah. Just saw a great cow,' says Mack. 'And a not-bad possum.'

When they are finally checked into the Peabody Hotel, it is already late afternoon. Their room is a little stuffy and lit in a strange, golden way. Mack flops on the bed.

Quilty, beginning to perspire, takes his jacket off and throws it on the floor. 'Y'know: what is wrong with you?' he asks.

'What do you mean, *me*? What is wrong with *you*?'

'You're so distracted and weird.'

'We're traveling. I'm sight-seeing. I'm tired. Sorry if I seem distant.'

' "Sight-seeing." That's nice! How about me? Yoo-hoo!'

Mack sighs. When he goes on the attack like this, Quilty tends to head in five miserable directions at once. He has a brief nervous breakdown and shouts from every shattered corner of it, then afterward pulls himself together and apologizes. It is all a bit familiar. Mack closes his eyes, to sail away from him. He floats off and, trying not to think of Lou, briefly thinks of Annie, though the sudden blood rush that stiffens him pulls at his stitches and snaps him awake. He sits up. He kicks off his shoes and socks and looks at his pickled toes: slugs in a box.

Quilty is cross-legged on the floor, trying to do some deep-breathing exercises. He is trying to get chi to his meridians – or something like that. 'You think I don't know you're attracted to half the people you see?'

Quilty is saying. 'You think I'm stupid or something? You don't think I feel your head turn and your gaze stop everywhere we go?'

'What?'

'You're too much,' Quilty finally says to Mack.

'*I'm* too much? You are! You're so damn nervous and territorial,' Mack says.

'I have a highly inflamed sense of yard,' says Quilty. He has given up on the exercises. 'Blind people do. I don't want you sticking your hitchhiker's thumb out over the property line. It's a betrayal and an eyesore to the community!'

'What community? What are you talking about?'

'All you sighted people are alike. You think we're Mr Magoo! You think I'm not as aware as some guy who paints water towers and's got cysts on his dick?'

Mack shakes his head. He sits up and starts to put his shoes back on. 'You really go for the juggler, don't you?' he says.

'Juggler?' Quilty howls. '*Juggler*? No, obviously, I go for the clowns.'

Mack is puzzled. Quilty's head is tilted in that hyperalert way that says nothing in the room will get past him. 'Juggler,' Mack says. 'Isn't that the word? What is the word?'

'A juggler,' says Quilty, slowly for the jury, 'is someone who juggles.'

Mack's chest tightens around a small emptied space. He feels his own crappy luck returning like a curse. 'You don't even like me, do you?' he says.

'Like you? Is that what you're really asking?'

'I'm not sure,' says Mack. He looks around the hotel room. Not this, not any room with Quilty in it would ever be his home.

'Let me tell you a story,' says Quilty.

'I don't like stories,' Mack says.

It now seems to have cost Mack so much to be here. In his mind – a memory or a premonition, which is it, his mind does not distinguish – he sees himself returning not just to Tapston but to Kentucky or to Illinois, wherever it is Annie lives now, and stealing back his own-blooded boy, whom he loves, and who is his, and running fast with him toward a car, putting him in and driving off. It would be the proper thing, in a way. Other men have done it.

Quilty's story goes like this: 'A woman came to my office once very early on in my practice. Her case was a simple divorce that she made complicated by greed and stubbornness, and she worked up quite a bill. When she got the bill, she phoned me, shouting and saying angry things. I said, "Look, we'll work out a payment plan. One hundred dollars a month. How does that sound?" I was reasonable. My practice was new and struggling. Still, she refused to pay a cent. I had to take out a loan to pay my secretary, and I never forgot that. So, five years later, that very same woman's doctor phones me. She's got bone cancer, the doctor says, and I'm one of the only German Jews in town and might have the same blood type for a marrow transfusion for her. Would I consider it, at least consider having a blood test? I said, "Absolutely not," and hung up. The doctor called back. He begged me, but I hung up again. A month later, the woman died.'

'What's your point?' says Mack. Quilty's voice is flying apart now.

'That that is the truth about me,' he says. 'Don't you see—'

'Yes, *I* fucking see. I am the one here who does the seeing! Me and Guapo.'

He pauses for a long time. 'I don't forgive anybody anything. That is the point.'

'Y'know what? This whole thing is such a crock,' says Mack, but his voice is thin and diffident, and he finishes putting on his shoes, but without socks, and then grabs up his coat.

Downstairs, the clock says quarter to five, and a crowd is gathering to watch the ducks. A red carpet has already been rolled out from the elevator to the fountain, and this makes the ducks excited, anxious for the evening ritual, their clipped wings fluttering. Mack takes a table in the back and orders a double whiskey with ice. He drinks it fast – it freezes and burns in that great old way: it has been too long. He orders another. The pianist on the other side of the lobby is playing 'Street of Dreams': 'Love laughs at a king/Kings don't mean a thing' the man sings, and it seems to Mack the most beautiful song in the world. Men everywhere are about to die for reasons they don't know and wouldn't like if they did – but here is a song to do it by, so that life, in its mad belches and spasms, might not demolish so much this time.

The ducks drink and dive in the fountain.

Probably Mack is already drunk as a horse.

Near the Union Avenue door is a young woman mime, juggling Coke bottles. People waiting for the ducks have gathered to watch. Even in her white pancake makeup, she is attractive. Her red hair is bright as a daylily and through her black leotards her legs are taut as an archer's bow.

Go for the juggler, thinks Mack. Go for the juggler. His head hurts, but his throat and lungs are hot and clear.

Out of the corner of his eye, he suddenly notices Quilty and Guapo, stepping slow and unsure, making their way around the far edge of the crowd. Their expressions are lonely and distraught, even Guapo's. Mack looks back at the fountain. Soon Guapo will find him – but Mack is not going to move until then, needing the ceremony of Quilty's effort. He knows Quilty will devise some conciliatory gift. He will come up and touch Mack and whisper, 'Come back, don't be angry, you know this is how the two of us get.'

But for now, Mack will just watch the ducks, watch them summoned by their caretaker, an old uniformed black man who blows a silver whistle and wields a long rod, signaling the ducks out of the water, out onto the carpet in a line. They haven't had a thing to say about it, these ducks, thinks Mack, haven't done a thing to deserve it, but there they are, God's lilies, year-round in a giant hotel, someone caring for them the rest of their lives. All the other birds of the world – the mange-hollowed hawks, the lordless hens, the dumb clucks – will live punishing, unblessed lives, winging it north, south, here, there, searching for a place of rest. But not these. Not these *rich, lucky* ducks! graced with rug and stairs, upstairs and down, roof to pool to penthouse, always steered, guided, welcomed toward those golden elevator doors like a heaven's mouth, and though it isn't really a heaven's mouth, it is maybe the lip of all there is.

Mack sighs. Why must he always take the measure of his own stupid suffering? Why must he always look around and compare his own against others'?

Because God wants people to.

Even if you're comparing yourself to ducks?

Especially if you're comparing yourself to ducks.

He feels his own head shrink with the hate that is love with no place to go. He will do it: he will go back and get Lou if it kills him. A million soldiers are getting ready to die for less. He will find Annie; maybe it won't be that hard. And at first, he will ask her nicely. But then he will do what a father must: a boy is a father's. Sons love their fathers like nothing else. Mack read that once in a magazine.

Yet the more he imagines finding Lou, the more greatly he suspects that the whole mad task will indeed kill him. He sees – as if again in a vision (of what he must prevent or of what he cannot prevent, who knew with visions?) — the death of himself and the sorrow of his boy. He sees the wound in his own back, his eyes turning from fish-gray jellies to the plus and minus signs of a comic-book corpse. He sees Lou scratched and crawling back toward a house, the starry sky Mack's mocking sparkled shroud.

But he will do it anyway, or what is he? Pond scum envying the ducks. All is well. Safely rest. God is nigh.

~ ~ ~

As the birds walk up the red carpet, quacking and honking fussily, a pack of pleased Miss Americas, Mack watches them pause and look up, satisfied but quizzical, into the burst of lights from the tourists' cameras, the hollywood explosion of them along the runner. The birds weave a little, stop, then proceed again, seeming uncertain why anyone would want to take these pictures, flash a light, be there at all, why any of this should be happening, though, by God, and sometimes surely not by God, it happened every day.

Quilty, at the edge of the crowd, holds up his fingers, giving each person he passes the peace sign and saying, 'Peace.' He comes close to Mack.

'Peace,' he says.

'People don't say that anymore,' says Mack.

'Well, they should,' says Quilty. His nostrils have begun to flare, in that way that always signals a sob. He sinks to the floor and grabs Mack's feet. Quilty's gestures of contrition are like comets: infrequent and brilliant, but with a lot of space garbage. 'No more war!' Quilty cries. 'No more devastation!'

For the moment, it is only Quilty who is devastated. People are looking. 'You're upstaging the ducks,' says Mack.

Quilty pulls himself up via Mack's trousers. 'Have pity,' he says.

This is Quilty's audition ritual: whenever he feels it is time for it, he calls upon himself to audition for love. He has no script, no reliable sense of stage, just a faceful of his heart's own greasepaint and a relentless need for applause.

'Okay, okay,' says Mack, and as the elevator closes on the dozen birds and their bowing trainer, everybody in the hotel lounge claps.

'Thank you,' murmurs Quilty. 'You are too kind, too kind.'

ANNIE PROULX

BROKEBACK MOUNTAIN

Ennis del Mar wakes before five, wind rocking the trailer, hissing in around the aluminum door and window frames. The shirts hanging on a nail shudder slightly in the draft. He gets up, scratching the grey wedge of belly and pubic hair, shuffles to the gas burner, pours leftover coffee in a chipped enamel pan; the flame swathes it in blue. He turns on the tap and urinates in the sink, pulls on his shirt and jeans, his worn boots, stamping the heels against the floor to get them full on. The wind booms down the curved length of the trailer and under its roaring passage he can hear the scratching of fine gravel and sand. It could be bad on the highway with the horse trailer. He has to be packed and away from the place that morning. Again the ranch is on the market and they've shipped out the last of the horses, paid everybody off the day before, the owner saying, 'Give em to the real estate shark, I'm out a here,' dropping the keys in Ennis's hand. He might have to stay with his married daughter until he picks up another job, yet he is suffused with a sense of pleasure because Jack Twist was in his dream.

The stale coffee is boiling up but he catches it before it goes over the side, pours it into a stained cup and blows on the black liquid, lets a panel of the dream slide forward. If he does not force his attention on it, it might stoke the day, rewarm that old, cold time on the mountain when they owned the world and nothing seemed

ANNIE PROULX (born 1935): Proulx's books include the novels The Shipping News, Postcards, Accordion Crimes *and* That Old Ace in the Hole *and the collection* Close Range: Wyoming Stories. *She has three sons and lives in rural places.*

wrong. The wind strikes the trailer like a load of dirt coming off a dump truck, eases, dies, leaves a temporary silence.

~ ~ ~

They were raised on small, poor ranches in opposite corners of the state, Jack Twist in Lightning Flat up on the Montana border, Ennis del Mar from around Sage, near the Utah line, both high school dropout country boys with no prospects, brought up to hard work and privation, both rough-mannered, rough-spoken, inured to the stoic life. Ennis, reared by his older brother and sister after their parents drove off the only curve on Dead Horse Road leaving them twenty-four dollars in cash and a two-mortgage ranch, applied at age fourteen for a hardship license that let him make the hour-long trip from the ranch to the high school. The pickup was old, no heater, one windshield wiper and bad tires; when the transmission went there was no money to fix it. He had wanted to be a sophomore, felt the word carried a kind of distinction, but the truck broke down short of it, pitching him directly into ranch work.

In 1963 when he met Jack Twist, Ennis was engaged to Alma Beers. Both Jack and Ennis claimed to be saving money for a small spread; in Ennis's case that meant a tobacco can with two five-dollar bills inside. That spring, hungry for any job, each had signed up with Farm and Ranch Employment – they came together on paper as herder and camp tender for the same sheep operation north of Signal. The summer range lay above the tree line on Forest Service land on Brokeback Mountain. It would be Jack Twist's second summer on the mountain, Ennis's first. Neither of them was twenty.

They shook hands in the choky little trailer office in front of a table littered with scribbled papers, a Bakelite ashtray brimming with stubs. The venetian blinds hung askew and admitted a triangle of white light, the shadow of the foreman's hand moving into it. Joe Aguirre, wavy hair the color of cigarette ash and parted down the middle, gave them his point of view.

'Forest Service got designated campsites on the allotments. Them camps can be a couple a miles from where we pasture the sheep. Bad predator loss, nobody near lookin after em at night. What I want, camp tender in the main camp where the Forest Service says, but the HERDER' – pointing at Jack with a chop of his hand – 'pitch a pup tent on the q.t. with the sheep, out a sight, and he's goin a SLEEP there. Eat supper, breakfast in camp, but SLEEP WITH THE SHEEP, hunderd percent, NO FIRE, don't leave NO SIGN. Roll up that tent every mornin case Forest Service snoops around. Got the dogs, your .30–.30, sleep there. Last summer had goddamn near twenty-five percent loss. I don't want that again. YOU,' he said to Ennis, taking in the ragged hair, the big nicked hands, the jeans torn, button-gaping shirt, 'Fridays twelve noon be down at the bridge with your next week list and mules. Somebody with supplies'll be there in a pickup.' He didn't ask if Ennis had a watch but took a cheap round ticker on a braided cord from a box on a high shelf, wound and set it, tossed it to him as if he weren't worth the reach. 'TOMORROW MORNIN we'll truck you up the jump-off.' Pair of deuces going nowhere.

They found a bar and drank beer through the afternoon, Jack telling Ennis about a lightning storm on the mountain the year before that killed forty-two sheep, the peculiar stink of them and the way they bloated, the need for plenty of whiskey up there. He had shot an eagle, he said, turned his head to show the tail feather in his hatband. At first glance Jack seemed fair enough with his curly hair and quick laugh, but for a small man he carried some weight in the haunch and his smile disclosed buck-teeth, not pronounced enough to let him eat popcorn out of the neck of a jug, but noticeable. He was infatuated with the rodeo life and fastened his belt with a minor bull-riding buckle, but his boots were worn to the quick, holed beyond repair and he was crazy to be somewhere, anywhere else than Lightning Flat.

Ennis, high-arched nose and narrow face, was scruffy and a little cave-chested, balanced a small torso on long, caliper legs, possessed a muscular and supple body made for the horse and for fighting. His reflexes were uncommonly quick and he was farsighted enough to dislike reading anything except Hamley's saddle catalog.

The sheep trucks and horse trailers unloaded at the trailhead and a bandy-legged Basque showed Ennis how to pack the mules, two packs and a riding load on each animal ring-lashed with double diamonds and secured with half hitches, telling him, 'Don't never order soup. Them boxes a soup are real bad to pack.' Three puppies belonging to one of the blue heelers went in a pack basket, the runt inside Jack's coat, for he loved a little dog. Ennis picked out a big chestnut called Cigar Butt to ride, Jack a bay mare who turned out to have a low startle point. The string of spare horses included a mouse-colored grullo whose looks Ennis liked. Ennis and Jack, the dogs, horses and mules, a thousand ewes and their lambs flowed up the trail like dirty water through the timber and out above the tree line into the great flowery meadowss and the coursing, endless wind.

They got the big tent up on the Forest Service's platform, the kitchen and grub boxes secured. Both slept in camp that first night, Jack already bitching about Joe Aguirre's sleep-with-the-sheep-and-no-fire order, though he saddled the bay mare in the dark morning without saying much. Dawn came glassy orange, stained from below by a gelatinous band of pale green. The sooty bulk of the mountain paled slowly until it was the same color as the smoke from Ennis's breakfast fire. The cold air sweetened, banded pebbles and crumbs of soil cast sudden pencil-long shadows and the rearing lodgepole pines below them massed in slabs of somber malachite.

During the day Ennis looked across a great gulf and sometimes saw Jack, a small dot moving across a high meadow as an insect moves across a tablecloth; Jack, in his dark camp, saw Ennis as night fire, a red spark on the huge black mass of mountain.

~ ~ ~

Jack came lagging in late one afternoon, drank his two bottles of beer cooled in a wet sack on the shady side of the tent, ate two bowls of stew, four of Ennis's stone biscuits, a can of peaches, rolled a smoke, watched the sun drop.

'I'm commutin four hours a day,' he said morosely. 'Come in for breakfast, go back to the sheep, evenin get em bedded down, come in for supper, go back to the sheep, spend half the night jumpin up and checkin for coyotes. By rights I should be spendin the night here. Aguirre got no right a make me do this.'

'You want a switch?' said Ennis. 'I wouldn't mind herdin. I wouldn't mind sleepin out there.'

'That ain't the point. Point is, we both should be in this camp. And that goddamn pup tent smells like cat piss or worse.'

'Wouldn't mind bein out there.'

'Tell you what, you got a get up a dozen times in the night out there over them coyotes. Happy to switch but give you warnin I can't cook worth a shit. Pretty good with a can opener.'

'Can't be no worse than me, then. Sure, I wouldn't mind a do it.'

They fended off the night for an hour with the yellow kerosene lamp and around ten Ennis rode Cigar Butt, a good night horse, through the glimmering frost back to the sheep, carrying leftover biscuits, a jar of jam and a jar of coffee with him for the next day saying he'd save a trip, stay out until supper.

'Shot a coyote just first light,' he told Jack the next evening, sloshing his face with hot water, lathering up soap and hoping his razor had some cut left in it, while Jack peeled potatoes. 'Big son of a bitch. Balls on him size a apples. I bet he'd took a few lambs. Looked like he could a eat a camel. You want some a this hot water? There's plenty.'

'It's all yours.'

'Well, I'm goin a warsh everthing I can reach,' he said, pulling off his boots and jeans (no drawers, no socks, Jack noticed), slopping the green washcloth around until the fire spat.

They had a high-time supper by the fire, a can of beans each, fried potatoes and a quart of whiskey on shares, sat with their backs against a log, boot soles and copper jeans rivets hot, swapping the bottle while the lavender sky emptied of color and the chill air drained down, drinking, smoking cigarettes, getting up every now and then to piss, firelight throwing a sparkle in the arched stream, tossing sticks on the fire to keep the talk going, talking horses and rodeo, roughstock events, wrecks and injuries sustained, the submarine *Thresher* lost two months earlier with all hands and how it must have been in the last doomed minutes, dogs each had owned and known, the draft, Jack's home ranch where his father and mother held on, Ennis's family place folded years ago after his folks died, the older brother in Signal and a married sister in Casper. Jack said his father had been a pretty well-known bullrider years back but kept his secrets to himself, never gave Jack a word of advice, never came once to see Jack ride, though he had put him on the woolies when he was a little kid. Ennis said the kind of riding that interested him lasted longer than eight seconds and had some point to it. Money's a good point, said Jack, and Ennis had to agree. They were respectful of each other's opinions, each glad to have a companion where none had been expected. Ennis, riding against the wind back to the sheep in the treacherous, drunken light, thought he'd never had such a good time, felt he could paw the white out of the moon.

The summer went on and they moved the herd to new pasture, shifted the camp; the distance between the sheep and the new camp was greater and the night ride longer. Ennis rode easy, sleeping with his eyes open, but the hours he was away from the sheep stretched out and out. Jack pulled a squalling burr out of the harmonica, flattened a little from a fall off the skittish bay mare, and Ennis had a good raspy voice; a few nights they mangled their way through some songs. Ennis knew the salty words to 'Strawberry Roan.' Jack tried a Carl Perkins song, bawling 'what I say-ay-ay,' but he favored a sad hymn, 'Water-Walking Jesus,' learned from his mother who believed in the Pentecost, that he sang at dirge slowness, setting off distant coyote yips.

'Too late to go out to them damn sheep,' said Ennis, dizzy drunk on all fours one cold hour when the moon had notched past two. The meadow stones glowed white-green and a flinty wind worked over the meadow, scraped the fire low, then ruffled it into yellow silk sashes. 'Got you a extra blanket I'll roll up out here and grab forty winks, ride out at first light.'

'Freeze your ass off when that fire dies down. Better off sleepin in the tent.'

'Doubt I'll feel nothin.' But he staggered under canvas, pulled his boots off, snored on the ground cloth for a while, woke Jack with the clacking of his jaw.

'Jesus Christ, quit hammerin and get over here. Bedroll's big enough,' said Jack in an irritable sleep-clogged voice. It was big enough, warm enough, and in a little while they deepened their intimacy considerably. Ennis ran full-throttle on all roads whether fence mending or money spending, and he wanted none of it when Jack seized his left hand and brought it to his erect cock. Ennis jerked his hand away as though he'd touched fire, got to his knees, unbuckled his belt, shoved his pants down, hauled Jack onto all fours and, with the help of the clear slick and a little spit, entered him, nothing he'd done before but no instruction manual needed. They went at it in silence except for a few sharp intakes of breath and Jack's choked 'gun's goin *off*,' then out, down, and asleep.

Ennis woke in red dawn with his pants around his knees, a top-grade headache, and Jack butted against him; without saying anything about it both knew how it would go for the rest of the summer, sheep be damned.

As it did go. They never talked about the sex, let it happen, at first only in the tent at night, then in the full daylight with the hot sun striking down, and at evening in the fire glow, quick, rough, laughing and snorting, no lack of noises, but saying not a goddamn word except once Ennis said, 'I'm not no queer,' and Jack jumped in with 'Me neither. A one-shot thing. Nobody's business but ours.' There were only the two of them on the mountain flying in the euphoric, bitter air, looking down on the hawk's back and the crawling lights of vehicles on the plain below, suspended above ordinary affairs and distant from tame ranch dogs barking in the dark hours. They believed themselves invisible, not knowing Joe Aguirre had watched them through his 10x42 binoculars for ten minutes one day, waiting until they'd buttoned up their jeans, waiting until Ennis rode back to the sheep, before bringing up the message that Jack's people had sent word that his uncle Harold was in the hospital with pneumonia and expected not to make it. Though he did, and Aguirre came up again to say so, fixing Jack with his bold stare, not bothering to dismount.

In August Ennis spent the whole night with Jack in the main camp and in a blowy hailstorm the sheep took off west and got among a herd in another allotment. There was a damn miserable time for five days, Ennis and a Chilean herder with no English trying to sort them out, the task almost impossible as the paint brands were worn and faint at this late season. Even when the numbers were right Ennis knew the sheep were mixed. In a disquieting way everything seemed mixed.

The first snow came early, on August thirteenth, piling up a foot, but was followed by a quick melt. The next week Joe Aguirre sent word to bring them down – another, bigger storm was moving in from the Pacific – and they packed in the game and moved off the mountain with the sheep, stones rolling at their heels, purple cloud crowding in from the west and the metal smell of coming snow pressing them on. The mountain boiled with demonic energy, glazed with flickering broken-cloud light, the wind combed the grass and drew from the damaged krummholz and slit rock a bestial drone. As they descended the slope Ennis felt he was in a slow-motion, but headlong, irreversible fall.

Joe Aguirre paid them, said little. He had looked at the milling sheep with a sour expression, said, 'Some a these never went up there with you.' The count was not what he'd hoped for either. Ranch stiffs never did much of a job.

~ ~ ~

'You goin a do this next summer?' said Jack to Ennis in the street, one leg already up in his green pickup. The wind was gusting hard and cold.

'Maybe not.' A dust plume rose and hazed the air with fine grit and he squinted against it. 'Like I said, Alma and me's gettin married in December.

Try to get somethin on a ranch. You?' He looked away from Jack's jaw, bruised blue from the hard punch Ennis had thrown him on the last day.

'If nothin better comes along. Thought some about going back up to my daddy's place, give him a hand over the winter, then maybe head out for Texas in the spring. If the draft don't get me.'

'Well, see you around, I guess.' The wind tumbled an empty feed bag down the street until it fetched up under his truck.

'Right,' said Jack, and they shook hands, hit each other on the shoulder, then there was forty feet of distance between them and nothing to do but drive away in opposite directions. Within a mile Ennis felt like someone was pulling his guts out hand over hand a yard at a time. He stopped at the side of the road and, in the whirling new snow, tried to puke but nothing came up. He felt about as bad as he ever had and it took a long time for the feeling to wear off.

~ ~ ~

In December Ennis married Alma Beers and had her pregnant by mid-January. He picked up a few short-lived ranch jobs, then settled in as a wrangler on the old Elwood Hi-Top place north of Lost Cabin in Washakie County. He was still working there in September when Alma Jr., as he called his daughter, was born and their bedroom was full of the smell of old blood and milk and baby shit, and the sounds were of squalling and sucking and Alma's sleepy groans, all reassuring of fecundity and life's continuance to one who worked with livestock.

When the Hi-Top folded they moved to a small apartment in Riverton up over a laundry. Ennis got on the highway crew, tolerating it but working weekends at the Rafter B in exchange for keeping his horses out there. The second girl was born and Alma wanted to stay in town near the clinic because the child had an asthmatic wheeze.

'Ennis, please, no more damn lonesome ranches for us,' she said, sitting on his lap, wrapping her thin, freckled arms around him. 'Let's get a place here in town?'

'I guess,' said Ennis, slipping his hand up her blouse sleeve and stirring the silky armpit hair, then easing her down, fingers moving up her ribs to the jelly breast, over the round belly and knee and up into the wet gap all the way to the north pole or the equator depending which way you thought you were sailing, working at it until she shuddered and bucked against his hand and he rolled her over, did quickly what she hated. They stayed in the little apartment which he favored because it could be left at any time.

~ ~ ~

The fourth summer since Brokeback Mountain came on and in June Ennis had a general delivery letter from Jack Twist, the first sign of life in all that time.

Friend this letter is a long time over due. Hope you get it. Heard you was in Riverton. Im coming thru on the 24th, thought Id stop and buy you a beer. Drop me a line if you can, say if your there.

The return address was Childress, Texas. Ennis wrote back, *you bet*, gave the Riverton address.

The day was hot and clear in the morning, but by noon the clouds had pushed up out of the west rolling a little sultry air before them. Ennis, wearing his best shirt, white with wide black stripes, didn't know what time Jack would get there and so had taken the day off, paced back and forth, looking down into a street pale with dust. Alma was saying something about taking his friend to the Knife & Fork for supper instead of cooking it was so hot, if they could get a baby-sitter, but Ennis said more likely he'd just go out with Jack and get drunk. Jack was not a restaurant type, he said, thinking of the dirty spoons sticking out of the cans of cold beans balanced on the log.

Late in the afternoon, thunder growling, that same old green pickup rolled in and he saw Jack get out of the truck, beat-up Resistol tilted back. A hot jolt scalded Ennis and he was out on the landing pulling the door closed behind him. Jack took the stairs two and two. They seized each other by the shoulders, hugged mightily, squeezing the breath out of each other, saying, son of a bitch, son of a bitch, then, and easily as the right key turns the lock tumblers, their mouths came together, and hard, Jack's big teeth bringing blood, his hat falling to the floor, stubble rasping, wet saliva welling, and the door opening and Alma looking out for a few seconds at Ennis's straining shoulders and shutting the door again and still they clinched, pressing chest and groin and thigh and leg together, treading on each other's toes until they pulled apart to breathe and Ennis, not big on endearments, said what he said to his horses and daughters, little darlin.

The door opened again a few inches and Alma stood in the narrow light.

What could he say? 'Alma, this is Jack Twist, Jack, my wife Alma.' His chest was heaving. He could smell Jack – the intensely familiar odor of cigarettes, musky sweat and a faint sweetness like grass, and with it the rushing cold of the mountain. 'Alma,' he said, 'Jack and me ain't seen each other in four years.' As if it were a reason. He was glad the light was dim on the landing but did not turn away from her.

'Sure enough,' said Alma in a low voice. She had seen what she had seen. Behind her in the room lightning lit the window like a white sheet waving and the baby cried.

'You got a kid?' said Jack. His shaking hand grazed Ennis's hand, electrical current snapped between them.

'Two little girls,' Ennis said. 'Alma Jr. and Francine. Love them to pieces.' Alma's mouth twitched.

'I got a boy,' said Jack. 'Eight months old. Tell you what, I married a cute little old Texas girl down in Childress – Lureen.' From the vibration of the floorboard on which they both stood Ennis could feel how hard Jack was shaking.

'Alma,' he said. 'Jack and me is goin out and get a drink. Might not get back tonight, we get drinkin and talkin.'

'Sure enough,' Alma said, taking a dollar bill from her pocket. Ennis guessed she was going to ask him to get her a pack of cigarettes, bring him back sooner.

'Please to meet you,' said Jack, trembling like a run-out horse.

'Ennis –' said Alma in her misery voice, but that didn't slow him down on the stairs and he called back, 'Alma, you want smokes there's some in the pocket a my blue shirt in the bedroom.'

They went off in Jack's truck, bought a bottle of whiskey and within twenty minutes were in the Motel Siesta jouncing a bed. A few handfuls of hail rattled against the window followed by rain and slippery wind banging the unsecured door of the next room then and through the night.

~ ~ ~

The room stank of semen and smoke and sweat and whiskey, of old carpet and sour hay, saddle leather, shit and cheap soap. Ennis lay spread-eagled, spent and wet, breathing deep, still half tumescent, Jack blowing forceful cigarette clouds like whale spouts, and Jack said, 'Christ, it got a be all that time a yours ahorseback makes it so goddamn good. We got to talk about this. Swear to god I didn't know we was goin a get into this again – yeah,

I did. Why I'm here. I fuckin knew it. Redlined all the way, couldn't get here fast enough.'

'I didn't know where in the *hell* you was,' said Ennis. 'Four years. I about give up on you. I figured you was sore about that punch.'

'Friend,' said Jack, 'I was in Texas rodeoin. How I met Lureen. Look over on that chair.'

On the back of the soiled orange chair he saw the shine of a buckle. 'Bullridin?'

'Yeah. I made three fuckin thousand dollars that year. Fuckin starved. Had to borrow everything but a toothbrush from other guys. Drove grooves across Texas. Half the time under that cunt truck fixin it. Anyway, I didn't never think about losin. Lureen? There's some serious money there. Her old man's got it. Got this farm machinery business. Course he don't let her have none a the money, and he hates my fuckin guts, so it's a hard go now but one these days –'

'Well, you're goin a go where you look. Army didn't get you?' The thunder sounded far to the east, moving from them in its red wreaths of light.

'They can't get no use out a me. Got some crushed vertebrates. And a stress fracture, the arm bone here, you know how bullridin you're always leverin it off your thigh? – she gives a little ever time you do it. Even if you tape it good you break it a little goddamn bit at a time. Tell you what, hurts like a bitch afterwards. Had a busted leg. Busted in three places. Come off the bull and it was a big bull with a lot a drop, he got rid a me in about three flat and he come after me and he was sure faster. Lucky enough. Friend a mine got his oil checked with a horn dipstick and that was all she wrote. Bunch a other things, fuckin busted ribs, sprains and pains, torn ligaments. See, it ain't like it was in my daddy's time. It's guys with money go to college, trained athaletes. You got a have some money to rodeo now. Lureen's old man wouldn't give me a dime if I dropped it, except one way. And I know enough about the game now so I see that I ain't never goin a be on the bubble. Other reasons. I'm gettin out while I still can walk.'

Ennis pulled Jack's hand to his mouth, took a hit from the cigarette, exhaled. 'Sure as hell seem in one piece to me. You know, I was sittin up here all that time tryin to figure out if I was –? I know I ain't. I mean here we both got wives and kids, right? I like doin it with women, yeah, but Jesus H., ain't nothin like this. I never had no thoughts a doin it with another guy except I sure wrang it out a hunderd times thinkin about you. You do it with other guys? Jack?'

'Shit no,' said Jack, who had been riding more than bulls, not rolling his own. 'You know that. Old Brokeback got us good and it sure ain't over. We got a work out what the fuck we're goin a do now.'

'That summer,' said Ennis. 'When we split up after we got paid out I had gut cramps so bad I pulled over and tried to puke, thought I ate somethin bad at that place in Dubois. Took me about a year a figure out it was that I shouldn't a let you out a my sights. Too late then by a long, long while.'

'Friend,' said Jack. 'We got us a fuckin situation here. Got a figure out what to do.'

'I doubt there's nothin now we can do,' said Ennis. 'What I'm sayin, Jack, I built a life up in them years. Love my little girls. Alma? It ain't her fault. You got your baby and wife, that place in Texas. You and me can't hardly be decent together if what happened back there' – he jerked his head in the direction of the apartment – 'grabs on us like that. We do that in the wrong place we'll be dead. There's no reins on this one. It scares the piss out a me.'

'Got to tell you, friend, maybe somebody seen us that summer. I was back there the next June, thinkin about goin back – I didn't, lit out for Texas instead – and Joe Aguirre's in the office and he says to me, he says, "You boys found a way to make the time pass up there, didn't you," and I give him a look but when I went out I seen he had a big-ass pair a binoculars hangin off his rearview.' He neglected to add that the foreman had leaned back in his squeaky wooden tilt chair, said, Twist, you guys wasn't gettin paid to leave the dogs baby-sit the sheep while you stemmed the rose, and declined to rehire him. He went on, 'Yeah, that little punch a yours surprised me. I never figured you to throw a dirty punch.'

'I come up under my brother K.E., three years older'n me, slugged me silly ever day. Dad got tired a me come bawlin in the house and when I was about six he set me down and says, Ennis, you got a problem and you got a fix it or it's gonna be with you until you're ninety and K.E.'s ninety-three. Well, I says, he's bigger'n me. Dad says, you got a take him unawares, don't say nothin to him, make him feel some pain, get out fast and keep doin it until he takes the message. Nothin like hurtin somebody to make him hear good. So I did. I got him in the outhouse, jumped him on the stairs, come over to his pillow in the night while he was sleepin

and pasted him damn good. Took about two days. Never had trouble with
K.E. since. The lesson was, don't say nothin and get it over with quick.'
A telephone rang in the next room, rang on and on, stopped abruptly in
mid-peal.

'You won't catch me again,' said Jack. 'Listen. I'm thinkin, tell you
what, if you and me had a little ranch together, little cow and calf operation,
your horses, it'd be some sweet life. Like I said, I'm gettin out a rodeo. I
ain't no broke-dick rider but I don't got the bucks a ride out this slump
I'm in and I don't got the bones a keep gettin wrecked. I got it figured,
got this plan, Ennis, how we can do it, you and me. Lureen's old man,
you bet he'd give me a bunch if I'd get lost. Already more or less said it –'

'Whoa, whoa, whoa. It ain't goin a be that way. We can't. I'm stuck
with what I got, caught in my own loop. Can't get out of it. Jack, I don't
want a be like them guys you see around sometimes. And I don't want a
be dead. There was these two old guys ranched together down home, Earl
and Rich – Dad would pass a remark when he seen them. They was a joke
even though they was pretty tough old birds. I was what, nine years old
and they found Earl dead in a irrigation ditch. They'd took a tire iron to
him, spurred him up, drug him around by his dick until it pulled off, just
bloody pulp. What the tire iron done looked like pieces a burned tomatoes
all over him, nose tore down from skiddin on gravel.'

'You seen that?'

'Dad made sure I seen it. Took me to see it. Me and K.E. Dad laughed
about it. Hell, for all I know he done the job. If he was alive and was to
put his head in that door right now you bet he'd go get his tire iron. Two
guys livin together? No. All I can see is we get together once in a while
way the hell out in the back a nowhere –'

'How much is once in a while?' said Jack. 'Once in a while ever four
fuckin years?'

'No,' said Ennis, forbearing to ask whose fault that was. 'I goddamn
hate it that you're goin a drive away in the mornin and I'm goin back
to work. But if you can't fix it you got a stand it,' he said. 'Shit. I been
lookin at people on the street. This happen a other people? What the hell
do they do?'

'It don't happen in Wyomin and if it does I don't know what they do,
maybe go to Denver,' said Jack, sitting up, turning away from him, 'and I
don't give a flyin fuck. Son of a bitch, Ennis, take a couple days off. Right
now. Get us out a here. Throw your stuff in the back a my truck and let's

get up in the mountains. Couple a days. Call Alma up and tell her you're goin. Come on, Ennis, you just shot my airplane out a the sky – give me somethin a go on. This ain't no little thing that's happenin here.'

The hollow ringing began again in the next room, and as if he were answering it, Ennis picked up the phone on the bedside table, dialed his own number.

~ ~ ~

A slow corrosion worked between Ennis and Alma, no real trouble, just widening water. She was working at a grocery store clerk job, saw she'd always have to work to keep ahead of the bills on what Ennis made. Alma asked Ennis to use rubbers because she dreaded another pregnancy. He said no to that, said he would be happy to leave her alone if she didn't want any more of his kids. Under her breath she said, 'I'd have em if you'd support em.' And under that, thought, anyway, what you like to do don't make too many babies.

Her resentment opened out a little every year: the embrace she had glimpsed, Ennis's fishing trips once or twice a year with Jack Twist and never a vacation with her and the girls, his disinclination to step out and have any fun, his yearning for low-paid, long-houred ranch work, his propensity to roll to the wall and sleep as soon as he hit the bed, his failure to look for a decent permanent job with the country or the power company, put her in a long, slow dive and when Alma Jr. was nine and Francine seven she said, what am I doin hangin around with him, divorced Ennis and married the Riverton grocer.

Ennis went back to ranch work, hired on here and there, not getting much ahead but glad enough to be around stock again, free to drop things, quit if he had to and go into the mountains at short notice. He had no serious hard feelings, just a vague sense of getting short-changed, and showed it was all right by taking Thanksgiving dinner with Alma and her grocer and the kids, sitting between his girls and talking horses to them, telling jokes, trying not to be a sad daddy. After the pie Alma got him off in the kitchen, scraped the plates and said she worried about him and he ought to get married again. He saw she was pregnant, about four, five months, he guessed.

'Once burned,' he said, leaning against the counter, feeling too big for the room.

'You still go fishin with that Jack Twist?'

'Some.' He thought she'd take the pattern off the plate with the scraping.

'You know,' she said, and from her tone he knew something was coming, 'I used to wonder how come you never brought any trouts home. Always said you caught plenty. So one time I got your creel case open the night before you went on one a your little trips – price tag still on it after five years – and I tied a note on the end of the line. It said, hello Ennis, bring some fish home, love, Alma. And then you come back and said you'd caught a bunch a browns and ate them up. Remember? I looked in the case when I got a chance and there was my note still tied there and that line hadn't touched water in its life.' As though the word 'water' had called out its domestic cousin she twisted the faucet, sluiced the plates.

'That don't mean nothin.'

'Don't lie, don't try to fool me, Ennis. I know what it means. Jack Twist? Jack Nasty. You and him –'

She'd overstepped his line. He seized her wrist; tears sprang and rolled, a dish clattered.

'Shut up,' he said. 'Mind your own business. You don't know nothin about it.'

'I'm goin a yell for Bill.'

'You fuckin go right ahead. Go on and fuckin yell. I'll make him eat the fuckin floor and you too.' He gave another wrench that left her with a burning bracelet, shoved his hat on backwards and slammed out. He went to the Black and Blue Eagle bar that night, got drunk, had a short dirty fight and left. He didn't try to see his girls for a long time, figuring they would look him up when they got the sense and years to move out from Alma.

~ ~ ~

They were no longer young men with all of it before them. Jack had filled out through the shoulders and hams, Ennis stayed as lean as a clothes-pole, stepped around in worn boots, jeans and shirts summer and winter, added a canvas coat in cold weather. A benign growth appeared on his eyelid and gave it a drooping appearance, a broken nose healed crooked.

Years on years they worked their way through the high meadows and mountain drainages, horse-packing into the Big Horns, Medicine Bows, south end of the Gallatins, Absarokas, Granites, Owl Creeks, the Bridger-Teton Range, the Freezeouts and the Shirleys, Ferrises and the Rattlesnakes, Salt River Range, into the Wind Rivers over and again, the Sierra Madres, Gros Ventres, the Washakies, Laramies, but never returning to Brokeback.

Down in Texas Jack's father-in-law died and Lureen, who inherited the farm equipment business, showed a skill for management and hard deals. Jack found himself with a vague managerial title, traveling to stock and agricultural machinery shows. He had some money now and found ways to spend it on his buying trips. A little Texas accent flavored his sentences, 'cow' twisted into 'kyow' and 'wife' coming out as 'waf.' He'd had his front teeth filed down and capped, said he'd felt no pain, and to finish the job grew a heavy mustache.

~ ~ ~

In May of 1983 they spent a few cold days at a series of little icebound, no-name high lakes, then worked across into the Hail Strew River drainage.

Going up, the day was fine but the trail deep-drifted and slopping wet at the margins. They left it to wind through a slashy cut, leading the horses through brittle branchwood, Jack, the same eagle feather in his old hat, lifting his head in the heated noon to take the air scented with resinous lodgepole, the dry needle duff and hot rock, bitter juniper crushed beneath the horses' hooves. Ennis, weather-eyed, looked west for the heated cumulus that might come up on such a day but the boneless blue was so deep, said Jack, that he might drown looking up.

Around three they swung through a narrow pass to a southeast slope where the strong spring sun had had a chance to work, dropped down to the trail again which lay snowless below them. They could hear the river muttering and making a distant train sound a long way off. Twenty minutes on they surprised a black bear on the bank above them rolling a log over for grubs and Jack's horse shied and reared, Jack saying 'Wo! Wo!' and Ennis's bay dancing and snorting but holding. Jack reached for the .30-.06 but there was no need; the startled bear galloped into the trees with the lumpish gait that made it seem it was falling apart.

The tea-colored river ran fast with snowmelt, a scarf of bubbles at every high rock, pools and setbacks streaming. The ochre-branched willows swayed stiffly, pollened catkins like yellow thumbprints. The horses drank and Jack dismounted, scooped icy water up in his hand, crystalline drops falling from his fingers, his mouth and chin glistening with wet.

'Get beaver fever doin that,' said Ennis, then, 'Good enough place,' looking at the level bench above the river, two or three fire-rings from old hunting camps. A sloping meadow rose behind the bench, protected by a stand of lodgepole. There was plenty of dry wood. They set up camp without saying much, picketed the horses in the meadow. Jack broke the seal on a bottle of whiskey, took a long, hot swallow, exhaled forcefully, said, 'That's one a the two things I need right now,' capped and tossed it to Ennis.

On the third morning there were the clouds Ennis had expected, a grey racer out of the west, a bar of darkness driving wind before it and small flakes. It faded after an hour into tender spring snow that heaped wet and heavy. By nightfall it turned colder. Jack and Ennis passed a joint back and forth, the fire burning late, Jack restless and bitching about the cold, poking the flames with a stick, twisting the dial of the transistor radio until the batteries died.

Ennis said he'd been putting the blocks to a woman who worked part-time at the Wolf Ears bar in Signal where he was working now for Stoutamire's cow and calf outfit, but it wasn't going anywhere and she had some problems he didn't want. Jack said he'd had a thing going with the wife of a rancher down the road in Childress and for the last few months he'd slank around expecting to get shot by Lureen or the husband, one. Ennis laughed a little and said he probably deserved it. Jack said he was doing all right but he missed Ennis bad enough sometimes to make him whip babies.

The horses nickered in the darkness beyond the fire's circle of light. Ennis put his arm around Jack, pulled him close, said he saw his girls about once a month, Alma Jr. a shy seventeen-year-old with his beanpole length, Francine a little live wire. Jack slid his cold hand between Ennis's legs, said he was worried about his boy who was, no doubt about it, dyslexic or something, couldn't get anything right, fifteen years old and couldn't hardly read, *he* could see it though goddamn Lureen wouldn't admit to it and pretended the kid was o.k., refused to get any bitchin kind a help about it. He didn't know what the fuck the answer was. Lureen had the money and called the shots.

'I used a want a boy for a kid,' said Ennis, undoing buttons, 'but just got little girls.'

'I didn't want none a either kind,' said Jack. 'But fuck-all has worked the way I wanted. Nothin never come to my hand the right way.' Without getting up he threw deadwood on the fire, the sparks flying up with their truths and lies, a few hot points of fire landing on their hands and faces, not for the first time, and they rolled down into the dirt. One thing never changed: the brilliant charge of their infrequent couplings was darkened by the sense of time flying, never enough time, never enough.

A day or two later in the trailhead parking lot, horses loaded into the trailer, Ennis was ready to head back to Signal, Jack up to Lightning Flat to see the old man. Ennis leaned into Jack's window, said what he'd been putting off the whole week, that likely he couldn't get away again until November after they'd shipped stock and before winter feeding started.

'November. What in hell happened a August? Tell you what, we said August, nine, ten days. Christ, Ennis! Whyn't you tell me this before? You had a fuckin week to say some little word about it. And why's it we're always in the friggin cold weather? We ought a do somethin. We ought a go south. We ought a go to Mexico one day.'

'Mexico? Jack, you know me. All the travelin I ever done is goin around the coffeepot lookin for the handle. And I'll be runnin the baler all August, that's what's the matter with August. Lighten up, Jack. We can hunt in November, kill a nice elk. Try if I can get Don Wroe's cabin again. We had a good time that year.'

'You know, friend, this is a goddamn bitch of a unsatisfactory situation. You used a come away easy. It's like seein the pope now.'

'Jack, I got a work. Them earlier days I used a quit the jobs. You got a wife with money, a good job. You forget how it is bein broke all the time. You ever hear a child support? I been payin out for years and got more to go! Let me tell you, I can't quit this one. and I can't get the time off. It was tough gettin this time — some a them late heifers is still calvin. You don't leave then. You don't. Stoutamire is a hell-raiser and he raised hell about me takin the week. I don't blame him. He probly ain't got a night's sleep since I left. The trade-off was August. You got a better idea?'

'I did once.' The tone was bitter and accusatory.

Ennis said nothing, straightened up slowly, rubbed at his forehead; a horse stamped inside the trailer. He walked to his truck, put his hand on the trailer, said something that only the horses could hear, turned and walked back at a deliberate pace.

'You been a Mexico, Jack?' Mexico was the place. He'd heard. He was cutting fence now, trespassing in the shoot-em zone.

'Hell yes, I been. Where's the fuckin problem?' Braced for it all these years and here it came, late and unexpected.

'I got a say this to you one time, Jack, and I ain't foolin. What I don't know,' said Ennis, 'all them things I don't know could get you killed if I should come to know them.'

'Try this one,' said Jack, 'and *I'll* say it just one time. Tell you what, we could a had a good life together, a fuckin real good life. You wouldn't do it, Ennis, so what we got now is Brokeback Mountain. Everything built on that. It's all we got, boy, fuckin all, so I hope you know that if you don't never know the rest. Count the damn few times we been together in twenty years. Measure the fuckin short leash you keep me on, then ask me about Mexico and then tell me you'll kill me for needin it and not hardly never gettin it. You got no fuckin idea how bad it gets. I'm not you. I can't make it on a couple a high-altitude fucks once or twice a year. You're too much for me, Ennis, you son of a whoreson bitch. I wish I knew how to quit you.'

Like vast clouds of steam from thermal springs in winter the years of things unsaid and now unsayable – admissions, declarations, shames, guilts, fears – rose around them. Ennis stood as if heart-shot, face grey and deep-lined, grimacing, eyes screwed shut, fists clenched, legs caving, hit the ground on his knees.

'Jesus,' said Jack. 'Ennis?' But before he was out of the truck, trying to guess if it was heart attack or the overflow of an incendiary rage, Ennis was back on his feet and somehow, as a coat hanger is straightened to open a locked car and then bent again to its original shape, they torqued things almost to where they had been, for what they'd said was no news. Nothing ended, nothing begun, nothing resolved.

~ ~ ~

What Jack remembered and craved in a way he could neither help nor understand was the time that distant summer on Brokeback when Ennis had come up behind him and pulled him close, the silent embrace satisfying some shared and sexless hunger.

They had stood that way for a long time in front of the fire, its burning tossing ruddy chunks of light, the shadow of their bodies a single column against the rock. The minutes ticked by from the round watch in Ennis's pocket, from the sticks in the fire settling into coals. Stars bit through the wavy heat layers above the fire. Ennis's breath came slow and quiet, he hummed, rocked a little in the sparklight and Jack leaned against the steady heartbeat, the vibrations of the humming like faint electricity and, standing, he fell into sleep that was not sleep but something else drowsy and tranced until Ennis, dredging up a rusty but still useable phrase from the childhood time before his mother died, said, 'Time to hit the hay, cowboy. I got a go. Come on, you're sleepin on your feet like a horse,' and gave Jack a shake, a push, and went off in the darkness. Jack heard his spurs tremble as he mounted, the words 'see you tomorrow,' and the horse's shuddering snort, grind of hoof on stone.

Later, that dozy embrace solidified in his memory as the single moment of artless, charmed happiness in their separate and difficult lives. Nothing marred it, even the knowledge that Ennis would not then embrace him face to face because he did not want to see nor feel that it was Jack he held. And maybe, he thought, they'd never got much farther than that. Let be, let be.

~ ~ ~

Ennis didn't know about the accident for months until his postcard to Jack saying that November still looked like the first chance came back stamped DECEASED. He called Jack's number in Childress, something he had done only once before when Alma divorced him and Jack had misunderstood the reason for the call, had driven twelve hundred miles north for nothing. This would be all right, Jack would answer, had to answer. But he did not. It was Lureen and she said who? who is this? and when he told her again she said in a level voice yes, Jack was pumping up a flat on the truck out on a back road when the tire blew up. The bead was damaged somehow and the force of the explosion slammed the rim into his face, broke his nose and jaw and knocked him unconscious on his back. By the time someone came along he had drowned in his own blood.

No, he thought, they got him with the tire iron.

'Jack used to mention you,' she said. 'You're the fishing buddy or the hunting buddy, I know that. Would have let you know,' she said, 'but I wasn't sure about your name and address. Jack kept most a his friends addresses in his head. It was a terrible thing. He was only thirty-nine years old.'

The huge sadness of the northern plains rolled down on him. He didn't know which way it was, the tire iron or a real accident, blood choking down Jack's throat and nobody to turn him over. Under the wind drone he heard steel slamming off bone, the hollow chatter of a settling tire rim.

'He buried down there?' He wanted to curse her for letting Jack die on the dirt road.

The little Texas voice came slip-sliding down the wire. 'We put a stone up. He use to say he wanted to be cremated, ashes scattered on Brokeback Mountain. I didn't know where that was. So he was cremated, like he wanted, and like I say, half his ashes was interred here, and the rest I sent up to his folks. I thought Brokeback Mountain was around where he grew up. But knowing Jack, it might be some pretend place where the bluebirds sing and there's a whiskey spring.'

'We herded sheep on Brokeback one summer,' said Ennis. He could hardly speak.

'Well, he said it was his place. I thought he meant to get drunk. Drink whiskey up there. He drank a lot.'

'His folks still up in Lightnin Flat?'

'Oh yeah. They'll be there until they die. I never met them. They didn't come down for the funeral. You get in touch with them. I suppose they'd appreciate it if his wishes was carried out.'

No doubt about it, she was polite but the little voice was cold as snow.

~ ~ ~

The road to Lightning Flat went through desolate country past a dozen abandoned ranches distributed over the plain at eight- and ten-mile intervals, houses sitting blank-eyed in the weeds, corral fences down. The mailbox read John C. Twist. The ranch was a meagre little place, leafy spurge taking over. The stock was too far distant for him to see their condition, only that they were black baldies. A porch stretched across the front of the tiny brown stucco house, four rooms, two down, two up.

Ennis sat at the kitchen table with Jack's father. Jack's mother, stout and careful in her movements as though recovering from an operation, said, 'Want some coffee, don't you? Piece a cherry cake?'

'Thank you, ma'am, I'll take a cup a coffee but I can't eat no cake just now.'

The old man sat silent, his hands folded on the plastic tablecloth, staring at Ennis with an angry, knowing expression. Ennis recognized in him a not uncommon type with the hard need to be the stud duck in the pond. He couldn't see much of Jack in either one of them, took a breath.

'I feel awful bad about Jack. Can't begin to say how bad I feel. I knew him a long time. I come by to tell you that if you want me to take his ashes up there on Brokeback like his wife says he wanted I'd be proud to.'

There was a silence. Ennis cleared his throat but said nothing more.

The old man said, 'Tell you what, I know where Brokeback Mountain is. He thought he was too goddamn special to be buried in the family plot.'

Jack's mother ignored this, said, 'He used a come home every year, even after he was married and down in Texas, and help his daddy on the ranch for a week, fix the gates and mow and all. I kept his room like it was when he was a boy and I think he appreciated that. You are welcome to go up in his room if you want.'

The old man spoke angrily. 'I can't get no help out here. Jack used a say, "Ennis del Mar," he used a say, "I'm goin a bring him up here one a these days and we'll lick this damn ranch into shape." He had some half-baked idea the two a you was goin a move up here, build a log cabin and help me run this ranch and bring it up. Then, this spring he's got another one's goin a come up here with him and build a place and help run the ranch, some ranch neighbor a his from down in Texas. He's goin a split up with his wife and come back here. So he says. But like most a Jack's ideas it never come to pass.'

So now he knew it had been the tire iron. He stood up, said, you bet he'd like to see Jack's room, recalled one of Jack's stories about this old man. Jack was dick-clipped and the old man was not; it bothered the son who had discovered the anatomical disconformity during a hard scene. He had been about three or four, he said always late getting to the toilet, struggling with buttons, the seat, the height of the thing and often as not left the surroundings sprinkled down. The old man blew up about it and this one time worked into a crazy rage. 'Christ, he licked the stuffin out a me, knocked me down on the bathroom floor, whipped me with his belt. I thought he was killin me. Then he says, ("You want a know what it's like with piss all over the place? I'll learn you,") and he pulls it out and lets go all over me, soaked me, then he throws a towel at me and makes me mop up the floor, take my clothes off and warsh them in the bathtub, warsh out the towel, I'm bawlin and blubberin. But while he was hosin me down I seen he had some extra material that I was missin. I seen they'd cut me different like you'd crop a ear or scorch a brand. No way to get it right with him after that.'

The bedroom, at the top of a steep stair that had its own climbing rhythm, was tiny and hot, afternoon sun pounding through the west window, hitting the narrow boy's bed against the wall, an ink-stained desk and wooden chair, a b.b. gun in a hand-whittled rack over the bed. The window looked down on the gravel road stretching south and it occurred to him that for his growing-up years that was the only road Jack knew. An ancient magazine photograph of some dark-haired movie star was taped to the wall beside the bed, the skin tone gone magenta. He could hear Jack's mother downstairs running water, filling the kettle and setting it back on the stove, asking the old man a muffled question.

The closet was a shallow cavity with a wooden rod braced across, a faded cretonne curtain on a string closing it off from the rest of the room. In the closet hung two pairs of jeans crease-ironed and folded neatly over wire hangers, on the floor a pair of worn packer boots he thought he remembered. At the north end of the closet a tiny jog in the wall made a slight hiding place and here, stiff with long suspension from a nail, hung a shirt. He lifted it off the nail. Jack's old shirt from Brokeback days. The dried blood on the sleeve was his own blood; a gushing nosebleed on the last afternoon on the mountain when Jack, in their contortionist grappling and wrestling, had slammed Ennis's nose hard with his knee. He had staunched the blood which was everywhere, all over both of them, with his shirtsleeve, but the staunching hadn't held because Ennis had suddenly swung from the deck and laid the ministering angel out in the wild columbine, wings folded.

The shirt seemed heavy until he saw there was another shirt inside it, the sleeves carefully worked down inside Jack's sleeves. It was his own plaid shirt, lost, he'd thought, long ago in some damn laundry, his dirty shirt, the pocket ripped, buttons missing, stolen by Jack and hidden here inside Jack's own shirt, the pair like two skins, one inside the other, two in one. He pressed his face into the fabric and breathed in slowly through his mouth and nose, hoping for the faintest smoke and mountain sage and salty sweet stink of Jack but there was no real scent, only the memory of it, the imagined power of Brokeback Mountain of which nothing was left but what he held in his hands.

~ ~ ~

In the end the stud duck refused to let Jack's ashes go. 'Tell you what, we got a family plot and he's goin in it.' Jack's mother stood at the table coring apples with a sharp, serrated instrument. 'You come again,' she said.

Bumping down the washboard road Ennis passed the country cemetery fenced with sagging sheep wire, a tiny fenced square on the welling prairie, a few graves bright with plastic flowers, and didn't want to know Jack was going in there, to be buried on the grieving plain.

～ ～ ～

A few weeks later on the Saturday he threw all Stoutamire's dirty horse blankets into the back of his pickup and took them down to the Quik Stop Car Wash to turn the high-pressure spray on them. When the wet clean blankets were stowed in the truck bed he stepped into Higgins's gift shop and busied himself with the postcard rack.

'Ennis, what are you lookin for rootin through them postcards?' said Linda Higgins, throwing a sopping brown coffee filter into the garbage can.

'Scene a Brokeback Mountain.'

'Over in Fremont County?'

'No, north a here.'

'I didn't order none a them. Let me get the order list. They got it I can get you a hundred. I got a order some more cards anyway.'

'One's enough,' said Ennis.

When it came – thirty cents – he pinned it up in his trailer, brass-headed tack in each corner. Below it he drove a nail and on the nail he hung the wire hanger and the two old shirts suspended from it. He stepped back and looked at the ensemble through a few stinging tears.

'Jack, I swear –' he said, though Jack had never asked him to swear anything and was himself not the swearing kind.

～ ～ ～

Around that time Jack began to appear in his dreams, Jack as he had first seen him, curly-headed and smiling and bucktoothed, talking about getting up off his pockets and into the control zone, but the can of beans with the spoon handle jutting out and balanced on the log was there as well, in a cartoon shape and lurid colors that gave the dreams a flavor of comic obscenity. The spoon handle was the kind that could be used as a tire iron. And he would wake sometimes in grief, sometimes with the old sense of joy and release; the pillow sometimes wet, sometimes the sheets.

There was some open space between what he knew and what he tried to believe, but nothing could be done about it, and if you can't fix it you've got to stand it.

DAVID EBERSHOFF

LIVING TOGETHER

Alex Tuck wondered if he should return the cat, thinking he could no longer fit her into his life, and now here she was, Joan, the size of a small beagle and with a leathery ear ripped from an alley fight, coughing up a slimy ball of fur. He turned to Guy, whose lip was curling just then, his nose, a little boy's nose on the face of a man, twitching. See, this was why Alex shouldn't have taken Joan from his sister. He couldn't manage. He couldn't manage her.

Guy set down the last box. His knees cracked and the brittle sound of it made Alex think of how much older Guy was: more than fifteen years, Guy closer to forty than not, and hair dusted with gray, and bones that spoke, and a look in his handsome dimpled face of – how else could Alex describe it? – a powerful man who could break any heart he chose to fondle and squeeze.

'Does she always do that? Puke up like that?'

'No, not always.' Alex's hands were up in the air, protesting something.

'Don't you think you should've told me about it before you moved in?' Guy's face was still, his eyes rocks of gold, and Alex felt a jolt through him – had he already messed things up with his new roommate? – but

---

DAVID EBERSHOFF (born 1969): Ebershoff is the author of two novels, The Danish Girl and Pasadena, and a story collection, The Rose City. He is the publishing director of the Modern Library.

then Guy was laughing, winking, scratching Joan's black tail with one hand and his own head with the other. He touched the cat's whiskers and then the white patch on her belly. 'Hey, Alex, relax buddy.' A smile cracked Guy's face: lips, and the steak of a tongue, dimly purple. 'I had a roommate in college once who had a cat. She sort of looked like Joan, except her name was Betty, as in Ford. She loved to lick the wineglasses in the sink.'

Alex scooped Joan into his arms. She was purring, and her fur was damp from the mist greasing the city outside, and Alex just then noticed the hair on Guy's knees, hair like fur, already sun-bleached from the season's first days at the beach – Provincetown, Guy had told Alex; a beach town on the fist of Cape Cod where men wore swimsuits the size of cocktail napkins, Guy had explained, or nothing at all, and where anyone, yes, anyone, could find love for the night. 'You'll have to come along with me one weekend,' Guy had said, when they first met, just one week ago.

'What happened to her?'

'Who?'

'Betty the cat?'

'Oh, Betty? Oh god, it was awful. Oh god, I haven't thought about it for a long time. One day when my roommate and I were at our marketing class, Betty must have been playing around because when we got home we found her with her collar caught on the knob of a kitchen drawer. Poor Betty, hanging there, her neck snapped. Dead like that,' and Guy snapped his fingers, which were thick and backed by the same golden strands of fur.

Alex didn't know what to say. His eye wandered to the galley kitchen, where a lone frying pan hung on a rack. Would Joan do something like that here? She wasn't even his cat, really, but his older sister's. He'd taken on Joan only in the last year, after protesting about not having the time, about not being home enough, about not having room for her in his life. 'Just do me this one favor,' Nan had said, bandaged in her hospital room.

On a Boston street gripped by gentrification, at the top floor of a renovated brownstone, the apartment had plenty of room for the two men, one young, the other less so. Enough room for them and the cat, though they would have to share the bathroom, with its bin of skin-care products and its sink caked with white droppings of toothpaste. But the yellow pine floors and pale gray walls and the high ceilings added to the sense of space – certainly the two men would not stumble over each other here. Bay windows in the living room framed a view – if you stretched your neck – of the slim John Hancock tower, which just now was shimmering with sunlight needling through the mist. And then through the skylight more sun appeared, falling on Alex and Guy; the spitty rain was lifting, the green-and-blue burst of early summer returning, and there he was, Alex, just out of college, still, at twenty-two, filling in the gaps of his frame, all bone and angst, as he thought of it; and there was Guy, a man no taller than Alex but somehow more present, arms stretching the sleeves of his T-shirt, which read P-TOWN VOLLEYBALL over the breast, and one big toe, bony and tan, scratching the other, and the mesh of gym shorts catching, and displaying, the bulk and shift of Guy's thigh. Yes, there they were, Alex boiling up under his sweater buttoned to the throat and in the sun, which now flooded the skylight and shined down on them, the two of them, in that awkward moment when two people, two strangers, realize that indeed they will be living together.

It was only the second time they had met. Alex had lived through this moment once before with his freshman roommate – a scene of common hope showing up in their mutually tentative grins, in the way the two boys turned away from each other as they undressed that first night. Hope that this other person would remain reasonable. Hope that the stranger, whose bed sat four or five feet from Alex's, would not crack and lose it in the night, slouching in the direction of cruelty. Alex supposed married couples, his own parents for that matter, must also share this moment: After the honeymoon, after the romance, his mother must have looked at his bearded father at least once and thought, 'Don't turn on me.' Alex would've asked, but his father was dead, long dead.

A water stain, scaly and yellow, spread on the wall from the skylight to the floor. Rain must have seeped in during a winter past. At one spot the paint had blistered into a circle the size of a hand, and Alex was surprised to see it, puzzled that he hadn't noticed the damage when he'd first visited the apartment. He had also missed the urine stain on the carpet, and the flash of gold in Guy's molars.

'So, here we are,' said Alex, and he laughed, though Guy could have mistaken it for a gasp. It struck Alex that this was happening to him now, at last, that he was actually in the middle of this: a new apartment with a new roommate in a new city, and tomorrow he would start his first job; he thought of the empty desk waiting, with its silent phone, with the

Rolodex hanging limply with blank cards. It was a new life for a young man in search of a new life; it occurred to him just then that no one knew him or who he was or where he came from and no one had met his sister, thin in a nightgown, or his mother, with her hair swooped up like a meringue. He knew he would spend the next several months of his life introducing himself, and he knew – although he couldn't explain it, were you to ask – that it would never again be like this, never again would life feel like this, with so much sprawled ahead, life ajar. So this is how I'll be living, he thought, looking around, and there was Guy again, sitting on the steps that led to the roof deck, pulling on his gym socks, his legs agape.

Alex could feel the sweat on his forehead; he told himself he was too excited, and he wiped at the dew above his lip. He patted his brow with the handkerchief he had spent last night ironing, this one and his dozen others and his T-shirts, all white and blank, discarded at the first sign of yellow stain beneath the arm, and his gym shorts, which he had bought recently because a boy in college, not quite a friend, a boy with a wardrobe of sheer blousy shirts and an older boyfriend in New York, had said, 'You'll have to join a gym when you get to Boston. You were planning on joining a gym, weren't you, Alex?' But his own sweat bothered Alex, the clinginess, the lingering scent, the way it pasted his clothes to his skin and revealed the angles, the pink, of his somehow childlike body. 'A gym?' Alex had said. 'Yes, I've already signed up,' he had lied. But what would Alex do at a gym?

Yet Alex knew that soon, none too soon, he would find out. Was Guy on his way to the gym just now?

'You look hot,' said Guy, tying his sneakers and then standing and laying a hand on Alex's shoulder. 'How about something to drink?' And then, 'Hey, do you want to go to the gym with me? Go for a workout and then a steam?'

They had met through a service called Rainbow Roommates recommended by the boy in college, Patrick, whose hair was dyed a raspberry red. 'You fill out a form of what you're looking for in a roommate. You know, your likes, your dislikes. If you're a smoker or not. Be sure to put down how anal you are,' Patrick had said, giggling in that girlish way of his. To Alex the whole thing sounded like blind dating, something he had never done, but it excited him – the idea of calling someone, and then meeting him in his apartment, an actual stranger, just anybody who could afford the sixty-dollar fee. And then with limited information – the neatness of the part through his hair, the firmness of his handshake, the order of the pillows on the living room sofa, the potential stability that his job as a computer salesman implied, all of this plus any display of kindness, or cruelty, for that matter – a decision had to be made whether or not Alex could live with this man. It made no sense, really, that people could proceed this way, the risks were too high – *he could be an utter slob . . . he could go through my things and read my diary . . . he could ask me to join him in his sleigh bed late one night* – but what else could Alex do? Where else would Alex live? Back in California? Back in his mother's house? Back down the tiptoey hall that connected Alex's bedroom to his sister's? Alex needed to get on with his new life, he needed an apartment and a roommate, a place he could afford on his first-time salary, a roommate who would not only hand him a key but also make room for his cat, Saint Joan, as he sometimes called her, and Boston was about as far as he could hope from Pasadena, where his mother still lived, where his sister had returned to, and he knew no one in this city, in this state, no one except an ex of Patrick's, whom Patrick had urged Alex to look up – *you'll like Timmy, he reminds me of you* – which didn't turn out to be the case; Alex knew no one at all until now, no one but Guy, who was throwing his leather-and-mesh lifting gloves into his backpack and saying, 'Let's go to the gym. Joan'll be all right. Leave her and let's head out for a workout.' And then, 'Come on, Alex, everyone knows that the first thing you do after finding a place to live is sign up for the gym.' And then, finally, with a second hand on Alex's other shoulder, 'Hey, Alex. Is everything all right? Are you going to be all right?'

~ ~ ~

But Alex turned down the trip to the gym, and in his new room he tried to unpack. He hung what he could in the closet, but it was shallow, a single short pipe and two hooks, and he'd have to store most of his clothes in boxes beneath the bed. 'I've got some extra room in my closet,' Guy offered, standing in the door frame, his backpack hanging from a fist. Alex declined, saying he didn't really need any extra space. 'Most of this stuff I don't wear anymore.' This wasn't true, but might as well be, he realized, because he knew that part of piecing together this new life would come from buying a new set of clothes – a tank top for the summer, a pair of cargo-pocketed shorts – that would make him look more like one of *them*.

Then Joan padded between Guy's legs into the bedroom. 'How long have you had her?' She sat in the space between Alex and Guy, looking from one to the other and back.

'Just under a year.' Alex was rolling his winter socks and folding his cardigans into a pile. These he would store beneath the bed, in a box labeled BOOKS where he would also hide his diary and his thumbed stash of daddy-son fantasy magazines.

'Where'd she come from?'

'She used to be my sister's.'

'Why'd she give her up?'

Alex's room overlooked an alley, and through the window came the yelling of a man and a woman, a couple shrieking over a jealousy: 'Would you stop looking at my sister like that!'

'She almost died and couldn't take care of her anymore.'

Alex continued with the pile of sweaters. When Guy was gone he would begin folding his boxer shorts; he couldn't bring himself to fold his underwear in front of his roommate, not just yet. A second shriek came from the alley, this time a single heaving sob. And then, just barely, 'I can't believe you did that.' Almost a year had passed since Nan had tried to kill herself, and the note she left had asked him to take care of Joan. But Nan survived, and it never occurred to Alex that Saint Joan would become his, except that was what his mother decided would be best. 'She should live with you,' his mother had said, and at first Alex didn't know who she was referring to: Who was the *she*? 'She seems to really like you.' And then, 'It's like she's in love with you, that cat is.'

It was a year before that – a little more than two years ago – when Nan had first adopted Joan. She was living in Santa Monica at the time, writing copy for an advertising agency two blocks from the beach. Alex's mother liked to tell her friends that her daughter was practically famous: She had written those TV commercials for Pig Pig Bacon, the ones with the lovers nibbling opposite ends of a strip of ham, the one with the jingle that almost everyone in the country – or so it seemed to his mother, to Nan, even to Alex himself – was singing just then.

After Nan adopted the cat, Alex went home to visit his family. One night he decided to sleep on Nan's sofa rather than at his mother's, and there they were in Nan's apartment, Alex and Nan, separated by five years, the older sister a prettier version of her brother yet the two nearly identical in size: she the strong impressive woman, he the slight rail of a man; that night, that one night, during Alex's spring break, in the downpour of a

California March storm, the gutters overflowing above Nan's window, there in her living room, with the shelf of video boxes, each a clip of one of her commercials, there they spoke, the two siblings, about this and that, about the rain, about their mother, about the new cat. 'She's the size of a small dog,' Alex had exclaimed when he first tried to load her into his arms. 'She thinks she's a puppy,' Nan had said, her fingers, tan from a recent visit to the sun bed, raking Joan's fur, picking at a knot in her tail.

'I would have thought you would've wanted a Persian or some fancy cat like that.' And Nan – whose beauty no one in the world would argue with, not a soul in the world – had replied, 'What would make you say that?'

Yes, what would make Alex say that? 'What's that thing on her paw?'

'Oh, that?' His sister inspected the bald patch on the cat's front paw. 'She has this weird habit of chewing her own foot. Another indication that she thinks she's a dog.'

Sometimes when he closed his eyes, he couldn't remember what his sister looked like: She was a figure, alive and huge, with a blank oval of a face; someone had scratched it out. What made her beautiful? Sometimes he would ask himself, but he could never answer the question; he'd have to pull out an old photo – the two of them on a picnic in Lacy Park or hiking beneath the summit of Mount Wilson, alone, away from the world – to remind himself that her eyes were green, the green of late summer when the underside of a leaf, overturned in the wind, reveals itself as blue.

For many months Nan had been inviting Alex to visit her in her new apartment in Santa Monica. 'Whenever you come out, why not spend a night or two with me? Why spend all that time with Mom? She drives you crazy.'

'She drives you crazy, too.'

That night – that only night Alex slept on his sister's couch – they stayed up late. Joan (was this the first time he ever thought of her as Saint Joan?) moved from Nan's lap to Alex's and back. Nan proceeded with a conversation in which he added very little, or that was how it felt to Alex. How old was he that night? Oh, only twenty, just twenty, and yet at certain instances he felt like a child, as if he had no more experience with the grime of the world than an eight-year-old; and at other times, other nights, tonight perhaps, he felt old, a soul wise and sound and still. And perhaps he felt both at once, perhaps just then in his life Alex was beginning to perceive the doubleness, the inexhaustible doubleness, of his life. This and that, all at the same time; and here they were, Alex, twenty and still only shaving once a week, and Nan, with a curtain of blond hair falling around her face, in a sleeveless red sweater that shaped her breasts like the skin over the meat of an apple. Was she wearing anything beneath the sweater? He didn't think so, and then she cracked a window – *It's warm tonight* – and with the breeze faintly salty from the ocean running across their skin, her skin, Alex became certain that the answer was no. She was in a pair of khaki shorts, with a little side pocket where she would store, were she on a trek through a forest, an army knife and a small sack of raisins. Why did Alex have that thought about his sister just then, about what she might pack away in the side pocket of her shorts? He had never trekked with her, never shared a tent with her, never lain awake with her as the wind ran across their nylon sleeping bags. So why imagine her in shorts and hiking boots, with raisins stored away? Had he dreamed of this? Had this, all of this, flitted through his dreamer's mind?

They sat opposite each other on the two white sofas their mother had bought for Nan from a catalog. Alex curled his legs beneath him, and if he'd had a tail it would be tucked up too. Nan lay spread out on her back, her orange toenails dangling over the sofa and her arm flinging about as if it were searching for a box of chocolates on the coffee table. 'So, I've been dating this guy,' she began.

'That's great.' Alex pulled his knees to his chest. 'Who is he?'

'His name is Carter. He's a writer, a screenwriter. He just sold his first script.'

'That sounds great.'

'He is,' and Nan turned her head to her brother and smiled, and then shook herself almost imperceptibly, as if a shiver were creeping up her spine.

'How long have you been seeing him?'

'About four months.'

'Does Mom like him?'

'Mom? Oh, he hasn't met Mom.'

Sometimes he couldn't imagine talking to Nan if she weren't his sister. He felt that way about his mother, less often, but even so. They weren't people he naturally would want to get to know. At Christmas dinner a few years ago, when he was a little drunk on grog, he blurted out at the table that the only thing he had in common with them was food.

'Where'd you meet him?' Alex said.

'Who?'

'Carter?'

'Oh, Carter. Where'd I meet Carter? It's the funniest story. It's one of those times when you can't believe how small the world is, when you think you must be related to the whole world because it's just so small. But I'll tell you later. It's a long story. Such a *long* story.'

And then Nan said, with one hand buried in the fur of the cat, 'By the way, Alex, are you gay?'

'Yes.'

'Yeah, I thought so. I was just wondering.' She curled a strand of hair behind her ear. 'It doesn't bother me one bit.'

'It doesn't bother me, either.'

'But I wouldn't tell Mom. I'm not sure how she would take it.'

'She already knows.'

He stood, moving to the window. Her apartment overlooked an alley, and in the carport below Alex could see Nan's little red convertible and the garbage bins chained to a post. He didn't want to talk to his sister anymore, not about this. He was hot, and he opened the window further, and a veil of damp salt air fell across his face and he wondered why she would talk to him like this. He didn't like to move into the realm of intimacies with Nan. To tell the truth, he didn't trust her. When they were young, when Nan was twelve, she used to invite Alex to play dress-up with her whenever their mother was out on an errand. Together they'd put on old flowered gowns that their mother could no longer fit into. Alex would fix Nan's hair with yellow ribbons, and next Nan would clip into Alex's hair white barrettes painted with green butterflies. They would dance to the radio, and Nan always said it was all right, it's okay for you to play like a girl, Alex, it doesn't matter. And Alex loved the fun of pretending, he loved the crush of chiffon beneath him as he sat down to a make-believe dinner party. Then one night, as Alex and Nan stood in the kitchen with their mother, Nan proudly said, 'Alex likes to dress up with me. He likes to put on your dresses, Mom. Especially that old orange velvet one, the one you spilled chocolate pudding on.' Alex's mother quietly set down her pocketbook and took his wrists, one in each hand. 'You're not your sister,' she said, shaking. 'Why are you acting like your sister?'

~ ~ ~

That first night in the apartment, Alex and Guy ordered Chinese food. They carried the little white cardboard boxes to the roof, where there was a rotting deck and patio chairs chained to the chimney and pitted with rust. It was a few minutes past sunset, the sky bright at the rim, a half moon arranging itself for the evening. Just beyond was the Prudential tower, erect and poked with antennae, and over there the financial district, the offices twinkling with people uncertain if they should call it a night. On a deck down the block three women were tending a flaring barbecue. Beyond them a man and a woman, erased to silhouette, pressed together in embrace.

Guy was talking about his past boyfriends. 'Lewis was a copy-machine repairman. He came into my office a few times with smudges of toner on his nose and then we exchanged numbers. When we started dating I found out he wasn't really a copy-machine repairman but actually a poet. So I convinced him he had too much talent to be wasting his time fixing copiers. His poems were amazing; I can't describe them, but they were amazing. He started writing a collection of poetry with a poem about every tiny part of my body. You know, a poem on the skin at the cheekbone, one on the hair at the wrist bone, a poem about my second toe.'

Guy stopped, as if to give Alex a chance to comment, but Alex liked the story too much to interrupt. 'Anyways,' Guy went on, 'he quit his job and lived with me for nearly two years, writing poetry while I was at work. He used what's now your room as his study, setting up a little desk and everything. He said he was working on an epic. In fact, he said he was rewriting *The Faerie Queene*. I paid for everything, and he wrote during the day and did most of the housework, which was handy because I'm not so good with that sort of stuff. But I can't believe I put up with him, supporting him like that. I mean, without realizing it, all of a sudden I was keeping a man, which is definitely not the type of guy I am. But you know what? Sometimes I really miss his cooking. I mean, every night I'd come home to something different: sashimi, tacos.'

Alex considered the complexities of living together and the issues of money and chores and privacy and love. He could remember the days when he was very young and only his father's name appeared on the family's checking account. His mother sometimes could not take Alex to the grocery store because she had forgotten to ask his father to sign a check made out to El Rancho; she'd have to wait until the next day, unless she forgot again to ask his father to sign the two or three checks as he shuffled out of the house into the early-morning glare. His mother's face often tightened with nerves as she explained the checks: the grocery store, the shoe repair, tuition was due. Once Alex heard her say, 'But it's my money, for god's sake.' That was before he died; just before the car he and Nan were in swerved off the road.

'Finally, one day I came home from work,' Guy continued. 'And my so-called boyfriend said, "Honey, I've got something to show you," and he held up this little paperback book with a drawing on the cover of a boy in khaki shorts and no shirt and a yellow kerchief around his throat sitting on the knee of an older man, a scoutmaster, some guy with a chevron on his sleeve. The book was called *Boys Scout*. And I said, "What's that?" and he said, "It's mine, I wrote it. Go on, open it up," and then it hit me, like a big old frying pan on the head, that all that time he'd spent at home, all that time I'd paid for – *for the sake of literature*, as he kept putting it – during all that time, he'd been writing a porn novel. And you know what, Alex? With his first check – which wasn't so big, mind you – he up and moved. You know what he said? He said I don't understand a writer's mind. And then he was gone, didn't even take his little desk. That desk in your room, that was his. And every once in a while when I'm in New York on business I make a little side trip into a triple-X shop and buy one of his new books. He writes three or four a month now, and has a lot of pen names like Raymond Kenneth Hedgspoon III and Jack Luck.' Guy stopped to fish a sesame shrimp out of the cardboard carton. 'And you know what the worst part of all of this is?'

'What?'

'Those novels are pretty good. I try my best not to get horny when I read them. I mean, I'm still angry at him and everything, but by the second page, even before I know it, I'm sitting there with my old coconut in my fist.'

Alex mumbled something that Guy could have heard as, 'It was called *Boys Scout*?' But what Alex really said, or should have said, were he an honest fellow, was: 'I've read *Boys Scout*.'

But Guy seemed to trust Alex's awkwardness. He showed no distaste for the nervousness, for the mumbled words, for the way Alex's eyes would fail to meet his own. Alex supposed that this was what had first convinced him that Guy would make a fine roommate. He didn't seem like the type of man who would mind Alex and his ways. When he first came to see the apartment, Alex had flushed red as a wound when Guy asked a few questions people should know about each other before they move in. 'Do you sleep around a lot?' Guy had inquired. 'I'm not making any judgment calls, but I suppose I should know about it in advance if you think you'll be bringing home a different guy every night.'

'Oh, no. It's not like that. I mean. No, not every night, not . . . not . . . not –'

But he couldn't continue.

'Well, give me an idea of what to expect. On average, how many people do you sleep with a month?'

'I . . . I don't really know.'

'What do you mean you don't really know?'

'I mean, I don't know what you mean. What you're asking me.' And then Alex needed to sit on the sofa and he brought a pillow needlepointed with a lavender lambda to his chest.

'Are you all right?'

'No, I'm fine. Just tired is all.'

And Guy went to the kitchen and returned with a glass of water. With the first sip Alex felt better, and Guy seemed to know to talk about something else.

Except for one last comment: 'Of course, if you get a boyfriend, something long-term, that would be different. In that case, he'd be welcome to stay over. I wouldn't mind sharing the bathroom with someone if you're in love.'

'Of course,' Alex said. 'Of course that would be different.'

'And the same goes for me,' Guy offered. 'I won't be bringing home too many tricks. Just the ones where there's something indicating that first hint of love.'

~ ~ ~

For nearly a year Alex had lived by himself in Tokyo in an apartment with blue paper parasols hanging from the ceiling and a mouse that came up through the pipes to nibble on the bathroom soap. He was there studying history at Keio University, his junior year abroad, away from the little world of college and his half-friend Patrick, away from home, away from everyone he knew. It was a year when his telephone rarely rang, and he could lose himself in the orange brick library until closing and there was no one to ask him where he'd been. It was a year when he could meet a man, and then another, men sometimes twice his age, late at night at Kinsmen, the upstairs bar in Ni-Chome, and return to his apartment with the stain of dawn and no one would ever know how his evening had passed. With whom it had passed. Alex was alone, and he knew that never again would the world permit him to live so alone. For the first time he wondered if it was what he wanted, this isolation, or if some sort of attachment to another would one day appeal to him. Then late one summer night, when the humidity clung to his skin, Alex was taking a cold bath. The phone rang, and Alex ran to answer: '*Moshi moshi.*'

'Nan's gone and tried to kill herself,' his mother blurted out, as if she also wanted to say, 'So what do you think of that?'

Alex immediately felt repulsed by his nudity. How could he talk to his mother without any clothes on? About Nan? He crouched on the tatami mat like a bird dropping an egg. At his feet lay a glossy, thumbed magazine that he'd planned to use later that night. With a quick snap Alex closed his thighs, tucking away his genitals.

'Alex, oh, it's awful,' his mother cried. 'She flung herself through the front window of a restaurant. She just stood back on the sidewalk, took a running start, and flew through the air and then through the glass, crashing in on the tables. It was late at night. Something must've made her lose control.' His mother paused. 'I guess she cracked.'

He opened his mouth, as if he were about to scream, but nothing came out. Both at once it felt as if his heart were racing and coming to a halt. 'What do you suppose made her do it?'

'I was hoping you might have some idea,' she said, sniffling, and Alex imagined her nose against the shoulder of her robe.

'But something must have caused it.'

'How am I supposed to know? She's all stitched up now and can't talk.'

'How is she?'

'It looks like she's going to be all right.' Again the doubleness of life: relief and regret flooding his chest simultaneously. Was it possible to love his sister in more than one way? he asked himself, he had often asked himself. To love her and hate her and love her yet again, all in the same compressed instant of his life. Where did it come from, the doubleness, the perpetual flip-flopping of emotion? Would it ever relent? What was it Patrick used to say? The man you love will build you up and ruin you all at the same time, so just get used to it, my sweet Alexandra.

Then Alex heard his mother *tisk*ing at Joan. She continued rattling into the phone and at Joan: *And who's going to take care of this sweet old cat?* Again Alex strained to picture his sister, to imagine her hurling herself through the window. Yet all he could see was the body of an athletic woman sprinting down the sidewalk, a naked muscled physique like that of an Olympic swimmer topped off with Alex's own shallow, overheated face.

His mother wanted him to come home at once. 'Won't you come back to see her? It would cheer her up. She's buried in bandages, and she can't move yet and she can't speak because she has so many stitches in her lips. It would make her so happy to see you, I just know it. Right now, you're the only thing she has. You and me.'

'Mom, I can't. My courses are really tough and I can't skip any lectures. I still have a lot of research to get done before I leave here. I'll be home in five weeks.'

'But couldn't you come home for a week? Oh, Alex, please. For once won't you change your plans?'

'I can't.'

And he didn't.

But every day his mother would call from the hospital room and give her account of what she thought Nan would like to say to him. 'You know, I was thinking, Alex. When Nan gets married – the music can make or break a wedding – and I was thinking about what we should have at Nan's wedding.'

'But is Nan even dating anyone?' Alex said, worried about the cost of the telephone call.

'A mother has to be prepared to take care of the details of her children's lives. Isn't that right, Nan? Your sister just nodded in agreement with me, Alex. Besides, Nan just recently began dating again one of her old boyfriends, a nice young man who wants to be a writer. A boy named Carter.'

'How is she feeling today?'

'Carter is such a nice boy. And handsome, too. You know how they met? This was over a year ago, but do you know how they met?'

'But how is Nan today? Is she any better?'

'It's the funniest story. Don't you want to hear it?'

'But is she any better? Have the doctors said anything today?'

'Oh, she's the same but a little better I suppose. Less' – and this she whispered – 'sedated.'

'Did the doctors tell you anything?'

'Anyway, you'll never believe where they met.'

Alex gave up. 'Where'd they meet?'

'In your bedroom.'

'In my bedroom?'

'Well, you know how I sometimes rent out the house to film crews and television producers and the like. Well, one day I got a call asking if they could film a commercial for a mortgage bank, and they needed a boy's bedroom – you know, something real boy-boy, with pennants on the wall and stuff. They asked if I had a son and if his room was available. I said I sure do and it sure is and so on the day of the shoot I had to be out of town so Nan agreed to watch over things and the young man who wrote the commercial's script is Carter, and that's why they met in your bedroom. Isn't that funny?'

'Not really.'

'Oh, Nan thought it was. She knew that would wind you up.'

'Well, it doesn't.'

'Oh, Alex, why do you have to take everything so seriously?'

'What else have the doctors told you?'

'One last thing, Alex,' his mother said. 'Nan and I are stuck on something.'

'What's that?'

'What's that organ march by Krebs, you know the one, the one that goes *dum dum dum dum*. Oh, what's that called? Nan and I were talking – well, I was the one doing the talking – about her wedding, in the event she would ever marry Carter one day, and we were talking about music and what should be played at the ceremony and right at the same time we both thought of this piece by Krebs but we couldn't think of what it's called. Shoot, you know the one I'm talking about, *dum dum dum dum*. Her doctors think she'll be out of here by the time you get back from Japan. She has this terrific lady plastic surgeon. *Dum dum dum*, damn it, Alex, help me. It starts with a *W*.'

But what was Nan thinking just then, lying there beneath the gauze, IV drip to her right, her eyes peering out? His sister, now faceless in a body bandage. He couldn't bring himself to tell his mother that the piece she was thinking of was called 'Wachet auf.' Instead, this somehow reminded him of the dinner table of his youth and the time his mother announced, 'Nan is going to love having a playmate this summer.' Without informing anyone, Mrs Tuck had invited a girl with chapped shins from the South of France to live with them for June and July. When Nan, who was twelve at the time, found out, she sulked for a week, until the girl's plane landed, and then Nan started to scream. 'I thought Nan would've loved you, Nathalie,' Mrs Tuck had to eventually say as she drove the bony child back to the airport after only eleven days in America. 'I must have been wrong.' But Alex never got the chance to say that *he* would have loved to have had the little girl stay and help him by sharing the daily alarm of living with Nan.

~ ~ ~

After dinner on the roof, Alex set out for a walk in his new neighborhood. He wanted to find the market, the florist, the coffee shop, the video store. On Columbus Avenue, in the yellow cone of a street lamp, he stopped to watch a young woman juggle sacks of groceries, her dry cleaning dangling from a pinkie and her mail between her teeth as she struggled with her keys. Cars were parked, some of them waving neon orange tickets beneath their wipers. Diners filled the window of the Japanese restaurant, conductorly chopsticks in the air. Men passed, men in nylon running pants with snaps at the ankles, men in tank tops stretched across their shaved chests, men peering out beneath baseball caps, beneath tidy haircuts, beneath eyebrows pruned and shaped by the tweezer. There were many men, most a few years older than Alex and some Alex's age, moving up the street, headed somewhere with their back-packs, with their thick-soled sneakers, with their shoulders meaty with muscle and tattooed. To the gym, Alex knew, and he followed them, although in truth there weren't that many, just four or five, but it felt to Alex, on that first night, as if there were more, as if he'd seen the world that would become his, and indeed it heaved and sighed with the fullness of a world: a street, a market, a neighbor with her groceries, a parking ticket, a pack of men, all like Alex, he sensed – all with the past swirling about them like litter on the street, all with their faces scrubbed and shaved and their hair gelled up or down, all heading onward to the future, believing blindly that what lay ahead must surely rank above what lay sprawled behind.

She recovered, Nan did, the pink wisps of scars around her face like a wreath. The scarring was worse on her arms, where the weltish tissue buckled; and she reported how her breasts and belly were puckered by the purple memory of all those gashes. When she left the hospital, she checked into a psychiatric retreat in North County San Diego, on a former rancho twenty miles inland from Carlsbad. Alex visited her once, just after he returned from Japan. They sat in wrought-iron rocking chairs on a veranda that overlooked a lemon grove. It was early September, before the start of his senior year, and the rancho's hillside was gold, and in the distance, through the smog, they looked toward the ocean. He was adjusting to being back, and it shocked him how quickly his life in Tokyo, his little life, was receding into the trunk of his past. 'It's hard to believe I'm back for good. I miss Japan sometimes. A lot, in fact. There was still so much I wanted to do there.'

'Like what?'

'I never went to Hokkaido; I just never had the time or money. Other stuff, too.'

'Like what?'

'I made a few good friends, but now I wish I'd spent more time with them.'

'Like who?'

'I knew a really nice woman named Tamiko who worked in the bookstore near my university. Other people, too.' Wind ran through the lemon grove. There on the breeze was the scent of autumn, and just beyond it, or above it, was the powdery scent of Nan, in silk pajamas and a kimono patterned with lily pads that he had bought her at Mitsukoshi. The salesclerk had asked, 'For your special lady, yes?'

'Who else did you meet there?'

'This guy named Yosei. He and I sometimes went to the movies together.'

'Did you like him?'

'Well, sure,' but then Alex realized what she meant. 'Not like that. He was just a friend. Not with Yosei. He's a pal, but not like that.'

'Anyone else?' She stared out: Beyond the lemon grove was a swimming pool that was off-limits to the retreat's residents. But someone was swimming in it, bouncing on the diving board. One of the nurses, Nan explained. Her afternoon off. 'Isn't there anyone else you want to tell me about?'

He never told his sister about any of the boys and men who passed through his life. They came and went, and he didn't want her to know, didn't want to hear the judgment – or was it something else? – in her voice: *Where'd you meet him? What does he do? How old is he?*

But something had changed, Alex believed. In the quiet of the afternoon, with the sun dazzling the lemons and the swimming pool and burning Alex's arm hanging beyond the veranda's shade, Alex felt certain that his sister had somehow changed. There she was, the knot of her kimono tight, her fist supporting her chin, her hair shorn down like a little boy's. A pensiveness filled her sewn-together face, and Alex barely recognized her.

'During my last month there I met a guy named Jun. I guess I liked him a lot. I suppose you could say we were dating, that we were boyfriends. It's just my luck that my first real boyfriend would live in Tokyo. I met him only four or five weeks before I came home. We met at a coffee shop in Yoyogi, right by my apartment. He asked me if I was from New York because he was going there on vacation. He's a doctor, a young doctor, a gynecologist in fact. Just finished medical school and he was going to New York before he started up his residency. And we spent nearly every day together, during that last month. It was nice. Nicer than I ever thought it could be. I met him on the same day you –' but Alex stopped himself. That detail he shouldn't add.

Instead, maybe he should tell Nan about the time Jun took him hiking on Mount Fuji. About the Buddhist temple in the foothills. He looked to his sister, wondering if she wanted to know more. She had asked, after all. Hadn't she asked? But Nan remained quiet in her rocker; she stared out, surveying the vista, the ranchland, the red tile roofs of the ever-creeping suburb. 'Oh, Alex,' she said finally. 'I don't want to hear about you and your fags.'

~ ~ ~

He scratched his key at the lock, and at first it didn't take; Alex realized just then that this was the first time he was returning to his new home. He imagined how familiar this gesture would become – key sliding into slot – and shortly he'd do it without thinking, without any recognition of the turning bolt. His life would become that automatic. But not yet tonight, when the street and the apartment and the handsome heft of Guy still glittered, all part of a dream he hadn't realized he was having. All part of something that had yet to fully take shape. As he entered the apartment a strange wheezing greeted him. At first he thought that a window was open or that a rag was somehow caught over the air-conditioning vent. But the air-conditioning wasn't on, and the windows were closed. The gasping continued, and now Alex heard Guy's voice: 'Oh, shit. Oh, shit. Oh, come on, don't do this. Come on, you stupid shit.'

It was coming from the kitchen, and when Alex reached the doorway he saw Guy sitting cross-legged in the corner next to the garbage pail. At first he didn't see Alex, and he continued: 'Come on, you stupid cat. Don't do this to me.' In his lap lay Joan, croaking for air. Every few seconds her body shook, flopping like a fish on a dock, her head reaching up. And there she was: in Guy's lap, a lap already lodged into Alex's fantasies, the cat that he never thought of as his own, the cat that his sister had left to him, but then Nan hadn't gone anywhere, Saint Joan the cat with a rat trap pressing into her skull. The sweep of the trap's arm had torn through the leathery skin of her ear and lashed out an eye. Blood black as her fur drowned away the expression on her face. It ran over Guy's legs, catching in the hair of his thigh.

Finally he noticed Alex. 'She got her head caught in the trap,' Guy said, trying – only halfheartedly – to make a joke of it, as if they could laugh it away. And if he could have, Alex would have laughed, too, because surely something about this was funny, but then Alex couldn't think what. Guy stopped, as if the weight of Saint Joan was becoming too much. 'I can't get her out.'

Alex stood calm. He steeled himself against the pangs that might rise in his chest. He didn't want to become intimate with this crisis; he'd do his best to disallow it. Disasters happen, deaths occur. Skulls are crushed. His sister, when she was twelve, built a playpen for her hamster Ginnie on the porch outside her window. One day, when Alex and the other children in the neighborhood refused to let Nan join their game of sprinkler tag in the backyard, she stormed up to her room and yelled from her open window, 'I hope you all die! Every last one of you!' And with that, Nan slammed her window, crushing into its white frame the small bones of the hamster. This story hovered over the family; it was retold often to the pitiful amusement of a large gathering at the dinner table. Oh, how they would laugh at this one now. His mother wiping the corners of her eyes with a monogrammed napkin, and Nan herself giggling about the child she once was. You couldn't help but laugh about it now. But there was another story from that time that wasn't retold. His sister, when she was twelve, one rainy afternoon lay down in the dark hollow of their mother's dressing closet. She had told Alex to enter the blackness after two minutes, and when he did she guided his hands over the soft mounds of her chest. She led his fingers to her warm sticky inside and then made him lick his hand. Alex's heart had stopped at the taste; he felt as if he had taken his last breath.

'I don't understand where it came from,' Alex said.

'What?'

'The trap. What was it doing there?'

'I keep one down in that little hole by the dishwasher. Sometimes mice come through it.'

'But it's such a big trap. I've never seen a trap that big.'

'I once saw a rat. I got a big one just in case.'

Alex hadn't asked about rats or mice before he moved in. But why should he have thought to? So much to know about someone before you live with him; so many things you'll never know.

'Can you get it off her?' He squatted next to his roommate, and their knees touched, and Alex felt something like a pilot light spark and try to catch in his chest.

'I'm trying.' Guy's voice cracked, approaching panic. 'Give me a hand.' And then, 'Alex, I'm sorry. It never occurred to me . . . I just never thought that she would . . . that you would –' But Guy couldn't finish.

And Alex, too, was slow to move. All he could do was stare and recall and forget and look ahead. He thought about tomorrow: That was when his new life would start, tomorrow. The empty desk where he'd open his day calendar; the Rolodex he'd begin to fill with typewritten cards; the first telephone call home to Guy to tell him he was running late, he couldn't meet him at the gym. 'You'll have to go on without me,' Alex imagined himself saying to someone – if not to Guy, then to someone. Yes, tomorrow, after the trap was removed and the body of poor Saint Joan, who just now passed from living to dead, was discarded in the trash bin in the back alley, after that his life, the one he'd been planning his whole life, would begin, and how would it feel to Alex Tuck? How would it feel to this young man, twenty-two, a teetering mass of bone and hurt, to finally feel the catch take hold in his chest, the rise in his throat, and the regrettable burn of coming to life?

DAVID LEAVITT
CROSSING ST. GOTTHARD

It was the tunnel – its imminence – that all of them were contemplating that afternoon on the train, each in a different way; the tunnel, at nine miles the longest in the world, slicing under the gelid landscape of the St. Gotthard Pass. To Irene it was an object of dread. She feared enclosure in small spaces, had heard from Maisie Withers that during the crossing the carriage heated up to a boiling pitch. 'I was as black as a nigger from the soot,' Maisie Withers said. 'People have died.' 'Never again,' Maisie Withers concluded, pouring lemonade in her sitting room in Hartford, and meaning never again the tunnel but also (Irene knew) never again Italy, never again Europe; for Maisie was a gullible woman, and during her tour had had her pocketbook stolen.

And it was not only Maisie Withers, Irene reflected now (watching, across the way, her son Grady, his nose flat against the glass), but also her own ancient terror of windowless rooms, of corners, that since their docking in Liverpool had brought the prospect of the tunnel looming before her, black as death itself (a being which, as she approached fifty, she was trying to muster the courage to meet eye to eye), until she found

DAVID LEAVITT (born 1961): Leavitt is the author of five novels (two of which, The Lost Language of Cranes *and* The Page Turner, *have been made into films), three collections of short stories, a book of novellas, and, most recently, a meditation on Florence for Bloomsbury's* The Writer and the City *series. He teaches at the University of Florida.*

herself counting first the weeks, then the days, then the hours leading up to the inevitable reckoning: the train slipping into the dark, into the mountain. (It was half a mile deep, Grady kept reminding her, half a mile of solid rock separating earth from sky.) Irene remembered a ghost story she'd read as a girl – a man believed to be dead wakes in his coffin. Was it too late to hire a carriage, then, to go *over* the pass, as Toby had? But no. Winter had already started up there. Oh, if she'd had her way, they'd have taken a different route; only Grady would have been disappointed, and since his brother's death she dared not disappoint Grady. He longed for the tunnel as ardently as his mother dreaded it.

~ ~ ~

'Mama, is it coming soon?'

'Yes, dear.'

'But you said half an hour.'

'Hush, Grady! I'm not a clock.'

'But you said –'

'Read your book, Grady,' Harold interrupted.

'I finished it.'

'Then do your puzzle.'

'I finished that, too.'

'Then look out the window.'

'Or just shut up,' added Stephen, his eyes sliding open.

'Stephen, you're not to talk to your brother that way.'

'He's a pest. Can't a fellow get some sleep?'

Stephen's eyes slid shut, and Grady turned to examine the view. Though nearly fourteen, he was still a child. His leg shook. With his breath he fogged shapes onto the glass.

'Did I tell you it's the longest in the world? Did I tell you –'

'Yes, Grady. Now please hush.'

They didn't understand. They were always telling him to hush. Well, all right, he would hush. He would never again utter a single word, and show them all.

Irene sneezed.

'Excuse me,' she said to the red-nosed lady sitting next to her.

'Heavens! You needn't apologize to *me*.'

'It's getting cold rather early this year,' Irene ventured, relieved beyond measure to discover that her neighbor spoke English.

'Indeed it is. It gets cold earlier every year, I find. Judgment Day must be nigh!'

Irene laughed. They started chatting. She was elegantly got up, this red-nosed lady. She knitted with her gloves on. From her hat extended a fanciful aigrette that danced and bobbed. Grady watched it, watched the moving mountains outside the window. (Some were already capped with snow.) Then the train turned, the sun came blazing into the compartment so sharply that the red-nosed lady murmured, 'Goodness me,' shielded her eyes, pulled the curtain shut against it.

Well, that did it for Grady. After all, hadn't they just told him to look at the view? No one cared. He had finished his book. He had finished his puzzle. The tunnel would never arrive.

Snorting, he thrust his head behind the curtain.

'Grady, don't be rude.'

He didn't answer. And really, behind the curtain it was a different world. He could feel warmth on his face. He could revel in the delicious sensation of apartness that the gold-lit curtain bestowed, and that only the chatter of women interrupted. But it was rude.

'Oh, I know, I know!' (Whose voice was that? The rednosed lady's?) 'Oh yes, I know!' (Women always said that. They always knew.)

Harold had his face in a book. Stephen was a bully.

'Oh dear, yes!'

Whoever was talking, her voice was loud. His mother's voice he could not make out. His mother's voice was high but not loud, unless she shouted, which she tended to do lately. Outside the window an Alpine landscape spread out: fir groves, steep-roofed wooden houses, fields of dead sunflowers to which the stuffy compartment with its scratched mahogany paneling bore no discernible relation. This first-class compartment belonged to the gaslit ambience of stations and station hotels. It was a bubble of metropolitan, semipublic space sent out into the wide world, and from the confines of which its inmates could regard the uncouth spectacle of nature as a kind of *tableau vivant*. Still, the trappings of luxury did little to mask its fundamental discomforts: seats that pained the back, fetid air, dirty carpets.

They were on their way to Italy, Irene told Mrs. Warshaw (for this was the red-nosed lady's name). They were on their way to Italy for a tour – Milan, Venice, Verona, Florence, Rome (Irene counted off on her fingers), then a villa in Naples for the winter months – because her sons ought to see the world, she felt; American boys knew so little; they had studied French but could hardly speak a word. (Mrs. Warshaw, nodding fervently, agreed it was a shame.)

'And this will be your first trip to Italy?'

'The first time I've been abroad, actually, although my brother, Toby, came twenty years ago. He wrote some lovely letters for the *Hartford Evening Post*.'

'Marvelous! And how lucky you are to have three handsome sons as escorts. I myself have only a daughter.'

'Oh, but Harold's not my son! Harold's my cousin Millie's boy. He's the tutor.'

'How nice.' Mrs. Warshaw smiled assessingly at Harold. Yes, she thought, tutor he is, and tutor he will always be. He looked the part of the poor relation, no doubt expected to play the same role in the lady's life abroad that his mother played in her life at home: the companion to whom she could turn when she needed consolation, or someone to torture. (Mrs. Warshaw knew the ways of the world.)

As for the boys, the brothers: the older one looked different. Darker. Different fathers, perhaps?

But Irene thought: She's right. I do – *did* – have three sons.

And Harold tried to hide inside his book. Only he thought: They ought to treat me with more respect. The boys ought to call me Mr. Prescott, not Cousin Hal, for they hardly know me. Also, he smarted at the dismissive tone with which Aunt Irene enunciated the word *tutor*, as if he were something just one step above the level of a servant. He deserved better than that, deserved better than to be at the beck and call of boys in whom art, music, the classical world, inspired boredom at best, outright contempt at worst. For though Uncle George, God rest his soul, had financed his education, it was not Uncle George who had gotten the highest scores in the history of the Classics Department. It was not Uncle George whose translations of Cicero had won a prize. Harold had done all that himself.

On the other hand, goodness knew he could never have afforded Europe on his own. To his charges he owed the blessed image of his mother's backyard in St. Louis, his mother in her gardening gloves and hat, holding her shears over the roses while on the porch the old chair in which he habitually spent his summers reading, or sleeping, or cursing – my God, he wasn't in it! It was empty! To them he owed this miracle.

~ ~ ~

'And will your husband be joining you in Naples?'
  'I'm afraid my husband passed away last winter.'
  'Ah.'
 Mrs. Warshaw dropped a stitch.

~ ~ ~

The overdecorated compartment in which these five people were sitting was small – four feet by six feet. Really, it had the look of a theater stall, Harold decided, with its maroon velvet seats, its window like a stage, its curtain – well, like a curtain. Above the stained head-rests wrapped in slipcovers embellished with the crest of the railway hung six prints in reedy frames: three yellowed views of Rome – Trajan's Column (the glass cracked), the Pantheon, the Colosseum (over which Mrs. Warshaw's aigrette danced); and opposite, as if to echo the perpetual contempt with which the Christian world regards the pagan, three views of Florence – Santa Croce, the Duomo, the Palazzo Vecchio guarded by Michelangelo's immense nude David – none of which Harold, who reverenced the classical, could see. Instead, when he glanced up from his book, it was the interior of the Pantheon that met his gaze, the orifice at the center of the dome throwing against its coffered ceiling a coin of light.

~ ~ ~

He put down his book. (It was Ovid's *Metamorphoses*, in Latin.) Across from him, under the Pantheon, Stephen sprawled, his long legs in their loose flannel trousers spread wide but bent at the knees, because finally they were too long, those legs, for a compartment in which three people were expected to sit facing three people for hours at a time. He was asleep, or pretending to be asleep, so that Harold could drink in his beauty for once with impunity, while Mrs Warshaw knitted, and Grady's head bobbed behind the curtain, and Aunt Irene said she knew, she knew. Stephen was motionless. Stephen was inscrutable. Still, Harold could tell that he too was alert to the tunnel's imminence; he could tell because every few minutes his eyes slotted open, the way the eyes of a doll do when you tilt back its head: green and gold, those eyes, like the sun-mottled grass beneath a tree.

He rarely spoke, Stephen. His body had the elongated musculature of a harp. His face was elusive in its beauty, like those white masks the Venetians wear at Carnival. Only sometimes he shifted his legs, in those flannel trousers that were a chaos of folds, a mountain landscape, valleys, passes, peaks. Most, Harold knew, if you punched them down, would flatten; but one would grow heavy and warm at his touch.

And now Harold had to put his book on his lap. He had to. He was twenty-two years old, scrawny, with a constitution his doctor described as 'delicate'; yet when he closed his eyes, he and Stephen wore togas and stood together in a square filled with rational light. Or Harold was a great warrior, and Stephen the beloved *eremenos* over whose gore-drenched body he scattered kisses at battle's end. Or they were training together, naked, in the gymnasium.

Shameful thoughts! He must cast them out of his mind. He must find a worthier object for his adoration than this stupid, vulgar boy, this boy who, for all his facile handsomeness, would have hardly raised an eyebrow in the age of Socrates.

～ ～ ～

'Not Captain Warshaw, though! The Captain had a stomach of iron.'

What were they talking about? The Channel crossing, no doubt. Aunt Irene never tired of describing her travel woes. She detested boats, detested hotel beds, hated tunnels. Whereas Harold, if anyone had asked him, would have said that he looked forward to the tunnel not as an end in itself, the way Grady did, but because the tunnel meant the south, meant Italy. For though it did not literally link Switzerland with Italy, on one side the towns had German names – Göschenen, Andermatt, Hospenthal – while on the other they had Italian names – Airolo, Ambri, Lurengo – and this fact in itself was enough to intoxicate him.

～ ～ ～

Now Stephen stretched; the landscape of his trousers surged, earthquakes leveled the peaks, the rivers were rerouted and the crust of the earth churned up. It was as if a capricious god, unsatisfied with his handiwork, had decided to forge the world anew.

～ ～ ～

'Ah, how I envy any traveler his first visit to Italy!' Mrs. Warshaw said. ('Because for you it will be new – what is for me already faded. Beginning with Airolo, the campanile, as the train comes out the other end of the tunnel . . .'

Harold's book twitched. He knew all about the campanile.

'Is it splendid?' Irene asked.

'Oh, no.' Mrs. Warshaw shook her head decisively. 'Not splendid at all. Quite plain, in fact, especially when you compare it to all those other wonderful Italian towers – in Pisa, in Bologna. I mustn't forget San Gimignano! Yes, compared to the towers of San Gimignano, the campanile of Airolo is utterly without distinction or merit. Still, you will never forget it, because it is the first.'

'Well, we shall look forward to it. Grady, be sure to look out for the tower of . . . just after the tunnel.'

The curtain didn't budge.

Irene's smile said: 'Sons.'

'And where are you traveling, if I might be so bold?'

'To Florence. It's my habit to spend the winter there. You see, when I lost the Captain, I went abroad intending to make a six-months tour of Europe. But then six months turned into a year, and a year into five years, and now it will be eight years in January since I last walked on native soil. Oh, I think of returning to Toronto sometimes, settling in some little nook. And yet there is still so much to see! I have the travel bug, I fear. I wonder if I shall ever go home.' Mrs. Warshaw gazed toward the curtained window. 'Ah, beloved Florence!' she exhaled. 'How I long once again to take in the view from Bellosguardo.'

'How lovely it must be,' echoed Irene, though in truth she had no idea where Bellosguardo was, and feared repeating the name lest she should mispronounce it.

'Florence is full of treasures,' Mrs. Warshaw continued. 'For instance, you must go to the Palazzo della Signoria and look at the Perseus.'

Harold's book twitched again. He knew all about the Perseus.

'Of course we shall go and see them straightaway,' Irene said. 'When do they bloom?'

~ ~ ~

When do they bloom!

It sometimes seemed to Harold that it was Aunt Irene, and not her sons, who needed the tutor. She was ignorant of everything, and yet she never seemed to care when she made an idiot of herself. In Harold's estimation, this was typical of the Pratt branch of the family. With the exception of dear departed Toby (both of them), no one in that branch of the family possessed the slightest receptivity to what Pater called (and Harold never forgot it) 'the poetic passion, the desire of beauty, the love of art for its own sake.' Pratts were anti-Paterian. Not for them Pater's 'failure is forming habits.' To them the formation of habits – healthy habits – was the very essence of success. (It was a subject on which Uncle George, God rest his soul, had taken no end of pleasure in lecturing Harold.)

Still, Harold could not hate them. After all, they had made his education possible. At Thanksgiving and Christmas they always had a place for him at their table (albeit crammed in at a corner in a kitchen chair). 'Our little scholarship boy,' Aunt Irene called him. 'Our little genius, Harold.'

Later, after Uncle George had died, and Toby had died, and Toby the Second as well, Irene had come to him. 'Harold, would you like to see Europe?' she'd asked, fixing his collar.

'More than anything, Aunt Irene.'

'Because I'm planning a little tour this fall with the boys – following my brother's itinerary, you know – and I thought, Wouldn't it be marvelous for them to have a tutor, a scholar like yourself, to tell them what was what. What do you think, Harold? Would your mother mind?'

'I think it's a capital idea.'

'Good.'

So here he was.

So far, things hadn't gone well at all.

In Paris, Harold had decided to test the boys' receptivity to art by taking them to the Louvre. But Grady wanted only to ride the métro, and got infuriated when Harold explained that there was no need to take the métro: the museum was only a block from their hotel. Then they were standing in front of the Mona Lisa, Harold lecturing, Grady quivering with rage at having been deprived of the métro, Stephen leaning, inscrutable as ever, against a white wall. Harold spoke eloquently about the painting and, as he spoke, he felt the silent pressure of their boredom. They had their long bodies arranged in attitudes of sculptural indifference, as if to say, we have no truck with any of this. Curse our mother for pulling us out of our lives, and curse our father for dying, and our brother for dying, and curse you. To which Harold wanted to answer: Well, do you think I like it any more than you do? Do you think I enjoy babbling like an idiot, and being ignored? For the truth was, the scrim of their apathy diffused his own sense of wonder. After all, he was seeing this for the first time, too: not a cheap reproduction, but *La Gioconda*. The real thing. How dare they not notice, not care?

Yes, Harold decided that morning, they were normal, these boys. They would never warm to art. (As if to prove his point, they now gravitated away from his lecturing, and toward an old man who had set up an easel and paints to copy a minor annunciation – their curiosity piqued by some low circus element in the proceedings: 'Gosh, it looks exactly like the original!' an American man standing nearby said to his wife.) Why Aunt Irene had insisted on bringing them to Europe in the first place Harold still couldn't fathom; what did she think was going to happen, anyway? Did she imagine that upon contact with the sack of Rome, the riches of Venice, some dormant love of beauty would awaken in them, and they would suddenly be transformed into cultured, intellectual boys, the sort upon whom she could rely for flashes of wit at dinner parties, crossword solutions on rainy afternoons? Boys, in other words, like their brother Toby, or their uncle Toby, for that matter, who had kept a portrait of Byron on his desk. Grady, on the other hand, couldn't have cared less about Byron, while Stephen, so far as Harold could tell, liked only to lean against white walls in his flannel trousers, challenging the marble for beauty. Really, he was too much, Stephen: self-absorbed, smug, arrogant. Harold adored him.

~ ~ ~

There was a rapping on the compartment door.

'*Entrez*', announced Mrs. Warshaw.

The conductor stepped in. Immediately Grady pulled back the curtain, splaying the light. Stephen's eyes slotted open again.

'Permit me to excuse myself,' the conductor said in tormented French, 'but we are approaching the St. Gotthard tunnel. I shall now light the lamps and make certain that the windows and ventilators are properly closed.'

'*Bien sûr.*'

The conductor was Italian, a handsome, sturdy fellow with a thick black mustache, blue eyes, fine lips. Dark hairs curled under his cuffs, rode down the length of his hands to the ends of his thick fingers.

Bowing, he stepped to the front of the compartment, where he got down on his knees and fiddled with the ventilator panel. As he knelt he winked manfully at Grady.

'Oh, I don't like tunnels,' Irene said. 'I get claustrophobic.'

'I hope you don't get seasick!' Mrs. Warshaw laughed. 'But never mind. When you've been through the St. Gotthard as often as I have, you shall sleep right through, as I intend to do.'

'How long is it again?'

'Nine miles!' Grady shouted. 'The longest in the –' He winced. He had broken his vow.

'Nine miles! Dear Lord! And it will take half an hour?'

'More or less.'

'Half an hour in the dark!'

'The gas jets will be lit. You needn't worry.'

The conductor, having finished with the ventilators, stood to examine the window latches. In securing the one on the right he pressed a wool-covered leg against Harold's knees.

'*Va bene,*' he said next, yanking at the latch for good measure. (It did not give.) Then he turned to face Harold, over whose head the oil lamp protruded; raised his arms into the air to light it, so that his shirt pulled up almost but not quite enough to reveal a glimpse of what was underneath (what *was* underneath?); parted his legs around Harold's knees. Harold had no choice but to stare into the white of that shirt, breathe in its odor of eau de cologne and cigar.

Then the lamp was lit. Glancing down, the conductor smiled.

'*Merci mesdames,*' he concluded merrily. And to Harold: '*Grazie, signore.*'

Harold muttered, '*Prego,*' kept his eyes out the window.

The door shut firmly.

'I shall be so happy to have my first glimpse of Milan,' Irene said.

Why French for the women and Italian for him?

～ ～ ～

They had been traveling forever. They had been traveling for years: Paris, the gaslit platform at the Gare de Lyon, a distant dream; then miles of dull French farmland, flat and blurred; and then the clattery dollhouse architecture of Switzerland, all that grass and those little clusters of chalets with their tilted roofs and knotty shuttered windows, like the window the bird would have flown out on the cuckoo clock . . . if it had ever worked, if Uncle George had ever bothered to fix it. But he had not.

Really, there was nothing to do but read, so Harold read.

Orpheus: having led Eurydice up from the Underworld, he turned to make sure she hadn't tired behind him. He turned even though he had been warned in no uncertain terms not to turn; that turning was the one forbidden thing. And what happened? Exactly what Orpheus should have expected to happen. As if his eyes themselves shot out rays of plague, Eurydice shrank back into the vapors and died a second death, fell back down the dark well. This story of Orpheus and Eurydice Harold had read a hundred times, maybe even five hundred times, and still it frustrated him; still he hoped each time that Orpheus would catch on for once, and not look back. Yet he always looked back. And why? Had love turned Orpheus's head? Harold doubted it. Perhaps the exigencies of story, then: for really, if the episode had ended with the happy couple emerging safely into the dewy morning light, something in every reader would have been left slavering for the expected payoff.

Of course there were other possible explanations. For instance: perhaps Orpheus had found it impossible not to give in to a certain self-destructive impulse; that inability, upon being told 'Don't cross that line,' not to cross it.

Only God has the power to turn back time.

Or perhaps Orpheus, at the last minute, had changed his mind; decided he didn't want Eurydice back after all. This was a radical interpretation, albeit one to which later events in Orpheus's life lent credence.

Harold remembered something – *Huck Finn*, he thought – you must never look over your shoulder at the moon.

~ ~ ~

Something made him put his book down. Stephen had woken up. He was rubbing his left eye with the ball of his fist. No, he did not look like his brother, did not look like any Pratt, for that matter. (Mrs. Warshaw was correct about this, though little else.) According to Harold's mother, this was because Aunt Irene, after years of not being able to conceive, had taken him in as a foundling, only wouldn't you know it? The very day the baby arrived she found out she was pregnant. 'It's always like that,' his mother had said. 'Women who take in foundlings always get pregnant the day the foundling arrives.'

Nine months later Toby was born – Toby the Second – that marvelous boy who rivaled his adopted brother for athletic skills, outstripped him in book smarts, but was handsome, too, Pratt handsome, with pale skin and small ears. Toby had been a star pupil, whereas Irene had had to plead with the headmaster to keep Stephen from being held back a grade. Not that the boys disliked each other: instead, so far as Harold could tell, they simply made a point of ignoring each other. (And how was this possible? How was it possible for anyone to ignore either of them?)

'Be kind to your Aunt Irene,' his mother had told him at the station in St. Louis. 'She's known too much death.'

And now she sat opposite him, here on the train, and he could see from her eyes that it was true: she had known too much death.

Harold flipped ahead a few pages.

Throughout this time Orpheus had shrunk from loving any woman, either because of his unhappy experience, or because he had pledged himself not to do so. In spite of this there were many who were fired with a desire to marry the poet, many were indignant to find themselves repulsed. However, Orpheus preferred to center his affection on boys of tender years, and to enjoy the brief spring and early flowering of their youth: he was the first to introduce this custom among the people of Thrace.

Boys of tender years, like Stephen, who, as Harold glanced up, shifted again, opened his eyes, and stared at his cousin malevolently.

And the train rumbled, and Mrs. Warshaw's aigrette fluttered before the Colosseum, and the cracked glass that covered Trajan's Column rattled.

They were starting to climb at a steeper gradient. They were nearing the tunnel at last.

~ ~ ~

From the *Hartford Evening Post*, November 4, 1878: Letter Six, 'Crossing from the Tyrol into Ticino,' by Tobias R. Pratt:

As we began the climb over the great mountain of San Gottardo our *mulattiere*, a most affable and friendly fellow within whose Germanic accent one could detect echoes of the imminent South, explained that even as we made our way through the pass, at that very moment men were laboring under our feet to dig a vast railway tunnel that upon completion will be the longest in the world. This tunnel will make Italy an easier destination for those of us who wish always to be idling in her beneficent breezes . . . and yet how far the Palazzo della Signoria seemed to us that morning, as we rose higher and higher into snowy regions! It was difficult to believe that on the other side the lovely music of the Italian voice and the taste of a rich red wine awaited us; still this faith gave us the strength to persevere through what we knew would be three days of hard travel.

To pass the time, we asked our guide his opinion of the new tunnel. His response was ambivalent. Yes, he admitted, the tunnel would bring tourism (and hence money) to his corner of the world. And yet the cost! Had we heard, for instance, that already one hundred men had lost their lives underground? A hint of superstitious worry entered his voice, as if he feared lest the mountain – outraged by such invasions – should one day decide that it had had enough and with one great heave of its breast smash the tunnel and all its occupants to smithereens . . .

And Irene thought: He never saw it. He had been dead two years already by the time it was finished.

And Grady thought: Finally.

And Mrs. Warshaw thought: I hope the *signora* saved me Room 5, as she promised.

And Harold watched Stephen's trousers hungrily, hungrily. Glimpses, guesses. All he had ever known were glimpses, guesses. Never, God forbid, a touch; never, never the sort of fraternal bond, unsullied by carnal need, to which epic poetry paid homage; never anything – except this ceaseless worrying of a bone from which every scrap of meat had long been chewed, this ceaseless searching for an outline amid the folds of a pair of flannel trousers.

Yes, he thought, leaning back, I should have been born in classical times. For he genuinely believed himself to be the victim of some heavenly imbroglio, the result of which was his being delivered not (as he should have been) into an Athenian boudoir (his mother someone wise and severe, like Plotina), but rather into a bassinet in a back bedroom in St.

Louis where the air was wrong, the light was wrong, the milk did not nourish him. No wonder he grew up ugly, ill, ill-tempered! He belonged to a different age. And now he wanted to cry out, so that all of Switzerland could hear him: I belong to a different age!

～ ～ ～

The train slowed. Behind the curtain Grady watched the signs giving way one to the next, one to the next: GÖ-SCHE-NEN, GÖ-SCHE-NEN. GÖ-SCHE-NEN.

> By such songs as these the Thracian poet was drawing the woods and rocks to follow him, charming the creatures of the wild, when suddenly the Ciconian women caught sight of him. Looking down from the crest of a hill, these maddened creatures, with animal skins slung across their breasts, saw Orpheus as he was singing and accompanying himself on the lyre. One of them, tossing her hair till it streamed in the light breeze, cried out: 'See! Look here! Here is the man who scorns us!' and flung her spear –

Darkness. Harold shut his book.

～ ～ ～

As soon as the train entered the tunnel the temperature began to rise. Despite the careful labors of the conductor, smoke was slipping into the compartment: not enough to be discernible at first by anything other than its dry, sharp smell; but then Harold noticed that no sooner had he wiped his spectacles clean, than they were already filmed again with dust; and then a gray fog, almost a mist, occupied the compartment, obscuring his vision; he could no longer distinguish, for instance, which of the three little prints across the way from him represented the Pantheon, which Trajan's Column, which the Colosseum.

Mrs. Warshaw's head slumped. She snored.

And Grady pressed his face up against the glass, even though there was nothing to see outside the window but a bluish black void, which he likened to the sinuous fabric of space itself.

And Irene, a handkerchief balled in her fist, wondered: Do the dead age? Would her little Toby, in heaven, remain forever the child he had been when he had died? Or would he grow, marry, have angel children?

And Toby her brother? Had *he* had angel children?

If Toby was in heaven – and not the other place. She sometimes feared he might be in the other place – every sermon she'd ever heard suggested it – in which case she would probably never get closer to him than she was right now, right here, in this infernal tunnel.

She glanced at Stephen, awake now. God forgive her for thinking it, but it should have been him, repairing the well with George. Only Stephen had been in bed with influenza, so Toby went.

Punishment? But if so, for what? Thoughts?

Could you be punished for thoughts?

Suddenly she could hardly breathe the searing air – as if a hundred men were smoking cigars all at once.

~ ~ ~

Midway – or what Harold assumed was midway – he thought he heard the wheels scrape. So the train would stall, and then what would they do? There wouldn't be enough oxygen to get out on foot without suffocating. The tunnel was too long. Half a mile of rock separated train from sky; half a mile of rock, atop which trees grew, a woman milked her cow, a baker made bread.

The heat abashed; seemed to eat the air. Harold felt the weight of mountains on his lungs.

Think of other things, he told himself, and in his mind undid the glissando of buttons on Stephen's trousers. Yet the smell in his nostrils – that smell of cigars – was the conductor's.

~ ~ ~

Light scratched the window. The train shuddered to a stop. Someone flung open a door.

They were outside. Dozens of soot-smeared passengers stumbled among the tracks, the visible clouds of smoke, the sloping planes of alpine grass. For they were there now. Through.

The train throbbed. Conductors, stripped to their waistcoats, took buckets and mops and swabbed the filthy windows until cataracts of black water pooled outside the tracks.

People had died. Her brother in Greece, her child and her husband in the backyard.

There was no heaven, no hell. The dead did not age because the dead *were not.* (Still, Irene fingered the yellowed newspaper clippings in her purse; looked around for Stephen, who had disappeared.)

And meanwhile Harold had run up the hill from the train, and now stood on a low promontory, wiping ash from his spectacles with a handkerchief.

Where was Stephen? Suddenly she was terrified, convinced that something had happened to Stephen on the train, in the tunnel. 'Harold!' she called. 'Harold, have you seen Stephen?'

But he chose not to hear her. He was gazing at the campanile of Airolo, vivid in the fading light.

~ ~ ~

In Airolo, Harold looked for signs that the world was becoming Italy. And while it was true that most of the men in the station bar drank beer, one or two were drinking wine; and when he asked for wine in Italian, he was answered in Italian, and given a glass.

'Grady, do you want anything?'

Silence.

'Grady!'

He still wasn't talking to them.

Aunt Irene had gone into the washroom. She was not there to forbid Harold from drinking, so he drank. Around him, at tables, local workers – perhaps the same ones who had dug the tunnel – smoked and played cards. Most of them had pallid, dark blond faces, Germanic faces; but one was reading a newspaper called *Corriere della Sera*, and one boy's skin seemed to have been touched, even in this northernmost outpost, by a finger of Mediterranean sun.

Italy, he thought, and gazing across the room, noticed that Stephen, darker by far than any man in the bar, had come inside. One hand in his pocket, he was leaning against a white wall, drinking beer from a tall glass.

Apart.

He is from here, Harold realized suddenly. But does he even know it?

Then the conductor came into the bar. Harold turned, blushing, to contemplate his wine, wondering when the necessary boldness would come: to look another man straight in the eye, as men do.

~ ~ ~

Aunt Irene had at last emerged, with Mrs. Warshaw, from the washroom.

'Harold, I'm worried about Stephen,' she said. 'The last time I saw him was when we came out of the —'

'He's over there.'

'Oh, Stephen!' his mother cried, and to Harold's surprise she ran to him, embraced him tightly, pressed her face into his chest. 'My darling, I've been worried sick about you! Where have you been?'

'Can't a man take a walk?' Stephen asked irritably.

'Yes, of course. Of course he can.' Letting him go, she dabbed at her eyes. 'You've grown so tall! You're almost a man! No wonder you don't like Mother hugging you anymore. Oh, Stephen, you're such a wonderful son, I hope you know, I hope you'll always know, how much we treasure you.'

Stephen grimaced; sipped at his beer.

'Well, we're through it,' Mrs. Warshaw said. 'Now tell me the truth, it wasn't so bad as all that, was it?'

'How I long for a bed!' Irene said. 'Is Milan much further?'

'Just a few hours, dear,' Mrs. Warshaw said, patting her hand. 'And only short tunnels from now on, I promise you.'

DAVID LEVINSON

A PERFECT DAY FOR SWIMMING

In December, I went to visit my father in Austin because Alex had just left me, I'd quit my assistant editing job at *Glamour*, and I wanted to be someplace that wasn't New York in winter. I went because my mother wasn't an option. She and her creepy husband, Ted, were traveling to Jekyll Island off the coast of Georgia, where Ted's family had a house. I went because I had no other place to go.

'Spend Christmas with us, Kate,' my father had said and I'd thought, Why not? Sun, margaritas, *and* a heart-shaped swimming pool.

He sprung for my ticket, and arranged for a car to pick me up at the airport. He sounded strange on the phone, as if he hadn't slept in days. Because my father's an attorney, hard-working and harder-drinking, I didn't think anything of it. I simply thought he was immersed in a case.

I arrived at the house, knocked on the door, rang the bell. Nothing, no one. I sweated like a tropical forest in my black cable-knit, turtleneck sweater, black wool pants, black boots. A fixed, hot sun, and the tempera-

---

DAVID LEVINSON (born 1969): A true Texan, Levinson grew up in the hot, muggy and beautiful city of San Antonio. As a boy, he spent most of his time playing Missile Command at his uncle's pool hall, Tiffany Billiards, and reading Encyclopedia Brown, *which saved him. This short story is part of a collection –* Most of Us are Here Against Our Will *– published by Viking UK.*

ture in the low eighties. Winter days in Austin. I called out, 'Dad? Howard?' I called out, 'Matthew? Jason?' (Howard's kids from his first marriage.) No one came to the door or the windows or zoomed around from behind the house. 'Jesus,' I mumbled.

Suitcase in hand, I headed around to the back yard and tried the deck door, which was locked. Inside, the kitchen glimmered, white and spotless. A bottle of Chivas Regal, a red velvet bow tied at its throat, sat on the tiled counter. A defrosting turkey, probably thirty pounds, perched on the table, drops of oily water catching the falling slants of sunlight. 'Howard? Dad?' I said again, tapping the glass. Two o'clock in the afternoon, I thought. Where the hell is everybody?

I called the house on my cell phone and Howard's deep voice emanated from the answering machine. 'Howdy-ho,' he said cheerily. 'We can't come to the phone . . .'

'No doubt,' I said, and sank down into one of the deckchairs, removing my sweater and unzipping my boots.

It had been snowing in Brooklyn, drifting by our fourth-story windows, when Alex had announced he was moving out. I'd thrown the bottle of wine I'd been drinking at him and said, 'Something I said?' I knew it was more than that; I was just being a bitch. We'd been living together for three years and I expected a little more from him, like not breaking up with me when we're scheduled to spend the holidays in Cancun.

Opening my suitcase, I found my hot-pink, string bikini and stripped. I gathered up my Walkman and headed to the pool. The sun made me feel babyish and stiff, as if I'd recently emerged from a coma. I laid out on one of the loungers for about half an hour. The sun roasted the air, flies buzzed, my head spun. I saw Alex carrying boxes out, shaking his head as I'd sat on the couch, smoking and drinking. I knew why he was going. At one point, he'd sat down beside me and said, 'You could've done anything else, Kate, anything at all. But you didn't.' He was talking about his maps, which I'd ripped to shreds the night before. Alex collected maps: old maps, rare and expensive maps. Maps of Africa and Asia and Russia. Gorgeous maps with blues and greens and browns. Hundreds of maps.

Sufficiently fried, I went to the lip of the pool and dabbed my foot in the tepid water. I plucked off my sunglasses, kneeled down, and let out a little gasp, which in turn became a series of hard giggles. Because there, lying on the bottom, was Santa Claus.

A shiny red Explorer pulled into the driveway, windows down. Singing cut through the patchy suburban quiet: *If you stay, it'll get better/Wherever you go it's bound to rain.* Matthew and Jason bolted out of the car, hooting, and fell onto the grass, clutching their necks. 'Country music sucks,' they said in unison.

Howard called, 'Boys, straws suck, country music does not. Now, take the bags inside, please.' The sun had fallen behind the trees, shading the pool, as I climbed off the raft, forgetting about Santa. My foot hit a corner of the plastic and I winced, though I felt nothing acutely. I wrapped myself in a towel and headed up to the house. The boys sang, 'Kate's here, Kate's here,' then darted off. Howard met me on the wooden deck, sweating lightly.

'Kate,' he said, wrapping me in a bear-hug, 'so good to see you. Have you been here long?'

'Long enough to take a dip in your heart,' I said, shaking my hair loose of the remaining water. 'And long enough to find Santa. Howard, what's going on?'

His face became a bundle of untidy energy, which on some men might have been interpreted as excitement; on Howard, it seemed nervous. We went into the cool kitchen. His meaty hands reached into the brown-paper bags, extracting steaks, bacon, rice cakes. Sweat clung lightly to the pock-marked skin around his ears. Beneath his T-shirt, his cannonball-like shoulders and barrel-chest professed hours spent in the gym. He wore a green fatigue T-shirt with the word SEAL, in bold black piping. The shirt, like Howard, had seen a lot. He might've been handsome if he weren't my father's lover.

'So that's where you father dumped Santa,' Howard said sadly. 'Kate, Doug and I had a falling out. He moved into the Four Seasons in town. He was supposed to have telephoned you.'

'No telephone,' I said.

Howard walked over to the turkey, poked it with a finger. 'God, I knew I should've bought fresh this year,' he said, noticing something on the floor. He turned around and said, 'Kate, are you bleeding?'

I looked down at a couple of blotchy red footprints. I lifted up my right foot and there, on the soft fleshy arch, a tiny crooked gash. I laughed a meandering laugh; honestly, I felt nothing.

'Boys,' Howard called, 'take Kate upstairs and show her where the antibacterial soap is.' He squeezed one of my shoulders. 'You'll be all right, kiddo. Not life-threatening.'

The boys were playing *Star Wars* on the stairs. Matthew was Yoda; Jason, Luke Skywalker. Matthew, the younger, said, 'You're a coward, Skywalker.'

Jason replied, 'Up yours, Yoda.'

In the living room, on the mantel, there was a picture of me at Lost Maples National Park, in a pair of wet shorts, with long hair. I'd taken the photo beside it, of Howard and my father kissing, a few years back. Beneath the photographs, four oversized stockings tacked up. An unadorned giant Christmas tree stood in the corner by the door. The whole room smelled of pine and popcorn. Other than the picture, no further signs of my father anywhere.

~ ~ ~

Matthew said, 'I broke my foot once.' He smiled and touched my big toe. Then he leaned down and planted a tiny kiss there. Although the accident had occurred a few months ago, Matthew measured its passing in adventure – trips to the zoo, the circus, the Ice Capades. The minutiae of his life fascinated me, mainly because it all unfolded in the same sweet earnest way. There was no trying, only the glory of play. To be six years old again, I thought.

'I remember,' I said. 'But that was an accident and you were such a big boy.'

Jason grimaced. He'd had longer to process the nasty world of adults and knew that Matthew's 'accident' might not have been an accident at all. The jury was still out on exactly what had happened; only Matthew knew for sure. I could sense Jason's burgeoning rage as he moped around the room, picking up a neon-green toy water gun cracked in two.

'I broke this,' he said grinning. 'Doug gave it to me on my birthday but I can't use it anymore. I asked Santa Claus for a new one but he's dead.'

Matthew said, huffily, 'Nuh-uh, Jathon. Santa's not dead. He'th just – not there.'

I couldn't help smiling at Matthew; when I was his age, I'd had the same trouble controlling my esses. Especially when I was frustrated.

Jason shrugged, dropped the gun on the carpet amid a pile of clothes and ratty *X-Men* comic books. His restlessness was abstracted. I wanted to grab him by the shoulders and hold him still. I said, 'Jason, why don't you come over here and play with us?'

His brown eyes turned toward the window with light expectation, as a car turned into the driveway. When the car pulled out again a moment later, the expectation fizzled into anger. He fidgeted at the window, tapping it absently with his fingers, a drummer banging out a song.

'Hey, guys. I have a great idea. Why don't you surprise your dad and clean up your rooms?' I said, trying not to sound like a game-show hostess, the mother they didn't have and probably needed. My voice felt stagy, full of booby prizes and trapdoors. Just play the game, boys, and see how much you can win.

'Only if I can have some Nerds,' Matthew said.

'I'll see what I can do,' I said, rising.

Jason tugged at my back and indicated for me to kneel down. Then, he whispered, 'When Matthew broke his foot, Doug gave him these little blue pills. Want me to get some for you?'

I looked over at the plaster cast of Matthew's tiny foot on the shelf, displayed between his World Series baseball signed by Bernie Williams and his Little League trophy, third place.

'No thanks,' I said. 'I'm perfectly fine.'

Jason grimaced again. Of course you're not fine, his face said. I turned my back on him. When the pain finally did come, there would be something comforting in it, something useful and familiar.

~ ~ ~

Downstairs, Howard spoke quietly on the phone. He held up a hand, motioning to the refrigerator, nearly hidden behind a collage of decorations and drawings made by the boys. Happy-face magnets of shellacked bread dough, stick figures in different colored pencil, with glitter for lips and sequins for eyes. Warped and blotchy watercolors of dead deer and rifles. Two lists, both to Santa, each an entire page long. On my own fridge at home, there was simply an ancient black-and-white wedding photograph of my mother and father.

The coffee still too hot, I added some ice, a lot of sugar and cream. I went outside to the deck. I heard, 'No, Doug, we've talked about this already. You can stay to trim the tree and *then you go*.'

Howard came out, face tight, hands shaking as he stirred his coffee. 'How's your foot?' he said.

I nodded that it was all right as he reached over to examine it. 'Your father's on his way.' He massaged my foot absently. I sat there, letting him, because really, why not? It felt great. Howard gave great massages, better than anyone. Once, a couple years ago, I told Alex this and he said, 'Of course. Being a fag makes him sensitive that way.' I didn't know. Things like that were hard to say. Howard drank beer, played softball, worked out in the yard. He also gave incredible foot rubs. It seemed to me that my father had it pretty good.

'How are the boys holding up?' I said.

'Oh, well, they're confused,' Howard said. 'Like me. Like the entire world when something like this happens. Don't let anyone tell you that men are from Mars and women are from Venus, Kate. Everyone's from Pluto.'

Tentatively, I said, 'What about Jason?'

'What do you mean?' Howard said. 'Did he – oh, God, he didn't do anything to Matthew again, did he? I've told him a thousand times not to be a bully. I'm so afraid he's going to turn into –' There was real surprise in his voice and behind that, something pinched and strained.

'No, no, nothing like that. He's just, well, he seems a little angry to me,' I said.

'He's angry, Kate. We're all angry. The only one of us who isn't angry is Matthew and he's not old enough yet to realize it. When your father –'

'Howard, that was an accident,' I said. 'Wasn't it?'

'You mean like Santa in the swimming pool,' he said, shaking his head in earnest. 'If you only knew, Kate.'

I knew a little. I knew my father came home drunk and stayed drunk the entire evening. I knew that he let his law practice run itself, which meant he wasn't paying his bills or employees. I knew he'd been calling me, his only daughter, at all hours of the night, crying.

Unable to sit still, Howard rose and wandered over to a potted geranium. He buried a finger in it. 'I really have to water this more or it's a goner.'

I sat in silence, sipping my coffee. 'What did he do this time?' I said.

'Nothing,' Howard said. 'Everything. You know Doug's drill, Kate. Two months of flowers and kindness and then *wham!* we're back in the trenches with him.'

The door flew open and Jason and Matthew tore out of the house.

Their light-sabers, one orange, one green, iridescent in the crepuscular dark. 'Boys, for heaven's sake,' Howard said.

'I cleaned my room,' Matthew said. 'Can I have my Nerds now?'

Howard frowned. 'Bribery went out with Barney the Dinosaur,' he said to me. I smiled tensely. 'Sugar is our new war,' he said as my father pulled his truck into the driveway.

The boys lost their sabers and raced over to it. A couple of minutes later, they flanked my father, swinging his arms back and forth. Without his beard, his face looked sunken and lost.

'Doug's here,' Matthew said.

Jason let go my father's hand and stood away from them, holding up his little hands, as if trying to keep something from falling on top of him. He made a series of squeaks.

'Jason, stop that please,' Howard said.

'I'm trying to locate Santa,' he said. 'I think I picked up his signal. It's very weak . . .'

'I don't care if you're speaking to Ghengis Khan, cease and desist right this minute,' Howard said, smiling. Look at my boy, his face said. Tell me he's not going to be all right.

'Hello, Doug,' Howard said, neither warm nor pleasant.

'Howard,' my father said, peering past him into the house.

'I'll get started on dinner,' Howard said, smoothing out his I GET A KICK OUT OF YOU apron. 'Boys, set the table for dinner please.'

'No need,' my father said. 'Rudy's BBQ to the rescue.'

'Then I guess I'll go and take a shower,' Howard said and went inside.

I said, turning to my father, 'How are you holding up?'

'About as good as I can be,' he said, 'considering this is the third day in a row I've thought about hanging myself with my own entrails.'

'That isn't funny,' I said. And then, 'Why didn't you call me?'

'I thought I could fix it before you got here,' he said. 'And you're right. That's not funny.' He paused. 'Not nearly as funny as your fifty-two-year-old father staring at himself in the mirror on Christmas Eve and wondering how the hell he's made such a mess of his life.'

His speech was warm and liquid and I wondered if he'd been drinking. I leaned into him, only to catch the whiff of garlic, and behind that, peppermint.

'Well, even if Howard isn't glad you're here, I am,' I said, the pain in my foot livid. I went to the door.

'Kate, what's with the limp?' he said.

'I stepped on Santa Claus in the pool,' I said.

My father wrinkled up his face. 'Yes, that's one of the casualties,' he said. 'Are you all right?' I nodded. 'It's good to see you, daughter. I'm looking forward to our little outing on Sunday.'

'Me, too,' I said. We'd planned a camping trip to Lost Maples, a place I hadn't been since girlhood.

'Well, then, I'll get the spare ribs – hickory-smoked, your favorite – out of the car,' he said.

I gave him a great big smile, teeth and all. I didn't feel like reminding him I hadn't touched red meat in years.

～ ～ ～

During dinner, the phone rang twice. My father excused himself and I heard him above us, creaking across the hardwood floors. I was on my third gin and tonic when he reappeared and said, 'Howard, Jerome beeped in. He said something about bridge next week. I told him you'd call him back.'

Howard said, 'Bridge. Don't make me laugh.'

My father rubbed his hands together as if he were about to perform a magic trick. And now here's Douglas Burnett, HOUDINI'S HOMO-SEXUAL COUSIN. He said, 'Which of my big boys wants to help me trim the tree?'

'Me, Doug, me. I do, Doug. Let me. I'm older,' Jason said.

'But I'm Yoda,' Matthew said, face stormy. 'That maketh me older by a thousand yearth!'

'Say years,' Jason said, taking the initiative, goading. Something Jason had obviously heard before. 'Say it, Matthew. Years, not yearth.'

Matthew shook his head, lowered his eyes. 'No.'

'Please, boys, enough. Go help Doug,' Howard said, massaging his temples.

I looked at him, this worn-out man, who for ages had endured the bloody, damaged Burnett heart next to him. Almost as a reflex, my father placed a hand on Howard's shoulder. The boys' faces, like my own, waffled between consternation and wonder. My father leaned down and planted a kiss on the bald crown of Howard's head.

'Doug,' Howard said, 'come on.'

'Angel angel angel,' the boys sang, racing around the table.

I sat silent, taking in this unsettling tableau.

'Stay close to your father,' Howard said. 'And Doug, the light's out in the garage so take this.' He handed my father a flashlight. As he held it out and my father took it, Howard's eyes gently drifted over his face, his own face changing incrementally, from disappointment to acknowledgement to something else entirely. It said, *I see you're trying but it's not enough.*

With my father and the boys outside, Howard said, 'Your father looks . . .'

Like a train wreck, I thought. 'He still loves you, Howard,' I said.

'Oh, I know that,' he said. 'But that isn't the point. Love can't keep this marriage from imploding.'

'What about counseling?' I said.

'Tried it,' he sighed. 'But after Doug punched Father Louden and broke his glasses, I asked myself why in the heck I was going through this with him. Your father's not an easy man to get along with.'

'No offense but that doesn't sound like him,' I said, running a finger around the lip of the glass. 'He was never violent with me or –'

'Well, like it or not,' Howard said, face flushed in the light, 'that's what happened.'

Somewhere, beyond the perimeter of the house, the boys scattered as my father called them back. I finished my drink, poured another, and then went down to the steamy, heated pool.

~ ~ ~

Howard and my father gathered around the tree, while Matthew sat on the floor working on a string of cranberries. His little fingers, stained red, waved up at me. Jason, his breathing insistent through a Darth Vader mask, marched from fire to tree, tree to kitchen, kitchen to fire again.

'Kate, you're just in time for the angel,' my father said. 'Howard, the angel, please.'

Howard looked around him. 'I thought you brought it in,' he said.

'I must've left her in the car,' my father said. 'Kate, how about –'

'No, no, no,' Howard said. 'You stay here. I need to grab some cranberry sauce out of the freezer in the garage.' My father tossed Howard the keys. 'Jason, if I've told you once, I've told you a thousand times, get your butt away from the fire.'

Mesmerized, his entire body finally at rest, Jason watched the logs break apart. The flue sucked up the glowing embers in a dazzling swirl.

'You know, this is the first time since I've been here that you've actually stopped moving,' I said, tousling his hair.

'He's a mover and a shaker,' my father said. 'No harm in that.'

I said, 'What happened to the star we used to have?'

'Up in flames,' my father said. 'Last year.'

'I made that star,' I said.

'Wait until you see the angel,' my father said. 'Howard's grandmother's. I had it cleaned.'

'Thugar, thugar, thugar,' Matthew said and shook the bag of Nerds I'd found for him hidden in the pantry.

'Say sugar,' my father said. 'S-u-g-a-r.'

'That'th what I thaid,' he said. 'Eth-u-g-a-r.'

'Where in the heck one of these boys picked up a lisp, I'll never know,' my father said.

'Maybe you'd like to blame that on me, too,' Howard said, standing in the door, angel in one hand, an empty bottle of whiskey in the other. His face was missing its usual out-in-the-yard tan. 'Doug,' he said, 'I'd like you to go now.'

The air in the room tautened and I shifted uncomfortably. Matthew stopped threading the cranberries and threw them at Jason, who launched them into the fire. Too hot, they exploded, like bullets.

'Howard, what are you babbling about?' my father said.

Howard set the angel down on the coffee table. 'I found this,' he said, 'on the floor in the back of your truck.'

My father's face registered a frown. 'That's an old bottle, Howard,' he said. 'Now, will someone please hand me the angel?'

'No, Doug,' Howard said. 'You have to go.'

Jason picked up the angel and turned it over, while Howard and my father's bickering grew operatic. Their voices rose, heavy, muscular, each word lifting the hairs on my neck. Matthew scooted up against the couch and covered his ears. I kneeled down beside him and stroked the smooth skin of his cheek. The melodrama unfolded like a bad TV movie. Howard stormed out of the room and went into the kitchen. I heard him speaking on the phone, though I had no idea with whom.

My father, still on the ladder, rested his head against a rung, staring off at the pool, unaware of Jason below him. Standing at the ladder's foot, Jason reached up to hand my father the angel, opened his hands, and let it go. I tried to yell, 'Dad,' but my voice wouldn't leave my body. My father reached for the angel, which slipped out of his fingers, somersaulted to the floor and shattered. My head filled with the staged gasps of a live TV audience.

Howard rushed back in and said, 'Ooh, my angel,' and turned to Jason, who was halfway up the stairs.

My father scrambled down the ladder, stepping over the broken, jagged pieces, fury in his eyes.

'She's ruined,' Howard said.

'Get back here,' my father said, and lunged for Jason. He snagged the boy in his paws.

Matthew burrowed his brown head into my shoulder and shuddered, his little body going rigid. Staring at my father, whose hands were on Jason's shoulders, both faces slack and blank, Howard said, 'Get. Your. Hands. Off. My. Child.' His voice, doused in gasoline, needed just another word from my father to help it combust.

My father let go Jason, who bolted up the stairs. 'This is my house,' my father roared. 'My house, Howard. My landscape, my pool, my furniture.'

Without saying a word, I led Matthew out of the room and then went to check on Jason. In the dark, he sat on his bed, clutching a Luke Skywalker doll in one hand, a Princess Leia doll in the other.

'You really screwed up this time,' Leia said. 'It wasn't me,' Luke said. 'It was the dark side.'

'Jason,' I said, entering his room.

'Go away,' he said. 'I'm busy.'

'Jason, it wasn't your fault,' I said. Howard and my father's voices sifted up to us. Something smashed, something else was knocked over, a door slammed. 'This has nothing to do with you.'

'But I did it on purpose,' he said.

Throwing the dolls against the wall, his little body shook and then he was crying. I sat down next to him and wrapped him in my arms. Matthew came in and then the three of us huddled together on the bed in the dark until my father's truck screeched out of the driveway.

~ ~ ~

Sometime during the night, Howard had laid out all the boys' presents. A plate of chocolate chip cookies, half-eaten, sat on the sideboard beside a half-drunk glass of milk. The tree lifeless, unlit lights and silver balls, strings of cranberries, popcorn, tinsel. I plugged the cord in. I drank the rest of the milk.

Standing at the window, I looked toward the pool, wisps of steam curling into the chilly night air. There was my father swimming laps, the bottle of Chivas resting on the pool's lip, glinting in the moonlight. The house lay silent, holding its breath as I made my way to him. I waited while he swam up and down the length of the heart. When he saw me, he said, 'This is my house, daughter. My pool, my fucking business.'

'Dad, what about the restraining order?'

He laughed and climbed out, shivering. He dried off his naked body, surprisingly well maintained. 'Let Howard try,' he said, cinching the towel about his waist and staring up at the house. 'I love that guy, you know. And those kids.'

'I know,' I said. 'They love you, too.'

'They shouldn't,' he said, and reached for the Chivas. 'Share a drink with your old man?'

He took a swig and passed me the bottle. I took one, too, a healthy gulp. The flavor of it, strong and medicinal, exploded in my mouth. 'Only the best,' he said, 'for my Kate.'

I smiled. How could I possibly be angry at my poor wreck of a father? There he was, charming and defective, life's incongruities playing their sad melodies in his head. I knew this, because life's incongruities were playing in mine as well.

'It's freezing out here,' I said, rising.

Inside, we sat at the kitchen table, speaking in whispers. My father played with the pieces of the angel spread out before us. 'What a Christmas,' he said, lifting up one of the blue porcelain wings. 'What a disaster.'

It was then that I thought of Alex and the butterfly, which I'd stayed up all night gluing together out of the pieces of his maps. He'd left that behind as well.

'Nothing's unfixable,' I said.

He said, 'Ah, but is it worth the fixing? Now that I think is the real question.' He gulped from the bottle, his big horsy brown eyes staring past me to the refrigerator. I knew he was weighing the possibilities, the maybes, the if-thens. His face grew stern, a complexity of motion in his head. Then he rose and went rifling through the kitchen drawers. 'That Krazy glue's in here somewhere,' he said.

'No, dad,' I said. 'I was thinking more of Target, you know.'

'Target,' he said, forgoing the search. 'Kate, you're a genius.'

I am my father's daughter, I thought. While he dressed, I called my voice mail: a message from my mother and Ted wishing me a merry Christmas. Nothing from Alex. My father returned and said, 'Okay, so how're we going to get there?'

'Let's take your truck,' I said. 'I'll drive.'

He shook his head. 'Can't,' he said. His face went flaccid and he brought the bottle to his lips. 'It's resting out on Highway 2222. Nothing major, but it won't run. No gas.'

'How did you get here, then?' I said in disbelief.

'Walked,' he said.

~ ~ ~

At two o'clock in the morning, we stepped into Target. Bright and antiseptic but soothing, with its familiar buzz of fluorescent lights, its holiday Muzak. Everything glowed that underwater blue, as silent sirens announced sudden holiday specials. The beauty and calm of this place were matched only by my own, helped along by the Chivas, which my father had managed to smuggle in. He was an extraordinary specimen.

Needing to use the bathroom, I said, 'Don't go wandering off, dad.'

He smiled, raised three fingers, and said, 'Lawyer's honor.'

By the time I got out, he was gone of course. I headed directly to the Christmas tree ornament aisle. No luck there. I scanned the rows of ornaments, gold stars with fake peridots and Plexiglas stars with green sand and *Joyeux Noël* in red. I took one of the gold stars and left the aisle. I called out his name, softly at first, then louder. The instrumental chorus to 'O Come, All Ye Faithful' jammed my head as I wandered from aisle to aisle, up one and down another. He was nowhere.

Twenty minutes later, after having him paged without result, I found him behind the wheel of the Explorer. Another gold star sat on the seat beside him, glittering in the sodium lamp's orange halo. He said, 'Toss me the keys, Kate,' and I fought the urge to remind him that he'd already lost one car that night.

'Where'd you disappear to?' I said, placing the gold stars on the back seat.

'I thought you said to meet you here,' he said.

'Dad,' I said and climbed in. Perhaps out of exhaustion, perhaps out of some misguided notion I had of fathers and daughters, that safety was inherent in the deal, I handed the keys to him and said, 'Nothing fancy, just drive.'

He grinned and crossed his fingers over his chest. I should've flexed what little authority I had, since I was the one who'd left Howard the note telling him that I'd borrowed his car. Yet the idea of arguing with my father, the defense attorney, at this late hour, seemed moot.

'How about we stop off for a teensy-weensy little drink to toast my daughter's brilliance?' he said, maneuvering Howard's car down South Congress, the capital building at our backs. My father, the lush, I thought. He took a right onto Fourth Street and headed over to Colorado. We passed a bar, the Boathouse, and he turned into the alley. 'No sense paying to park,' he added.

Once inside, it became clear my father was a regular. The men nodded and grinned at him as we passed. Some leaned on the mirrored walls, others danced on the tiny, elevated dance floor. Catching me, their faces went slack, their eyes glazing over, as if they'd never seen a woman before. Immediately, I resented my father's choice in venues, almost as much as I resented myself for having been coerced. I said, 'One drink, and then we're out of here. Right?'

'Anything, daffodil,' he said, cozying up to the bar.

The bartender, a big-boned man in overalls, smiled when he saw my father and said, 'I swear on the ghost of Norma Jean Baker, counselor, I'm innocent.' He held up his hands in mock surrender.

'Howdy, Sid,' my father said. 'Sid, my lovely daughter, Kate.'

'Delighted,' Sid said and poured out three shots of peppermint schnapps, two of which he slid to us. 'Pleased to make your acquaintance.'

We lifted our glasses, clinked in succession, and downed the schnapps, which tasted corrosive, like fermented mouthwash. I asked for a glass of water and a beer while my father ordered a scotch, neat, and said, 'I'll be right back.'

He wobbled toward the back of the bar and disappeared through a door marked COXSWAINS. Then, it was simply me and my beer and the thrashing men who stared at themselves in the mirrors. At one point, Sid said, 'Doug tells me you're from Brooklyn?'

I shook my head, having only caught the last part – from Brooklyn. I said, 'Me and the boyfriend broke up,' as if this might explain the reason I was standing in a gay bar on Christmas morning.

'Terrible news,' Sid said. 'He cheat on you or something?'

'Alex was faithful,' I said, the words working their way out of me like splinters.

'Because you know, that's what men do: they cheat,' Sid said. 'I come from a long line of cheaters myself. It's in my blood, I suppose. Hard to change it once it's there, you know what I'm saying.'

I nodded. Yes, I knew. As I drank my beer and searched the faces of these good-looking, well-dressed men, I saw something new, some inexplicable sadness. As if for a moment, drunk and twirling, the future had opened up to them, full of empty rooms and emptier beds. I'd caught this same expression on my face sometimes, in the mirror at work, a darkened window, and it frightened me. It was my father's face.

Minutes later, my father returned with a boy who couldn't have been more than twenty years old. 'Daffodil, I'd like you to meet . . .' He leaned in and whispered something into the boy's ear.

'Chad,' the boy said, extending his hand. 'I'm on the university's swim team.'

We all laughed nervously at his non sequitur. His hand, festooned with silver rings, curled dense in my own. The air around him smelled of chlorine and potato chips. My father finished his drink and ordered another for himself and one for Chad, who'd taken up a position between us. He was a tall, gaunt boy, with blond spiky hair, the hoops in his ears glinting in the dim light cast by the eruption of lighters. I liked him, though I couldn't say why.

My father stared at him, enraptured, and compassion rolled over inside of me. I felt it then, what it must've been like to be my father, going from one failed relationship to the next, his last one moribund, if not already dead. I knew then there were worse things than infidelity, worse even than skipping out on love: the surrender of what you had for the promise of what you didn't. A tighter fit, a more winning smile. Someone else, someone better. I thought of Alex, the challenge and bliss of being with someone who'd put up with me for three years, his persistence as foreign as the names of the cities covering his maps.

At some point, Chad and my father drifted away, let loose upon a whorl of passion. I stood there, sipping my beer, while my father danced with this boy less than half his age. Something appalling and beautiful in it, the way their bodies met in that space. My father's big and burly, the boy's unrestricted and severe. I thought of Lost Maples, the giant trees with their golden leaves. There'd be no camping trip, no hiking, no swimming. There'd only be what there'd always been: my father and his heart.

Chad appeared beside me and said, 'Come dance with us,' and I shook my head no.

'I hurt my foot,' I said, though this wasn't it at all.

'Your dad's really fun,' he said. His wide, freckled face held the most pleasant and knowing of grins. 'We're going to take off pretty soon, I guess. Nice to meet you.' And then he drifted off again.

I shifted all my weight to my foot, to feel the pain, resplendent and alive, to feel anything but the abstraction of a much fiercer longing. As a familiar song came on and the dance floor filled up, I ordered another beer, while my father and this lovely boy, this swimmer, spun each other around, dizzying and graceful. They made it look so easy, this coming together. Maybe that's all there is, I thought, moving from the bar toward the perimeter of the floor, where I joined the crush of handsome men who glanced right through me.

MICHAEL CARROLL

MIDAIR

Though he always flew coach, Rob still idealized commercial flight. He'd only been off the Continental flight from Hopkins International for twenty minutes, with his carry-on bags in tow (like a businessman, he never checked luggage), when he noticed the man looking like his father before he'd gotten sick all that time ago – with that same anxious and defeated mien. The man sat across from Rob watching him riffle through his free copy of *USA Today*. It was Rob's thirtieth birthday. The commuter terminal was practically empty, and on an overcast autumn Friday seemed filled with the ghosts of weary travellers.

He'd been staring at a wire-service photo of the current Republican presidential candidate, John Mars Babcock (not a bad looker), when an icy heat began to spread inside him – the feeling he always had when a man took notice of him. The man kept looking up from his book, a cheapo volume with the giant drastic-discount sticker still on it. His eyes were hollow in the weak fluorescent airport lighting, the spooky washed-out light of an aquarium that sits murmuring and glowing in a darkened room.

Though no client had ever used the term in front of him, Rob was a

MICHAEL CARROLL (born 1964): Carroll's fiction has appeared in Ontario Review, Chattahoochee Review and Reading Room Journal, among other publications. He has taught in Yemen and the Czech Republic, and now lives in New York City.

hustler. Since he'd turned nineteen, he'd spanked mayors for a living, topped think-tank eggheads, and sat up listening to boring explanations of the Oriental-sounding NASDAQ and Dow by some of its most successful gurus and devotees: the same men who only minutes before had fellated Rob while he repeated his sonny-boy cant (That's it, Daddy. Take it all the way. Baby likes it like that . . .), or played the cowboy or the trucker or the candle-bearing acolyte for them, or some other role from Rob's vast repertoire.

And he may have been imagining things, but hadn't the man been watching Rob since the moment they'd both dragged their carry-ons up to the gate? Briefly Rob fantasized having seen him on the flight from Cleveland. He almost seemed to know him, with his shrunken appearance made punier by his considerable height, and his pasty complexion thrown off balance by a tawny kitchen-sink dye job in his thinning hair, fading eyebrows and a wiry mustache through which the real silver was trying to express itself, though it glinted off-color like tarnished brass.

And then it came to him: this was Red Perkins, the singing Chevy dealer of Youngstown, who strummed his ukulele and caterwauled a jingle on local TV spots, luring car shoppers out from Cleveland. Without his makeup, Hawaiian shirt, a plastic lei and the studio lighting that gave him his name, he looked more like a fly-by-night used-car huckster about to make his deceptive pitch, and twenty years older than his telethon-trotting self.

Rob needed to take a leak and was debating with himself whether or not to ask Singin' Red to watch his bags so he could duck into the men's room. Singin' Red looked up from his Grisham, smiled and nodded, confirming Rob's suspicions. Rob could just see him now, about to fast-talk, gearing up to wheel and deal. 'Hey there, folks. This is Singin' Red Perkins beamin' to you live from right straight offa I-80! Man have I got a deal for you!'

Before they got too big, Red Perkins used to pull his children in front of the camera with a shiny new Camaro in the background, croon to them off-key about his great Chevy buys, and beg them to sing along. He had them wave at the camera at the end of each spot and shout his motto: 'If you like what you see now, Ohioans, you'll love whatcha get!' Red twanged hillbillyish and people said he came from over the border in West Virginia, though this was one of the few things he didn't make public. He was big on the family values circuit, charged for speaking engagements at churches and seminars, and circulated a 'scorecard' with his dealership logo printed on it rating state and national politicians. Now he sat across from Rob staring hard and looking lustful.

Rob spotted the men's room nearby and got up. With just the right amount of controlled enthusiasm, a faked Good Samness, the man said, 'I'll watch that for you, if you like.'

'That's okay,' Rob said. 'I'm just going to the restroom.'

'You never know,' the man suggested.

'Thanks. I probably shouldn't worry, anyway. The place is pretty deserted.'

'I wonder why,' the man said dryly. 'With a record of delays like this . . .'

Rob slipped away to the men's room and was pissing when the man came in and sidled up to the urinal next to him, his Cleveland Browns mini-duffel slung over his shoulder, and unzipped with an earnest look on his face.

'Yep,' said Red Perkins, splashing the porcelain audibly, 'the Waiting Game.'

Rob said, 'Well, I don't see what's causing the delay. And hey, what about my bags?'

'They're okay. Like you said, nobody's in the damn place.'

Rob nodded, but was now in a hurry to get back to his things.

'Yep,' said Red, standing there, 'FAA's riled up over safety, slowing things down. Too many planes taking off and landing. Goddamn nosy federal regulators. You on business or vacation?'

'Vacation.'

'Nantucket, or Hyannis?'

'Nantucket.'

'Me, I'm going to Hyannis. Got a suite at the Radisson – two hundred a night, uh-huh!'

Rob skipped washing his hands. He whistled tunelessly on his way out of the restroom and settled back to wait for their flight to be called. The video monitor above their heads keeping track of flights read 'Delayed.' He looked around and saw a predominantly well-dressed set of people, looking unbothered by the delay – or unsurprised.

He closed his eyes, leaned back in the chair, and got a gnawing reminder that he'd missed lunch. When he opened his eyes and sat up Red Perkins was in his seat again, sulking into his legal thriller. Rob pulled from his laptop case a bag of the peeled baby carrots that were the key to his dieting strategy. His mantra – My body's a fiery furnace – came from a late-night juicer infomercial. 'That looks healthy,' said Red, looking up from his book and grinning. Big dentures.

'It is,' said Rob, chewing ruefully. Why was a man like Singin' Red Perkins flying to Cape Cod? He chewed some more, then stopped. He looked up at the food court across the terminal.

My mind is the steady hand of the sure-fire stoker.

'Better than some old junk food,' said Red Perkins.

'That's what I thought,' said Rob. He leaned back and tossed the last of the carrots into the trash bin behind him. The package boomed reproachfully when it hit bottom – echoing across the terminal.

'Score,' Red Perkins said, nervously chuckling. 'Made it. Basket.'

'You know what?' Rob said to him, smiling and rising. 'I think I'll head up to that snack stand and get something to drink. You want anything?'

The man started in his seat, closing the book on his finger. 'Sounds like a plan,' he said. He was about to stand up.

'Uh, actually,' said Rob, 'I was thinking of asking you to stay here and watch my stuff, then bringing you something back. Whatever you want. My treat.'

'No thanks.'

'You sure, Singin' Red?' Rob winked.

The man chuckled awkwardly. 'Heh-heh, you from Cleveland?'

'I am,' Rob said. 'And I watch a lot of TV.'

Singin' Red pivoted his head back on his long wiry neck and raised a pair of ventriloquist doll's automated, dyed fuzzy eyebrows, mugging 'Get you.' And then, 'Hey, what's the deal?'

'I've always enjoyed those commercials,' Rob said. They looked at each other a while.

'Yeah, they're kinda fun,' said Singin' Red. 'I'm kinda pulling back, getting out of the biz. It's a hard racket. I'll tell you. All these foreign autos. I drive a Nissan Z.' He waggled his eyebrows again for Rob.

Rob knew how it worked. The men he serviced usually had money, and money was their closet door. After sex they became different, more conservative. One john had even assured Rob that taxation had likely been the cause of his father's death – even though Rob knew it was cancer, brought on by a life of smoking and working long, hard hours for a penny-pinching company. Yet it wasn't just fiscal-mindedness haunting some of them. One client, a therapist for an unusually enlightened-sounding Christian organization in Charlotte, suggested Rob's chosen profession had come out of a childhood in which Rob had held back his affections from a father who hadn't been able to afford enough toys for him. Hustling for men like this Sunday school teacher and father-of-three was a way of working through Rob's belated feelings of remorse, when in fact he should have been blaming Big Government and a regulation-cosseted economy. This from a man wearing a poker expression he could have swindled Vegas with, minutes after Rob had tied him naked to a hotel bedstead with a pair of skinny leather belts, and spanked him to orgasm with his deceased mother's silver hairbrush.

'You like Zs?' asked Red.

'Yeah,' said Rob. 'What color?' Zs had been his weakness before they were discontinued; nonetheless the incongruous but totally middle-age-crazy image of Red Perkins peeling rubber and shifting gears in the cockpit of his space-vehicle sports car amused Rob. Don't say red, he thought.

'Cherry-bomb red!'

'Well, good luck,' said Rob. 'You mind watching my stuff? A Coke? Nothing?'

Red studied him and let an easy smile appear on his face. He eyeballed Rob up and down and sucked his teeth.

'So what's a long, cool drink of water like you heading up to Nan-tucket for?'

'Same as you. Have a vacation.'

'Uh-huh. I got your number.'

'I wonder how,' said Rob. He wasn't listed with any service, and he didn't go on the Internet. Everything was handled, informally, by Harry in Orlando.

The guys in New York, he'd heard from several clients, worked much harder. 'Boys' who worked for agencies earned five times what Rob made by turning their métiers into assembly lines of specialized kink. They ran coy ads on-line and in the Manhattan meat-market rags, posting aggress-ively captioned photos of themselves stripped to the waist, body-waxed to nubility, holding phone receivers in their hands. From what he'd heard, the pictures were usually out of date. Clients told him that if you confronted them on this, they'd get defensive and demand half the money before clearing off your doorstep. That wasn't Rob's scene. He ran a friendly service. Real.

As he made his way to the food court, he was already fighting the impulse for a pizza slice or fries. It wasn't really a vacation for him. Before long he would have to make a decision, to cut bait or rededicate himself to the cause. He'd never spent more than a half-hour in any gym. He'd only ever jogged to keep the boyish figure Harry's contacts liked. Overnight, his metabolism had started betraying him. Some of the men were starting to make comments. Less and less could he get away with full lobster dinners with half a bottle of wine and dessert.

He'd learned from some of them, men like Harry, it was better to concentrate your yens into higher, more developed tastes. To savor one good single-malt, to order once from the top shelf instead of going headfirst into a series of watered-down well brands and ending up broke with a hangover that just wouldn't quit. Or to pluck, if you were in a mall with a guy or the two of you were strolling the esplanade of some refurbished waterfront, a single expensive European chocolate. Harry, an Orlando developer, was probably Rob's mentor. A not unattractive sixty-plusser, he took great care of himself, had a belly packed in tight but not washboard, didn't try to make himself look like he was in a boy band. He got a lot out of life. Harry was ever ready to uproot from Mousetown for a weekend, to fly off to New Orleans or Savannah, or some part of Florida Rob had never been to – Sanibel Island or Key Largo or Naples. They fished, went snorkeling, beachcombing, and sightseeing. They planned their weekends fourteen days ahead of time to take advantage of the lower fares, and with what Harry saved (he was semi-retired) they ate well, drank the good stuff, sat in hot tubs at straight resorts or upscale gay B&Bs and smoked Cuban cigars.

They'd met when Rob was nineteen, during a trip Rob took back to Jacksonville, the city where he had been born and had lived up through high school. It had been a soul-searching tour, a backpack on his back and in his jeans pocket a ticket to Mexico bought with money he'd earned bussing tables in a bagel restaurant on Euclid Avenue. He took the slow city buses everywhere. After a dry-eyed turn in the old neighborhood, his shiver-inducing look at the boarded-up restaurant his father had managed, and a nervous pilgrimage to the weed-infested graveyard where they'd buried him, he boarded a bus at the downtown station and headed for Miami, to catch a plane to Merida.

And it was in the American Airlines terminal at Miami International that he met Harry: a good-natured, tanned, silver-haired smiler with a deep ex-chain-smoker's chortle and a young pair of pale-green eyes.

It had been no problem starting a conversation. Harry did all the work. They were sitting at a gate not too different in feel from this one. Harry said right off he was treating himself to the Yucatan for going a year without smoking. What was he doing? Rob opened his mouth. Though he wanted this man's approval, he felt suddenly confused. He said something about his crazy screwed-up mother, his dead dad, the old haunts up in Jacksonville he'd just visited, and now this trip – all the things he had to do before he could make any more important decisions in his life. 'I guess I've been reading too much Salinger, or watching *The Breakfast Club* too often,' Rob said. 'Or something like that.'

Without condescending, yet conveying an obvious fidgety jones for a cigarette to help him negotiate this, Harry squeezed an eye shut as if squinting might enhance his powers as a seer, and said soberly, 'Sounds like you got a lot on your plate.'

Rob could tell in this one quick exchange that something was about to happen, there was some chemistry between them. It was awkward at first, but soon he settled in and felt comfortable around Harry. The truth was, he hadn't made any important decisions in his life. He'd been paralyzed by fear and procrastination since graduating from high school, when he and his mother had finally packed it in and headed home to her native Cleveland. 'College is your ticket,' she'd told him. 'Stay in school.' But his mother didn't have a dime to help out.

Harry laughed and said, 'I always wished I'd had a little comfort zone like that of farting around when I was your age. Always had to work. Good thing about working, though: if you're smart and arrange it correctly, build on your natural talents, you can make yourself a cushion.'

Harry did the work by getting you to talk and put things in perspective on your own. He never patronized. His sense of humor floated just below the surface, trawling for laughs or smiles of self-recognition giving him an excuse to laugh or smile along. You knew it was there because a bright bobber played up top: a jolly head, a high and dry wit, his expression as he let things wash over him (even as the current appeared to be getting rougher) – these were Harry's graces.

He was fun in bed, too, quick to take flame and giving off an exuberant heat as he kindled and built exactly the fire he needed, never too roaring or out of control, always with a smile when he kissed Rob and got started. The sex never lasted long, and was preceded and followed by lots of great, interesting adult talk. Rob liked taking his clothes off in front of Harry, in front of most men. For him that was the excitement. Just the idea of it.

One night on Cozumel, as they were perfecting batches of margaritas, and swatting back mosquitoes, and figuring out it was the sugary lime attracting them, Rob let himself get a bit out of hand. He tasted the salt on his tongue and the backwash of the cocktail in his gut – and for an instant he let the bile run. They were sitting on the balcony of their rented condo and Rob let fly a sudden, unsolicited denunciation of the upper class. He didn't stop to consider the possibility he'd offended his host, who was footing the bill. Nor did it occur to him that Harry was himself well-heeled. He'd be the last man on earth to advertise it.

'They don't care about anybody but themselves,' Rob said. 'They make money off men like my father then let them die when they're done wringing them dry. People like my dad never get a break.'

'But you could have a break,' Harry said, leaning forward to give the batch of margaritas a freshening stir.

Rob didn't have a clue what Harry was referring to, but it was the first time any adult had ever expressed an interest in what happened to him.

Rob said, 'What do you mean?' He was all ears.

'I mean, smart-ass, use your assets. They're frozen. They're going to waste.'

Rob looked puzzled.

Gently Harry tilted the pitcher of margaritas above Rob's waiting glass, pouring him one more. 'Right now all you're doing is sitting on them,' he said with mock disgust. He tisked. He let a smile cross his thin, dry lips, raised his thin, elegant eyebrows dryly. He winked, training his eyes downward to Rob's lap.

Harry said, 'When you and I met last week I felt very comfortable with you.'

'And so did I, with you.'

'See,' said Harry. 'We could've been old friends, or even father and son. It was all very natural, and at the same time I was very attracted to you.'

Rob pinched back the urge to thank Harry. Since then he'd learned to deflect compliments politely, the way men expected him to. Not coyly. They wanted someone they felt at ease with, the boy-next-door who wasn't stuck on himself, who let them do the sexing-up to get their fantasies started – until the middle of things, when the tables turned and the boy inside of the john had permission to be vulnerable and cry out for love and punishment, fury and consolation. Sometimes after they came they nuzzled against his chest and rested there like babies.

'And,' said Harry, 'you didn't seem to be repulsed by me.'

'Why would I?'

Here Harry sighed, somewhat irritably – as if not quite convinced by Rob's performance. He said, 'I have loads of friends like me, men who've got money and are horny as hell. All over the country. All they want's a guy like you to spend a little time with them. They don't have anybody. They're busy with their work or still in the closet. Or they live out in the middle of nowhere where people can't know. It'd be too dangerous, they'd lose business. Get it?'

'Sure.'

'Besides, you're a smart kid. Never will forget that speech you made to me in the Miami airport . . .' He laughed harmlessly, and something in Rob shifted. Brightened.

Out in the pirate sky, tattered clouds were crouched low against the curving coast. Above them stretched sprays of stars studding the clear midnight-blue. The lamp in a distant lighthouse glowed an eerie yellow-orange, making the scene look more like a stage set, a Disney World model of the old Spanish Main. Containable. Scenic, not overwhelming.

～ ～ ～

The flight was delayed again. They kept rolling back departure times. Rob wandered the corridor having polished off a fried chicken sandwich with mayonnaise, no fries, and a diet Coke.

He wondered if he should call his contact in Nantucket. When he looked down to check his cell phone, there were already two more messages from his mother. That morning as he stood at his kitchen sink drinking a protein shake, she'd called his answering machine and sung the happy birthday song she sang every year. He hadn't picked up and he hadn't called her to thank her. She didn't know what he did for a living, of course. He'd told her he worked in software and that helped explain his travelling.

She drove him nuts, but Rob had been keeping up with her on a nearly daily basis. She'd finally achieved the stability in Cleveland that had eluded her in Florida, having gone from the upside-down life of waitressing to the regular hours of a court stenographer. He was proud of her. He could still see her sitting at their little kitchen table in their roach-infested apartment in Jacksonville, her hair sun-streaked from all those times when she'd pulled him out of junior high and driven him to the beach for their hooky picnics together. She was still pretty then, and thin. She was crying and dabbing at a wet nose and red eyes and trying to find money in her checkbook for the rent.

~ ~ ~

Harry had tried teaching him how to save and invest. And more than once he'd promised himself he'd start school the following fall. But then the falls came and went, and each season he found an excuse for putting it off. 'I'm just not ready,' he'd tell Harry. 'I don't know what to study.' Harry always told him to stop stalling and give school a try.

As he walked back from having his snack, he could see Red watching him from over the top of his barely raised book. The overhead video screens shuffled their departure times and suddenly, just in time, there it was – the announcement for Nantucket: 'Boarding.'

'Hey, this is it,' Red called as he approached the gate. He was getting up.

'I really appreciate it,' said Rob, offering the man a smile.

Red stretched before gathering his things. 'I'll just be glad to take off.'

They proceeded to the gate together. Fewer than a dozen people were gathered for the flight.

It was the wrong part of the year for sunning, and Harry said the island would be deserted in October. His new client, Don, was in the construction business and did most of his work on Nantucket out of season; the rich developer for whom he worked subcontracted rooms in a 'boatel' to Don, to put his workers up in. Rob was getting the room and, as usual, the ticket for free, but nothing else money-related had been discussed. Harry knew he needed a rest.

The commuter they were on was a prop. Twenty seats with a row of single seats on his side of the aisle and a row of cozy-looking pairs on the other side. He sat looking out at the wing from his solitary place, Red directly across from him. Now he was quieter than he'd been at the gate, staring straight forward, so that for an instant Rob felt sorry that he'd been so sarcastic and remote.

While the passengers were settling in, Rob's cell phone went off, chirping cricket-like in his computer tote. It was Harry.

'You there yet?'

'Nope.'

'Goddamn La Guardia. Hey, happy birthday. How's it feel?'

'Not too bad.'

'You're as old as you feel. When I was your age, I felt my life just beginning.'

The stewardess came down the aisle. 'Can I have your attention?' she asked. 'We're getting ready to take off, so I need to ask you all to turn your phones off.'

Rob nodded her way. 'Oops,' he said, suddenly not wanting to hang up, 'looks like we might start to taxi now.' They shared a skeptical chuckle. 'I'll call when I get there.'

All the people on board except Red were on their phones, wrapping up their calls.

'Hurry back down,' said Harry. 'Want me to go ahead and make you a reservation?'

'Why not?' He hated saying it. Part of him believed he was going to return to his garage apartment in Cleveland a somehow new and different Rob. The other part, the realistic one, saw that nothing happened overnight in this life, except death.

'Love you, boy.'

Rob paused. He turned to the window, lowering his voice, and said, 'Well, I love you.' He could feel the stare of Red pass over him like the shadow of a cloud. 'Bye, now.'

'Girlfriend?' asked Red, moving one eyebrow ironically up and out of place.

'Not exactly.'

'Yeah.' Red nodded. He kept nodding to himself, a faint smile on his lips.

In the next moment they were caught up in the rituals of buckling up, bracing for takeoff. The props stirred to life and churned. The plane taxied to the end of the runway then turned, jerked forward and rolled until it had worked up a rumbling, bone-shaking speed. They were pulled up from the macadam with a rocketing swing-set momentum.

Mercifully, during the strain and moan of the plane's climb the engines made it too noisy for intelligible conversation. When it broke through the cover of stratus, Rob turned his body to the window and looked out toward the coast where they were headed. He got a Pepsi from the stewards as the sea came mistily into view, the water barely distinguishable from the ether above it. Suspended amid it all were huge cumulus clouds, silvery around the edges and gilt-shiny where they reflected the first sun he'd seen in days. He could identify all their shapes and portents now – although soon, going into the Cleveland winter, there would be a low-hanging day-to-day blanket of inversion to suffer under.

The captain came on and said, 'A little weather report for you folks. We're getting word from the Cape and Islands the temperature's staying at right about sixty-six degrees, with no rain on the horizon. Light breeze, partly cloudy, with occasional sunshine.' The passengers cheered.

As the plane changed directions and followed the coast northeast, they rounded an anvil-shaped cumulonimbus in an upward corkscrew spiral. It was bunchy and mountainous, glowing like honey with a thin silver foil around the nooks and curves, then taking on the autumn afternoon colors of rose and cornflower when he looked down at it from greater height. It could turn to rain and become a thunderhead with the slightest cool draft from the north.

A heathery green-and-gray crescent rimed in sparkling radium beaches listed up out of the blue. They swooped down steeply and made for it like a wasp zeroing in on a patch of flesh. He shook hands with Singin' Red, who'd fallen asleep after takeoff and dozed all through the pilot's announcements, then been bumped into an open-eyed stupor as they touched down. Singin' Red didn't say anything at first but looked at Rob strangely, panicked, and said, 'Not Hyannis?'

The Nantucket airport was the size of a 7-Eleven, and felt as crowded as a 7-Eleven does even when it has only half a dozen customers waiting in line. A tall man with sandy hair, ruddy skin, and crow's feet behind aviator shades came up to Rob and stuck out his hand. 'Rob?'

It was hard to tell his age – Don could have been forty or fifty. His work shirt and jeans were dusty, and sawdust clung to his tan work boots. 'I've heard a lot about you from Harry,' he said. 'I like Harry, a fine man. A gentleman.' His words came confidently but slowly. He carried one of Rob's bags out to his pickup.

He said he was from a family of carpenters and fishermen on the Cape. Leaving behind the world of unions and layoffs, he'd built his business from the ground up. He cocked an eye at Rob while he drove and said,

'Boy, you're cute. Just like Harry described you. And sexy.' He let his look linger. 'Yeah, real sexy . . .'

Rob smiled. 'That's good news,' he said.

Don asked him about Cleveland, the flight, and the weather, and even though Rob answered everything, by the time they were halfway to town, they'd exhausted their subjects.

After a silence, Don said, 'I want to know more about you.'

At the boatel, he showed Rob into the kitchenette and said he would be back in an hour to collect him. The unit looked out from the harbor end. Motorboats and yachts gleamed on glass in the harbor, and around it rose the town catching the light. Buttressing the skyline were a pair of steeples, the whitewashed lance of one church and another's gold-domed cupola. A breeze scrubbed at the stagnant halide smell of low tide. He went inside and unpacked, wondering if a drywall hanger or a roofer had been moved to give the boss's boy-toy a nicer view. He called Harry to say everything was fine, that he liked Don, but only got his answering machine, and left a message. He washed his face, brushed his teeth.

A horn sounded out front.

In the truck Don put his hand on Rob's knee, moving it up Rob's leg to his crotch as they rattled over cobblestones across town. It was a village right out of high school American lit class. Pilgrims and witches. They whizzed out the other end of town past cranberry bogs, crossing the countryside in its glow of autumn, then began to smell the brine of the sea again. Don wanted to show Rob his favorite beach, which was deserted at this time of year. They walked together for a long time through the sand, not talking. Once Don touched Rob's shoulder and smiled at him. The sun was going down.

~ ~ ~

On the ride home Don flipped open the glove box and reached in for a baggy and a set of rolling papers. Then he reached down and touched Rob's crotch. Steering one-handed, he opened the Ziplock bag in his lap and sifted and sorted the Jamaican ganja that Don told him a pipe fitter had brought him from Kingston. He creased the paper and filled and rolled the joint as if it were a miniature burrito. 'We'll wait,' he said, without another word till they got inside.

They smoked it in Don's bedroom overlooking the moonlit jetties below their cliffs. Rob was watching the sweep of a lighthouse beam as

Don unzipped and yanked his jeans down to his ankles, turned him away from the scenery, and went down on him.

Rob tried to drain his mind. He was excited but uncomfortable; he could have been raised here and been the exact same person, only things would have been nicer and less difficult. What if he'd met a guy like Don, who got him hot and interested him, ten years ago?

'You know what I feel like doing?' Don said as he came up for air; he started to unbutton their shirts then stopped and got up from his knees to stroke Rob's hair.

'What's that?'

Don edged in close, his breath warm and herbal. Then, delicately tucking back a lock of Rob's hair, he whispered in Rob's ear. There was nothing Rob had not been asked to do, but sometimes, doing some of them again felt like the first exciting time.

But then, in the pickup a couple of hours later, Don was suddenly and unbearably silent.

'Something on your mind?' Rob asked.

Don focused on the streets, the finger of his left hand resting on the scratchy yellow stubble of his upper lip. 'Babcock's visit,' he said.

'Babcock? He's coming here?'

'Saturday, and I've got to go and show my support.' He chuckled, wiping his mouth with the back of his hand as if he were wiping beer from his lips. 'Yeah, I knew ol' Johnny way back when.'

'Wow,' Rob said, considering it all.

'You won't be coming along, of course,' Don said. 'You can wait back at the apartment or walk into town.'

'Of course.'

'Yeah,' Don added, 'can't wait to see the look on his face when he gets a load of me.'

~ ~ ~

For the next few days Rob sampled the town with its charming Yankee frame houses and shingle-sided shops – as well as its ice cream, pancakes with real maple syrup and sweet-churned butter, its cream pies, fish and chips, clam chowder, deep-dish pizza and micro-brewed lager. He was strangely relaxed. He knew it was all borrowed time, but debts were not something he'd ever worried much about in the past.

In the apartment, with the curtains pulled, he drew long lavendertinctured baths and sat in them smoking a cache of illegal Cuban cigars Harry had gotten him through Mexican channels.

Don stayed away, working his men past sundown, pressed by a deadline. That was just as well, but Rob couldn't clear from his mind the sex they'd had together. Sometimes he would fantasize about somebody else when he was with clients. Not in this case. Don was full of lust and incendiary need. He seemed secure. Rob wondered how many guys like him Don had imported from the mainland.

When the phone rang and pulled Rob from his smoky, aromatic bath one afternoon in the middle of the week, it was Harry asking how things were going.

'You two getting along?'

'Great,' Rob replied, trying not to give away his giddy daydream mood.

'Well, you're a hit with Don – that much I know. He's been on the phone to me three times this week. Can't get him off.' Rob wondered if that wasn't a hint of jealousy he was hearing in Harry's voice.

'That's funny. I can't get him to stay on. He just comes over at night for a couple hours or shows up on his lunch break, and doesn't talk much. I thought at first he didn't like me.' That last remark was fudging things a bit.

'He's an odd bird. Had to quit drinking a while back. Guess it got out of hand. Has two kids in college.'

All of this news, which he sensed Don would never have volunteered, came as a shock to Rob.

'Now he's talking about taking you to this Babcock fundraiser thing.'

'You're kidding.' Rob had to sit down and let this development sink in.

'I think he might get a kick out of showing you off. In a quiet, reserved, not-too-obvious way.' Rob heard Harry chuckling in his big echoing kitchen he only ever made coffee in.

'Right,' said Rob.

'I never would've figured Johnny Babcock the presidential type. I mean, the balls of his even running! His daddy always wanted to run, of course, and now he's backing Junior all the way. There are a few little complications – some lavender skeletons in the closet, you might say. The incumbents have something on him, answers to questions like why the family-values poster boy took so long having kids.'

'I don't believe it.'

'It's been known for years. But everybody's so desperate to have a man from a friendly business dynasty on their side, they'll believe just about anything. Now for my money we don't need assholes like that gunking up the party – but that's just my two cents' worth.'

Harry unrolled possible scenarios for how it might get out in a calculated 'leak' to the press, even though it seemed the elephants had something on the donkeys just as big and damning to the incumbent. It was just a matter of time, Harry thought, before polls loosened tongues and sacrificial lambs took the fall for their parties. Yes, it was a war of nerves on both sides, but Babcock was especially vulnerable. The Democrats had a Scottish man, once a fetching kilt-wearing rent boy, to testify to everything – and photos.

'Daddy's boy did what he could to bury it. Everybody in the seventies snorted so much coke and crawled off to bed with each other, they didn't think anybody could possibly be paying any attention. But somebody's always paying attention, and making little souvenirs.'

'That's sick,' said Rob. 'It's cheap and dirty.'

'Johnny was always such an oily groveling type, anyway, trying to get everybody to like him. But to be honest, I don't really think he was ever gay. He always just wanted to please too many people at the same time. Still does.'

Before they hung up Harry said, 'Well, have a good time. You relaxing?'

Perhaps he'd detected some of Rob's nervous uncertainty. Rob said, 'I've been thinking about my mom. And how I won't call her for some reason.'

'Oh Lord,' Harry said. 'You and your mother again.' Though he'd never met her, he knew what was going on. 'You know I've been thinking of asking you something,' he went on. 'You mother knows about you in one way – what if you let her know about me? I don't mean about this and what you do for a living – but let her know I exist and there's something between us. Doesn't have to be the whole truth . . .'

At first Rob said nothing. It was an overture he'd felt coming for a while, one that was so overdue he didn't know how to reply. It was coming just as Rob was about to get desperate.

'Tell her you're going to come to live with me in Orlando and start college,' Harry said. 'She'll get it, she'll respect you. She'll be glad for you, and this time you'll really do it.'

'Okay,' Rob said. 'Yeah. Sure. I'll think about it.'

Don called deep into the evening, as Rob was getting into bed, and said he wanted to talk dirty. He was high, he said, but it had taken a scotch to smooth out the buzz he had going so that he didn't have any reason to move from his picture window. Rob wondered if Don had heard of the controversy brewing. He wondered if he should ask Don about his drinking, but the distance of Don's voice suggested otherwise.

'Talk to me, Robbie,' Don said calmly. 'Tell me your nastiest fantasy.'

When it was over, Don sprang the invitation on him, testing him for signs of gratitude. 'How do you like them apples?' he asked. Of course Rob was excited and said so – he was meeting his party's candidate. He knew Babcock was going to cut taxes, build up the army and set this country straight. All the men Rob liked believed in Babcock.

~ ~ ~

Saturday dawned damp and overcast, but cleared slightly as Rob made a sensible oatmeal breakfast, listened to the radio (the polls were favoring Babcock), struggled over the first chapter of *Rabbit is Rich*, and waited for Don to call. He was still reading when the phone rang.

'Be over in half an hour,' said Don, sounding frantic but 'up.'

Good to his word, Don arrived thirty minutes later in a navy jacket, pressed khakis, and a blue-and-gold repp tie. He let himself in and said, 'Have you got anything nice to wear?'

'Just a pair of khakis and a decent shirt,' Rob said. He was moving to the closet, shirtless and in his briefs.

'Better be careful, boy – you'll get a big butt.' Rob froze in place, then snapped out of it. He hurried to get dressed. 'Well, don't worry. We'll grab a jacket from my place on the way,' Don said, standing in the doorway. 'And a nice tie.'

Outside, the sun was starting to shine again with a vengeance.

They drove to a part of the island where the houses looked like three-storied, upturned wooden ships – beached and landscaped all around. In the front lawn of one, a huge tent was set up, with caterers and bartenders scurrying. A helicopter landed on a leafy clearing behind a dune, sending sandstorms up and over and into people's eyes, clothes and hair. Then Babcock and his entourage marched into view and the crowd began uproariously to applaud and whistle. 'New money,' Rob heard one man muttering behind him – a man dressed casually in the island colors of distressed kelly-green and a pink Rob remembered from the screw-tops of calamine lotion bottles where the lotion had dried and caked.

He could feel the heat and energy shooting off Don as the entourage drew closer – Babcock himself not quite in view yet. The crowd wriggled in their shoes, giggling and whispering.

The TV crews and reporters toward whom Babcock seemed to be moving steadily, for optimal coverage, at first blocked the view of everyone under the tent top. Then, suddenly, they all got their first look at him. From a distance he was handsome, fit, appealing.

Under the tent but obscured by so many people was a single banner, hung over the place where the bartender was set up and working:

THANK YOU, JOHN MARS BABCOCK!
(from the NANTUCKET ISLAND DEVELOPMENT
COMMITTEE)

He and Don were standing near a group of businessmen who'd formed a receiving line, toward which Babcock now headed. Don cocked his eyebrow at Rob, then moved in the direction of the line. Rob got the message and receded farther out of view.

Closer up, Babcock looked tired and, from what Rob could tell, was hiding the bags under his eyes with what looked like touches of Nantucket-pink spackle. He stepped up to the receiving line to shake hands and then, when he came to Don, stopped, did a double-take, averted his eyes even as Rob watched him moving his lips. He smiled before pushing on to the next person in the line, without looking back at Don.

Don grinned and tried to lean in and say something cheerful and funny to Babcock but the candidate moved his face away from Don and muttered something to one of his aides, who turned to the other aides and passed it on. Rob heard an exchange between Babcock and the next person in line about Martha's Vineyard, how they were looking out at the enemy from right there.

Babcock laughed, shaking the man's hand. They turned to the camera together, hands clasped, and their grins froze.

Out on the blue ocean, a giant white ferry chugged in from the Cape or the Vineyard.

Everyone including Babcock was dressed in polo shirts, windbreakers and loafers. Their chinos billowed in the breeze. As the photo ops began to fire more and more rapidly, Babcock's army of casual collegians took over and began moving folks around and posing them quickly and efficiently, letting Babcock linger just long enough to exchange best wishes or one-liners.

Don, looking surprised, made his first tenuous steps back to the photo line. Two of the aides moved in to block him, even raised their hands halfway as a tentative safeguard. Don retreated, his face confused. Minutes later Rob saw him at the edge of the tent with a drink in his hand talking to a bartender, rocking on his heels, looking felled.

And then, suddenly, there was Singin' Red. Pushing through the crowd, his brassy whiskers dipping down into the drink he held up to his lips, he saluted Rob. It was a scene out of a Saturday TV matinee – *Creature Feature*, Channel 17, Jacksonville. Zombies in Paradise. Night of the Living Gay Republicans.

Singin' Red turned to catch Don at the instant Don leaned calamitously into an aluminum tent pole. The tent shook and flapped over their heads, and the bartender rushed up from behind to support Don and pull him away. Another man, the host, trying to be discreet, hurried up to the miserable, stricken-looking Don with a shit-eating grin. The man was followed by his wife and one of the security guards who, Rob could see, had an earpiece with a coil of wire coming out of it tucked into the collar of his polo shirt. The host was a perma-tanned, rugged-looking, weekend-sailing type. He put his scotch on the ground as the security guard touched his earpiece and nodded. He took one of Don's arms, the host took the other and they led him toward the house. When Don tried to break away, they strong-armed him, jerking him through the door and leaving the wife to float about the scene and smooth everything over.

'Christ,' someone in the crowd said, 'Donald's been drinking again. It's a shame, but he really needs to get that under control . . .'

Singin' Red crossed to Rob's side of the tent and grazed his elbow. Looking at no one in particular, his gaze cheerful, he stopped at the edge of the tent and turned to face the crowd. He lifted his drink. Rob could hear the ice clinking in his glass.

A speech was starting up in the shade of an immense droopy pine, pulling the crowd out from under the tent. Singin' Red looked put out by this and signaled for the people around him to listen to him. He left his unfinished drink on one of the gingham vinyl-covered tables to free his hands up for clapping. By now the crowd's attention was directed towards the shade under the pine, and they shushed each other so everyone could hear the sharp metallic voices coming over the P.A. system.

Rob began to back out from under the tent. Ducking behind the banner, he spotted a path that led away from the house and the lawn through the dunes, and headed toward it. The host, who had slipped a yellow cardigan on and now held a drink in his hand, was watching from the porch, telling a joke about the Democrats' obsession with passing laws and collecting taxes. When he noticed Rob passing by, he grimaced so that some of his fillings glinted. He didn't say anything, just panned his head like a surveillance camera, taking it all in.

Rob picked his way over the soft sand between the dunes, past beach plums and thorny rose hips growing thick on the ground. When he got to the top, he saw a TV van that was stuck in the sand on the other side, its crew trying to get itself out.

He ran toward them and yelled over the steely din reverberating from the other side of the dune, 'Hey! You guys need help?'

A woman, looking dressy and standing by with a notebook and microphone tucked under her arm, was giving the other two directions. She turned to Rob with her hand on her hip, shaded her eyes, and said, 'Well, has he cranked up the old Babcock wind machine yet?'

'He's about to.'

'We better get over there, Jimmy,' she called, and the cameraman left the van for the driver to worry about. 'Sorry, Gary, we'll give you a hand later.'

'I can give you a hand,' Rob told the driver.

'Would you? I'll set some flattened-out cartons down for traction and push, and you can get behind the wheel so you don't mess up your clothes.'

'Oh I don't care. You think you can give me a lift into town?'

'Fuck yeah.'

On the way, Rob sat up front and asked the driver if he'd heard Harry's rumors about Babcock. 'Is it true, about him being gay in the seventies, and all the coke?'

'From what we've heard, and the people we've talked to, hell yeah.'

'Does he have a chance?'

'The way they're throwing money at him, you bet. He'll sandstorm voters with tax cuts. And when everybody's done wiping their eyes they'll see what they wanted to see, and if he keeps his nose clean for a term they'll ask him back.'

Rob knew that if Babcock slid by and won, Harry would end up happy. Finally one of ours back in, he'd say. He'd criticized Babcock, but in the end he rooted for any GOP candidate who made it through and whipped a Democrat.

As he was clearing out of the kitchenette back at the boatel, Rob left the sandy blazer and tie on the table for Don, but didn't write him a note. Harry would get upset, say it was discourteous and reflected poorly on him, but Harry would forgive him – especially since Rob had made his decision.

~ ~ ~

Hours later on the plane, he unbuckled his tight seatbelt right after takeoff. Coming down the aisle, the stewardess frowned on this infraction of air safety rules, but he gave her a smile, and she softened.

'That's a crazy place,' he said as the island tilted out of view below them.

She lifted a circumspect eyebrow and nodded as she passed up the aisle. Then she stopped and turned, resting a hand on his shoulder gently – even erotically.

'Buckle up for now, if you don't mind. It's bumpy on the way in, but if it clears up any I'll let you know.'

And what would he do? He pictured cement-block college buildings surrounded by palms.

'Half of all the weathermen in the world are queer,' he remembered Harry telling him.

He turned his head to look out the window: high gauzy cirrus saying high pressure and no rain. He wondered dizzily and sleepily if on a day like today he couldn't see all the way down to Florida.

PATRICK ROSE

THE VIEW FROM THE BALCONY

I left Vincent once. Just days after our third – and what turned out to be our last – anniversary, I left him for someone else: a handsome, journalist drunk who had been flirting with me for months, mumbling promises of a better life over stolen lunches and warm martinis, who looked down more than he looked into my eyes and who picked up the check consistently. And for a time my life became something different. For a time I became a handsome, novelist drunk. I had a job as a paralegal and had never published a novel but I *felt* handsome, anyway, and was drunk, and the two of us painted Richmond a scandalous red while our friends stepped aside like pedestrians avoiding a pair of lunatics.

During that time I spoke to Vincent only twice. The first time, he dialed my new number and the drunk answered, and after listening to the drunk banter, 'No, no, no, who is *this*?' several times I wrestled the phone out of his hand and said hello. I was drunk, too.

Vincent was sobbing. 'I shouldn't have called,' he said.

'No,' I said, 'you should have. I'm glad you did.' And suddenly I meant

PATRICK ROSE (born 1965): Rose was born in Washington, D.C. and grew up on Merritt Island, Florida. Among other jobs, he has worked as a house-painter, a bartender, an English teacher, a janitor, a ghost writer, a supply room clerk, a book reviewer, and a reader for a blinded Argentinian soldier. His fiction has been published in numerous literary journals, including Ontario Review. *He lives in New York City.*

it with a conviction that surprised me, that lay beneath my drunkenness like the cement foundation of a swimming pool. We talked for a while, and eventually the drunk stole an entire pack of expensive cigarettes from my bureau and left in a fury. I didn't care. I said to Vincent, 'Listen, I've fucked up.'

'Are you?'

He'd misunderstood and I didn't correct him.

The drunk and I stayed together for another two months. He had a book coming out from a university press – a study on Tolstoy's use of slapstick – and being an unpublished writer, I lacquered him with reverence. But as it turned out, we never talked about writing (and we never wrote). We drank, and our affair followed a predictable curve: we went through a lot of money and a lot of Skyy vodka, we were barred from two restaurants for fighting, we eventually stopped using each other's names, and while we often lay passed out together, we stopped having even the most disentangled sex.

'Do you love me?' I asked him one soupy morning.

'Does it matter?'

Destitute in my new wreck of an apartment, I called Vincent. I rambled into his answering machine for a full minute before he picked up and said, 'I hope you're alone.'

'I am.'

'Are you fucked up?'

'You mean at the moment, or in general?' I missed him terribly and was afraid to say so. He was generous. He didn't ask me why I'd called, or what I wanted from him, or even what the status was between me and the man I'd left him for. He asked if I wanted to have lunch the next day.

Vincent was and always had been a stable, predictable person. He'd held down the same job – as a deed-researcher in the Henrico County court system – for the past nine years; he never missed his annual physical; he changed the oil in his car every ten thousand miles without fail. We'd met in the candy-strewn wake of Richmond's meager Gay Pride Parade, match-made by a mutual friend who'd placed us on the same square of sidewalk. Both of us having just turned twenty-seven. Both of us having made previous, doomed attempts at long-term relationships. We shared a pack of Smarties, and by the end of it we were dating. A month later, in our apartment, we were having friends over for dinner and nostalgically recounting the story of how we'd met over a pack of Smarties. Our life together, as Vincent told me more than once over the next few years, was the ideal he had always dreamed of, because we were 'like any other normal, domestic couple' – which I took to mean that we paid our bills on time and had monogamous, weekly, and very vanilla sex with the shades pulled down and the lights turned off, and that the two of us – who had started out as scrawny boys – had plumped up some, like bulbs nestled into rich soil.

When we met in the diner that day, two months after our break-up, I saw immediately that he'd shed his excess weight under some heavy gym work and was starting to put on muscle. He'd grown a Van Dyck. He was drinking coffee, which he'd never drunk before, and he was leaning away from the table like a man about to wager a cautious deal. I was contrite and demure. By the end of the meal we'd agreed to make an appointment with a counselor, and I'd sworn I would never drink again.

~ ~ ~

The counselor's name was Lola and her office looked like the inside of a hunting lodge. She sat across from us in a chair that swivelled in all directions, with her arms – and sometimes her legs – knotted around her body in a way that made her appear more tortured by what we were saying than we were. Vincent and I sat at either end of a leather couch long enough for a dysfunctional family of six. For the fifteen weeks that we saw her, Lola was perpetually nursing a cold. With a tissue knotted in one hand and the box wedged between her legs, she zeroed in on me: What was *happening* in my mind during that last leg of our relationship, just before I left? Where *was* I?

I lied. Slumped on one end of the leather couch, I told Lola – and Vincent – that I hadn't known where or who I was, when in fact I'd known exactly where I was and no longer cared for it, and exactly who I was and hated that person. I had thrown myself headlong into the idea of being a writer, sold myself on the notion that domestic stability was the key to accomplishing this, and had written a stack of novel manuscripts without trying very hard to publish any of them. A single rejection slip became a communiqué to me from the entire publishing world: *fat chance*. And while I'd been busy failing, my frustration had grown like kudzu around every other part of my life. But I didn't want to talk about my writing.

'I just got . . . restless,' I said.

Lola stared at me with wide, viral eyes. Vincent looked forward into the fish tank. These fish – counselor's fish, meant to soothe and calm the patient – looked drugged, catatonically meandering through a forest of bubbles rising up from a treasure chest, a broken ship's bow, a collapsed skeleton. I envied them. They had no sense of history, didn't care where they were or what they hadn't accomplished.

Not long after our first session, I decided counseling wasn't for me. But one afternoon, I cracked. 'You want the truth? I'm a failure. I'm thirty years old and I've got five unpublished novels sitting around in boxes. I feel completely isolated in my ambitions, worthless when I'm not writing and like a nobody when I sit down to work. I hate my stupid job. I hate my life. And I've failed *you*,' I said, turning with tears in my eyes to stare down the length of the couch into Vincent's startled face.

It became known as the day of the breakthrough.

We bumped our appointments up to twice a week after that. Lola wanted to know about these manuscripts – how I *felt* about them now – and I admitted that I'd spent a fair amount of money on sturdy, mail-order boxes from a company called 'The Writer in You', and had spent nearly as much time typing up labels for each boxed draft of each novel as I had submitting my work to agents and editors. 'What's more important to you?' she asked. 'Writing or publishing?'

'Both,' I said.

'Well,' she smiled as she touched a tissue to her nose, 'they can't *both* be "more important."'

'Writing,' I said. 'And then publishing. I mean, they're both a big part of who I am – who I want to be.'

'You believe success will make you happy?'

'Well,' I said. 'Success would *help*.'

'Why?'

'Because it would validate me.'

'It's interesting that it's something you want so badly, and yet you seem almost . . . *invested* . . . in your discouragement.'

Wrong, I thought. *Wrong, wrong, wrong*. But all I could think to say was, 'It's a very cut-throat business.'

'One you want to succeed in. And you felt like your life with Vincent wasn't helping things any.'

'No!' I said, 'That's oversimplifying things. It's not like *that*.' Though it *was* like that, somehow, and I shuddered as this ugly realization slammed up against another, seemingly contradictory thought: in the three months that I'd spent away from Vincent – free of him – I hadn't written a word.

Lola let me wallow in my own silence for a minute, then swivelled an inch to the right and looked at Vincent. 'Let's focus on you for a while.'

Vincent said he had never known how to get close to me, the writer. Feeling suddenly ganged-up on I told him he could have started by *reading* what I wrote, by showing an ongoing involvement in what I did. Then he said that he'd read every draft word for word, and that we'd discussed it, and I realized he was right. 'I just don't interest you,' he said, 'because I'm not a writer,' and for two consecutive sessions we both seemed to forget that *I* was the one who had gone berserk and run off with a booze-hound, and concentrated instead on how to make him feel 'complete' in relation to me. As Lola explained it, it was a problem of logic: A) he felt he didn't interest me; B) I insisted that he *did*, and always *had*; and yet C) I had left him. Why? 'I was just so *restless*,' I said again, helplessly.

'That may be true,' Lola said, 'but what we're trying to do right now is focus on Vincent.'

'I can't focus on just Vincent,' I said. (At that moment, I couldn't even look at him.)

'If B,' Lola said, 'then why C?'

'Maybe it was because I didn't interest *myself* anymore,' I said.

'Bingo,' she said. 'And what does that say about Vincent?'

Under Lola's direction, we played a game called 'I Don't Understand.' Vincent would try to articulate a feeling he was struggling with, and when the time came I would say outright, 'I don't understand,' and it was understood that I wasn't trying to be difficult, or sarcastic, but was honestly letting him know he wasn't getting through. He was then required to rephrase whatever he was trying to say, leaving himself open to the likelihood that I might once again reply, 'I don't understand,' until whatever he was trying to say was made crystal clear. 'Communication,' Lola told us, 'is everything.' But what I learned from the 'I Don't Understand' game was that communication *wasn't* everything. I began to appreciate Vincent for the mere struggle alone: the way he leaned forward without looking at me; the way his gym-chiseled hands twisted around each other, squeezing the digits; the way he began a sentence three, maybe four, different ways, and then abandoned it altogether with an exasperated huff of air. I wanted to be appreciated for the same struggle.

'What's important is that we're trying,' I said – to both Vincent and

Lola, as if the three of us were attempting to mend a damaged *ménage à trois*. 'I can't always say what I mean, but it's the attempt that matters.'

Vincent glanced toward the fish, then slowly shook his head no. 'I don't understand.'

'I can't *make* you understand. What should matter is that I *want* you to understand.'

He realigned his shoulders against the leather back of the couch. He blinked and said, 'I'm sorry, but I still don't understand.'

'Don't apologize,' Lola said, clutching herself.

'I don't understand,' Vincent amended.

I glared at her. 'Am I communicating *anything*?'

'Oh, yes,' she said. 'We're making progress.'

~ ~ ~

The journalist (Lola had recommended I stop referring to him as 'the drunk') called me one afternoon weeks after I'd stopped seeing him and told me he never wanted to see me again. By then, I was only thinking of him in the early mornings when I was alone and most susceptible to guilt. I'd taken the one snapshot of him I possessed – in which he was clutching a martini, a twenty-dollar cigar angling up from his lips like one half of a drawbridge – and thrown it away; there was no visible evidence of him left in my apartment, just as there was no longer any booze. 'You're a total dick,' he said into the phone. We'd done a lot of fighting in the last days – arguments that fizzed up without warning and bubbled without end – and this had become one of his favorite euphemisms for me.

'All right,' I said. Lola had told me not to indulge him.

'I just want you to know that. You told me you were sick of that guy. You told me you hated him.'

(In fact, I had told the journalist almost nothing about Vincent or my past. Once I'd broken up with Vincent I thought about him all the time, but it made me nauseous to discuss him – especially with the journalist.) 'He must have been a wimp,' the journalist had smirked drunkenly around a cigar one night. 'He must have been one big killjoy.'

'No,' I'd said, 'he wasn't.'

'Well, then, what *was* he to you? I mean, if he was Mr Wonderful, why are you with *me*?'

'Because,' I'd said. (But by that time the sex had gone out of it, the fun had been drowned, and I wasn't sure why I'd done anything.)

'You totally led me to believe you cared about what we had together,' the journalist barked now into the phone. 'You made all these promises. You're a total dick.'

Had I stabbed *him* in the back, as well? It may have been true; all I knew for certain was that I could no longer be around him, and that I wanted only to make things right with Vincent. Maybe I *was* a total dick.

'*Total*,' the journalist said, as if underscoring my thought process. '*Dick*.'

I bought Vincent flowers. I showed up at the door of the apartment we used to share and whisked him off to dinners and movies. I had been invited, during our separation, to join friends the following month for a week in the south of France, and I made the suggestion to Vincent one night, as we were walking out of a theater, that he join me.

It was as if I'd suggested we adopt a child together. He stopped dead in his tracks. 'We should think about that,' he said. 'We should think about it hard. It might not be the best idea.'

'But it might. We could get out of here completely. Neither one of us has been to France before, so we could share it together.'

'They're writers,' Vincent said, referring to Andrew and Garth, the couple who had invited me.

'So?'

He started walking again. 'So everyone would be a writer but me.'

'That doesn't matter.'

'Plus,' he said, 'Andrew's very successful. It might only frustrate you to be around him.'

'I *like* Andrew,' I said. 'And I've known Garth for years. It would do me good to be around other writers. Besides, I'm not going there to work and neither are they. It's a vacation. It's Provence.'

'It sounds like Tension Territory,' he said (one of Lola's expressions).

'Well, what do you want to do – avoid that part of my life?'

'I'm not saying that. But it might not be the best idea to *embrace* it right now, either.'

'You think I'd be happier if I quit writing, don't you? If that's what you're thinking, I wish you'd just come out and say it.'

'I'm not comfortable with this conversation?' It was another game we'd learned from Lola as a means of being open with each other. It was called the 'Level of Comfort,' in which one of us said something dicey, and the other one stated clearly that he wasn't comfortable with the topic, and tagged a question mark onto the admission so that it wouldn't sound evasive or bossy. 'But don't mix the games,' Lola had warned us. 'If one of you says he isn't comfortable with a certain topic, the other shouldn't respond with "I don't understand." Levels of comfort should always be respected.'

We'd reached my car and I unlocked and opened the passenger door for him. He stared at the dark interior as if it were a cave of commitment he wasn't quite ready to venture into. Finally he said, 'I think we should discuss this with Lola.'

Lola, the next time we saw her, smiled and rubbed her jaw against her shoulder, rocking back and forth enthusiastically in her chair. A new glaze layered itself over the cold in her eyes and she said, 'It sounds like your second honeymoon.'

For the first time, Vincent disagreed with her. 'I'm not so sure.'

'Why?'

'Because there's something I can't get out of my mind,' he said. Then he told us about a gay couple in their mid-forties he knew − friends he'd made while we were separated − one of whom had been dying of liver cancer and the other of whom, it turned out, was a perfect donor match and had given fifty percent of his liver in a surgical procedure they both had pulled through successfully. 'I can't get it out of my mind.'

'I don't understand,' I said. 'You can't get *what* out of your mind?'

He sucked in a shot of air through his nose, wrung his fingers together, and said, 'I would have, before. But not now.'

Lola shifted in her chair and said, '*I* don't understand.'

Vincent looked at me down the length of the couch. His eyes were dry; the whites were perfectly white. 'I wouldn't give you half my liver.'

Well, then, I thought, staring forward at the mindless, meandering fish. Well, then.

~ ~ ~

For several days I became a blubbering idiot. I missed work and stopped answering my phone. I even missed one of our meetings with Lola, begging off on her answering machine at the last minute. Vincent left me several messages which I didn't return, and when I finally called him − only to let him know I was still alive − he said, 'Look, I didn't mean I'd feel that way *forever*. It's just where I am right now.'

I told him not to worry about it. I understood.

'Don't do anything stupid,' he said.

I understood that comment, as well. I'd already driven to the liquor store and sat in the parking lot fuming, and then crying, and had finally shuffled inside to buy a bottle of Skyy – only then realizing I'd left my wallet at home.

I was convinced I had ruined what little good was left in my life. Vincent, I decided, was the most decent person I had ever known, and I'd ruined *him*, as well. Before I left him, he would have given his liver to anyone. I stopped eating, cried constantly, slept badly, and for several mornings in a row was awakened by a pounding in my chest I felt certain was the beginnings of a heart attack.

Finally the phone rang, and wanting desperately to talk to Vincent, I scooped up the receiver and said hello.

'My book's out,' the voice said.

I swallowed. I thought about hanging up. 'Congratulations.'

'Remember what we'd planned for this day? We were going to eat lobster at Byram's and drink Dom.'

'Well,' I said, 'it's really great that your book is out.'

'Yeah. There's a store in Charlottesville that's going to carry it. We were going to have Grand Marnier in the rotunda at the Jefferson. Remember talking about that?'

'I'm really happy for you.'

'No, you're not. What you are –' he said, and I hung up before he could say it, then unplugged the phone.

It was as if I'd piled the worst of me into a dinghy and cut the towline, for the more I thought about that person I was no longer to refer to as 'the drunk,' the more buoyant and sea-worthy I began to feel.

I went to the gym and sweated for an hour on a contraption that had oscillating poles and roaming pedals. I got an expensive haircut. When I met Vincent next – this time in the food court at the local mall – I said, 'Come to France with me. We owe it to ourselves to take this trip, to prove that we can make this work.'

He told me I looked pale. He told me he regretted the liver remark, what a stupid comment it was to make, even if it was true. Then he said yes, he would go.

~ ~ ~

Garth and I had met in college in the early eighties, back when we could talk about little more than our eminent indoctrination into the ranks of

Capote, Kerouac and Carver. Over the years, we'd both continued to write, and we'd kept each other fortified with literary postcards inscribed with encouragement, but for all our intentions of causing a splash in the publishing world, neither one of us had made so much as a ripple. Our combined frustration, perhaps more than anything, had become the glue of our friendship. Then, just before I started dating Vincent, I received an envelope from Garth postmarked Vienna. Inside were two small sheets of what looked like very expensive stationery. 'You will not *believe* who I'm dating,' it read. 'You will be astounded. Sit down.' And then, 'Sitting down? See page two.' On page two were the words 'ANDREW DUNCAN.'

I had never heard of Andrew Duncan. He turned out to be a writer who was prolific, rich and, outside of my limited scope of the world, famous. By the time I'd read his seven novels, his half-dozen plays and his collection of essays, I was sick with envy of Garth's new life and feeling privately miserable about my own. It wasn't that Andrew Duncan's writing moved me. In fact, it was too smart for me, too 'heady'; it made me feel stupid. But I was jaundiced, nonetheless, with the thought of Garth's sudden proximity to glamour, of what this might do for his career, of how 'literary' his life had suddenly become. When Andrew Duncan's next novel hit the bookstores and I opened it to the dedication page to read the words '*For Garth – of course*,' I became seeped in despair, convinced that my life was one big, stinking bomb.

'How about that?' Vincent had said that evening, having heard all about Garth and his new, famous friend, gazing at the page that bore Garth's name.

'Yep.' I'd pasted a smile onto my face. 'Isn't that something?'

This ultra-literary couple had met at a writer's conference in Key West which Garth had tried to talk me into attending but which I'd decided I couldn't afford. He and Andrew had spent that first night together and every night since. They lived in various places around Europe, cavorting with other writers, and I'd kicked myself over and over wondering how different my life would have been if only *I'd* gone to Key West and had been standing in that spot (was it next to a book display, or in a reception line, or in the corner of some dark strip-bar over highballs?). A year after they'd become a couple, they passed through Washington, D.C., for a book-signing and I drove over from Richmond and met them for dinner. I watched them smile at each other, flirt, get cuddly. There was a twenty-four-year age difference between them; Andrew had a solid, mid-fifties belly, and his hair was wiry and gray. Vincent and I were the same age. Could I picture myself with an older man?

The very question racked me with guilt, as did the answer: *In a heartbeat*.

But at that time the drunk – or, rather, the journalist – was still two years into my future, and I did my best to resign myself to the fact that confronted me each morning like a cold glass of water thrown into my face: This (not *that*) was my life. Look at it sideways, or through half-cocked eyes. Look at it from years down the road, where you will no doubt be standing in line at a grocery store in Richmond, Virginia, steeped in your own bad posture. This, my friend, is your life.

～　～　～

We pooled our money and bought Vincent a very expensive, last-minute ticket. Before training down to Provence, we stayed a day and a half in Paris, where we walked around the Marais district and the Île de la Cité with little knowledge of what we were seeing, preoccupied with what was at stake between us. I made a fool out of myself, or felt like I did, bursting into tears as we shuffled through the candle-lit dankness of Notre-Dame. 'What's wrong with you?' Vincent asked. He sounded both surprised and annoyed.

'Nothing,' I said. And then, 'It's that statue of Joan of Arc. I just didn't expect to see it.' I tried to laugh and dragged a hand across my face. In truth, I was crying simply because we were there, together; we felt as if we might be whole again.

The next morning we took the train south to Avignon. The car was hot, and a young girl in a short, light-brown dress ran up and down the aisle like a hamster for most of the trip, so that I was nauseous by the time we pulled into the station. But it was Vincent who said, 'I could throw up, if I gave it any thought.'

'Are you in a bad mood?'

'I'm just hungry,' he said.

'Maybe it's your nerves.'

'You say that like I should be nervous. Should I be?'

I shook my head no – almost frantically – and smiled.

Garth and Andrew were standing at the end of the platform. They waved enthusiastically, and as we lumbered toward them with our bags, they began talking at the same time.

'Welcome!'

'Isn't it hot? Isn't it awful?'

'We've rented a car, but there's no air conditioning.'

'But we have a pool!'

'The house has a pool fed by a spring, but you have to walk through a field of dead snails to get to it.'

'The snails are *alive*, Booty. They're hibernating.'

'They're *dead*, Booty. And they *kee-runch* under your sandals.'

'You have to wear sandals.'

'The shells would cut your feet.'

'Booty.'

'*Booty*.'

It was something they hadn't done when I'd first met them: talked to each other – in front of anyone, it seemed – like a pair of feral twins who had raised themselves in the forest and developed their own language.

'And you must be the *very* cute Vincent,' Andrew said, shaking Vincent's hand.

Vincent rattled his head in a kind of bewildered affirmation. 'Thanks for inviting us.'

'Well, how could we resist?' Andrew dropped his eyes down Vincent's torso, as if to verify that the item ordered matched the catalogue picture to a tee.

Garth drove. From the passenger seat, Andrew played tour-guide, and we deferred to him for all the necessary information about what we were seeing. 'Those,' he said, twisting around to point at the mountains with a wavering finger, 'are the Southern and the Northern Alpilles. The pass cut through them used to be the main route that linked Spain and Italy. It ends here, and that's why the Romans chose this spot to build Glanum.'

'What's Glanum?' I asked.

Andrew turned around again and spoke to Vincent. 'The ancient city. The ruins. They're right across from the house. They're Gallo-Greek, or Hellenistic, but they're Gallo-Roman, too. Fascinating, really.'

'How's Booty?' Garth asked, and Andrew grinned and responded, 'Bootific.'

I was jealous all over again: not just of their lifestyle (this small wedge of which we'd been invited to share for a few days), but of the dynamic that existed between them, this private language which it embarrassed me to witness, but which clearly implied a bounty of affection and mutual enthusiasm. It seemed a kind of natural adjustment for a literary life so weighted with intellect that it needed senseless babble to balance itself out. I reached across the hot seat and squeezed Vincent's leg beneath his carry-on bag. He pulsed his thigh muscle once, but didn't look at me.

I said, 'We can't wait to see the house.'

Andrew looked at Vincent again. 'It's the *perfect* writer's retreat.'

Before long we rolled off the paved road and onto a path that wound through the dry brambles. We passed a plastic sign that read '*Privée*,' and another, wooden sign upon which the letters appeared to have been burned: '*Mas de la Fé.*'

'Tell them what it says, Booty.'

Andrew pronounced carefully, '*House of Faith.*'

They knew what was at stake here. I'd written Garth a letter explaining what had happened between Vincent and me (a milquetoast version that circumvented the 'issue' of my failed writing career and managed to omit the drunken journalist completely) and he'd sent a note back that sounded less like advice and more like a slogan for Canyon Ranch: 'Come to the country, woman; get healed.'

The *Mas* was of mottled, gray stone with blue shutters and a blue, rounded front door. 'Late seventeenth-century,' Andrew told us, 'a *villa*, if you want *haute couture*,' though to us it was just a beautiful country house. There were stone tables out front, a stone patio on one side, and across a field of either dead or sleeping snails, the swimming pool. Andrew gave us a tour of the inside. 'This is the nookie suite. Mm-mmm,' he said, as if tasting something delicious. 'It's the biggest, softest bed in the house, and we saved it just for the two of you.' I offered him a smile that felt like it would crumble right off my jaw.

The four of us took naps soon after we arrived. Our room was small and meager, but charming in the way we would have expected, with rough walls that looked carved out of soap, a wardrobe, and a ceiling grooved with knotty beams. The bed, as Andrew had promised, was soft. Next to it was a waist-high, gilded statue of the Virgin Mary. 'You'll want to cover her face when you *engage* each other,' he'd said, 'unless you're into the idea of a third party joining you.' But we didn't engage each other at all. Vincent fell asleep almost instantly, and I lay next to him flat on my back, staring up at the ceiling and trying to match my breathing rhythm to his.

Andrew cooked dinner that night and they opened a bottle of local wine, which I declined, while Vincent, who had never been much of a drinker before we'd split up, downed two large glasses like water. It went to his head, I could tell; he sat blinking languidly at the three of us throughout the meal. Afterwards we perched in the living room on furniture that felt like church pews, and Andrew told us about the novel he'd just finished writing. 'It's set in Segovia, ages ago. There's a story – supposedly true – about a nurse who lived in the castle there (have you seen it?), and one night while the family was away she was holding the baby on the balcony and accidentally dropped it over the railing, ker-splat, and she was so filled with remorse, she threw *herself* off, as well. So I got to thinking, what if she had an old vendetta against the family, and psychologically she *wanted* to kill the child, but then she became so wracked with guilt, she did herself in? I mean, who knows how many minutes, or *hours*, passed before she jumped? I wanted a challenge, so I put myself in the mind of the nurse. It really seems the only challenge left in literature: to tell the story from the point of view least in common with your own personality. I mean, I'm not a woman, and I've never been a nurse, and I don't even *like* children. There's this big, long, interior monologue near the end, of course; very self-indulgent on my part. Can you imagine? A historical novel *and* it's from the point of view of a woman? They'll hang me for it.'

'They won't hang you, Nubby,' Garth said. 'It's brilliant. If there's any backlash, it'll be plain old jealousy.'

'They haven't been kind to Gore,' Andrew said.

'*Gore* hasn't been kind to *them*, either. But you, Nub–Nub, are a sweets, and they love you.'

'Garth's my biggest cheerleader,' Andrew told us, hooking his smile to one side and waving a thumb toward Garth. 'But anyway, I can't really worry about it. You have to write what you have to write, right?'

'Which is why I,' Garth said, ' – not that it's under contract, of course – but *I* am writing an epic about an intensely Baptist family outrageously populated with homosexuals. And I've taken Booty's suggestion: I'm telling it from the point of view of the straight, Puritanical, asshole father. I have almost three hundred pages so far.'

'And it's wow-some, Boots.'

'Let's hope your friends in high places think so.'

'They will.'

'They'd better,' Garth said, 'or I'm cashing it in this time and doing a swan dive off something very, very high.' Then he added, 'Smooch,' winking at Andrew, and turned toward me. 'What are *you* working on?'

'Oh, not much,' I said. 'An old story that I never got around to finishing. I'm just playing with it.'

'You should read it to us.'

'Do what?' I said. 'Oh, gosh no. This is a vacation for us. But thanks.' I glanced at Vincent, whose eyes were half-lidded.

Andrew, I think, took note of this, and shifted on his pew, speaking more to Vincent's body than his placid face. 'It must be so *boring* to hear people talk about their writing – especially for people who don't write. Even *I* hate to hear people talk about their writing, but I end up courting it because it's the only way I can talk about my own.' He laughed, and I thought about nudging Vincent to solicit some kind of response, when his eyes suddenly sprang open and he said,

'It's fascinating. Really.'

I was cleaning up the narrow kitchen with Garth later that night when he asked, 'You think Vincent's glad to be here?'

'Oh, totally. He's wild about it.'

'He looks bored, and I can't say I blame him.'

'What's to be bored with?'

'Oh, please,' Garth said, dropping a clean plate onto a shelf. 'One more *quaint* little villa where there's nothing to do but sit around and yammer.'

'It's wonderful,' I said. 'It's a real *thing* for us – to be here while we're, you know, trying to patch things up.'

'You're lucky he doesn't write.'

'Oh, come on. You've got it pretty good.'

'Yeah, I do. But think about it: what *am* I, if I don't publish this novel? His secretary. His *date* for conferences and award ceremonies.'

'You're his lover,' I said. 'Or husband. Or partner. Whatever term you want to use.'

'I think I'd use the phrase "traveling companion and occasional fuck-buddy."'

I rinsed the last dish under the tap and glanced at him. 'That makes it sound like – I mean, do you two . . . play around?'

Garth snorted. 'Yes, *Virginia*, there is polygamy. He's Andrew Duncan, for Christ's sake. People want that celebrity booty and he's more than happy to give it up. He believes in couples, emotional bonding, all that, but he doesn't believe in monogamy for *anyone*. He wrote about it in *The Stagnant Pollen*.'

'Oh, yeah,' I said, though I could remember almost nothing about the book.

'You ought to watch him around Vincent. I recognize that look in his eye, that little curl in his voice. He wants that handshake.'

'Handshake?'

Garth quoted: '"Some people say sex is nothing but an intimate conversation. I say, sex is the handshake; let the conversation come later."'

'He knows Vincent and I are trying to work things out here.'

'Of course he does. And that has nothing to do with his wanting to get into Vincent's pants.'

'I don't think I have anything to worry about,' I said.

'No? All right.'

'What about you? Are you okay with Andrew's . . . philosophy?'

Garth shrugged. 'I say, go to town. It's where *I'm* going every chance I get.'

'But – you love each other, right?'

'I'm crazy about him. And he'd be lost without me. But if I can't publish this book, I'm going to go postal.'

It was a sudden jump in topic – from lover stability to career angst – but it made complete sense to me.

We heard the padding of feet overhead, and then Andrew's voice down the stairwell: 'Coming, Nipper?'

'Coming, Nipper,' Garth said, his tone sugar-sweet but his face void of expression.

~ ~ ~

Later, as I showered upstairs, Vincent took it upon himself to finish unpacking our bags. I was wrapped in a towel when I came back into the bedroom, and as I looked up he was standing next to my suitcase and holding the manuscript I'd said I had no intention of bringing. 'I can't believe you brought this,' he said.

'You know,' I said softly, pushing the door closed behind me, 'I shouldn't feel guilty about writing.'

'Of course not,' he said. 'You should feel guilty about *lying*. You told me you weren't going to bring any work. You said this was a vacation.'

'I just threw it in there at the last second,' I said. 'Something to fiddle around with, in case we got held up at the airport,' which sounded pathetic even as it tripped out of my mouth. 'Tell me what you're really angry about,' I said. 'It's not that I brought the story. It's the *issue* in general, right?'

He sucked in a mouthful of air and held it for several moments. Then he said, 'I'm not really comfortable with this conversation? So maybe we should just drop it.'

It was as if, having logged enough hours in Lola's office, we were free to bring up any topic in the name of honest confrontation, and then we were free not to pursue it in the name of mutual respect. 'All right,' I said in a voice so meek it nauseated me. I looked about the carved walls of the room, desperate to change the subject. 'That virgin's staring at us, you know. I really think Andrew's got a camera mounted in her eye – probably trained on you.'

'Uh-huh.' He glanced down at the funnel of pages in his hand. 'Where do you want me to put this?'

~ ~ ~

The next day the four of us walked down to the pool, which was little more than a concrete rectangle sunk into a field of dry crabgrass. Vincent and I wore sandals, as instructed, and the snails that clung like miniature cotton balls to the weeds crunched under our feet, though whether they'd been dead or alive beforehand still remained undetermined. Andrew and Garth stripped naked and eased into the cold spring water, and I followed their lead. 'Show us that gym-buffed body,' Andrew said to Vincent. But Vincent kept his suit on. While the rest of us sloshed around aimlessly, he did breast-stroke laps with his gaze held forward, away from everyone's nakedness, including my own. I couldn't read his mood – and couldn't ask about it, either – so in the best playful voice I could muster I said, 'Don't you want to get naked? We're in Provence, for God's sake,' as if the region were renowned for its skinny-dipping.

He considered the question as he stiff-armed past me through the water. 'Not really,' he said. 'It must be a writer thing.'

He made an overlapping stitch from one end of the pool to the other as if he had some place he needed to get to. I drifted alongside him uselessly, like a pilot fish.

'Look at that booty, Booty,' Garth said to Andrew, of Andrew, as Andrew climbed out of the water.

Andrew feigned embarrassment and pretended to cover his ass with one hand, chiding, '*Booty*.'

'Look at *your* booty,' I said beneath my breath as Vincent swam past me.

He looked at me incredulously, as if I'd just gargled out a sentence of Provençal French.

I wanted the impossible. I wanted a focused picture of how things were now between us, a clearly labeled dot on the map of our recovery: *You Are Here*. Back in the room, as he was getting dressed, I lay down flat on the bed and said out of the blue, 'Look, I'm sorry. I'm sorry I left you for someone else.'

He was buttoning his shirt with the same precision that had carried him up and down the length of the pool. 'You don't have to tell me that again.'

'I *want* to tell you that again. You know, I didn't sleep with him before you and I broke up.'

'You've said *that* before, too.'

'I don't think you believe me.'

'I've told you I do believe you,' he said.

'Have you forgiven me?'

'Forgiveness is a process.' (A sentence straight from Lola's mouth.)

'Well, are we all right? I mean, what we're trying to do here. Are we . . . all right?'

'We must be,' he said, tucking in his shirt. 'We're in Provence.'

He stared at me, waiting for me to speak next, and I could feel the words rise up like chlorine-tinged bile in my throat: *I'm not really comfortable with this conversation . . . ?* I rolled over and eased my face into the pillow.

That night, Andrew read to us from his new manuscript. The writing was beautiful, what I heard of it; I spent much of the time watching Vincent, who was slouched in a wooden chair clearly making an effort to look pleasant and entertained, but I knew him well enough to recognize his discomfort. Shamefully, I tried to imagine the journalist in his place. I overcame the guilt of this by then imagining myself sitting in front of Lola and hearing her say, *Why did you do that? Don't be ashamed. Take your time.*

Well, I might have said, *I thought the journalist would have been enjoying it more. I was concerned for Vincent, who looked self-conscious and miserable.*

Maybe he was just tired.

He was self-conscious. He couldn't let himself appreciate it.

And the journalist would have appreciated it more – as a writer?

No. The journalist would have been drunk. And in fact, *Vincent* was drunk, having egged Garth into opening a second bottle of wine at dinner. Andrew read for over an hour, and by the end of it Vincent had sunk down to a forty-five degree angle in his chair, his hands locked over his ribs.

'So you liked it?' Andrew asked the three of us.

Garth was applauding. I shook my head and brought my hands together.

'That was the part the lawyers want me to change,' Andrew said. 'I mean, *yes*, I based it on a woman I used to know at Berkeley, and *yes*, she *did* express her pug's anal glands once while wearing a pair of dinner gloves, but not in the seventeenth century and not in Spain, so what's the big deal?'

'Why don't *you* read to us now?' Garth said to me.

'Absolutely!' Andrew said. 'Read us that story you've been working on.'

I glanced at Vincent. I watched his chest expand and contract steadily beneath the clasp of his hands. 'Oh, no,' I said. 'Thanks, but I shouldn't.'

'Go get it,' Garth said. 'It's not like we have anything else to do.'

'Really,' I said, 'thanks. But I shouldn't. I mean, it isn't finished yet, and we came here to relax. You know, get away from work.'

'Our loss, then,' Andrew said. 'So – you really liked it?'

'Beautiful.' This came from Vincent, who uttered the word without a change in his sloped posture or expression, his gaze fixed on the floor that stretched out between the four of us. 'Just beautiful.'

The next morning we sat down to a breakfast of coffee and *sacristans*. It was another clear day, intensely bright outside the windows and burning by ten o'clock. Refilling our plates with doughy twists, Andrew announced that Garth was going to read to us a chapter from his novel.

'Oh, I'm not,' Garth said, thumbing a smear of powdered sugar from the corner of his mouth.

'*Yes*, Nipper,' Andrew said. 'We can't wait a minute longer.'

Garth grinned sheepishly at each of us in turn, then got up from the table and went for his manuscript. I cringed inside. This was exactly what I had longed for during those dreary days of life back in Richmond: to be among other writers, to hear what they were working on; at the same time, I felt something slipping away with each word that was read aloud. Garth read for over an hour, as had Andrew. I barely followed a sentence of it, so intent was I on Vincent's posture, his placid eyes, the abbreviated line of his mouth. Afterwards we applauded gently and lauded Garth's use of imagery. 'Well, enough of *that*,' Garth said, pushing the pages forward across the table. 'Now let's hear some *real* literature. Go get your story.'

I declined politely. And declined again when they became insistent. Vincent blinked at me and said. 'Go get it. Read the story.'

'I don't want to,' I said evenly.

'Why not?'

'Audience awareness,' I said, then forced a smile into my face and displayed it for the room.

~ ~ ~

Vincent and I walked through the nearby town of Saint-Rémy the next afternoon and barely said a word to each other. The streets were narrow and beautiful, strung with laundry and lanterns. I pointed at things without commenting, and this seemed fine with him. When we stopped into a store that made its own soaps, we walked among the giant vats of boiling lavender and almond and smelled dozens of tiny bars, holding them up to each other's noses without commenting on them, like a pair of mutes. I thought, maybe we no longer need to think about fighting. Maybe the fight is a constant, a truth binding us like a vow; our own secret language. If only Lola could see us now.

On the way back to *Mas de la Fé*, we passed the asylum that had once housed Van Gogh. I swallowed the last mouthful of silence I could endure and said, 'Can you imagine being locked up like that, looking out one of those windows and painting as much as he did?'

'Why did we come here?' Vincent said in a cracked, dry voice.

I felt my stomach catch just beneath my heart and thought of a million things to say, and then nothing. I imagined cutting off not my own ear, but my penis, and lobbing it over a balcony after Vincent's receding body. 'Let's go back to Paris early,' I said. 'We can walk along the Champs-Élysées and go up to the top of the Arc de Triomphe; you said you wanted to do that.'

'Did I?'

'*Yes*,' I said a little too forcefully. 'You told me you wanted to do that, and we didn't get a chance.'

'You really ought to read them your story. I think you'll resent me if you don't – unless you're afraid they won't like it.'

'I'm not going to read the fucking story. I'm going to tear the fucking story up and throw it in the fireplace.'

He listened to this staring forward at the asylum. He shook his head yes, gently, and said, 'What fireplace?'

~ ~ ~

Andrew prepared another meal for us – four sizzling hens, a pot of ratatouille and green beans, two different kinds of bread and five different cheeses he'd purchased that afternoon in Saint-Rémy. The three of them had drinks before dinner and passed the wine around the table, and I almost held up my glass, but didn't. Halfway through the meal Vincent found a bottle of Merlot, asked what it was, and opened it.

'And then I thought, fuck 'em,' Andrew said. 'If they're afraid of the book that much, I'll take it somewhere else. I mean, the day after I got the proofs in the mail, the *lawyer* – not the editor, but the *lawyer* – started calling me about references to this character and that character, wanting to know who each of them was based on, and whether that person might sue because I made some reference to her undersized breasts or his beady eyes. Finally I said, "Look, I'll add a sentence to the last page: *By the way, they were all midgets*. Will that satisfy you?" And he took me seriously! Apparently, they have a history of midget lawsuits.'

'So what now?' I asked, watching Vincent throw back the Merlot.

'I don't know. My agent wants me to switch houses for my next book. "Bidding war." That's her favorite phrase.'

'Would be mine, too,' Garth said around a mouthful of hen.

'But I feel terrible,' Andrew said. 'I feel like I've been blathering on about myself for days. Won't you please read us this mysterious story?'

It took me a moment to realize he was talking to me; my eyes were still on Vincent, who was swirling his glass around now, staring into its oily bottom while his free hand reached for the bottle of Merlot. 'It's not going to happen,' I said.

Andrew smiled at Vincent. One of his eyelids flickered in what may or may not have been a wink. 'Too bad *you* don't have a story.'

'You know what?' Vincent suddenly spoke up. 'I do.' He gave the nearly empty bottle a slight push, as if decidedly finished with it for the moment, and it swivelled, and tipped. I lunged for it. Catching it just before its side met the table, I jerked it upright, and a fine, crimson thread of Merlot launched out as if from a jugular and landed across the wood –

and across the white surface of Andrew's shirt front. I was opening my mouth to apologize when Vincent's voice plowed forth: 'I have a story, just like the rest of you. And I'll read it, if you'd like.'

He was looking at none of us. From where I sat next to him, I could see only the bulbous slope of his eyelids, as if he were talking in his sleep. His mouth hung open between sentences.

Cautiously, Andrew said, 'We'd love to hear it.'

'It isn't actually written down,' Vincent said. 'But it's in my head.' He lifted his empty glass to his lips and drained the air from it. 'What I've done is put myself into the mind of the character who least resembles *me*. You know the technique. It's the only way to do it – tell the story from the point of view of someone who's *nothing* like you, because everything else has been done, and blah, blah, blah. So what happens is, my life – speaking as this other person, this character – my life is going nowhere. I've got a lover, and I've got a home we made together, and I've got this living room I just *had* to paint "wet terracotta" –'

'Stop it,' I said.

'All these things I said I wanted, these things I talked about, they're all there in front of me . . . like a drawing. Like if you tried to put together a picture of what your life *should* be, and there it is, it's perfect . . . only you don't quite like it. So what do I do? Well, the critics will hate me for this part, because it's really going to seem unrealistic. I mean, totally *stupid*. But you've got to write what you've got to write. And I hate my life, in this story. I mean, I'm going out of my fucking skull. I could work on it, you know, try to improve my life, like anyone with common sense would. But rather than do the *work*, rather than try to *fix* the picture –'

'Stop it,' I said again.

'– I just tear it up.'

My elbows were on the table, and without my deciding to put them there, my thumbs were pressed against my forehead – hard enough, it felt, to break through my skull. I wanted to stand up but couldn't move. I heard the chary current of breathing over the surface of the table, and when I finally looked up Vincent was moving his eyes over the three of us. He looked livid.

'It's not a very good story, is it?' he said in a voice suddenly winded. 'I mean, who in his right mind wants to read about a character so spineless, so –' His jaw worked soundlessly around his tongue. He looked at Andrew and at Garth, and finally at me, and said, '– unlikeable?'

My face burned. I tried to swallow. After a moment, I said, 'We should clean up.'

But Vincent stood up from the table. 'I'm going swimming.'

'I'll come with you!' Andrew said, rising from his chair with a sudden buoyancy.

Vincent glanced at Andrew, then made his way to the stairs – for his towel, I assumed – his hands against the walls as he mounted the first step. Andrew was trailing a finger over the vein of Merlot on his shirt as he followed.

I sat staring at the empty bottle. The room was filled with the creaks and moans of the ceiling as the two of them moved about the floor above us, and not until those sounds died out, not until all movement seemed to have ceased overhead, did I lift my eyes to look at Garth.

Garth opened his mouth, but then closed it without saying anything.

What felt like five minutes passed, broken only by a single creak in the floor above.

'Celebrity booty?' I managed to say, my eyes turning damp.

Garth shrugged. 'I didn't think he was much of a reader.'

A short while later Vincent came back down the stairs wearing a white towel around his waist. His face was flushed red, as if the sun he'd absorbed into his body over the past few days were suddenly concentrated there. He didn't look into the dining room but walked straight to the front door, opened it, and disappeared into the night. There was no sign of Andrew.

'You need to go after him,' Garth said.

'I think he wants to be alone.'

'He's drunk. He's going down to the pool. You need to go after him.'

Slowly, I pushed up from the table.

It was almost midnight, but the sky was azure, back-lit with more stars than I'd ever fathomed, and the field was luminescent with the snails that clung like bits of phosphate to the dry grass. I saw Vincent long before I reached him. He was sitting at the edge of the pool with his back to me, his legs pulled up to his chest. The towel had fallen from his waist and lay around him like a puddle of milk from which he had emerged. He was naked.

I stood behind him listening to the impossibly dense silence that surrounded us, a silence so oppressive and drowning I thought I would choke, until at last the sound of a blatting motor – a tiny car, maybe, or a Vespa – announced itself far off down the road and then receded into the distance. As if the sound were that of a zipper pulled open on my lungs, I started to breathe again, feeling suddenly and strangely optimistic: I didn't care what had just happened in the house between Vincent and Andrew. If anything, I was thankful for it. Vincent and I, we were just a couple of people, and this was what couples did. They had their fights, their adventures. They fucked up, and they mended. 'You know,' I said, in a voice barely above a whisper, 'we can still make this work.'

Immediately he stood up. In one drastic motion – I thought he would tumble into me – he swung around and closed his hands over my elbows and pulled me against him. He was trembling, and he had an erection. His mouth pressed against my neck. His hands pulled at the waist of my shorts and yanked up my t-shirt, until I was fumbling to help him and, naked, we were bending down to lie on top of my clothes. He nearly fell into the pool and I grabbed him. He made a small gasp – of surprise, maybe, of anger – and then pressed his mouth against my collarbone and bit down as if to silence it.

It was nothing like us. He moved with a force, an intention, to which I deferred – awkwardly, at first, and then willingly. He had learned things, or gone places, with someone else, I thought (possibly only minutes before), and he was suddenly determined to go there with me. For the first time in our history of making love, he brought his tongue to my armpits, to my nostrils, to my ass. He pushed my shoulders to the cement and took me into his mouth. I told him I was close, then told him I was going to come, and he didn't stop but took in everything, swallowing audibly even before I was finished.

~ ~ ~

We didn't speak on the walk back to the house, or as we settled into bed; Vincent, in fact, didn't look at me. But we slept that night wrapped around each other for the first time since we'd left Richmond.

The next morning I was awakened – though initially I wasn't sure by what. For a few moments I lay motionless on my side, facing the wall, aware only that it was daylight and that my mind had fixed itself on something I was about to forget. Then I felt his hand on the back of my head. He was stroking my hair. And layered over this feeling was the sound of his voice.

'I hope you have it.'

His hand curled gently around the back of my skull. *I hope you have it.*

I was dreaming, I thought, and I placed myself in the texture of the wall, the light coming from the window, the returning memory of the previous evening.

'I hope you have success.'

Then I heard his breath trembling in the wake of his words, and I turned over.

His face was bathed in tears.

'What did you say?' I asked.

He was dressed. His shirt was buttoned to the collar. He removed his hand from my head and drew his face, suddenly so close to my own, away. 'I'm a monster,' he said. 'And so are you.'

'What are you talking about?'

'Nothing. I'm going for a walk.'

'No you're not. Tell me what's bothering you.'

'Nothing.'

'What's *wrong*?' I asked.

He was wiping away the dampness on his face, pulling at the skin around his eyes with his fingertips. 'Please talk to me,' I said, but he shook his head.

'We don't have to.'

'Why not?' And then, with no thought of our therapy in mind, with an utter helplessness that formed the words, I said, 'I don't understand.'

But I think we both did.

~ ~ ~

I told Garth and Andrew later that morning that we would be returning to Paris in the afternoon. Across the table from each other, they exchanged the most serious look I'd seen pass between them, and Andrew's face crimped inward like that of a boy being admonished. He took his coffee cup and walked into the kitchen, and a moment later stuck his head out of the doorway and waved for me to follow. 'I hope this isn't, you know, because of –' His voice, already a whisper, unraveled into soundlessness. I assured him it wasn't. 'Well, here,' he breathed, digging into his back pocket for his wallet. He took out a stack of French money and pushed it toward me.

'I'm not taking your money,' I said.

'You should. Do you know how much it's going to cost to change your train ticket? And the hotels in Paris are a fortune. You probably didn't count on spending that much.'

'We're fine.'

'Yes, but I'm loaded. My last advance was a bundle. *Please* take it.'

I stared down at the money he was pinching not an inch away from my chest. It was tempting, but I couldn't decide whether he was offering it simply because he was generous, or because he felt guilty. And if it was guilt, it meant he was offering me payment for whatever he'd done with Vincent, and not even Lola could have turned that one into a healthy transaction.

I thanked him again, declined, and we carried our mugs back into the dining room.

After a long stretch in which the four of us shredded our pastries, Andrew's eyes made cricket jumps around the room and he broke the silence. 'You *have* to see Glanum before you go!' he said, sounding almost panicked. 'It's beautiful. It's romantic. I mean, you should do it, if it's your last day here.'

Vincent didn't respond. I tried to smile but couldn't, and nodded my head slightly in thanks.

Later we walked across the property to the road, and following Andrew's directions, we reached a gravelly path and a sign marking the entrance to Glanum. The sky was unbroken save for the enormous, burning eye of the sun. I pinched the dampness out of my eyes and felt sweat run in steady, narrow streams down my legs and down my torso inside my shirt. We bought tickets and were handed brochures at a small, aluminum pavilion, and we followed the path to a clearing in the dry trees and brush, where the stone city opened before us like the skeleton of a fallen giant. Nothing before us was whole or intact. There were places where only the lowest of existing walls, sometimes just enough to cut the surface of the dirt, gave evidence to what had once been a curia, a bathhouse, a forum; places where walls and balustrades had been reassembled to resemble their former selves; places where the fragments were left to lie where they had fallen. Amidst a decimated rib cage of columns, a wide, stone promenade traced the uneven ground like a broken spine. I thought that I should have been thinking about the people who had once lived here, about their lives and the struggles they had known, but I couldn't picture any of them. I couldn't *place* anyone – other than me and Vincent, here in the present moment. The city seemed made for us.

~ ~ ~

That last day and a half we spent in Paris passed like a blending of hours without seams, almost without moments, though not entirely.

We did climb to the top of the Arc de Triomphe to gaze out over the city under a hot, open sky. Vincent handed his camera to another American tourist and asked her to take our picture – a picture I have never seen. Afterwards, we sat down at a table in a café on the Champs-Élysées. He ordered a cup of coffee. I ordered a beer without looking at him. And when it came, and when I'd stared down at its foamy top and finally brought it to my lips and swallowed, and felt it burn like the blade of a knife down the inside of my throat, I got up from the table and walked, and then ran, to the back of the café – only to find the men's room door locked. In a panic, I pushed past a woman about to enter the ladies' room and slammed the door behind me a second before I vomited across the toilet and the tiled wall. I fell to my knees and was sick for the next five minutes.

When I was finally able to stand, my hands and my legs and even the muscles of my face trembling, I opened the door and let the stench trail behind me. The woman was still waiting. I stepped around her, avoiding her eyes, and she uttered something in French – a wet, biting sound, as if she were tearing meat.

MARK DEVISH

IS IT HOT? DOES IT RAIN?

I had no idea where to find a public bathroom. I wasn't sure that hospitals even had public bathrooms. I followed this lady to the elevator – she was leaning on a walker, pulling along both her IV stand and her little boy. When she got off I followed her again. The little boy orbited around her, walking backwards, talking to her as he circled. I stood watching from a water fountain as they moved down the hall. I leaned over, closed my eyes, and drank. A drop of water stuck in my throat, and I tried to imitate the phlegmy hum of the old man in the bed next to Bobby's. We had been trying to decide if the guy was singing or if he was in pain. It sounded like he was trying either to cough or to come.

A sign pointed out Oncology to the left, Waiting Room and ICU to the right. Two couples sat in the waiting room. The TV set rattled above them. The women had eyes rimmed with water, the men shoulders that sagged from the weight of arms crossed in front of their chests. They looked at me expectantly. 'Is there a bathroom around here?' I asked.

'Down past ICU,' one of the men said. 'Go right. It's one of them unisex jobs. You might have to wait,' he said, looking at me.

MARK DEVISH (born 1968): Devish did most of his growing up in Memphis, Tennessee and Richmond, Virginia. As a child, he played the French horn. He has an MFA in fiction from the University of Florida and currently lives in Gainesville, Florida, with his long-time feline companion, Garp.

The PA occasionally crackled static. I understood the words *Doctor*, *call*, and sometimes *OR*. Whole sentences floated out and I didn't understand even a single syllable. I passed by a cluster of rooms whose walls were giant windows that showed patients – obviously bad-off patients – in various states of disrepair. A woman, her head half-shaved, a line of stitches running up her cheek from right below the ear, was watching TV. Sewed her up just like a baseball, I thought, and chewed the inside of my cheek to keep from giggling. The florescents were fucking with my head. Out of place, I thought. I'm seriously out of place here.

A man in a blue coat stood looking at a body buried beneath gizmos and pumps and bloody gauze. I heard the thin sound of music from across the hall. It sounded familiar, and I had suspicions. I stepped towards a door that stood open by about six inches. Just launching the transition from 'Scarlet' into 'Fire.' Sometime in the '80s. 'Eighty-five, maybe. I looked through the window and saw a guy lying in the green light cast by the monitors that hung over his head. No one else was in the room.

I listened from the hallway, my ear in front of the door. We are everywhere, just like the bumper stickers say. Where's the strangest place you ever heard the Dead? This was it, hands down, the strangest. Once, in Hampton – '86, I think, but maybe it was '87 – the McDonald's near the Coliseum had been playing 'Terrapin Station' on the intercom. That was cool. This was fucked up.

I knocked on the doorjamb but he didn't move. 'Hello,' I tried, tentative, pushing open the door, knocking again. From the cricket chirp of the heart monitor I was pretty sure he wasn't going to answer. I stepped towards him and felt a shudder run up through my body. A high sour taste, like the smell of burnt orange, touched the back of my throat. My eyes twitched so fast I could almost hear them in their sockets. I hadn't experienced a sensation like it since my ten-year-old self had snuck into my parents' bedroom and found *The Joy of Sex*.

'Hello,' I said again, just to be sure, but he didn't move. A small boom-box sat on a cheap pressboard dresser – white surgical tape stuck to the handle had been markered *Property of ICU*. 'I'm Elmore,' I said to him. 'What's going on?' I had to stifle a giggle. It sounded silly.

He was about my age. He had curly black hair that ringed his face like a frame – he'll be able to pull it back into a ponytail soon, I thought. His skin was like marble. Smooth. I could see the sharp outline of his collar-bones above the neckline of his light-blue hospital smock. The hollow spot below his Adam's apple – the unprotected hole where a pencil could be pushed into the trachea – was shaped like the tip of a tongue. I imagined it could hold at least a teaspoon of liquid.

I had seen guys like him at shows all over the country. Peace, love, happiness, Jerry-jams and drugs. He didn't look hurt. He looked good. He looks OK, I thought. Uninjured. He looks fine. I pulled at my own black hair, tightening the curls that somehow escaped the tieback to hang in my face. I tried not to stare at him but I could not stop myself.

You're supposed to talk to people in the hospital, I finally thought. It's good for them even to hear your voice. I had read that somewhere. It felt silly. I had been there for almost fifteen minutes and not a muscle had moved.

'Did you go to the show last night?' I said to him. I didn't know what else to say. The green monitor above his bed showed the mountain/valley beat of his heart. His heart rate was 75, which seemed somehow fast, and his blood pressure was 110/60, which seemed like it might have been low. I really didn't know.

'A hometown show,' I said. I shrugged at him. 'For me, at least. Imagine that. Took about twenty minutes to get to the lot. A good show, too.' A sheet of paper was taped to the wall above his bed. Handwritten notes of some kind: spiked2x–LPR good:clr;xray hd trma?unrspnsve.

'The Fire' ended its homestretch and the drums pounded out the beginning of 'Samson.' Jerry sounded pissed, shredding chords, his fingers blurring lines, Phil behind him throwing bombs into the bass. One of those moments. I couldn't help nodding my head. 'Hell yeah,' I said to him. 'This tape sounds good.' I looked for a tape case but didn't see one. 'Wish I knew where it was from,' I said. I noticed the padding of bandages, stomach to thighs, underneath the shape of his sheet.

'I was thinking how fucked up it got after the show last night,' I said. 'For us, you know, for me and my friends. But I guess if you were at the show last night it got even more fucked up for you. I mean, shit, you know.' I motioned at the room, the monitors, the bed. 'Hey. You ain't contagious or nothing, are you?' I asked. I was kidding, trying to make a joke, but I was afraid for a second it didn't sound funny. For a second I was scared it might be true.

His fingers were long, tapered, segmented by knuckles the size of gumballs. I kept expecting them to move. Fingers like that should. The chart at the foot of his bed had a piece of masking tape on the cover that said Mr. XA. 'X-A,' I said. 'Zah?' He wasn't any help. 'Mr. Zah?' I said again. I liked saying it. I wondered if it was Russian, some sort of Anglicized spelling of something I couldn't pronounce.

I just kept talking. I was being charming. I didn't want to leave. I told him about Bobby's accident. 'It was after the show, last night,' I said. 'We had just got back from the lot. He rolled right between Julian and Teresa on the way down the stairs,' I said. 'We all heard the bone snap.'

First aid had been relatively simple: try to calm everyone down, call 911, and clean out everyone's pockets. Teresa handled the phone and our various stashes. I tried to keep Bobby warm, treated him for shock the best I could. I had been a Boy Scout, so I was in charge. Bobby looked grateful, even though I didn't do much but lay a blanket over him and pat the sweat from his face. Julian and Teresa did the things I asked them to do. It was actually kind of cool.

'The cops just sort of showed up with the ambulance,' I said to the guy in the bed. He still hadn't moved. 'Things got pretty ugly. Julian gave them a hard time, you know, just being an asshole –' 'He fell is all. He fucking slipped. We don't need no cops, there wasn't any crime' '– until they finally asked him for ID. I think they were just trying to scare him, you know, but when he pulled his wallet from his pocket a baggy with about three bong hits in it came plopping out. He had forgotten all about it. He got a ticket for possession.'

He was doing nothing but lying there. I wondered how he'd look different if he were dead. There was something between us. I could see it in the way the air was in the room. It filled me up. I wanted to hold him and make cooing sounds. I wanted to make it all better.

I touched him on the forehead first, like my mom used to do when she was checking to see if I had a fever. It happened even before I knew I was doing it. He was warm. His skin was dry.

I don't know what I intended to do. It wasn't meant to be sexual. It was maternal. Fraternal. I traced the outline of his face like a blind man making friends.

But then I couldn't stop myself. I felt his skin, the way it moved around on his skull underneath his eyebrows. I felt the ridges of bone in his Adam's apple. When I touched the tip of his nose, his lips pulled up into a sneer.

'See?' I said. 'He's alive.' I had just picked up his hand when a nurse walked through the door.

'Oh,' she said stiffly. 'A visitor.'

'Yeah,' I said. 'Hi.'

I was terrified. Embarrassed. Electric. I had been caught playing doctor. I was holding a man's hand. Suddenly I had an erection. I could feel my pulse in the way it was folded in my jeans.

She looked at me like she knew I knew I shouldn't be there. Panic, dark-brown and leathery, fluttered up inside me. A crap spasm made me stand up straight. I'd forgotten about the bathroom.

'Are you family?' she asked.

'No,' I said, 'just a friend.' I cupped my hand and coughed, hoping I didn't smell like beer.

'You're not supposed to be in here,' the nurse said. 'Samson' came to an end and the audience roared and cheered. I stared at the floor, played with a hole in my shirt. My face felt hot. I didn't know what to say. 'Oh,' was finally all I could manage.

She stepped right up next to me and opened the chart. I could feel her shoulder against mine. I moved away. She copied some numbers off the monitor above his head. I thought about walking out but then I just stood there. She wrote something down and turned to me, her expression questioning but concerned. 'I've got to change his dressings,' she said. 'Why don't you come back in half an hour?'

'Oh,' I said. 'OK.' My brain felt loose in my head. I didn't know what was happening.

'I'm serious,' she said. 'We need to talk.'

'OK,' I said again. 'Sure.' I walked out into the hall. Walked as quick as I could to the bathroom. I wasn't going to go back there.

~ ~ ~

The nurse on Bobby's floor said that visiting hours were over. She glared at me, and I felt uneasy just standing there talking to her. On the elevator an orderly with an empty gurney raised his eyebrows and looked at me. When the doors closed he asked me what floor I wanted. He rode all the way down to the lobby with me, and for a second I was afraid he was going to talk, maybe ask me who I had been visiting, or if I had been up to the ICU. But we were both quiet.

A man stood by the Admissions desk, holding a boy who was already dressed in a hospital gown. The orderly pushed over to them and the man laid the boy down. They wheeled the boy over to the elevators, and the orderly pushed a button. Then they stood there and waited. A few people stood behind them and waited, too.

I tried to remember where we had parked, but then wasn't sure whose car we had come in. It had been a long day. I had to trace it back to figure out it was my car. I drove.

Teresa and Julian were waiting for me. Julian was standing there with his arms crossed, a cigarette bit down into his teeth. 'Where the fuck have you been?' he asked as I climbed into the car. I started the engine and ran the idle high, my foot on the gas, one glance at Teresa to see her eyeing me. I picked a tape off the seat and plugged it in at random. It was Teresa's Cornell '77, cued right to the beginning of 'Estimated.' I dug my bowl from my pocket and used a tape case as a tray to pack one up. 'You coming?' I asked them, and they both got in the car.

Julian started to say something and I turned the volume up, my speakers rattling. I handed him the bowl and then just sort of shrugged when either of them spoke to me. I pointed us towards home and then lost myself in Keith's organ, that simple stepping buzz behind Jerry's fiery noodling. Nah, Nah, nah nah. The sun glinted off the windows of the buildings that we passed. I continued to drive. Donna's vocals were surprisingly pitched and tasteful. Phil, off in the zone, slid long, perfect notes up the fretboard and popped leads all over the place. A perfect choice. I pursed my lips like I was sucking through a straw. The air tasted like water after being in the sickness of the hospital. Julian and Teresa were nodding along, all of us in the car, listening to the tune. We were on the interstate with the windows rolled down.

When we pulled up in front of Julian's, Teresa popped the tape from the deck. She was probably going to spend the night. I turned the radio off and rummaged the floorboards for something to listen to.

'Seriously, man,' Julian said before he got out. 'Where were you for so long?'

I didn't want to tell them. It felt like a secret. My fingers itched. It was easier not to tell. 'I had the runs,' I said to Julian. 'It was awful,' I said. 'Can hummus go bad?' I said. 'I bought that sandwich from that sketchy chick after the show.'

'Something did you wrong, huh?' Julian rested his chin on the passenger-side headrest. He was looking at me in the rearview mirror.

'I don't know,' I said. 'Maybe it's just nerves.'

'Yeah, well, you should go see Bobby tomorrow morning. He seemed a little miffed that you disappeared so quick.'

'Okay,' I said, and I could feel that I was nervous. 'You want to come with me?'

'I got to work. We'll probably go later.'

'Yeah,' I said. 'I'll go in the morning, before class.'

Teresa gave me Bobby's keys, and said that he had asked if I could go by to check on his plants. He had five scrawny pot plants clinging to some sort of synthetic soil in a wading pool filled with a supposedly nutrient-rich solution. Whatever it was, it stank. And with his 60-watt florescents I doubted he was going to get anywhere.

The tapes in my car were all over-listened to. I put in Alpine '85, the first night, but I couldn't stand it. I knew it too well. It couldn't surprise me at all. I turned the radio on but could only find commercials the rest of the way home.

I was too keyed to read, but I had a hundred pages to get through for class. I couldn't sit still. The day kept replaying itself. Zah, I would think, and I would lose my place. He was lying there, right now, in the hospital. I wondered if he had woken up, if he had moved, if anyone else was in his room. It was wrong that someone my age was sick enough to be in intensive care.

I took a couple of bong hits and stretched out on the couch. I was going to take one more stab at the reading. I didn't get through thirty pages before I burned out and nodded off hard, the book rising and falling on my chest.

～ ～ ～

'They say I'm going to be here a while,' Bobby told me. 'In traction. For at least a week.'

'Bummer,' I said. His leg was up in a sling. It had been a pretty jagged break, the bone threatening to come through the skin, one of the big muscles all torn to hell. He'd be in a cast for six months or more.

'You're telling me,' Bobby said. 'You ever have to shit in a bedpan?'

'Can't say that I have.'

'It's embarrassing,' Bobby said. I wondered for a second how Mr. XA would take care of that. Probably with tubes of some sort. It had to be automatic. 'Especially handing the thing over when I'm done. Like it's a trophy or something.'

'It's natural,' I said. 'Everybody does it.'

'Whatever,' he said. 'It's still embarrassing.'

The old man in the next bed was watching a talk show. A woman I assume was his wife sat next to him. He made his sound, an ambiguous rasping like maybe he was scratching an itch. When the commercials started she touched him on the hand. 'Henry,' she said, but he stared intently at the screen. 'Hey, Henry.'

'Listen, man,' Bobby said to me. 'Would you mind bringing some tapes? Some early stuff, huh? I'm sick of the '80s.'

'I can do that,' I said. 'I'm gonna check on your plants this afternoon. I'll be back tonight.'

The old man turned the TV up and his wife took her hand away from his. For a minute we all sat there, watching commercials. A man pushing a cart full of laundry squeaked by in the hall. When the show came back on I shook my head. 'I have to go to class,' I said.

'Yeah,' Bobby said. 'Guess I'm gonna take a nap.'

I kept telling myself that I wasn't going to go up there, but once I got to the elevator I couldn't stop. She won't be here, I thought. Her shift would have been over long ago. A quick peek, I thought. Just to see if he's alone.

The hallway was clear down to his room. I walked all the way to the bathroom. He appeared to be alone. I tried to pee but couldn't. I washed my hands and splashed water on my face. Nurse be damned, I thought. I'm going in there. I'm going to see him one more time. I looked at myself in the mirror. I tightened my ponytail. I walked back down the hall.

The same tape was playing, only quieter. 'Samson' again. I wondered who kept flipping it for him. 'You doing any better today?' I asked. I brushed my knuckles down the side of his face. His legs were in slightly different positions. His knees had more of a crook to them.

'I can't stay,' I said to him. 'I've got a class.'

I kept looking out at the hallway. I expected that nurse to walk in. I expected her to have a security guard or a cop with her. A man was looking at a woman in the room across the hall. He slid a chair next to her bed and sat down. He reached under her sheets and fumbled around. He pulled out her hand and kissed it. It made me want to cry.

'Samson' came to an end and the audience roared and cheered. 'Is this the only tape you have?' I asked Mr. XA. 'You must be sick of it.' He looked like he had been carved, like he was a statue made of skin. I touched the inside of his elbow. I felt a spark on my fingers. There was tuning and then Jerry strummed the beginning of 'Terrapin.' I looked in the top dresser drawer. Inside was a plastic bag filled with bloody clothes. 'Holy fuck,' I said. 'Are these yours?'

The intercom came alive and I heard a doctor paged to ICU. A nurse – not *the* nurse, but still my blood stuck a second in my veins – ran by the door. A nest of voices, laced with professional panic, came from a room two doors down. 'I got to go,' I said. 'Take care.'

I looked at him from the doorway. He could have been a child in an oversized crib. It felt wrong to leave him. He was like nothing I had seen.

When I got to my car I realized I only had twenty minutes to get to class. I wasn't going to make it. I wanted to go back and see him instead. It made me feel sick. I started my car but then looked at the tapes scattered on the floor and on the seat. I grabbed the first ones that I knew sounded good. Philly 4–6–82 set II. RFK 7–6–86 set II. Hershey Park 6–28–85 set I. I rewound them all to their beginnings and debated whether or not I should. 'Fuck it,' I said. 'Fifteen minutes.' No matter what happens, I promised myself, this is the last time you're going up there. This is it, I thought. You've got to say goodbye.

The man who had been with the woman across the hall got off the elevator as I was getting on. He looked around the lobby. He didn't seem to recognize me. There was no reason he should. As the doors shut he was walking towards the exit.

The hallway was quiet when I got off. Whatever had been happening had happened. I walked straight into his room. No one was there but him. 'Listen,' I said. 'I brought you some tapes,' I said. I popped Philly in and 'Shakedown' filled the room. 'Check it out,' I said. 'Jerry cooks during this jam.' I held his feet through the sheet and wiggled them in time to the music. I stroked him on the shoulder. It felt like I was petting a cat. I picked up his hand and his fingers curled around mine. I wondered if he knew what he was doing, or if it was a reflex, like a baby does when you poke a finger into its fist. I could feel his heart in his chest. I could feel his nipple under my hand.

'This is fucked up,' I said. 'Jesus.'

I had to get out of there. For a second the world was frozen. 'Goodbye,'

I finally said. 'Good luck.' Then I leaned over as gently as I could and I kissed him on the cheek. Then I kissed him on the forehead. I had my fingers in his hair. 'Jesus,' I said again. I rushed for the door, sweating. All the way to my car I kept looking over my shoulder, looking back to see who had seen.

~ ~ ~

That night I took the stairs to Bobby's room. I was avoiding the elevators. It seemed safer that way.

'This Demerol is kicking my ass,' Bobby said to me. He looked up and laughed. 'I recommend it,' he said. 'Goddamn.'

The man in the next bed was staring at us. He muttered under his breath. He made his sound – hmmmmuhhh – and Bobby asked him if he needed a drink of water. 'I could call the nurse,' he said. The man grunted at us and turned away.

I gave Bobby the tapes I'd brought. 'I don't know how that Avalon from '68 sounds,' I said. 'But the Winterland '74 kicks ass.'

'Holy fuck,' Bobby said to me, half sitting from his waist. 'Did you hear about that shit? After the show?'

'What shit?' I asked.

'Some kid got mauled after the show,' he said. 'It was in the paper.'

'Mauled?' I asked. 'What do you mean?'

'I mean fucked up,' Bobby said. 'Mangled all to hell. They think it was a dog.'

'A dog? What?'

'They found some kid bleeding to death in the lot after the show. Julian told me about it. He saw it in yesterday's paper. Some kind of animal, it said. They think it was a dog. Evidently the kid had no ID. No one knows who he is.'

'Holy shit,' I said. I was thinking of Zah. Bobby adjusted himself through the sheet that covered his crotch. He wasn't wearing underwear because of the cast. I looked away and the old man caught my eye.

'Hey,' he said. 'You. Visiting hours are over.'

'Give me a break,' Bobby said.

'*I* could call the nurse,' the old man said. 'If that's what you want.'

'Man, what'd I ever do to you?' Bobby asked. 'You been on me all day.'

I knocked on the bottom of Bobby's cast. 'I should go,' I said. 'It's getting late.'

'Don't let him run you off,' Bobby said. 'Stay a while.'

'I should go,' I said again. 'Visiting hours *are* over.'

'Whatever,' Bobby said. 'You coming back tomorrow?'

I looked at the old man. 'I'll be here,' I said. 'Julian's going to get me in the morning. We can hang all day.'

The hallway was deserted. My footsteps echoed off the stairs. My car sat alone in a puddle of light. On the way home I stopped and bought the paper. I found a story about the show and the trash and a handful of arrests, but nothing about a guy found bleeding in the lot. Zah, I thought. It could be. I lay in the dark. It took almost an hour to fall asleep.

~ ~ ~

I was walking down the hall towards ICU. The intercom crackled on and a voice said that my party was waiting at Will Call. Through one of the windows, I could see Jerry Garcia sitting on the edge of a bed, an acoustic guitar in his lap. In another room two old women hovered over a naked boy. I kept an eye out for that nurse. I kept going until I reached his room.

He smiled at me and opened his eyes. They were the lightest blue they could be without being gray. His hair had grown. It was fanned out behind his head, reaching down till it just touched his shoulders. The sheet was pulled down to his belly button, and he was naked underneath. He glistened like the flank of a horse. Shiny, soft skin covered his muscles. His voice was throaty and sweet. 'You came back,' he said.

'I never left,' I said. I was proud of him. He had fought it. He had won. 'You were asleep,' I said.

'I had the weirdest dream,' he said. 'You were in it.' His hands floated up towards me. They moved like drunken birds on the ends of his arms. His fingers waved at me gently, moving like they were underwater. One snaked out and brushed me lightly on my cheek. I could see the outline of his body under the sheet, the trim of his legs, the fork they made at his hips. The shape of his erection stood out as plain as if he was wearing spandex. I was embarrassed, but I couldn't stop looking at it. I hoped he wouldn't notice. He was smiling at me.

The nurse walked in and looked at his chart. 'I knew you'd be back,' she said to me. 'I can always spot your kind.'

'He's my brother,' I said. 'What's wrong with that?'

'Nothing,' she said. 'Nothing's wrong with that.' She was swabbing my arm with a cotton ball and alcohol. I hadn't seen her coming. She held the needle up, checking it in the light. She squirted the air-bubbles out. Some of the liquid made a splash on the floor by my feet. 'Relax,' she said.

Whatever it was made me sleepy. I could feel it in my blood, making it sluggish and thick. She picked me up like I was a baby, my head in one hand, my legs draped over the other. She laid me next to him on the bed and then turned off the lights. 'Sleep tight,' she said.

He waited until it was quiet in the room, the heart monitor slowing into silence. I could hear her footsteps in the hall. 'You're not asleep,' he whispered to me. His fingers touched the corner of my mouth, the corner of my eyes. He rolled over on top of me, his collarbone biting into the hollow of my neck. 'My brother,' he said. He giggled. 'Don't go to sleep,' he said. 'Stay with me,' he said. 'Please stay with me.'

I could feel him pushing down into me, the mattress giving way with the consistency of sand. He knocked the air right out of me. I hugged him back, hugged him hard, trying all the while, trying just to breathe.

~ ~ ~

I knew what had happened even before I was awake. I could feel it in the sheets and on my skin. Jesus, I thought. He's not even conscious. I felt like a pervert. I felt nauseated. It was 5 a.m. I could hear thunder in the distance. I took the hottest shower I could stand.

The note I put on the door told Julian to meet me at the hospital. The street lights faded as the sun came up. I had to see Zah, I had to say I was sorry. I didn't expect to get past the lobby, but I made the stairwell before the security guard saw me. As the door swung shut I thought I heard her whistle.

I took the stairs two at a time. The nurse – *that* nurse – and a man with a hat were standing in the hall. I ducked into the Waiting Room before they saw me. The TV was off. It hung over the room like an eye. I sat down in a plastic chair and tried to make myself look small.

A few minutes later the man with the hat walked in. A woman was with him. They wore regular clothes. They tried to whisper but I could still hear them. The woman said to the man, 'I think you'd better call. I haven't spoken to her in five years.'

'She's your sister,' the man said. 'Jake's her son.'

'Yeah,' she said. 'Some mother she turned out to be.'

I shifted in my seat, looked out at the hall. They saw me sitting there, but they didn't stop. The man murmured something I couldn't hear.

'You're right,' the woman said. 'I know.'

'I'll get you some coffee,' he said. He touched her on the hand. 'It's going to be okay.'

The woman dug through her purse, found an address book, flipped through it. 'I don't even have their number,' she said. 'Not the one in Phoenix.'

'Call information,' he said. She was starting to cry. He patted her on the back, touched her once on the back of her head.

'I'll be back,' he said. 'Don't worry.' He walked out into the hall.

'Phoenix,' the woman said into the pay phone that hung on the wall. 'Last name Wells. First name either Debbie or John.' She was composing herself, searching her purse for paper and pen. 'Bustelo Drive?' she said. 'I'm not sure.' She wrote a number down. 'Thank you,' she said.

I could hear her sniffling as she dialed the number. 'I'm sorry to wake you,' she said. 'It's me.'

She had her back to me. She was leaned forward, her head against the wall, the phone buried under her hair.

'I've missed you, too,' she said. 'Of course.'

'I'm still up north,' she said. 'I'm still here.'

Her voice couldn't hide that she was upset. I wondered who she was talking to, how they sounded on the other end of the line. She took a breath that I heard shudder in her lungs.

'Yeah,' she said. 'You're in Phoenix. I know. How is it?'

She shifted against the wall, turned towards the door.

'Really?' she said. 'Is it hot? Does it rain?

'It's Jake,' she said. 'There's been an accident.'

I didn't want to stay for that. In the hallway the man was returning, a styrofoam cup in his hand. The rest of the way was clear.

The silence in his room struck me first. The heart monitor was off, the tape deck quiet, the bed empty. I couldn't believe he was gone.

The sheets was thrown over the foot of the bed. The outline of his body was pushed down into the mattress. I will, I thought, I will. I was lying in it before I could change my mind. I snuggled my head in the hollow his had left in the pillow. I tried to find the position of his legs. I pulled the sheets up over me.

Out in the hall, the elevator opened with a ding. I could hear the rustle of cloth, the clatter of feet. I closed my eyes. There were voices that I couldn't understand. They're out there, I thought, walking past. I lay in his bed and waited for someone to find me.

ACKNOWLEDGEMENTS

Grateful acknowledgement is made for permission to reprint the following copyrighted works:

'The Point of It' from *The Eternal Moment* by E.M. Forster. Reprinted by kind permission of The Provost and Scholars of King's College, Cambridge and the Society of Authors as the Literary Representative of the E.M. Forster Estate.

'Local Colour' from *The Child of Queen Victoria and Other Stories* by William Plomer. Copyright © 1933. Reprinted by permission of the William Plomer Trust.

'A Visit to Priapus' by Glenway Wescott. Reprinted by permission of Harold Ober Associates Inc. Copyright © 2003 by Anatole Pohorilenko.

'Me and the Girls' from *Star Quality: The Collected Stories of Noël Coward* by Noël Coward. Copyright © 1939, 1951, 1963, 1964, 1965, 1966, 1967, 1983 by the Estate of Noël Coward. Used by permission of the publisher, Dutton Signet, a division of Penguin Books USA Inc., and Michael Imison Playwrights Ltd.

'Momma' from *The Gallery*, by John Horne Burns. Reprinted by permission of Secker & Warburg. Copyright © 1947.

'Gerald Brockhurst' from *Private View*, by Jocelyn Brooke. Copyright © 1954.

'Servants with Torches' by Donald Windham. First published by Sandy

Campbell in a limited edition illustrated by Paul Cadmus, 1955. Later collected in *The Warm Country*, Rupert Hart-Davis, 1960; Scribner's, 1962. By permission of the author.

'May We Borrow Your Husband?' from *May We Borrow Your Husband?* by Graham Greene. Copyright © 1962 by Graham Greene. Used by permission of Viking Penguin, a division of Penguin Books USA Inc., and David Higham Associates.

'Some of These Days' from *The Candles of Your Eyes* by James Purdy. Copyright © 1975, 1976, 1978, 1979, 1984, 1987 by James Purdy. Reprinted by permission of Curtis Brown Ltd., and Peter Owen Publishers, London.

'Torridge' from *Lovers of Their Time* by William Trevor. Copyright © 1978 by William Trevor. Used by permission of Viking Penguin, a division of Penguin Books USA Inc., and Peter Fraser & Dunlop Group Ltd.

'The Cinderella Waltz' from *The Burning House: Short Stories* by Ann Beattie. Copyright © 1979, 1980, 1981, 1982 by Irony & Pity, Inc. Reprinted by permission of Random House, Inc., and International Creative Management, Inc.

'Jimmy' from *Diamonds at the Bottom of the Sea* by Desmond Hogan. Copyright © 1979 Desmond Hogan. First published by Hamish Hamilton and reprinted by permission of the author and Rogers, Coleridge & White Ltd.

'Jump or Dive' from *One Way or Another* by Peter Cameron. Copyright © 1985 by Peter Cameron. Reprinted by permission of the Irene Skolnick Agency. First appeared in *The New Yorker*, June 17, 1985.

'My Mother's Clothes: The School of Beauty and Shame' by Richard McCann. Copyright © 1986 by Richard McCann. Originally appeared in the *Atlantic Monthly*. Reprinted by permission of Brandt & Brandt Literary Agents, Inc.

'Good with Words' by Stephen Greco. First appeared in *Advocate Men*. By permission of the author. Copyright © 1987, 1992.

'Nothing to Ask For' by Dennis McFarland. First appeared in *The New Yorker*. Copyright © 1989 by Dennis McFarland. Reprinted by permission of Brandt & Brandt Literary Agents, Inc.

'Dramas' from *Lantern Slides* by Edna O'Brien. Copyright © 1990 by Edna O'Brien. Reprinted by permission of Farrar, Straus & Giroux, Inc., and Aitken & Stone Limited.

'Atlantis,' 'Capiche?,' 'Sudden Extinction,' 'Leaving,' 'The Origin of *Roget's Thesaurus*,' and 'Childless' (re-titled 'Six Fables') from *Maps to Anywhere* by Bernard Cooper. Copyright © 1990 by Bernard Cooper. By permission of the University of Georgia Press.

'The *Times* as It Knows Us' from *The Body and Its Dangers* by Allen Barnett. Copyright © 1990 by Allen Barnett. By permission of St Martin's Press, Inc., New York, NY.

'Adult Art' from *White People* by Allan Gurganus. Copyright © 1991 by Allan Gurganus. Reprinted by permission of Alfred A. Knopf, Inc., and International Creative Management, Inc.

'Perrin and the Fallen Angel' from *Dangerous Desires* by Peter Wells. Copyright © 1991 by Peter Wells. Used by permission of Viking Penguin, a division of Penguin Books USA Inc., Reed Publishing (NZ) Ltd., and Michael Gifkins & Associates.

'Self-Portrait in Twenty-three Rounds' from *Close to the Knives: A Memoir of Disintegration* by David Wojnarowicz (Vintage Books, 1991 USA; Serpent's Tail, 1992, Great Britain). Reprinted by permission of the Estate of David Wojnarowicz.

'Reprise' by Edmund White. Copyright © 1992 by Edmund White. Reprinted by permission of the author.

'The Whiz Kids' by A.M. Homes (originally titled 'Duck Duck Goose') by A.M. Homes. Originally published in *Christopher Street* magazine. Copyright © 1992 by A.M. Homes. By permission of Donadio & Ashworth, Inc.

'Gentlemen Can Wash Their Hands in the Gents' from *Such Times* by Christopher Coe. Copyright © Christopher Coe (1992), by kind permission of the author and The Sayle Literary Agency.

'Scenes from the Fifties' from *Licks of Love* by John Updike (Hamish Hamilton, 2000). Copyright © John Updike, 2000. First published by Penguin Books.

'What You Want to Do Fine' from *Birds of America* by Lorrie Moore. Copyright © 1998. Reprinted by permissioin of Faber & Faber.

'Brokeback Mountain' from *Close Range* by Annie Proulx. Copyright © Dead Line Ltd. 1999 by kind permission of Annie Proulx and The Sayle Literary Agency. First published by Fourth Estate.

'Living Together' from *The Rose City* by David Ebershoff. Copyright © 2001 by David Ebershoff. Used by permission of Viking, Penguin, a division of Penguin Group USA Inc.